— A RAGNAROK PUBLICATIONS ANTHOLOGY —

Blackguards

TALES OF ASSASSINS, MERCENARIES, AND ROGUES

EDITED BY
J.M. MARTIN

RAGNAROK
PUBLICATIONS
CRESTVIEW HILLS, KENTUCKY

BLACKGUARDS: Tales of Assassins, Mercenaries, and Rogues
Ragnarok Publications | www.ragnarokpub.com
Editor In Chief: Tim Marquitz | Creative Director: J.M. Martin

Published by Ragnarok Publications
206 College Park Drive, Ste. 1
Crestview Hills, KY 41017

ISBN (hardback): 978-1-941987-16-2
ISBN (trade paperback): 978-1-941987-06-3
ISBN (ePub): 978-1-941987-05-6
Worldwide Rights
Created in the United States of America

Editor: J.M. Martin
Copy Editor (select stories): Roger Bellini
Publicity: Melanie R. Meadors
Social Media: Nick Sharps
Publishers' Assistant: Meaghan Mullin
Cover Illustration: Arman Akopian
Interior Illustrations: Oksana Dmitrienko & Orion Zangara
Cover Design & Interior Layout: Shawn T. King

Blackguards *is dedicated to—and in memory of—the 'big man,' David Gemmell (1948 – 2006), who wrote in the Drenai novel,* Waylander, *about his tormented assassin:* "There is evil in all of us, and it is the mark of a man how he defies the evil within."

Blackguards
CONTENTS

FOREWORD

"Poorly Calculated Randomistics"
GLEN COOK

Wow! So there I was, all excited because Joe Martin asked me to do the introduction to an anthology of stories about lovable rascal anti-heroes. Or maybe lovable not so much. But…I'd never done anything like that before. People do not ask me to because folks who do know me believe that I don't take this writing business nearly serious enough for their taste. Folks who don't know me but have heard a thing here and there generally own the notion that I am some kind of grumbling apostate who will not take literary posturing seriously.

Well, yeah, that's me. They're right. None of it will make a lick of difference a thousand years from now. Or even a hundred.

Oh. The black collywobbles almost got me there.

But, dude! Here came a grand new adventure!

Then, after several sweaty hours of stewing with no production, I began to sag and drift off toward the blue deeps.

Point the First: My beloved mother-in-law passed, leaving ten thousand real world details to be handled, hammered, served, saved, disposed, all stuff that takes precedence over writing.

Then the more critical Point the Second: What could I actually say, the quotidian demons conquered? I had no clue. Intros I recalled kind of stroked the reader (cynical Cook suspecting that he was the only reader on the planet who actually dipped into forewords, anyway, they not being the red meat a reader wanted to gnaw) but tended not to say anything useful.

Too, I came to the task proudly wearing a major lower working class anti-intellectual, anti-academic bias. I loved a rousing good story but those guys (the gender neutral third person collective that my wife so loathes from the wait staff at any restaurant where said staff does not pretend to be French), the ones who talked about writing, were just older versions of the kids in high school who inflated the curve and were too athletically challenged to walk and chew gum. Not that they would be caught with a stick anywhere but up their butts.

Even today my cape is a conviction that most people who find a place in literary academia do so in order to get out of having to go to work for a living.

(You chance on me in person sometime, and care, ask how my best friend from college and I brewed up a huge ration of bullshit to wow his thesis committee by proposing that Don Quixote's horse, Rosinante, gained the name because Cervantes may have shared his cell with a Catalonian for a while.)

I wander. I ramble. I become self-indulgent and do not address the topic at hand. I am near mad in my lack of focus because while I was traveling I reread two R. A. Lafferty books, neither of which honored in the least the conventions of plot that constrain the rest of us. I need to get a hand on the tiller and steer a straighter course.

So after one try at begging off the job I promised I would take an honest shot at introducing this collection, which looks like is going to be kick-ass, just based on the track records of those guilty of contributing to it.

During my beg off phase I proposed that maybe Cook wasn't the guy with the chops to engage the intellect of that unusual reader who does take a moment to peruse the foreword. I protested that I am not clear on what an anti-hero is, outside what the dictionary says. My own world view divides people into us guys and them guys, with most everyone steadfastly occupying the moral low ground. Them guys are bad guys because they won't do what us guys want them to do. Which means that, for me, good and bad are extremely dependent upon where I am standing. I am always the good guy and hero in my own saga. Every anti-hero is exactly that in his.

Joe begged me to give it a real try. You might surprise yourself, he said.

That has proven to be true, but perhaps not with a positive spin.

I began by brooding (an excellent, if brief, means of escaping the uncomfortable real world consequences of the passing of my mother-in-law: hope you and Romy are enjoying that better place, Peg) not so much on anti-heroes and anti-heroism but on what makes for interesting characters in shorter fictions. What made a memorable person who never existed outside the imagination of a pervert like me?

And it did seem that the most memorable creatures were less than shining good when you got up close enough to smell them. They gained shining status like a patina of time.

Think Arthur, the once and future king. He has warts all over him when you get up close. He had a son with his sister, not commonly accepted heroic behavior…though maybe it started out being fun. Later he had a war with that son. And his golden circle of Camelot guys were mostly not such squeaky clean actors, either. Old Art couldn't keep his wife from cheating with some of them. The Knights of the Round were pretty much all anti-heroic in some way.

Flaws. Some of them huge. I began reflecting on characters who touched me when I was younger, Fafhrd and Mouser, Elric and Hawkmoon, Conan the Barbarian (R. E. Howard's Conan), and so many others. They all had something in common: they were flawed. Even damaged. Definitely somewhat less than ideal human beings. They all had, to say the least, shadows at the edges of their dubious characters. In our oh so politically correct and sensitivity-burdened 21st Century North America every last one of them would be locked up and the keys chucked into the Crack of Doom, with one key ring to bind them. They committed murders, thievery, shoplifting, pickpocketry, smuggling, counterfeiting, tax evasion, even pederasty. And yet they were what we all wanted to be when we grew up. They were interesting. Their bad behavior and ability to get away with it, most of the time, made them interesting.

Of course, it helped that their antagonists were more wicked and distasteful than they were. Usually.

Still more thinking (brain cramps threatened) led me to conclude that it is all about character. Interesting people doing interesting things, though an excellent character can carry a feeble plot by making you care about him. And people battling the darkness within them while coping with the enemy without are more interesting than those who line up bad guys and cut them down only because they own the mickle-sharp scythe of moral superiority.

Thus do I find most Batman iterations more interesting than the various versions of Superman. Batman is a homicidal psychopath savagely struggling to keep his mania under control. He goes into battle as much to save himself as he does to save the world.

(Aside, I do feel that if Batman had let the evil run free at certain critical moments, Joker and other serial escapees from Arkham would not have placed nearly so much stress on him, and Gotham could have saved billions in reconstruction costs.)

We do become fascinated by evil, even infatuated with evil. Why do women chase after and even marry life-serving killer convicts? And are we not unfathomably infatuated with evils already overcome? There are about six genuine Nazis remaining alive in the whole wide world yet still we dote on conspiracy stories which allow us to splash a swastika across a book cover.

But maybe we do that knowing that it is only a story now. We can get a little thrill without having to truly dread a horror already put down. We can have fun, knowing that a particular evil can no longer strike back. Boogerman stories for grownups.

The triumph over evil achieved, we can even make that evil the hero in its own song, as Norman Spinrad did in *The Iron Dream*, where Adolf Hitler immigrates to America and becomes a famous science fiction writer.

The small evils in us all, and our endless contests with and sometimes surrenders to them, are what define us as people. The quirks of the characters we conjure in the minds of our readers (always, really, more part of who they secretly are than part of us who give them their shadows) help make them worth accompanying on their adventures. The anti-hero would be that character with a little extra, special quirkage that makes you think, "Oh, that rogue Mouser. I wish I could be like him. What's he gonna do next?"

Glen Cook
October, 2014

INTRODUCTION

J.M. MARTIN

In sixth grade I read *The Hobbit* as a class assignment. I was 11 years old and a whole world had opened up to me. Thinking about Bilbo Baggins, he was an interesting fellow, sure, but he really captured my imagination as soon as the grey wizard labeled him a thief. Soon after that he acquired the One Ring, outfoxed Gollum, and became a truly canny little twit. It wasn't just the ring, but also the magical, orc-sensing blade called *Sting* that transformed Bilbo from a mere sneaky hobbit to a bona fide blackguard.

Blackguard, by the way, is actually pronounced 'blaggard,' as in haggard. The term seemingly originated from scullions and kitchen-knaves, in particular those in courtly caravans who were in charge of the pots, pans, utensils, and the conveyance of coal. They were called as such for often being a sullied and rag-tag assembly in comparison to the livery of the guard at the head of the convoy. They have been defined as 'the lowest menials in a royal or noble household,' and the works of one Ben Jonson in *Love Restored* (dated 1612), declares:

'In all great houses, but particularly in the royal residences, there were a number of mean and dirty dependents, whose office it was to attend the wood-yard and sculleries. Of these the most forlorn wretches seem to have been selected to carry coals to the kitchens and halls…and to this smutty regiment who rode in the carts with the pots and kettles, which, with every other article of furniture, were then moved from palace to palace, [and] the people, in derision, gave [them] the name of black guards, a term since become sufficiently familiar, and never properly explained."

Even more interesting to note is the French word 'blague,' which today means more of a prank or joke but, in 18th century France, meant "to lie," more or less, a 'blageur' being someone who speaks pretentiously. Therefore one could extrapolate that a 'blaggard'— also 'blagger' in some texts — is a 'rag-tag deceiver with grandiloquent habits.' Some learned men might debate that this extrapolation is a bit of a stretch, but it certainly seems to fit the bill as far as I'm concerned.

So Bilbo Baggins could be pinned as a blackguard of sorts, but a well-meaning one on an estimable quest, rather unlike the goals and general misconduct of a true blackguard; that is to say those encompassing the rank and file not only of thieves but all manner of mercenaries from hucksters and devil-may-care cheats to narcissistic cutthroats and rapacious slave traders that populate the emerging fantasy subgenre called 'grimdark,' an amalgam of the adventure novel in gritty attire, cloaked in fool's motley, vitriol, and the picaresque.

Indeed, the seeds were planted and my imagination sprouted in early bloom. At a young age I became entranced by fantasy fiction, particularly to the rag-tag, outcast, grandiloquent, cunning blackguard. Tolkien's hobbits, dwarfs, and wizards were just the beginning. Throughout my teens and twenties I devoured entire series of blaggardly anti-heroes. R.E. Howard's Conan and Red Sonja. Michael Moorcock's Elric and Moonglum. Fritz Lieber's Fafhrd and Gray Mouser. Glen Cook's The Black Company. Robert Lynn Asprin's Thieves' World. Karl Edward Wagner's Kane the Mystic Swordsman. Bob Salvatore's Drizzt Du'Orden. Robin Hobb's FitzChivalry. David Gemmell's Druss the Legend and Waylander. Stephen King's The Dark Tower. And in my thirties I went on to discover such indisputable innovators of the anti-hero movement as Rafael Sabatini, Alexandre Dumas, even Gene Wolfe, and more recently the brilliant works of Scott Lynch's Gentleman Bastard series and Brandon Sanderson's Mistborn titles.

Blackguards: Tales of Assassins, Mercenaries, and Rogues is rooted in all of the above and more. I am so proud of this book with its 27 brilliant stories by the industry's leaders in speculative fiction, with tales of 'forlorn wretches' and 'smutty regiments,' most set in their own proprietary worlds. This was my goal from the beginning, to gather a collection of proprietary works, and I started with some of my writer chums who I'd come to know through an online group I started in 2010 called 'The Writers of the Storm.' Among these, I hit up Django Wexler, Mark Lawrence, Jon Sprunk, Kenny Soward, John Gwynne, Tim Marquitz, and David Dalglish. I knew they would make a solid core to build from, and after greasing those knaves' sweaty palms, the ripple effect took over. It's a cool feeling, going from reading the works of Carol Berg and Paul Kemp and Richard Lee Byers to actually *publishing* them (I sometimes pinch myself), and I'm well pleased with the table of contents herein.

But none of this could have happened without our Kickstarter benefactors. *Blackguards* was crowdfunded by 1,237 generous contributors (kickstarter.com, search: Blackguards) who invested their ducats and enabled us to pay the authors, artists, and printer, as well as produce some dandy add-ons like posters, magnet calendars, and collectible coins. It overfunded so far beyond the target goal — and my expectations — that I almost feel like a highwayman brigand myself. Like a blaggard!

Hmm. In fact…I feel less a highwayman and more a grandiloquent guild captain! Aye, the godfather of 1,237 well-favored rogues…you know, being that the rewards reaped by their deft and timely positionings are so damned bloody rich, after all. Why, upon possession of such goods I daresay those Kickstartians fancy themselves bona fide blue bloods, the very aristocracy of blackguards!

And you, Reader, whether you backed the Kickstarter campaign or acquired this book afterward, I hope you savor this fat 750 page grimoire the authors, artists, and folks of Ragnarok have cobbled together. I daresay you will; after all, you, too, are a blackguard. You've swept up something and secreted it away, put it in a space you've kept alive from the very moment you first discovered fantasy fiction. What is it? Look. There is something you've got hidden away in your pocket! It's your love for the rogue! And why shouldn't you keep it? It's yours. Your special sanctuary. And, therein, all your favorite dastards and ne'er-do-wells, mercenaries, thieves, and the like are indulging in their trade, taking what they will but also, in doing so, giving something back, deliberate or not.

Adventure.

Indeed, there's a bit of Bilbo Baggins in each and every one of us.

And *that* is an encouraging thought.

J.M. Martin
February, 2015

MAINON

JEAN RABE

Jean Rabe is the author of 30 fantasy and adventure

novels and more than 60 short stories. When she's

not writing, which isn't often, she edits…two dozen

anthologies and more than a hundred magazine issues.

Her genre writing includes military, science-fiction,

fantasy, urban fantasy, mystery, horror, and modern-

day action. She lives in central Illinois near three train

tracks that provide "music" to type by.

Visit her website: www.jeanrabe.com.

Blackguards

T HE ROASTED PIKE WITH green sorrel *verjuice* was amazing; Mainon held a piece on her tongue and relished the flavor. The scents from the other dishes arrayed on the table—artistically prepared marine and freshwater fish—competed for her attention. It had been quite some time since she'd dined in so lavish a place.

The chairs were thickly padded and covered with expensive red brocade, the floor was gleaming marble, and the table made of a polished wood so dark it looked like a patch of a starless night sky come to ground. Soft music drifted from behind a silk curtain, a reed instrument and a harp, and a third instrument she couldn't identify. Everything seemed carefully designed to delight all the senses.

She thought to compliment her host, but remained silent, not wanting him to know she was pleased and impressed. If she'd been in her home city she would have made arrangements to talk to the chef and urge him to share a recipe or two, for the pike in particular. But she was a full day's ride from home, visiting the port

"MAINON"

Illustration by **OKSANA DMITRIENKO**

city of Nyrill. So she simply continued to savor the meal, take in the surroundings, and scrutinize her host.

Ilarion was a noble of the merchant house of D'multek, a handsome man with oiled, dark hair, even olive skin, and wide, dark eyes that caught her stare and held it. Despite his voluminous robe, she could tell he had a muscular build. She'd researched him, a man born to wealth who in his relatively short life had managed to considerably increase his family's holdings. Even his upcoming wedding would further expand his business and influence. He had chosen a bride from the nearby country of Crullfeld, from a family nearly equal to his own in riches. Mainon learned of the bride, too—Erleene Hawe—who, at twenty-two, was a dozen years younger than Ilarion. She was said to be the oldest daughter of a cloth merchant. Erleene was not present at this feast.

Mainon was far from her own beautiful self this day. Her long black hair was coiled around her head in a tight braid and tinted by a simple magical glamor that rendered it a flat earthen brown. The same spell made her brilliant green eyes a dull gray and gave her a scar that ran from the base of her right ear down her neck. She wore ash-colored silk robes with a faint green trim, making her appear almost drab.

"I nearly did not come to this meeting, Ilarion," Mainon said. She took a sip from a crystal goblet filled with a pale gold wine. The wine was a little too dry; the only spot of imperfection in the elaborate meal. "I prefer to meet clients on my own terms and in places of my choosing. It is rare I make an exception. And I did not appreciate dealing with messengers upon messengers to set this up." She took another sip and found it a little better. Perhaps it was an acquired taste.

Ilarion quietly regarded her before speaking, creases forming in his brow as if he measured what to say. "There was no choice regarding the situation, the messengers upon messengers, milady."

His voice was rich and deep and Mainon wondered if he sang.

"Given my position in this city, this meeting had to be on my terms, and with my requirements." He leaned forward, elbows resting on either side of his plate. "But obviously my messengers intrigued you just enough. You are here, after all."

Mainon allowed herself a slight smile. "I am here until I finish this meal. Speak quickly."

Before he could continue, the waiter brought desert, and Mainon did not hesitate to sample it. A mashed pear tart, baked in butter, rose water, and sugar, it was dusted with cinnamon and ginger and served in a small pie shell.

Ilarion watched the server depart. "I've a need to hire you, milady."

"And the target?"

"I have a seer in my employ who I consult on various matters. Three days past he relayed to me a vision most disturbing. He warned me that an assassin has been hired to kill me before my wedding to Erleene. She is not at this dinner because I do not want her to know about the assassin. I wish no worries on my new bride." His once musical voice was strained now. "The seer believes someone does not want our houses joined and my power expanded. Thus I had my messengers find you, she who is said to be the best assassin in this part of the world. I want you to kill the one who has been hired to kill me. Kill the killer, so to speak." He leaned back in his chair and waited for Mainon's response. "You haven't much time. The wedding ceremony is in two days. Please, milady, help me."

She glanced at the men around the table and stationed in corners; considerable security for Ilarion. It would be difficult for an assassin to get past them. With a silent spell, she discerned the noble wore magical baubles to further protect him, as did some of his guards. She wondered why such a man with so many layers of insulation would fear that an assassin could succeed.

Could she succeed?

"I have no faith in seers, Ilarion. Oracular magic is unreliable, and most who claim to command it are fakirs. Prophecies speak only to possibilities. The future is not guaranteed."

Could she succeed in assassinating Ilarion?

Perhaps, she decided, that would be the way to approach it. How would she go about killing Ilarion? That might lead her to the one sent to kill him.

"Nonetheless, Ilarion, consider me hired."

NYRILL'S POOREST LIVED NEAR the docks. Mainon saw that the colors were dreary, the air filled with the scent of fish and filth, and many of the people looked beaten down by their own misfortune. Some had no homes and wore and carried all their possessions; it was the same in her home city, they were just spread out in various districts there, not concentrated in one place.

Farther from the sea, the view improved and the air smelled cleaner. As the land rose, so did the level of society. Like cream, the wealthy floated to the top.

Ilarion's manse was perched high atop the bluffs that overlooked Nyrill. The richest of the city's residents built their homes on the bluffs; the higher their elevation, the more wealth they commanded. Only a few mansions were farther up than Ilarion's.

A veritable palace, she considered his manor house, for it was that lavishly decorated. She spotted crystal and gold in every room, expensive incense burning, and not the smallest speck of dust anywhere. She shook off the unaccustomed envy of his great wealth; she'd been in several such dwellings before, though admittedly none were quite this opulent.

Mainon decided to make a much more thorough inspection of the manse and grounds when she finished meeting Ilarion's staff. She was introduced to advisors and guards, accountants, librarians, poets, artists, musicians…so many people she could recall only a few names and conjure up flashing images of faces.

Xeno Icculus, however, she had no trouble committing to memory.

The seer politely bowed and extended his hand. "I told Ilarion to hire the very best assassin his coin could buy." Xeno's voice was commanding, but raspy, and that coupled with a yellow tinge to his thin fingers and the corners of his lips showed that he indulged in smoking water pipes. "My incantations revealed that to be you."

"Then reveal something of yourself to me," Mainon returned almost too quickly. "It would only be fair."

The pair sat in a room filled with gilded harps and other musical instruments that appeared to be more for show than intended for use. The walls were painted a dark burgundy, matching the rugs on the floor, but enough light spilled in through the window to reveal the faint lines on the seer's patrician face.

His brown hair and beard were cut short, a little gray showing throughout, but mostly at his temples. Well into middle years, she judged, but striking in appearance. His fair skin, made all the paler by rich brown robes so dark they appeared black, suggested he was from a faraway land, and his thin arms and long neck made him look birdlike.

"I am a true seer," he began, waving a hand with a theatrical flourish.

Or a good actor, Mainon thought. He had the voice and manner of a thespian. Did he really see Ilarion's demise? Could he in truth foresee the future?

"I work the caravan routes occasionally, not wanting to limit myself to any one city for an extended length of time. Ilarion would like to consider me one of his employees, but this is not the case. While I accept coins from the man—for my services—it is not a formal or permanent arrangement. I spend a fair amount of my days in Crullfeld…and in a few nearby countries as well."

A silence settled between the two, Mainon studying Xeno's eyes. They didn't blink. He didn't look away. There was no nervous twitch, only a steady gaze, and she swore she saw herself mirrored in his pupils. She pulled in a deep breath, casting an enchantment at the same time, and scenting the magic about him.

"And I am a more powerful wielder of the eldritch energies than most in this city," he continued. "Certainly more practiced than those in Ilarion's steady employ. Stronger in the arcane arts than you. But no doubt you've just discovered all of that."

She cocked her head. There indeed was that much magic about him.

"Are you still skeptical of me, Mainon?"

She released a breath she'd been holding and turned to look out the window. "I am always skeptical of seers."

"Safer that way," he said. "But safer for Ilarion that he is not so skeptical and believes my vision. Had he not believed me, he would not have hired you. Had he not hired you, there would be no wedding, only a funeral."

"You might actually be genuine." There was hesitation in her voice.

He didn't reply.

"So I will take this threat against Ilarion very seriously."

"Safer that way for him." Xeno stood and brushed at the folds in his robe until the garment hung straight. "As I said, my spells revealed that you are the best. This evening I will show you my vision that led to your hiring. First, I trust you'll want to more closely explore the grounds. I understand that you've been to the city before, but never so high up on the hill."

———◆———

ONE DAY TO GO until the wedding, and the kitchen buzzed with hushed conversations from a dozen men and women working to prepare complicated pastries that were being kept chilled by a wizard in Ilarion's employ. Castles made of sugar, swans sculpted of various confections, lilac-tinted pie crusts that would hold…what? Berries? Chocolate? Something deadly for the groom?

Mainon's sense of smell was acute and her eyes keen, but she did not pick up anything amiss. Spell after spell revealed nothing poisonous…nothing poisonous at this particular moment in time. Did Ilarion have tasters who would first be sampling everything on the wedding plate? Of course, she told herself. Still, poison remained a possibility; it was a method she would have considered were the contract to kill him hers.

The laundry was next, an oppressive, hot, stone room below ground where the steam swirled as thick as fog on an early-morning river bank. Here only women toiled, hair plastered to the sides of their heads and sweat stains deep in their garments. From time to time a long-nosed man came in to observe and bark orders. Mainon found no trace of poison in the soap or water, nothing anywhere.

She spiraled up and out, discovering magical wards that nearly caught her, guards stationed in shadowy niches, paintings with false eyes where more guards peered through to watch those who traipsed the halls. In the courtyards beyond she found enchanted snares—nothing lethal, but all of them designed to catch and firmly hold a trespasser. A good assassin could get by them all, she noted. She had. And no doubt many of the wards would be rendered ineffective on the wedding day, Ilarion not wanting any guests to be offended.

A good assassin could get onto the grounds and into the manse, especially someone well dressed and appearing to have an invitation.

She strolled by neighboring manor houses, pressing herself against garden walls and listening to pieces of conversation when "Ilarion" or "Erleene" were mentioned.

"He marries not for love," someone said. "He marries only to add to his wealth."

"She is beautiful. I could spend the rest of my days living in the glow from her smile."

"Ilarion wants to own the very top of the bluff, to have no one perched above him. This wedding will guarantee that."

"There were local women he could have had his pick from, beauties all of them. And from good families, too."

"Our daughter…he once considered her." Mainon made note of this particular residence. She would discover who lived here and if there was animosity between them and Ilarion. "Too close to his own age, our daughter. Not young enough."

"Ilarion will put on a display the likes of which this city has never seen. I've heard they've been preparing cakes for weeks."

"He'll not live to see his first child born. There's talk of an assassin." Mainon found more than one home where this rumor flowed.

A good assassin could indeed succeed, she decided as she picked her way back to Ilarion's manse. But it would take a very good assassin to get back out undetected. The assassin would have a masterful disguise, perhaps looking like one of the groom's close friends or guards, and would need a considerable amount of magical talent.

Mainon's mind churned with the possibilities of how she would approach it. Perhaps Xeno's "vision" would give her a clue.

———◆———

"WELCOME, SKEPTICAL MAINON." XENO gestured to a velvet-covered cushion in the center of a small room.

There were no pieces of traditional furniture, just cushions spread across thick rugs. The room was heavily draped and lit by lamps that hung from the walls at regular intervals. Oil residue streaks extending up the walls from the lamp bowls hinted that the drapes were rarely opened.

She sat cross-legged on the cushion he'd indicated, back straight and shoulders square. He took up a position opposite her on a cushion that was not so plush. One he sat on often and had mashed down over time? She noted his eyes were glossy, and she detected a trace of flowery tobacco scent on his robes. Xeno had been smoking a water pipe recently. Did he need them for his visions?

"I trust you completed a most thorough inspection of the grounds?"

She continued to study him and the surroundings. The room seemed out of place compared to the rest of those in the manse, dark and nothing outwardly valuable in it. She hadn't noticed the door to it on her first two passes through Ilarion's home. Perhaps it had been magically masked. She would have to take another walk through the residence, this with a more careful eye and enchantments at hand to discover if there were other such secret rooms where an assassin might find a secure hiding place.

Xeno said something else, but she missed the first several words, caught up in thoughts about the manse.

"I came here to see this vision of yours," she answered. She drummed her slender fingers against her arm, making no attempt to disguise her impatience.

"My time is limited, too. Shall we begin?" He closed his eyes and rested his elbows against his knees, arms outstretched and palms up, fingers splayed wide.

Theatrical, she judged, a true wielder of magic needed few gestures or special poses; she needed only her mind and an occasional bauble to augment her natural talents. She peered at him closer, finding all four rings on his right hand pulsing with a steady, but faint dweomer. There was a magical pendant around his neck, and something under his robe that she couldn't see.

His lips moved and he spoke an archaic language that sounded vaguely familiar. An incantation, certainly, and when he finished an image formed between them.

"Ilarion," Mainon said.

"As he will be dressed tomorrow on his wedding day."

"You've seen the cloak and shirt?" They were shot through with gold thread, the fabric a creamy silk that shimmered in a light that cut through swirling shadows and came from somewhere within the vision.

The seer shook his head. "His wedding garb is secret, only seen by himself and his closest attendants. I merely know this to be a piece of time plucked from tomorrow."

"Before the ceremony?"

He shrugged. "Yes, but how soon before I cannot say. This sort of magic is not so precise…as I believe you've pointed out to Ilarion and myself before. Continue to watch, please."

Shadows deepened around Ilarion, whether from candles and lamps flickering or people moving around close, but out of range of the vision. Curtains fluttering? A cape billowing? Mainon strained to make it out, but instead locked onto Ilarion's face. His once handsome visage suddenly contorted in pain and his mouth opened. He screamed, but no sound came from the image. It was long, and she imagined shrill, his agony obviously intense. He twitched and dropped to his knees, writhing and contorting in ways his limbs weren't designed to move. Sweat beads blossomed on his skin and dampened his wedding garb. A moment later tiny blossoms of blood erupted on the creamy fabric, as if invisible darts had been thrown at him from all directions.

The gyrations continued for uncomfortable long minutes before Ilarion stopped breathing. A line of black blood spilled from his mouth.

A quick death, she favored dispensing. More dignity in it for her and her target. But this assassin? There was malice involved. This assassin didn't just want Ilarion dead, but to suffer mightily.

Mainon stared at her client's face, frozen in torture. A shudder danced down her spine, chasing away the last of her skepticism in Xeno's arcane skills.

"And Erleene?"

Xeno drew his lips into a thin line. "I've had no visions of her. I believe she is safe from the assassin's wrath. She is the eldest of five girls, so killing her would not prevent the houses from merging. Ilarion would simply choose the next daughter in line, then the next. The marriage is for power, milady." His breath whistled out between his teeth. "But slaying my friend Ilarion ends the potential merger. Ilarion is an only child. Can you stop this? Prevent my vision from becoming real? Can you save my friend?"

"That is what I have been hired to do." She rose from the cushion and padded toward the door.

"Then hopefully his coin is being well spent."

Where would Ilarion be when the attack would come? When? Her repeated questioning of Xeno yielded no more information. He'd said if he could provide that information, Ilarion wouldn't have needed to employ her.

"And…milady…please find something more appropriate to wear for the ceremony tomorrow."

She glanced down at her ash gray robes and left Xeno's hidden room.

An hour later, she pinned one of Ilarion's guards to the floor outside the kitchen. He was wiry and squirmed beneath her, legs bucking and sending her off him and against the wall. Mainon's head struck hard and she bit down on her bottom lip to keep her focus. Then she leaped at him again, drawing a knife from a sheath on her calf and going for his throat.

He'd done nothing suspicious, said nothing to alert her that something was amiss. But she'd seen him two days past at the inn where she dined on the delicious pike, and again yesterday during her tour of the grounds. She spotted him moments ago after making another pass through the laundry when she searched for the garments she saw Ilarion wearing in the seer's vision. And she saw him heartbeats past outside the kitchen. He could not be in two places at the same time, and she doubted he was a twin. He'd used magic to borrow a regular guard's visage. A quick incantation confirmed that he wore a spell to mask his appearance—similar to the one she wore to color her hair and give her a scar.

The man was graceful as a cat, and stronger than his lithe frame hinted. He rolled to the side and jumped to his feet as she came at him again. A knife flashed from the folds of his tabard and met hers in a deft parry. For an instant his face blurred, as if he had trouble both maintaining his illusory image and fighting her. She didn't worry that he might have an associate sneaking up behind her; assassins with very few exceptions worked alone.

"Who paid you?" she hissed, knowing full well that if he was good at his trade, he wouldn't answer.

His reply was a gob of spittle aimed at her face. She blinked, and in that instant he lunged at her, dropping in a crouch and slashing up with his knife. The blade looked wet. Poison, she suspected, as she spun out of its path and managed to come up to the man's side.

He was fast, definitely skilled, she judged. Not her equal, but close. They danced in the hall outside the kitchen, the fight making little noise—the swish of his tabard and cloak and her silk robe, the soft clank of their knives meeting. But suddenly a crash intruded, the sound drawing his eyes away from Mainon for just an instant. A woman had emerged from the kitchen. She'd been carrying a tray heavy with crystal goblets. Startled, she'd dropped the tray and the resulting crash gave Mainon the edge she needed.

Mainon pivoted away from the assassin and slipped up behind him, rammed her knife into his back, the blade sliding between ribs and finding his lungs. He dropped to his knees as the kitchen woman screamed.

"Stay back!" Mainon warned as a trio of workers emerged from the kitchen, all of them gasping and pointing, one flailing at the air with a big wooden spoon. The assassin was dying, but remained a threat.

He tried to suck in a breath, but instead made a gurgling, wheezing sound. The woman with the spoon screamed when blood bubbled from his lips. In a last measure of defiance, he swung his knife wildly, catching Mainon's robe. She twisted the fabric and tugged the blade out of his grasp, then stabbed him in the throat with it. The woman who had dropped the goblets fell in a swoon.

Within moments, the sound of rhythmic footsteps filled the hall as real guards arrived. Mainon retrieved her knife and wiped the blade on the dead assassin's cloak. His face was much different now, thickly lined around the eyes, as if he'd often squinted into the sun, his hair thin like a wispy cobweb. She found a pouch of empty vials on him and discretely pocketed it, along with a ring that had the tingle of magic to it—her prize from the encounter. Then she edged away as more curious workers gathered.

Mainon had smelled something about the assassin—coriander, nutmeg, and other spices. He'd been in the kitchen, and that's where she went now. She focused her magic through her senses, fingers playing along the outside of the vials as she went, thumb rubbing against one like it was a worry stone.

"There and there and there." Poison in one of the wedding cakes, in the swan-shaped confection, and in a pastry boat that was taking shape. She found four more deadly delicacies before she pronounced the rest of the food safe. Poison was a method she would have considered to kill Ilarion, though she would not have used such a virulent, slow-acting one as this assassin had employed. Where had he acquired it? Who paid him to do it? Though she'd been in the city a few times before, she didn't know enough of its shadowy places to ferret out those answers quickly.

"Mainon." Xeno had entered so silently she hadn't heard him.

She whirled and pointed to the tainted treats.

"Indeed, my friend hired the best in you, milady. The vision of Ilarion dying before his wedding? I can no longer conjure it." He released a deep breath, and the lines on his face relaxed. "The threat is passed. My thanks to you. My friend will survive and enjoy his wedding."

Mainon, however, knew she would not consider herself successful until after Ilarion was married and the houses legally joined.

ERLEENE WAS BEAUTIFUL. TALL and thin, with a heart-shaped face ringed in golden curls, she was escorted across the grounds on the arm of her father. Her dress was pale yellow, the shade of the sun dappling on a still pond, and it glistened in artful patterns where tiny gems and seed pearls had been sewn. Flowers were woven in her hair; more flowers circled her wrists and waist.

The late afternoon ceremony was in the principal garden, and the weather cooperated. Mainon perched herself on a balcony where she could overlook everything. She didn't want to take the chance that on the ground she might miss some nefarious activity in the press of guests and attendants. Athletic, she could leap to the ground without hesitation should trouble arise.

"I shouldn't worry," she whispered. She'd inspected the grounds twice, the manse until her feet ached. Xeno and she cast spells that would make it almost impossible for someone to magically disguise themselves as the assassin had outside the kitchen. She'd even dropped her own guise and wore an appropriately stunning gown—though not one so voluminous it would slow her movements.

But she worried nonetheless. She was being paid too well not to worry.

Music filled the courtyard as Ilarion arrived at the altar. Mainon continued to watch the crowd, not allowing herself to enjoy the pageantry, though both her client and his seer had encouraged her to. And then before she realized it, the wedding was over. A cheer erupted, crashing toward her like a wave. The guests—she estimated three hundred—followed Ilarion and Erleene inside. Music filtered out of a window below her, followed by the clink of glasses, gentle laughter, and the murmur of well-wishers. The scents of roasted meat and spiced vegetables drifted out and made her mouth water. Mainon had never cared for weddings, but she always enjoyed a good wedding feast.

One final meal at this fine, fine residence, and then she would gladly head home.

The festivities lasted well into the evening, the guests consuming more food and drink than she thought possible. Couples, some of whom had overindulged, tottered on the dance floor and stepped on each others' robes and skirts.

Later, Mainon, who had also overindulged, stood before Ilarion and Erleene, Xeno hovering behind the couple and beaming.

"I bid you farewell," Mainon said, nodding to her client. "And I wish you both a good, long life together." She said nothing else, guessing that Ilarion still had not mentioned the threat of an assassin to his bride.

"And I give you my gratitude." Ilarion bowed deeply, his smile reaching his eyes. "Safe journey home." He paused and gave her a wink. "You'll find something in the stable with your horse." Softer: "What we agreed upon…and a little more." Then Ilarion turned to face his wife. "And now let us retire to our chamber, my sweet. The night is not through with us yet."

Mainon wove her way between a portly man and his even portlier wife who were trying to keep up to music that had just turned lively. Once outside, she breathed deep, taking all the flowery scents of the garden far into her lungs, the fragrances more preferable to the warring perfumes of the guests.

She'd nearly reached the stable when she spun and ran back to the manse. She hadn't been able to enjoy any of the day, not the meal or the music or the expensive wine. Something had been festering at the back of her mind, something she couldn't place and something that wouldn't go away. She'd been turning all of the possibilities over and over.

The threat passed.

The threat passed?

She'd caught the assassin with his poison outside the kitchen yesterday.

The poisoned food discarded.

The ceremony finished and the houses joined.

The seer's vision quashed.

The seer.

The threat passed?

She'd come to know his many expressions, and the one he displayed several minutes ago was new to her. He was beaming, his face practically glowing, and his eyes were on Erleene. Xeno gazed at the young girl with deep affection. *Covetously so.*

Mainon cursed herself for not remaining skeptical about oracular magic and the seer himself and urged herself faster still.

She dashed through the main hall, narrowly avoiding a throng of guests who were leaving, and once past the dining room she vaulted over a maid scrubbing at something that had been spilled on an ornate carpet. She took the stairs three at a time, skirt hiked up above her knees and dagger sheaths on her legs showing.

Within a handful of heartbeats she was outside Ilarion's bedchamber door. A moment more and she was in, eyes adjusting to the darkness. Only a single candle burned by the bed.

"Xeno!" She shouted the seer's name to get the attention of Ilarion and his bride. "Xeno, show yourself!"

Shadows shifted near the bed, then a curtain a few feet away fluttered in a slight breeze. The shadows drifted closer to her.

"What outrage!" Ilarion said. He'd been in the process of taking off his exquisite cream-colored garment, the one in the seer's vision. "What is the—"

The shadows reminded her of what she'd seen around Ilarion in that vision.

"Xeno!"

"How did you know?" the shadows asked.

Before she could answer, the shadows swirled around her and took her breath. She scented the poison, like had been in the empty vials and on the assassin's knife, the same virulent stuff that promised a long, horrible death. She kicked out, connecting with something solid in the shadowy mass, the impact chasing away the shadow-spell Xeno had been maintaining.

"Xeno!" This time it was Ilarion who cried the seer's name. "Traitor!"

"The real assassin," Mainon said when she regained her breath. She pressed her attack, hands and feet furiously pummeling the seer. She had to keep him from casting another spell, as she feared he was indeed more skilled with magic than she. Her attacks were not so masterful as usual, they were desperate, almost maniacal, but it worked to achieve her purpose.

He was not her match physically, and she wore him down before turning his own dagger upon him and driving it in his chest. Mainon looked away as the scene in the seer's vision played out in the meager candlelight…only with Xeno, not Ilarion, the victim of the horrid, slow-acting poison.

"I don't understand." Ilarion hovered over his young bride, smoothing at her face. The girl was pale, her lips quivering, and her eyes wide with terror—and filled with something else.

Loss, Mainon knew. She shook her head and glanced back at the quivering Xeno. For the briefest of moments Mainon considered slitting the seer's throat to end his suffering. Her fingers tightened around her dagger. She could…she should—

Then all thoughts of mercy fled as Mainon felt the hot, fiery sensation of a blade thrust in her back and swiftly and painfully removed. Whirling and dropping to a crouch, she saw Erleene step back, holding a thorn knife dripping with blood, its curving and scalloped edges intended to inflict serious damage going in and worse coming out.

The agony centered in Mainon's back had a pulse to it, and she felt her clothes grow warm and sticky with her blood. Erleene smiled slyly and shifted so she could keep watch on Mainon and Ilarion.

"What? What is the meaning?" Ilarion shouted. Out of bed, he put his back up against a wall, glancing fearfully between the two women.

"Xeno and your bride, they hatched the plan to have you assassinated," Mainon said. A wave of weakness crashed through her and she concentrated to stay on her feet. "It would be expected, really, someone trying to prevent your houses from joining and from you becoming more powerful."

"By hiring you," Erleene spat, "and by you catching an assassin yesterday, my beloved Xeno could convince you any threat was passed." She swept in and lashed out, revealing she had a reasonable skill with the weapon.

But she was not as skilled as the assassin. Mainon gathered her magic and focused it on her wound. She possessed no healing enchantments, but she could mask at least some of the hurt. In that same instant she twisted and avoided Erleene's lunge, twisted again and got behind her, slashed down to hamstring the bride.

Erleene screamed in pain and outrage, fell to her knees and waved the knife in front of her in an effort to keep Mainon at bay. But the assassin continued her assault; she had to be quick, before the blood loss felled her. She whirled and came up on Erleene's side and drove the dagger forward, aiming for the bride's arm and striking her near the wrist, the force of the blow sending the blade in bone deep and lodging it there. A shriller scream and Erleene's fingers opened and the thorn knife clattered to the floor. Mainon swept up the knife and backed toward Ilarion as she caught her breath.

"Quite the wife you have," Mainon hissed.

The noble stared blankly, his face pale, eyes wide with surprise, sweat thick on his forehead. "I...I thought the threat had vanished," he said weakly. "By the gods, I was blind. The real threat was Xeno and Erleene. They wanted me dead *after* the ceremony."

"When we'd think the threat had been dealt with," Mainon said. She was feeling stronger, likely because the magic was tamping down more of the pain. She needed the aid of a healer—very soon, and she knew of one in the city below.

"Help me, husband," Erleene said. She tried to stand, but instead collapsed onto her side. "Help, please. You're wrong. I meant you no harm."

Ilarion shook his head. "She would inherit all my holdings, making her house unrivaled in power. And she would still have... *him*." He looked at Mainon. "So I hire you again, assassin. Finish my wife while she is down. An easy kill." His lip curled. "I will not be married to someone who wants me dead."

Erleene sobbed. "No! Please..."

Mainon looked from Ilarion to Erleene. The young woman should be able to recover from her wounds given time. Then she glanced at Xeno, his body still twitched in agony from the lethal poison, albeit barely. The would-be killer took his last gasp and stilled.

"My obligation to you is over," Mainon said. "You hired me to kill one assassin, and only one. As for your wife, I think you can manage the task yourself."

It was time for her to leave while she still could.

Mainon tucked the thorn knife in her belt, padded to the sobbing Erleene, who looked up with wet, fearful eyes. She stepped on the bride's hand for leverage and pulled her dagger free. Erleene screamed and wept.

"An easy kill," Mainon said. She certainly would welcome more gold from the noble for doing the simple task herself. But in all the years Mainon had worked as an assassin, she'd never made a man a widower; she had a personal code. "Too easy."

She slipped from the chamber and down the stairs, still losing blood, feeling the warm stickiness against her back growing. Crossing the grounds was laborious, despite all traces of her pain gone it did nothing to diminish her weakness. Climbing onto her horse—and securing the bag of gold from the noble—was onerous. Mainon fought to stay conscious as she led her mount into the city and toward the harbor.

A healer lived there, one who was not terribly expensive.

One who had helped her a few times before.

Mainon would regale the healer with a tale of the wedding.

She had never cared for them, too much fuss, too many people, though the feasts were typically good. From her vantage she could look back and see the manor, its lantern lights aflicker.

"'Til death do they part," she said, and looked toward the sea.

IRINDAI

-The Song of the Shattered Sands-

BRADLEY P. BEAULIEU

*The desert surrounding the city of Sharakhai is filled
with mysterious and wondrous creatures. Some are ages
old, and secret themselves into the forgotten corners of
the Great Shangazi. Others hide among humanity,
toying with them even as they envy their short, bright,
candleflame lives. They envy the myriad things they do,
the things they accomplish, alone and together. They
wonder what it would be like to be one of them instead
of some undying creature forged by the hands of gods.
This is the story of Çeda, the hero of* Twelve Kings in
Sharakhai, *a story sparked when her path crosses that
of one such creature. I hope you enjoy it.*

CEDA FOUND BRAMA BY the river.

She watched from within a stand of cattails, where she was hunkered low, cool river water lapping at her ankles.

Brama was playing in the water with a dozen other gutter wrens—playing!—apparently without a care in the world after he'd nicked her purse. She felt the anger roiling inside her like a pot boiling over. He'd probably come straight here to brag to his friends, show them what he'd done and challenge them to do the same, then demand tribute like some paltry lord of mud and fleas.

The lot of them were playing skipjack along the Haddah's muddy banks. One by one, boys and girls would run to the lip of the bank and leap onto a grimy piece of canvas pulled taut as a skin drum by seven or eight of the older children, who would then launch them into the air. They would flail their arms and legs mid-flight, screaming or yelling, before splashing like stones into the Haddah, water spraying like diamonds in the dry, desert air.

Her lips curling in disgust, Çeda watched as Brama was launched in turn. He barked like a jackal and flew through the air to crash into the water, arms and legs spread wide. After, he waded back to the

"IRINDAI"

Illustration by ORION ZANGARA

canvas and relieved one of the others so they could make a run of their own—the same pattern he'd followed every other time he'd jumped into the river.

When he reaches dry ground, Çeda told herself.

Moving with a pace that would keep her position concealed, Çeda pulled out a locket on a silver chain from inside her dress. She pried the locket open, its two halves spreading like wings to reveal a dried white petal with a tip of palest blue. After taking the petal out, she clipped the locket closed and placed the fragile petal beneath her tongue. Spit filled her mouth. A shiver ran down her frame as the flavor of spices filled her. Mace and rosemary and a hint of jasmine and other things she didn't have words for.

The petal had been stolen from the adichara, a forbidden tree that bloomed only once every six weeks under the light of the twin moons. When gathered on such nights, they were imbued with breathtaking power. Part of her hated to use even one of the petals on Brama, but her anger over what he'd done was more than strong enough to smother any distaste.

As the effects of the petal spread, granting a barely contained verve to her limbs, she stuffed the locket back inside her dress and scanned the river. Colors were sharper now. She could *hear* more as well, not just the children in the river but the very breath and rattle of the city. It took effort in the early moments of imbibing the petals to concentrate, but she was used to doing so, and she focused her attention on those near and around Brama. A clutch of children were playing downriver, some trying to spear fish, others wading and laughing or splashing one another. Most likely they wouldn't interfere. There was one who gave her pause, though, a dark-skinned Kundhunese boy with bright blue eyes. He stood apart from the others, and seemed to be watching Brama and the children with almost as much interest as Çeda. She would swear she'd seen him before, but just then she couldn't remember where or when it might have been.

She worked at the memory, scratching at it, but like a stubborn sliver it only sank deeper in her mind, and soon Brama was handing over his section of the canvas to a girl with a lopsided grin.

The moment Brama gained the bank, Çeda parted the cattails and marched forward. "Brama!"

He turned, staring at her with a frown. Her identity was still hidden by her white turban and veil, so he wouldn't know who she was, but she could see in his eyes that he recognized the flowing blue dress she'd been wearing early that morning.

He scanned the area to see if anyone else was with her. "What do you want?"

"There's something you stole from me," she called, "and I mean to have it back." Çeda didn't know Brama well. He was a boy who liked to traipse about Sharakhai's west end, bullying some, shying away from others. He was an opportunist, and a right good lock-slip if rumor was true. She might have gone all her days and never thought twice about Brama but that morning he'd stolen something from her: a purse she was meant to deliver for Osman—a shade, as it was known in Sharakhai. It was as simple a task as Osman had ever given her—hardly more than a prance across the city—and she'd bungled it, but she'd be damned by Bakhi's bright hammer before she'd let a boy like Brama get away with it.

Brama's eyes flicked to the children in the river. They were watching, not yet approaching, but it wouldn't take long before they came to back him up. The moment his eyes were off her, Çeda drew her shinai, her curved wooden practice sword, from its holder at her belt. She didn't like walking around Sharakhai with a real sword—girls of fifteen, even tall as she was, attracted notice bearing steel—but few enough spent more than a passing glance at a girl wearing a shinai, especially in the west end where children practicing the dance of blades could be found on any street, alley, or open space one cared to look.

Brama's eyes were only for Çeda now. He looked her up and down, perhaps truly noticing her frame for the first time. She was tall. She had more muscle than he might have noticed earlier. She was holding a sword with a cozy grip—a *lover's* grip, the bladewrights called it, the kind that revealed just how intimate a sword and its master were with one another—and with the magic of the petal now running through her veins, Çeda was itching to use it.

Brama's friends were stepping out of the water now, and it seemed to lend him some confidence, for he swelled, not unlike like a man who'd had one too many glasses of araq might do, or the dirt dogs in the pits often did when they knew they were outmatched. He stuffed one hand down his still-dripping pants and pulled out a short but well-edged knife. "I've got nothing of yours"—he smiled as the other children fanned around and behind Çeda—"so why don't you run off before that pretty dress of yours is stained red?"

Brama had muscle as well, but it was the rangy sort, the kind that felt good to thump with the edge of a wooden sword. "You stole a purse, cut from my belt as I strode through the spice market."

"A thousand and one gutter wrens wander that market day and night. Any one of them might have stolen your purse."

"Ah, but it *wasn't* any one of them." She lifted the point of her shinai and thrust it toward Brama's chest. "The nick from your little knife wasn't nearly as clean as you thought, Brama Junayd'ava. I saw you running like a whipped dog down the aisles, and I *know* you heard me calling."

She thought he might be put off by the use of his familial name, but instead he squinted, as if he recognized her voice and was trying to place it. "I don't know who it might have been, but you're a fool if you think it was me."

The circle around her was closing in now, some with river stones clutched in their scrawny hands.

Çeda took a half-step closer to Brama and dropped into a fighting stance. "This is your last warning, Brama."

Brama merely smiled. "You should have run while you had the chance."

Çeda didn't wait any longer. She charged.

She brought her sword swiftly down against his hastily raised defenses. The wooden blade cracked against his forearms, then his rib cage, then his knee, not enough to break bones—though she could easily have done so—but certainly more than enough to send him crumpling to the ground.

Other children rushed in, but if her time in the pits had taught her anything it was how to maintain distance with the enemy, even many at once. She rushed past Brama's fallen form, twisting and striking a girl every bit as tall as Brama across the face. Another came barreling after, but Çeda dropped and snapped her leg out, catching the girl and sending her tumbling off the bank and into the river.

The ones with the stones loosed them at Çeda as two more boys braved the range of her sword. One stone struck a glancing blow against her shoulder, another squarely against her ribs, but the effects of the petal deadened the pain. Four quick strokes of her shinai and the boys were howling away, shaking pain from their knuckles and wrists.

She was alone now. None would come near. Even the boy with a rock the size of a lemon held in each hand remained still as a statue, the fear plain on his face.

Brama lay at her feet, cringing.

"Where's the purse?" she asked him.

His face grew hard, his teeth gritting away the pain. "I don't have it."

"That wasn't what I asked you, Brama." She grabbed a hunk of his hair—"I said, *where is it?*"—and slammed his head onto the ground.

"I don't have it!"

Somehow, his refusal made her go calm as the night's cool winds. She let go of Brama's hair and stood, staring down at him with her shinai still held easily in her right hand. "When are you going to learn, Brama?" She raised her sword, ready to give him something to think about before asking him the question again, but she stopped when she heard a piercing whistle from somewhere along the riverbank. She turned, but not before laying the tip of her sword over Brama's kidney, a warning for him to lay still.

A man with broad shoulders wearing laced sandals and a striped kaftan was standing near the edge of the river, staring at her. The sun glinted brightly off the lapping waves behind him, so she didn't at first recognize him—and why by the gods' sweet breath would he be here in any case?—but soon she *did* recognize him.

Osman.

The very man she should have delivered the purse to this morning. But she'd failed to, because of fucking Brama.

She was half-tempted to bring the sword down across Brama's thieving little face. He flinched, perhaps sensing the brewing sandstorm within her, and that made her want to strike him even more, but she stayed her hand when Osman shouted, "Enough!" in that clipped tone of his. And then she saw what he was holding in his right hand, dangling like a fish.

The purse. *Her* purse, a small, red leather affair, the very one he'd asked her to pick up and bring to him at the pits.

"Come," he said, and turned to walk along the dusty bank of

the Haddah.

Çeda had no difficulty understanding the command was meant for her, so she left, but not before kicking dirt over Brama's quivering form. As she walked toward Osman, she realized the Kundhunese boy with the blue eyes was watching her intently.

Not Osman. Just her.

"Hurry up," Osman said.

She refused to run, but she quickened her pace until they were walking side by side. She glanced back only once, and found that the Kundhunese boy had vanished. She scanned the river, curious, but she was so intrigued by Osman's sudden possession of the purse that she gave up after too long. How by the hot desert winds could Osman have learned not only that the purse had been stolen but that Brama had been the one to do it? And after learning it, how could he have found it so quickly?

The answer came to her in little time, but before she could say anything about it, Osman said, "Why confront him?"

"What?"

"Why challenge Brama while he's playing with his friends along the Haddah?"

Çeda shrugged. "Because I had to know where the purse was."

"You knew where the purse was."

"No, I didn't."

"Yes, you did. I saw you watching him as he hid his clothes and other things in the cattails. You could have taken it while they were splashing in the river."

He'd seen that, had he?

She tried on a dozen different answers, finally settling on, "He deserved it."

"A lot of boys like Brama deserve a beating, but you can't be the one to give it to them, Çeda. People in Sharakhai have long memories, and sooner or later, the city will end up the master and you the student, and I'll wager you're old enough to know how that lesson is likely to end."

"I thought you'd be grateful. It was *your* package I was protecting."

"First of all, the only time you'll find me grateful is when none of my packages go missing. Second, that was no favor you were doling out back there. Not for me, at least. You were nursing a wound to your precious ego. You fight in the pits, and if I'm being truthful, I've rarely seen someone with the gifts the gods themselves surely bestowed upon you, but don't think that trading blows with dirt dogs helps you at all in the shadows of this streets. You're shrewd enough when you put your mind to it, but you'd better start putting that quality to better use before I find that you've been given back to the desert."

Given back to the desert, a phrase that spoke of bleaching bones, of men and women forgotten and swallowed by the Shangazi's ever-shifting dunes…She was so angry she wasn't sure she wouldn't still give *Brama* back to the desert. "You do this to everyone, then?" Çeda asked as a wagon train rumbled past. "Set them up to see how they dance?"

Osman shrugged, not even looking at her. "I had to know what you'd do if you lost a package."

"And?"

"And what?"

"How did I do?"

"Poorly. It's the *package* I care about, Çeda. Let *me* decide who needs a beating and who doesn't. Understand?"

"Yes," she said, forcing the words through her teeth.

Osman stopped walking. They were on a small lane now, a well-worn one used by laborers to head to and from Sharakhai's sandy northern harbor. Men and women passed them by like the Haddah's waters around a pair of particularly surly stones. "Tell me you understand."

She stared into his eyes, ready to answer with another petulant, barking reply, but she stopped herself. This was no small thing he was asking. Osman might have been a pit fighter once, but he was a shademan now. He'd taken Çeda under his wing, but he would toss her to the dogs if he thought he couldn't trust her.

She'd been foolish with Brama. She saw that now. She needed to watch out for Osman's interests, not her own.

"I understand," she said.

"Good, because there's something a bit more delicate we need to discuss."

"*That* doesn't sound good."

Osman shared a wolfish smile and bowed his head like old Ibrahim the storyteller did before beginning a tale. "How astute of you to notice."

They passed out of an alley and onto the cobblestone quay surrounding the northern harbor. A line of eight sandships were just setting sail, their long runners carrying them swiftly over the amber sand toward the gap between the two tall lighthouses. "Two days ago," Osman continued, leading them over a meandering rank of stones that marked the dry yard around the lighthouse, "a man named Kadir came to me. He works for someone who is…Well, let's just say she's a powerful woman, indeed. Kadir's visit was regarding a package that was delivered to him three weeks ago, a package delivered by you." Osman came to a stop short of the door to the lighthouse. Beside them lay an old mint garden that years ago had been well-tended but had since lain forgotten, so that its contents looked little better than a forgotten pile of brown twine. "He also claimed that the contents had been poisoned."

Suddenly Çeda felt very, very small. She felt under scrutiny, like a dung beetle crawling over open sand. "Poisoned?"

"Poisoned."

"By whom?"

"That's the question, isn't it?"

"Well, it wasn't me! I remember that package. It was delivered as you asked!"

"I know."

"I didn't tamper with it."

"I *know*, or we'd be having a very different conversation."

"Is this why you had Brama steal the purse?"

Osman shrugged while waggling his head. "I would've done it sooner or later in any case." Çeda opened her mouth to deny it again, but Osman held up his hand. "Kadir wishes to speak with you. He believes he knows who sent the poison but would like to find more clues from you if there are any to be found."

Çeda stared deeper into his eyes. "And you told him I would? What if he thinks I *did* poison the contents of that drop? What kind of fool would I be to simply walk into his arms?"

"As I said, he works for a powerful woman. If *she* thought you had done so, she wouldn't have done me the courtesy of having Kadir ask to see you. He and I spoke for a long while. I believe him, Çeda, and you will be under my protection. You'll be safe enough, though I'm sure it won't be a comfortable conversation to have."

"And if I refuse?"

"Then Kadir doesn't get what he wants and life goes on."

"With no repercussions?"

A sad simulacrum of a smile broke over Osman's broad, handsome face. "None for *you*."

"But you would lose her as a client."

Osman shrugged. "In all likelihood, yes."

Çeda took a deep breath. She didn't like this. She didn't like this one bit. She knew her shading with Osman would get her into some trouble sooner or later. She just hadn't expected it would come from Osman himself. Still, she owed him much, and if this Kadir really *did* wish to speak of clues to the one who'd meddled with the package, then it seemed safe enough.

"Very well," she said.

Osman nodded, then put his fingers to his mouth and whistled sharply. From the lighthouse came Tariq, a boy Çeda had grown up with and who had joined the ranks of Osman's shades around the same time she had.

"Bring them," Osman said.

Tariq nodded and ran off down the quay before ducking into an alley. Soon, a rich, covered araba led by two horses was trundling up the quay toward the lighthouse with Tariq hanging off the back. When it had swung around the sandy circle in the yard and pulled to a stop, Tariq dropped and ran back to stand in the lighthouse doorway. Osman swung the araba's door open and Çeda climbed inside.

"Come see me when it's done," Osman said, closing the door and knocking twice upon it. "I'll stay until you return."

As the araba pulled away, Çeda saw someone standing on one of the empty piers in the sandy harbor—again, the Kundhunese boy with the bright blue eyes. He had a scar running near his left eye and down his cheek. Strange she hadn't noticed it before, as it was long and puckered in places. The pier and the boy were both lost from sight as the araba passed a long train of wagons loaded high with cord after cord of bright white wood. When the wagons had passed, the boy had vanished.

IN A TASTEFULLY APPOINTED room Çeda sat in a high-backed chair of ornamented silk. The estate to which she'd been brought had surely been built centuries before. She could tell not only from the architecture, but from the paintings on the walls, the vases on their pedestals, the occasional weapon. They were elegant, all, but had clearly been born of another age.

Ashwandi, the beautiful, dark-skinned woman who'd led Çeda here, lingered in the arched doorway, staring at Çeda with a strange mixture of piqued curiosity and contempt. "Kadir will see you soon," she said, and bowed her head. No sooner had she left than a slender man strode in scanning a sheet of vellum. As he swept behind an opulent desk, Çeda stood and bowed her head, for this was surely Kadir. He ignored her, his eyes continuing to scan the tightly scripted words while holding his free hand at attention behind his back, the pose a steward would often take while standing at attention. His brow creased as he finished. Only then did he set the vellum down and regard Çeda with a critical eye. He hid a frown as he looked her up and down. "Osman sent you?"

This was a man who took his position seriously, Çeda could tell, and it made her even more curious to know who his master was. "He did."

"It was you who delivered the package, then?"

"Yes."

"Your name?"

"Çedamihn Ahyanesh'ala."

He nodded as if knowing her full name had incrementally raised her status in his eyes. "Osman was to tell you our purpose here. Did he?"

"To a degree."

A frown appeared on Kadir's refined face. "Tell me what he told you."

"That the package I delivered had been poisoned. That it had been discovered early. That I was not under suspicion."

"The first two I'll grant you. As to the third"—he swept the back of his damask coat as he sat—"let us see what we see."

Çeda bowed her head once more. "Forgive me if I overstep my bounds, *hajib*, but my master informed me that I had come to help you find the one responsible. Was he mistaken?"

Kadir gave her the smallest of smiles, but it seemed genuine. "He said you were direct."

"My mother always told me there's little point in waiting when a hare needs chasing."

"There are times when that's *exactly* what needs to happen, but your mother was wise. So tell me, do you remember much from that day?"

Çeda shrugged noncommittally. "I remember it, but I recall nothing amiss. I came for the box at Osman's estate at nightfall as he'd bid me and, after the moons had set and full night had come, brought it to the drop near Blackfire Gate."

"Did you notice anyone following you?"

"No, or I would have delayed and come the following night."

"Did you notice anything strange in the days before the drop?"

Her mind went immediately to the strange, blue-eyed Kundhuni boy. She remembered where she'd seen him now: at the spice market just before Brama had nicked her purse. She'd seen him again at the river, and then a short while ago at the harbor. How many times had she missed him? Had he been watching her for days? Weeks?

"What is it?" Kadir asked, his dark eyes suddenly sharper.

"It's nothing to do with your package. At least, I don't think it is."

"Just tell me."

"There was a boy. I've seen him several times these past few days."

"He's been following you?"

Çeda shrugged. "I suppose he must be, though I have no idea why. I've never seen him before."

Kadir seemed eminently unfazed by this. "He's a head and a half shorter than I, with closely shorn hair and cinnamon skin and bright blue eyes. And a scar"—he ran his little finger down the left side of his face, neatly bisecting the skin between temple and eye—"just here."

"Yes…But how did you know?"

Kadir pursed his lips, staring down at the desk for a moment, then he took in Çeda anew, his eyes roaming her form, lingering not only on her face, but on her hands as well, which were riddled with small scars from her time in the pits. She balled them into fists and held them by her side, which only seemed to draw *more* notice to her scars. Kadir smiled a patronizing smile. "The boy you saw is from Kundhun, and the poison on the package you delivered was not meant for my mistress, but for Ashwandi, the woman who delivered you to this room."

Ashwandi had been beautiful, but she had also eyed Çeda uncharitably from the moment she'd stepped foot in the estate.

"Why?" Çeda asked.

"My mistress hosts social gatherings, and in these she has had cause to take on protégés. In her wisdom she took on a Kundhuni girl named Kesaea, a princess of the thousand tribes. Years ago Kesaea had come to Sharakhai with her sister, Ashwandi, and here the two of them have remained, vying for my mistress's attentions. When Kesaea left our employ, there was some, shall we say, *acrimony* over the decision."

"She was forced from her lofty position…."

Kadir nodded, granting her the smallest of smiles. "Just so, and as you might have guessed, Ashwandi took her place. You can see how this might cause more than a little bit of strife between siblings, especially one—may my mistress forgive me for saying it—as petulant as Kesaea."

"But to poison her sister?"

Kadir shrugged. "Surely you've heard worse stories in the smoke houses of Sharakhai."

In point of fact, she doubted Kadir would be caught dead in a Sharakhani smoke house. "Yes, but from a princess?"

"Are not those who wield the scepter most likely to strike?"

"I suppose," Çeda said. "What of the boy, though? Why should I still find him following me?"

She left unsaid the fact that the boy had likely been following her for quite some time, a logical conclusion that bothered her greatly, not merely for the fact that she hadn't noticed him before today, but because she hadn't a clue as to the reason behind it. If she was to become the unwitting accomplice to this boy's plans, why follow her at all and give Çeda the chance to become wise to it? And for that matter, how would they even have known that she would be the one to take the shade from Osman that night?

Kadir steepled his fingers. "Now that *does* give me pause. Have you no guesses of your own?"

Çeda shrugged. "None," she said. And then the strangest thing happened. A moth flew into Çeda's field of vision. Where it had come from she had no idea, but it landed on her sleeve and sat there, wings fanning slowly. The top of its wings were the deepest indigo Çeda had ever seen, with a bright orange mark akin to a candle flame.

Çeda was loath to shoo it away, partly from the sheer surprise of it, but more so from the realization that Kadir was staring at it as if it were about to burst into flame and take Çeda with it.

"They're called irindai," Kadir said with an ease that made Çeda's hackles rise. "Some call them cressetwings, and consider what just happened to you a sign of bountiful luck."

"Others call them gallows moths," she replied, "and consider them a sign of imminent death."

"Well," he said, standing and motioning to the way out, "as with so much in the world, surely the truth lies somewhere in between." As Çeda stood, the moth flew away and was lost in the fronds of a potted fern in the corner. "I'll only ask you for one more thing. Keep an eye out for the boy. I would not recommend you approach him—there's no telling how Kesaea might have armed him—but if you discover that he's following you still, return to this estate and inform me."

Çeda might have granted Kadir that if she'd been planning to leave this matter alone, but she refused to allow some Kundhuni child to use her as his plaything. She couldn't tell that to Kadir, though, not leastwise because it might get back to Osman, so she nodded obediently and said, "Very well."

As Kadir joined her at the arched entryway, he held his hands out to her, as if asking her to dance. It was such an odd and unexpected gesture that she complied, lifting her hands for him to take. He did, then considered her with deliberate care. "They say scars have tales to tell, each and every one." He examined not just her hands, but her face, her body, her legs, even her ankles, which somehow made her feel unclothed. "What would yours tell, Çedamihn Ahyanesh'ala?"

"Tales are not told for free in this city, Kadir."

"If it's money you want"—he leaned toward her—"you need but whisper the price."

"The price of their telling is something you cannot afford."

Kadir laughed. "You'd do well not to underestimate the size of my mistress's purse, nor her will to follow a scent once she's gotten wind of it."

"My tales are my own," she said finally.

For a moment, Kadir seemed prepared to press her, but then he raised her hands and bowed his head. "Forgive my boldness. A habit most foul, formed from years of service."

"Think nothing of it," Çeda said, though somehow she doubted he would heed her words. No matter what he said, his eyes were too hungry, too expectant of submission.

Kadir raised his hand high and motioned to Ashwandi, who stood further down the hall. She came and put on a smile, motioning for Çeda to follow her. Her smile vanished, however, when the moth fluttered out from Kadir's office to flitter around the two of them. As they walked toward the entrance to the estate, the moth continued to dog them, and it became clear it was fluttering around Çeda much more than it was Ashwandi, a thing that appeared to please the Kundhunese woman not at all.

———— ◆ ————

THE CLACK FROM THE strike of wooden swords filled the desert air, strangely deadened by the surrounding dunes where Çeda and Djaga, her mentor in the pits, fought. The sun shined off Djaga's dark, sweat-glistened skin. The sand shushed as they glided over it, a strangely calming sound amid the rattle of armor and the thud of their shinai as they engaged then backed away.

Çeda fought with abandon, hoping to impress, pushing herself more than she had in a long while. When Djaga retreated, Çeda closed the gap. When Djaga pressed, Çeda countered as soon as the flurry had ended. When Djaga ran backward, Çeda flew after her. She thought she'd timed her advance perfectly, but just as she was lunging forward, Djaga did too, beating aside her blade and sending a nasty swipe of her shinai over Çeda's thigh.

Çeda, thinking Djaga was going to press her advantage, slid quickly away as the pain blossomed, but instead the tall black woman stopped and stood, chest heaving, her face a sneer of disgust. "You invite me to spar," she said in her thick accent, "and this is what I get? You're not watching *me*."

Çeda opened her mouth to explain, to apologize, but Djaga abruptly turned away and headed for the skiff they'd sailed from Sharakhai's western harbor. Together they stepped over the runners of the sandship to reach the ship's side, at which point Djaga leaned over the gunwales, popped the top of their keg of water, and filled a gourd cup. "You're distracted," Djaga said after downing the cup and running the back of her hand over her mouth. She refilled the cup and held it out to Çeda. "Why?"

There was no sense denying it. She *was* distracted. Çeda took the offered cup and drank down the sun-warmed water.

"Tell me it's a man," Djaga went on, a smile making her full lips go crooked. "Tell me you've decide to take your Emre to bed. He's disappointed you, hasn't he? I knew he would. Haven't I always said it? No man as gorgeous as that knows his the way to the promised land."

Çeda laughed. She shared a home with Emre, and he meant much to her, but not *that*—they'd probably never be *that*—yet it never stopped Djaga from digging her elbow into Çeda's ribs every chance she got.

"Come, come. What's there to think about? He's a pretty boy… You're a pretty girl…."

"Well, if you must know," Çeda said, desperate to move the conversation beyond these particular grounds, "it *is* about a boy."

"A boy…"

"A Kundhunese boy."

"Well, well, well...A *Kundhunese* boy..." Djaga laughed, then bowed and flourished her arms to the desert around them. "Then know this, oh Çeda the White Wolf. The desert is wide enough to hold your secrets. Tell us both your tale if you're bold enough."

Where to begin? In the days that had followed her meeting with Kadir, she would swear by her mother's own blood that she'd seen the blue-eyed boy a half-dozen times, but always from the corner of her eye, and when she looked with a keener gaze, she found someone or some*thing* else entirely—boys or even girls with similarly dark skin, lighter-skinned boys wearing dark clothes, even the simple swaying of shadows beneath the odd acacia tree. Once she'd even spotted him in the ceaseless flow of traffic along the Trough, but when she'd caught up to him and spun him around, it had been a Sharakani boy with closely shorn hair who looked nothing like the bright-eyed Kundhuni. The mother had shoved Çeda away, and Çeda had retreated under the angry glares of those standing nearby, wondering what was happening to her.

She'd spent the next few days wallowing in confusion and fear while a small voice whispered from the corners of her mind—*you're going mad, mad, mad, you're going mad*. A fury born from her own helplessness grew hotter by the day, but what good was fury when there was nothing to direct it against? She needed a change. If the winds were blowing across one's bow, one didn't simply stay the course. One turned and tacked until the safety of port was reached once more.

And who better to help steer this strange ship than Djaga? So much of this tale seemed to be wrapped up in the people of Kundhun, their customs, their norms, and Djaga was Kundhunese. She might see any number of things Çeda was blind to. So she told Djaga her tale. She spoke of the shade, of Osman's confession after, of her visit with Kadir. She spent a long while describing the strange blue-eyed boy with the cinnamon skin, hoping Djaga would somehow know him, but there was no glimmer of recognition in her eyes.

When she was done, she asked Djaga, "Have you heard of her, this princess Kesaea?"

"No," Djaga replied, "but you know what we say in the backlands. If you stand our princesses shoulder to shoulder with our princes, they will drown the land like blades of grass."

It was true. There were as many kings and queens as there were hills in Kundhun, or so it seemed. "It was so strange," Çeda went on. "When I left, a moth followed me."

Djaga smiled her broad smile. "Good luck be upon you."

But Çeda shrugged. "So they say, but it was a gallows moth."

"An irindai? A cressetwing?"

"Yes. Why are you making that face?"

"Who did you say is this Kadir's mistress?"

"I don't know her name."

Djaga's expression pinched from one of confusion to outright worry. "There's a woman who hides in the shadows of the lords of Sharakhai. A drug lord named Rümayesh. Have you heard the name?"

"I've heard it," Çeda lied.

"I can tell you don't know enough, girl. Not nearly enough. Those who enter her house pay fistfuls of rahl to do so—not the silver of the southern quarter, mind you, nor the coppers of the west end, but *gold*. Her clientele is exclusive. The lords and ladies of Goldenhill, those of noble blood, rich merchants and caravan masters that paid their way into Rümayesh's good graces, and in return she feeds them dreams, dreams she summons and all share in. Dreams taken from the souls that Rümayesh herself selects."

"Why did you think of Rümayesh?"

Djaga's face was staring out at the sand, her eyes distant, but now she pulled her gaze away and stared down at Çeda. "Because she uses irindai, Çeda."

Someone, somewhere danced over Çeda's grave. "How can you know?"

"There was one in the pits, the one who taught me, as I teach you. Her name was Meliz, and one day she disappeared. For weeks we searched for her. She was found at the bottom of a dry well two months later, still alive, the crushed body of a cressetwing stuffed inside her mouth. We nursed her back to health, but she was never the same. Her mind was gone. She remembered nothing—not why she'd been taken, nor who had taken her. She couldn't even remember who she was, not much of it, anyway. It had all been taken from her. She did whisper a name, though, over and over."

"Rümayesh."

"Just so. She took her own life two months later"—Djaga drew her thumb across her neck—"a crimson smile, drawn with her favorite sword." She looked Çeda up and down, as if she were in danger even here in the desert. "You say he's left you alone, this Kadir?"

"As near as I can tell."

"Then make no mistake, girl, the gods of the desert have shined upon you!" Djaga took the gourd cup from Çeda and set it onto the keg. In unspoken agreement, they strode away from the skiff and began loosening their limbs. "Watch yourself in the coming days, and when we return to Sharakhai, go to Bakhi's temple. Give him a kind word and show him a bit of silver, or gold if you can manage, lest he take it all back."

Çeda had no intention of doing so—she didn't believe in filling the coffers of the temples any more than she believed in giving the

Kings of Sharakhai their due respect—but she nodded just the same.

"Now come!" Djaga brought her blade quickly down across Çeda's defenses, a swing Çeda beat aside easily. "You've a bout in two weeks." She swung again, and again Çeda blocked it, backing up this time. "People know we spar with one another, girl." A third strike came, a thing Djaga put her entire body into, but Çeda skipped back, avoiding the blow. "I'll not have it said the White Wolf is some poor imitation of the Lion of Kundhun!"

Çeda retreated and bowed, arms and shinai swept back while her eyes were fixed on Djaga. "Very well," she said, and leapt in for more.

⎯⎯⎯•⎯⎯⎯

THE DAYS PASSED QUICKLY after that.

Çeda saw the boy again—several times, in fact, and now she was sure it was him. Once, she was sure she'd caught him in the Well, the quarter of the city that held Osman's pits. She chased after him, yelling for him to stop, and when she'd turned the corner, her hand nearly upon him, she found the alley ahead empty. He'd disappeared. At a whistle, she'd looked up and found the boy staring down at her with a wide smile. And then he was off, leaving an awkward knot inside her she couldn't untie, a knot composed of anger and impotence and foolishness.

He must be a warlock, she decided—it ran thick in some areas of Kundhun—and now for some reason he was toying with her. She vowed to find him, but for the life of her she had no idea how she would manage it. Every time she tried to lie in wait, she ended up spending hours with nothing to show for it.

She lost herself in preparations for her upcoming bout instead— running in the mornings, sparring in the afternoons, lifting Djaga's stone weights beneath the pier in the western harbor in the evenings. Osman had told her she'd have no shading work until after her day in the pits, a thing that had bothered her at first, but given that there was nothing she could do about it she threw herself into her training with an abandon she hadn't felt in months.

Djaga noticed, and even allowed a grudging nod once or twice for how focused Çeda's technique had become. "Good, girl. Good," she had said. "Now keep your rage bottled up. Release it in the pits, not before. It's not so hard as you might think."

Çeda thought she understood, but as the day for her bout approached, she found herself becoming more and more nervous. It wasn't because of her opponent—some Mirean swordmaster who'd had some success in Sharakhai's pits before. It was because she couldn't shake the feeling that she was being watched, that something was about to happen.

And it wasn't from the Kundhunese boy this time. She kept seeing men or women watching her. When she looked, however, they seemed to be doing completely innocent things, apparently oblivious to her presence. The experience so unnerved her that, despite her plans in the desert, she took Djaga's advice and went to Bakhi's temple and dropped three golden coins into the alms basket at the foot of Bakhi's altar. She thought to speak with the priestess, but she looked down at Çeda's kneeling form so uncharitably that Çeda just stood and left the temple.

It was all in her mind, she decided. Her mind and her worries were conspiring to play tricks on her. Yet slowly, the strange calmness she'd shown with Djaga began to slip as the day of the bout approached.

"Enough," Djaga said two days before the match. "We've practiced enough. Too much, in fact. There are times when you can overtrain, and I think I've done it with you, girl. Take this time before your match. Stay away from the pits, think of anything but fighting, and you'll return to the pits a new woman."

"And if I don't?"

"Then you'll be no worse off than you are now. You're in your mind too much. Go to your Emre. Fuck him like you should have done long ago. Or take another to your bed. But for the love of the gods, let your sword lay untouched."

Near dusk that evening, as Çeda wended her way through the tents of the bazaars, waving to those who had stuck throughout the dinner hours hoping to catch a final few patrons, she felt someone watching her: a woman who Çeda could tell was thin and lithe, but little more than this, for her head was hidden in a deep cowl, her hands within the long, flowing sleeves. Çeda had no idea who the woman might be, but she wasn't about to lead her toward the home she shared with Emre.

She kept her pace, moving along a narrow street that would head down toward the slums of the Shallows, and when she came to the next corner and turned, she ducked into an elaborate stone archway, the entrance to a boneyard that looked as though it had stood longer than Sharakhai itself.

She glanced over the yard for the telltale glow of wights or wailers—one didn't treat boneyards lightly in the desert—then peered out through the arch from behind a stone pillar marking one of the graves. She saw the form soon enough, a shadow in the deeper darkness. The woman slowed, perhaps realizing she'd lost her quarry. She pulled her cowl off her head and turned this way, then that, then continued down the street.

Çeda hadn't seen her clearly, but she knew it was Ashwandi, the woman who'd led her to speak with Kadir, who'd led her out of the estate when they were done. What by Tulathan's bright eyes would she be doing chasing Çeda through the streets? And why was she doing it so clumsily?

Çeda drew the knife from her belt and followed, padding carefully in time with Ashwandi's footsteps but with broader strides, until she was right behind her. Ashwandi turned, eyes wide as she raised her hands to fend Çeda off, but she was too late. In a blink Çeda had slipped her arm around Ashwandi's neck and pressed the tip of her knife into her back—not enough to draw blood, but certainly enough to make Ashwandi intimately familiar with just how sharp Çeda's blades were kept.

"You might get away with such things east of the Trough," Çeda whispered, "but not here." She pressed the knife deeper, enough to pierce skin, drawing a gasp from Ashwandi. "Here, women like you are as likely to end up on the banks of the Haddah staring sightless into a star-filled sky as they are to make it home again."

"I'm not the one you should be worried about," she rasped.

"No?" Çeda asked, easing her hold on Ashwandi's throat. "Who, then? Your mistress, Rümayesh?"

"I am no *servant* of Rümayesh! I am her love, and she is mine." Her Kundhunese accent was noticeable, but more like a fine bottle of citrus wine than the harsh, home-brewed araq of Djaga's accent.

"She wants me, doesn't she? That's why I'm being followed."

"You begin to understand, yes? But I tell you, you have no idea the sort of trouble you're in."

Çeda shoved Ashwandi away. It was then that Çeda realized that a bandage was wrapped tightly around her left hand. With a pace that spoke of self-consciousness, or even embarrassment, she used her good hand to tug her sleeve back over her bandaged hand, then pulled her cowl back into place. Only when her face was hidden within its depths did she speak once more. "Do you know who Rümayesh is? She has *seen* you, girl. She is *intrigued*…And nothing will draw her attention away now, not until she tires of you."

Çeda felt suddenly exposed and foolish, a fly caught in a very intricate web. "What would she want of *me*?"

"You're a tasty little treat, I'll give you that. She's taken by this girl who shades at night but fights in the pits by light of day." Even in the dying light, Çeda was sure Ashwandi caught her surprised expression. "Yes, she knows of your *other* pursuits with Osman, and now she's taken by the pretty thing that came to her estate, by the White Wolf who sank her fangs into the Malasani brute."

This implied much…That Rümayesh likely knew of Çeda's time with Djaga, her training for her coming bout, her time in the pits, perhaps. Çeda didn't merely feel off-balance; she felt like the world had been tipped upside down, and now the city was crashing down around her. "I came to Kadir to speak of a *package*. That was all."

"You've been set up, girl, as have I."

Çeda closed the distance between them with one long stride. "Make some bloody sense before I rethink how very nice I've been treating you."

"Kadir told you of my sister, Kesaea. For years *she* held the favored position at Rümayesh's side, longer than any other, if the stories I've heard are true. But Rümayesh grew bored of her, as I knew she would, and *I* stepped into her place." Ashwandi shrugged. "Kesaea was angry. With Rümayesh, with me. But after a week of her typical petulance, she returned home to Kundhun, and I hoped that would be the end of it."

"But it wasn't, was it? *She* sent the boy."

"Boys. There are two of them. Twins. And she didn't *send* them. She *summoned* them. Our mother has the blood of witches running through her veins, and Kesaea inherited much of it. Their names are Hidi and Makuo. Hidi is the angry one. He has a scar running down his cheek, a remnant of the one and only time he disobeyed his father, the trickster god, Onondu, our god of vengeance in the savannah lands."

By the desert's endless sand, *twins*…And born of a trickster god. It explained, perhaps, why she'd been unable to do any more than see them from the corner of her eye. They'd been toying with her all along. "But why?" Çeda asked. "What would those boys want with me?"

Ashwandi looked at her as if she were daft. "Don't you see? They were sent by my sister to harm *me*. They've been sent to find a way for me to fall from grace, and in you, they've found it, for if Rümayesh becomes entranced with you…"

"She'll what, forget about you?"

Ashwandi shrugged. "It is her way. There isn't room in her life for more than one obsession."

"You wish to be that? An obsession?"

"You don't know what it's like…It's wondrous when she turns her attention to you, if you don't fight it, that is. To be without it…"

Çeda's head was swimming. "Tell Rümayesh what your sister has done! Surely she'll see that she's being manipulated."

"I have"—Ashwandi turned, as if worried someone was watching—"but it isn't Rümayesh that's being manipulated. It's us. All of us. You, me, Kesaea, even Onondu, which surely pleases her to no end. Don't you see, girl? Rümayesh *enjoys* this, seeing us squabble and fight."

"She acts like a god herself."

Even from within the cowl, Çeda could see Ashwandi's eyes growing intense, and when she spoke once more, her words were very, very soft. "You aren't far from the mark, but there's something you might do."

"Out with it, then."

"The boys, Hidi and Makuo. I know how to bind them."

"And how might you do that?"

The tall Kundhunese woman reached into her robes. "I've already done it." She held out a small fabric pouch for Çeda to take. "Search for them. And when you are near, use this to send them home."

Çeda stared down at the pouch. "What is it?"

Her only response was to take Çeda's hand in hers—the bandaged one—and forcibly press it into her palm.

Staring at the bloody bandages around her left hand, Çeda had a guess as to what was inside. "Why don't *you* do it?"

"Because they're not here for me. They're here for Rümayesh, and now you, and they will avoid me when they can, for the blood of my mother runs through my veins as well." She nodded toward the pouch. "Onondu will listen to this, and so will Hidi and Makuo."

Çeda had heard how cruel the gods of the savannah were. They demanded much for their favors. Blood. Fingers. Limbs. Sometimes the lives of loved ones. How desperate Ashwandi must be to do such a thing just to remain by Rümayesh's side...

No, Çeda realized. This was no fault of Ashwandi, nor even Kesaea, but rather the one they both longed for. How strong the lure of Rümayesh to make them both do this, for surely Kesaea had gone through a similar ritual on her return to Kundhun.

Rümayesh had cast a spell that had utterly bewitched them both, these princesses of Kundhun.

Çeda stuffed the pouch, heavy as a lodestone, into the larger leather bag on her belt. "What do I do?"

"Wear it in their presence. They will listen to you, and they will grant you one favor."

"A *favor*? What am I to do with that? Can I ask them to simply leave?"

"Perhaps, but that would be unwise. They must be turned to Rümayesh now, to make her forget about you. I fear that is the only way for you to survive this."

"And for you to return to her good graces…"

Ashwandi shrugged. "We want what we want, and I've given up much for that to happen." She began stepping away, her eyes still on Çeda. "The twins are drawn to water. You'll find them along the Haddah, often at dusk or dawn."

And then she turned and was gone, swallowed by the growing darkness over Sharakhai.

———————◆———————

WITH THE EASTERN SKY a burnished bronze and the stars still shining in the west, Çeda pulled the black veil across her face and crept along the edge of the Haddah, watching carefully for signs of movement along the riverbank. She had arrived hours ago, hoping to catch the godling twins either in the night or as the sun rose. She still hadn't found them, and soon the city would be waking from its slumber. She didn't wish to be skulking along the river when it did, but the desire to find them was palpable as a canker, and every bit as maddening.

The talk with Ashwandi had so shaken Çeda she hadn't gone home last night, preferring to sleep in a hammock at the rear of Ibrahim the storyteller's tiny mudbrick home. She'd unwrapped the rolled bandage and found Ashwandi's severed finger resting there with a leather cord running through it like some depraved version of thread and needle. She'd held it up to the starry sky, looked at it beneath the light of the moons, Rhia and Tulathan, wondering if she would feel the magic bound to it, or through it that of the twin boys. She'd felt nothing, though, and after a time she'd slipped the cord over her neck and worn the finger like a talisman, which was surely what Ashwandi had meant for her to do.

It rested between her breasts, a thing she was all too conscious of, especially when she walked. It tickled her skin like the unwelcome touch of a man, and she longed to be rid of it, but she couldn't, she knew. Not until this was all over.

She parted the reeds and padded further down the Haddah. She passed beneath a stone bridge, looking carefully along its underside, which the boys might use to hide, but when she found nothing she moved on, heading deeper into the city.

Above her, beyond the banks, a donkey brayed. A woman shouted at it, and the sounds of a millstone came alive, dwindling and then replaced by burble of the river and the rattle of stones as Çeda trekked onward. The sky brightened further. Carts clattered over bridges. Laborers trudged along, lunches bundled in cloth. A boy and a girl, both with wild, kinky hair, headed down to the banks of the Haddah with nets in hand. She even saw one of the rare Qaimiri trading ships rowing toward a pier, her lateen sails up, catching a favorable wind.

But of the twins she saw no sign.

She was just about ready to give up when she saw movement near an old acacia. Half the branches were dead, and the thing looked as though it were about to tip over and fall in the water at any moment. But in the branches still choked with leaves she could see two legs hanging down, swinging back and forth. The skin was the same dark color she remembered, and when she looked harder, she saw movement in the branches above—the second twin, surely, sitting higher than the first.

She took to the damp earth along the edge of the bank to silence her footsteps, then pulled her *kenshar* from its sheath at her belt, whispering a prayer to fickle Bakhi as she did so. Reaching past her mother's silver chain and locket, she slipped Ashwandi's severed finger from around her neck, whipping the leather cord around her hand with one quick snap of her wrist.

She stood twenty paces away now.

As she approached the godling boys, she wondered how vengeful the god Onondu might be. She hoped it wouldn't come to bloodshed, but she'd promised herself that if they wouldn't listen to her commands, she would do whatever she needed to protect herself, even if it meant killing his children. Her identity was her most closely guarded secret, after all—no different than a chest of golden rahl, a chest these boys had tipped over with their mischief, spilling its treasure over the dirt for Rümayesh and Ashwandi and perhaps all of Sharakhai to see.

Ten paces away.

Then five.

The nearest twin faced away from her, looking downriver to the trading ship, which was just mooring, men and women busying themselves about the deck, a few jumping to the pier. She'd grab him first, drag him down and put her knife to his throat, then she'd grip the finger tightly and speak her wish. The moment she took a step forward, though, something snapped beneath her foot.

She glanced down. Gods, a dried branch off the acacia. How could she have missed it?

When she looked up once more, Hidi, the one with the scar, was turned on the branch, looking straight at her with those piercing blue eyes. In a flash he dropped and sprinted up the bank.

Çeda ran after him and was nearly on him, hand outstretched, ready to grab a fistful of his ivory-colored tunic, when something fell on her from behind. She collapsed and rolled instinctively away, coming to a stand with her *kenshar* at the ready, but by the time she did both of the boys were bounding away like a brace of desert hare.

She was up and chasing after them in a flash. "Release me!" she called, gripping Ashwandi's finger tightly. "Do you hear me? I command you to release me!"

But they didn't listen, and soon they were leading a chase into the tight streets of the Knot, a veritable maze of mudbrick that had been built, and then built *upon* so that walkways and homes stretched out and over the street, making Çeda feel all the more watched as men and women and boys stared from the doorways and windows and balconies of their homes.

Çeda sprinted through the streets, wending this way, then that, coming ever closer to reaching the boys. She reached for the nearest of them—her hands even brushed his shoulder—but just then a rangy cat with eyes the very same color of blue as the boys came running out from behind a pile of overturned crates and tripped her. She fell hard onto the dirt as the boys ahead giggled.

She got up again, her shoulders aching in pain, and followed them down the alley they'd sprinted into. When she reached the mouth of the alley, however, she found not a pair of twin boys, but a strikingly beautiful woman wearing a jeweled *abaya* with thread-of-gold embroidery along cuff and collar and hem. She looked every bit as surprised as Çeda—almost as if she too had been following someone through the back-tracked ways of the Knot.

"Could it be?" the woman asked, her voice biting as the desert wind. "The little wren I've been chasing these many weeks?"

Çeda had never seen this woman before—tall, elegant, the air of the aristocracy floating about her like a halo—but her identity could be no clearer than if she'd stated her name from the start.

"I'm no one," she said to Rümayesh.

"Ah, but you are, sweet one." From the billowing sleeve of her right arm a sling dropped into her hand. In a flash she had it spinning over her head, the sound of its blurred passage mingling with Rümayesh's next words. "You certainly are."

Then she released the stone.

Or Çeda *thought* it was a stone.

It flew like a spear for Çeda's chest, and when it struck, a blue powder burst into the cool morning air. She tried not to breathe it, but she'd been startled and took in a lungful of the tainted air. As she spun away its scent and taste invaded her senses—fresh figs mixed with something acrid, like lemons going to rot.

Çeda turned to run, but she'd not gone five strides before the ground tilted up and struck her like a maul. The world swam in her eyes as she managed with great effort to roll over. Blinking to clear her eyes of their sudden tears, she stared up at the blue sky peeking between the shoulders of the encroaching mudbrick homes. In the windows, old women and a smattering of children watched, but when they recognized the woman approaching Çeda, they ducked their heads back inside and shuttered their windows.

Çeda's *kenshar* was gone, fallen in the dusty street two paces away, though it might as well have been two leagues for all her leaden limbs would listen to her. She'd somehow managed to keep Ashwandi's finger, though; its leather cord had surely prevented it from flying away like her knife. Her throat convulsed. Her tongue was numb, but she chanted while gripping the finger as tightly as her rapidly weakening muscles would allow. "Release me, Hidi… Release me, Makuo…release me, Onondu…"

The only answer she received was the vision of the beautiful woman coming to stand over her, staring down with bright eyes and a wicked demon grin.

———◆———

ÇEDA WOKE STARING AT the ceiling of a dimly lit room.

She was lying on something cold and hard. She tried to sit up, tried to *move* but was unable to. Her legs felt as though the entire world were sitting atop them. Her arms were little better. Even her eyes moved with a strange listlessness, brought on, no doubt, by the powder that had erupted when the sling stone had struck.

The light in the room flickered strangely.

No.

The ceiling itself…

It was covered in some strange cloth, undulating like the fur-covered skin of some curious beast.

No.

Not cloth…

Wings. By the gods who breathe, they were *wings.*

She was lying in a room, and above her, covering the ceiling as far as the lamplight revealed, moths blanketed its surface, their wings folding slowly in and out, flashing their bright cresset flames over and over and over. They did so in concert such that waves appeared to roll across their surface, as if they were not thousands upon thousands of individuals at all, but a collective that together formed some larger, unknowable consciousness. She couldn't take her eyes from them, so hypnotic were they, not even when she heard footsteps approaching, the sound of it strangely deadened.

It was cool here. And humid. She was underground, then, in a cellar, perhaps, or one of the many caverns that could be found beneath the surface of Sharakhai.

The footsteps came nearer. "Do you like them?"

Rümayesh…

Soon the tall woman was standing over Çeda, staring down with an expression not so different from what a caring mother might share with her sick daughter. The urge to reject the very notion that this woman held any similarities whatsoever to Çeda's mother manifested in a lifting of Çeda's arm in an attempt to slap the look away. Her right arm shifted, but no more than this, leaving

Çeda to fume as Rümayesh reached down and brushed Çeda's hair from her forehead.

"They're wondrous things," she said, looking up to the ceiling, to the walls around them, every surface awash in a landscape of slowly beating wings. "Do you know what they do?"

Çeda tried to respond, but her mouth and tongue felt thick and rigid, like hardening clay.

Rümayesh went on, apparently unfazed by Çeda's silence. "They are taken by the mouth, eaten, in a manner of speaking, but when one does, she is changed, drawn into the whole of the irindai, drawn into a dream of their, and your, making. Some think they're connected, all of them, anywhere in the world, like threads in a grand weave, though I doubt it goes so far as that. These, though... My lovely brood..." She stopped near the wall and stretched out her forefinger until one of the moths crawled upon it, then walked slowly across the room until she was standing once more at Çeda's side. "*They* are certainly aware of one another, as you will soon see."

"Wuh..." Çeda tried forming words. "Wuh...Wuh..."

Rümayesh stared at the moth as if she hadn't heard Çeda's graceless attempts at speech. "The effects of the powder will wear off in time, certainly soon enough for you to select the irindai you wish to consume"—she flicked her hand and the moth took wing, fluttering in the air for a moment, circling her, then flying back and returning to the very same location it had roosted before crawling onto Rümayesh's outstretched finger—"though if experience has taught me anything, it's the irindai that choose *you*, not the other way around.

"Relax, now. The ritual will start soon. I'd ask that you choose a memory for us to share. My patrons wait years to partake of someone as captivating as you, so choose well. Make the memory dear. I wouldn't want them to leave disappointed." She strode away, heading for the arched entrance to the room. "And I hope you're not thinking of denying me this small request. If you refuse, I'll simply find one on my own, but it's less special for my patrons when I do. The memory is dimmed. More importantly to you, the experience will, I'm afraid, leave your mind ravaged, possibly beyond repair."

When she reached the archway, she stopped and turned until she was staring sidelong at Çeda. "Perhaps the tale of the White Wolf's first fight in the pits. Yes, I think that would please them a great deal. There will be plenty of time for the rest in the coming weeks."

Dear gods, it was true then. It was all true. Rümayesh was going to force her to take one of these moths and relive her past. Like a dream, except her *patrons* would dream them as well. How many? A dozen? Two dozen? They'd witness her trips out to the blooming fields to harvest adichara petals. They'd see how she dried them and used them in service of Osman's shades or her own needs. Either was a high crime in Sharakhai, punishable by death.

But that wasn't the worst part.

She didn't wish to die, but she was horrified by the thought of someone forcibly taking her memories from her. By Tulathan's bright eyes, would she still have them when they were done with her? Or would they rob her memories and leave her some useless husk like Djaga's mentor, Meliz? Would she go to the farther fields not knowing her mother? She couldn't bear it. She'd lost her mother eight years ago, but at least she still had her *memories* of her. At least she'd *know* her when they were reunited in the world beyond.

As a door somewhere boomed shut, she commanded her muscles to move. She felt her legs shift, her arms twitch, but they would do no more than this. She tried over and over and over again, and soon it was bringing on a dull pain that grew with each attempt.

She saw movement to her right and managed to loll her head

in that direction. Gods, a *mound* of irindai were rising, pulling away from their brethren. It was vaguely man-shaped, she realized.

Or *boy*-shaped.

As the form came forth, the moths began fluttering away, returning to their previous positions, and a second form began to emerge. Whole flocks of moths peeled away, revealing two boys with dark skin and bright blue eyes, and one of them, Hidi, with his terrible scar running down his cheek.

Hidi glanced to the archway where Rümayesh had recently went. Makuo came straight for Çeda, a gentle smile on his lips. "You are here," he said in a Kundhunese accent so thick Çeda could barely understand him.

"Yuh…" Çeda licked her lips and tried again. "You wuh-wanted me here…"

Hidi came and stood next to Makuo. "Yes, and now you come."

"Buh…But I commanded you. Ashwandi…"

"Yes," said Makuo, "and we are bound. We listened."

"I s-said to release me."

Hidi tilted his head, as if speaking to a child. "And we will obey. We will give you the keys."

"What do you mean?"

"You must release yourself," said Hidi in a sharp tone. "Rümayesh is not so easy to move as that."

"H-how?"

Hidi ignored her, choosing to step around the perimeter of the cellar, while Makuo reached into Çeda's black *thawb* and pulled out her mother's locket.

"Luh-leave that alone!"

"Calm yourself, girl." He pried it open, revealing the two petals Çeda had placed inside. She'd normally have nothing inside, or perhaps one if she was expecting trouble, but she'd started carrying two for the fear that was constantly running through her.

Makuo took them, then whistled two sharp notes. A flurry of cressetwings descended from the ceiling, one of them alighting on Makuo's outstretched finger, the rest continuing to fly around and above his head. With care, Makuo set the two petals onto the wings of the moth. The petals remained there, as if they'd been a part of the moth from the moment it crawled from its chrysalis. Makuo whistled again, and the moth on his finger flew to join her sistren.

Bit by bit, the swarm retook their positions, but in doing so Çeda completely lost the one with the petals. She searched frantically, but couldn't find it. "Where is it?"

At this they both smiled and spoke in unison, "And what fun would we have by giving you that?" They glanced to the archway, and Hidi began backing away. Moths flew toward him, landing on him, layering his form as if consuming him.

Makuo touched his hand to Çeda's cheek. "Look to the flames," he said while backing away. "Look to the flames and you'll find it." Soon both of them had been consumed by the irindai.

And all was still.

She could hear her own heartbeat, so complete was the silence.

She looked among the irindai, one to the next to the next, trying to find the one to which Makuo had fixed the petals, but it was so bloody dim she couldn't tell if one merely had a bright mark of flame or if it was indeed the one she needed.

While she searched, she worked her muscles—her legs, her arms, her neck, her torso. It was slow in the coming, but she managed to bend her limbs, to regain some sense of normal movement, even if it was slow, even if it felt as though her muscles were made of bright, molten metal.

Just when she was ready to sit up, she heard the door opening, and this time many sets of footsteps approached. Kadir came first, but others followed, men and women dressed in white thawbs or full-length kaftans, and with them came the reek of the sort of tabbaq that would make one high. Some wore *niqabs* or veiled turbans to hide their faces, but most were unadorned, and came holding flutes of golden wine in their hands or stubby glasses filled with araq. Others still held nothing at all, preferring to cross their arms or hold them behind their backs as they stared at the irindai or Rümayesh or Çeda.

In her desperation, Çeda tried to lift herself from the cold slab upon which she lay, but before she could do more than curl her head and shoulders off the slab, Kadir came rushing to her side and pressed her back down. Those gathered watched with jackal eyes, hyena grins, as Kadir leaned in. "Stay where you are until spoken to," he whispered, "and perhaps you'll leave this place whole." Unlike Rümayesh, who was soft velvet, a knife in the dark, Kadir was a cold, bloody hammer, every bit as blunt and every bit as deadly.

She grit her jaw and stared up, not wanting to give Kadir the satisfaction of seeing the fear in her eyes, and that was when she noticed it. Makuo's irindai, slowly fanning its wings almost directly overhead. How could she have missed it earlier? Now that she *had* seen it, though, it was like a bloody great beacon. A fire on the horizon.

With care, praying Kadir wouldn't notice, she averted her gaze and lay still. Kadir did glance up, but then retreated to one corner of the room. From a pedestal he picked up a heavy bronze cymbal and a leather-wrapped rod of the same metal. He ran the rod around the edge of the cymbal, creating a strangely hypnotic sound. The irindai responded immediately, their wings moving at a slower pace in time to the rhythm of the cymbal.

"The festivities are over," Rümayesh said. "I trust you'll enjoy what I've found for you, a rare little bird indeed. A Sharakhani through and through, with mystery upon mystery we can unravel together. Please"—she motioned around her to the walls, to the low ceiling—"choose, and our young maid will follow."

Those gathered began walking about the room, looking up to the ceiling, plucking a single moth from the writhing mass. Çeda tried as well as she could not to stare at the moth with the adichara petals, but she was so worried that someone would take it that she found her eyes flicking there every so often. One of the women noticed. Eyes glazed, she stared up at the ceiling where Çeda's gaze had wandered. Her hand wavered near Çeda's cressetwing, but the gods must have been watching over Çeda, for the woman chose another less than a hand's-breadth away.

One by one, those gathered opened their mouths and placed the moth within, taking great care to prevent harm to the delicate wings. Without exception, their eyes flickered closed as soon as the irindai was taken within them. Their lids opened and closed like the wings of the irindai, then they stood still, watching Çeda or Rümayesh or one another in a half-lidded daze.

Rümayesh strode to Çeda's side.

"Choose," was all she said.

Çeda stared defiantly, as if she were conflicted, as if she might very well do something desperate at any moment. She would take the cressetwing the boys meant for her but, when she did so, she wanted Rümayesh's eyes on *her* and nowhere else. With care, Çeda stood. She felt strangely alone with Rümayesh, even with so many of those gathered staring dazedly at the two of them. With as much speed as she could manage, she grabbed the cressetwing with the petals and stuffed it into her mouth.

She had planned to chew it immediately, to devour it, but the moment the moth's delicate wings touched her tongue, a rush of euphoria welled up from somewhere deep inside. It brought with it a rush of thoughts and memories, all flickering like the surface of a sun-dappled river.

Her mother raising her wooden shinai in the air, waiting for Çeda to do the same.

Running through the dusty streets of Sharakhai with Emre, each with a mound of stolen pistachios cradled in their arms, shells dripping like rain as they sprint along.

Peeking through the parted blankets of a stall in the spice market late at night as Havasham, the handsome son of Athel the carpetmonger, thrusts himself over and over between the legs of Lina, a girl three years Çeda's elder who is not beautiful but has a way of talking with the boys with that sharp tongue of hers that makes them want her.

Çeda felt her consciousness attempt to expand to encompass all of who she was, all she'd experienced. She wondered, even while her mind raged, whether everyone experienced this same thing or if it was to do with the petals she'd also consumed. She could feel it now—the verve the petals granted her, the strength, the awareness.

Through the irindai she could feel others' minds as well: those closest, their eagerness to feel more from Çeda; those beyond, who had done this many times before but hungered for more; and Rümayesh, who was someone different altogether.

Where Rümayesh stood, there were two, not one.

Two minds, sharing the same body. One, a lady of Sharakhai, highborn, a woman who'd lived in her estate in Goldenhill her entire life.

And the other…

A chill rushed down Çeda's frame even as more of the memories jumbled past.

The other was something else. Something Çeda had never seen or experienced before. How could she have? This mind was deep, foreign, and by the gods *old*—not in the way Ibrahim the storyteller was old, nor even in the way the Kings of Sharakhai, who'd seen the passage of centuries four, were old, but in the way the city was old. In the way the desert was old.

This was no human, but some creature of the desert, some vestige of the desert's making, or one of the *ehrekh* that haunted the forgotten corners of the Great Shangazi.

Çeda knew immediately that few others had ever felt this being's presence, for it now awoke in a way it hadn't been moments ago. It grew fearful, if only for the span of a heartbeat, and in the wake of that realization, Rümayesh—or the woman Çeda had *thought* was Rümayesh—strode forward and placed her hand around Çeda's neck, gripping it tightly enough to limit Çeda's breath. She leaned down and stared into Çeda's eyes, imposing her will, sifting through Çeda's memories.

Çeda couldn't allow this.

She couldn't allow Rümayesh to have her way. Çeda would be lost if she did.

This was the gift of the adichara petals that Hidi and Makuo had granted her—the ability to remain above the effects of the irindai, at least to some small degree.

But what to do about Rümayesh?

As more memories were examined, then tossed aside like uncut jewels, Çeda thought desperately for something that might divide these two, something that might give the highborn woman a reason to throw off the chains Rümayesh had placed on her.

She found it moments later. A memory flashed past—of stepping into the blooming fields to cut one of the adichara flowers. It was discarded immediately by Rümayesh, but the woman huddling beneath that greater consciousness, a highborn woman of Sharakhai, flared in anger and indignation. Rümayesh tried to settle on Çeda's first fight in the pits, but Çeda drew her mind back to the twisted trees that grew in a vast ring outside the city's limits. Had Çeda not had the effects of the adichara running through her, she would surely have succumbed to the onslaught Rümayesh was throwing against her defenses, but with the petals she was able to focus on that memory, to share it with all those gathered within the cellar.

She pads along the sand as the twin moons shine brightly above. The adichara's thorned branches sway, limned in moonlight. They click and clack and creak, a symphony of movement in the otherwise still air. Çeda looks among the blooms, which glow softly in the moonlight, a river of stars over an endless sea. She chooses not the widest, nor the brightest, but the bloom that seems to be facing the moons unshrinkingly, then cuts it with a swift stroke of her kenshar, tucking it away in a pouch at her belt.

Çeda had expected anger from the woman Rümayesh controlled. What she hadn't expected was anger from all the others as well. She should have, though. Nearly everyone gathered here would have the blood of Kings running through their veins; they would know every bit as well as Çeda the sort of crime they were witnessing. A woman stealing into the blooming fields to take of the adichara insulted not only the Kings, but all who revered the twisted trees.

They began to mumble and murmur, more and more of their number waking from the dream they shared. At first they stepped forward like boneyard shamblers, but with every moment that passed they seemed to come more alive.

Behind them, the highborn woman Rümayesh controlled railed against her bonds. She was more angry, more aware of herself, than she'd been in years, but she was buoyed by the anger of those around her. Rümayesh's will was still strong, however. She held against the assault, the two of them at a stalemate. Soon, though, the woman's anger would ebb. Soon Rümayesh would regain the control she'd had over this woman for so long.

Çeda had lost track of those around her. She realized with a start that one of the men was holding a *kenshar*. A woman on Çeda's opposite side drew a slim knife of her own. A remnant of Çeda's earlier lethargy still remained, but fear now drove her. She rolled backward, coming to a crouch, waiting for any to approach.

A moment later the man did, the woman right after, but they both gave clumsy swipes of their blades. Çeda leapt over the man, snaking her arm around his neck as she went. She landed and levered him so that he tipped backward, then controlled him, moving him slowly toward the door.

He tried to use his knife to strike at her arm, but she was ready. She released his neck at the last moment and snatched the wrist holding the knife with one hand, closed her other hand around his closed fist, the one wrapped around the weapon. Then she drew his own knife toward his neck. He was so surprised he hardly fought her, and by the time he realized what was happening, it was too late. The knife slipped into his throat like a needle through ripe summer fruit.

For a moment, everyone stared at the blood running hot over Çeda's hands.

They were not only *witnessing* his death; they *felt* it through their shared bond. As his heart slowed and finally stopped, the irindai burst from the walls and from the ceiling. The air became thick with them, fluttering, touching skin, batting eyes, becoming caught in hair.

Çeda's mind burned in the thoughts and the emotions of all those gathered. They were of one mind, now, sharing what they'd known, what they hoped to be, what they feared in the deepest recesses of their minds. It was too much, a flood that consumed them all, one by one.

Çeda screamed, a single note added to the cacophony of screams filling this small space, then fell beneath the weight of their collected dreams.

ÇEDA OPENED HER EYES, finding a dark-skinned boy with bright blue eyes staring at her.

"The sun shining bright, girl," Makuo said. "Time you return to it, let it see your face before it forget."

"What?" Çeda sat up slowly, her mind still lost in the land of dreams. She remembered who she was now—her name, her purpose here—but it seemed like an age and a day since she'd fallen to the weight of the minds around her.

Across the floor of the cellar, bodies lay everywhere like leaves tossed by the wind. Layer upon layer of dead moths covered their forms. Hidi stood by a sarcophagus, staring into its depths. It was what Çeda had been lying upon, she realized. The lid had been removed and now lay cracked and broken to one side.

Çeda stood and took one step toward the sarcophagus, but Makuo stopped her. "This isn't for you," the boy said.

Within the sarcophagus, she saw the crown of a head, wiry black hair, two twisted horns sweeping back from the forehead.

She thought of pressing Makuo. They'd won, she knew. They'd beaten Rümayesh with her help, and until now they'd considered her their ally, but that could change at any moment.

Steer you well wide of the will of the gods, old Ibrahim had always said after finishing one of his tragic stories. She'd heard dozens of those stories, and none of them ended happily. She'd always thought it a trick of Ibrahim's storytelling, to end them so, but now she wasn't so sure.

"What of Ashwandi?" Çeda asked.

Hidi looked up from whatever it was that had him transfixed, his scar puckering as he bared his teeth. "She free now. Her sister's wish was always for Ashwandi to leave the *ehrekh's* side, to return to the grasslands."

An *ehrekh*, then…

Rümayesh was an *ehrekh*, a twisted yet powerful experiment of the god, Goezhen. Few remained in the desert, but those that did were powerful indeed.

"Is she alive?"

"Oh, yes," the boys said in unison, their eyes full of glee.

"What will you do with her?" Çeda asked, tilting her head toward the sarcophagus.

At this they frowned. Hidi returned his gaze to Rümayesh's sleeping form, while Makuo took her by the shoulders and led her away. "The sun shining bright," he said. "Time you return to it."

Çeda let herself be led from the cellar, but her tread was heavy. Rümayesh may have tricked Çeda, may have wanted to steal her memories, but something didn't feel right about leaving her to these godling boys.

Makuo led her up a set of winding stairs and at last to a metal door. Çeda paused, her hand resting above the handle.

Steer you well wide of the will of the gods.

There was wisdom on those words, she thought as she gripped the door's warm handle. Surely there was wisdom. Then she opened the door and stepped into the sunlight.

THE SUBTLER ART

-Serendib-

CAT RAMBO

This is the second time I've written about Serendib (the first story featured the antagonist from this one), but the world's been floating around in my head for a couple of decades now, originally as a game setting, and I can tell more stories and a possible novel are lurking within it as well. I chose a middle-aged married couple as my protagonists because I don't see much heroic fantasy with characters like that, and it seems like a definite lack to me.

A NYTHING CAN HAPPEN IN Serendib, the city built of dimensions intersecting, and this is what happened there once.

The noodle shop that lies on the border between the neighborhood of Yddle, which is really a forest, houses strapped to the wide trunks, and Eclect, an industrial quarter, is claimed by both, with equally little reason.

The shop was its own Territory, with laws differing from either area, but the same can be said of many eating establishments in the City of a Thousand Parts. But the noodles were hand shaved, and the sauce was made of minced ginger and chopped green onions with a little soy sauce and a dash of enlightenment, and they were unequaled in Serendib.

It was the Dark's favorite place to eat, and since she and Tericatus were haphazard cooks at best and capable of (usually accidentally) killing someone at worst, they often ate their meals out. And because the city is so full of notorious people, very few noted that the woman once known as the best assassin on five continents on a world that only held four and her lover, a wizard who'd in his time achieved wonders and miracles and once even a rebirthed God, were slurping noodles only

"THE SUBTLER ART"

Illustration by ORION ZANGARA

an elbow length's away at the same chipped beige stone counter.

Though indifferent cooks, both were fond enough of food to argue its nuances in detail, and this day they were arguing over the use of white pepper or golden when eating the silvery little fish that spawn every seventh Spring in Serendib.

"Yellow pepper has a flatness to it," the Dark argued. Since retirement, she had let herself accumulate a little extra fat over her wiry muscles, and a few white strands traced themselves through her midnight hair, but she remained the one of the pair who drew most eyes. Her lover was a lean man, sparse in flesh and hair, gangly, with long capable hands spotted with unnatural colors and burns from alchemical ventures.

"Cooking," said another person, newly arrived, on the other side of her, "is an exceedingly subtle art."

"Cathay," the Dark said, recognizing the newcomer. Her tone was cool. Cathay was both acquaintance and former lover for both of them, but more than that, she was a Trickster mage, and you never knew what she might be getting into.

Tericatus grunted his own acknowledgment and greeting, rolling an eye sideways at the Dark in warning. He knew she was prone to impatience and, while Tricksters can play with many things, impatience is a favorite point to press on.

But the conversation Cathay made was slight, as though the Trickster's mind was elsewhere, and by the time the others had tapped coin to counter in order to pay, most of what she'd said had vanished, except for those few words.

"A subtle art," the Dark repeated to Tericatus, letting the words linger like the pepper on her tongue. "It describes what I do, as well. The most subtle art of all, assassination."

Tericatus leaned back in his chair with a smile on his lips and a challenging quirk to his eyebrow. "A subtle art, but surely not the *most* subtle. That would be magery, which is subtlety embodied."

The Dark looked *hard* at her mate. While she loved him above almost all things, she had been—and remained—very proud of her skill at her profession.

The argument hung in the air between them. So many words could go in defense of either side. But actions speak stronger than words. And so they stood and slid a token beneath their empty bowls and nodded at one another in total agreement.

"Who first?" the Dark asked.

"I have something in mind already, if you don't care," Tericatus murmured.

"Very well."

SERENDIB HAS NO CENTER—or at least the legend goes that if anyone ever finds it, the city will fall—but surely wherever its heart is, it must lie close to the gardens of Caran Sul.

Their gates are built of white moon-metal, which grows darker whenever the moon is shadowed, and their grounds are overgrown with shanks of dry green leaves and withered purple blossoms that smell sweet and salty, like the very edges of the sea.

In the center, five towers reach to the sky, only to tangle into the form of Castle Knot, where the Angry Daughters, descended from the prophet who once lived there, swarm, and occasionally pull passersby into their skyborne nests, never to be seen again.

Tericatus and the Dark paid their admittance coin to the sleepy attendant at the entrance stile outside the gate and entered through the pathway hacked into the vegetation. Tericatus paused halfway down the tunnel to lean down and pick up a caterpillar from the dusty path, transferring it to the dry leaves on the opposite side.

The Dark kept a wary eye on the sky as they emerged into sunlight. While she did not fear an encounter with a few Daughters, a crowd of them would be an entirely different thing. But nothing stirred in the stony coils and twists so far above.

"This reminds me," she ventured, "of the time we infiltrated the demon city of S'keral pretending to be visiting scholars and wrestled that purple stone free from that idol."

"Indeed," Tericatus said, "this is nothing like that."

"Ah. Perhaps it is more like the time we entered the village of shapeshifters and killed their leaders before anyone had time enough to react."

"It is not like that either," Tericatus said, a little irritably.

"Remind me," she said, "exactly what we are doing here."

Tericatus stopped and crossed his arms. "I'm demonstrating the subtlety with which magic can work."

"And how exactly will it work?" she inquired.

He unfolded an arm and pointed upward towards the dark shapes flapping their way down from the heights, clacking the brazen, razor-sharp bills on the masks they wore.

"I presume you don't need me to do anything?"

Tericatus did not deign to answer.

The shapes continued to descend. The Dark could see the brass claws tipping their gloves, each stained with ominous rust.

"You're quite sure you don't need me?"

A butterfly fluttered across the sky from behind them. Dodging to catch it in her talons, one Daughter collided with another, and the pair tumbled into the path of a third, then a fourth...

The Dark blinked as the long grass around them filled with fallen bodies.

"Very nice," she said with genuine appreciation. "And the tipping point?"

Tericatus smirked slightly. "The caterpillar. You may have noticed that I moved it from one kind of plant to another…?"

"Of course."

"And when it eats jilla leaves, its scent changes, attracting adults of its species to come lay more eggs there."

"Well done," she said. "A valiant try indeed."

———•———

THE HOME FOR DICTATORS is, despite its name, a retirement home, though it is true that it holds plenty of past leaders of all sorts of stripes, and many of them are not particularly benign.

"Why here?" Tericatus said as they came up Fume and Spray and Rant Street, changing elevations as they went till the air grew chill and dry.

"It grates on me to perform a hit without getting paid for it," the Dark said, a little apologetically. "It feels unprofessional."

"You're retired. Why should you worry about feeling unprofessional?"

"*You're* retired too. Why should you worry about who's more subtle?"

"Technically, wizards never retire."

"Assassins do," the Dark said. "It's just that we don't usually get the chance."

"Get the chance or lose the itch?"

She shrugged. "A little of both?"

Tericatus expected the Dark to go in through the back in the way she'd been famous for: unseen, unannounced. Or failing that, to disguise herself in one of her many cunning alterations: an elderly inmate to be admitted, a child come to visit a grandparent, a dignitary there to honor some old politician. But instead she marched up the steps and signed her name in bold letters on the guestbook: THE DARK.

The receptionist/nurse, a young newtling with damp, pallid skin and limpid eyes, spun the book around to read the name, which clearly meant little to him. "And you've come to see...?" he said, letting the sentence trail upward in question as his head tilted.

The Dark eyed him. It was a look Tericatus knew well, a look that started mild and reasonable but which, as time progressed, swelled into menace, darkened like clouds gathering on the edge of the horizon. The newtling paled, cheeks twitching convulsively as he swallowed.

"Simply announce me to the inhabitants at large," the Dark said.

Without taking his eyes from her, the newtling fumbled for the intercom, a device clearly borrowed from some slightly more but not too advanced dimension, laden with black-iron cogs and the faint green glow of phlogiston. He said hesitantly into the bell-like speaking cup, "The, uh, Dark is here to see, uh, someone."

The Dark smiled faintly and turned back to the waiting room.

After a few moments, Tericatus said, "Are we expecting someone?"

"Not really," the Dark replied.

"Some *thing*?"

"Closer, but not quite," she said.

They glanced around as a bustle of doctors went through a doorway.

"There we go," the Dark said.

She tugged her lover in their wake and up a set of stairs where they watched the doctors gather in a room at the head. An elderly woman lay motionless in her bed there.

"The Witch of the Southeast," the Dark murmured. "She's always feared me, and her heart was as frail as tissue paper. Come on."

They drifted further along the corridor. The Dark paused in a doorway. A man in a wicker and brass wheelchair wore an admiral's uniform, but his eyes were unseeing, his lips drawn up in a rictus that exposed purple gums.

"Diploberry," the Dark said. "It keeps well, and just a little has the effect one wants. It is a relatively painless means of suicide."

Tericatus looked at the admiral. "Because he heard you were coming?"

The Dark spread her hands in a helpless shrug, her grin fox-sly.

"And you're getting paid for all of them? How long ago did you plant some of the seeds you've harvested here?"

"The longest would be a decade and a half," she mused.

"How many others have died?"

"Three. All dictators whose former victims were more than willing to see their old oppressors gone."

Tericatus protested, "You can't predict that with such finesse!"

"Can I not?" She pointed at the door where three stretchers were exiting, carried by orderlies in the costume of the place; gold braids and silver sharkskin suits.

She smiled smugly. "Subtle, no?"

Tericatus nodded, frowning.

"Come now," she said. "Is it that hard to admit defeat?"

"Not so hard, my love," he said. "But isn't that Cathay?"

The Dark felt another touch of unease. You never know what a Trickster Mage is getting you into. And there indeed stood Cathay at the front desk, speaking sweetly to someone, a bouquet of withered purple blossoms in her hand, more of them in her hair, exuding a smell like longing and regret and the endless sea.

The Dark murmured, "She always loved those flowers, and yet did not like contending with the Daughters."

Tericatus said, "She had lovers here, I know that. No doubt she has five inheritances coming."

Cathay turned and smiled at them. The Dark bowed slightly, and Tericatus inclined his head.

———◦———

"BUT," THE DARK FINALLY said into the silence as they walked away, headed by mutual accord to the bar closest to the noodle shop, "we can still argue over which of us exercises the second most subtle art."

SEEDS

-The Sanctuary Duet-
CAROL BERG

The scoundrel hero of my Lighthouse Duet, Flesh
and Spirit *and* Breath and Bone, *is a renegade
sorcerer with a serious addiction problem and a unique
outlook on life. My new Sanctuary Duet,* Dust and
Light *and* Ash and Silver *(2015), is a parallel
story set in the same world as the Lighthouse books.
But* Dust and Light *involves a very different sorcerer,
an upright young portrait artist who is, to his disgust
and humiliation, contracted to a testy, common man of
the law with shady doings in his past. "Seeds" recounts
a chance encounter between my scoundrel and my
lawman some five years before the cataclysmic events
of these two duologies—a civil war, a disastrous winter,
rampaging fanatics, and the roots of myth in a realm
just beyond the world we can see.*

Blackguards

I F ANY HIERARCH, PRIESTESS, monk, or practor were to ask me where I choose to worship my gods, I would have to say a friendly sop-house. I take no preference among the Elder Gods, the Karish upstart Iero, or anyone else's divinity, offering libations, prayers, and oaths equally to them all as the occasion demands. But in all this wretched world there's naught to compare with a fine bath, a barrel of mead, and a merry melee of pipes, dancing, and new friends to put me in mind of the sacred.

The piper gave a final flourish to the galliard just as I led the chain of dancers in a leap from the trestle table nearest the fire.

"Don't weaken," I yelled, heat pulsing in my blood, the world spinning cheerfully as I clamped my hands atop those at my waist to ensure the rosy-breasted girl followed me. Or perhaps it was the delicate young man with perfect skin that stank of a tannery had ended up my choice of second for the dance. Five years on the run had taught me that delights could be found in all sorts of interesting forms.

Alas, the piper yielded to a boy with a soft-strung lute, and the chain broke and scattered. Some dancers collapsed on the floor. The sop-house girls filled cups from the casks or dragged partners up the

"SEEDS"

Illustration by OKSANA DMITRIENKO

stair. A man in a swirling black cape danced his partner into a dark corner, where they appeared to be continuing the dance. Or wrestling. Or finding more serious amusement.

I grabbed my second's wrists and sagged onto a bench by the door, twirling her around and pulling her onto my lap. It was neither the rosy girl nor the delicate, stinking young man, but the tall, bony girl with teasing eyes.

She pecked my cheek and pulled away. "Do come again morrow-night, sweeting. 'Tis fine to dance with such a long-legged fellow instead of the runts grown up around Wroling."

I plunged fingers into her oat-hued curls and drew her back for a better kiss. Her lips were not at all bony and her breath was sweet. "But the night's not half gone," I whispered, "and winter's come early again. How's a lone soldier to stay warm?"

Her fingers traced my bristly chin and I took advantage. They tasted of honey.

"Oh, that I could," she sighed. "But I must be off to my mam. I could ask her could you sleep in the byre…"

Few offers could so chill a man's parts as aught to do with mothers and cows. So I let go. "The goddess mother bless your mam, but straw gives me sneezing fits. We'll dance again tomorrow."

My turn to sigh. I'd hoped for a hearth fire and a night's companionship. Though to be honest, I shouldn't complain. For a man released from the king's legion only that morn, with three coppers to his name in a town where he knew not a soul, I'd had a most exemplary day. This holy sop-house had provided me a mutton pie as I'd not seen in half a year, a merry evening, and, less delightful but more important, another few months before I disintegrated into a pain-wracked lunatic.

The man who had solved my annoying problem was yet hunched over the little table in the shadows. A slight fellow with a dark greasy tangle of hair, and eyes like burnt-out hollows. The tremors in his hands had drawn me that morning, as I sought the means to soothe my perverse affliction.

A fumble in my waist pocket retrieved not three but only a single coin—the last copper from the year of soldiering for good King Eodward. I flipped it to a passing girl—the rosy one with a sheen of sweat glistening on her skin. "Fill that fellow's cup, Katie. I think he needs it more than I do."

"Bek the corpse-cutter?" Her shudder chilled my own skin. "Wish he'd drink somewheres else. Were my own arm dangling off, I wouldn't have him sew it back on. Not when I know what he does with those hands. At least he don't try to touch the girls no more. We taught him that right off."

She tucked the coin between her rosy breasts and bustled off to fill the man's cup. She must have told him who paid, as when she moved away he raised the cup in my direction.

My soul shivered. Surgery was a nasty, lonesome business at best. Every soldier heard the best ones cut up bodies to learn how we were put together. But a wounded man always kept a friend about to make sure the surgeon didn't steal his liver or leave a demon sign inside him. And once the wound was sewn, no man wanted to see the surgeon again, lest the fellow had taken a liking to his body and decided to make a study of it. No wonder such a man took refuge in a bit of unsavory pleasure. We all did what we had to do to soothe the pain of living.

I sipped the dregs in my own cup, putting my mind to where I might sleep and what work I might find hereabouts till the king needed his soldiers again. I'd certainly no means to travel elsewhere.

Angry voices rose from the caped man and his partner—clearly male—in the back corner. It seemed their dance had turned unpleasant. Perhaps I should leave. A man in my position could not afford to linger in the neighborhood of a brawl. Those who hunted me were ever alert.

I reached under the bench for my rucksack, only to shove it back again straightaway as the sop-house door flew open. One might have thought my mother, the ever-drunk diviner, had whispered warning in my ear, for a broad-chested man with a thatch of rusty hair and beard near filled the doorway not ten paces from my bench.

"Hold your places and heed my saying!" he bellowed. His thick, hairy hand tapped the worn sword hilt at his hip. "I'm First Constable Bastien, come to make an arrest for violation of the laws of the kingdom of Navronne and the town of Wroling."

No way to slip past him. If I could have made my excessive height less noticeable, I would have done it years ago. All I could do was keep still and quiet, and beg the gods he'd come for someone else. Surely if he knew what I was, he'd have brought a pureblood sorcerer to deal with me, no matter that I was the least capable spellcaster in Navronne. As for the simpler matter from earlier in the day, I was sure I'd got away clean.

"Everyone here is to empty his pockets."

The terse command eased my greater fear. But the lesser matter loomed larger, and a glance at the corpse-cutting surgeon sent my spirit plummeting. Constable Bastien had fixed his eye on the man in the shadows and the shaggy head nodded straight at me.

The constable pivoted smartly in my direction. "We'll begin right here."

Two annoyingly stalwart henchman in leather jerkins followed him inside.

"What might your name be?" said the constable. "Don't think I've seen you round here."

"Name is…Valen," I said. "Man-at-arms to good King Eodward, Sky Lord bless our doughty sovereign."

Daren't lie about it; comrades from the legion might have found their way to Wroling. But I certainly didn't tell him the whole of my name. Aurellian names were sorcerers' names. Sorcerers masked half their faces and wore wine-colored cloaks and *never* danced in sop-houses…unless they were *recondeurs*. Renegades.

"Released from service, I understand," said Constable Bastien, confirming that he'd spoken to the damnable surgeon. And here I'd used my last coin to buy the corpse-cutter mead. How stupid could a man be to trust a twistmind? No matter I was one, too, I kept my oaths.

"Aye, noble constable, the king—our mutual employer, one might say—has given his legion leave," I said, calm and comradely, "allowing us to find decent shelter for the winter. Don't you find it troubling how the weather's so much worse these last few years? Makes a man wary of offending the gods. Which part do you take in the saying—is it the gods' anger with our dissipations or is it the bowl of the sky slipped from its moorings that's caused this demonish winter? I've heard—"

"Perhaps you'd best listen instead of babbling, Armsman Valen. I said turn out your pockets. You'll see the rest here have done so. They know how Magistrate Maslin dislikes it when a suspect disobeys his officers. A felon plies his trade in Wroling at his peril."

Indeed, every man had emptied his waist pocket and every woman her apron and her bodice. The tables were a litter of luck charms, toothpicks, thread spools, pebbles, bits of string, and a pitiful few coins.

Uneasy, I turned out the pocket I'd emptied for the cursed surgeon. "A *suspect*, you say? A *felon*? What have I done but serve my king in the miserable northlands? A man comes home after so long with seeping wounds…grievous sorrows…debts to the gods…boot rot…"

The unmoved constable cocked his head and skewered me with a stare. "Boot rot, eh? Perhaps you should remove those boots."

"Before a civil company? I'm sure the bath ladies could testify I've had them off—"

"Now." He twitched a finger at his two men.

Frenzied resistance availed naught before such odds.

Thus one henchman yanked off my boots while I lay prostrate with the other cur seated on my backside and the constable's boot on my neck. And of course, the little pouch tucked in my boot was found to contain *nivat* seeds—the hard black creations of Magrog the Tormentor that had been my salvation and my devilment since I turned fourteen. The henchmen fetched rope and shackles as Constable Bastien called Bek, the corpse-cutter, to witness that I was indeed the man who'd sought the most out-of-the-way purveyor of nivat in the district.

"Just after dawn this very morning. He even said he'd see to the business straightaway." Bek's trembling hands shoved his greasy hair aside. "Didn't imagine he meant to *steal* the goods." Despite his tremors, the surgeon was clear spoken, neither mead nor simpleton's ignorance blurring his testimony.

The constable admirably restrained his gloating, as he displayed the little mound of seeds to all who were paying attention—by this time that was only the landlord and the horrified bony girl, who was fanning herself in relief that she'd not dragged me to her mam's byre.

"As it happens, Seedsman Fitch reports that exactly six-and-thirty nivat seeds vanished between dawn and ninth hour. Unfortunately for Seedsman Fitch, no one left payment. Unfortunately for you, Magistrate Maslin sees thieving as a public plague and has vowed to cleanse it from our noble town."

All my favored stories and pleas died unspoken. This Magistrate

Maslin sounded like the obstacle. Perhaps if we could get somewhere more private, I could budge the constable from this public posturing. Sadly, somewhere private looked to be a lockup.

My stomach clamored in revolt. Sweat broke out on brow and back. No enemy swordsman, no archer, no whip or blow could set my spirit gibbering as could a locked room—a relic of a hateful childhood and my own perverse nature. The prospect was almost enough to make me contrive some magic to escape. But if a Registry servitor or any other pureblood lurked in the vicinity, use of magic could spell my doom.

Failing some compromise with Constable Bastien, I could survive a whipping or a tenday in the stocks, even the hateful lockup if worse came to worse. I'd done so plenty of times. But I'd need that nivat soon.

"No need for chains, good constable," I said, as they bound my hands at my back. It was all I could do to keep still. "I'll behave. I swear it on my life. I'll work off the debt, do hard labor willing, whatever's necessary."

"Magistrate Maslin will decide. But were I in your place, I'd start practicing my armsman's skills with my off hand."

"My off—" Horror choked my throat entire and set the evening's mead and mutton pie into a maelstrom. "A *hand?*"

King Eodward had halted the lopping of hands for thieving years ago, saying that destroying a thief's chance of honest work made no sense. He was right. Fighting, laboring, tending iron smelts, tanning hides, I'd done them all and more—I wasn't particular how I kept from starving—but no work available to an ignorant lout like me could be managed with but one hand. And what of lovemaking, one of the gods' dearest graces to humankind? Arrosa's mercy, I was only twenty!

And then there was magic. I'd given up magic almost completely when I ran away from my family, as pureblood sorcery was easily detectable, especially in the low places I frequented. I'd never been good at spellwork, thus it was no great sacrifice. But from time to time when running or hiding, and most especially when dealing with nivat...

Fingers were the conduit of magic. To take a sorcerer's hand was unthinkable, forbidden by every law of crown and temple. And yet the very last thing these people could know of me was the truth of my blood. *Great gods of Idrium, Heaven, and Hell!*

I fought to quiet my belly before I retched on the constable's boots. No one seemed to be watching us anymore. The patrons had loaded up their coins and combs and crowded about the scuffle grown louder in the back corner. The surgeon had taken his tattler's fee and slunk back to his seat in the shadows.

"I'll do whatever you want to make amends, noble constable," I said as the henchmen locked the shackles and hauled me to my feet. "I'm a loyal servant of the king. I even met him once after a battle and he commended me." No need to feign desperation. "But my da is dead, my family's vegetable plot withered. We need nivat seeds for feast bread to lure the holy Danae to heal—"

"Best not waste breath." His detestably unthreatened finger thumped my chest to silence me. "None of that matters in Wroling. Only the law and punishment. What in Magrog's hells is going on back there?"

This last he bellowed above the rising din. The sop-house patrons had broken into whistles and drunken cheers as if they watched a dog fight.

The crowd parted and the delicate young man with the tanner's stink stumbled straight toward the constable and me, one eye a swollen wreck, tunic ripped, and netherstocks flapping at his knees. His hand gripped a bloody knife, and his face reflected a desperation as profound as my own.

"Come back here, you gods-cursed catamite!" A snarling fellow threw an arm around the young man's neck and dragged him backward.

The bloody dagger dropped to the floor as the smaller man clawed at the choke hold and tore at his assailant's long cape, exposing garb wholly out of place in a sop-house. Silk brocade, indigo velvet, ruffles of very expensive lace, rings of rubies and sapphires, and, far worse, fresh blood—whether his or his attacker's it wasn't clear.

The bigger man wore no mask and his cape was black, not the hue of good wine, thus he was no pureblood, which was a small grace for my part. But he was certainly noble born, which for the delicate young man meant serious trouble.

"Denys." The name was spoken with such quiet horror, I almost didn't hear it above my own rattling fear. But it drew my gaze to the man beside me. For one instant was Constable Bastien's soul laid bare, before he shuttered dismay and anger with unfeeling duty. A servant of the law could not afford to care about anyone but nobles and magistrates.

The constable bowed deeply. "Lord Felix, what's happened here?"

Blood soaked the lordling's sleeve, which did not seem to hamper his grip. A gory trickle leaked from his mangled lower lip. The latter looked more like a bite than a stab wound. Any reasonable judge with two eyes would understand clearly what had gone on.

"This scrap of offal tried to steal my dagger," said the pudding-faced noble, tightening his choke grip. "When I objected and told him that a beggar who stank so vilely could never be a proper sneak thief, he went wild and stabbed me. I need a message taken to my father."

Three men scrambled forward, bowed heads, and bent their

knees. The young lord chose one with his boot.

"Tell the edane I am direly wounded, but have apprehended the murderous fiend. He must send our physician and three men-at-arms. Tell them to bring a gelding knife."

Denys near fainted. Bastien did not even blanch.

On any other night, I'd feel sorrier for the lively, handsome fellow who'd shared the dance with me. But faced with confinement, my own mutilation, and the sickness that would come upon me in the next hours without enchanted nivat, it was difficult not to envy him a quick death. Coals already smoldered in my belly, ready to take fire and consume my body and soul.

The constable waved at one of his henchmen. "Transfer the shackles from the thief to this sniveling wretch. I'll alert Magistrate Maslin that we've two felons to bring before him in the morning."

Yet again he bowed to the noble. "My Lord Felix, please to take a seat to preserve your strength. Yonder fellow Bek is a decent surgeon and can see to your wound."

"A sop-house surgeon? Are you mad, constable? My father's physician is a pureblood." He shoved the slender Denys to his knees and spat on him. "You will inform Magistrate Maslin that he must deal with this murderous weasel *this* hour. I intend the wretch to spend a most unpleasant tenday in our dungeon before he dies."

"Bas," whispered Denys, fumbling at his clothes to cover his nakedness. "'Twasn't my fault. He tried to—"

The constable slapped the bruised young man in the mouth. "Silence, villain," he snapped. "Thieving from this noble lord. Drawing his blood. Seems you've pissed your bed, eh? Now lie in it."

As the henchman hobbled me with a length of rope, the constable shackled young Denys. His harshness was not feigned. Yet that singular moment unmasked had been unmistakable, so a person might hope Bastien was not so cursed righteous as he seemed. Alas, the world had taught me elsewise.

———◆———

MAGISTRATE MASLIN COULD HAVE been my father all over again. Squat, venom-tongued, and wholly unwilling to listen to argument or reason. Yet I'll say he was a brave brute, not intimidated in the least by Lord Felix's bluster, or perhaps he was simply enraged at being dragged out of bed near midnight.

Maslin ruled that Bastien's two felons would remain confined in the cells until tenth hour of the morning, so that the official verdicts could be posted in Wroling's square for the ten hours crown law specified. At that time Denys de Verte, tanner's assistant, clearly guilty of attacking his better, would be turned over to the Edane of Wroling and his son Felix for their choice of punishment. To the young noble's frothing frustration, that punishment excluded death, as "the young lord's wounds were nowhere approaching mortal."

At that same hour Valen of nowhere, former man-at-arms in the king's legion, clearly guilty of stealing nivat seeds from a reputable seedsman, would have his right hand lopped off. Cautery would be supplied at the prisoner's own expense, to be worked off with indentured labor, as the prisoner had nothing of value on his person.

For once in my life, I kept my mouth shut. I was deathly afraid I'd start blathering that I was pureblood and that the magistrate would die horribly for taking my hand. But even life with one hand would be better than what my own kind had in store for me were I to be captured after six years on the run. Never again would I be allowed to make a choice for myself—whether to eat, speak, sleep, dance, sing, or marry. I could be contracted to the most unscrupulous of masters, kept deaf or forbidden ever to see the sun or breathe the air of the world. I could be whipped or put on public display as an affront to the gods for rejecting the divine gift of magic and the life it laid out for me. There had to be another way out of this mess.

———— •—•—— ————

THE CELLS CONSISTED OF four windowless iron boxes below the Magistrate's Hall. The hulking second constable Hugh dragged me down the stair and shoved me into one already occupied by an ancient jolly drunkard named Elfun, who stank of piss, and immediately began spewing nonsense stories. Elfun would have been a fine companion were we holed up in an alleyway in a storm with a barrel fire and skin of ale, but on this night I'd no good humor to share with him.

Bless the builders of the Hall, the cell door was not solid, but a grillwork of bars. I clung to it, willing the single weakling lamp never to burn out and pretending I could breathe. Matters could have been much worse. A cell was a damned sight better than the oubliette where they were going to stow poor Denys. The testy young Lord Felix had squeezed that concession from old Maslin. Constable Bastien had pronounced it a fine idea.

The stair spat out a pair of Lord Felix's men-at-arms, a stumbling, shackled Denys, and the constable. "Your master needn't fret," Bastien snapped at the two guards as he yanked open a trap in the floor of the cell across from mine. "None's going to escape from here."

A cackle from behind me spewed the scent of rotted teeth my way. "I've a tale about a prisoner what let a rat eat him bit by bit. He thought the most of him could escape that way, though he never figgered how to get his bones out…"

"Stop your rattling, lunatic!" The constable's irritation quieted old Elfun's babbling, but didn't stop it.

"…and then there was another feller what chewed off his toes, thinking to slip his shackles…"

They lowered Denys, shackles and all, into the hole without benefit of the wooden ladder that was propped against the wall, and dropped him when he was scarce halfway down. He made not a whimper as the trap door fell shut, trapping him in the pitch-dark hole. Even the imagining gave me the shakes, though I had my own share of those already.

"Constable, please," I said, once the growling Bastien had locked the trap and the cell door. "I'm going to die in here. 'Tis murder to leave me. I beg you…"

Between the confinement and the lurking fire in my gut, I'd no need to feign desperation. Shuddering, I licked my lips and scratched my arms, then blotted my forehead with my sleeve. My hands would not stay still.

"None dies in my cells. If they're judged deserving, they die clean and proper on the gallows. The law is the law." Bastien dragged his gaze from their fix on the trap door and scowled at me. The signs of a nivat slave were known to any who walked the streets. "Then again, if they've murdered themselves with unsavory pleasure, 'tis on their own head."

"If I could change it, I would," I blurted. "But I was young and sick when I started. Pain eats your soul."

Why did I tell him that? I needed to make a plan before thought became impossible. "There's a halfblood in town will do the spellwork for me. All I ask is twelve seeds and an hour's freedom to get it done. On my mam's life, I'll come back."

He burst into decidedly unmerry laughter. "Naturally an honest fellow like you would come back. Oh, but then, you're not honest, are you? You'll need more than spelled nivat paste in the morning when they take an axe to your thieving hand…or will the pain just make the pleasure finer?"

It would. Gods save my raddled body, it would...for about ten heartbeats. "Better to lose the hand than my mind."

"Go to sleep. I'll see Bek's here with his cautery iron tomorrow. His fees are low and I'm sure he can find some way you can work off the debt. Even one-handed. Mayhap it will help that he knows what you'll endure as your perversion takes its vengeance. He threw off nivat's claws years ago."

His disdain rubbed me raw. The blackguard constable had no way to know what had driven me to the seeds. "Your friend the corpse-cutter's already made his coin off me today. Do you collect a tithe when you get him work cauterizing stumps or tending young nobles whose brutish pricks get them into sop-house scrapes?"

The constable rammed his arm between the bars of my cell and about my neck, jamming my face to the grillwork. "Hear me, twistmind. Bek's work is more honest than stealing a seedsman's stock. Maybe you fought honestly for the king, maybe you didn't, but you, at least, are guilty of your crime. The law demands you pay. *Justice* demands you pay."

"True enough," I croaked, low enough the edane's men could not hear. "But how just is law that punishes one who *suffers* the crime? None'll whip the seedsman, but they're going to geld a merry young man who's done no wrong—the *friend* you've just thrown into yonder pit. Will you summon Surgeon Bek to cauterize *that* wound? Law is not so simple as you pretend. Perhaps this Magistrate Maslin should let you study it."

Spewing a disgusted breath, he released my head and shoved me backward. On his way to the stair, he doused the lamp. "I do study it," he said from the dark. "Now sleep."

———•———

I DIDN'T. I COULDN'T. At first, fury at the callous constable held me together. But as the night crawled onward, it became more difficult to think beyond the chaos inside my skin. I clung to the bars, shaking and sweating as sickness and my damnable terror of confinement tightened their hold on my sinews. Despair taunted me. How could I imagine that a man who served the law cared for anyone? The law would have both Denys and me half men by the next nightfall.

I was almost desperate enough to rouse the snoring Elfun to strangle me when soft footsteps descended the stair. The muffled jingle of keys, then hinges, keys again, and a quiet clank sounded from the cell across the way. A deeper darkness yawned in the pitchy lockup.

"Denys." Only practiced skill enabled me to hear the whispered name. "Are you awake?"

Even pureblood hearing could not detect an answer from the pit.

"Move aside. Ladder's coming down. Yes, you will. You've no say in this."

Sky Lord's mercy, was he going to turn the man over to Felix beforetime?

Evidently Denys didn't believe so. His shackles rattled as he climbed.

"You're ruined if you let me go, Bas." Denys's steady voice put me to shame, while at the same time stirring my dead hopes. "I can't allow it. I won't. Five years you've worked to erase the past. They're going to offer you the position in Palinur because even this maniac magistrate can't find fault with you."

"We'll go north. I'll start over. Find another post. I'll not build my life on your grave."

"They're not allowed to kill me." This time Denys's voice quavered…but only a little. "I'll survive a few scars…"

And as if some impish godlet shot an arrow of starlight through the clouds to sting my backside, their honest care for each other gave me an answer.

I mustered every shred of calm and reason I could manage. "The way I see it there are several ways we three can end up at the end of this coming day. One has handsome Denys a eunuch, the constable a guilt-ridden prick, and me a one-handed lunatic peeling his skin away. A second has Denys and his studious constable become fugitives—which, let me tell you, is not at all a cheerful way to live—and me the same lunatic as the first. But a third possibility has Bastien's position preserved, Denys owning all the parts he was born with—albeit needing a home other than Wroling—and I, Valen, confirmed in my depravity, but carrying forward the knowledge of a good deed which might someday redeem me."

"Are you gone mad already?" snarled the constable. "There's no possible—"

"Hear me out." The plan had come together near full blown. "The entire cost would be the favor owed me by a lowlife halfblood, whose name will remain secret, and twelve nivat seeds, which Denys could hand over only when he is safely away. Sadly, I've no wherewithal to pay the seedsman for his lost property else I'd never have stolen them in the first place, but perhaps one or the other of you might see to it in return for the help I'll give. For certain, Wroling's tender justice will suffer. But perhaps the balance of right will outweigh the balance of wickedness in this case: I will forever reap the punishment of my sins, and Constable Bastien, who studies the law, will be left free to uphold the good."

The silence from the other cell was profound. I liked to imagine I heard the sound of wrestling consciences, rather than insane disbelief.

"Holy, holy, holy…hee, hee, hee…now *that's* a wild tale." The cackling clattered like a fistfuls of pebbles thrown at the iron walls. "Though I don't remember new tales so well. The next tankard of sack will wash this'n all-l-l-l away."

"Hush, Elfun," I said. "Or I'll give you something wild to remember."

Biting, undecipherable argument emanated from the dark. I begged Serena Fortuna for a bit of grace.

"How would you get me out of here without compromising Bastien?" said Denys, admirably calm.

I clenched my hands to keep from wrenching the bars from their mortar. "I've long experience with locks and hiding, as long as we're fast." Really and truly fast. "And Bastien will need a solid alibi…"

The constable took some convincing. And he utterly refused to allow Denys to hold the seeds that would be my payment, believing I'd kill his friend to get them. But eventually they both agreed. One thing about being backed up in a wretched corner with the howling wolves' saliva dripping on your toes: There is only one way to go. Straight through them.

———•◆•———

"UP, THIEF, SHOW YOURSELF!" Like clockwork, Bastien's man rattled my cell door and tested the lock. Lord Felix's man bawled at Denys to show himself below the opened trap. Twice, the pair of them had done the same. Twice they'd left, satisfied that all was secure. During the visits and for every moment in between Bastien remained in his workroom upstairs with the rest of his men and Felix's—well observed.

For the third time, the guards were satisfied. Their footsteps faded up the stair.

Before beginning his hourly surveillance, Bastien would have scratched a number above the sop-house door, indicating to my mysterious *halfblood friend* that he was to meet me outside the lockup at fourth hour of the night watch. That meant it was time for us to go.

The cell lock was not so different than the myriad I'd met before. With a breathed prayer to Erdru, Lord of Vines and Drunkards, I laid my fingers on it and called up magic. Pins snicked inside the lock. Levers fell. And stuck. I tried to jar it loose...to no avail. Gods, only an hour till they'd return.

A slight adjustment to the spell, and the cursed mechanism fell open, spitting orange sparks. I shoved the gate open and cast a soft light. The lock was halfway melted.

Tittering broke out behind me. "Something wild for sure. Who's done that?"

"Valen's halfblood friend," I said. "Tell that to all who come and they'll let you out come morning." No help for it. My incompetent spellwork removed all question as to how the locks were broken, further reducing the time we had to get away.

Another burst of sparks opened the cell in front of me. A third that trembled the floor opened Denys's pit. I shoved the ladder down. "Quickly!"

Once he was up, I set to work on Denys's shackles. *Spelled* locks. *Damnation!*

Forcing patience I didn't have, I peeled away the simple spell on his left shackle and burst the lock. Denys sucked in his breath.

"Does Bas know?" he said softly, as I began working magic on the right side.

"No," I said. "And he cannot. Not ever."

Another burst and I breathed again.

Only when Denys climbed the stair in front of me did I note the charred stocking and burnt flesh on his right ankle.

"Sorry that was rough," I said. "Truly I'm not good at much of anything. Though I could have shown you a fine evening if *I* had partnered you in the galliard."

His quiet laugh and his hand on my shoulder had me grinning as I doused my light and we darted across the courtyard of the Magistrate's Hall and into the lane.

I pressed Denys into the shadows. "Wait."

Kneeling on the deserted street, I closed my eyes, laid hands on the filthy cobbles, and drew on the reservoir of magic that lived in my blood. My drunkard mother was a diviner, but it was my father's bloodline magic lived in me. The Cartamanduas were a line of cartographers—mapmakers, route finders, and guides. My particular bent, pitiful as it was, allowed me to read a road.

Magic flowed through my fingers. Iron-wheeled carts and farmers' barrows had laid down tracks here, as had every kind of shoe from crudest leather to fine slippers, as well as naked feet, mules and pigs, geese and horses. Fewer threads had woven this road than others I'd known, and hope permeated the dirt and stone more than enmity or sorrow. Wroling was a newer town and had never seen war.

Heaving a full breath, easier now that no walls confined me, I sank deeper into the magic, stretching my awareness beyond the plot I touched. Soggy waking here and there, sleepy lovemaking that tempted me to linger, anxieties about empty market stalls… hunger…wariness at hungry soldiers wandering so near daughters and bringing worries of the world inside the town walls. No signs of lurking spite or ready knives. Magistrate Maslin's town felt safe. *Our* safety depended on my sense of his town.

"All's well for now," I said, popping to my feet. "Let's move."

"You're no halfblood."

"No."

"A renegade, then."

"Best if you don't question. I'm going to save your balls."

Denys laughed again and stuffed a small green bag into my waist pocket. "If you trust me enough to show me this, then I'll trust you to honor your promise."

I tried not to think what he'd given me. I wasn't worthy of that kind of trust. Though it was too late, anyway. Once I fed my perversion, I was useless for a day, thus certain to get caught.

We raced through Wroling's quiet streets. Even if we could sneak through the city gates—wholly unlikely—we'd no time to get far enough away. So we would keep moving, laying down a confusion of tracks for the edane's hounds and any purebloods they brought in. I blessed the low clouds that spat freezing rain on us as it kept people late in their beds. Half an hour more and our escape would be discovered.

In a nearby alley, Bastien had left Denys a thick wool shirt and a good cloak that quieted my slight companion's shivering. The cloak he'd left for me scarce reached my knees, and the moth-eaten woolen scarf would have done better to wrap fish, but they would serve to disguise my garments.

He'd also left my rucksack that contained my every possession. A touch assured me that its false bottom was intact. I stuffed Denys's little green bag in beside the shard of mirror glass and the silver needle and refused to think more of them. Cramps already tormented gut and limbs. A few hours and the craving would begin to devour my senses. Eventually we'd have to go to ground.

———◦———

WE DIDN'T NEED THE tolling bell to know when they'd discovered us missing. We kept running, traversing every street and alleyway, slowing only when we encountered other people. Every little while, I would lay my hands on dirt or cobbles and use my bent to judge where we needed to go next. I felt the hunt spreading out from the Magistrate's Hall. Determined at first… and then furious…murderous. Lord Felix must have joined them.

"Are you all right, Valen?" Denys steadied me as stabbing fire in one thigh set me stumbling. "We should stop."

"Not yet." I couldn't say more without heaving.

From time to time we'd trade cloaks or scarves. I hunched my shoulders hoping to disguise my height. Sometimes we separated, rounding a block of houses in opposite directions, but never far enough a cry would fail to bring us back together. The coal in my gut burst into flame. Raindrops felt like small hammers that left bruises of acid. But we could not stop.

Again, I knelt and poured out magic. The hunt had moved north. We moved south. Bless all gods that Denys knew the streets. I had warned Bastien not to hold back in the chase, swearing that my disreputable friend would see to Denys's safety. And so I would. I did not fail my oaths.

In late afternoon weak magic joined the hunt. If I used magic again, we were lost. But it was yapping hounds threatened to end us first.

"We're done!" A panting Denys gaped at the moldering mountain of foulness that choked the narrow alley—fifty years, at least, of Wroling's refuse, rotting carcasses, ashes, and slops.

"Not yet." I gasped as a belly cramp speared my gut. "Crawl under. Deep as you can bear. They won't let the hounds dig too deep. I've done this before."

I dug in, too, and held still for an eternity of demonic howling, expecting slavering jaws to drag us out at any moment. My incessant shivering must not give us away. Must not. Would not…

"VALEN? CAN YOU HEAR me? They're gone."

I couldn't move. Couldn't speak. Surely a fiery dagger was slitting the skin along my spine. The foulness that buried me had triggered a wrenching nausea, and every heave felt like a giant knotted my gut and crushed it in his fist. The world was naught but pain and need.

A century of unidentifiable muck fell away, exposing my shame.

"What next? We've covered every part of the town. You've got to move or it's all for naught."

Of *course* it was all for naught. My mother had told me I'd end in a midden, burning my feet or clawing my eyes out to supply pain enough to trigger nivat's release. Bastien was right to scorn me.

"You made a bargain, Valen. It's almost sunset. You have your seeds. Come…I know where we'll be safe."

Reed-like Denys, who scarce came to my shoulder, dragged me up. Hunched over my clenching belly, muzzling groans, I staggered onward. Deeper into the alley. Down a narrow stair. Steam billowed from a door with hinges that scraped like claws on steel. Torchlight seared my eyes, and the cacophony of reedy scraping that might once have been music filled them with tears.

Hands shoved my stinking body to a hard bed and crammed a stick in my teeth. "Bite this so you won't scream."

My hand! Please gods, no! I tried to fight them off, but every muscle seized.

"They're in his rucksack…the seeds."

"Get out, Denys." A dry reasoned voice spoke softly as if he knew every word shrilled like Iero's trumpeting angels. "Ludo will hide you in a tub until the caravan leaves tomorrow. Gatzi spawn, did you two spend the whole day in a sewer?"

"Valen kept them off. He risked everything. Is he going to die?"

"He might wish so, but I've a notion what's needed. Bastien doesn't know he's here?"

"He thinks we're hid at your place."

"Go."

Pain splintered my bones. I could do naught but shiver, weep, and await the ax.

But then, a crunching noise released a scent of spice and earth that near stopped my heart with hunger. "Please," I mumbled. "Let me enspell them, then you can cut it off."

"You'll have to provide the blood and the magic," said the dark-haired man, stabbing my finger with a lance that masqueraded as a silver needle. "I'll do the rest. But I only cut parts off corpses, and you're not there yet."

———✦———

LAZY AND WARM, DELICIOUSLY clean from the bath, I settled deeper in the pillows, enjoying a bit of eavesdropping.

"God's bones, Bek!" said the man beyond the wall. "The edane's sorcerer said this Valen was surely pureblood—very likely the Cartamandua renegade that's stayed free so long. We could have made our fortune had we turned him in."

"You've kept Denys alive and whole," said Bek, dry as dust, "even if he can't be with you, and the pureblood's vanished."

"Aye. Worth the price." Sadness laced Bastien's growl. "I'm thinking someday I'll buy me a pureblood contract. Could be useful for the Coroner of the Twelve Districts of Palinur to have his own sorcerer. Gods save me from a twistmind, though. A drunkard surgeon is bad enough."

Their laughter faded down the passage.

I burrowed my face in Katie's rosy breasts and smiled to think of Denys safe. And I'd twenty-eight days before I'd need the seeds again.

From below, the sop-house music called me to the dance. Too bad the taproom wasn't safe and my legs weighed like lead. Instead I'd sleep a while, and then, if Katie pleased, we would celebrate the holy rites.

JANCY'S JUSTICE

-GnomeSaga-
KENNY SOWARD

Jancy is a secondary character in the GnomeSaga series, but for Blackguards *I felt she deserved a bit of the spotlight. "Jancy's Justice" takes place some years prior to the Battle of Hightower (as told in GnomeSaga). Working as a barmaid in the rough-and-tumble city of Half Town, 'Jancy the Quick' keeps her true profession a secret, but is poised to respond whenever injustice is found. In this instance, injustice has found her, but this time, Jancy may have bitten off more than she can chew.*

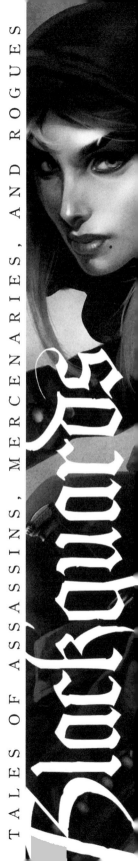

TALES OF ASSASSINS, MERCENARIES, AND ROGUES

Blackguards

J ANCY TIPPED HER SERVING tray as she wove through the crowd. Four dented, pewter cups filled with Laureen Pimpleton's best watered down swill leaned dangerously over the heads of her drunken patrons. A single spilled drop could ignite a wall-shattering brawl, and Laureen knew it.

"Walk straight and keep your tray up, Jancy, or you'll be eating outside with the dogs tonight!" The squat, black-haired proprietress belted out from behind the chipped oaken bar where she scrubbed dirty cups in a barrel of sudsy water.

Jancy smiled and gave the tray an extra twist as she spun between Rex Knuckleminder and Friar Beltonis. Her lithe form swam in her skirts. Her feet danced. Yet, she was never in danger of spilling anything; in fact, she'd never spilled a drop throughout her employment at the Broken Dog Tavern, never in the ever-crowded great room, and *never* in front of (or on) the patrons, many of whom were Half Town regulars with their toothy grins and sly hands, others just passing through on their way to Pelore or Vrath.

But let Laureen think I'm some was a clumsy, yellow-haired twit. That's me. Just your average serving wench.

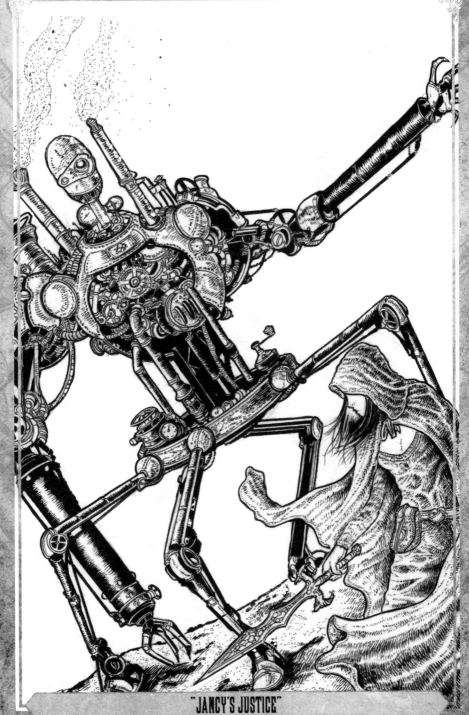

"JANCY'S JUSTICE"

Illustration by **ORION ZANGARA**

Despite Laureen's bawling (a noise these patrons were used to), everyone's attention focused on the traveling bard, Hopper. The gangly fellow sat splay-legged on the lip of the stone hearth, and his long fingers trilled delicately across the strings of his worn, wooden harp. Words sprung from the man's buck-toothed mouth in golden tones at odds with his bucolic persona, and his ridiculous feathered cap seemed to dance upon his head. The crowd was rapt. Even rowdy Billben Hardhand's jaw hung open as Hopper's tale unraveled. A somber yarn about the arrival of the gnomish race from far across the Dawnbreak Ocean, had them enthralled.

"Exiles," Hopper crooned, "from some faraway land, the race of sharp-brained folk arrived on Sullenor's west coast, wet and bedraggled, in wood ships banded with steel and brass and copper, driven by tremendous steam engines, autonomous paddles beating mercilessly at the ocean waves. Wherever gnomes settled, the sky above swarmed with a flotilla of aeroships buzzing like giant wasps—*bzzzzzz*. Armored plates covered wooden hulls, kept aloft by clusters of brawny, air-filled teats, sails driven by conjured gusts—"

"You talkin' about teats? Ain't seen any in *my* bed!" Rodge the drunken glass worker shouted (a fixture at the Broken Dog Tavern) and fell forward into his ale.

"Go home, Rodge," someone yelled. "We want to hear Hopper's tale, not stories about your teatless bed!"

Laughter rippled through the crowd, and then Hopper continued: "In this time there was but a thousand gnomes left in the *entire* world. And just as fast as they made land, they were turned away by the humans of Teszereth, and so they drove south down the coast to the shores of what would one day become the Pelorian capital; there, the gnomes found their respite, however brief. They gathered themselves, salvaging and modifying their ships and engines, sinking the rest, and then ventured inland, seeking a place to burrow, some place deep and dark and well-protected. An aerostat scout led them on one final trudge through the Cogspine Mountains to its highest peak, Kubalesh, named so by the thick-headed barbarians who dwelled there." Hopper growled that last part like a severely malnourished bear—(the bard was so damn scrawny). "Not for long though, because the gnomes were ruthless and cunning in their desperation, and their hands were soon steeped in blood."

Rodge's head rose. "Gnome bastards," he complained, then hiccupped. "How big do you think their gnomewoman's *teats* are?" Spittle flew from his mouth as he made a smallish gesture with his thumb and index finger.

"More than what you're getting!" That might have been Rex.

The crowd bent and swayed with raucous laughter. Even Jancy cracked a smile. Like clockwork, nearly every night, Rodge would start his mouth up and the others would tear him down.

"Now SHUT UP before I smash your face in!" And that was *definitely* Rex.

"Deep within the mountain," Hopper proceeded yet again, "like a great stony helm above their gnomish heads, they dug. The city they forged there in those cavernous halls was called Thrasperville.

"With their safety ensured, the gnomish Mayor was re-established, and the King and Queen from the old world, who had lived in the shadows for two dozen years to protect their gnomish line, were to be re-seated in the glorious new throne room made from the parts of broken machines, a new foundation built on iron and steam and steel, cogs and gears, and bone-numbing voracity.

"The gnomes had survived…"

Rodge clapped weakly and nearly rolled off his seat. Someone shoved him straight again.

"…yet, too much time had passed, and the Thrasperville gnomes were too distant from their original home in the old world. Many did not feel bound by the old ways; it was a different time, and their recent hardships had carved out a new type of gnome. Rebellious *cogweavers* and powerful *thaumaturges* made their claims to power. Old royal families, far removed from their lofty places, thought to regain their lost glory.

"One such gnomestress, a *machineweaver* called Vilka, sought the gnomish crown for her family, the Stillbrights. She marched into the throne room surrounded by a small army of whirring automatons and threatened to take the crown by force.

"It was a sad moment for gnomes," Hopper's voice had turned melancholy and droll. "One of the few times when greed surpassed the curiosity of invention." He strummed a mournful chord for emphasis.

"Jancy!" came a cry from the kitchen. Five seconds passed, and then again, "Jancy!"

Damn, Laureen!

Jancy reluctantly got back to work just as the story was getting good. She knew better than to ignore the proprietress twice. She resumed serving mutton and carrot stew, and more ale, while receiving a few well-placed slaps on the backside because she was too enthralled listening to Hopper to dodge them. Finally, turning her hip to avoid yet another grabby hand, she gave up on the story and focused on finishing her job and dodging deviant patrons.

That evening, when the patrons had all gone home (either on their own two feet, or dragged out by their less drunken friends), she found Hopper at the hearth with a flagon of wine for company. She usually found him there after a performance, except on overly rowdy nights, in which case he made a hasty exit, but tonight he'd left them thoughtful and melancholy, and they'd gone quietly home to their ale-spun dreams. His demeanor, shoulders slumped and eyes filled with weariness, conveyed how much energy he'd expended during his storytelling.

He put on a buck-toothed grin at her approach. "Hello, luv. I was just gathering myself for a good, long sleep."

"What room are you in?"

"Oh…can't stay here, dear. I'll be out in the stable with my pony."

"You outdid yourself tonight. The drink is on me. For that matter, let me get your room and board for the night."

Hopper's thin red face lit up, his smile large and even a bit frightening in the low tavern light. Then he sobered, cocking his head. "What's the catch?"

"Finish the story."

"Already done, dearie. Finished 'bout an hour ago."

"No…for *me*. I didn't get to hear it all."

His head sunk, and his eyes studied her from a lower angle. Jancy could tell he'd been taken for a fool before, and probably paid dearly for it, too. "So's you're sayin' if I finish, you'll buy this flagon….the *wineskin* the flagon was poured from, *and* you'll have me put upstairs where it's warm?"

"That's the deal."

The bard sighed, nodded, and re-arranged his expression. It was a miraculous transformation, one Jancy had seen several times before. His chest puffed up before her eyes as all traces of weariness slipped away, as if he was sucking life from the fire, the candles, and even the lingering smells of mutton and fried potatoes, and feeding off it. He worked his jaw around and puckered his lips. Twisted them. Squeezed his eyes shut. Then loosened everything into a visage of happy contentment, complete with a big, dumb grin plastered on his face, buck teeth still as gargantuan as mill stones, but far less pronounced.

"Yes, dearie," he said, his voice markedly higher, happier, and a touch mischievous. "I saw you whisked away by your duties 'bout the time I was telling what Vilka did after bursting into the throne room with her steel soldiers."

"Yes! That's it. What happened next?" Jancy said, as she pulled a chair over and sat facing the bard.

"Well," Hopper began, edging forward, "she demanded her crown, that's what she did. She demanded half the metal in the mountain and her choice of suitors to start her bloodline fresh and new and full; yes, that was what she wanted the most. A *child*… wooooeeeeeooooo…a child." Hopper sung that last part in a lilting falsetto that made the hairs on the back of Jancy's neck stand on end. He picked up his harp and launched into the tale's finale.

"The high-ranking gnomes in attendance called their swordsmen to them, realizing their sure doom should they remain divided. They banded together and shouted down Vilka and her claims; wizards and tradesman alike joined the fray.

"But Vilka did not back down, ruthless and cunning as she was. She ordered her stiff-legged, clankity-clank automatons forward. They marched to a song of spinning cogs and glowing eyes, steel hides deflecting all brave blades.

"And rather than christening the great hall with laughter, the place rang with steel and cries of horror as the already bedraggled colony suffered even more horrible deaths. Fathers and sons, young gnomes and even gnomelings just come of age perished in the desperate fighting.

"The throne room was bathed in blood and oil."

Jancy felt a little sick at the thought. "Oh no. I don't like this Vilka gnomestress at all. Not one little bit."

"As well you shouldn't," Hopper continued, standing now, his arms open wide in oratorical ecstasy. He fairly shouted, "Vilka has forever been the thorn for Thrasperville gnomes, stuck in their side, even to this day."

"Quiet down in there!" Laureen shouted from the kitchen.

"Never mind her," Jancy said. "Go on. *Please.*"

"Just when it seemed Vilka would win her throne by bloody battle, a young gnome named Frank Grundzest carted in a mighty magnetic stone they'd used to lift machines across great chasms on their path through the mountains. With a few quick words and the flick of a lever, he removed the spell that bound the stone's power and loosed its magnetic effect upon the throne room.

"The defenders encircling the throne gaped in awe as the automatons ground to a halt, toppling backwards at the mercy of the stone's pull!"

"Oh, but what about the gnomes? Their *armor?*"

"Fortunately for them, most of the gnomes in attendance wore leathers and tradesman's garb, yet the pull from the magnetic stone stole the weapons right out of their hands and yanked any loose metal from the walls and ceiling in a deadly rain. The center of the throne room was a heap of twisted, twitching metal, and a floor greased with the blood of their kin.

"With the motorized clatterers incapacitated, the gnomes went after Vilka. But she was impossible to kill. Once she saw the battle lost, she simply vanished."

"That's strange." Jancy bit her lip. "But I'll bet everyone was quite pleased with that."

Hopper shook his head vigorously. "Not so, dearie. You see, Vilka the Damaged, as she later came to be known, had absconded with the royal child."

Jancy's stomach twisted. "She took their *child?*"

Hopper nodded. "Thrasperville's scryers caught up with her

soon enough. A hundred furious gnomes plunged down through the Cogspires in pursuit, stopping before a deep valley that twisted through a flock of knobby hills. A dozen went in, never to return. A dozen more, with the same result. Of the last dozen, one returned, crawling up the barren hillside to his kin. His lips raced with incoherent babbling, his eyes bulging with distant terror. He died in their arms, against the wishes of the company cleric, whose gods seemed to have abandoned them in the face of the evil sorceress, Vilka.

"Full of rage and sorrow, what remained of the Thrasperville gnomes left the valley and returned to their new home under the mountain, more haunted now than ever before."

"That's terribly unfair." Jancy was disappointed the story had taken such a melancholy turn. She was even more upset about the fate of the stolen child, the little prince or princeling who might have had a wonderful life and ruled the gnomish subjects with a fair and just hand.

"That's not all, lass. No. Upon hearing news that her child had not been retrieved, the Queen threw herself from a high peak."

Tears welled up in Jancy's eyes and spilled down her cheeks (the first thing she'd ever spilled at the Broken Dog).

"What's wrong, lass? You look like you just lost a friend to a river dragon."

Jancy wasn't entirely surprised to find herself furious and heartbroken. She often got this way whenever she experienced some sort of mindless injustice, especially when it came to children. Only most of the time there was something she could do about it… and she often did. It was the '*itch* to move,' she called it, a feeling that she needed to act, to be in sudden motion, sudden *emotion*.

She sputtered. "It was a wonderful tale, Hopper. Really. I'm just sad for the child, is all. Taken from its mother and carried away by some complete stranger. Poor thing was probably dead before dawn."

"That's a thing, isn't it?" Hopper giggled. "You might think Vilka and the child passed away, victims of time and the natural order of death. Never mind magick elixirs and youth-altering spells..."

Jancy cocked her head, shifted in her chair. She started to speak, stopped, started again. "She's not still alive, is she?" Jancy was incredulous, but curious too. "That was hundreds of years ago. Even with magick, there'd be no way anyone could stay alive *that* long, could they?"

Hopper grew suddenly quiet, a mere whisper of the personality that been ringing through the tavern for the past half hour. He leaned forward, his wormy lips twisting. "I know she's alive, because I've *seen* her, luv. I've sang for her...in her tower at the foot of the Cogspire Mountains."

"Hopper..." Jancy threatened him with a look. She was in no mood to play.

"Aye, she is alive." He gulped. "And she still has the child. I've heard its cries. I've heard it *wailing*..."

JANCY STALKED SWIFT AND low across the night-blackened field of thigh-high razor grass with a knot in her stomach and a nervous sheen of sweat covering her skin. She held a shadow stick in front of her, its trailing plumes of *non-dark* flame and smoke shielding her, she hoped, from scrying eyes. The Pelorian vendor had guaranteed the crude stick's worth, and Jancy had accepted his word with all the coin she had left.

If the shadow stick failed, there would be no getting her money back.

Looming south, the Cogspire Mountains. Not the largest or

most far-ranging she'd ever seen, but as spiny and prickly as they came; dangerous and close, stone protrusions covering the odd-shaped hills and valleys like a pox, gnarled fingers of rock through which strange currents of wind sang. The ostentatious lowing of beasts—*giants?*—vibrating through the star-speckled sky.

Standing somewhere in all that tremendous power; Vilka's tower.

Jancy had gotten herself into some precarious spots before, but this one was looking worse by the minute. *You knew that, though. Didn't you? You heard Hopper's story. But, the child!*

Yes, indeed, the child. This *specific* child, who, if Hopper's story could be believed, remained trapped in some sort of sorcerous time bubble, never having felt its true mother's touch, never able to grow up, never to grow old.

How, then, do you justify yourself this time, Jancy? It was true. She had no mental category for this particular jaunt. Usually, it was "if I can just make this one child's life better, it will be worth the danger," or "I may die doing what I'm about to do, but this family won't be bothered by collectors anymore," or "putting my blade through that wretch's throat will be the best thing that ever happened to them. He was their father, yes, but with a father like that, who needs enemies?"

A bad life for a good life. A chance to make the world a better place when the *'establishment'* failed—a far too common occurrence for Jancy's liking. Her methods seemed like a solid approach. And, in a strange way, it was as if every life she freed from the yoke of injustice seeded for her a little family of her own. They may never remember her, of course. She was just a shadow, some flicker of movement passing through their lives in the blink of an eye, cutting out all the bad things like…like…well, like, any *good* mother would do.

But this child. *This child.* Isn't it long past helping? Wouldn't it be a deranged soul by now, whatever mental and spiritual growth it may have attained in a normal home now stunted by magick and the selfish wishes of a cruel sorceress? Jancy had no real appreciation for wielded magick. Too wild to control, it corrupted even the wisest of wizards.

What does magickal imprisonment do to a child so exposed over the course of hundreds of years?

Still, she had to see, had to be sure, even though Death's attention was turning her way once more; even as she stalked the landscape and carefully picked her way south into the teeth of the unknown, Jancy found herself grinning. It was not an unfamiliar thing. It was the itch.

The *itch* to move.

———•———

JANCY HAD HATED BREAKING Hopper's trust—especially with the business end of her dagger—but she minced nothing when it came to things like this. From the pointed end of her blade, she'd wrung the directions from the bard. He'd been reluctant at first, fearing Vilka's wrath for his indiscretion, but when given a choice between dying now and dying later, Hopper had wisely chosen to extend his life a little while longer. She hoped the bard would forgive her as he rested comfortably on the stuffed wool mattress in the cushiest room in the Broken Dog.

Probably thought of it as his last good night's sleep.

In any case, her course was set.

The dilapidated dock was right where he said it would be, next to the slow-rolling mountain river. Smelled like moss and mold and old wood. The thing was so rickety she was surprised it still stood. *But that's what you want someone to think, isn't it, Vilka? This is where Hopper would be expected. But not me.*

Jancy followed the lazy river upstream several miles to a small lake surrounded by sloping rock walls on three sides. A waterfall gushed an icy cascade over a weak lip of rock across the way, drenching leafy branches that sprouted from seams and cracks.

Jancy crouched behind a clutch of brush and two moping trees and gazed at her surrounds. Another dock perched at the lake's edge with a wide, flat-bottomed boat moored to it. It was amazing, this secret, this clandestine operation at the northern edge of the Cogspire Mountains, just a hundred miles from the original crime. Aside from Hopper, Jancy wondered who else visited Vilka in her remote tower? Who else knew this criminal remained alive? Surely, someone in Thrasperville? Maybe they did, and there was nothing they could do about it. She had to believe, if they knew, they would have finished her if they could.

Jancy shuddered. This was no ale-swilling brute of a parent, or even an uncommon thug. This was an evil older than she could imagine. Vilka was a thick rod of might…a master witch…who'd laid low a small army of trained gnomish fighters and mages.

I'm a fool. What can I hope to do that they could not?

Jancy clutched the hilt of the dagger at her side, her teeth grinding as she imagined the poor *wailing* child kept prisoner in that tower. She could turn around now knowing this was likely too much for her to chew. Good chance she'd die; who could she help then? But another part of her said this was the perfect time to stand true, to leap from the edge of the precipice and fly, kicking, at the face of doubt. To prove her justice reached far…even for someone as heinous as Vilka. But even then what would it prove if she could pull off what so many others could not?

That I'm quicker, that's what.

Her clear emerald eyes scanned the hills and rises, cliff edges bathed in star light and the glow of a fat, somber moon. The wind was up, shifting branches and carrying leaves across the surreal landscape, stirring up the scents of musty fall.

She didn't *feel* watched, yet the air rang with tension. Or maybe *she* was the tension. Yes, that must be it. *Quicker.*

Jancy found the path, a track of dirt wide enough for a horse, and followed it around the lake and up into the rolling hills, steeper, deeper, toward the heart of her mad obsession. She moved swiftly, resting only to grab a bite of food and to stretch like a cat. As she jogged along, courage and doubt competed inside of her, fighting for control, twisting her stomach into nervous knots. At the head of a long, stone path flanked by obsidian posts, she stopped, eyed the subtle etchings—*wards*—presented on the smooth surfaces.

"I think not," she chimed, softly.

Shadow stick held high, Jancy leaped off the path and into a lightly forested area, hoping it would shield her from watchful eyes. She made pace with her steady breathing, hypnotic, as she fed off the chill air. Ahead, through gaps in the claw-fingered branches of trees, she spied a spire of darkness rising from a distant hill. A thrill ran through her, and dread, too; Hopper had spoken true, and the reality of Vilka's legend struck her in the face like ice water, a sobering reminder that this was no ordinary foe. Doubt edged up again, but she forced it down. Her legs propelled her onward, strong and fleet, undeterred by her mind's wavering confidence. She pushed the pace, sticking to gullies and wooded areas where she could, rebellious against common sense, until sweat beaded her brow. She'd exhaust herself reaching the tower if she must, but she'd not be a coward. Sure enough, the effort of tackling the rugged terrain soaked up the nervous tension like a sponge soaking up water.

Soon she was beyond worry, beyond fear. A bit worn out but soul-fired. For a long time, her feet on the ground and her quickened breathing were the only sounds, but then came something else. A series of hums and metallic screeches, interspersed with loud clangs that echoed through the hills, growing louder as the tower loomed larger. The echo of *machinery*.

Jancy approached a low wall at the base of a gently sloping rise. Dilapidated and in ill-repair, missing whole sections in places. The black, mossy stone marked the edge of Vilka's fortress. At the top, rose a curtain wall and a gate made of the same stone.

Vilka's main tower was a beast of an edifice, a thick and imposing hunk of rock and steel…moving and glinting mechanics in the sheer moonlight.

What kind of place is this? More importantly, Jancy, what's your plan?

She skirted the edge of the wall, looking sharp. If she went up the hill, they'd surely see her. *They? Who?* It didn't matter who. She felt the scryer's roving eyes, felt *other* eyes, too. But then she came to a place where the short wall had crumbled inward, followed by a thick patch of brush and grass intruding up the hill and well into the outer courtyard. The wall was only twenty or thirty yards distant at that strategic point.

Without another thought, Jancy charged silently through the brush, keeping low, then sprinted across the open ground to the wall, slammed her back against the slimy stone, and listened for signs she'd been detected.

Too quick.

She took the shadow stick in her mouth. Its *non-fire* burned her nose and eyes like a smoldering soot as she proceeded to search for purchase up the wall. Her thin fingers found cracks, her toes crevices, and then she was scaling…the inhuman or *unhuman* part of her taking over, an instinctive skill she'd had since she could remember.

At the top, Jancy slipped over and crouched on the battlement, eyes searching. Within the inner yard, she spied a squat tower, its veined, domed ceiling, like translucent skin pulled taut over a brazier, pulsed with a pale, sickly glow. She sprinted down the battlements toward the gate and then angled toward the tower. Leaped…soared…her eyes half-lidded in the gusting wind…until she met the wall. Her fingers gripped the lip of a protruding window sill, her feet knocking gently against the stone below.

She listened for a moment, pulled herself up, and spied inside. The scryer at his work bench, head buried in a contraption made of metal framework and lenses, a scrying stone suspended from wires beneath it. The pale, worm-skinned gnome used handles to maneuver the contraption over a map of the surrounding lands.

Didn't see me, did you?

Jancy crept into the room, drawing one of her twin blades from her hip. Her heart thudded in her chest, her eyes narrowed in focus, her breathing all but silent. She hung close to the wall. Circling…circling…

The gnome jerked up from his divinations and slung a splatter of molten energy where Jancy *used* to be; the scalding magick struck the wall in a sizzling spray. But Jancy had already spun away, appearing in a quiet rush of air to stand beside the surprised wizard. He gasped and fell backward, knocking the contraption from the scrying table, clasping at the blood bubbling hole in his neck.

Jancy wiped her blade on his dingy robe and crept down the spiraling steps of the tower into a single large room. The scryer's living quarters, sparse and bookish, accoutered with the tarnished remnants of some bygone era. She spied the door to the inner courtyard and made for it, hoping the scryer's death had gone unnoticed by the tower's occupants.

Midway into the chamber, she stopped. What was that scuttling? What was that squeak? Her eyes scanned the dark corners, ears strained. There was nothing else alive in the room, she was sure of it.

But then came a thin, quiet *clink*, a slow hiss of steam, and Jancy looked up.

Two spider-like automatons clung to the ceiling, their bulging brass eyes fixed on her. She dove away as they dropped, a cacophony of ear-shattering noise, wiggling torsos flipping, legs flailing as they scrambled to bring her down.

Realizing she couldn't make it to the door before they were on her, Jancy turned and faced the snapping, hissing machines. They were a mass of legs, pincers, and claws, each with a stinger-tipped tail. A burnt oil smell rode blasts of hot steam, nearly choking her. Fast but crude things, stupid and ungainly, they pinched, snagged, and pummeled Jancy before she was able to hold her ground with a flurry of desperate parries, both daggers flashing in sparks against the patchwork appendages.

Most nimble fighters would *never* have chosen daggers so heavy or long, each blade the length of her forearm, yet Jancy found she loved the weight of her weapons in her hands. They were balance and counter-balance, sharp as sin, and when they met their mark, they could punch right through even plate armor, much to more than one armored assailant's surprise.

She leapt above a darting stinger and landed atop one of the wiggling, dog-sized things, burying a blade into a crevice between the head and thorax, pinning it to the ground. Rolled away just as the other crashed through, tearing into its brother in haphazard confusion. Jancy circled, waiting for a proper opening between the snapping, jittering forms.

Breathe. Wait for the itch…

And there was the opening she needed. Jancy reached out and snagged the thing's tail at the base of the stinger, heaved the squealing thing off the pile. Its brass eyes rolled around to find her. It twisted, biting, slicing with an assortment of deadly implements affixed to flexible segmented appendages. Jancy deflected two buzzing saws and buried her remaining blade into its head assembly—ping, ping, *crunch!*—parting the metal plate and cutting through cogs and gears and cables.

The thing crashed limp to the floor, although some internal mechanisms continued to whirr and click in broken confusion.

Jancy sighed. A dull pain in her side screamed. Something warm and wet soaked her shirt. She looked down, although she already knew; the sliver of a hooked leg had buried itself into her flesh.

Damn.

It came out easily enough, had only penetrated a couple of inches, thankfully. Superficial, but it hurt like hell. She dressed the wound with a poultice of herbs and a patch of *sticky leaf* from her light pack. She'd not wanted to waste time doing it, but the bleeding had to be mitigated before she moved on.

Moving to the door, she took a peek into the inner courtyard. Clear, as far as she could tell. Nothing but the sing-song of mechanics coming from the tower, and a slight vibration beneath her feet. Had that been there before? The strange, shifting edifice rose up before her, massive at its base, hardly tapering at all toward the top; three-hundred feet of stone and steel with pinwheels and cogs set flush into the wall or rising and descending through slits. Her curious eyes roamed the moonlit construction, wondering at its marvel. She began to hear a cadence to the cacophony, a *shurr, shurr, clink, click, clink, click, thwack!* Over and over.

It must be some kind of war machine, something to thwart an army. Her mind drifted back to Hopper's tale, and she wondered how many Thrasperville gnomes had lost their lives assaulting Vilka's fortress. *Good thing I'm not an army.*

And then another sound made her pulse quicken; the

unmistakable, warbling cry of a baby. The child's squall echoed down from the top of the tower, somehow louder than anything else, filling her head with agitation. In Jancy's mind, the child sounded unhappy. Urgent. Alone.

"Bitch," Jancy murmured through pursed lips. On an impulse she opened the door and sprinted across the courtyard. She'd already traced her path up the three-hundred foot tower, and it wouldn't take long for her to get to the top. Then she'd deal with Vilka.

She leapt to clutch one of the steel beams that made a frame at the base of the tower, but a firm hand grasped her foot and jerked her down. She met the ground with mind-numbing force, crushing the air from her lungs, and snapping her teeth together. Her vision went black. Her head rang. Even in her dazed state, having her senses knocked flat out of her, she knew. Something wanted to kill her.

Move...roll...crawl...up...up on your knees...up on your feet! It was all she could think to do until her brain righted itself. All the while, something heavy smashed the ground in pursuit. She tasted dirt and machine oil. Sounded like a giant bashing a tree trunk on the ground!

A moment more...and her vision crawled back; she was in the courtyard, yes.

The violent crashing stopped. She'd outdistanced it.

Another moment...and her head quit ringing; the baby's hiccupping wail cut through.

Jancy turned to meet the thing—a brute of a machine, all chest and piston-thick arms, greased parts flexing, glinting moonlight. It positioned itself between her and the tower with thumping footfalls.

"I could just run around you," she told it, striding forward. "I'm quicker."

The bulk sunk into a crouch. Something inside thrummed with

growing intensity.

"But where's the fun in that?"

Jancy burst ahead in a blur of motion. She swung both blades left across her body, allowing their weight to throw her off balance and into a careening stagger. The stuttering, sibilant roar of the automaton burned her ears as it reached out a paw to snatch her up. Jancy's right foot planted itself, stiff-legged, breaking her momentum, reversing her body in a dizzying, slingshot spin. She lost sight of the machine for an instant...until it popped back into view. But by this time, the girl was committed, pitching forward headlong, blades held together, stiff-armed, above her head.

Her momentum carried her off her feet. For an instant, she was airborne. A feeling of weightless elation passed through her before her blades slammed home to the hilt: the joint at the machine's hip, a sliver of hope. A weak spot. Steam ruptured from a sliced pressure line, bathing her face in hot agony. Tiny metal fittings trickled downward out of the wound. Something snapped. The machine's leg buckled, then lifted, and Jancy saw a shred of opportunity. She planted her shoulder into its crotch, gathered her legs, and shoved. Her back screamed, muscles quivering with the effort. If the boys at the Broken Dog could see her now, they'd never take another swipe at her backside again. No, this wasn't something even a very large man would attempt, much less a waif of a girl. Not even a waif, but a *wisp*.

It was the *unhuman* in her.

She gritted and grinned as it pitched...backwards...in a fall that seemed to take an eternity. It shook the ground in a violent crash, arms flailing helplessly. Jancy spied a tiny window on the breast facing, leaking a soft, green light. She leaped atop it and plunged her blade through the glass. The machine stopped moving.

For her own curiosity, she pried open the faceplate with the tip of her blade, and found another gnome inside. Like his kin, that same cold, pale skin, and luminous green eyes that stared up at her, *past* her, at the twinkling sky.

Were these the gnomes who'd supported Vilka in the centuries-old fight for the gnomish throne? Had she blessed them with unusually long life, too? Jancy curled her lip at the gnome's pasty, dead skin. "Some price to pay…"

The wailing baby ripped her attention upward, and soon Jancy was scaling the wall of Vilka's tower.

———•—•———

THIS IS IT. THIS is the window.

Jancy had followed her ears to the right spot, or so she thought. Wouldn't know for sure until she pulled herself over the jutting, angled ledge to see what awaited her. And would that be Vilka? Yes, certainly. The shadow stick, lost. The scryer, dead. The fight in the yard. The sorceress could *not* have felt Jancy's presence.

So be it.

Jancy took one glance over her shoulder—the breathtaking view from this dizzying height as she clung to the sill's underside like a spider, fingers and thin leather climbing boots locked into the tiniest of crevices, arms and legs bent at rigid angles to keep her from plunging down, down—and took a deep breath of night air.

And then she pulled herself up and over the ledge to land lightly on a plush, animal skin rug. Light oozed from brass wall sconces holding clear domes of glass. A smell like old garments and machine oil tickled Jancy's nose. The room was wide, spanning the tower's full diameter. A set of stairs spiraled up along the wall, another set spiraled down.

Jancy was hardly an expert in valuable antiquities, but even her untrained eye could fathom the pricelessness of the artifacts displayed on the walls, bureaus, and tables all around the room. In a far niche stood a cluster of exotic, pale dolls, clockwork beauties with skin made of porcelain and brass plates, nearly seamless rivet work and clear, vibrant eyes that looked down or away; some right at her.

"Waaaaaa!"

Heart racing, senses piqued to screaming, Jancy darted to an ornate bed in the center of the room, slid across the golden quilt, and landed softly beside a gently rocking cradle. The child's prison swayed of its own volition, the *click, click, click* of mechanisms inside as the machine wheel turned and the rocker arm gently labored.

Jancy stood over it, looking down. She pursed her lips in disappointment. The baby wailed again and Jancy nodded to herself—*dumb, dumb, dumb, Jancy. You are so dumb. A fool, even, for coming here.*

She shook her head and reached inside to touch it, see if it was real. Its skin was cold and unyielding, tarnished, marred with faint, circular scratches from what must have been centuries of polishing. Eyes made of azure-tinted crystal shifted around, looking at nothing. Brass eyelids blinked with soft *claps*. Its hinged mouth flopped open, and that discordant cry came again. "Waaaa!"

"Damn it." *You should have known not to trust a bard's tale. Only half right, it was. He said he'd* heard *a child, but you never thought to ask him if he'd actually* seen *it. And you're a fool for not noticing it sooner, so blind…*

"I'm trying to discern what you are." The voice reached her from another part of the room; a child's voice bathed in callousness.

Jancy froze.

"A human? An elf? No, I think neither of those."

Unhuman. Jancy pulled her hands out of the cradle and turned.

The owner of the voice separated herself from the other dolls with slow, easy steps for one so small. She came to just above Jancy's waist but seemed taller. Must be her elegant posture; back straight, shoulders up and stiff, weight balanced perfectly on her hips.

"You're Vilka."

"I am." No hesitation. "But that still doesn't answer my question. What are *you*?" The sorceress lingered in the shadows at the edge of the light, playing.

"Don't you want to know my name?"

Vilka made a dismissive noise. "It hardly matters." She crossed to Jancy's right, passing behind a sitting chair, her pallid hands tracing gently across its back. The sorceress moved in and out of the shadows, exposing her features a little at a time. She wore a simple black gown, slippers on her feet, and bracelets that jangled as she moved. Hair the color of ink fell in tiny ringlets around her brow and down over her shoulders. A sharp jaw was set in something like anger, softened by glowing skin. A startlingly blue eye flashed in the light and then dimmed as the sorcerous found another pocket of darkness.

It was unnerving the way she moved, especially since Jancy had thought herself something of an enigma in that category. "What happened to the baby?"

"The baby? Oh, you mean my son, Nurthrik? He's been gone a very long time, both from this tower and from the face of Sullenor, too. Dead, I'm afraid. But he lived a very long life."

Jancy shook her head in confusion. "I don't understand. Hopper..." *Damn!* She hadn't meant to expose the bard. Well, no use in protecting him now. *That* squirrel was on the spit. "Hopper told me you took the child from the throne room in Thrasperville. That you *stole* him."

Vilka's chuckle was a wicked stab. The sorceress turned and

crossed back the other way, toward the window, showing Jancy, quite plainly, the other side of her face. Jancy gasped, stepped back, stomach turning with revulsion. Vilka's face was…it was…skinless… no, plated. No, an assembly. Delicate rivets ran across her forehead, encircled her ear, and plunged beneath her chin. Her jaw was hinged with a finely-grooved bolt. A blue stone blazed from her lidless eye socket. Brass teeth clicked when she spoke, and her voice no longer feigned at kindness or even curiosity. It was cruel. "Is *that* what he said?"

"Yes, and he said you killed so many good gnomes. That you slaughtered them for no other reason than ambition."

"Well, yes. I did the stealing of the child, and the slaughtering. Well, some of it, anyway. But, as usual, the scribes and bards only have one side of the tale. The side that is the most compelling and cruel and pointedly *not* in my favor, no doubt." Vilka was standing not fifteen feet from Jancy, staring out the window. She sighed, cocked her head. "You do know there's always *two*…sides."

"Yes, of course." Jancy sought her itch, longed for it. But it was gone. She was frozen to the spot, unable to move. Barely able to breath. She gulped. "What's your side, then?"

"The truth!" Vilka's chin jutted in defiance. "Hopper painted the Thrasperville colony as the perfect picture of victory over great odds, yes? Pure of purpose?"

Jancy nodded.

"The last of our kind?"

Again, Jancy nodded.

"Hah! No, Thrasperville was founded by criminals and miscreants, necromongers and polymagickians, who fled across the sea to this insipid rock you call Sullenor. We were prisoners of the cogweavers in the old world. Entire generations of us, slaves. Entrapped so long no one remembered why we'd been imprisoned in the first place. So we broke free, killed hundreds of them, stole what we could, and trudged across the sea.

"Who knew that when we came here, we'd turn against one another?" Vilka shrugged. "Looking back, it shouldn't have come as a surprise, I suppose. We all had our egos, and our pride. We all wanted to rule in the new world with the others at our feet. What happened in the throne room at Thrasperville was nothing short of chaos. Bloodshed. Brother against sister. Father against son.

"My stealing that child got their attention. It bound them together. It gave them a common cause. You see, I *saved* that city. They came after me rather than destroy themselves."

"They couldn't defeat you."

"No, they couldn't. And my dear son, Nurthrik, grew up to be quite normal. A great cogweaver in his own right. A decent wizard, even. In fact, he got very bored of this tower and sought his fortune elsewhere, out there in the world." She waved her hand absently at the window. "Met some of our Thrasperville kin who were not happy with the current Mayor, or whatever they called it at the time, and struck out eastward to begin a new city. They called it Hightower, I believe."

Jancy's nerves began to calm as she sensed the truth in Vilka's story. Jancy knew the hearts of men, had witnessed their cruelty and malice firsthand, and she figured they weren't too far removed from the hearts of gnomes. She could picture the slaughter in the throne room; a combination of her and Hopper's tales, the truth lying somewhere in between the tellings. It didn't matter, though, because there was no child in danger. There was no *child*. Jancy had no reason to be here, no reason to trouble this gnomestress, strange as she may be, any longer.

"Why do you keep this?" Jancy nodded to the hulk of metal in the cradle.

A flash of sadness passed over the Vilka's face, a quick sprinkle of sorrow, and "because it reminds me of him. My son."

Someone else's son. But Jancy didn't press the point. "I'm sorry for coming here. I shouldn't have. I didn't know—"

"Yes, assumptions. They always get us into trouble, don't they? I find it ironic that a *baby stealer* came here to accuse me of the selfsame thing."

"I don't *steal* them."

"Oh? What would you call it, then? Did you come all this way because you thought it was hungry?"

"No!" Jancy bit her tongue. That itch wiggled inside her belly, that tease of premonition she always got when something was about to go horribly wrong. "I'll just be going, if you don't mind." Jancy started to slide across the bed, since Vilka was directly in her path if she wanted to go around it, but the sorceress stepped quickly and quietly toward the window, blocking the way out. Her gaze remained outside, though, leaving that awful side of her face for Jancy to consider.

"You won't take the stairs? Don't you trust me?"

Jancy stopped, put her feet back on the ground. "I don't even know you."

"That's right," Vilka's voice dripped venom. "And you broke into my home."

Jancy shifted nervously from one foot to the other. She'd already taken stock of every possible escape route, but the only sure exit was out the window, *through* the sorceress. "I…I apologize for that. My intentions were—."

Vilka faced Jancy, smiled, half honey, half horror. "Apology *not* accepted. You see, if I let everyone simply stroll in here, have a cup of tea, and then leave, I fear my reputation would suffer. I might even seem somehow *vulnerable* to those wobbleheads up in

Thrasperville who, for the most part, have forgotten all about me."

Jancy's body became taut for a nervous moment and then relaxed into state of calm resignation. It would be a fight. She could feel it.

"Plus I have a collection to keep up." The sorceress gestured to a large tank behind Jancy, a massive block of glass so opaque that not even Jancy's superior eyes could pierce it. Now, though, it was crystalizing, clearing, so that she could see what was stored there…

Jancy gasped, unbelieving.

Heads.

In ornate glass jars.

Bloated things in some murky brine. Humans and elves, dwarves with their beards spun around at the bottoms, trolls in the bigger ones. But mostly gnomes. Old ones, to be sure; flesh sloughed and floating in that putrid slosh. Jancy felt their eyes on her. Accusing! They all knew what she'd been doing these past few years. *Fixing* those poor fathers and wretched mothers, killing, no, *murdering* anyone that didn't fit her sense of right and good. Whispers in Half Town's taverns spoke of a misguided vigilante. She knew then that hers would be the next head in a jar. And probably Hopper's soon after.

She returned Vilka's wicked stare, blue eyes against green, her fingers brushing the hilts of her knives.

And then Jancy got the itch to move…

PROFESSIONAL INTEGRITY

-Riyria-

MICHAEL J. SULLIVAN

"Professional Integrity" is set in the world of my Riyria Revelations, which centers around two rogues, Royce Melborn (a cynical thief/assassin) and Hadrian Blackwater (a more idealistic ex-mercenary). No prior knowledge of the Riyria books is required to enjoy this story to its fullest. This team makes a living taking "jobs" for various nobles. Usually that means stealing something, but when a young heiress asks them to steal her…well that's a first for the pair. The name of the person being Tuckerized in this short couldn't have been a better choice. While I'm playing it coy as to avoid spoilers, I think you'll come to understand why it fits this particular story so well.

Blackguards

SAY THAT AGAIN," HADRIAN said.

"I want you to kidnap me." Red-headed, freckled, with deep green eyes as fresh as the leaves of trees after a hard rain, the young woman sat, or more accurately perched, on a stool. Holding a purse on her lap, she was all smiles.

Royce, who had been watching the passing carriages, chose that moment to shut the tea shop's door. He also closed the adjoining room's partition, sealing the three of them in a world of doilies, crumb cakes, tiny cups, and parasol stands.

"We're thieves," Royce told her in a quiet voice. "We don't kidnap."

"It's the same thing, really," the young woman insisted, maintaining her blinding grin.

"Really—it isn't," Royce said.

"No, seriously. You're just stealing, you know…a person—me."

"Fine," Royce said. "Consider yourself stolen."

"No, not now. You have to kidnap me *tomorrow* night."

"Why?" Hadrian asked, leaning forward carefully.

He sat across from the young woman—who'd said her name was Kristin Lamb—at a little table with an untouched teapot and three

"PROFESSIONAL INTEGRITY"

Illustration by OKSANA DMITRIENKO

cups. He was certain a good bump would send the whole thing over. The entire room was like that, filled with glass and porcelain.

"Because that's when he's coming, and he needs to think I've been abducted."

"Who's *he*?"

The woman's bright grin stretched to a full-on beam. Kristin looked up and then closed her eyes, lost in a moment of memory or dream. "Just the most wonderful man on the face of Elan—the Viscount Ianto Don Speakman."

"And why do you want him to think you've been kidnapped?"

Kristin's eyes popped open, and she shifted in her seat. "Is it really necessary for you to know?"

"No, it's not, because we don't kidnap heiresses," Royce jumped in. He was hovering halfway between the table and the door to the street. "Now if you know a neighbor you don't like who has a jeweled tiara she keeps in a dresser drawer, we can do business, otherwise—"

"Yes, it's necessary," Hadrian said, and turned to face her more directly, the scabbard of his bastard sword dragging across the rug.

"Well, you see, we're going to be married."

"Okay, so why do you want your *fiancé* to think you've been kidnapped?"

"Well…" Kristin's fingers played self-consciously with the heart-shaped silver locket hanging from a chain around her neck, her face blushing. "He's not *exactly* my fiancé."

"How much *not* your fiancé is he?"

She looked away, her sunbeam smile growing cloudy. "He doesn't know I exist." Her white-gloved hands came up to cover embarrassment.

"Not going to make much of an impression on him if you disappear then, is it?" Royce took advantage of the woman's covered face to glare at Hadrian and jerked his head toward the exit.

Royce wasn't the sociable sort. Most of their jobs were set up through a liaison which avoided this shortcoming, but after their last arranged venture, which resulted in the two being trapped in the roots of a mountain by a long dead dwarven jester, Royce had insisted on handling this meeting personally.

"No, it will!" Kristin's head popped out of her hands. "When he's heard I've been taken, he'll rush to my rescue. And tomorrow will be perfect. Ianto and Parson Engels come every month. They spend their nights drinking with my father until they all pass out."

"Oh, yeah, definitely sounds like *the most wonderful man in Elan.*" Royce moved behind Kristin and, with an earnest expression, pointed at the door.

"Oh he's not a drunkard. He's a man of honor and only partakes to please my father. He's much too polite to say no."

"Luckily we don't suffer from the same malady. Hadrian? Shall we? No need to keep wasting this lady's time and we really—"

"I'll pay fifteen sovereign tenents." Kristin pried the mouth of her purse open. The coins poured onto the delicate table with a clatter. One rolled off, hit the floor, and spiraled around before ramming into Royce's foot. "See!"

Royce plucked the coin with a look of amazement. "You *brought* the money with you?"

"Ah-huh." Kristin nodded, making her ponytail bounce. "I thought you might not believe me."

"Oh, trust me, I don't *believe* you."

"What?" She patted a gloved hand on the pile she'd just poured. "This *is* real coin."

"I know—I'm not referring to the money," Royce said. "I honestly can't believe you made it this far."

"*Oh.*" She threw a dismissive hand at him and smirked. "Well,

I only live a few miles outside of Medford." Kristin pointed toward the window, which framed their view of the crowded plaza of Gentry Square where scores of nobles strolled in the midday sun. "I could have walked. Really I could have, but these are new shoes..." She stomped a dainty foot on the rug, making a muffled *thump*. "And Daddy is always saying the horses need exercise."

"I meant in *life*," Royce said. "I can't believe you've *lived* this long. You're what? Twenty-five? Twenty-six? By now I would have bet gold you'd have drowned by looking up in a rainstorm."

Kristin's eyes widened. "Don't you dare insult me!" She squared her shoulders and straightened the sleeves of her gown. "You make it sound like I'm an old hag. I'm only *twenty-two*!"

Royce looked at Hadrian and rolled his eyes. Turning back to Kristin, he made a ridiculous bow. "Oh—well, my apologies."

Kristin's face became a beacon of hope as she leaned forward. "So you'll do it?"

"No!" Royce's tone echoed with finality.

"But Royce—" Hadrian started.

"Listen," Royce stopped him. "Aside from the fact that we don't kidnap—or even pretend to—tomorrow is a full moon, which adds additional risk to an already stupid idea."

Hadrian ignored him and leaned toward Kristin, careful not to put his weight on the table. *If I get out of here without breaking something it will be a miracle.* "Let me get this straight. You're willing to pay fifteen tenents just in the hope your disappearance will be noticed by this Ianto fellow?"

The woman wiggled her eyebrows. "Clever, right?"

"Not if clever means the same in your world as it does in ours," Royce said.

"My father will panic when I disappear. And Ianto—being the daring, brave, and wonderful man he is—will offer to find me. And when he does, I'll throw my arms around his neck and thank him with kisses. *Oh*—he'll notice me."

"And then you two will live happily ever after, I suppose?" Royce stared at the woman, his disgust replaced by pity. Hadrian had seen the same expression after his partner's bay mare broke her leg stepping in a woodchuck hole.

"Absolutely." Kristin bounced once more in her chair.

Hadrian picked up the woman's empty purse and began putting the coins back. "Listen, I'm sorry, but I have to agree with Royce. You don't need us. Save your money. If you really think your disappearance will work, just sneak out and *pretend* you were kidnapped."

"I can't do that."

"Why not?"

"Because he locks me in."

"Who does?"

"My father."

"So? Climb out a window."

"I can't."

"You're bedroom doesn't have a window?"

"He doesn't lock me in my bedroom."

"Where does he lock you?"

"In a steel box…in the basement."

Hadrian stopped gathering up the coins, opened his mouth, and then closed it. He glanced at Royce, who failed to offer any help, but appeared genuinely interested in the conversation for the first time. "Your father…wait…" Hadrian forgot himself and leaned on the table with his elbow, causing the thing to tilt and creak or possibly crack; he wasn't sure which. Jerking his elbow nearly took out the porcelain teapot. He watched to make certain the table wouldn't collapse, composed himself, clasped his hands, and leaned toward her again. "Why in Maribor's name would your father lock you in a box?"

Kristin shrugged, making the lace of her dress dance.

"Have you asked?"

She looked at Hadrian with a smirk.

"So what did he say?"

"He just says it's for my own safety and won't say anything else."

"And your mother? What does she say? Why does she go along with this?"

"My mother died when I was five, and I'm certain that's part of it. After what happened to her, he's overprotective."

"What happened to your mother?"

Kristin focused on the teacups. "We were attacked by wolves just a few miles from home. She was killed. He's always saying he won't let it happen again."

"So he locks you in a steel box every night?"

"No. Just when Ianto and the parson visit, which, of course, is why Ianto hasn't noticed me."

"Yeah." Royce nodded his head. "I can see that being a problem."

"Exactly," Kristin nodded along with him. "So all you have to do is come in after they've passed out, go downstairs, and steal me. You can leave a note telling them where to leave some ransom money…you can keep that too, by the way. Then just tie me to a tree or something and send another note saying where they can find me."

"You know, that really doesn't sound too hard," Hadrian said.

"Don't encourage her." Royce pushed away from the chair.

"Royce, the poor woman is being locked in a box whenever suitors visit, I think maybe she could use a little help, don't you?"

"Oh, she needs help all right, but we're not in the *helping* business."

Hadrian pointed at the purse. "But she's also paying fifteen gold tenents. You like gold tenents."

The door to the tea shop opened, ringing a small bell, and a splash of sunlight hit the floor as three elderly ladies entered while closing their parasols. They were warmly greeted by the owners who rushed out of the side office—a husband and wife, Hadrian guessed; he wasn't sure. He and Royce had been working out of Medford for years, but this was the first time they'd set foot inside the tea shop. Most of their meetings were conducted in the far less affluent Rose and the Thorn Tavern. That wasn't possible this time. Kristin couldn't be expected to go to the Lower Quarter, much less Wayward Street. It's likely she didn't even know such places existed.

The three ladies glanced suspiciously in their direction. Two surly looking men with a young, well-to-do woman trapped between them raised suspicion. Especially Royce. His all-enveloping cloak and piercing glare screamed malevolence. He was the sort of man mothers described to keep children from wandering. And Hadrian wasn't much better. Dressed in worn leather and totting three swords along with a three-day-old beard, he made the perfect accomplice. In most places they frequented, their don't-bother-us appearance was a good thing—not so much in a gentry tea shop. At least the money had been put away.

Hadrian lowered his voice. "Come on, Royce, it's an easy job. I've seen you do more on a dull night just for kicks."

"So you'll do it?" Kristin asked, that brilliant smile back again, all hope and butterflies.

Hadrian looked at Royce.

Royce glanced at the elderly women as they took seats across the room. He sighed, threw up his hands in resignation, then turned away.

"It doesn't look like it," Hadrian explained, "but that's a yes."

"Can I just leave the money with you, then?" Kristin asked.

Royce turned back and loomed over the little table and the young woman. "I was going to insist on that, even if we *didn't* take the job." This whispered statement was delivered with all the sinister foreboding known to make grown men shiver.

"Oh good!" Kristin jumped up, clapping her hands—her smile wider than ever. "And you'll be there tomorrow night? Ridgewood Manor, about half a mile past the mill with the waterwheel."

Hadrian glanced over at the trio of ladies openly watching. "We'd be happy to accept your invitation."

RIDGEWOOD MANOR AND THE surrounding estate was a plot of land provided to the Port Minister as part of his compensation by King Amrath, ruler of Melengar. At one time it may have been grand, but the place was showing its age and wasn't much to look at, at least from the outside. Two stories of mismatched stone, moss, and ivy, Hadrian might have mistaken it for a rustic inn or a once-fine tavern that had fallen on hard times. Three dormers jutting out of the gabled roof suggested a third story, and the two chimneys spouting on either side hinted at the owner's indulgence for comfort. But the soot-stained manor wore an abandoned expression, a lonely melancholy reflected in the many unadorned windows that peered out on an empty countryside and an encroaching forest.

Royce and Hadrian had found the Lamb estate right where Kristin said it would be, some five miles southeast of Medford, just past the waterwheel of Abner's gristmill. The house was nestled so far back from the King's Road that a sign was needed. The simple plank, cut into the shape of an arrow and mounted on a listing post, was weathered to the point of uselessness. Following the arrow's suggestion, they walked up a dirt road that faded into a two-track path as it wandered through a dense forest. After what Hadrian guessed to be a quarter mile, they found a clearing with a lonesome duck pond where a forgotten rowboat rotted. Beyond it stood the moss blanketed wall, the wrought iron gate, and the manor.

"What kind of person locks their daughter in a box?" Hadrian asked, staring at the house.

Royce settled in behind a thick patch of blackberry bushes near the eaves of the forest. The summer wind was somewhere else that evening, and nothing moved except the occasional flight of birds and a pair of mallards dunking their heads in the leaf-strewn pond. The sun was still high enough so that shade was welcomed, but the shadow of the manor was long enough to reach the rotting rowboat.

"People do strange things. For instance—you took this job."

"I didn't hear you say 'No.'"

Royce knelt down, peering through the leaves, his sight methodically panning the grounds. "Actually I did. You just weren't listening. You were swayed because she's cute."

"She is cute. People like cute things: puppies, kittens, babies—not you, of course, but most people. The fact that you hate puppies is really disturbing, by the way."

Royce showed no sign of listening.

"If you really didn't want to do this, we wouldn't be here," Hadrian said. "In fact, we could have just kept her money. Not like there was anything she could have done about it. So if it was such a stupid idea, why are we here?"

"Professional integrity."

Hadrian laughed.

"Quiet," Royce scolded, his head turning, eyes darting around.

Hadrian covered his mouth, the laughter reduced to airy snorts.

Royce scowled.

"Do you even know what the word *integrity* means?"

Royce sighed and shifted a foot to get a better look at the yard near the gate.

"No seriously," Hadrian said. "Why are we here?"

Royce shrugged. "Curiosity."

"So you want to know why he locks her in a box too?"

"That…and other things."

"Oh? *Ooh.*"

Royce looked over. "What?"

"This isn't about the woman at all. This is about her father."

Royce pointed up at the house. "Lord Darren Lamb all but killed Medford's underground trade when Amrath appointed him Port Minister. For more than a year, nothing moved in or out of the city."

"Nothing *illegal*, you mean." Hadrian struggled to find a safe place to sit among the thorny tendrils of the dense thicket, then he removed his left boot. While the trip from Medford was a generally pleasant walk along country lanes, somewhere near the gristmill Hadrian had discovered a pebble near his heel.

"Right—and he actually enforced the king's tariffs."

"The man was clearly insane."

Royce smirked. "The point is he successfully corked the flow of contraband for the first year after his appointment, and then everything went back to business as usual. You don't find that interesting?"

"You heard Kristin. The man's wife died—and not from some fever. Think about it—*wolves*. That kind of thing can mess some people up. Do you really think he was concentrating on his work after that?" He paused holding his boot absently and looked once more toward the house. "I didn't even think there were wolves around here anymore."

"Maybe it wasn't wolves."

Hadrian turned the boot upside-down and began shaking it. "What do you mean?"

"Any man who shuts off the flow of contraband is going to have a lot of nasty enemies."

"You know, not everything is a conspiracy."

Royce turned and looked squarely at him. "And the steel box?"

Hadrian looked up. "Okay, you've got me there. But as you said, people do strange things. Maybe Kristin is right. Her father could just be overly protective."

"Overly protective fathers threaten suitors with a thumbscrew by saying it won't be used on their thumbs. They don't lock their daughter in a steel box." Royce pulled back a branch to give them both a clear view of the front gate. "I think something else is going on in that house after dark."

"Like what?"

Royce smiled. "*That's* why we're here."

As the sun was about to set, a carriage carrying two men rolled past Royce and Hadrian. It entered the gate and the door to the house opened before it came to a stop.

A richly dressed man rushed out. "Finally!" His voice carried easily across the duck pond to the blackberry thicket. "I thought you might not be coming."

Two men stepped out. "Sorry. Too many last minute things. Lost track of the time," said the larger man.

"Well, I had Leta save dinner for you."

"Kristin?"

"She's safe. I locked her in for the night a few minutes ago. I don't take chances anymore."

They went inside. The door closed with a distant clap, and as

Royce and Hadrian waited in the forest, the sky darkened and night fell.

——◆◆——

THERE WERE TIMES HADRIAN wondered if Royce was actually a cat that some mischievous witch had turned into a man and then lost track of. The similarities were too numerous to be coincidental. An irritatingly-superior aloof nature, fastidiousness, a habit of roaming at night, and his general propensity for solitude were all evidence. But it was when he was hunting, as he was that night, that Hadrian really saw the cat in Royce. The man could sit perfectly still, eyes wide, for hours. He even breathed differently, as if smelling his prey.

Hadrian crawled from the brambles and walked beneath the eaves for a time before finally just lying on the lawn and staring up at the stars. He used to gaze at the night sky often as a kid. Having grown up in a tiny manorial village there wasn't much else to do at night—and it appeared there still wasn't. These stars were different than the ones he had grown up with. The manor was too. Difficult to form a precise thought, the place had a lonely, sad feeling. It was impossible to imagine someone as alive as Kristin living there.

Hadrian fell asleep, and when he woke a full moon was in the sky. He crept back to Royce who remained just as he'd left him—a cat on the hunt.

"Have a nice nap?" Royce asked.

"How long was I sleeping?"

"Few hours."

"Anything happen?"

His answer was a howl that rang through the night.

"Was that a...?"

"A wolf," Royce said.

"But we're only five miles outside of Medford."

Royce shrugged.

"First time you heard it?"

Royce shook his head. "Off and on for a while now."

"Getting closer or farther away?"

Royce peered thoughtfully toward the house. "Neither."

While Hadrian was pondering this, Royce stood up. "Getting late. Time to steal an heiress."

The wall around the manor was only four feet, and they hopped it, landing in a small front-yard garden. Despite the season, no flowers bloomed. The hedges were ragged and grew over the stone walk. The bird bath was dry, filled with only old leaves and a water stain. Royce peered in the dark windows, then looked up toward the roof.

"Just wait here," Royce said as he moved to the corner of the house and began climbing the irregular edge stones. Designed as a pretty border, they made an excellent ladder for the likes of Royce. Hadrian waited among the overgrown beds and empty planters watching the ghostly form of his partner creep along the roof to one of the dormers where he slipped inside an open window.

Another canine howled, closer this time but muffled—*behind the house perhaps?* The night had turned chilly, the ground wet. Morning would be coming soon, and Hadrian wondered—if only for a moment—if Royce had let him sleep out of kindness. He still made the mistake of thinking of Royce as a normal person, at least what Hadrian thought of as normal. The two had debated the nature of what *normal* was on far too many nights. Royce won those arguments because he had a way with logic which eluded Hadrian, unless Hadrian was drinking. At those times, at least in his own mind, Hadrian declared himself the victor. Royce hadn't been giving Hadrian his rest out of kindness; he was waiting for the right time. This was the witching hour, the small of the morning when the living left the world to ghosts, goblins, and thieves. Everyone inside would be asleep.

The front door opened and a shadow waved him to enter.

"Three of them asleep in the big room." Royce pointed into the darkness. "Drunk, I think. Stairs are this way. Stay close. Be quiet."

Oouuuwwoo.

The wolf howled again—much louder.

Hadrian stopped Royce by grabbing his arm. "That's—it's…"

"In the house—yeah."

"Can't be a wolf then. Has to be a dog."

Royce only shrugged. "Heiress," he said, and led the way down a hall into the kitchen. Walls of stone with an obstacle course of pots and pans on the floor and dangling from overhead beams, it smelled of smoke and grease. Royce led Hadrian to a set of stairs beside a barrel and a pile of wood. Down they went, leaving most of the light behind. Only a single shaft bled down the steps to a cellar filled with racks of wine. In the center of the basement floor, Hadrian could barely make out a trapdoor with a metal ring and a big brass padlock, holding it fast.

"Kristin?" Hadrian called softly.

Oouuuwwoo.

The thieves stared at the metal door, then at each other.

The trapdoor had a jailer-style peek window that Royce slid back.

All Hadrian saw was a pair of vicious eyes and bright canine teeth that caught the light as a wolf snarled and snapped.

They both stepped back in shock as the caged animal growled and yipped louder than before. Hadrian heard the sound of feet rushing across the floor above them.

"Damn it!" Royce said, pulling his dagger from beneath his cloak. "Let's get out of here." He moved toward the stairs.

Hadrian took one last look at the wolf. It lunged at the opening, a long snout punching through the hole. When it drew back, the light glinted on a silver chain and heart-shaped locket around the animal's neck.

———————

"WHO ARE YOU? WHAT are you doing in my house?" Lord Darren Lamb was short, plump, in his late forties, and still in possession of his own hair. He stood just outside the kitchen, blocking their path with a spear and struggling to wipe his eyes clear of sleep.

With him were two others. A thin fellow with a burning candelabra in one hand and a long dagger in the other. He dressed in the black and scarlet robes of a Nyphron priest. The other was a tall man with a bald head and goatee, wearing a stiff-collared doublet and holding a saber.

"Nobody and, oddly enough, absolutely nothing," Royce replied. His voice was cool, relaxed, but the cat was crouched, claws out, fur high.

Hadrian moved to his side where he stared at his lordship and the spear. The blade was bright silver.

"Nothing?" Lord Darren said incredulously. "What are your names? Why are you here?"

"Misunderstanding," Royce said. "And if you'll move aside, we'll be leaving."

"I don't think so," the tall man with the saber growled. "You're a pair of thieves, come to steal from his lordship."

"King Amrath will take your hands for this," the thin priest with the bouquet of candles said.

"Is that true?" Lord Darren asked Royce.

"Which part?" Royce asked.

"Are you thieves who've come to steal from me?"

Royce rocked his head from side to side. "Sort of—but as you can see, we didn't. Changed our minds."

"I'm Lord Darren, Port Minister of Medford, and officer of the king's justice. Do you know that?"

"Actually, yes."

"I have the power to execute you right here."

Royce smiled. "You can try. Wouldn't advise it."

"Your lordship." The saber-bearing, bald man raised his weapon. "Do I have your permission to—"

"Your daughter is a werewolf?" Hadrian asked.

Everyone looked at him—even Royce.

Lord Darren's eyes grew wide, and he stepped back as if Hadrian had threatened him, but while he carried three swords, he hadn't drawn any of them.

His lordship shot a nervous look at the priest. "You swore—"

"I didn't tell anyone," the priest replied quickly. He had a sharp whine to his voice.

His lordship turned to the bald man.

"Don't look at me." The tall man lowered his blade to a less awkward position, but still kept the tip pointed at Royce.

"So she *is* a werewolf," Hadrian concluded.

"You're not serious," Royce said.

"You saw what was in the box."

"I saw a wolf."

"That wolf is wearing a heart-shaped silver locket around its neck."

"Drop your weapons," Lord Darren declared in a commanding,

although less confident tone.

Royce looked puzzled. "Why?"

"The two of you are under arrest for attempted burglary."

"No, I meant why should we put our weapons down?"

"Put them down or we'll make you drop them," the tall man said, and raised his blade once more.

"Don't do that," Hadrian said quickly, and laid a restraining hand on Royce's shoulder, drawing him back. "Threats just make him grouchy. But I'll tell you what—how about we *all* put the blades away and discuss the situation in a friendly manner. What do you say?"

"I say we've already talked too much." The tall man took a step forward.

Hadrian saw the attack coming, read his feet and shift of weight. The bald man knew how to use a blade. He had experience but no talent. Hadrian, having positioned himself in front of Royce, became the default target. Stepping close, Hadrian ignored the sword and blocked the man's arm. He caught him by the wrist, twisted, took the weapon away, and shoved him to the floor. Then Hadrian turned on the priest who shuffled deftly forward with his dagger ready to stab. He stopped as Hadrian pointed the saber at him.

"Drop it," Hadrian ordered.

The priest hesitated.

"Drop it or *you'll* be the one to lose a hand." Hadrian was lying. He wouldn't cut off a man's hand when he only had a dagger any more than he'd hit a woman brandishing a shovel. The priest didn't know that, and years spent with Royce had taught Hadrian intimidation was a useful tool in saving lives. This wasn't the lesson Royce intended him to learn, but Royce wasn't the best teacher.

The priest dropped the dagger.

"Your lordship…you don't look like much of an expert with a

spear," Hadrian said. "What do you say we just talk?"

Lord Darren set the spear on the floor and took a step back.

The bald man was on his feet again and Hadrian tossed the saber back to him. He caught it as shock washed over his face.

"I hate when you do that," Royce said.

"WHO ELSE KNOWS?" LORD Darren asked Royce and Hadrian. "How many people have you told?"

They had moved to the drawing room, where his lordship placed the spear above the fireplace and invited Royce and Hadrian to join him at a small mahogany table dressed with a dark wine bottle surrounded by cut-crystal glasses. On the walls were paintings of people and landscapes; the most prominent hung opposite the windows and depicted a beautiful woman wearing a silver heart-shaped locket.

Hadrian shrugged. "*We* didn't even know until five minutes ago."

"Technically we still don't know," Royce said. "And we don't need to know. Our business here is done."

"What business is that?" the priest asked.

"What part of *our* business don't you understand?" Royce responded with his usual quiet voice and fixed stare that caused the man to lean back in his chair.

"If you're still curious"—Hadrian looked at Royce—"why not just ask them?"

"Ask us what?" The bald man looked awkward on the couch, his hands gripping the cushions. Hadrian recognized that uncomfortable pose from when he was sitting in the tea shop.

"How about we begin with why there is a wolf in that box?"

There was a silence, then Lord Darren stood up and walked to the fireplace. "My wife was killed. I was staying in town to inspect the docks, and I sent her and Kristin home in a carriage driven by a man named Roy—Roy Westin. Good man, I thought."

"You really couldn't know," the priest said, leaning forward with sad understanding eyes.

"Turns out Roy Westin had a secret."

"His name wasn't Roy Westin," the bald man took over. Hadrian realized he had a slight accent—southern in nature, but he couldn't pinpoint it. "His real name was DerVoy Brickle. Comes from my homeland—a place of jungles and wild things, overrun with black magic and curses. Brickle had one of these curses. Every full moon he changed into a monstrous wolf driven by bloodlust to kill. I tracked him many miles until he got on a ship bound for Vernes."

"You're from Calis, then?" Hadrian asked.

The bald man nodded. "I'm the Viscount Ianto Don Speakman of Tel Dar. Brickle was part of a pack of cursed men who roamed the forests and hills near my estate. They killed many of my people, and I've made it my life's work to see this curse ended. I hunted and killed each of them, but Brickle slipped away. I ran into difficulty catching his trail in Vernes. By that time, he was already in Medford and working as a carriage driver. I arrived too late to save his lordship's wife. The night he drove her and the child home there was a full moon."

"They were coming through the forest." Lord Darren pointed out the windows. "When Roy *changed*. It sent the horses into a panic, and the carriage crashed. The beast tore my wife apart and turned on Kristin just as Ianto arrived. He used that spear"—he pointed to the silver weapon mounted over the mantle—"and killed it. But the damage had already been done. My beautiful wife was dead, and the wolf had bitten Kristin."

Lord Darren got up and poured himself a glass of wine, then

paused, looked at the two of them and sighed. "Would you care for a glass?"

"Gracious for a man to entertain thieves," Royce said.

"I have a cellar full of this stuff, left by the previous owner. And I find it less humiliating to offer rather than have it taken."

"We really weren't here to steal from you," Hadrian said.

Royce waited until Lord Darren drank, then poured himself a small glass.

"Just visiting without an invitation, then?" his lordship asked. "In the middle of the night after slipping in—where?" He looked around. "A window? The garden door?"

"So how did *he* get involved in all this?" Royce pointed at the priest.

Ianto said, "When I saw the girl had been bitten and the wolf I had just killed turn back into a man, I tried to speak to Lord Darren, but in his grief he wouldn't see me. So I sought out Parson Engels to arrange a meeting. We sat in this very room, and I explained his daughter might have the same curse."

"I have seen such things before in the service of the church," Engels added. "The viscount wanted the girl killed, but I begged him to stay his hand. She was an innocent, and certainly Novron wouldn't want to take the life of one of his own who was cursed through no fault of her own. I convinced Ianto if appropriate precautions could be made the child could live."

"When they told me of Claire's death, and what would happen to Kristin, I didn't believe them. Who would accept such a tale?" Lord Darren was still holding his glass, staring off toward the fireplace. "The viscount gave me the spear and insisted I lock Kristin up the night of the next full moon. I thought they were crazy, but the parson insisted. If I didn't do as he said, he would have no choice but to tell the bishop of Medford, who would go to the king. They agreed to stay silent only if I could prevent her from harming anyone else."

"And on the next full moon?" Hadrian asked.

Lord Darren nodded, then swallowed the last of his wine. "I planned to lock Kristin's bedroom door, but they insisted on a more secure place. Leta, my housekeeper, told us about a steel safe in the basement that the previous Port Minister, Lord Griswold, had installed to keep his valuables in." Lord Darren poured himself another glass.

Royce hadn't tasted his drink yet. He was still swirling the wine, watching it spin inside the glass.

Lord Darren noticed and smirked. "It's not poisoned, and it's good wine. Don't know where Griswold got it. No labels on any of the bottles." His lordship took another swallow, then retreated to the hearth and leaned on the mantle before continuing. "Poor Kristin. She had no idea why I was locking her in that dreadful place. Thankfully she was only five. We made a game of it, but later that night when I heard the howling…" He took another swallow of wine, a big one. His eyes staring off unfocused. "When we drew back the plate she had changed. My darling daughter had turned into a vicious, snarling, fanged beast. Only then did I believe."

"So you two come here every full moon?" Hadrian asked Engels.

The parson nodded. "It's necessary to contain Uberlin's minion, and I couldn't live with myself if she escaped in that dreadful form and killed, or worse, passed the curse to others. It was either this or destroy the child."

"What do you do all night?" Hadrian asked.

Lord Darren pointed at the bottle on the table. "We drink. I do at least. Have to once she starts howling."

"So, you know all about us," Ianto said. "Now what about you? Who are you, and why are you here?"

Royce finally tasted the wine. "Just visiting."

"I think I know who you are," the parson said. "Two men, one big with three swords, one little dressed in a dark hood."

"I'm not *that* little," Royce protested with a dash of menace.

"You're Riyria."

"Riyria?" Ianto asked, and Lord Darren's expression showed the viscount had only barely beaten him to the question.

"A pair of thieves that work in Medford," Engels explained. "Contract workers. Only do special jobs—that's how they co-exist with the local thieves' guild, the Crimson Hand."

Royce smiled at him. "Amazingly well informed for a clergyman. Tell me *Pastor* Engels, what are the twelve tenents of the Nyphron Church?"

"I wouldn't waste my time ministering to the likes of you two."

"But you do know them?"

"Of course."

Royce continued to smile until Engels poured himself a glass of wine.

"The sun!" Lord Darren crossed the room and threw back the curtains, revealing the morning light. He took a step toward the kitchen, then turned. "You have to promise me not to breathe a word of this to my daughter. She doesn't know, and I don't want her to—not yet. One day she'll have to learn the truth, but I want her to have a few more years of innocence, a few more years of happiness. Promise me."

"You have my word," Hadrian said.

Lord Darren looked at Royce.

"Oh, yes. You have mine too."

The Port Minister rushed out of the room.

"Your lordship!" Engels shouted after him, glanced at Ianto, and sighed.

Hadrian looked to Royce who remained relaxed in his chair taking another sip of wine. The man appeared all too comfortable for one who, moments before, had been eager to leave.

When Lord Darren returned, he had a drowsy Kristin at his side. The woman was yawning and running fingers through her hair. She wore a simple white nightgown with a burgundy robe tied at the waist with a gold cord. Her eyes grew wide at the sight of Royce and Hadrian.

Lord Darren led her toward the stairs to the second story when Kristin stopped and addressed the pair, "You were supposed to kidnap me!"

This caught everyone's attention.

Lord Darren hesitated, confused. "You *know* these men?"

"I hired them to abduct me."

"To what?"

The woman stood rigid, arms straight, hands in fists, her lips rolled up in a painful frown. "Why didn't you steal me? I paid you!" She looked at Ianto. "This is *sooo* embarrassing! You two are absolutely lousy thieves!"

"You *paid* them?" Lord Darren was still trying to understand.

"We couldn't kidnap you," Hadrian said.

"Why not?" Kristin's voice was near screech level.

"Because, apparently, you're a werewolf," Royce said.

Kristin blinked. "What? I'm a what?"

"Werewolf. You turn into a vicious wolf every full moon. That's why your father locks you in the box."

"You gave me your word!" his lordship shouted.

"And you actually believed me." Royce shook his head. "I can't believe the king appointed you to enforce his tax and tariff laws. It's little wonder the black market is thriving."

"I'm not a werewolf!" Kristin said.

Hadrian offered his most sympathetic smile. "I'm afraid you are. You still wore your locket."

Kristin touched the necklace. "And…" The woman's eyes darted back in forth in thought. "And was this wolf wearing this nightgown as well? This robe?"

Hadrian glanced at Royce. Both shook their heads.

"Because this is what I woke up in. Do my clothes magically disappear and reappear as well?"

This caught even Lord Darren by surprise and he looked to Ianto. "How does that work?"

"I hunt werewolves, I'm not an expert in their enchantments."

Eyes shifted toward Engels, who waved his hands before his face. "Look, that doesn't matter. We've all seen her change."

"Have you?" Royce asked. He looked at Lord Darren. "Have you actually *witnessed* your daughter change into a wolf?"

He shook his head. "No—and I would never want to."

"I'm not a werewolf!" the woman repeated, then stared at Ianto. "All this time—all these years—you've been coming here because… because…"

"He wanted to kill you," Royce told her. "But as long as your father stays here, looking over you, Ianto won't go to the king and demand your execution or just stab you with that pretty silver spear. Still want to marry him?"

"I wish I was a wolf," Kristin said. "I wish I was a wolf right now!"

"So each full moon, while you sleep in a steel box, he's here having a party." Royce raised his glass.

"We aren't having a *party*," Lord Darren said through clenched teeth.

"No. More of a small social gathering, I suppose. But you do enjoy a very fine wine."

"I drink to cope with the fact my daughter is howling through a steel grate! I drink to fall asleep before I go mad. I don't care about the quality of the wine."

"Pity, this is Montemorcey, one of the finest wines in the world."

Lord Darren looked puzzled. "Can't be. Montemorcey is banned in Melengar by the king's edict."

"And yet you have one of the largest collections I've ever seen. You are an *excellent* Port Minister, aren't you?"

Lord Darren glanced at the bottle on the table.

"Trust me," Hadrian said. "If it wasn't Montemorcey, he would have spit it out. That's the only thing I've ever seen him drink."

Lord Darren continued to look at the bottle.

"Can we get back to the werewolf thing?" the woman asked.

"I'm sorry, Kristin," her father said. "But it's true. I wanted to spare you that horror until you were a little older, but…well now you know."

"It's not true!" She stood glaring at him defiantly as tears filled her eyes. "It's not!"

Lord Darren reached out to hold her, but Kristin recoiled. She looked at Engels and Ianto and drew away from them as well. Finally she faced Hadrian. "I brought you here. You work for me. Tell the truth!"

"There *was* a wolf in the box you spoke of, and it was wearing your necklace." He pointed at the silver locket. "Were you bitten by the wolf that killed your mother?"

The woman began to sob. Lord Darren put his arms around his daughter, and this time she let him hug her.

A tall slender woman in a servant's gown appeared from the corridor. Her hair was pulled back, showing threads of gray. She held out her hands. "There now, come child. Let's get you washed up and dressed."

"Thank you, Leta," Lord Darren said, releasing Kristin.

Hadrian felt awful as he watched the once hopeful woman shuffle out, head bowed. "Isn't there anything that can be done? A cure of some sort?"

"His lordship has investigated everything possible," Engels said. "Nothing short of death will free her."

Lord Darren faced Royce and Hadrian. "As my daughter admits to hiring you to break into my house, and since you made no attempt to steal anything—other than her—I can find no cause to arrest either of you. I don't think there's a law against paying someone to kidnap yourself…so you're free to leave."

Royce raised an eyebrow and smirked.

"My lord," Engels protested. "If they talk—if the king learns—your daughter will be executed."

"First," Royce said, "I'm not the sort to talk."

Engels frowned. "You've proved your word means nothing."

"I'm not giving my word. Don't even know what that stupid saying means. Just pointing out I'm naturally quiet. Second, what's you're alternative? Want Hadrian to take your weapons away again?"

"It doesn't matter," Lord Darren declared. "Now that Kristin knows, I'll go to the king and explain the whole thing. I—I just can't keep living like this, and what happens to Kristin when I die? Now that she knows, we'll face this together. One more night in the box, then my daughter and I will throw ourselves on the mercy of his majesty. Maybe he can help us out of this nightmare." He looked at Royce and Hadrian once more. "I can't say I'm pleased you came, but perhaps it was for the best."

———•———

ON THE ROAD HEADING back toward Medford, Royce and

Hadrian stopped at the Gilded Lilly public house where they shared lamb stew, heavy bread, and some light ale for Hadrian. Royce, who normally didn't linger, showed no desire to hurry, and they enjoyed a rare leisurely afternoon on the open porch overlooking the King's Road.

"We aren't going back to Medford, are we?" Hadrian asked when Royce ordered a third round of drinks.

"You can if you like."

"And what will *you* be doing?"

Royce grinned.

"You're going back? Why?"

"Professional integrity."

"You keep saying that. You're starting to scare me."

Royce put his feet up on one of the empty chairs at their little table. All the furniture at the Lilly was old-fashioned rustic—sturdy, the sort Hadrian could trust.

"You can say I'm still curious." Royce stripped a splinter from the table and used it to clean his teeth of lamb.

"About what?"

"For one thing"—he used the splinter to point at the sky—"there aren't twelve tenants of the Nyphron Church."

"There aren't? How many are there?"

Royce looked at him shocked. "How should I know? I just picked a number at random. Either I'm incredibly lucky or Engels is lying. And he knows too much about the underbelly of Medford to be alive, much less a minister of the church. He works for the Hand."

Hadrian wasn't surprised. While servants of the church usually made him uneasy, as if he were guilty of something, Engels had a comfortable brown-bread-and-beer way about him. "So, I guess you'd be interested to know Engel's isn't the only one being dishonest. Ianto isn't a viscount of Tel Dar, either."

Royce shifted his shoulders to look at him, displaying raised eyebrows. "What makes you say that?"

"Tel Dar is a little Tenkin village on the eaves of the Gur Em. They don't have viscounts there, just a chief and a warlord. But if they did have a viscount his title would be Pansoh. I suspect the closest old Ianto has been to Calis is Wesbaden or possibly Dagastan." Hadrian took a swallow of his ale. "That saber he was swinging is a seadog cleaver, and I suspect you'll find a dirk tucked in his belt somewhere. Real popular among sailors of the southern seas."

"Something is definitely going on," Royce said. "That something involves the Hand and crates of Montemorcey wine. And since knowledge is power, I want to know what."

"And how do you plan to find out?"

"By doing what our client asked us to. We're going to steal Lord Darren Lamb's daughter."

"Royce." Hadrian paused, holding his mug halfway to his mouth. "There's another full moon tonight, and the woman has a habit of turning into a killer wolf after sunset. I'm thinking this might be a bad idea."

"It was your poor judgment to take this job in the first place. Now it's my turn."

THE TWO SLIPPED IN right after dark, and knowing exactly where to go, they crept through the house with ease. Hadrian imagined Royce wanted to reach Kristin before the moon rose— before the change. Why, he wasn't sure. He doubted even Royce knew. Maybe he just wanted to witness the transformation. Royce wasn't one to believe in anything he didn't see, smell, and touch.

The Ridgewood Manor's kitchen still smelled of pork, and Hadrian guessed there was one less pig running around the estate that evening. Lord Darren had likely held a farewell feast. No sense saving anything, his rainy day had come. He would abide by Amrath's judgment, and it wouldn't be good for him or his daughter.

Just as the previous night, Hadrian dodged pots, pans, and kettles as he followed Royce down the stairs.

"Kristin?" Hadrian called out softly as they touched down on the cellar's bricks. The basement was dark except for the single shaft of weak light spilling down the stairs. He took a step around the wine racks when Royce's hand stopped him.

"The box is open."

Hadrian peered through the gloom and spotted the open top. Set in the floor, it appeared as a huge drain with its lid flipped back on metal hinges.

"Why is it open?" he whispered. "Is she in there?"

Together they crept closer. Hadrian couldn't see anything but darkness.

"Empty," Royce said.

"Maybe they didn't put her in tonight, or maybe they're about to."

Something caught Royce's eye, and he knelt down near the wall and picked it up. "Interesting."

"I can't see. What is it?"

"The lock for the box and a cup."

Hadrian heard Royce sniff.

"Wine?"

"Milk."

"Milk?"

"They put Kristin in the box, but someone intentionally failed to lock it."

"But then where—" Hadrian looked back up at the stairs, at the brightening shaft of pale light—the light of a rising moon. He took the steps two at a time.

"What are you going to do?" Royce called after him.

"Going after her. Isn't that why we came?"

Hadrian could see better once he surfaced in the kitchen, where windows cast elongated squares. Better wasn't good; better wasn't even mediocre. Too many shadows and dark places surrounded him. Unlike Royce, Hadrian always fumbled his way in the dark. As he moved into the corridor, things only got worse, even darker. Every doorway, every niche was capable of concealing a lurking beast. He tried to remember what he saw their first night.

A black wolf? A gray wolf? Too bad it hadn't been white.

As he moved even deeper into darkness, he touched his swords. He had three: a hand-and-a-half on his right hip, a short on his left. Fast and agile, they were what he used most often when fighting men. He didn't have experience fighting wolves. Maybe the big two-handed spadone on his back would work best. Using the flange, he could wield it like a spear. A spear would be a fine weapon against a wolf. Against a werewolf, a *silver* spear would be even better. He headed toward the drawing room…and the mantle.

I'm not going to kill her. She's just a young woman. A young woman with two inch fangs and four sets of claws.

Hadrian spotted candlelight up and to his right. A moment later, from the same direction, he heard a growl, a snap, claws on wood, and the cry of a man.

Damn it!

Hadrian ran into the drawing room where Lord Darren and Pastor Engels shuffled backward in horror as a large black wolf attacked Ianto. Before Hadrian was fully in the room, the animal had pinned the bald man to the floor. In a burst of blood that sprayed the little table and the cut-crystal glasses, the wolf ripped his throat out.

Ianto had been on the far side of the room. The wolf had passed by the others to attack him.

He wanted to kill you... Still want to marry him?

Hadrian guessed this was her answer.

"Kristin! No!" Lord Darren shouted at her.

With blood dripping from her jaws, the wolf turned, crouched with raised fur and flattened ears, and crept toward him, growling.

Hadrian rushed in, but the wolf took no notice, eyes fixed on her prey. Engels had his dagger out, backing away. Lord Darren gave a glance toward the mantle. He'd never reach it.

"Kristin!" Hadrian shouted and waved a hand, but the wolf had no interest.

"Dear Maribor, Kristin, no—don't," her father begged.

Engels made the first move. He bolted for the front door.

The wolf gave a yip, claws raked the polished wood floor, and a hundred pounds of animal slammed into the parson.

Lord Darren saw his chance, and running to the mantle, he ripped down the spear. Hadrian charged the wolf, whose teeth were buried in Engel's shoulder, jerking him wildly.

"No!" Hadrian cried as the screaming pastor lashed out with his dagger and stabbed the wolf in her side.

Kristin let the man's shoulder go and bit into his throat. Just like Ianto, Pastor Engels died in a burst of blood.

"Stay back!" Lord Darren shouted, coming forward with the spear in both hands. "Your blades are useless against her. Only silver can kill a werewolf."

Hadrian knew this to be true. He had spent years in the jungles of Calis and had heard many tales of werewolves and other far worse creatures. And yet…the wolf was bleeding badly from the dagger still jammed in her ribs. She was also wavering. Kristin continued to growl, but her haunches collapsed. The snarl faded from her lips, and a tongue began to hang as she struggled to breathe.

Lord Darren came to Hadrian's side and together they watched as the wolf lay down in a growing pool of blood. The growl became a whimper.

"Kristin." Lord Darren put down the spear, and he, too, lowered himself to a squat. Tears spilled down his cheeks.

The wolf laid its head on the floor and the animal's breathing grew shallower.

"My beautiful girl. I'm so, so sorry."

The wolf's eyes closed and Lord Darren crept forward placing a hand on her head. Her eyes opened, a weak flutter. The pupils focused on his lordship, and Hadrian thought he saw appreciation there. Lord Darren continued to stroke the wolf's fur long after it stopped breathing.

Hadrian picked up the silver spear, then sat down at the little table and poured himself a glass of wine, taking the only glass which wasn't covered in Ianto's blood. Normally he didn't care for wine, but he would have swallowed turpentine if it was the only thing available.

"Why'd you do it?" Lord Darren asked Hadrian, still petting the dead wolf. "Why'd you come back? Why'd you let her out?"

"Let her out? We didn't let her out. We came back because we realized Engels and Ianto were lying about who they were."

"Lying?"

"You didn't know, then?"

"Know what?"

Hadrian glanced at Ianto's body sprawled on the floor. "I suppose it doesn't matter now."

Lord Darren wiped his cheeks. "She was such a good girl. Such a very good girl."

Royce entered from the same corridor Hadrian had and paused to look at the bodies.

"Where have you been?" Hadrian asked.

"Exploring."

"Exploring? While I was hunting a werewolf in the dark? Didn't you think I could use your help?"

Royce looked once more at the bodies. "You did fine."

"You call this fine? Engels and Ianto were torn to pieces, and Lord Darren's daughter is dead."

Royce paused in thought. "Maybe, but I doubt it—wouldn't make sense if she was."

This caught Lord Darren's attention and the man looked over skeptically. "What are you talking about?"

"Royce," Hadrian said in exasperation. He pointed at the dead wolf. "She's right there."

The thief glanced at the animal. "That's a wolf."

"I know, but it's also Kristin."

"No, that's just a wolf. If that was a werewolf, wouldn't we be seeing a dead woman right now? Or was Ianto lying about that as well?"

Hadrian was stunned. "No...he was right, at least that's what's supposed to happen. When a werewolf dies, the body reverts to its original form."

"What are you saying?" Lord Darren asked, rising to his feet.

"I'm saying we could sit around here and chat, or we can go find your daughter. I'll assume you prefer the latter."

———✦———

LORD DARREN LED THEM to the barn and Hadrian was impressed his lordship knew how to saddle a horse. That was good, it would save time.

"Where are we going? Where is Kristin?" the lord asked while tightening the saddle's strap.

"Don't know exactly, but I don't think she's gotten too far. Not in her condition."

"Condition? What condition?"

"Drugged, I imagine. I found footprints and drag marks." Royce jerked his head to the right. "See anything missing?"

Lord Darren looked over. "My carriage!"

"And your housekeeper. I'm guessing Leta always helped tuck Kristin in on those full-moon nights. Gave her some warm milk to help her sleep, perhaps?"

"She put something in the milk?"

"That'd be my guess."

"But why?"

"That's what we're going to find out. All I can tell you right now is they're gone, and the box in the basement isn't Lord Griswold's secret safe. I know a few things about safes, and no fool puts a safe in plain sight. They're always hidden by drapes or under floorboards. That one has a false back, behind which is a tunnel that leads outside. That's a pretty poor design for a *safe*, don't you think?"

"A smugglers hole?" Lord Darren asked.

"Now you're starting to catch on. How do you think all that wine got into the cellar? I think Lord Griswold would object to smugglers making deliveries to his front door. Can't blame him, given he was Port Minister and all."

"And that's not all I found. There's a cage on wheels that can butt up against that false back. Along with discarded bones and hay. Your daughter isn't a werewolf. Someone just wanted you to think she was. Tonight the cage was left open. I imagine the smells from the kitchen led it upstairs and then…well you and Hadrian saw the rest."

"But why would someone let the beast out? And what about Kristin?"

"I believe we'll discover all that once we find the carriage."

THE THREE MEN RACED beneath the full moon. They found the two track road and followed it southeast as it cut an overgrown trail through dense brush and deep woods. Intermittent shadows of tree trunks and pale light flickered past, disorienting Hadrian as he lay low across the horse's back and let the chill wind blow over him. They stopped at mud puddles where Royce dismounted to examine ruts. Then off they flew again with Hadrian trusting to Royce and the horse he rode, whose name he didn't even know. He kept his mind focused on Kristin, the woman with the beaming smile who wanted to be kidnapped and finally got her wish.

The sky was lightening with the dawn when at last the carriage came into view. Stuck in a mud puddle, Kristin was out in front pulling the horse forward while Leta struggled to push the carriage from behind, legs covered in mud. She let out a startled cry as they rode up and stood wide-eyed, staring into the face of Lord Darren.

"Daddy!" Kristin let go of the bridle and sprinted across the puddle to her father. "Daddy! You're alive! You're alive!"

Lord Darren leapt down from his saddle and threw his arms around his daughter, spinning the young woman so her feet whirled behind her. "Of course I am—and so are you. So are you!" He was half weeping, half laughing as he clutched Kristin to his cheek and kissed her hair.

Leta started to inch to the side, glancing at the trees.

Royce slipped off his horse, and looking dead at her, shook his head.

"What were you doing?" the lordship asked his daughter. "We thought you were kidnapped. Why were you helping? Where were you going?"

"Leta told me you were dead, that I'd killed you. All of you." Kristin wiped her tears. "When I woke up, I begged her to take me back…to see you. But she said there was nothing to be done. If I returned, I would be killed. Leta was taking me to Aunt Edna's. She's going to keep me from hurting anyone else. She promised to lock me up on full moons."

"Clever." Royce nodded, then turned to Leta. "You served Lord Griswold, didn't you?"

She didn't answer until he took a step closer and let a hand slip inside his cloak, then she nodded. "Been housekeeper at Ridgewood for decades."

"You knew he was taking bribes from the smugglers, so he gave you a cut to keep you quiet. Is that right?"

"We had a nice thing going until he came." Leta turned toward Lord Darren. "You shut everything down right tight you did."

"So, you came up with a plan," Royce said.

"Wasn't me. Shawn got the idea of kidnapping her ladyship and Kristin. They planned on taking 'em to Shawn's boat. They'd keep 'em there and force his lordship to resume the same deal they had with Griswold."

"Shawn is Ianto's real name?" Hadrian asked.

Leta nodded. "He's captain of the *Medusa*, used to be Griswold's best shipper."

"And Engels?"

She hesitated.

Royce took another step. "He's dead. So is Shawn. That part of your plan worked. So who was he?"

She hesitated only a moment more, then shrugged. "Clyde Davis. Dock chief for the Crimson Hand."

Royce looked at Hadrian. "Told you." Then he asked Leta, "But something went wrong, didn't it?"

"When Shawn and his men chased the lady's carriage, Roy whipped the horse and made a run for it. Killed himself when the carriage flipped. Her ladyship was busted up bad too. There was no saving her. But she told Kristin to run, and she did, right into the forest. Clyde and Shawn had to borrow Blake Everett's hounds to find her. Mean dogs they are. One bit the girl."

"So why didn't Shawn just take Kristin and run?" Royce asked.

"Might have been better if he did. But two people were dead, and one was the Port Minister's wife. No getting around that. There was going to be a crackdown and business would suffer. The king would have the high constable poking around. It would be a big mess."

"And how did the whole werewolf thing come about?"

"That was Shawn's idea too. Little girl thought Everett's hounds were wolves. So Shawn tells her that's exactly what they were— said the beasts killed her mother, but he saved her. Then he got to thinking about stories he'd heard in Calis, and since the girl had been bitten…"

"And how do you fit in?" Royce stared at Leta.

She took a step back. "I didn't do much. Griswold had a smugglers' hole Lord Darren didn't know about. Shawn had his men take the *Medusa* up north to catch a wolf, a big one. It was my job to drag Kristin out and get the wolf in. Just needed a little food to lure it. After a while, it was sort of trained, although Shawn used to beat it to keep the animal vicious. Then just before dawn,

I'd put Kristin back. Was easy when she was little—a lot harder as she and I got older."

"But why?" Lord Darren asked. "Why do all this?"

"Best time to navigate the Galewyr is when there's a full moon," Royce said. "And if you can be sure the Port Minister will be home looking after his 'poor daughter' you can move a lot of black market goods."

Leta nodded. "Shawn would unload his ship at Roe and send his long boats up the river to Medford. Clyde bribed the port watch and his crew off-loaded right at the dock. Two nights of work was all that was needed to clear Shawn's hold. Then they'd have a month to trade before the next shipment."

"So why did you let the wolf out?" Lord Darren asked.

"Because you were going to go to the king," Royce said.

Leta looked at them both. "Shawn and Clyde could just disappear, but me? Where would I go? How would I make money? How could I survive?"

"You were going to keep Kristin thinking she was a monster and feed off her like a leech?" Lord Darren glared at the housekeeper.

"She was all I had!" Leta cried. "I—I was desperate, don't you see?"

Lord Darren shook his head in disgust. He took several breaths to calm down, then focused on Hadrian and Royce. "And how about you two? Why'd you come back?"

Hadrian stared at his partner, mirroring his lordship's quizzical look.

"Professional integrity," Royce said.

Hadrian rolled his eyes.

Royce glared at him. "It's true. I knew someone was deceiving me, maybe using me. Thought it might have been your daughter, could have been part of a group. Maybe the Hand trying something.

Easy mistake to make, the way she tried to hire us with such a sickly-sweet, wide-eyed, wholesome act. I was positive it was a swindle or game of some sort. No one is that cute." He shook his head and turned to Kristin. "I was wrong. You're just a freak of nature."

Kristin smiled back. "Better than being a werewolf."

"True." Royce nodded. "Anyway, I don't like being used. I go to great lengths to make certain those who try regret it. It would hurt business if I let something like that slip. So I needed to know what was really going on and, if possible, make certain those responsible never did it again."

Lord Darren nodded. "Well, thank you—both of you." He was still holding his daughter like he was terrified of ever letting go. "But—well, who are you? Who are you really?"

Royce smiled. "Riyria."

"Riyria? I don't understand?"

"Why would you? It's elvish for two."

TROLL TROUBLE

-*Balathex*-

RICHARD LEE BYERS

I've written several stories about Selden and plan to write many more. A former mercenary, he gave up war to settle in Balathex, the City of Fountains, and set up shop as a fencing master. But old habits die hard, and a man can use a secondary source of income when he has a habit of picking losing horses at the hippodrome. So he still hires out his sword on occasion and generally finds himself enmeshed in supernatural mysteries and fighting sorcerers, demons, and the like. "Troll Trouble" is set before the other published Selden stories and is an origin of sorts. It relates how he first got himself established in Balathex.

T HE FOREST OF THORNS is well named. Briars scratched and snagged me with every step, or at least it seemed that way. Meanwhile, the soft ground mired my boots, and cold rainwater dripped on me from the weave of branches overhead.

In other words, this little excursion into the wild was unpleasant enough to remind me of one reason why I'd abandoned the life of a mercenary—marching in the snow and heat, eating half-spoiled rations or none at all, and sleeping rough—to set up shop as a fencing master in Balathex, City of Fountains. I strove to stay alert lest discomfort distract me.

Yet despite my caution, when I first glimpsed the troll peeking out at me, he was only a few strides away. It seemed unfair that a creature so large could nonetheless hide so successfully, even behind the broad, mossy trunk of an ancient oak.

Truly, though, there was no reason why he shouldn't, because he wasn't as tall as a tree. Such towering specimens may have existed long ago. They may still, in far corners of the world. But in all my wandering, I've never seen one.

No, his long arms knotted with muscle, hide mottled brown and gray,

"TROLL TROUBLE"

Illustration by OKSANA DMITRIENKO

red eyes shining under a ridged brow and fanged mouth smirking and slavering at the prospect of cruel sport and fresh meat, this fellow merely loomed half again as tall as I was. That was still big enough to make a sensible man turn tail.

I didn't, though. Nor did I reach for my broadsword in its scabbard, though my fingers itched for the hilt. Instead, as the creature shambled into the open, I gave him a nod and said, "Hello. My name is Selden. I come as an envoy of the August Assembly of Balathex."

Then I studied his brutish face in an effort to determine whether he believed the lie, and if so, whether it mattered.

MY ERRAND BEGAN THREE nights earlier, in the shop I'd rented and through hard and fumbling work—I'm no carpenter— transformed into a space suitable for teaching swordplay and associated arts. Effort wasted, it seemed, for no students had presented themselves to study there.

The problem was that I was a stranger. No one in Balathex knew me as a successful duelist or an instructor capable of raising others to proficiency. The obvious remedy was to pick a few quarrels, but I was reluctant to go down that path.

I'd grown tired of killing for no better reason than to put silver in my purse, and besides, I was loath to start my new life by instigating feuds. I didn't need vengeful brothers, sons, and friends of the deceased leaping out at me for years thereafter.

Unfortunately, that unsatisfactory scheme was the only plan I'd been able to devise. Thus, on the night in question, I sat alone drinking cheap Ghentoy red laced with raw spirit, and never mind that I'd squandered coin originally intended for next week's rent to purchase the jugs. Morose as I was, I had more immediate needs.

Someone rapped on the door.

My first half-tipsy thought was that I'd lost track of the date, and the landlord had come for his due, but a moment's reflection assured me that couldn't be so. Perhaps here was my first pupil, then, unlikely as that seemed at this late hour.

I straightened my jerkin, smoothed down my hair, and hurried to answer the knock. When I did, a stooped old woman squinted at me from the other side of the threshold.

She wore charms, talismans of made of bone and feathers and other items hidden in little cloth bags, dangling around her wrinkled neck. But had you seen her, you wouldn't have thought *sorceress*. You would have thought *witch*.

For there was nothing about her to suggest the sort of citified mage who pores over grimoires, compounds elixirs from rare ingredients, and commands devils via complex ritual and force of will. Rather, she was manifestly a village wise woman who knew only the patchy lore her mother passed down to her, brewed dubious remedies from whatever happened to grow nearby, and dickered with goblins in a manner little different than she'd haggle with a neighbor.

Surprised, I said, "Mother Elkinda."

She sniffed twice. "You stink of drink."

"Whereas you stink of the usual." It was true. There are rustic folk who give the lie to the insult *dirty peasant,* but she wasn't one of them. "And I suppose that, as we both smell already, a hug won't make it any worse."

We put that to the test, and afterward, I ushered her inside.

"How did you know I was in the city?" I asked.

"The wind whispered it to me, and then I dowsed my way to your door." She hefted a gnarled walking stick.

"Well, it's good you came when you did," I said. "In a week or two, I'll likely be gone." Soldiering again, if I could find a captain to take me on this late in the season.

I don't think she even registered the glumness in my tone. "I need your help," she said. "I…may have done a bad thing."

Concern nudged aside my self-pity. I waved her on toward the rickety table.

She stumbled before she got there. It was a long hike from her little forest village to the city, and she'd exhausted herself making it. I caught her, got her into a chair, poured her a cup of wine, and sat back down across from her. "Tell me," I said.

She took a long drink first. When she set the goblet down, she said, "There are trolls in the wood."

More concerned now, I nodded. "I know."

"Well, what you may not know is that sometimes they need blessings and medicine just like people do. Then they come to me."

I frowned. "That's like trafficking with outlaws, only worse. People would hang you if they found out."

She glowered. "I give the trolls things they need, and in return, they leave the village alone. We couldn't live where we do, otherwise."

"I can believe it," I said. "And I wasn't condemning you, just worried for your sake. Please, go on."

"Well…two of the trolls who came to me were Skav Hearteater, their chieftain, and Ojojum, his mate. Their problem was, she couldn't conceive."

"And that upset them?"

"Yes. In some ways, trolls and people are alike. Through my craft, I discovered the fault lay with Skav, but when I tried to quicken his seed with the usual remedies, nothing happened."

"So you tried something unusual?"

"Once I was fool enough to tell the trolls the notion that had come to me, they insisted. Had I refused, how do you think it would have ended?"

"With your flesh in their bellies," I said. "So what did you do?"

"I called a spirit of lust and fertility and put it inside the Hearteater. My thought was that he would share the imp's vigor the next time he and Ojojum coupled." She smiled. "And I was right. She's with child."

"Then what's the problem?"

The smile disappeared. "Skav changed. He'd always doted on Ojojum. But afterward, he started beating her until, fearful she'd lose the baby, she ran away."

"Ran away and came to you. Because she suspected your magic was to blame? More to the point, do *you* think it's to blame?"

Elkinda sighed. "Perhaps. When the spirit came, I sensed it was something crueler and less biddable than I meant to catch. Something from the netherworld and not just out of Nature."

"You should have tossed it back and tried again."

"That's easy to say now, but I'd had trouble summoning anything. I didn't know if I'd be lucky a second time, and with the trolls watching and waiting…"

"I understand," I said. "Well, partly. Do you believe the spirit's touch poisoned Skav's mind?"

"Worse. I fear it didn't leave his body when it was supposed to. I need you to find out if it's still inside."

"What, now?"

"I can fix it so you're able to see the incubus once you're close enough. I need to know for a fact that it's there and how it looks before I can set about casting it out."

"Then go peer at Skav yourself. You're the one who's friendly with him."

She shook her head. "The spirit would be suspicious of me."

"Whereas the trolls will eat me simply because they're hungry."

She grimaced. "I know what I'm asking. But dangerous as trolls are, the ones hereabout mostly leave people alone. They won't do that much longer if a demon has possessed their chief. They'll start hunting humans every chance they get, and you're the only one I can ask to help me keep it from happening."

She didn't add that I owed her my life. Apparently she trusted me to remember that for myself.

I came down with the plague called the Bloody Noose when my mercenary company was chasing bandits on the fringe of the Forest of Thorns. For fear of contagion, my comrades abandoned me. Mother Elkinda found me a day later.

She always claimed the foul potions and gruels she gave me cured me of my affliction. I had my doubts. But I didn't doubt that after the delirium passed and I was breathing normally again, my lingering weakness would still have killed me had she not nursed me through the two long months of my recovery.

Now the debt had come due. I poured us each another drink and said, "Tell me how I'll be able to spot the imp."

———— ⁘ ————

NOW YOU KNOW HOW I came to find myself deep in the woods facing a troll. But you may still wonder why I approached the creatures openly when I might have spied on them instead.

This was my thinking. Mother Elkinda knew the trolls; she watched the trails in the heart of the wood, but not where they laired. I could have crept around for days before I found the place, and even when I had, I might not recognize Skav. I'd never seen him before, and to human eyes, one naked beast-man tends to looks like another. And once I did identify him, I'd still need to come close to discern the incubus inside, close enough to make concealment problematic.

Thus, passing myself off as an emissary seemed a better option. Or at least it did until the troll roared and rushed me with ham-sized, jagged-clawed hands outstretched.

I jumped aside, and he lunged past me. As he lurched back around, I snatched my sword out. He hesitated, but not, I judged, because the blade frightened him. He was simply considering how to contend with it.

At least that gave me another chance to talk. "I know where Ojojum is," I told him. "I think the Hearteater will want to hear, don't you?"

"Yes," he growled, then instantly swatted at the sword in an attempt to knock it aside.

I twitched the blade above the arc of the blow and sliced him across the knuckles. He snatched his hand back, and in that instant, I lunged closer and set sharp steel against his dangling, warty genitals. He froze.

"Give me your word," I said, "that you'll take me to Skav without any more nonsense. Or I swear I'll geld you."

"I'll take you," he said. His voice still sounded like growls and coughs. It reminded me of the lions I'd seen in the grasslands of Lazvalla.

I shifted my sword away from his maleness and returned it to its scabbard. I didn't like doing it, but it seemed unwieldy to approach Skav as an envoy and a hostage taker, too.

To my relief, the creature before me didn't try another attack. Instead, he led me on down the path. Evidently the feel of a blade against his tender parts had made a lasting impression.

His cooperation notwithstanding, I never dropped my guard. But eventually I relaxed somewhat, and then I asked, "What sort of mood is the Hearteater in today?"

My guide gave me a glower. "Angry. Hungry." Then he stepped into a spot where the tangle of branches overhead was thin and winced at the wan light leaking down from the sky.

That's how trolls are. It's a myth that sunlight turns them to stone, but they're sensitive to it. Had my companion not been charged with keeping watch on the trail, he might well have opted to sleep by day and roam around at night.

Certainly, that was the case with the majority of his fellows. They lay snoring in heaps of leaves and pine needles in a particularly shady portion of the forest floor.

Despite the crudity of the sleeping arrangements, the place had the air of a home and not just a camp where nomads had stopped for a day. The trolls had taken the trouble to wedge racks of antlers and skulls, some of them human, in the crotches of trees and to scratch crude drawings on the trunks.

That was all I had time to take in before one of the wakeful trolls noticed me. He roared a warning, whereupon his fellows roused and, glaring and slavering, came shambling to surround me.

I didn't realize when one reached to grab me from behind. Fortunately, my guide noticed. He snarled, slashed with his claws, and sent my would-be assailant reeling backward with a gashed face.

It was more assistance than I had any right to expect. But I'd entered the trolls' home at the side of my reluctant escort, and maybe that meant an attempt to harm me implied disrespect for him.

The balked troll swiped at his flowing blood and gathered himself to lunge. Fearing that a general brawl was imminent, I shouted, "I speak for the lords of Balathex, and I can tell you what's become of Ojojum!"

Some part of that was surprising or intriguing enough to make the creatures around me falter. Then another troll, one who hadn't rushed to encircle me with the others, prowled out of the gloom.

Upon observing him, I decided I'd been wrong about one thing. I would have recognized Skav Hearteater on sight. He was even bigger than the others and had dried blood and yellow earth streaked on his face and chest.

I couldn't tell if he also had an incubus riding him. I hoped Elkinda's witchcraft would answer that question in due course.

"What do you know about my mate?" Skav demanded.

"One thing at a time," I said. "Do you understand that I speak for Balathex?"

He flicked his hand in an impatient gesture I chose to interpret as *yes*.

"So do you promise to receive me hospitably and allow me to depart in peace," I persisted, "as the rulers of men deal with one another's envoys?"

"Tell me where Ojojum is!" he bellowed, "or my people will tear you to bits!" The trolls surrounding me poised their hands to rip and snatch.

"Kill me," I said, "and you won't find out about your mate. More, if I don't come home in one piece, Balathex will avenge the affront to its sovereignty by sending an army to scour the forest clean of trolls, as many of my folk believe we should have long ago."

Skav glared at me. I stared back while trying to look like a dauntless idiot who'd enjoy nothing more than dying hideously for the sake of the Whispering City.

Finally the Hearteater said, "I promise not to hurt you. Why not? What does a little turd like you matter either way?"

"Thank you for your courtesy," I replied. "May I approach?"

"Come," he said, and, looking disgruntled that I might not be supper after all, the other trolls opened the way for me. I walked forward until I was near enough to converse comfortably, which in this circumstance wasn't comfortable at all.

Without taking my eyes off Skav, I bowed. "My lord—"

"Ojojum!" he snapped. "Where?"

"Balathex," I replied.

"You captured her." His clawed fingers flexed, and growls and muttering sounded from the trolls behind me.

"No," I said. "She came to the city of her own free will seeking sanctuary, and the August Assembly gave it to her."

He hesitated. Then: "You're lying!"

I certainly was. Had his mate presented herself at a city gate, the guard would have attacked her on sight. But I hoped ignorance of human society would prevent Skav from realizing how preposterous my claims actually were.

"Admittedly," I said, "it's a novel situation. But your mate's petition came to the attention of the Hand Maids of Rendeth. The welfare of mothers and children is their particular concern, and they pleaded on Ojojum's behalf."

"For a troll! And the leaders heeded them?"

"Yes. They respect the temples, and honestly, I think the very strangeness of it all intrigued them." Trying to look casual about it, I drew a handkerchief from my sleeve, ostensibly to wipe sweat from my face. In reality, Mother Elkinda had soaked the cloth in something she'd brewed in an iron pot, and I needed to get the fumes into my eyes.

When I did, my eyes burned, and tears dissolved the world into blur. I daresay blindness is never desirable, but I can attest that unexpectedly losing your sight in the midst of a mob of man-eating brutes is particularly disconcerting.

Fortunately, none of the trolls availed itself of the opportunity to attack me before the stinging faded and I blinked and wiped the tears away. Instead, Skav asked me, "What ails you?"

"Pardon me," I said. Meanwhile, inside my head, I was cursing Elkinda for not warning me. "Apparently something's blooming hereabouts…"

Suddenly, midway through my excuse, Skav's face changed. A second set of features shined through it like firelight glowing through a paper lantern, and remarkably, the one underneath was even more disturbing. With his crooked fangs and piggy crimson eyes, the troll chieftain was ugly and intimidating but not unnatural. In contrast, the long, narrow visage of the incubus twitched, oozed, and flickered from moment to moment in a way that was both wrong in some fundamental manner and sickening to behold.

But I couldn't let the demon know I beheld it. I held myself steady and finished my thought: "…that disagrees with me."

"I'll disagree with you," said Skav, jumping back to the actual point of the conversation, "unless you prove you're telling the truth."

"Just think about it," I replied. "If Ojojum didn't come to Balathex, how do I even know her name, let alone that she's gone missing?"

Apparently he couldn't think of an alternative explanation. For after another pause, he snarled, "Send her back! Or I'll kill every human in the forest!"

Now that I had the information I'd come for, I would have liked nothing better than to assure him Balathex would bow to his wishes and make a speedy departure. But alas, the emissary I was pretending to be wouldn't behave that way.

"We've been over this," I said. "If you trolls make pests of yourselves, the August Assembly will do whatever is required to exterminate you. But it needn't come to that. Ojojum wants to return home."

Skav grunted. "What's stopping her, then?"

"You are. She says you've been beating her for no reason, and she's afraid she'll miscarry."

He hesitated. Then: "There are reasons. But maybe I've been too strict. I don't want to hurt the child." Behind its mask of flesh, the incubus grinned.

"Good," I said. "But it won't be quite that easy. When Ojojum returns, six Hand Maids will accompany her. They'll ask you to swear on a lock of Rendeth's hair that the abuse will stop."

The incubus's leer stretched until it split his seething face in two. "If that's what it takes."

After negotiating the details of the fictitious rendezvous, I took my leave and, once I was a little way down the trail, quickened my pace. Shortly after that, I had to stop and puke. The devil's face had been that upsetting.

───◆·◆───

WHEN I TOLD MOTHER Elkinda about the palaver, she said, "You didn't tell me you were going to talk to them. It's a wonder you're still alive."

I shrugged. "I made Skav believe he had to let me go to seize a bigger prize, namely, Ojojum at his mercy once more, six nuns to eat, and a sacred relic to defile. What I don't understand is why he and the tribe aren't rampaging through the woods killing people already."

The witch shifted on the only chair in her hut. "Maybe the incubus wants to get used to being Skav first," she said. "Or spend more time enjoying it. The spirit may believe that once the slaughter starts, an army truly will come running to wipe out the trolls, its host included."

"Too bad that isn't so."

When the residents of Balathex thought about the forest

dwellers at all, it was as poachers, runaway indentured servants, and mad hermits whose welfare was of trifling importance. In time, I supposed, the August Assembly might send sufficient troops to put an end to the trolls, but by then, whole settlements would lie dead.

"No use crying about it." Throwing her head back, Elkinda emptied her jack of the bitter beer they brewed there in her village, then used her walking stick to heave herself to her feet. "I'll just have to clean up my own mess." She started hobbling around gathering the ingredients for a spell, a clump of moss from this shelf, a piece of stag horn carved with a rune from the table in the corner.

I stood up from the earthen floor so I could stay out of her way. My head jostled a dried lizard hanging beneath the thatched roof.

When Elkinda had collected everything she needed, she carried it outside to the crackling yellow fire she'd built, and I followed. She gazed up at the moon and stars, or what we could see of them through crisscrossing branches and wisps of cloud, then motioned for me to stand in a particular spot.

I couldn't tell what made that bit of ground special. She hadn't scratched a circle of protection in the dirt or anything like that. But I obeyed without asking the reason why. Once mages set to work, it's dangerous to distract them.

With me positioned to her satisfaction, the wise woman started chanting words in a language I didn't recognize. Periodically, she tossed one of the items she'd collected into the flames until they were all gone. Afterward, the incantation droned on.

Then, in an instant, the fire turned from gold to scarlet and shot up high over Elkinda's head. At the top, the pillar of flame spread into a fan shape in a way that reminded me of a hand poised to swat a fly.

Elkinda gasped and jerked backward. She recognized the threat as quickly as I did, but that didn't mean she was spry enough to avoid it.

I lunged, threw my arms around her, and drove onward until balance deserted me and we fell. Behind us, fire hurtled earthward with a hiss like a cataract. A wave of heat washed over me.

But when I checked, neither Elkinda nor I were burning, nor had the plunging blaze left a sheet of flame licking at our feet. Some tufts of grass were charring and smoking, but mostly, the fire was gone. In the pit where the witch had lit it with a word of command, only coals remained.

I stood up, offered my hand, and hauled her to her feet. "Are you all right?" I asked.

"No," she said.

"Did I hurt you? I didn't want to knock you down—"

"I'm fine!" she spat. "But don't you understand what just happened? I can't cast out the incubus! It's protected. Too much darkness stuck to it when I pulled it up from the places underneath."

"Maybe if you try again?"

"I will. I owe everyone that, no matter what the danger. But it won't work."

"Then don't be foolish. Think of a different tactic."

She shook her head. "There's only one. I'd need to attack the incubus close up, with Skav in front of my eyes. That might tip the balance in my favor. But how could I do it without the trolls spotting me?"

How indeed?

Curse it, it wasn't fair. I'd called on the trolls once and lived to tell about it. That should have been sufficient.

But there isn't much in life that counts for less than *fair* and *should.* I took a breath and said, "Well, plainly, you can't creep up on them, not tottering along with a cane. We'll need to hide you where the creatures will come to you. And then I'll need to distract them."

MY SECOND MEETING WITH the trolls was set for dusk. Plainly, that was stupid. Even if a man survived the parley itself, he'd start the night in the deep forest for the man-eaters to stalk as the temptation seized them. But when Skav and I negotiated the details of the rendezvous, I hadn't imagined I'd actually be keeping it.

As Ojojum and I advanced up the trail, I resisted the urge to look for other trolls. It didn't matter if they were already shadowing us. The important question was, had the creatures stumbled across Mother Elkinda in the thicket where I'd hidden her that morning?

Unfortunately, there was no way of knowing, and perhaps Ojojum realized as much, for she, with her tangled steel-gray tresses and unborn child swelling her belly, looked as nervous as I felt. After a while, I noticed she was shivering.

It sounds asinine to say I felt sympathy for a troll, but perhaps it was because we were comrades in a dangerous venture. I touched her on the forearm, above the spot where some animal's teeth or horns had scarred her, and said, "It's going to be all right."

She shook her head. "I didn't tell Mother Elkinda everything Skav did to me. Beatings weren't the worst of it."

"It wasn't truly him," I said. "That's why we're here, to bring the real Skav back."

"I know." She spat in the dirt as a soldier will try to spit away fear. I shifted my hold on the chest tucked under my arm, and we headed onward.

I'd carried the box around through years of campaigning, and though I'd done my best to clean it up, it still looked like the scratched, utilitarian article it was. But I hoped that to troll eyes, it would pass for a reliquary.

After another bend, the trail widened out to make a clearing. Concealed by brush, a stream gurgled nearby.

Skav was waiting with much of his tribe but not, I was relieved to see, with a killed or captured Elkinda. Upon sighting Ojojum and me, he asked, "Where are the Hand Maids of Rendeth?"

"I apologize," I said. "When the time to set forth arrived, it turned out that even holy sisters are susceptible to human frailty. By which I mean, they were afraid to meet trolls. But surely that doesn't matter. You see Ojojum is with me. I also brought the relic." I held out the chest.

Meanwhile, I prayed my nattering had fixed everyone's attention on me. That Elkinda had lit her fire—she'd said she could manage with a small one, but the exorcism required at least a bit of flame— and started whispering her incantation without anyone noticing.

Skav glowered as though pondering whether there might be some way of forcing me to produce the absent nuns. Finally his red eyes shifted to Ojojum. "Have you truly come back to me?" he asked.

She hesitated, and the thought came to me that our deception was about to fail because she was too afraid to lie convincingly. But then she said, "You hurt me and shamed me, but a child needs a father. I'll come back if you take the oath."

"Good." The Hearteater looked back to me. "Open the box."

"As you wish." I set the chest on the ground slowly, feigning reverence. Then I slipped the iron key into the lock and tried to twist it.

It wouldn't turn. Since I'd previously broken the lock with the point of a dagger, that didn't surprise me.

But I did my best to feign surprise. As I jiggled and shifted the key, I said, "I'm sorry. I didn't try this before I left the temple. The Hand Maids didn't warn me the lock sticks."

Skav endured my clicking the key back and forth for a bit

longer. Then a clawed hand gripped my shoulder and flung me backward. The troll chieftain dropped to one knee beside the chest and started trying to turn the key himself.

Why, you may wonder, did he bother? He surely intended to end this farce by giving Ojojum the most vicious thrashing yet and telling his fellow trolls to tear me apart. Why not get on with it, then?

I can only speculate, but maybe the incubus simply wasn't very clever. With the right bit of mummery, you could fix its attention on something insignificant.

Or maybe it enjoyed toying with its victims and so didn't care to reveal its true intentions just yet. It wanted Ojojum and me to enjoy false hope a while longer.

While Skav fiddled with the key, I silently implored Elkinda to hurry and fought the urge to glance in her direction. I wanted to know if there were at least wisps of smoke rising from the thicket, but I couldn't risk some troll looking where I was and spotting them, too.

Skav eventually snarled, sprang to his feet, and grabbed the chest. His claws digging into the wood, making it snap and groan, he swung it over his head.

"Please, don't!" I cried. "The chest is sacred in its own right!"

Ignoring me, he dashed the box to the ground. It smashed apart to reveal the emptiness inside.

The Hearteater rounded on me. "What does this mean?" he growled.

It meant I needed to improvise a new stalling tactic.

"It's a miracle," I said. "Rendeth whisked the lock of hair out of the chest and back to the temple."

Ridiculous as that assertion sounded, it gave Skav pause. His true plans for the relic had surely been impious to say the least, and perhaps in his mind, that bad intent lent my claim a trace of plausibility.

As before, his hesitation didn't last long. Then he said, "The hair was never in there."

"It was," I insisted. "I saw it myself before the Hand Maids closed the chest. And I know what this means." I turned to Ojojum. "You said you had to return to Skav for the baby's sake and so we could never be together. But the Bright Angel has given us a sign that our love is meant to be."

The trolls gaped at me. The notion of romance between one of their kind and a human was as bizarre to them as it is to you and me.

But grotesquerie was helpful. Anything to keep Skav off balance.

Ojojum was as surprised as everyone else and needed a moment to reply. When she did, though, she followed my lead: "Yes. You're kind, and Skav's cruel. You're clever, and he's stupid. You'll make a better mate and a better father."

Seemingly furious and dumbfounded in equal measure, Skav looked like he was struggling to work out a suitable response. Eventually he opted for the obvious.

"Enough of this!" he roared to his followers. "Come eat." He sneered at Ojojum. "You're going to eat his face, eyes, and pizzle, and afterward, I'll fix it so you never run off again."

Some of the trolls, the hungrier or less befuddled ones, started toward me. I drew my broadsword. The blade glowed white in the gathering gloom.

"Another miracle!" I cried. "Rendeth charged the sword with holy power."

I wished. The humbler truth was that Elkinda, loath to send me back among the trolls without some semblance of a magical defense, had muttered over the weapon and then set it outside for the better part of a day, during which time it had soaked up sunlight like a sponge holds water.

The trolls balked. The radiance stung and dazzled them, and maybe they feared the Bright Angel truly was watching over me.

But then Skav decided she wasn't. Or else the infernal spirit inhabiting him was game to try its luck against an agent of the divine.

The troll chieftain advanced on me. I came on guard, my sword held high to shine as much light in his eyes as possible.

This was pretty much the situation all my trickery and lies were supposed to avert. The sole difference between it and my grimmest imaginings was that I was only fighting Skav. For the moment, his followers were holding back, but it was far from certain that would change the outcome in my favor, especially when I couldn't even try for the kill. I still hoped that, given enough time, Elkinda would cast the demon out.

Squinting against the glow, Skav came closer still, then, with a quicker, lunging step, snatched for the broadsword. Though I didn't want to kill him, I was willing to wound him if that would slow him down, and I spun the blade to avoid the grab and slice his hand as I'd previously cut the watcher on the trail.

Skav spun his hand, too, and swept the sword out of line. He sprang and raked at my chest with his claws. The other trolls roared in anticipation of the killing stroke.

I leaped backward, and the attack fell short by a finger-length. He kept charging and slashing, and I continued my scrambling retreat. I tried to open up the distance so I could interpose my blade between us again, but he was pressing too hard.

Then I attempted a shift to the side that would cause him to blunder past me. He compensated.

In desperation, I suddenly reversed direction, advancing instead of retreating. That spoiled his aim, and his talons slashed harmlessly behind me. I bashed the broadsword's pommel into his jaw. If the impact stunned him, it would win me the instant I needed to separate myself from him and come back on guard. If not, I'd positioned myself perfectly for him to gather me into a flensing, bone-breaking bear hug.

The attack did stun him. Even so, simply by stumbling on forward, he nearly knocked me to the ground. But I wrenched myself out of the way and even managed to cut the back of his thigh as I did.

Unfortunately, though, when Skav shook off the daze produced by the clout on the jaw and whirled in my direction, he moved as fast as before. The leg wound didn't hinder him.

The thing that was hampering him was the sunlight stored in the sword. That became apparent when it dimmed and disappeared.

The trolls bellowed and howled to see the enchantment exhaust its power, and Skav came at me even harder. He could now see me better.

Whereas I was seeing him worse. With the glow in the blade extinguished, I discovered that if the sun hadn't quite set yet, it might as well have with the trees obscuring it.

Curse you, Elkinda, I thought, and curse my stupidity, too. Why had I staked my life on a second exorcism succeeding when the first one had been an abject failure?

I belatedly decided I should try to kill the Hearteater. If I succeeded, the trolls wouldn't have a demon for a leader anymore and presumably wouldn't go on a rampage. That would be victory of a sort even if I doubted the creatures would let me survive to celebrate it.

Since I'd been fighting defensively, when I came on the attack, it surprised Skav. A stop cut met a clawing hand and left the little finger dangling. He hesitated. I stepped in, feinted high, then low, then spun my blade high again to deliver the true attack at the juncture of his neck and shoulder. The cut landed where I'd aimed it.

But Skav drove at me once more. Leathery hide and dense muscle had kept the sword stroke from shearing deep enough to kill.

I jumped back. His claws still grazed my chest, though, and that was enough to dump me on the ground.

Skav threw himself on top of me. The hand I'd maimed retained sufficient strength to pin my sword arm, and the Hearteater raised his other hand to rip me to pieces.

Then Ojojum rushed in behind him, grabbed his wrist, and strained to keep him from clawing me. Her intervention roused the rest of the trolls from their passivity, and they charged forward, too. I had no doubt it was to pull her off Skav and enable him to get on with butchering me.

But that was when the incubus finally came swirling up out of the troll chieftain's head like steam from a kettle.

The spirit's long, rippling face seemed even ghastlier than before, because now it was full of rage and the rage was directed at me. Its cloudy arms stretching, it reached down and plunged its fingers into my head.

Its touch felt like what it was, filth slithering into me, but there was even more to the unpleasantness than that. Every nasty thing in my mind—emotions it had shamed me to feel, perverse impulses I didn't even realize I had—welled up to join with the intruder.

Given time, that dual onslaught would surely have crushed my will. But when Elkinda dragged the spirit out of him, Skav had gone limp. His grip on my sword arm had relaxed, and I was able to jerk it free.

I thrust the blade through the demon's torso and felt nothing. It was like stabbing fog.

Still, perhaps because Elkinda's magic rendered it susceptible, the incubus screeched, a shriek heard not with the ears but with the mind, and disappeared. To my relief, the vile sensations in my head vanished along with it.

Afterward, the trolls stood flummoxed by astonishment and, conceivably, even horror, for it seemed to me that the incubus's appearance had appalled them, as well.

In that moment of quiet, Elkinda emerged from her thicket. "There," she declared, "all better."

Still heedless of his various wounds, Skav got up off me and embraced Ojojum. "I couldn't help it," he growled. "The spirit had me in its grip."

"I know." She ran her talons through his greasy black hair, dislodging a nit or two. "I know."

Skav rounded on Elkinda. "I should have said," he growled, "the spirit had me in its grip thanks to *you*."

I clambered to my feet. "You're right," I panted. "The wise woman's magic didn't work precisely as intended. But she and I risked our lives to save you, and at the end of it all, you and Ojojum have the child you wanted. That being so, I ask you to let us go in peace."

Scowling, the troll mulled it over. Then he asked, "All the things you said before. About being an envoy, the relic, and loving Ojojum. Was any of it true?"

"Not a bit," I said.

He laughed a grating laugh. "The demon believed, but I didn't. All right. Go."

I took a long breath and strode toward Elkinda.

Then Skav said, "Wait."

Heart thumping, I turned.

"We have gold," said the troll. "Some our fathers took fighting your fathers. Some, we took from city fools who hunt too deep inside the forest. Do you want some?"

I did. I knew just what to do with it.

With gold, I could rent a more fashionable space for my school, buy elegant clothes, and cut a stylish figure to attract the notice of Balathex's gentry. I could stage fencing exhibitions and demonstrate my skills. Gold was a second chance to achieve the life I wanted.

I smiled at Skav. "Well, if you're offering," I said.

A BETTER MAN

-Egil & Nix-

PAUL S. KEMP

Egil and Nix feature in my sword and sorcery novels,
The Hammer and the Blade, A Discourse in Steel,
and the forthcoming, A Conversation in Blood. *Their
stories are pacy, filled with action and wit (I hope). I
think of them as a cross of Fafhrd and the Gray Mouser,
spiced with a bit of Conan and Indiana Jones. I hope
you enjoy reading their stories as much as I do writing
them.* "A Better Man" *takes place after the events of* A
Discourse in Steel *(though it is entirely standalone).*

S UMMER HEAT SMOTHERED DUR Follin in humidity so heavy that Nix fancied he could twist his hands in the air and wring out a tankard of water. The Slick Tunnel's common room steamed in a fog of body odor, pipe smoke, stale puke, and Gadd's eel stew. Even the walls seemed to sweat.

Nix watched a half-drunk slubber from one of the farms outside the city stagger up the stairs with one of Tesha's working girls.

"In this heat?" he said. "They're going to slip right off each other."

Egil eyed the farmhand hob over the rim of his tankard. "Eh, you just dislike hard work."

"It's *hard* work by definition, yeah?" Nix waited for a response, received none from the big priest, then added, "No doubt that galloped unnoticed past what passes for your wit."

"It wasn't funny, is all," Egil said, swirling his tankard. "It's the heat. It's turned your wit flaccid."

Nix inclined his head, warming to the game. "'Flaccid,' is well played, priest, especially for one of your otherwise stunted intellect."

"'Limp' would've worked just as well," Egil said with a nonchalant shrug. "Both pinion the point. To wit, that your wit is lacking in wit."

"A BETTER MAN"

Illustration by OKSANA DMITRIENKO

"I guess you're in a mood, then," Nix grumbled.

Egil shifted in his chair, the legs groaning under his weight. "I want for something to do, is all."

"You're a priest. Go pray or something."

"To whom?" Egil said absently.

"Fair point," Nix conceded. "But that's your own fault for worshipping a dead god. And did you say, 'whom,' now?'"

"I did."

"Fak, man. 'Flaccid' and 'whom' within moments of each other? You're prohibited from reading henceforth."

The two men shared a table in the corner of the common room, near a window that looked out on Shoddy Way. Egil's glare, notorious ill-temper, and hulking frame kept the other patrons at a reasonable distance, and that suited Nix fine. Less stink, he figured. Sweat covered the priest's bald head, turning the tattoo on his pate teary eyed—the eye of Ebenor, the Momentary God, divine for only a moment, dead ever since. Nix pulled restlessly at his shirt and shifted in his seat, unable to get comfortable.

"Here sit men of flaccid wit, to whom the heat is shite," Nix said. "The two, they want for ought to do, but only naught in sight."

"Fak's sake, man," Egil said, shaking his head. That makes everything more terrible."

"It does," Nix agreed, and eyed the common room to distract himself.

Patrons thronged the room's tables, sipping at Gadd's warm ale, while the working women and men of the Tunnel did a brisk, sweaty trade, but everyone did everything at a languorous pace, as if they could stave off the heat by moving slowly enough to avoid its notice.

Nix took a gulp of ale, more out of habit than thirst, and grimaced. "Gods, it's like drinking spit. Not even Gadd's excellence makes this tolerable. Fakkin' summer."

"We ought to leave," Egil said, suddenly animated, the movement of his massive body testing his chair's construction. "Get out of Dur Follin. Head north, maybe. We could search out the Tomb of the Wraith King."

Nix was already shaking his head. "It's too fakking hot to move. And the Wraith King is a legend. No, I submit that we sit here until the sooner of our deaths or the arrival of autumn. Done?"

Egil slouched in his seat, the liveliness in his eyes gone as fast it had appeared. He raised his tankard in surrender. "Done. But no more fakking limericks."

"Done."

A few moments passed in silence.

"I'm bored of this course already," Nix said.

"Likewise."

"Fak."

"Likewise."

"I heard the Night Blade's in town," Nix said after a moment, just to say something.

Egil harumphed and made a dismissive gesture. "The Night Blade. Bah."

"As skilled an assassin as they come, is what I hear."

Egil burped and somehow infused the sound with contempt. Nix waved away the stink of the expulsion.

"A skilled assassin is as contradictory a term as a virginal whore," Egil said. "Assassins sneak about and stab from the dark unseen. Cowards, the lot. Even you, my small friend, with all your faults in things martial—"

"Faults! Small!"

"Even you, my diminutive friend, with all your failings—"

"Diminutive, now? You *are* done with reading, priest. I will burn every book you own. So vowed. And you're soon to get another terrible limerick."

Egil chuckled. "Even you, my quick, stabby friend, don't take the coward's path and at least face your foes."

"Well…" Nix began, thinking of the many times events ran afoul of Egil's characterization, but the priest continued on, his opinion untroubled with facts.

"This Night Blade is just a more skilled coward than most."

"You realize we're tomb robbers and not knights, yeah?"

"Noble work, nobly done," Egil pronounced somberly.

"No argument from me," Nix said.

Chairs propped open the double doors to the Slick Tunnel in a futile attempt to lure a breeze inside, but the opening just seemed to draw in more heat. Nix was about to call for them to be closed when a silhouette darkened the space between the jambs.

She stood a bit taller than Nix and wore a wide brimmed hat, riding boots, a faded green tabard to mid-thigh, and sharpened steel of various lengths. Long dark hair fell out from under her hat to reach a strong jaw. A crossbow hung from a shoulder sling.

Nix nodded at the doorway. "Could be something to do just stepped in the door."

Egil turned in his seat. "Hmm."

The woman's gaze scoured the common room, moving from table to table.

"That's an old uniform, but not one of the Lord Mayor's," Nix said.

"One of the noble houses, maybe?"

"Nothing I've ever seen," Nix said. "Looks threadbare. Shite, are we wanted men?"

"Usually," Egil answered. "But not at the moment."

Nix ran a hand over his stubble. "She looks grim of purpose, no?But I'd wager not a bounty hunter."

"Agreed."

"Shite," Nix swore.

"Shite, indeed," Egil echoed.

"A Road Warden," they said together. "Former."

Her eyes reached them, narrowed, and stuck them to their seats.

"I don't like the look of that," Nix muttered.

"I think maybe I do," said Egil, with a smile.

"She's not hard to look upon, I'll concede," Nix said.

She strode toward them, drawing eyes as she went. She stopped when she reached their table.

"Egil and Nix," she said, not a question. "May I sit?"

Nix smiled as best he could. "Not with so serious a look on your face. And how is it you're not sweating in this heat?"

Egil stood and pulled out a seat for her. Her eyes might've widened a touch at the priest's hulking form. "Sit, please."

"Gods, man," Nix said, tsking. "She's pretty so you're pulling out a chair just like that? What if she was here to arrest us?"

"Ignore him," Egil said.

"I'd ignore you both if I could," she said, and sat. "But that's not my decision."

"Egil, I think she walked through that doorjust to hurt our feelings."

She looked Nix in the face, her lips pursed. "Do you always talk so much?"

"See?" Nix said to Egil. "Another blow to my feelings. And with all that I still feel she's about to ask a favor."

"Not a favor," she said. "An offer."

"A drink?" Egil asked her.

"No. So—"

"So you're a Road Warden," Nix said, interrupting. "Or were

once. You probably hail originally from…oh, I'll say, New Dineen?"

"Cooler there," Egil said wistfully.

She looked surprised, then intrigued. She put her elbows on the table and interlaced her fingers. Nix went on.

"You're here looking for someone or something in Dur Follin and need our help. Close?"

She half smiled. "So you're not the hobs I thought you might be. Well enough. I was a Road Warden, true. But I'm protecting someone, not looking for him."

"Who's the *him*?" Egil asked.

"It's too soon for that," she said, and her half-smile lost the war to a frown.

"I'm not interested," Nix said. A lie. He was interested in just about anything at the moment. He wore boredom with no style.

"I am," Egil said.

"Of course you are," said Nix, rolling his eyes. "Because you are an oaf."

She removed her hat, letting her dark hair fall free to her shoulders. Egil was already smitten, Nix could see.

"How can we help?" Egil asked.

"Shall I continue?" she asked Nix. "Or are we done?"

Nix waved her on, and she dove right in.

"Imagine that an important person from New Dineen had an unofficial meeting with an important person here in Dur Follin. Imagine further—"

"This is a lot of imagining to demand of my priest friend," Nix said. "We were just discussing his limitations in that—"

"I can imagine punching your nose," Egil said. "Twice."

"That's twice more than I imagined you able, then," Nix said.

"*Imagine further,*" she went on, irritated, "that a party or parties very much wanted to ensure that this meeting did not occur and had retained a party or parties to ensure that the party, or parties, coming from New Dineen would be killed here."

Nix frowned, looked to Egil. "Is this what it's like to listen to me talk?"

Egil tilted the bucket of his head. "Mostly. But you're not as pretty."

"I most assuredly am," Nix said, then leaned forward in his chair and stared into her face. "That was a lot of words to say so little. Party of this, party of that. We still don't know your name."

"Sairsa is my name," she said, "and I've told you all I can for now."

"Except why you're here and what you really want," Nix said. He sighed, reached down to the satchel in which he kept his needful things, from lockpicks to magical gewgaws, and removed a black candle.

"What is that?" she asked, eyes narrowed in suspicion.

"A gewgaw," Egil said contemptuously.

"My priestly friend has limited use for things magical," Nix explained.

"As do I," she said cautiously.

Nix slammed the rest of his warm ale in one long gulp and placed the candle in the cup to prevent its falling over. He removed a match from his satchel and lit the taper. An orange flame danced on the wick.

"See this? If any of us speak a lie while this burns, the flame will turn from orange to green, like so." He cleared his throat. "I think Egil is highly intelligent."

The flame remained orange.

"Fak," Nix cursed. "Must not be working."

Egil leaned back in his seat and crossed the tree-trunks of his arms across his chest. "The truth is made plain, you mean."

Nix ignored him and said to her, "You understand the point?"

She stared at the candle, at Nix, at Egil, and Nix could see thoughts moving behind her eyes.

She nodded. "I understand. You don't know me. I have no one to vouch for me, and it will take too long to check with anyone you might know back in New Dineen. I take it then that I at least have your interest."

"At this point you're just helping us pass the time," Nix said, then to Egil, "Who do we know in New Dineen?"

The mountains of Egil's shoulders rose in a shrug. "Two or three slubbers, a couple fakkers."

"All we know are fakkers and slubbers," Nix said, shaking his head. "Why is that?"

"I blame you," Egil said.

"Accepted," Nix said.

"Do you two try to unbalance everyone with your banter?" she asked.

"Oh, I like her," Egil said.

Nix smiled. "Let's start again, then. From the beginning. You can tell us what we ask and maybe get our help, or you can walk out now.""

She held her seat.

"Mind the flame's color, Egil."

"Aye."

"Well enough," Sairsa said. "We'll do it your way. I'm in the employ of a wizard of Ochre Order."

Nix let out a whistle. The Ochre Order and its Arch Magister had a dark reputation and were the true power in New Dineen.

"Name?" Egil asked.

"Oorgan," she said, and the name meant nothing to Nix. "He is...finalizing a pact with one Kerfallen the Grey."

Nix kept his face expressionless, though he knew the name Kerfallen well. Nix purchased many of his gewgaws in the Low Bazaar from Kerfallen's agents. Kerfallen himself was a recluse, a mysterious wizard whose walled manse was rumored to be filled with all manner of magical traps and automata.

"What kind of pact?" Egil asked. "We've had bad experiences with pacts."

"You don't need to know that," Sairsa said, and eyed the candle flame sidelong. "I'm not sure I understand it anyway."

"Wizard shite," Egil said, nodding in sympathy. He took a slug of ale. "Best not understood."

"Sounds boring so far," Nix lied, sitting back in his seat.

Sairsa frowned in irritation. "The Night Blade's been hired to kill Oorgan before the pact can be concluded."

"Now that's something," Egil said.

"By *whom*?" Nix said, and winked at Egil.

"And how is it that you know the Night Blade's been hired?" Egil said.

"Not so boring, now?" Sairsa asked.

"Wizards and assassins deserve one another," Egil said. "Still...."

"I concede some slight interest," Nix said, "but what does this have to do with us? And where's Oorgan now?"

"He's en route from New Dineen. A day out. I'm here in advance of his arrival."

"So you're protecting him but left him behind?" Nix asked.

She reddened. "I'm scouting Dur Follin. And he won't come to harm. I left him well-protected."

"You still haven't told us what this has to do with us," Egil said. "You've a reputation."

Nix smiled. "For good looks, intelligence, and charm, of course."

"For competence," she said. "You know Dur Follin and its

players but are independent of them. That's what I need. Oorgan will have to remain in town two days before the meeting with Kerfallen."

"Two days? Why's that?"

She shrugged. "Something to do with the timing of the pact, preparations, I don't know."

"Wizard shite," Egil repeated.

She clasped her hands and looked them in the eye, each in turn. "So?"

Egil eyed Nix, bushy eyebrows raised. "We wanted something to do. This is something."

"What's the pay?" Nix asked her.

She didn't look surprised by the question, though Egil did.

"This is a damsel in distress, Nix," the priest said.

She gave Egil an obscene gesture. "Hardly."

"Hardly it is, then," Egil said, smiling.

Nix pointed a finger at Egil. "Recall the last damsel in distress we helped. No, recall the last *two*."

"Once again," she said. "I'm not—"

Egil's brow furrowed and he inclined his head. "That's a fair point."

"Pay?" Nix asked Sairsa.

"I"ll pay you more if you vow to talk less."

Nix laughed.

"Twenty five terns each," she said. "Seem fair?"

Egil looked at Nix, eyebrows raised.

"It's light but I'm bored," Nix said. "Done," He and Egil didn't want for coin, and he was too sweaty to haggle.

"Dawn tomorrow at the North Gate, then," she said. "You get ten terns then. The remainder when the meet is over two days hence."

She stood, turned, and walked out without another word.

After she'd gone, Nix leaned back in his chair and tapped the table top with one finger. "Well, that's about half a story."

"You had the candle burning," Egil said, nodding at the taper and its orange flame.

"It's just a candle," Nix admitted. "There's no magic in it. I wanted to encourage truth. Like she said, we've got no time to check her story."

Egil ran a hand over Ebenor's eye. "She never looked at it and never hesitated in her responses, so I'd say she spoke truth. Me, I like her. You're too distrustful."

"Being distrustful keeps me alive. Keeps you alive, too, often enough. Besides, you trust and like too readily, especially when it comes to pretty women."

"Bah."

"You can't help every woman who walks through these doors, you know."

"Maybe not all," Egil answered quietly. "But many."

Nix knew that was the end of the conversation, at least on that subject. Egil had failed his wife and daughter years earlier, and both had died. He seemed determined to never fail another woman in his life.

"Well," Nix said, clearing his throat to clear the air. "I was bored and now I'm not."

"I guess the gods hear our words at times," Egil said. "Let's gear up."

"Aye," Nix said. "I hope we get to meet this Night Blade."

———✦———

NIX AND EGIL MET Sairsa on the cobble paved road just

within the North Gate. A dozen or so other people stood around them, stinking in the pre-dawn heat, yawning, eyes bleary with hangovers or sleeplessness. Nix made most of them as caravaneers who hadn't gotten out of Dur Follin before the gates closed for the night and so had gotten stuck inside. Most were probably late for their posts in the caravan yards outside the walls.

The sky lightened with dawn and the eight watchmen, looking as hungover as the caravaneers, went through the routine of opening the gate. The crowd edged forward as they slid bolts and turned gears.

"Back off," one of the watchman barked.

The routine ended with the turning of a great spoked wheel, the slow clink of wrist-thick chains, and the gate swinging open.

A half dozen donkey or oxen-drawn open-topped wagons lined the road outside, farmers and farmhands milling around them. Several tents were pitched in the grass in the shadow of the walls.

"This Oorgan's a farmer-wizard, then," Nix said.

Sairsa pushed through the throng, brow furrowed. "They should've arrived last night if they'd kept to the schedule I set. Stay here," she said, and hurried away.

"I guess we'll stay here," Egil said.

"Aye."

The farmers avoided eye contact with Egil and Nix as they drove or walked past, no doubt made uncomfortable by their hard looks and sharp steel. A short time later Sairsa returned, leading a train of three saddled horses.

"Oorgan's a horse, then?" Nix said.

"Probably just the ass," Egil said.

"Shut your holes and mount up," she said. She swung into the saddle with practiced grace.

"I don't ride," Nix said.

Sairsa glared at him. "You do today. I—"

"I don't ride," he repeated, eyeing the horse nervously. "Look at the shifty eyes on this beast. No one should trust him."

"It's a her, Nix, a mare, and I gave Oorgan a particular travel schedule to follow. That he's not here when he should be means something happened to delay him. We need to go find him. Right now. And that means you ride."

Nix shuffled his feet. "Listen, I can't ride, is what I mean to say. I never learned."

Her look could have spoiled milk. "City bred slubber."

Nix affected indignance. "I'm just particular about the reasons I'll part my legs."

She shook her head. "You'll ride with me, then. I'll help you up."

Nix could feel Egil's grin, a giant smile that stretched from one end of the city to the other.

"Come on," she said and extended a hand.

"Not a fakkin' word, Egil," he said and surrendered to the inevitable.

He took her hand, she lifted him up, and he sat behind her.

"I feel a bit unstable," he lied, and wrapped his arms around her. She might have been slim, but she was all gristle.

Egil mounted the larger of the remaining two horses, and Sairsa spurred the mare into motion. Nix kept his mouth shut and held on tight as the horses tore down the northbound road out Dur Follin. Keeping the Meander to their left, they devoured the miles. Soon they were clear of the hamlets and farmsteads that dotted the landscape around the city. Open road extended before them.

"Maybe he turned back?" Nix asked.

Sairsa shook her head. "Not possible. Something's gone amiss."

They topped a tall rise and the dark ribbon of the road stretched out below them. Figures moved on it, two groups. Sairsa cursed.

A group of four horsemen armed with bows harried a nobleman's carriage pelting down the road toward Dur Follin. The horsemen, clad in leather jerkins and plumed helms, rode like experts. Nix made them as Jafari, easterners noted for their horsemanship. Cavalry cutlasses hung from their belts, but their bows were their weapons of choice. They drew as they rode and shot at the driver and the team of four horses. The driver ducked and crouched at every shot, sometimes veered the carriage toward the riders to foul their aim. The carriage bounced, jostled, and tilted wildly left and right, nearly toppling at one point. Nix was sure it would soon lose a wheel.

Perhaps a fifth of a league behind the carriage, another two groups of horsemen fought a pitched battle.

"That's them," Sairsa said, and spurred her mount down the rise. "Those are the bodyguards back up the road. They must have tried to hold off the attack while the carriage fled."

"Aye, but four of the Jafari broke ranks and followed."

"Protecting the carriage is the priority," Sairsa said. "The bodyguards knew the risks."

"Get me within throwing range," Nix said, drawing a throwing dagger, then called to Egil. "We take out those four first, yeah?"

"Aye," Egil called, and drew a hand axe from his belt

Sairsa noticed the dagger Nix he held. "You can't hit anything from horseback with that!"

"Milady, it's been a long time since I've missed *any*thing. Just get me close."

As they tore down the rise, the distant melee ended with four of the carriage's guards falling to Jafari blades and the sole surviving bodyguard bolting in the other direction. The six surviving Jafari attackers spurred their horses and rode hard after the carriage.

"See it?" Nix called to Egil.

"I see it," Egil shouted back. "We work fast before they catch up. I'm to the right."

"Aye, that," Nix said to himself. To Sairsa, he said, "Go left."

She did. The four Jafari horseman saw them coming, turned their horses, bent their bows, and fired. Sairsa veered hard to the left to avoid the shot, and Egil turned his mount hard right. Two of the Jafari snarled, drew their cutlasses, and spurred their mounts at Egil, Nix, and Sairsa.

"A bit closer now," Nix said in Sairsa's ear as they bore down on the Jafari. Sairsa drew her blade and the Jafari had eyes only for her.

Nix could see his face, tanned and wrinkled from the sun, silver ringlets in his dark beard, long hair bouncing behind him, cutlass raised high, yellowed teeth bared in a snarl.

"That'll do," Nix said to her, leaned out a bit, and hurled his dagger at the Jafari. The blade hit him in the throat and sank to the hilt. His eyes widened, and he fell from his mount, choking on steel and blood.

Nix checked on Egil, saw that the big priest had no intention of closing with a Jafari cavalryman either. At fifteen paces distant, Egil hurled his handaxe, not at the rider, but at the mount. The axe hit the horse in the head and it staggered once and dropped, taking the rider down with him. Dazed and wounded, the Jafari rose on wobbly legs. Egil drew one of the two large hammers he carried, closed the distance, and slammed it into the stunned cavalryman's head, sending a plume of blood skyward along with the plumed helmet.

Nix looked ahead and saw an arrow finally catch the driver in the side. The driver at it, sagged, and dropped the reins. The carriage started to slow.

"Get me to the carriage," Nix said.

"What are you going to do?"

"Drive it," he said. "At least I'll be off this fakking horse."

Sairsa goaded their mount on. Nix called to Egil.

"Occupy them both!"

Egil nodded. He ducked low in the saddle, using his mount as cover, hammer hanging from his ham fist as he charged toward the carriage and the two Jafari. One of them broke off and rode at him, cutlass in hand. They closed on one another rapidly and the Jafari slashed downward with his cutlass. Egil caught his arm at the wrist with his free hand while at the same time slamming his hammer into the hapless man's chest. Bones shattered and a spray of blood exploded from out of his mouth as he careened backward off his horse.

Meanwhile the other Jafari fired at Sairsa and Nix. The arrow whistled by Nix's ear. Sairsa veered to the other side of the carriage.

"A kiss for luck?" Nix asked.

She sneered.

"Worth a try," he said. He timed his dismount as best he could, though he didn't so much leap from the horse as lean toward the carriage and heave himself awkwardly out of the saddle. He barely got his hands on the driver's bench side rail. The rest of him dangled free, his boots skidding along the road, as Sairsa galloped off and wheeled around.

"Shite, shite, shite," he said, skipping along the road.

An arrow thunked into the wood beside his left hand. He pulled himself up to the bench with a grunt, frantically grabbed the corpse of the driver in both hands, and twisted the body in front of him, using it as a shield. He felt an arrow slam into it.

"Someone kill that bunghole!" he shouted, peeking out from behind the driver's body.

One of Egil's hammers flew across his field and vision and slammed into the ribs of the Jafari's horse. The mount whinnied with pain and collapsed, throwing the rider who tumbled to the hard earth and didn't rise.

Nix tossed the carriage driver's body over the side with a hurried apology, grabbed the reins, and snapped them on the horses. They lurched into a gallop.

"You alive in there?" Nix called over his shoulder into the passenger compartment.

"Just drive!" said a gruff voice.

"Not even a thanks? Nix grumbled. "Fakkin' wizards."

Egil and Sairsa fell in to either side of the carriage.

"Oorgan, do you live?" Sairsa called. "Are you hurt?"

"Yes and no," shouted the wizard.

"As him if he's polite," Nix shouted. "That'll get a no, too."

Oorgan ignored him. "It took you far too long to return, Sairsa!"

Arrows started to fall down around them in twos and threes. Nix stood on the bench for a moment and looked back. The six Jafari cavalrymen from the second group rode hard after the carriage, firing as they came. They were at the limit of their range and the carriage was maintaining its distance.

Nix grinned, but the grin failed as an arrow sank into the haunch of the right rear horse. The beast screamed with pain, stumbled, and fell, fouling the whole team. The carriage lurched to an awkward stop. The two front horses stomped and whinnied. Behind them, the Jafari closed.

Sairsa leaped from her horse on top of the carriage's roof.

"Cut the traces and get them going, Nix."

Nix did exactly that, freeing it from its trace. "Sorry, beast," he said to the wounded horse, and guided the other three away.

Egil slammed a hammer into the wounded horse's head, ending it's pain.

"Hurry," the priest said, bouncing his hammer in his fist and watching the Jafari close the distance.

"Come on, you oafs!" barked Oorgan from within the carriage. Sairsa's crossbow sang.

"Nice shot," Egil said, and Nix assumed she'd felled a Jafari.

Nix leaped back onto the bench and whipped the reins. The three remaining horses lurched into motion.

"Hyah! Hyah!"

Soon the horses were once more at a gallop. Sairsa's crossbow continued its rhythmic song and the rain of arrows soon stopped as the Jafari soon gave up the chase.

"We clear?" Nix called.

She slid down from the roof of the carriage and took a seat beside Nix on the bench.

"We're clear," she said, "but I lost some good men."

"Not *that* good, obviously," Nix said.

Egil, riding beside the carriage, said, "So this Night Blade uses Jafari hireswords to do his work? A coward, Nix, just as I said."

Nix couldn't but agree.

Sairsa thumped a fist on the carriage's passenger compartment. "All right in there?"

"Just get me to Dur Follin," the wizard answered.

THE LOW RUMBLE OF distant thunder vowed rain, and soon. Nix shook his head.

"Been waiting on rain for weeks and we're going to get it tonight of all nights. Fak."

"Aye, that," Egil said, hefting the weight of the new hammer he'd procured. "Roads will be a slog."

They'd been holed up with Oorgan and Sairsa at a rented manse waiting for the appointed night, all while anticipating the Night

Blade's attack, but nothing had happened, and now Nix just wanted to get things over with. The two days had passed at an interminable pace and they'd seen almost nothing of Oorgan, who remained upstairs doing whatever it was that wizards did.

"I'd rather be bored in the Tunnel's common room than bored here," Nix said.

Egil nodded. "There's good drink there, at least."

Nix looked over his shoulder at Sairsa, who sat alone with her thoughts and blades in a wooden chair near the large hearth.

"Be better if he'd travel on foot or horseback," Nix said to her.

"He won't," she said. "Beneath him, he'll say."

"Then I hope it's not beneath him to help push the carriage out of the mud," Nix snapped.

Sairsa only shrugged.

"Fakking wizards," Egil said half-heartedly.

Nix nodded. "True words."

They watched the sun set, the rain begin, and passed the time with small things while Ool's clock tolled the hours of night. An hour past midnight, Oorgan emerged from seclusion and swept down the stairs, his robes like an ochre tent around his corpulence. The runes and symbols embroidered along the robe's seams shimmered as he moved. His long black hair was pulled into a topknot that hung to his sash. A bone mask covered in tiny mystic runes hid his face from view.

"I'd wager five terns he's appallingly ugly," Nix whispered.

"I'd not take that bet," Egil said.

"We have a half hour to reach Kerfallen," the wizard said, his voice muffled behind the mask.

"A half hour to get across town in this weather will take some magic indeed, wizard," Egil said.

Oorgan didn't deign to respond.

"Just stay alert," said Sairsa. "If the Night Blade is going to make a play, it'll be while we're on the road."

They'd hired an old man to drive the carriage and found him dozing on the bench, hood pulled up against the rain. Nix nudged him awake.

"Time to go, granther."

Oorgan disappeared into the passenger compartment, Nix took point, Sairsa and Egil took position to either side of the carriage, and they rolled through the unmanned gates of the manse. Nix felt exposed the moment they hit the road. They hadn't gone a block before the rain turned to a full-on downpour. The road soon became a slog. They walked the streets at as brisk a pace as the rain and mud allowed. Visibility was shite. Buildings crowded close on all sides, creaking in the wind, windows and porches dark.

Nix darted ahead from time to time to check alleys and side streets. Egil and Sairsa kept eyes on the rooftops. The rain prevented Nix from hearing much. He thought he caught the sight of movement in an alley. He crouched low and darted ahead, falchion in hand. He peeked around the alley's corner, but saw nothing, so signaled the all clear.

And so they continued, block after block through the rain and dark.

As they rounded the next corner, Nix sensed something amiss.

"There!" Egil called, and pointed to a rooftop.

Nix saw movement there, just a flash.

"Cover!" Nix shouted, as the first crossbow bolt whistled down from the rooftops. A shaft struck the driver's bench next to the old man's thigh, another struck the board at his feet, another two thunked into the body of the carriage behind him. The old man cursed and jumped from his perch as fast as his age allowed. He hit the mud, slipped, and fell face down in the road. The horses slowed, stopped.

Nix and Egil and Sairsa crowded close to the carriage, scanning the rooftops. Nix wound up his sling and fired at motion atop a nearby roof, but couldn't tell if he hit anything. Sairsa fired, too, and immediately reloaded.

"Get back up there and drive, slubber!" Egil shouted at the driver, but the old timer was already crawling through the mud under the wagon.

"Fak's sake," Nix said, and climbed up onto the bench. "Get on," he called to Sairsa and Egil, and snapped the reins.

The horses pulled and Egil and Sairsa clambered onto the side rails. Nix whipped the horses as much as he dared, leaving the old man behind in the road, all the while trying to make himself small on the bench. A bolt slammed into the carriage and vibrated in the wood, three, six, a dozen. He thought about turning around, but it would have taken too long and exposed them to too much fire. There was nothing to do but drive through it as fast as they could.

"Can you two kill someone please?" he shouted. "I'm taking a lot of fakkin' fire!"

"Hurry," Oorgan called from the passenger compartment. "I cannot be late."

Sairsa's crossbow twanged and a body fell from a rooftop, but the bolts continued to rain down. Nix made at least a dozen men on rooftops on either side of the street. He simply stayed low and kept the horses moving.

"Egil, two on the porch to the right. See 'em?"

"I see them," Egil said, and bounded off the carriage toward the building.

"Cover him, Sairsa!" Nix shouted, and she fired at the two men atop the porch. They ducked and by the time they poked up their heads, Egil had slammed his hammers into the support posts holding up the roof and the whole of it came crashing down, carrying the two men with it. Egil stomped on one's head with his boot and slammed his hammer into the other, finishing both men.

Curses and shouts and more shots came from the rooftops across the street from Egil. The priest picked up one of the corpses and used it as a shield as he stumbled and ran back toward the carriage.

"Cover the other side!" Nix said to Sairsa, as Egil climbed aboard.

They came around a corner and found the road blocked by three farm wagons plainly set there intentionally.

"Shite!" Nix said. He considered forcing the horses to ram through, but didn't think they could make it.

"You're going to have to get out, wizard!" he said to Oorgan.

"I'm not getting out. I'm paying you to handle this!"

"Suit yourself," Nix said, and bounded off the wagon. "Cover me," he said, and Sairsa did. So did Egil, hurling a hammer at a man on the rooftop and felling him with a single blow.

Nix zig-zagged his way through crossbow fire until he reached the side of the building where Egil had felled his target. He leaped up and scaled the wall with the practiced ease of one used to using the Thieves' Highway. Once he reached the top, he found the dead man, his chest caved in by Egil's hammer. Bolts skittered off the roof tiles around him. He grabbed Egil's hammer, pausing a beat to appreciate its weight, and heaved it back down to the priest with grunt.

"How in the Hells do you even swing that thing?" he shouted down.

"I'm not diminutive," Egil called back, darting out into the road for a moment to retrieve his weapon from the mud.

Nix crouched along the roof's eave, loaded a lead bullet in his sling pouch, and wound it up as he sought a target. He spotted movement on the rooftop across the street, a man rising and taking aim with a crossbow at Egil. Nix stood and loosed. The lead bullet struck the man in the face, and he fell back with a shout. A crossbow bolt thudded into the roof next to Nix's boot and vibrated there.

"Fakker," Nix said. He grabbed the crossbow from the corpse at his feet, grabbed a bolt, and prepared to load. Nix glanced at the corpse's face, did a double take, and cursed—the dead man was Varnel, a member of Dur Follin's Thieves' Guild.

"Egil," he shouted down and across the street. "These here are guild slubbers."

"What?"

Egil knew as well as Nix that they had a truce with the guild.

"Hey, you fakkers," Nix shouted. "Hold your fakkin' fire. Do you know who we are? Egil and Nix. You hear me? Are you all guild boys? The Upright Man knows us and owes us."

"Come on out," someone shouted from one of the rooftops across the way. "We'll give you what you're owed."

Another voice shouted from another rooftop. "Nix? That really you?"

Nix recognized the voice. "Trelgin, that you?"

"Aye. What are you doing out here? "

"Me? What the fak are you doing out here?"

"Muscle work, we thought. Delay a carriage was the goal."

Nix and Egil shared a look.

"Delay?" Nix asked. "Shite. Listen, how about you go your way, and we'll go ours. We'll call this a misunderstanding, yeah?"

"Yeah," Trelgin said. "Apologies." Then, to his fellows, Trelgin said, "Night's done, boys."

Nix leaped from the rooftop onto a bale of hay, rolled, came to his feet, and jogged out to the carriage.

"Fak," Egil said.

Nix turned to Sairsa. "You see what's happened?"

Her expression told him she didn't, so he explained.

"The Night Blade played you. This was all set up. First the Jafari and now these guild boys."

"What are you on about?"

"These boys were paid to delay the carriage. *Delay.* The Night Blade is on his way to Kerfallen's manse right now, probably in a carriage not unlike this one, probably dressed in robes and a mask, too. Oorgan was never the target. Kerfallen was."

"What?" she said, coloring. "How do you know that?"

"Because it fits," Nix said. "And that's how I'd do it." .

"Shite," she said, looking off in the direction of Kerfallen's manse.

"Seconded," Nix said.

"Done is done," said Egil, and slung his hammers. "I didn't sign on to save two wizards. One was one too many."

Oorgan's masked face poked out of the window of the lacquered carriage, his voice a hiss from under the mask.

"I need him alive to renew my pact, you shiftless, ignorant asses! Sairsa, save him. I'll double your pay. Go!"

She eyed Egil and Nix, eyebrows raised in a question. "He doubles mine, I'll double yours."

"Now!" Oorgan said.

"Shut your hole," Egil said to the wizard. "You talk too much for someone who can't even cast a spell."

"We wanted a run at this Night Blade anyway," Nix said to Egil.

"True," Egil said. He frowned, looked from Nix to Sairsa then back to Nix. "Fine. Done." To Sairsa he said, "But this is just to help you. Fak Oorgan and his mask and pacts and the rest of the wizard shite. We know where we're going?"

"I know," Sairsa said with a nod.

"Hurry!" Oorgan said. "Where's that old man? I'll follow in the carriage."

"That's very comforting," Nix said, as the three sprinted along Dur Follin's muddy roads.

———•———

THEY WERE WINDED AND coated in road grime by the time they reached the gate of Kerfallen's walled, two story manse. The metal gate stood open. The Night Blade was probably already through.

Two of the wizard's sexless, hairless, humanoid-looking automatons stepped out from the gatehouse to arrest their approach. The constructs, stitched together by Kerfallen's magic, were made mostly of metal and hide and wood, their forms covered in straps and buckles. Some bound spirit or demon or elemental must have animated them.

"Stop," one of the automatons said. "You are unwelcome here and are trespassing at the residence of—"

Egil slammed his shoulder into it, driving it hard against a gate post, then spun and slammed his hammer into the head of the second automaton, knocking its metal and leather head from its shoulders. Meanwhile Nix drew a poniard and drove it through the chest of the automaton Egil had driven against the post. Nix pushed the blade through the construct's body and into the wooden post, pinioning it in place.

"Stop," the automaton said without inflection, grabbing for Nix. "Stop."

Nix slipped the construct's grasp and fell in with Egil and Sairsa, who were sprinting toward the porch that wrapped Kerfallen's manse. A carriage sat not far from the grand stairs that led up to the porch and rune-inscribed doors of the wizard's home.

"You are betrayed, wizard!" Egil shouted, his voice booming over the sound of the rain.

Nix took the stairs of the porch three at a time, Egil at his side, Sairsa trailing. He stopped Egil at the door and felt it with the tips of his fingers, trying to sense of the tingle of a ward. Sensing none, he nodded at Egil and the priest shouldered the huge doors open.

They stood in a large foyer, tiled in stones scribed with symbols of power. Hundreds of colored crystals hung from the ceiling on metal filaments as thin as hairs. Dozens of birds or bats flapped off in the darkness. The home smelled of spice and decay. A dim green light suffused the room, but Nix could discern no source. A stairway snaked its way up into an upper floor that was lost to darkness. The stairway turned at an odd angle that made Nix's eyes hurt.

"Wizard!" Egil called. "Speak!"

The deep bass of Egil's voice caused the hanging crystals to chime softly and, as they did, they showered motes of light, a rain of red, green, and blue fireflies.

"Kerfallen!" Nix shouted, summoning more motes. "Beware!"

A carved wooden door that Nix was certain hadn't been there a moment before opened to their right and robed figure emerged. He stood only the height of a young boy. He threw back his hood to reveal a man's face, though: a sharp, lined mien covered in tattoos of tiny magical symbols, not dissimilar from those on Oorgan's mask. Three silver studs pieced his protuberant nose, and his stern eyes missed nothing.

"I'm Kerfallen the Grey," he said, his voice much deeper than Nix would have expected, given his stature. "Who dares this intrusion?"

Nix opened his mouth to speak but the words gave way to a

scream. Agonizing pain lit up his back. Metal scraped a rib and warm fluid soaked him. A word jumped to his mind: kidney. He'd been stabbed and he'd bleed out in moments. He tried to say Egil's name but the priest was already down, too, on all fours, bleeding from his back, the blood already pooling on the floor. A figure was standing over him: Sairsa, two bloody blades in her fist.

"The High Magister sends his regards," she snarled and bounded at Kerfallen.

The wizard stumbled backward, fumbled at an amulet at his throat, and managed to utter only a single word in the Language of Creation before Sairsa was on him, driving him to the tiled floor, her blades rising and falling so fast and often that she'd punctured his chest and abdomen a dozen times in two breaths. He spat blood once, feebly, then died.

Sairsa seized the amulet he wore on a chain around his neck, wiped her blades on his robe, stood, and turned to go.

"It was business, boys," she said to them. "Not personal."

Nix could barely hear her over the sound of his own slowing heartbeat. Flat on his stomach, he turned to look at Egil. The priest collapsed from all fours, slipping in his own blood.

"Fak you," Egil said to her, his voice breaking.

She sneered. "You wanted a run at the Night Blade. You had it."

With that, she stepped over them, past them, and left them to die.

Nix found it hard to breathe. He tried to reach for Egil but his arm would not answer his command. "A poor end to a good run," he said, unsure Egil heard him.

But Egil had. "Aye," the priest said. "Fak."

They lay there on the tiled floor of a wizard's manse, bleeding and dying. Nix realized of a sudden that the world would go on without him. It didn't seem fair.

"Shite," he said, his voice breaking. "Shite."

A door opened from their left, where a door hadn't been before, and slippered feet approached. Nix was too weak to turn. Egil groaned. The feet stopped outside the pool of blood in which Nix lay.

"Sorry about this," said a voice. "It will hurt, but you'll live."

Nix hissed with pain as something—a healing elixir, he realized—was poured on his back. He felt the skin knit closed, felt the magic of the balm restore his strength. The slippers moved off, did the same for Egil. Nix clambered to his feet, his clothes soaked with rain and blood and turned to face his savior. For a moment, he couldn't speak.

"Kerfallen?" he managed at last.

"What is this?" Egil said, as he, too, rose.

Before them stood what appeared to be a copy of the Kerfallen whom Sairsa had just stabbed to death—pierced nose, tattoos, all of it. Nix looked at the body, back at the person before him, back at the body.

"I don't understand," he said.

"Wizard shite," Egil said, but there was no conviction behind it.

Kerfallen grinned, showing a mouthful of silvery, metal teeth. "The High Magister of the Ochre Order stripped Oorgan of his magic, the worst punishment he can mete out, since members of the Order are prohibited from killing one another. He forbade anyone from helping Oorgan regain it, but Oorgan and I have a relationship that goes back…a long way. And I have a dislike of the High Magister. He's a prick, to speak plainly. "

Egil looked back at the corpse of Kerfallen, then to the living man. "But…what the fak is that, then?"

The tiny wizard beamed. "That? That's one of my finer works, quite unlike the crude constructs I use at the gates and in the Low Bazaar to sell my wares."

Nix marveled at the similarities. "It's a construct? Then how do we even know we're talking to the real you now?"

Kerfallen smiled. "I suppose you don't." He gestured at his form. "But that would be finer work still, don't you think?"

Nix put the pieces together. "So you knew she was coming for you?"

"The Night Blade? I knew the High Magister had retained her."

"Why not just kill her then?" Nix asked.

"Aye, that," Egil said, rubbing the spot on his back where he'd taken Sairsa's blade.

Kerfallen pursed his lips. "She bears a device that wards her against magic. She might as well be invisible to it."

"Go on and say it, Egil," Nix said.

"Fakkin' gewgaws," the priest said.

But Nix knew then why Sairsa had never worried about the candle back at the Tunnel. Ieve if it had been magical, it would not have detected her lies.

"She was easier to deceive than she would've been to kill," Kerfallen said. "She'll collect her fee before either she or the High Magister realize their mistake."

"The High Magister will come after you again," Nix said. "Won't he?"

Kerfallen shrugged. "Perhaps, or perhaps not. Oorgan will soon have his magic back. Why bother with me then?"

"Huh," Nix said, and looked at Egil. "Well, I've heard enough. You?"

"Indeed."

Nix bowed. "Our thanks, Kerfallen the Grey."

"You'll pay my agent in the Bazaar for the healing elixirs, of course. The next time you purchase a…gewgaw."

"Uh, of course," Nix said, knowing better than to argue a debt with a wizard.

The rumble of a carriage sounded from outside.

"Here comes Oorgan now," Kerfallen said. "And he and I must be about our business. Good evening."

———◆———

EGIL AND NIX TRUDGED in silence through the rain and the dark. Nix broke the quiet halfway to the Tunnel.

"So we got played by the Night Blade."

"And she got played by Kerfallen," Egil said.

Nix shook his head. "True, but Kerfallen played us, too."

"Aye," Egil said. "We got it coming and going." He cleared his throat. "Not our finest hour."

"No," Nix agreed. "But I bet you learned your lesson."

"And what lesson is that?" the priest asked.

"That you can't help every fakkin' woman who walks through the door of the Tunnel and asks for help. Gods, man. That's thrice now!"

"No," Egil said softly. "I think I'll keep doing just as I have."

Nix sighed, nodded, expecting no different. "I suppose you will. Makes you a better man than me."

"Drinks?" Egil asked.

"Several, aye. And remind me to buy some of those elixirs from Kerfallen next time I'm in the Low Bazaar."

THE FIRST KILL

-The Shadow Campaigns-
DJANGO WEXLER

---

*"The First Kill" is a bit of backstory for the universe
of The Shadow Campaigns. It's always hard to give
a proper spotlight to the villains in a novel where they
don't get a POV, so I wanted to take this chance to
explore that a little.* The Shadow Throne *implies a
connection between Andreas, Duke Orlanko's brutally
efficient go-to killer, and Sothe, the Gray Rose, his best
agent turned bitter enemy. In this story, we get to see
these two at an earlier point in their careers, and take a
look at how that relationship got started.*

Blackguards

I T WAS AN HOUR before dawn, and the heat was already stifling. Andreas stared at the water-stained plaster of the ceiling, gray and shadowed in the grimy light filtering through the curtains. His pillow was damp with sweat.

Damn the Deslandai, he thought, *for building their God-damned city in a swamp.*

He was suddenly eager to be moving, in spite of the early hour. The bedsheets were already in a tangled pile on the floor, the night too hot for even thin linen. Andreas rolled off the scratchy mattress, hit the floor in a noiseless crouch, and padded silently to the window. It was cheap glass, bubbly and yellow in an iron frame, and the latch squeaked as he tugged it open and pushed the panes wide.

The air outside wasn't much better. A trifle cooler, perhaps, but what it lacked in temperature it made up for in smell. The little room, on the fourth floor of a crumbling brick apartment block that catered to thieves, whores, and rivermen, overlooked one of the Free City of Desland's famous horse markets, and the stench of the by-products of thousands of nervous horses was omnipresent. Even Andreas, no stranger to foulness, found himself wrinkling his nose.

"THE FIRST KILL"

Illustration by OKSANA DMITRIENKO

The only virtue of the place was that it was anonymous, somewhere no one would remark on two foreigners staying for a few days. If, as he'd been warned, the Komerzint really was on guard, they would be unlikely to peg the poorly-dressed travelers as Concordat assassins.

There was a murmur from the bed as Beth rolled over and sat up, woken either by the squeal of the window or the pervasive stink. She yawned, her dark hair puffed around her head like a frizzy halo.

"Sir?" she said. "Is something wrong?"

"Just the heat," Andreas muttered, turning away from the window.

"Is it time?"

"We've got another hour. Go back to sleep, if you like."

"Too hot to sleep." Beth flopped back on the bed, staring at the ceiling. "Are you nervous, sir?"

Andreas glared at her. She was just past her twentieth year, a compact, graceful woman whose small size belied a surprising amount of muscle. She'd been assigned to him for her final training for the last six months, the latest in a string of apprentices the Last Duke had given to him when they were finally ready to get their hands dirty. He hadn't asked to her to climb into his bed as well, but she'd taken to it as eagerly as to her official duties.

"Nervous?" he said. "Why? We don't even know the job yet."

"About the meeting. The Gray Rose."

The Gray Rose. Andreas had been trying not to think about that. *Am I nervous?*

After a moment of self-examination, he decided he was, a little. It was an unfamiliar feeling, but not an entirely unpleasant one, a tingle of anticipation in the pit of his stomach, like the best moments just before a kill.

After all, there was no way around it. The Gray Rose was a

legend. The greatest agent in the history of Duke Orlanko's Ministry of Information; a spy and assassin absolutely with equal. Some of the stories told about her in the canteens of the Cobweb veered into the absurd: she could walk through walls, kill men with the merest touch, disguise herself as anyone from a beggar-child to the King of Vordan.

Andreas had taken pains to find out the truth, or as much of it as was in the archives, and it was almost as impressive. Orlanko turned to the Gray Rose when a mission required daring, skill, and ruthlessness, and she had more kills to her credit than any other Concordat agent. Most of the techniques the Cobweb now taught to new recruits, the Gray Rose had invented. She'd been with Orlanko almost since the beginning, since he'd taken over the moribund Ministry of Information and converted it into the most feared secret police on the continent, and her hands were drenched in blood.

And I will meet her in an hour. No one he knew at the Ministry had been afforded that singular honor. Andreas stood staring a moment longer, staring through the horse market as though it were a curtain of fog.

He turned, abruptly, and went back to the bed. Beth raised her head.

"Sir?" she said. "I'm sorry if my question offended. I thought—"

His hand slid across her skin, up from her ankle and along the curve of her inner thigh.

"Oh." Her small chin lifted in response to his touch. "Are you sure—?"

"We have," he said, kissing her breast and feeling her give a little shiver, "an hour."

Beth raised no further protests. As she gasped and wrapped her arms around his shoulders, Andreas closed his eyes and thought, *the Gray Rose. At last.*

———◆·◆———

THE RIVER VELT, LIFEBLOOD of the Free Cities, flowed broad and deep through Desland. Above the city, the river narrowed as it descended from higher ground, the rushing water providing power to the cities innumerable waterwheels. The wide, flat stretch just below the rapids was as far north as deep-bottom ships could come, and Desland had grown up as the gateway between ocean-going traffic and the ox-drawn barges that plied the waters upstream.

The east bank of the Velt was higher here, and so the business of loading and unloading cargo stayed on the west side. The opposite heights were lined with the houses of the wealthy, square three- or four-story stone mansions belonging to merchants and city burghers who'd grown rich off the river trade. They were lined up like soldiers on parade, facing the river with broad terraces and enormous windows to take in the view. At the base of the crumbling red stone cliff, private docks jutted out into the water, with the pleasure craft of the quality tied up beside them.

Andreas sat on the west bank, across the river from these fortresses of privilege, studying them over the tin rim of a coffee cup. The coffeeshop was only a wooden stall surrounded by a few rusting cast-iron tables and chipped wooden chairs, the whole thing ready to be stacked on the back of a wagon and hauled away at a turn in the weather. The owner had set up on a stretch of muddy grass flanking a brick warehouse, only a few yards from the riverfront. All around was the business of the city, just getting into full swing now that the sun was well and truly risen, a chorus of shouts and rattling wheels and the sounds of horses.

A shadow fell across the table. Andreas didn't look up.

"Hello." A woman's voice. "Three-aye-five-one."

"One-dee-three-seven," Andreas said. Today's code, memorized from the table printed in tiny type on a scrap of foolscap sewn into his breeches.

"Hello, Andreas," the Gray Rose said. "Welcome to Desland."

"Thank you," Andreas said. "Please sit down, ah …"

"Call me Rose." There was a touch of humor in her voice. She pulled out the chair across from him, which creaked in protest, and sat.

Andreas had carefully schooled himself to have no expectations regarding her appearance. Rumor had it, of course, that she was a great beauty, but he'd known better than to believe that. The woman facing him was plain, unremarkable. She had dark hair, tied back and coiled behind her head, and a thin face with a hatchet of a nose. He guessed her age at thirty, or a little past. Like him, she had looks that would not draw attention in a crowd and would be easily forgotten. She wore a dark brown dress with brass buttons, and could have passed for a local, a dockworker's wife or a fisherwoman.

"It's an honor to meet you," Andreas said. He had to concentrate on keeping his tone casual.

"Still telling stories about me in the canteen, are they?"

"They are. I didn't know what to believe, so I went looking in the archives."

Her eyebrow went up. "And what did you find?"

"A lot of missing files. But enough to know how good you are."

Rose chuckled. "And I, in turn, have read the files on you. The Duke thinks very highly of you, you know."

"I'm honored by his grace's trust." He couldn't help a slight smile. "And what did *you* find?"

"I found a man who seems to enjoy his work." Her tone didn't make it clear whether she approved of this or not. "The girl in the blue dress. Your partner?"

"My…assistant. I'm training her." Beth was acting as lookout at another table, behind the coffee stall.

"Well, tell her there's not much point to standing sentry if she makes it obvious by staring at everybody."

"I'm sure she'll appreciate the feedback."

"Are you two ready to move?"

"Everything is in place." He'd spent the last week accumulating the tools he might need and securing an escape route for a quick getaway; standard procedure for a mission in unfriendly territory. "We can go on your word."

"Good." She scraped her chair halfway around the table, until she was sitting beside him and they could both look out at the river. "See the house with the blue marble, second from the left?"

"I see it." Andreas sipped his coffee. It was a three-story manor house, much like the others. A huge semi-circular balcony jutted out from the second floor, supported by stone buttresses sunk into the cliff face.

"It belongs to the Baronet di Ninevah, and he has a special guest tonight. The Secretary-Treasurer Sepulveda of the Knights of the Far Shore."

Andreas nodded slowly, taking in every detail of the building.

"The Knights have considerable business interests in the far east," Rose went on. "They are expanding their concern westward, and negotiations have been ongoing with several potential partners. One of them is the House of Nachten, out of Hamvelt."

While not an expert on commercial dealings, Andreas recognized the name. The Nachten were one of the High Families of Hamvelt, the elite who supplied the commercial and political rulership of the mountain city. He cleared his throat.

"I take it that the Duke would not approve of this partnership."

"Emphatically," Rose said. "His grace has several times suggested more suitable arrangements to the Knights, and they seemed amenable. Nevertheless, we discovered the Secretary-Treasurer had come here, in what he believes to be all secrecy, to meet with Hamveltai representatives. His Grace is not pleased. You are to visit Secretary-Treasurer Sepulveda and make this absolutely clear."

"Exactly how displeased *is* His Grace?"

"Extremely displeased. His instructions to me were, 'tell Andreas the leash is slipped.'"

Andreas fought back a grin. "I *see*. Very well. Tonight?"

"Tonight."

"Will you be joining us?"

"Only if something goes wrong. Otherwise, I will be… watching."

So this is a test. He'd guessed it was something of the sort. The mission was no doubt real—it wouldn't be much of a test if it wasn't—but there was more at stake than an order of puffed-up old windbags and their ambitions. Orlanko and the Gray Rose wanted to see what he could do. He felt his pulse quicken. *I'll show her what I can do.*

"Understood," he said.

Under the table, he felt the touch of her fingers against his hand, and she passed him a folded sheaf of paper.

"That's what we know about the layout and the guards," she said. "The Knights have brought a few people with them, but nothing serious. If there's real opposition, it will come from the Komerzint. There have been some hints that they're keeping an eye on this."

The Komerzint—Commercial Intelligence—had once been a private firm supplying information to highly placed Hamveltai concerns. In the last few decades, it had grown into the *de facto* clandestine service of the Hamveltai state; only natural, in a city where business and political interests were so intertwined.

"Any particular instructions as regards the Secretary-Treasurer himself?" Andreas said.

"Nothing elaborate necessary. The message will be received in the right places." Rose pushed her chair back and got to her feet. "Good hunting. His Grace looks forward to your report."

Andreas grinned. "His Grace will not be disappointed."

———✦———

A LESSER MAN MIGHT have been disappointed at not being given the opportunity to work side by side with the Gray Rose, but Andreas decided it was better this way. *She'll be watching me.* That was enough to make his heart beat faster, and it meant that he could work without risk of being overshadowed.

What *was* disappointing was that the first step in the proceedings was up to Beth. He didn't like trusting his apprentice with crucial matters, but she was smaller and lighter than he was, and a better climber. *And there's always a backup plan.*

After looking over the plan of the house Rose had supplied, he'd decided to approach from the river side. It was perhaps a trifle obvious as an opening move, but the front door of the house was on a well-lit, fashionable street which would have carriage traffic and patrols of watchmen all through the night. The di Ninevah docks boasted only a solitary watchman and his lantern, keeping an eye on the baronet's finely appointed pleasure galley.

Andreas had taken care of him with a single shot from a soot-blackened crossbow while their little boat was still fifty yards out. Not a bad shot, if he said so himself, from a rocking boat and against a target silhouetted only occasionally against his lamp. The guard had taken the bolt in the temple and pitched off the pier with a soft splash, inaudible amid the gentle creaking of the tied-up boats. No one raised the alarm when Andreas rowed their own boat in and settled it between the pleasure galley and a cargo barge, well-concealed from casual eyes.

Di Ninevah wasn't such a fool that he'd completely ignored the possibility of intruders getting in this way, of course. The stairway that led from the docks to the house was cut deeply into the rock, well-lit by oil lanterns, and blocked by a pair of wrought-iron gates with solid locks. It was also overlooked by a second-floor window, and any movement would be obvious to a watcher within.

To Andreas' trained eye, however, the twenty feet of cliff was not the obstacle that it might have appeared. The red stone was soft and crumbling—treacherous to be sure, but offering plenty of hand- and foot-holds. Beth was halfway up, moving slowly and carefully, a dark, spidery shadow in her soft gray working outfit. Andreas stood on the dock below, keeping watch, as she tested each new position with one hand before trusting it with her weight. A soft rain of pebbles below her testified to the necessity of these precautions.

In another twenty minutes, she'd reached the top. The baronet's enormous balcony, while no doubt ideal for dinner parties in the warm summer evenings, provided a perfect place to make the ascent shielded from any possible view from the house windows. Beth disappeared over the lip of the cliff in a final spray of pebbles, and a moment later Andreas could hear a metallic *clink* as she hammered a piton into the rock. A coil of rope fell toward him, unrolling as it went, and he caught it before it hit the dock.

With the knotted cord in his hand, the climb was quick and easy work, though his boots scraped more dirt and small rocks from the cliff. Beth was waiting for him at the top, crouched beside the anchored line, her face a pale oval in the light from the quarter-moon.

"Well done," Andreas said. Praise had to be given when it was due, that was a vital part of training. Beth smiled.

"Thank you, sir."

He nodded and moved deeper beneath the balcony, and she fell into step behind him. Around the sides of the house, there were gardens, but nothing would grow in the shadow of that overhang, so the space had been covered in flagstones and given over to the more mundane task of airing out old bedding and linens. Sheets hung from hooked stands, still as specters, and Andreas crept around them with utmost care. Stumbling into one and bringing the whole thing crashing down would lend the enterprise a comic-opera touch that he would *not* appreciate.

The door leading from the under-balcony space into the house was plain but strong, secured with a stout iron lock. Rose hadn't provided any information on its construction, so Andreas had decided not to rely on fiddling around with picks, which in any case had never been his strong suit. Instead, he took a small flask from his belt, uncorked the stopper, and tilted it gently into the keyhole.

The flask was full of gunpowder— not the ordinary coarse stuff one might use to propel a cannonball, but a much more finely ground variety sometimes called 'flash powder'. It burned faster and hotter than its common cousin, and it was so fine-grained that particles of it lingered in the air like an incendiary fog. A few pinches was enough. He restoppered the flask, motioned Beth to back off a step, and struck a match near the keyhole.

The powder went off with a soft *whumph*, producing a flash of light that would have ruined Andreas' night-vision if he hadn't already had his eyes tightly shut. As soon as he heard the noise, he grabbed the door-handle and turned it. Inside the lock, the tiny fireball would have blown all the tumblers outward; the handle resisted for a moment, then opened with a *click*, smoke still pouring out of the keyhole.

Andreas eased the door open. As Rose's plans had promised, it led into a servant's hall, just off the kitchens. It was late enough that the staff—except for the watchmen, of course—would have gone to bed for the evening. A back stair led up to the third floor, to the Secretary-Treasurer's room. *So far, so good.*

———⊶•⊷———

THE AMBUSH WAS WAITING in the third-floor hall, where a concealed door led out from the servants' passage onto a well-appointed hallway. Andreas opened the door and glanced in both directions, satisfying himself that the hall was empty, and slipped through, with Beth close behind him. Just after the door closed, though, he caught the sound of running footsteps, and then a squeal as an iron bolt slammed into place.

Someone had been waiting until they went through to block their escape. Something at the back of Andreas' mind, the part of him that kept him alive when missions went wrong, had him reaching for his weapons before his conscious mind understood what had happened. He drew a short sword in his right hand and a curved fighting knife in his left, and when the nearest bedroom door burst open to disgorge armed men, he was already moving.

The men were ready for a fight, but they were not expecting their opponent to come at them so quickly. Andreas got only an instant to assess the grim-faced, mustached fellows in fighting leathers, slim swords in hand and small round shields belted to their opposite forearms.

The first one through the door way stopped in his tracks when he saw Andreas coming, forcing his fellows to pull up short behind him. Andreas feinted high with his sword, bringing the man's shield up. Metal scraped on metal as the butt of Andreas' hilt hammered the shield, but he was already pivoting to bring his knife around into the man's belly. His opponent doubled up around the wound, exposing the next guard, wedged awkwardly in the doorway. There wasn't time or room for a proper swing, so Andreas punched him in the face with the hilt of his sword, sending him stumbling backward with blood streaming from his nose. The third guard, who'd had a moment to get clear, stepped aside and raised his sword, only to find Andreas shoving the man he'd stabbed out of the way and slamming the bedroom door.

Behind him, the hallway echoed with the stupendous *bang* of a pistol shot. Andreas looked over his shoulder to find three more swordsmen closing from the opposite direction. Beth had shot one in the chest, and she tucked the smoking pistol into her waistband and drew another from the leather strap at the small of her back. The remaining two guards hesitated, not eager to charge a loaded pistol, and Andreas decided to use that opportunity to seek a better tactical position.

"Beth!" he said. "With me!"

Beth fired again, and he winced—the shot had probably been more useful as a threat. Andreas ran flat-out at a pair of double doors that gave way before his shoulder with a wooden splintering sound. He pulled up short in the room beyond—a hexagonal, nearly empty space, some kind of performance chamber—and Beth trotted past him, pistol still held in one hand. Andreas slammed the door behind her. He'd broken the lock, but there was an iron bolt, and he drew it closed just in time for the first of the guards to reach the doors and start pushing.

"That won't hold," he muttered, casting about. A glass-fronted drinks cabinet looked heavy enough for his purposes, and he gestured to Beth. "Help me with this."

She dropped the pistol, and together they managed to get the solid piece of furniture off the ground, glass bottles inside rattling and tinkling wildly. They parked it across the doors, and Andreas stepped to one side of the doorway, drawing Beth after him.

Men on the other side were shouting in a language he couldn't follow—not Hamveltai. *Daciai, presumably. Those fellows have an Old Coast look.* The Knights might be more commercial enterprise than marital organization these days, but evidently they could still rustle up a few soldiers when the occasion called for it.

"Holy *shit*," Beth breathed.

"Are you all right?" Andreas said. He watched the door, which was shaking as the guards pounded on it from the other side.

"Fine." She gulped air and swallowed hard. "I'm fine. I just… *shit*. I barely saw them coming."

"It was neatly done. Block the way behind us, trap us in a corridor between two converging teams."

"They were waiting for us."

"Indeed. Rose's information is apparently not as good as she believes."

"Any idea who those guys are?"

"Knights, perhaps. More likely Old Coast mercenaries." He listened for a moment. "There's at least six of them out there."

Beth crossed to the other side of the room, where three big windows looked out over the river.

"We're right over the balcony," she reported. "But they've got a man down there."

"Of course they do." Andreas unshipped the folding crossbow from its harness and snapped the ribs into place. "Find something to tie a rope to."

Beth drew another coil of rope from her small pack. "There may be more inside. Over the balcony rail once we get down?"

Andreas finished drawing the crossbow, hearing the catch click, then paused. "Over the rail?"

"And back down the cliff. To the boat." She looked back at him. "Or did you have an alternate route in mind?"

Escape. That was the correct option, obviously. The mission was blown, had been blown from the beginning; they'd been expecting a couple of sleepy watchmen, not a house full of hornet-mad mercenaries. The best decision was to withdraw and wait for another opportunity.

But the Gray Rose is watching. Would *she* withdraw, under the same circumstances? *Or would she get the job done, and be damned to the opposition?*

Beth was staring at him. Her eyes were wide, he saw, and her breath came quickly, but she wasn't panicked. *Good.* That guard in the hallway had been her first kill, and every trainee reacted differently to a first kill. *I've done a good job with this one.*

"We're not pulling out," Andreas said. "We'll drop to the balcony and go in through another window. They won't be expecting it."

Beth blinked, swallowed, and nodded. She hadn't been privy to the mission briefing; if he thought it was important enough to carry on, in spite of the risks, that was his call to make.

"Okay," she said, with only a slight tremor in her voice. With a few quick movements, she opened the window and tied the rope to the iron crossbar. "We're good to go."

"You may want to take this chance to reload," Andreas said, indicating the pistol she'd dropped.

"Right."

Beth fumbled through her pocket for a paper cartridge, and Andreas moved to the window. He leaned out, just for a moment, to spot the armed figure waiting on the balcony, then ducked back and fitted a blackened metal bolt to his crossbow. The man down there would be alert—the whole house had probably heard the pistol shots—but he didn't know where danger might come from.

"Ready?" Andreas said.

Beth nodded, and as though to reinforce the need to move, a pair of shots came from the doorway. The wood around the bolt cracked and exploded, and the doors shifted against the heavy cabinets.

Andreas raised the crossbow to his shoulder. "I'll shoot, you drop. Go."

Beth took a deep breath, put her pistols back in her waistband, and jumped through the open window, knotted line in one hand. Andreas leaned out after her, sighting on the guard, who had turned to face the house at the sound of more shooting. *Perfect.*

The crossbow *thrummed*, and the guard sprouted a quarrel just above the bridge of his nose. He toppled, shield clattering against the stones. Andreas snapped the ribs of the crossbow closed, secured it to its harness, and followed Beth down the line. It was only a fifteen foot drop, and she was already on the balcony, pressed up against the wall between a pair of windows. Andreas joined her, trying to recall the layout of the parts of the building he hadn't expected to enter.

"That hallway leads out to the main staircase," he said. "Most of them are still breaking down the door upstairs, so we've got a minute or so."

"They'll still have guards on the stairs," Beth said, her tone professionally detached. Andreas hid an admiring smile.

"Shoot one of them, I'll handle any others."

"Got it."

"Ready to run?"

She nodded.

Andreas drew his sword and slammed the hilt against the windowpane, shattering the expensive glass. No point in stealth now, with the house full of shouting men breaking down doors. He vaulted through, avoiding the dangerous shards still stuck in the frame, and Beth followed. A heartbeat was sufficient to assure himself that the floor plan matched what he remembered; then he broke into a dead run, with his apprentice close behind.

A well-appointed hallway rushed past, doors to sitting rooms and drawing rooms tightly shut. Andreas noted, absently, that whoever had planned this ambush must have made sure the domestic staff were given the night off, or there would have been a good deal more panic. Then they were turning a corner, out into the main hall, where a staircase with crimson carpets led in both directions.

As Beth had predicted, there were guards on the landing, three more men with sword and buckler. They were looking the wrong way, though, up towards the excitement on the third floor. Andreas ran straight at them, sword extended like a lancer, and took the first through the kidney from behind with a clean thrust. He slid off the blade, gurgling, and the next man to turn dropped with a startled expression as Beth's pistol-shot found him. The third man backpedaled, shouting, but Andreas didn't give him a chance to get his footing. He swung his sword at the mercenary's right side, forcing him to parry, then stepped in and snaked his other hand around the man's shield arm. The guard pulled away, opening himself up, and Andreas kicked him in the groin. He doubled over, and his momentum carried his throat across the blade of Andreas' sword, placed neatly in his path. Blood spurted, soaking the rich carpet a darker shade of red.

Beth jogged up. "Nicely done, sir."

"Thank you."

Andreas looked up the stairs. The hall led in both directions at the top. The left was toward where they'd gone out the window, the right led to Secretary-Treasurer Sepulveda's bedroom. Not great, tactically—if they got bogged down, enemies could catch up from behind—but there was no way around it. He jogged up the stairs, peeked around the corner to the left, and swore.

Four men were heading back towards the stairs, weapons drawn. *They must have got the door down already, and figured out we got clear.* Or else they'd heard the shot from downstairs—he'd been hoping it was too noisy for that—and were coming to investigate.

"Go!" he hissed at Beth. "Third door on the right, get it open. Now!"

Beth nodded and threw herself forward, turning right at the junction. The guards saw her, and shouted in alarm, but she didn't hesitate. *Good girl.* Andreas sheathed his sword and grabbed the flask of flash powder from his belt. The container was stiffened leather, and it was the work of a moment to cut it in half with his knife. As the four guards came in front of the stairs, he hurled the mutilated flask into their midst, spraying powder as fine as milled flour in all directions. He followed it with a match, just as the men were turning to face this new assailant, and squeezed his eyes shut.

The powder went up all at once with a *whoomph* and a rush of heat that frizzled Andreas' eyebrow. The blast would blind and burn, but it wasn't enough to kill. Andreas would have liked to take a few moments to finish the guards off, but they still had their weapons drawn and flailing, and doing it safely would take longer than he could afford. Instead he slipped past them, following Beth. The door he'd indicated was open, and as he approached he heard a shot from inside. Wood exploded into splinters from the doorframe. Andreas spun through, exposing himself as little as possible, and dropped into a crouch.

The bedroom was a small guest suite, and he found himself in the receiving room, with a few armchairs and spindly tables. Another doorway in the opposite wall led to a dining room, and beyond that a closed door presumably concealed the bedroom itself. Beth was crouched behind a chair, one of her pistols lying on the floor beside her, trickling smoke. She had the other in her hand.

The guards would not be far behind him. Andreas pushed the door closed, paused a moment, then leapt across the line of fire from the inner door. A pistol shot rang out, the ball smacking into the plaster in a puff of dust. From his new position, he could reach the bolt, which he pushed home to buy at least a few minutes. That done, he squatted beside Beth, well out of sight of the dining room doorway.

"At least two of them in there," Beth said. "A pistol each."

"Two shots so far. We've got quite a few more behind us, too."

Beth grimaced. "We'll have to risk it."

Andreas nodded, picturing the two men inside frantically reloading. If they were fast—or if they had a second pair of loaded weapons—this was going to be extremely dangerous. Even a poor shot would have a hard time missing a target trapped in a doorway at this range.

"Okay," Andreas said. "Give me the pistol. You go first, move fast and stay low, try to draw a shot. I'll be right behind."

"Got it." Beth closed her eyes and took several deep breaths. Andreas could hear booted feet outside, and once again frantic pounding on the door. "Ready."

She reversed the pistol and handed it to him, then crouched by the edge of the doorframe. Andreas took a position behind her, ready to lean out as soon as she moved.

"Andreas…" Beth's voice was a bare whisper.

"What?"

"Nothing. Sorry, sir. Ready?"

"Go."

Beth pushed off, rolling through the doorway and throwing herself into a sideways dodge as soon as she was clear. Two pistols went off, almost simultaneously, roaring in the enclosed space. Andreas stepped into the doorway, drew a bead on a man crouching behind a long lacquered table, and fired. It wasn't a perfect shot, but the ball caught the guard in the shoulder and spun him to the floor. The second guard had discarded his pistol and drawn a sword, and Andreas did likewise. They stepped forward, the guard edging clear of the chairs tucked in around the table to get a clear space, Andreas giving ground slightly.

The mercenary snarled—he was an older man, with a badge sewn into his jacket, perhaps indicating his rank—and pressed forward. Then something went *thunk*; a throwing knife sprouted between his shoulder blades, as if by magic. It didn't sink deep enough to do real damage, but the guard turned to find the source of this new attack, and that was all the opening Andreas needed to drop into a neat lunge and put the point of his sword through the man's throat.

He hurried across the room to the other guard, in case he was still capable of offering any resistance, but the mercenary was only clutching his wound and moaning. Andreas finished him with a quick slash, sheathed his sword, and went back to check on Beth.

She was sitting up, with obvious difficulty, supporting herself with one hand and keeping the other pressed against her stomach. Blood, thick and red, welled between her fingers.

"Good throw," Andreas said. Recognizing good work was important for training.

"Thanks." Beth swallowed, the muscles in her throat working. "Not quite fast enough, though."

Andreas said nothing. Beth gave a weak smile and jerked her head toward the inner doorway.

"Go on," she said. "Finish the job. Then we'll see about getting out of here."

———•◆•———

THE DOOR TO THE Secretary-Treasurer's room opened with a creak, neither locked nor bolted. No lamps were burning, but by the light from the outer room Andreas could see dark shapes sprawled across the floor. He counted four of them—five, he corrected, seeing another curled up in one corner—all armed mercenaries, all dead. There was remarkably little blood. Each man had been killed by a single deep stab wound, to the head or to the heart. None of the five had managed to even draw a sword.

The bed, a big four-poster, was hung round with curtains. Andreas drew them back, already certain what he would find. Sepulveda was an old man, pale and liver-spotted, with wispy gray hair and long, quivering jowls. His mouth was open in a silent 'O' of surprise, and his cloudy eyes stared sightlessly at the ceiling. His hands were clutched over his heart, where a dark stain on his shirt marked the wound underneath.

"Rose?" Andreas said. "You're here, aren't you?"

A shadow extracted itself from the deeper darkness beside the bed. "I wasn't expecting you."

The guards in the outer room didn't know about this, Andreas thought. That meant that these men had died, not just without getting the chance to draw a weapon, but practically without a sound. *This wasn't a fight. It was a…dissection.*

"Did you know they'd be waiting for us?" he said.

Rose shrugged. "It was always a possibility. One of our local informants has been compromised by the Komerzint. Now that they've tipped their hand"—she gestured at the corpses—"we'll be able to find out who, and express His Grace's feelings on the matter."

"And you just decided to come in here and do the job yourself? You didn't think I'd make it?"

"I didn't think you'd try." She walked across the room to stand in front of him. "Retreat would have been the correct tactical option."

"But you waited here for me."

"As I said. I've read your file."

Rose slipped past him, out into the dining room. Andreas followed. The noise of the guards at the outer door had grown louder.

"If this is a test," Andreas said, as Rose knelt beside Beth, "did I pass?"

"That depends," Rose said. "Did you learn anything?"

Andreas looked down at the two women. Beth's eyes were closed, and her breathing was fast and shallow. Rose put two fingers to her throat, then gently pulled her hand away to examine the wound.

"I learned not to be the first one through the door," Andreas muttered.

"She may live," Rose said, straightening up. "If we can get her to a cutter soon."

"So what now? It sounds like there's at least a dozen of them out in the hallway. We won't have a chance if we have to carry her."

"Consider it another test. You're trapped in a room with a badly injured comrade and no escape route." Rose cocked her head. "What do you do?"

Andreas stared at her for a moment, then crouched beside Beth. He wasn't sure if she was conscious or not, but either way he moved so fast she had no time to make a sound. His knife went in to the soft spot under her jaw in a single, smooth motion.

Her legs kicked, weakly, and the breath went out of her with a sigh. Andreas withdrew his blade, wiped it on her shirtsleeve, and sheathed it again.

He looked up at the Gray Rose, and she looked back at him, her expression unreadable. He wondered if, in that moment, he had finally surprised her. Then she was turning away, drawing a long, curved blade as the door broke open, and a moment later men were falling around her like wheat before the scythe.

MANHUNT

-Sword & Barrow-
MARK SMYLIE

This story takes place in a thief-plagued city from the setting of The Barrow, *my first novel. Its main character, Otalo Galluessi, does not appear in* The Barrow *until literally its very last page, with only a single line of dialogue; but as with so many seemingly minor characters that appear fleetingly in either the novel or the associated* Artesia *graphic novels, in my head he already had a bit of back story and the potential to play a broader role down the line. Indeed, I enjoyed exploring his role in the events spilling out from* The Barrow *so much that this story will now be included as a prologue to its sequel,* Black Heart.

I hope you enjoy it as well.

THREE MEN MOVED SWIFTLY and silently through the courtyard, dressed for night work. Black neck stocks had been pulled up to mask their faces, and broad-brimmed tricorn hats were pulled low over their eyes. Loose, dark half-coats covered the long daggers stashed about their persons. Otalo carried a short, heavy-bladed cut-and-thrust sword, still in its wooden scabbard, holding it propped over his shoulder as though it were a club; while Lodrigo, a big broad-shouldered man, carried an actual club, the head of its long wooden shaft wrapped in iron, the grip wrapped in leather. Casseyo had one hand resting on a heavy chopping falchion tucked in its scabbard under his coat, while the other hand carried an unlit lantern. According to the city's law of arms, they could all be arrested for bearing weapons above their station, as only knights or the appointed members of the City Watch were allowed to carry anything larger than a dagger within the city walls. But as they were intent upon a long night of murder that was the least of their concerns.

Otalo spotted the arched doorway that they were looking for and moved towards it, boots soft on the cobblestones. Lodrigo and Casseyo took up a position on each side of the door as his hand rested on the

"MANHUNT"

Illustration by **ORION ZANGARA**

handle. Otalo held his breath, and his hand pushed on the door. Normally at this hour it would have been barred from the inside by the building's porter, but pains had been taken to assure that it wouldn't be. And thankfully it opened, albeit with a creak that sounded loud in the dark. He breathed out, and nodded to his companions. "Second floor, first apartment on the left, with the sign of a magpie drawn upon it," he whispered. He was pretty sure they'd have remembered the location of their target, but it paid to make sure. The two men nodded, steeling themselves.

"Right," whispered Casseyo as he drew his falchion. "Let's not tarry."

"Aye," whispered Lodrigo. His eyes had a perpetually sleepy expression about them, as though he was only half-awake. "King's Fortune smile on us. Time's a-wasting when there's someone needs killing."

Otalo grunted as he drew his sword and held it in his right hand, the wooden scabbard in his left. *Always bring the right tool for the job.*

━━●━━

THERAPOLI AS A CITY—while not as decadent or unmannered as the great cities of Palatia Archaia to the north, or the Hemapoline League of Cities to the east, or even Avella, the Immortal City, capital of the Empire of Thessid-Gola to the south—could on most nights have claimed to have at least presented itself well to the adventurous traveler. Even into the dawn hours there would have been lights and revelers and the smell of roasting meat and fried fish by the Forum. In the streets of the Foreign Quarter, the Old Quarter, and the University Quarter, streetwalkers, hustlers, johns and dandies, the bored and the busy would all have been out and about, each on their own mission of desire or need. The night patrols of the City Watch would have passed by, calling out "All's well!" to any that cared to hear them.

On most nights.

The command had come by whisper and rumor, filtering into the ears of the night patrols of the City Watch for the third evening in a row: *the Guild says stay off the streets.* And like the rats and cowards they were, most of his fellow Watchmen had exchanged glances with each other, and nodded silently, and stepped off the streets and into guardrooms and tavern halls and brothels, and shut the doors tight against the chill night air. And so for three nights in a row they'd left the city streets to the tender mercies of the very criminals they were charged with protecting them from, left them filled with tension and the whiff of fire and ash, the eerie silence punctured by distant shouts and screams. Most of those in the Old Quarter not forewarned by whisper and rumor as the Dusk Maiden rose and Night fell would still have felt it in the air, and locked their doors and the shutters to their windows, and cowered in the dark with candles and prayers and sharpened knives for company.

And they'd pop their heads up the next morning and survey the damage done, and listen to tales of squads of thugs and assassins breaking down doors and dragging men and women screaming into the night, a growing roster of the missing—and presumed dead, for their bodies had simply vanished. Even during the day everyone had been walking careful, past the gutted ruins of the Sleight of Hand, once the Quarter's most notorious brothel and now a shuttered, smoking wreck. A campaign of terror and murder and intimidation, operating right under the noses of the City Watch, indeed seemingly with the tacit approval of at least some of its commanders. An indictment of the corruption endemic to the Watch and to the city plainly visible for all to see, and yet most of his fellow Watchmen were content to shrug and drink their warm beer.

But not him. Oh no. Not Conrad Theorodrum.

"You've always been too proud for your own good, Conrad," said Baldwin, cheerily hoisting a glass. "I mean, it's too bad about the Sleight of Hand, I'll miss that place, but I guess that's what happens when you don't pay your dues to the Guild."

"We are charged with keeping the High King's peace," Conrad said. "And now we stand here and do nothing?"

World-weary Lars shook his head. "Look, compromise is how this all works. Otherwise, it'd be war between the Guild and the Watch." Baldwin nodded heartily in agreement.

"Compromise?" Conrad fumed. He looked around the bar of the Horn and Hound. Most of the other Watchmen avoided making eye contact. "*Compromise?* We're told to look the other way while the Guild murders and steals in the night with impunity? That's not compromise, that's *capitulation!*"

"Don't mess it up for the rest of us, you asshole," said Lars in a low growl. "Leave it alone."

"A pox take you all, gentlemen," Conrad said in reply, and he stormed out of the Horn & Hound.

He supposed he *was* proud, and what of it? He'd never be a knight, he'd been born into the wrong family for that, a minor line of Theodrum long separated from land or title; but like his father before him he had found the cause of service in the City Watch, and wore the colors of High King and city with the same pride as if they were a knight's sigil. And who knew what luck and fortune might bring, should he distinguish himself at the right moment, in the right company, in the view of a Peer of the Realm? Knighthoods had been granted before for bravery and action in the field; he'd heard the stories, seen men ride by that it had happened to. He had a flash of guilt, and of anger, for this was as much a cause of his discontent as any more high-minded purpose. Sitting stuck behind a locked door while just outside murder was being allowed to happen meant that he was being robbed of the chance to display his worth: an *injustice* layered on *injustice*.

Standing on the eerily deserted High Promenade by himself, however, and looking out onto the equally deserted High Plaza, he had to admit that suddenly he wasn't sure if this was such a good idea.

———•———

THE THREE MEN SLIPPING into the ground floor of the tenement building off of Poor's Square on the High Promenade were Amorans, and though dressed no differently than the Danians and Aurians who dominated Therapoli, they were part of an easily identifiable minority in the city: black and brown of skin in a sea of pale and tan, their black hair curled and kinky, with broad lips and strong noses. They were considered immigrants, though all three had been born in the city; Otalo was himself perhaps the closest to being a new arrival, as his parents had settled in Therapoli only a few years before he'd been born, but he spoke the Middle Tongue without a hint of accent. Casseyo's family had been in the city for two centuries, and lighter-skinned Lodrigo's father was a Danian, a sailor who'd fallen in love with an Amoran woman from an old merchant family on Old South Road and settled with her in the Foreign Quarter.

As Amorans they often had to be careful about where in the city they went and when, as in some Quarters their kind was not welcome; but they were all right in the Old Quarter, particularly as they were Marked Men, known to be part of the crew of Guizo the Fat, a Prince of the Guild whose writ extended far and wide in the city's underground. The Old Quarter belonged to Bad Mowbray and the Gilded Lady and their lieutenants and dependents, but they and Guizo were known allies and Guizo's men were often welcome there; and on this night they walked its streets by express invitation. A dozen of his bravos were back on Downland Street helping Petterwin Grim's men on a door-to-door, and a half-dozen more had helped Mowbray's men kick in the door of a tenement a hundred paces away on the High Promenade, almost by the Aqueducts.

Otalo was in the lead as they softly took the twisting stair up to the first floor, his eyes peering into the darkness above; there was a New Moon that night and no windows into the stairwell besides, so Casseyo had lit and hooded his lantern a few steps behind him. In some old tenements the stairs were made of stone or brick, but in this one they were wood, and he winced with every inadvertent creak. At each small landing he had to step over several sleeping bodies. Otalo scanned the sleepers quickly; it wouldn't do to be taken by surprise, but they looked right, smelled right (which was to say, all wrong, even through the stock).

He hit the first floor and spent a moment listening to the sounds from the halls stretching off on each side, before he turned onto the stairs twisting up to the inky darkness of the second floor. Several more sleeping drunks littered their path. He had almost reached the top of the steps when he paused. The last huddled body wrapped in a blanket was small, a child's body. He caught the glint of an open eye in the hooded lantern light. The tip of his sword came to hover for a moment a few inches from that open eye, and then he raised the blade upright.

"Are they still there?" he whispered through his stock.

The child nodded, and closed its eyes.

Otalo stepped onto the second and last landing. His eyes swept right and then left, but by the starlight from the open windows at each end of the hallways they were empty. Slowly Lodrigo and Casseyo joined him, Casseyo hanging back and looking behind them down the stairwells.

Otalo and Lodrigo crept down the hallway to the left until they reached the first set of doors. Casseyo finally came after, his hooded lantern bringing the hint of light. Faintly visible on the door to their right was a small chalk drawing of a bird. Otalo and Lodrigo frowned. Lodrigo cocked his head and quizzically indicated the door with the drawing. Otalo raised his shoulders in a confused shrug. *Second floor, first apartment on the left, with the sign of a magpie drawn upon it*; the report had been clear. But then it should have been the door on their left, not their right.

Otalo waved Casseyo closer, and as the lantern-bearer approached he stepped silently in front of the door on the left and inspected it closely. Despite the faint glimmers from the light he couldn't see for shit in the dark, but he tucked the wooden scabbard under his right arm and ran the fingers of his now free left hand over the surface of the wood, and they came away with the faint feel of chalk on his skin. *Someone switched the signs; but who and when?* His face scrunched in anger, wondering about the sentinel on the stairs. He stepped back and pointed at the left door and then at himself. He pointed at Lodrigo, then to his own eyes, then to the door on the right. Casseyo and Lodrigo nodded, hefting their weapons and the lantern.

He took a deep breath, shifting the wooden scabbard back into his left hand, happy at the feel of a weight in each grip.

The heel of his boot landed square where the latch-lock of the door would normally be, and the force was enough to splinter wood and send the door swinging open into the utter darkness of the chamber beyond. He barely had time to congratulate himself on getting it on the first kick when he was through the door and almost impaled on a blade thrust from someone waiting in the dark. He parried just in time and drove the point into the wood of the floor, his movement carrying him forward as he riposted automatically, the movements ingrained in him by years of practice, and the tip of his sword found a soft body. Someone screamed, a man, he thought. He heard a crash behind him and shouts and the sound of metal on metal, and he had time to think *we've walked into an ambush.*

There was almost no light, the lantern behind him was flickering and bouncing in all sorts of directions, but instinctually he suspected he was silhouetted in the doorway, and Otalo leapt forward, trying to get into the darkness, swinging the heavy blade furiously and blindly through the air around and in front of him, varying a figure-eight motion to fill every direction with whistling steel, waving the scabbard in his left hand more haphazardly to ward off any attacks. He struck something in front of him once with his sword, then twice, and it crumpled under the blows, the screaming man suddenly silent, then he caught something heavy and inanimate on his left that sent a shock up his arm—a wall? A post? Then a lot of empty air, then something nicked on his left, then again on his left, and then he connected with something softer on his right on the backswing as he drove forward, tripping over something on the floor.

He turned his trip into a rightward lunge with his head down, hands and arms and sword and scabbard crossed over his face, crashing blindly into someone staggering, and they both went down, his feet entangled in some sort of cloth, a dress or a long trailing cloak. He bounced off a wall with his right shoulder on the way down, slamming into wattle and daub and feeling it crush and give. His hat was knocked off his head. He landed on top of whoever it was, the scabbard spinning away, his left hand finding purchase on their throat and jaw to lift his upper body up and give his right arm some swinging room, and he brought the heavy blade of his sword down on the top half of their head in a short, torquing arc, again and again as hard as he could, until the hard cracks had turned soft and squishy.

The body under him was still twitching but he rolled off it and against the wall, and forced himself up until he was in a crouch, his sword waving wildly and blindly in front of him, panting heavily through the stock. He was about to cry out to his comrades when light suddenly bloomed in the room, and Casseyo finally leapt through the doors, his lantern's shutters opened in full. There was blood on Casseyo's falchion and his doublet glistened wetly, but the blood didn't seem to be his. Lodrigo, on the other hand, stumbled into the doorway, leaning against it and moaning in pain and anger. He was bleeding from his right thigh, his breeches slashed and ripped, and he clutched his right side with his left hand, while his right hand still held the iron-bound club; though somehow he'd managed to keep his hat on his head—more than Otalo or Casseyo could claim.

"How many?" Otalo gasped.

"Three," Lodrigo said, his eyes scrunched. "All on the Path, now."

Casseyo moved forward, shining his lantern light before them. There was a dead man, heavy-set, in the middle of the room—the man who'd first attacked him, Otalo thought—and Otalo was crouched against the wall over the body of a woman, the upper half of her face and head largely crushed in by his blows. "Is it her?" Casseyo asked eagerly, bringing the light closer.

Otalo crouched further, wiping the sweat from his eyes. "No," he said with a grunt. "Can't recognize her anymore, but her hair is dark, and naturally so, by the looks of it. She's Danian, not Aurian."

"Shit, it ain't even her? Was this a setup?" Lodrigo hissed. He pulled his neck stock down, revealing his round, fleshy face. "She was supposed to be alone, so who in the Six Hells are all these people?"

"The lookout," said Otalo with a sudden frown. "The little shit let us walk right into it." His expression grew grim when he thought about what he'd do to the little imp if he ever saw it again. *Corruption starts early in this part of town.* He paused, his mind quickly replaying the melee, his eyes taking in the details of the room now that he could see. *Something had been on my left.* He started to push himself back onto his feet, pointing to an open doorway on their left through which a blood trail disappeared. "Quick! In there!"

Casseyo and Lodrigo were through the doorway first, Otalo right behind them after grabbing up his scabbard from where it had scattered. The lantern light illuminated a pale Danian man on the floor, bleeding from a glancing head wound that had opened up his scalp. He was halfway across the room and moving slowly, feebly, his eyes having trouble focusing. Lodrigo half-stumbled to stand over him. The man sensed the danger looming above him and his struggles became more urgent. Lodrigo grunted heavily as the iron-shod club rose once, twice, each time resulting in a loud, sickening *crunch*.

But Otalo was already moving past them to the window. Carefully he peered out through the open shutters; there was no easy way down except a thirty-foot-plus drop to the stone cobbles of the courtyard, but he could see easy handholds to pull a body up onto the roof. He could smell something...a hint of jasmine, maybe? An exotic spice of some kind. *She was just here. I know it.* He turned to Lodrigo as he sheathed his sword and tucked the scabbard into his belt. "With your leg hurt you're too much at risk up on the roof. You two hit the street, head east along the Street of Furs, this building connects to the next one but she doesn't know we've got crew in there!"

"Right," grunted Lodrigo, and Casseyo nodded grimly.

"And if you see that fucking kid, cut its throat," Otalo hissed, and then he was pulling himself out the window and into open space.

FEAR WAS NOT SOMETHING that Conrad liked to admit to; no man ever did, even the smartest and most honest, but there was no question a palpable sense of dread, of something waiting and watching in the dark, permeated the city streets. Where normally the University Quarter would have been bright and bustling, all was instead dark and quiet, the watch lamps extinguished and the cobblestones deserted; and in the narrow alleys and tight corners where it would normally have been dark and quiet, well, there instead the echo of rustles and whispers seemed to play in the ear, as though a great black serpent were slithering from shadow to shadow just out of sight, murmuring to itself while seeking its prey.

Breathing was actually becoming difficult; the walls and alleys seemed to be closing in, and the intense desire to leave the streets soon became overwhelming as he wandered on his self-appointed rounds. He began to wonder if some enchantment lay over the city, and he briefly wished he had an amulet or talisman to ward off black magic. *Faith is your best protection,* he chided himself. *Faith, and a high vantage. Though a lantern would be useful as well.*

He turned the corner off of Mud Street and headed to a wooden gate inset in a stone wall; he knew that in the small alley behind it there was a stone staircase sometimes used by the Watch (as well as the Guild, he suspected) to get up to the roof of the buildings on that block, some of the oldest in the Quarter. The gate was never locked, and in a few short heartbeats he was bounding up the twisting stone steps until he reached a stone walkway that encompassed the peak of the slate-tiled roof. He leaned against the crenellated parapet, sucking in the crisp night air as though he'd been drowning.

When his head finally cleared of panic, he looked up and out over the rooftops of the city. He spotted the Sign of the Serpent, ruling in the First House of the Celestial Path; like many city dwellers he'd only rarely paid attention to the passage of the great signs in the sky above. He'd been born under the sign of the Dragon, he had, and he knew it had entered into the Third House, on the wane but still a reasonably propitious place for him on his endeavors. But he hadn't been to an astrologer in ages, considering their use to be a sign of poor moral character.

His eyes, accustomed now to the starlight, swept over the rooftops. The great bulk of the University building rose up to the south, its bell tower the highest point in the city except for the High King's Hall and the topmost spire of the Great Temple of the Divine King, both of which he could see in all their glory rising up out of High Quarter to the east. Another source of pride, that, to be part of the City Watch for the University Quarter, even if he himself had never attended the University; for it was one of the oldest in the world, a place of storied history, and of great power in the politics of the High King's Court and the Middle Kingdoms. *I am the Guardian of a High Order,* he liked to think.

He began to wander from rooftop to rooftop, following the stone walkways at some moments, and clambering up the peaked roofs to scan the nearby streets and building blocks from his perch. Even in the dead of night there should have been noises, lights— students and Magisters working late, or carousing loudly in the streets—but instead it was pitch black and silent. For a moment he could imagine that he was alone in an abandoned city, the world ended and him forgotten. Fear clenched his spine, and then he laughed and shrugged, drawing himself upright and throwing his head back. *And would that really be so terrible? This city is filled with deviants and criminals, the sick and the insane, and once-noble folk who have forgotten their proper place and now consort with the unclean and the impure. Let the Divine King send his Curse upon this place! Good riddance to bad rubbish, all.*

———— ✦ ————

IF NOTHING ELSE, OTALO had a gift for mayhem. Hearing of the growing Amoran community in Therapoli, his father and mother had braved the ship journey over the *Mera Argenta*. They'd opened up a small storefront serving street food from back home— the traditional stew-filled pastry called *tajina malsüka*, fried fish and vegetables, *m'gharetine* flatbreads, and a new creation, flaked pastry triangles filled with potatoes and spinach, which they had never eaten before—with him as the baker and her as the cook, singing Amoran folks songs as she bustled in the kitchen. And they'd certainly been well received by the Amorans who'd found a home in the Foreign Quarter.

The native Danians and Aurians had been a different matter. His father had weathered their japes and jokes, their cruelty and occasionally their beatings over the years. But his spirit had seemed unbroken. "You have to be patient with them, son," his father used to say when Otalo was very young. "This is a great city, a fine city, a place of marvels and opportunity. There's money to be made here, and a life to build." Even though he never seemed to make as much money as he hoped.

That optimism dimmed a bit after their shop caught fire mysteriously, and then their landlord, a Danian man, had accused them of being responsible for the fire. They had been forced by the merchant courts to work for their landlord to pay off the damages of the fire. After years of hardship the city had slowly broken his father down, at least physically; his spirit was now fortified by a love for the bottom of a bottle. Even when his mother had finally given up the ghost, and went to find her ancestors; even *then*, his father's optimism did not disappear entirely. "You have to be patient with them, son," his father would still whisper in between drinks. "Trust the King of Heaven to open their hearts."

Growing up watching the struggles of his father and mother, the straight and narrow had never appealed to Otalo. He'd grown up fighting on the streets, indeed he hadn't had much choice. He wasn't the biggest or strongest brawler; but he was certainly one that got the job done. He'd spent a fair portion of his misspent youth in and out of the city's jails. And when the great crew of a Guild Prince had beckoned (and one led by an Amoran no less), he had leapt at the chance, and found himself a tentative place in the city where his father, playing by the rules, had not. It wasn't a safe place, exactly; but it was a place where he could on occasion vent the anger and rage he felt inside him, and for that he was exceedingly grateful. Occasions like this night.

His heart beating fast, Otalo moved quickly over the peaked roofs of the tenement, his boots soft on the terracotta tiles. It was the night of the New Moon, the dark gate between the worlds open and tended by the goddess Djara Luna, a moon worthy of a night filled with murder. By starlight he followed the roof around to the eastern side of the building, and there the upper floors jutted out over Haggle Street and connected to the larger sprawling tenement next door, forming in effect a great arch or gateway into the dark heart of Bad Mowbray's territory with a fancy cupola built above the street. Otalo felt a grudging respect; it had taken some serious balls for their quarry to hide here by herself, under a Prince's nose as it were, though admittedly hiding more or less in plain sight was an old trick. He worked his way over the street—briefly wondering who lived in the chambers of the arching extension—and then stepped out onto the roofs of the next building. He scrambled to the top of the nearest peak, and studied the terrain. Up ahead of him the building shaped itself around a set of alleys, and beyond he could see the upper level of the Aqueduct and the looming rise of the University Quarter.

That's where she's going next. She's going to ground in the maze of the Quarter. He groaned at the thought.

He clambered forward and down until he was at the edge of the roof, peering off into the back alley that ran through the center of the building complex. He could see dormer windows on the roof where the building fronted on the High Promenade, and some appeared to be open; but he also knew that Bad Mowbray's men and others from Guizo's crew slid through its hallways, searching for their own quarry. He could hear the occasional muffled shout or scream from within the dark shape of the tenement. *Far better to be predator than prey—or worse yet still, bystander—on a night like this. If she went in there, she'll soon be caught.*

He glanced to his left, looking for ways to get off the roof, and spotted a drain pipe that led from the gutters down towards the alley. As his gaze followed the pipe to the ground, he spotted a furtive movement at its base—someone ducking around the corner and up the part of the alley that led to the Street of Furs. He was hit by that same scent from before. Otalo cursed quietly, and he scampered to that corner of the building complex, sheathing his sword as he went. "King of Heaven, help me," he whispered as he dropped onto his chest, feeling for the pipe, and then once he had his hand on it he swung his body over the edge of the roof into the air. His heart in his throat, he started working his way down.

He hit the alleyway with relief and set off in a crouched run, sword in one hand and scabbard in the other, wary of too much speed in the dark. He was on the Street of Furs in a few moments. The cobblestoned way was surprisingly quiet; even on a slow night the taverns and whores would have been indulging a lively trade there, but this night every door and window was shuttered, the street utterly silent except for his own heavy breathing. He paused, and then spied a shuttered light moving towards him from his left.

"Sorry," came Casseyo's whisper. "Lodrigo's moving slow." And sure enough Lodrigo lumbered up a breath or two later in a limping gait, ginger on his cut right leg.

Otalo scowled. *His wound's worse than I thought; perhaps poison?* "You didn't see anyone?" They shook their heads. He looked around; an alley opened north, and that was surely tempting, but the Street of Furs continued to the east where it met the Aqueduct and rose into the University Quarter. His every instinct said that was the direction she was headed. *Is that jasmine again? Is this a trick of some sort?* "This way," he grunted.

So that Lodrigo wouldn't fall too far behind, Otalo led the trio up the Street of Furs slower than he would have liked, and soon they were passing directly under the massive Aqueduct that brought water from faraway hills into the cisterns of the city. Artifacts from the Dürean Great Palace Period in the dawn of history, the great stone arches of the Aqueduct marched directly into the heart of the city, a stark reminder to its people of their debt to a long-lost culture that ruled the region long before the Divine King had risen to divinity. *Not the story you like to tell yourselves,* he grunted. Once past the Aqueduct, they officially entered into the University Quarter, and the street narrowed and became stepped as they bounded past staggered oaken doors recessed into the stone walls.

Otalo was a bit winded by the time he reached the top of the steps. The narrow street split left and right at the top, and he stopped and waited, catching his breath while Casseyo and Lodrigo caught up; Lodrigo was having trouble with the steps, and Casseyo had slowed to give him light and aid. The University Quarter was silent, unexpectedly so even at this hour; students did not behave like normal folks, by his observations. But he could hear nothing, and there were no lanterns lit and dangling above the street as would have been normal. The scent was gone, no longer lingering in the air.

Figures materialized on his left out of the dark. "Who goes there? Friend or foe?" came a voice.

"Depends on who's asking," Otalo replied calmly. Figures were also materializing on his right. He pulled the stock down from his face and rubbed his fingers through his sweat-dampened goatee.

"Otalo, is that you?" came the voice again. The figure came closer, became clearer. Otalo recognized the man as a Danian named Jonas the Grey, an independent operator who ran the closest thing the University Quarter had to a crew, now that the Lords of Book and Street (to whom Jonas had once belonged) were no longer counted amongst the rolls of the city's underworld. Several of his men—the brothers Cole and Ruvos Till, and "Little" Lucius, who was of course anything but—were behind him. Otalo glanced to his right, and saw the rest of their crew appearing: a dour but efficient man named Horne, and the inseparable pair Tall Myles and Little Myles (the Little in his case being, in fact, quite accurate). Dark leathers and doublets of fine cut were the standard here.

Otalo nodded and grinned. "Aye, it's me. Good to see you, Jonas."

"Hard to see you at all, Otalo, if you ain't flashing those pearly whites in the dark," said Jonas with a casual laugh as they shook hands. Otalo bristled a bit—he might have been Amoran, but he was a Marked Man and Jonas wasn't. He knew Jonas did not mean anything *mean* by it, at least not exactly. Lodrigo and Casseyo finally reached the top of the steps and the two groups mingled, shaking hands and grunting quick greetings.

"Has anyone come through this way?" Otalo asked when they were done with the preliminaries.

Jonas shook his head and shrugged. "Hard to tell. We've been chasing shadows up here all night. There ain't enough of us to seal it all up tight, we're all spread a little thin, and everyone's seeing shit moving in the corner of their eyes or hearing something from the next alley over."

Horne piped up. "We were just chasing what we thought was someone in the alley behind Drewson's College, but all we did was run into some of Red Rob's crew on the High Promenade. They're anchoring the southwest corner of the Quarter for us, and they're saying the same thing, they're jumpy as shit."

"The ghosts of the Quarter are acting up tonight," said Cole Till glumly, and to a man they all spat to the side and made warding signs in the air.

When he was done making his sign, Otalo's face was tight. "Red Rob Asprin has been blacklisted by the Guild."

Jonas shrugged. "I ain't in the Guild. And this is all-hands-on-deck, this is, has been since the night of Lord Arduin's Midnight Ride."

"Fine, no time to argue, and too much talk already." Otalo's face took on an even grimmer cast. "I swear on my bones our quarry fled this way." He turned to Horne. "You thought you saw someone in back of Drewson's; if you missed them, what other way could they have gone?"

Horne thought for a moment, but it was Little Myles that piped up first. "There's a stairwell, it's a shortcut through the wall up onto the University hill. They couldn't likely go towards the front of the University, the gate guards are there, so they'd have to cut around to the north side of the quads…"

They were all at a run even before Little Myles finished speaking, Horne leading Otalo south then east through the narrow streets while Jonas split some of his men off and took them the north way around. They came up quickly on the back of the College of the Globe, its massive cupola silhouetted against the night sky above them, and Horne led them left and around it to come up on the rear side of the main University building while the two Myleses went down towards Drewson's College and up through the stairwell in case someone was hiding in them.

Otalo never failed to be impressed by the exterior of the University. It was the second-largest single building in the entire city, second only to the Forum, and the Forum was just one ground level while the University loomed several stories high. He'd never been inside it; only a handful of Amorans from the city had ever been sponsored for study within its halls. He'd learned his letters—Guizo had made sure of that, easier now that the arrival of printing presses had meant the growing availability of books and broadsheets throughout the city—but he wasn't fool enough to compare his meager book learning to that of the men educated at the University. Great walls of smooth stone formed the base of the University quad, unbroken at ground level on most exterior sides except for small inset iron doors that were almost always barred from the inside, with great glass windows only on the upper levels of the building. The main entrance was on the southern side, stairs up into the interior quads through massive gates flanked by statues of some of the University's patron founders, but as Little Myles had noted, they were constantly guarded by reasonably vigilant constables and, if rumor was true, by spirits and magic as well.

The two Myleses rejoined them and they all jogged along the street alongside the wall, strung out a bit with limping Lodrigo still bringing up the rear, their eyes mostly on the buildings opposite the University: shuttered shops and storefronts on the ground level and what Otalo guessed would be apartments for students on the upper levels. Horne held up a hand; a great set of bronze-bound doors yawned open in the most imposing edifice on the block.

They slowed and approached it warily. "What is this building?" Otalo whispered.

Horne stopped by the open doors, and pressed himself into the stone lintel. "Quarters for many of the Magisters, owned by the University," he whispered back. He was frowning. "Doors should be barred for the night at this hour."

Otalo looked up the front of the building. Rosettes and other ornaments were carved into the stone facade; he stared for a moment at the head of a lioness. *A sign of Hathhalla, the Goddess of Vengeance and the jailor of Hell; strange for a University building.* He frowned. *This doesn't feel right. She didn't come this way.* "Right; find the night porter, find out why the door is open," he hissed. "We'll keep going, catch up with us when you can." Horne nodded and he disappeared inside the doors with the two Myles.

Otalo, Casseyo, and Lodrigo moved slowly up the street. When they reached the end of the block, his instincts said to turn left; and when they reached the next corner, left again. He started to wonder about where Jonas's territory ended; he knew they were very close to Mud Street where the Squire held sway, and once across the King's Road and into the High Quarter that would be the territory of the Red Wyrm, a full-fledged Prince of the Guild. The Squire had gained his Mark in the Guild from Bad Mowbray, and so could be counted on to do his duties, but the Red Wyrm was a rival to Mowbray and Guizo both, and—

Otalo was about to turn right when he froze, scabbard held out to the side to warn his fellows to stop. He sniffed the air deeply. *Jasmine, again. Or whatever it is. Strong this time.* He crept forward down a dead-end alley to a small square behind the Magisters' quarters, and a large carved door waiting in between two shuttered shop fronts. He looked at it for a moment, then reached out and gave it a small push. He stepped back to the side as it swung open silently, revealing a dark passageway. *Far too many open doors around here. Djara the Dark Moon, door between worlds, laughs at us.*

He turned back to Lodrigo. The man was sweating and grimacing, leaning against the shop shutters next to them. "Wait here for Horne, or Jonas, then come in with them to back us up, yeah?"

Lodrigo nodded glumly. "Sorry, boss."

Otalo pulled his stock back over his mouth and nose, and then moved slowly into the building's ground floor, Casseyo following and opening up the shutter on his lantern a little to light their way. The stone hallway slid off into the dark, and a stone staircase led up. The building was old; certainly as old as the Magisters' quarters next door. Otalo paused at the staircase, and with a nod of his head indicated that was the way they would go.

"How do you know which way she went?" Casseyo whispered.

"Do you smell it?" Otalo asked. "I think it's jasmine. Smelled it back where we got ambushed."

Casseyo frowned. "I don't smell anything."

Otalo sighed in exasperation. "Come on, then, just follow me."

He was certain of the scent now, faintly lingering before him, leading him on. A small voice in the back of his head said *trap*, but he pressed on regardless. The first floor landing was empty, short plastered hallways angling off to individual apartments. He wondered how many people lived in the building; it felt empty, *deserted,* like an ancient ruin, but rationally he knew that students and Under-Magisters would pay a pretty penny to live near the back of the University like this, so it should have had plenty of tenants. His nose and his instincts were telling him up, up again, and so he looped around to the staircase to the second floor and padded softly up the steps, Casseyo close behind.

They had stepped out onto the second floor landing when the scream saved them. The scream had presumably been intended to startle him, freeze him up, make him flinch or step back, *panic;* instead after years of fighting all he did was *react,* jabbing out with the wooden scabbard, catching the desperate man leaping out of the darkness with sword held high. Otalo's scabbard struck the man square in the apple of his throat, abruptly ending his scream with a squelch. And then the hall was filled with fury and clubs and daggers and fists. *Trap, again,* he had time to think.

Otalo laid about him with both sword and scabbard, not bothering with trying to aim, just intent on clearing some space around him as he was buffeted by bodies and blows. Casseyo's lantern hit the ground and rolled, sending a gout of oil flaring up; Otalo couldn't see what had happened to Casseyo himself and didn't have time to look, as someone was trying to get him in a headlock. He grunted as he took a couple of blunt blows across his back trying to drive him downward, and he sensed sharp steel dangerously close, questing for his innards. Urgently, he shook two bodies off, slamming one of them into the plaster of the wall, and then bringing his sword down repeatedly on the other before leaping forward to backhand a dark shape with his wooden scabbard.

The hallway behind was getting brighter; something was on fire. A shape plowed into him from the side, a sharp dagger slashing across his doublet but thankfully not getting much past the thick outer layer. He dropped his scabbard and grabbed and twisted, bringing the body across him and into the wall. His legs slid out from under him and he felt a sharp pain in his side, but he managed to wind up on top, and he brought the pommel of his short sword down twice onto a weeping eye socket before raising himself up and reversing the sword, pushing blade into throat. He rolled quickly, flailing his sword wildly in case someone was trying to get the drop on him, but he found himself temporarily and tentatively alone.

Behind him, part of the wall was aflame, silhouetting several struggling bodies as Casseyo tried very hard not to die. Otalo staggered to his feet, preparing to charge, and could only watch in relief as Horne came flying up the stairs and into the mass, a steel-hafted small axe flashing down onto someone's bald pate, instantly splitting it open. Tall Myles was bounding up the steps next, and he was already yelling out: "Fire! Fire! Stop the fire!"

Otalo knew without having to look that his quarry was not amongst the dead and dying sprawled around him; they were expendable, her *servants*. Hoping that one of the others might know a charm to douse the flames, he turned and staggered into the dark of the hallway, certain that he was on the right track. *She's close.*

A twist and a fumbling turn and he found himself opening a door out onto a covered stone walkway that ran around the inner wall of the building's tight, L-shaped interior courtyard. He shook his head, trying to get his eyes to focus in the faint starlight. A shape fled before him, and he began running in pursuit, passing shuttered windows and a door on his right, the drop over the parapet to the courtyard below on his left. Past the bend in the L it looked like the walkway terminated at a blank wall, part of the building projecting forward into its path, the onetime doorway there bricked over. His heart leapt into his throat even as he spotted the ladder down from the roof above, and someone descending it. He could hear shouts and cries from ahead.

He rounded the bend and came to a stop, panting.

———— •◦• ————

HE THOUGHT HE HEARD a scream and a commotion from somewhere below him, echoing up through an inner courtyard shaft, breaking the silence of the night. He turned away from the parapet and walked over the flat roof until he stood looking down at the dark courtyard below; it was like looking down into a well at night, into a pool of inky blackness that seemed to have no bottom.

Conrad frowned. *Did I imagine it?* he started to think. And then he heard something for sure; metal on metal, muted screams, a distant, thudding crash.

He spotted an open trapdoor and ladder down into the walkways that circled the walls of the courtyard. He moved with excitement, loosening his sword and dagger in their scabbards, and then climbing down as fast as he could manage on the rickety ladder.

As he stepped onto the stone of the walkway, he could hear someone moving at speed. A hooded figure appeared, a woman running around a corner towards him. "Halt! Who goes there?" he cried out, drawing his sword, but to his surprise the woman didn't stop running until she had thrown herself into his arms; if he hadn't turned his sword aside she'd have run herself through.

He had time to register piercing blue eyes filled with fear, pale skin, a flash of full lips that instantly commanded his attention. A heady perfume filled his nose, marking a Lady of rank and position. "Oh, sir!" the woman breathed, panic in her quavering voice. "Help me! They mean to kill me!"

Not on my Watch, he thought grimly.

———— •◦• ————

A MAN STOOD TALL and imperious several paces away, a red surcoat with a golden wyvern clutching a black starry circle in its claws over his gorget and mail hauberk—the sign of the night patrols of the City Watch. Short blond hair blew in the breeze. "Stand your ground, you black bastard!" the man yelled in a sharp voice, used to command. He had a heavy broadsword out, pointed at Otalo, while the other arm shielded a woman behind him, who peered furtively and intently at Otalo from under the hood of her cloak, her eyes narrowed to inscrutable slits. She was, Otalo realized with a pang, beautiful to look upon.

Where the fuck did he come from? Otalo wondered with a sinking feeling in his heart.

"That's one of them, my Lord!" the woman said breathlessly into the blond man's ear. "The most vicious of the lot! He intends to have my honor, and my life!"

The blond man scowled. "You brutish devil! Did you think the whole of the City Watch under the sway of your Guild? Did you really think someone like you could have the run of the city? Leave now, or die." He stepped forward, but the woman clung to him from behind, pulling him back.

Otalo raised his hands, holding the sword lightly in his right and opening the palm of his left and bringing it to his face. He tugged his stock down, revealing his nose and mouth, his neatly trimmed goatee. "Please," he pleaded quietly, gasping for breath. He was slowly aware of aches and pains, his back on fire, a wet feeling down his right leg and into his boot, sweat and maybe blood dripping into his eyes. "Please listen to me. She isn't who you think she is. She's one of the Nameless. An acolyte of Ligrid, a concubine to the Devil."

The blond man laughed. "Is that the best you can do? A baseless insult to an Aurian Lady from a black cur? Your words reveal you for the low character you are. On your knees, dog!"

Otalo heard a commotion from behind him, someone's boots moving quickly on the stone walkway. He felt very tired all of a sudden, and could only hope it was someone on his side. He heard Jonas's voice ring out angrily. "What are you doing, you fucking fool? King of Heaven, man, *she's one of the Nameless!*"

Otalo could see the blond man looking at Jonas behind him, frowning, confused, the wheels turning, comprehension slowly dawning on him. Otalo thought his heart would break. *No, please,* he thought. *Not like this.*

The hooded woman caught Otalo's eyes and held them. Hers were a piercing blue, and he thought them amongst the most striking that he'd ever seen. She smiled at him as her hand came up and around in front of her would-be protector's throat, and her sharp, glistening dagger cut him open from ear to ear right under his chin, right above the plate of his gorget. She started to laugh, a rich laugh of deep, ancient pleasure as blood sprayed from the cut in a high arc and the man's eyes went glassy. His broadsword clattered to the stones and he gurgled as he slumped and fell, his empty hands clawing at the parapet.

Otalo launched himself the last few yards, leaping over the struggling Watchman and slamming the woman back and up into the ladder bolted into the wall, her head cracking into one of the iron rungs, the force of the collision enough to send her dagger flying. He drove the tip of his sword up under her rib cage and towards her heart. She coughed blood into his face, and focused her eyes to sneer at him, still laughing. "I curse you to be my slave in the Six Hells, you f—" she started to hiss, but he pushed again, and her eyes went wide, and her face and body went slack, the last of the air in her lungs slipping out of her with a sigh.

After a long moment, he stepped back, and let her body fall to the stones, his sword still buried deep within her. He turned and looked down at the City Watchman. The man wasn't moving, a pool of blood slowly expanding on the walkway, his dilated eyes fixed on nothing. Otalo leaned his back against the wall, and slid down until he was seated, and held his head in his hands.

You have to be patient with them, son.

⬥

THE FIRE HAD THANKFULLY not been hard to put out, and their luck had held; no fatalities, but plenty of bleeders and bruises that needed closing and bandaging. Casseyo had somehow come out of the melee at the top of the stairs without a scratch. He was helping bandage up Otalo when they turned and saw the Gilded Lady stepping out onto the walkway, several of her ladies-in-waiting behind her, armed with rapiers and bearing torches. Jonas stood respectfully behind them. The Gilded Lady wore a high-necked brocade dress with puffed sleeves that glinted lightly in the torchlight with some sort of dark metal studs and a chain of office, made from gold coins from dozens of different cities, nations, and centuries. Gold eyeshadow and thick black eyelashes were the only makeup on her pale skin, her black hair pulled up into a braided bun and pinned with a broach. Under the collar of the dress Otalo could see a black choker over her apple, and he thought back on all the times he'd heard Guizo talk about the good old days, back when she was a man named Cole the Killer, back before she called herself the Gilded Lady. He and Casseyo bowed deep.

"Master Galluessi. Is it her?" asked the Gilded Lady in her deep, instantly recognizable voice. "The last of Lady Siovan's known acolytes?"

"Lady Allas Thorodur, if I am not mistaken," said Otalo grimly, coming up from his bow. Bad Mowbray and his men had gotten to the High Priestess herself on the first night, when the butchery had been hardest and fiercest, and it had been all cleanup ever since, hunting the Nameless they had slowly and secretly identified over the preceding weeks and months as their quarry went to ground. "Ariadesma said she'd be a hard one, and sure enough she'd had time to organize a couple of ambushes for us."

"Which you appear to have won through in your usual fashion," said the Gilded Lady with a demure nod of her head. "Well done, sirrah. If the reports from the other crews are accurate, then we've gotten as many of them as we're likely to get, and the rest will melt into the shadows. Your man Lodrigo will live, by the by; my Ladies are sucking the poison out." A not so demure smirk flashed across her face.

"Thank you, my Lady." Otalo nodded in relief, and then eyed the bodies with wroth and sadness. He shook his head as his gaze fell on the murdered Watchman, the man's pale throat a livid gash in the torchlight. "Doesn't it make you angry? I mean, we're hunting the fucking Nameless for them in the night, and here's the kind of man that would spit on us in the cold light of day."

The Gilded Lady smiled. "It would make me angry if we were doing this for them. But we're not. We're doing this for us. For me and mine, for you and yours. *No* man or woman is safe from the Nameless, but they stalk the margins and the shadows more than most, the places where *we* live and walk. When they want a child to play with, it ain't usually some nobleman's son that goes missing; when they're looking for fresh quim to work over, it ain't usually some high-born lady that winds up pulped and bleeding out. No, we're their natural prey: the peasant, the commoner, the dispossessed, the poor, the weak, the criminal, the *dregs*. And if we don't protect our own, we know sure as the Six Hells that *they* fucking won't," she said, kicking the dead Watchman in the shins for emphasis.

She turned away, and then looked back over her shoulder. "Do not spend another moment mourning that man. Jonas told me what happened. He made a choice, and he paid for it. It's no one's fault but his own. Dispose of his body as you wish. And give my best to Guizo."

She turned and disappeared back into the building as Jonas stepped out onto the walkway with the Tills in tow. "Right," he said cheerfully, rubbing his hands together. "No point fucking around. The dead aren't going to throw themselves away, and the night ain't getting any younger."

Otalo glanced at Casseyo, then with a baleful expression looked down at the dead Watchman.

———•———

IN THE END OTALO couldn't bring himself to simply disappear the man's body with those of the Nameless. So they left him there, his throat opened, his life's blood poured out in a great puddle around him, to be found by whoever came to investigate the noises during the night. At least then he'd get his funeral pyre, and the prayers of his family and temple and comrades-in-arms in the City Watch to guide him on the Path of the Dead. As to his fate when he reached the Place of Judgment and stood before the Judge of the Dead, well, there was nothing Otalo could do about that. If the man had been faithful to the Divine King, then an angel would appear and claim him for the Heavens. If he hadn't, then the Judge would send him to his appointed place in the Underworld, or in the Six Hells.

Celebrations of their purge of a coven of the Nameless Cults would have to wait. They'd left bodies scattered over a swath of the city, and it was darkest night by the time they'd been loaded onto wagons and trundled down to the barge that would take them out to the Harbor Wall; morning would find the smoke of fires hanging over the bay from the burning pits there for the third day in a row.

It was almost dawn by the time Otalo had reported to Guizo and headed home. As he trudged up the steps to his apartment, Otalo mused about his boss; Guizo the Fat was not known as "the Fat" without reason. His great bulk had not been seen outside the meeting house in the Forum in which he sat for many a year—perhaps even within living memory. Otalo had never seen Guizo anywhere else; his boss was there at the back table of the meeting house first thing in the morning, and still there deep in the night when Otalo left. He'd never seen Guizo sleep, or need to take a shit or a piss. *That's why he's so fat. He's just storing it all up for when the day finally comes that he decides to get up and try walking again.* He chuckled to himself but there was, in fact, something altogether uncanny about the performance that whiffed to Otalo of high sorcery.

But, in truth, there were worse bosses to have, and at least Guizo was one of his own. He'd started to feel like he was being worn thin, running out of patience, and at least with Guizo and his crew he didn't need to be constantly on edge.

He stepped inside the flat and closed the door as quietly as possible, intent on a soft bed and a dreamless sleep. But he heard someone stir in one of the bedrooms.

"Is that you, Otalo?" the old man's voice came, angry and petulant and still drunk.

"Yes, papa," Otalo said patiently. "I'm home."

BETTER TO LIVE THAN TO DIE

-The Faithful and the Fallen-

JOHN GWYNNE

The Banished Lands has a violent past, where men and giants clashed in a war for supremacy and near-extinction for the vanquished. Now men rule the land, giants little more than a memory, lurking in the wilds and dark places.

This tale takes place ten years before the events of Malice, *book one of the Faithful and the Fallen, within the Darkwood, a great forest that splits the western realms of Ardan and Narvon. It recounts a key moment in the life of a young bowman, Camlin, who is part of the Darkwood Brigands. A moment that has far-reaching consequences for the great conflict to come.*

TALES OF ASSASSINS, MERCENARIES, AND ROGUES

Blackguards

C AMLIN SAT AND WAITED, and as he waited, his mind wandered.

When he was a bairn his da would sit Camlin upon his knee and tell him to stay away from the Darkwood. He'd carry Camlin to their window and point at the ocean of trees just south of their Hold, stretching on and on to the ends of the earth, or so it had seemed to Camlin. Then his da would tell tales about the Darkwood brigands, how cruel and fierce they were, how they'd cut your throat for a handful of grain or a half-chewed copper.

Never thought for a moment I'd end up being one of 'em.

He concentrated on the road in front of him, looking down from an embankment shrouded in dense cover. A dozen black-fletched arrows were spiked into the earth before him, his bow of yew held loosely across his lap. In the canopy above, wood-pigeons cooed, further off a woodpecker drummed against a tree. Camlin's eyes drooped, head nodding, and with a jerk he sat straight.

"My da never told me how boring a Darkwood brigand's life was, either," he muttered.

"Shut up," a voice said close by—Casalu, his chief, words hissing

"BETTER TO LIVE THAN TO DIE"

Illustration by OKSANA DMITRIENKO

through a gap in his teeth. He couldn't see him, but he knew he was there, squat and hulking in the undergrowth like an old, surly boar.

"Sorry, chief," Camlin muttered.

"I said, shut. Up."

Camlin did. Upsetting Casalu was not how he wanted to start the day. Far better to be overlooked, as he usually was. Fifteen summers old he'd stumbled into the Darkwood. After a moon of wandering and starving he'd been found and taken in by Casalu's crew. Five years later he was still here, mostly because he had a knack for keeping his head down and his mouth shut. People that Casalu noticed didn't usually last too long.

He fixed his eyes back upon the road, a wide strip of crumbling flagstone that had seen better days. The giantsway, they called it. Built by giants, his da had told him, and Camlin reckoned that was true. All the giant relics were stone made, like this road, and there were enough of them littered about the land, most of them crumbling ruins now, a few of them taken and occupied by their conquerors. Moss and lichen grew on the giantsway, flagstones cracked and broken by countless years of freeze and thaw. It was still the best route through the Darkwood, though, linking the realm of Narvon in the north with Ardan in the south. And good roads meant travelers.

A fallen tree lay across the road before Camlin, branches splayed, roots twisting up to the heavens. To his left, further along the road, birds exploded from branches, squawking a protest.

Here they come.

Camlin reached for an arrow and nocked it loosely. Riders appeared around a far bend in the road, four, six, ten of them, behind them two wains pulled by shaggy coated oxen, and behind those another ten or twelve riders.

They drew closer, shifting sunlight dappling the road through the treetop canopy, details appearing upon the riders. All warriors, with thick-shafted spears and swords at their hips, iron torcs twisted around their necks, and their warrior braids tied with leather. Huge iron-rimmed shields were strapped to their saddles. Camlin saw all of this in a few heartbeats, but his eyes were drawn to their cloaks. Gray cloaks that marked them out as shieldmen of Brenin, King of Ardan.

This was wrong, supposed to be a merchant-train with a handful of mercenary guards. In Camlin's experience paid guards ran, sworn shieldmen didn't.

"Hold," Casalu hissed, continuing to mutter a string of unintelligible curses.

The riders reached the fallen tree. A few sharp words from one at the head of the column and a dozen warriors dismounted to move it, while the others sat tall in their saddles, their eyes scanning the trees about them.

Two wains were sat in the middle of the convoy—the first with a single chest in it, the second with three people, hands bound, and ropes about their necks.

Gently Camlin shifted his weight, muscles in his legs starting to burn.

"Be still," Casalu hissed at him.

Odds aren't good enough for Casalu, a score of Ardan shieldmen with sharp iron and fine war-gear against our ragged crew. We may outnumber them but I doubt we could out-fight them. Casalu will let them move the tree and go on their way. Too much of a fight for him.

A hissing sound from the far side of the road, a gray-cloaked warrior stiffening in his saddle, toppling backwards in a spray of blood, arrow through his throat.

There was a frozen moment. Camlin's heart lurched in his chest.

They were supposed to wait for Casalu's signal.

More arrows snaked from the trees. Horses screamed, warriors yelling, raising shields, drawing swords.

More swearing from Casalu, and Camlin heard the big man's bow creaking, saw an arrow fly into the chest of a stallion.

Camlin nocked an arrow, drew, felt the fletching tickle his cheek. Held his breath. Sighted. A warrior on foot by the tree, back to Camlin, scanning the far bank.

Release.

His bow-string thrummed, arrow flying true, sinking a handspan into the warrior's back, through boiled leather and wool padding and linen and into flesh. A grunt and the man was hurled forwards by the force of the bolt.

He reached for another arrow, nocked, drew, breathed, released, arrow slamming into the thigh of a rider, pinning his leg to his mount.

Another arrow, this one punching into a shoulder, spinning the warrior, dark blood spattering his gray cloak.

All of Casalu's crew could use a bow—had to if they wanted to lead this life—but none could wield it so well as Camlin. His instinct for it came right from the first, as little more than a bairn, when his da had put carved yew into his small, pudgy hands.

Another arrow, this one sinking almost to the fletching into a horse's neck, causing it to rear, screaming, sending its rider crashing to the ground.

By now their chosen victims were usually broken, fleeing in all directions. Not these men. A half-dozen of them were surging up the far bank, on foot or horse, yelling war-cries. They hit the undergrowth where Casalu's boys were lurking, fresh screams rising up as spears stabbed and swords hacked. Camlin saw old Annan flushed out of the bushes and ridden down, saw him tumble down the embankment in a tangle of boneless limbs.

A handful more of the gray-cloaks were forming up and facing towards Camlin. He felt a jolt of fear as he realized what they were doing, shields raised, thudding together as they charged up the embankment. Panic bubbled in his guts, and he sent an arrow thrumming into a shield. More arrows flitted from the bank, Casalu and the others. One gray-cloaked warrior staggered, a shaft skewering his calf, but the rest surged on up the slope. Twenty paces away now, then ten.

Beside him Casalu roared and rose from the undergrowth, hefted his heavy-bladed boar spear, and hurled it at the oncoming warriors. It crashed into a shield, blade pinning an arm behind it. Casalu shrieked wordlessly and ran at the gray-cloaks, knife and cleaver in his hands, chopping over the sagging shield-rim of the injured warrior.

Follow him, he's your chief, a voice screamed in Camlin's head. Before he realized what he was doing he was scrambling in the litter and soil, dropping his bow, and reaching for his sword.

Other figures burst from the undergrowth, more of Casalu's crew eager to be seen backing up their chief. Camlin ran down the slope, tripped on a root, and crashed into a gray-cloaked shieldman. They fell together, a glimpse of Casalu crouched and snarling over a bloody corpse, then Camlin was rolling, grunting, trying to drag his sword free of the tangle of limbs and shield, the warrior he'd collided with growling and spitting in his face.

With a crunch they hit the road and burst apart like a shattered barrel, flying in different directions. Camlin fell into a clump of mushrooms growing between crumbling flagstones, pushed himself to his hands and knees.

Get up, up, get up. He'd seen it before, a dozen times in a knife fight, first one to his feet was usually the only one. This wasn't a knife fight yet, but the principle was the same.

The gray-cloak hadn't been so lucky with his fall. He lay on the road, moving groggily, a pool of blood leaking from his head. Camlin searched for his sword, found it, and put it through the fallen man's throat.

Most of the fighting was happening up on the embankment now, the gray-cloaks taking the fight to Casalu's crew, the clash of iron and battle-cries echoing muted through the forest, telling him it wasn't over yet.

Brave men.

A sound on the road drew his eye. The wains were sitting still and unguarded. The first with a chest in its back and its driver slumped backwards with an arrow through his eye. The second was where the noise was coming from.

There were people in it, three of them, bound hand and throat, a cage of iron bars built into the back. The wain's driver was unlocking the cage door, a woodcutter's axe in his hand. The people in the cage were screaming.

Don't think he's searching for some firewood, or about to set them free.

Camlin pulled a knife from his belt, gripped it by the blade as his brother Col had taught him so many years ago, and threw it as the wain-driver swung the cage door open and raised his axe.

The knife caught him just below the ribs, buried to its hilt in flesh. With a confused look on his face the wain-driver staggered back a step, then slumped to the ground.

Camlin ran to the wain, looked in to see three people, a woman and bairn huddled before him, and further back a man, sitting calm as if he were waiting for his lunch to be served.

"Please," the woman said.

Camlin looked at her, squeezing a young lad tight, both

regarding him with pleading eyes. A memory flashed in his mind, so bright the world about him dimmed, of his mam and brother, Col, laying still and unseeing, blood seeping into the dirt of his Hold's yard. He blinked, banishing the thought and the sharp pain in his chest that accompanied it.

Cries echoed through the forest. Camlin peered up and saw Casalu and a few others hacking at a lone gray-cloak, the man retreating before them. As Camlin watched, the gray-cloak's sword snaked out, and one of Casalu's crew reeled back with blood spurting from his throat.

Fight's almost done. And Camlin knew what would happen to the woman and her bairn once Casalu and the others came down here, glutted with victory, blood still up.

"Run," he said to them, holding a hand out. The woman lifted her bound hands and he reached for his knife, remembered it was still in the wain-driver. He heard a noise from behind, started to turn, then an arm swung around his throat.

The wain-driver!

Apparently a knife in the belly was not enough to keep the man down. Camlin swung his elbow, threw his head back, felt cartilage crunch. His attacker only grunted and carried on squeezing. The woman and bairn shied away from them, the man in the wain just watching them.

Camlin braced his feet against the wain's iron wheel and threw himself backwards, wriggling like a worm on a hook, his attacker staggering a few steps, but then he was swung around and they crashed back into the wain, this time in reverse. The arm about his throat tightened. Sounds came out of his mouth, desperate, choking, spittle bubbling, a dark nimbus closing in on his vision, white dots exploding within it.

Then his attacker was grunting, making strangled sounds of his own, sour breath washing over Camlin. Abruptly the arm about his neck was gone and he staggered forward a step, dropped to his knees, sucking in huge gasping breaths. When he could breathe again he stood and turned, saw the wain-driver's face turning slowly purple, the prisoner in the wain with his bound hands around the man's throat, pulling the rope tight.

Camlin surged forward, grabbed his knife's hilt still protruding from his enemy's belly, ripped it free, and stabbed the man, again and again. Slowly he slumped in the prisoner's grip, arms sagging, face purple and bloated, tongue swollen. The prisoner loosened his grip and dropped the man to the ground, a sack of meat and bone.

Camlin rubbed at his neck, regarding the prisoner, who stepped back and resumed his place on a bench.

"Come on," Camlin croaked at the woman and her bairn, his throat burning. They stared at him frozen, so he grabbed the woman's wrists and cut her binds.

"Get out here," he grated, throat raw and swollen. She just looked at him as he sawed at the child's ropes.

He looked up at the embankments, heard Casalu shouting, saw others bending over fallen gray-cloaks, stripping them.

"Can you ride?"

The woman nodded.

"Then ride now, as fast as you ever have done, because if they catch you and your bairn…"

She hoisted her child and ran to a horse, a warrior's boot dangling from a stirrup. Without a look back she was pulling on the reins and kicking the stallion on, and in a clatter of hooves she and her bairn were gone.

Casalu heard them and came running down the embankment, snarling commands. He saw Camlin and strode to him, stopped when he saw the chest in the first wain. With his cleaver he shattered the lock and opened it. The look on his face flickered between greed and fear as he dug his hands in and let silver coins slip through his fingers.

"Too much," he muttered. "Brenin won't just walk away from this."

"It's yours now," a voice said, the prisoner from the wain.

Casalu snapped the lid closed and stalked over. He was thickset, all slabs of muscle, short-cropped hair and scars, with small intelligent eyes. His lower jaw jutted, too big for his face, making his bottom teeth stick out like tusks. Camlin often wondered if that was why he was called the Boar.

"Who are you?" Casalu asked the prisoner.

"Nobody."

"Answer the question, or you'll be a nobody with my cleaver in your skull."

"Name's Braith." He smiled, and despite the fact that Casalu had just threatened a quite unpleasant death the smile seemed warm and genuine.

Others started to join them, filtering out of the undergrowth laden with spoils—coin chinking in purses, boots, weapons, cloaks, the iron torcs of Brenin's fallen shieldman. One stepped over to the wain, Drem, Casalu's captain. He was one of the old-timers, streaks of iron in his black hair and beard. In his left hand he had a leather cord, threaded upon it the fresh-cut ears of dead shieldmen, still dripping blood. He liked his trophies.

"Out," he said.

Braith did as he was told, stood with his bound hands, still calm as if he were at the spring fair. He was tall, broad shouldered, a hint of gracefulness about him as he climbed from the wain. He didn't look much older than Camlin.

"So, Braith," Casalu said, stepping close. They were of a height, which was rare, Casalu usually looking down at everyone, though Casalu was wider, the muscle on his frame thick as an old, knotted oak. "Why are you a prisoner to Brenin's shieldmen?"

Braith held Casalu's eye a long, silent moment.

You don't want to do that.

"I'm being sent back to Narvon for trial," Braith said with a shrug.

"Trial for what?"

"Murder."

"Who?"

"One of King Owain's shieldmen."

"Why'd you do a fool thing like that?" Casalu asked, putting a boot upon the face of one of the dead shieldmen on the road. Laughter rippled about him.

"Self defense." Braith smiled his big smile.

"That's what they all say," someone called out.

Casalu stared at him again, sucked on his teeth.

"There were others," Casalu said, eyes fixing onto Camlin. "In the cage."

"Aye, chief. They escaped."

"How, when they were in a cage, hands bound?" Casalu looked about, saw the cut ropes of their bonds on the ground.

"They took off while I was busy," Camlin said, nodding at the dead wain-driver. His eyes flickered to Braith, but the man was picking dirt from a nail.

Casalu curled a lip at him but said no more. He hefted his cleaver, then gripped Braith's wrists and sliced his bonds.

"Welcome to my crew." He strode away a few steps, then paused and looked back. "And if I find out you're lying to me, I'll gut you."

CAMLIN WAS SAT WITH his back to a broad oak. Not for the first time this day he checked over his kit. It was a routine that calmed him when he was anxious. He'd put a fresh coat of wax on his yew bow, had a collection of hemp strings rolled in wax in a leather pouch. A quiver of thirty arrows stood wrapped in oiled doeskin—he'd killed and skinned the doe himself. He drew his sword with a whisper from the sheepskin-lined sheath he'd taken from one of the dead shieldmen the day Braith had joined them. He laid the blade across his lap.

Everything seemed to change from that day.

Braith had entered their camp almost a year ago, and since then the world had changed. He brought something with him, unseen yet influential and pervasive. Ambition.

He was a natural leader, Camlin finding that he would do things just in the hope to be noticed by Braith, and when a word of praise or a pat on the back was given, it would make him stand taller. Casalu ruled by fear, but slowly, incrementally the power balance began to shift. And Casalu saw it. He chose to send Braith on ever wilder and more dangerous raids, to Camlin's mind hoping that Braith would not come back. But he did, and always with that broad smile on his face.

Camlin looked about. Two score men were scattered about the dell. The last rays of the sun slanted through the canopy above, bathing the dell in an amber glow. A fire-pit crackled in its center, a deer carcass turning on the spit. Casalu was throwing dice with a few of his inner circle, men here and there attending to their daily tasks—stitching torn clothing, running a whetstone over a blade, skinning and salting meat for the morrow, piling wood for the fire-pit, fetching water from a nearby stream. Normal things, and yet something was in the air. A tension.

Camlin went back to his routine, running a whetstone along the blade of his sword, then oiling it with an old rag, sheathed it, and then went through the same process with his knife. He emptied his bag between his feet and checked over its contents. A copper box packed with dry tinder and kindling. A flint and iron. Fish-hooks and animal gut for the stitching of wounds. Various medicinal herbs—honey, sorrel leaves, yarrow, and seed of the poppy. A roll of linen bandages. An arterial strap. An iron to heat for the cauterization of wounds. A needle and hemp thread. And a pot.

Be prepared, he told himself. Or repeated what Braith had told him. Braith had taught him all of this, how to be disciplined, how to prepare as a warrior would. As a man.

He will come back.

Braith had been gone for four nights, sent with a small crew to scout and maybe raid near the northern border of the Darkwood, where a new fortress was being built to guard the giantsway. Casalu had insisted that Drem, his captain, go with them.

He should have been back by now.

He packed his bag, putting it all away neatly, in its place.

An owl hooted three times and he felt his pulse quicken.

They're back.

The soft footfall of feet on forest litter. All of them in this crew were woodsmen, knew how to move through the forest like a whisper. Whoever was coming was relaxed, not concerned about masking their approach.

Is Drem going to walk in with one of Braith's ears in his collection?

The footsteps grew louder, no more than three, maybe four people.

Seven men left here.

Men walked into the dell, Braith at their center, his warm

smile on his face. He saw Camlin and nodded a greeting, carried on walking, stopped a dozen paces from Casalu, who was still playing at dice.

Casalu had not moved, but his eyes flitted from Braith to the men with him.

"You looking for Drem?" Braith asked him.

Casalu said nothing.

Braith held up a leather thong, draped with ears. Most of them were dried out bits of skin, almost unrecognizable from their original form, but one was fresher, crusted blood still upon it.

"Drem and I had a little chat before he parted with his ear. He told me all kinds of interesting tales. Mostly about how you want me dead."

Camlin reached a hand inside his pouch and pulled out a string wrapped in parchment and wax. Slowly he set to stringing his bow.

"Help yourself to some bread and stew," Casalu said, looking back to his dice. "You can report to me later."

Braith threw the necklace of ears onto the throw-board.

"I call you out, Casalu ben Artair," he said, voice raised, filling the dell.

Casalu snorted. "Shut him up," he said, and one of his companions burst into life, Niall, a newcomer that Casalu had adopted. It was generally accepted that he was the best sword the Darkwood brigands had ever seen. He surged to his feet, drawing his sword at the same time and took a few running steps towards Braith, who stood still as stone, just watching him. Niall's head jerked back, he stumbled, then crashed to the ground, rolled and lay still, Camlin's arrow through his eye.

Men were on their feet everywhere now, iron scraping from sheaths, insults and challenges flying. Camlin had another arrow nocked, bow half drawn.

"Hold," Braith yelled, his voice drowning the others. "No need for more of us to die. Just one. Me or him." He pointed at Casalu, still sitting at his throw-board.

Casalu stood slowly, uncoiling like a wyrm from the old tales, all muscle and sinuous grace.

"We'll do this Darkwood style," Casalu said.

"Of course," Braith grinned.

Both men stripped to the waist, a circle forming around them. It was dusk now, the fire-pit sending huge shadows flickering against the trees lining the dell.

Braith and Casalu held their left arms out, together, and Camlin bound them wrist-to-wrist with a leather thong.

Casalu reached behind his back and drew his cleaver from its sheath.

"Darkwood style is knives," Camlin said, others around the dell muttering their agreement.

"If we're using our weapon of choice…" Braith rested his hand on his sword hilt.

Casalu glowered at Camlin, then cast a baleful glare at the rest of the crew. He threw his cleaver to the ground. Braith unbuckled his sword-belt and passed blade and sheath to Camlin.

"When I've gutted him you're next," Casalu growled at Camlin, patting the knife at his belt.

"That's a wager I'd bet against," Braith said, still smiling.

Then Camlin was stepping back and lifting a horn to his lips. He blew once, long and keening, and the fight began.

Both men pulled at their bound wrists, Casalu heavier, stronger, but Braith's feet shifting, body swaying, taking the power out of Casalu's attempts to drag him off balance.

Why haven't they drawn their knives?

They moved back and forth, sending wild shadows dancing

around the dell.

They're measuring one another.

Casalu gave another wild tug and Braith slipped to the side, hooked a foot behind Casalu's ankle and sent him staggering off balance; at the same time Braith's hand finally reached for his knife. Somehow Casalu righted himself and lunged forward, his fist smashing into Braith's mouth, sending him reeling.

Braith spat blood and teeth from split lips, waving his knife wildly to slow Casalu's charge. Then they both had a knife in their hands and were stabbing, slashing, iron sparking in the twilight, trailing incandescent arcs through the air, at the same time their tied arms pulling and pushing, lunging and dragging.

They staggered close to the fire-pit, Casalu trying to throw Braith into it, Braith using Casalu's momentum to swing them both in a half circle. For a moment they stood there, leaning into one another, silhouetted by flame and still as carven stone, wrists locked, knives grating above their heads, lips twisted and snarling, then Braith spat blood into Casalu's face and they were moving again, spinning, lunging, stabbing, blocking. Braith tripped and staggered, Casalu's knife plunging at his belly, Braith suddenly pulling backwards, falling, Casalu on top of him, the two of them rolling, punching and stabbing, then they were both on their feet again, crouching low, stepping away from each other.

Casalu was breathing hard, blood sluicing down his left arm, dripping from his fingertips, Braith's ear bleeding, mangled from what looked like a bite, blood running down his neck, another thin red line along one thigh.

They regarded each other for one long moment, the crackle of the fire-pit and Casalu's heavy breathing punctuating the silence, then they were moving together again, knives clashing, scraping, bodies slapping together, Camlin and the rest of the crew shouting and cheering.

Then Braith's knife was spinning through the air.

Casalu tugged Braith forward, wrapped his bound hand about Braith's waist, twisting Braith's left arm behind his back, holding him close. Braith grabbed Casalu's wrist with his free hand, both of them shaking with the strain, but Casalu's knife edged steadily closer.

Camlin felt a jolt of fear, both for Braith and for himself. He'd chosen his side, knew the consequences of that choice.

The knife moved steadily towards Braith's throat. Veins bulged in Braith's face, his neck, his arm. The knife a handspan from his throat. Sweat poured from Braith's face, dripped from his nose. The knife moved closer, now a finger's width from Braith's throat.

Casalu smiled.

Braith snapped his head forward, crunching into Casalu's face, a red explosion where Casalu's nose had been. And again, teeth flying. Casalu staggered back, knife hand falling, blade slipping from his fingers.

Braith followed him, brought a knee up into Casalu's groin, pushed the big man staggering back, and Braith dropped to the ground, rolled, came up with something gripped in his fist.

Casalu's cleaver.

Casalu blinked, opened his mouth, then with a wet thump the cleaver hacked into his neck. Blood spurted. Braith wrenched the blade free, chopped again, Casalu stumbling away, mouth flopping, Braith following. Another blow and Camlin heard the crack of bone splintering. Casalu dropped to his knees, swayed, fell onto his face.

Braith stood over him, chest heaving, nostrils flaring, blood splattering his face. Then he swung the cleaver again, severing Casalu's bound hand at the wrist.

A silence filled the dell.

"Looks like we've got a new chief," Camlin roared, and then men were cheering and yelling.

Camlin handed Braith his sheathed sword back.

"For a moment there, I was a bit worried," he said.

"Me too," Braith grinned. "But he forgot the first rule."

"The first rule?"

"Aye. The one that cancels out all others. The only rule, really."

"And what is that?" Camlin asked him.

"That it is better to live than to die." He nudged Casalu's corpse with his boot, then sucked in a deep breath and smiled through lacerated lips.

"Why so happy?"

"I have plans for this crew." Braith's smile broadened as he cleaned Casalu's blood from his cleaver.

THE SECRET

-The Broken Empire-

MARK LAWRENCE

"The Secret" is set in the world where my Broken Empire and Red Queen's War trilogies take place. I've been writing short stories based on the various members of Jorg Ancrath's 'brotherhood of the road', exploring their origins. When I saw that the Blackguards anthology was seeking tales of assassins...I thought it was time to write about Brother Sim.

Blackguards

*T*he moon shows her face and Sim crouches, low to the ground. On the castle walls, on the high towers, a dozen pairs of eyes hunt the darkness of the slopes outside, but only the wind finds Sim, tugging at his cloak, keening in his ears. He studies the battlements, the sheer expanse of stonework, the great gatehouse hunkered above the heaviest of portcullises. When the time comes he'll be fast. But now he waits. Sinking the teeth of his patience into the problem, watching how the guards move, how they come and go, where they rest their eyes.

"Every good story tells at least one lie and holds a secret at its heart."

The young man kept his head so still as he spoke that Dara thought of the statues in her father's hall. She watched his lips form the words, her gaze drawn by their motion amid the stillness of his face. All part of the storyteller's art, no doubt.

"The secret of this story hides in darkness, trapped behind the eyes of an assassin."

Dara let her gaze stray from Guise's mouth to encompass the rest of him, slight within his teller's tunic, buttoned to the top, his velvet tricorn rakishly askew, features fine, the light that had first lit her up

"THE SECRET"

Illustration by OKSANA DMITRIENKO

still burning in those gray eyes.

"Sim they called him. Perhaps it was his name. Assassins wear such things lightly. In any event Sim had been his name since the brotherhood took him in."

"A brotherhood? Was he a holy man?" Dara knew the pope kept assassins—the best that money could buy.

Guise smiled, a true storyteller doesn't bridle at questions. When questions are not welcome the story will not allow its audience to speak. "A holy man? Of a kind…he offered absolution, dealt in peace. Steel forgives all sins."

When Guise smiled Dara's heart beat faster and the lingering worry retreated. If her father discovered she'd snuck a man into her rooms, a mere commoner at that, he would double the guard—though she doubted the walls would hold more soldiers—have the bars at her window shackled together so no illicit key would open them, and worst of all, he would talk to her. He would summon her before the chair from which he spoke for all of Aramis and treat her not like a child, but like an adult in whom his trust had been misplaced. She would have to stand there, alone in that echoing expanse of marble, and explain the knotted curtain pulls she'd lowered as a rope, the alarm she'd had Clara raise to distract the guardsmen from their patrols…

"Brother Sim took his work seriously. The taking of a life is a—"

"Was he handsome, this Brother Sim?" Dara stretched on the couch, a languid motion, hot and sultry as the night. She felt sure a storm was building, the tree tops in the gardens had been thrashing in a humid wind when she opened the window for Guise, rain lacing the breeze. It would break soon. The distant thunder arrive and make good on its threats.

Dara half rolled to face the storyteller. He leaned forward on his small chair, close at hand, the story scroll unopened on his knee.

About his wrist he wore her favor, a silk handkerchief, embroidered with flower and tiny glass beads. "Was he handsome? Was he tall, this Sim?" she asked.

"Ordinary," Guise told her. "Unremarkable. The kind of face that might in the right light be anyone. Handsome in one instant, in the next forgettable. He stood shorter than most men, lacking the muscle of a warrior. His eyes though, they would chill you. Empty. As if he saw just bones and meat when he looked your way."

Dara shuddered, and Guise unrolled his scroll, fingertips floating above the characters set there, dark and numerous upon the vellum, crowded with meaning. "To find out why Sim watched those walls we have to journey, first many miles to the east, and then back through the hours and days until we find him there." Guise raised his voice, though still soft, for the guards outside the door mustn't hear him, and as he lifted his hand from the page, the story bore her away.

———•———

BROTHER SIM WAITED, FOR that is what assassins must do. First they wait for their task, then for opportunity. The brotherhood had made camp in the ruin of a small fortress, amid the wreckage and char-stink of whatever battle had emptied it. Sim had sought out the highest tower, as was his wont, and sat upon the battlements, staring at the point where the road that brought them became compressed between sky and land and vanished into a point. His legs dangled above a long drop.

"A name has been given." Brother Jorg spoke behind Sim. He'd climbed the spiral stair on quiet feet.

"Which name?" Sim still watched the road, leading as it did back into the past. Sometimes he wondered about that. About how a man might retrace his steps and yet still not return to the place he'd come from.

And Brother Jorg spoke the name. He came to stand by the wall and set a heavy gold coin beside Sim. In a brotherhood all brothers are equal, but some are more equal than others, and Jorg was their leader.

"Find us on the Appan Way when this is done." He turned and descended the steps.

Assassination is murder with somebody else's purpose. Sim reached for the coin, held it in his palm, felt the weight. Coins hold purpose, they bear it like a cup. A murder should always carry a weight, even if it's only the weight of gold. He turned the coin over in his scarred fingers. The face upon it would lead him to his victim.

SIM RODE FROM THE fort, beneath the gutted gatehouse, his equipment stowed, his weapons strapped about his person. The brothers saw him go and made no comment. Assassination is lonely work. They each feared him in their way. Hard-bitten men, dangerous with a sharp edge or a blunt instrument, but they feared him. Everyone sleeps after all. Every man is vulnerable.

Sim slowed his horse to a walk and set out along the trail that would bear him to a larger way, and thence to the Roma Road that led to Aramis. There was no haste in him, no eagerness. The assassin requires no passion. His work is not artistry, simply efficient. The very best assassin is no warrior, he doesn't achieve his ends through skill at arms. Instead he must know people, he must understand them, intimately. Sometimes it's the people who stand in his way, whose skin he must inhabit—sometimes the victims themselves.

Sim found an apple in his pocket, wizened but still sweet, and took a small bite, leaving a precise wound. The catch of course is that knowing the full depth of any human, knowing their hopes and frailties, the hurts of their past, the tremor with which they reach for the future…that knowledge is akin to love.

———•—————

"DO YOU THINK THAT'S true, Guise?" Dara asked the question into the pause the young man left. "Because who knows people better than a storyteller?" She drew herself up upon the couch so she sat opposite him, their knees almost touching. "You make your living telling our tales. And so many of them are about princesses…you must know *us* very well."

They shared a knowing smile, close enough now that Dara could see the rain's moisture still clinging to his hair. Dara laid her hand upon his knee—she could guess how this night's story would end. She had invited him to her chamber for more than old tales. Guise set his fingers above the symbols on the scroll, and began to speak again, not looking down but holding her gaze, as if he could read the story by drawing the words up through his hand.

———•—————

"SIM SAT AND WAITED and watched, as he had sat and waited and watched on each of ten previous nights, sometimes at the walls, sometimes in the city that washed up around the barren mount upon which the castle squatted. Always he listened, learning what could be learned, presenting a new face to each night, seeking his way in."

Dara frowned. "This Brother Sim came to Aramis to murder the man whose face was on the coin?" She shot Guise a sharp look. "My father—"

"Or some grandsire of his, my princess? Or perhaps just someone who might be found wherever the king might be? Or maybe Hertog the Second, that fearsome warlord who died in mysterious circumstances and whose brother, Jantis, inherited Aramis' throne three centuries back? Jantis proved somewhat inept in the business of armies and wore the crown for just two months before your family disposed of him upon the battlefield...Give the story space and it will tell itself."

Dara settled back, embarrassed at her outburst. Had she spoiled the secret? Was the story how her line came to reign in Aramis?

"We were discussing love, Princess Dara. The perfect assassin, the one who can reach anyone, anywhere, needs to know his target intimately, and such knowledge breeds love. So there lies a dilemma. The perfect assassin needs to be able to kill the thing he loves. Or, rather, to understand the emotion, but not let it stay his hand."

SIM NEVER STAYED HIS hand. Always seized his moment. When some alarm within the castle turned the guards from the battlements he advanced to the base of the wall, swift but smooth. He threw his padded grapple and the thin rope snaked out behind it. Within heartbeats he was climbing, drawing himself up along a line chosen after long inspection toward a spot where he stood least chance of being observed.

Arms burning he reached the battlement and crossed the parapet on all fours, quick as an eel, kicking free the grapple behind him and dropping into the tree he knew stood close to the wall at that spot. Below him the gardens seethed in the new risen wind. The castle walls enclosed several acres of garden, set to trees, shrub and bush, in chaotic profusion, capturing a manicured hint of the wild woods in which the nobility of Aramis so loved to hunt.

Sim waited, high in the arms of the elm, waited for whatever commotion had drawn the guardsmen's attention within the walls to die away. The wound on the heel of his palm had started to bleed again. He'd killed seasoned veterans without taking a scratch and somehow let a church librarian slice him with a letter opener. A half-inch lower and it would have opened the veins in his wrist, cut tendons perhaps. He touched his fingers to the wound and while he waited, cradled in the treetop, he let the recollection of the incident unfold behind his eyes.

The librarian, Honas, had proved useful in the end—providing maps from the days of the castle's construction and reading out the legends in a tremulous voice. A fair exchange all told. And when his store of information ran dry they sat looking at each other, the young man and the old.

"Brother Jorg said he might teach me to read," Sim told the churchman, folding the ancient map and slipping it into an inner pocket. "But he says a lot of things." Sim withdrew his hand and turned it over to reveal the short throwing knife on his palm, below it the cut Honas had scored him with still bled—an instinctive thing, a lashing out in fear as he turned from the table bearing his correspondence only to be surprised by Sim standing at his shoulder.

"It's a beautiful piece isn't it?" Sim turned his hand to let the candlelight slide along the blade. The weapon felt good in his hand, familiar. Strange to take comfort in the sharp edge of a little cross-knife, an instrument of pain and death…but he supposed the crosses that the faithful took their own comfort in were symbols of an instrument far crueller than his knife.

Sim slipped the blade between his middle fingers so an inch protruded like a gleaming claw, and with a swift motion cut Honas' throat. He caught the older man's head then, and held it, despite the thrashing, whispering into his ear, loud enough to be heard above the gurgles, but quiet enough that only they two would share the words.

"WHAT DID HE SAY?" Dara slid from the couch to sit at Guise's feet, his suede boots streaked with mud from his journey through the gardens.

"That's the secret, princess."

"You will tell me though?" She looked up at him, arching her brows.

Guise met her gaze. "Of course. Before the end. Nobody's story should end with the secret untold." He returned his eyes to the scroll before him. The low rumble of thunder reached them, vibrating in Dara's chest.

SIM WAITED IN THE tree, ripe with a purpose that was not his own. Many years before, his mother had tied all his purpose to a single coin, a lifetime ago, back when he'd been too young to know he was being sold. The brothel had taken him and held him until the brotherhood came with blood and fire and, seeing in him a different value, took the boy into their number. He'd been fourteen when they gave him a new life, and in the years since he'd come to accept a leader's direction to replace his own spinning compass; though, for each death, he took a coin, perhaps hoping in some deep and unspeaking recess of his mind that the coin his mother accepted would find its way to his hand, and give him back to himself.

———❖———

WHEN SIM'S MOMENT CAME he dropped, cloak fluttering behind him, two feet striking the back of a guardsman's neck. The man fell nerveless into a bush while Sim launched himself onto the second guard, punch knife in hand. In a heartbeat only Sim remained upright. He dragged the second man into the bush that received the first and, while all around him the leaves seethed beneath the wind, Sim whispered the secret to the men as their last moments came and went.

Beneath the shelter of the tree Brother Sim changed into his disguise. By the time he'd done up the last button a cold rain had begun to fall and the dark gardens bent and dripped. He advanced on the tall towers, the royal apartments, pausing only to set in place his equipment within the tall shrubs that marked the gardens' perimeter.

———❖———

"YOU DIDN'T JUST COME here to tell stories did you, Guise?" Dara moved her hand upon the young man's knee, feeling the firmness of his thigh. A flicker of lightning lit the room, mocking the lamps' illumination for a second, and burning in the storyteller's eyes. Three times in the past week she'd seen him in the houses of nobility, declaiming from the petty-stage to entertain the diners. Something about him had drawn her gaze, an almost delicate beauty, and he'd returned her frank attentions with something ambiguous, something more tempting than lust or admiration.

At Lord Garzan's presentation of suitors Dara had paid more mind to the storyteller than to the lordlings and minor princes her father had invited to seek her hand. Her father might have grand politics at the front of his thinking, alliances waiting to be sealed; Dara, however, had more immediate desires to satisfy and felt if she were to be sacrificed into some arranged marriage she may as well have a little fun first.

She'd thrown Guise her favor when his story ended and sent her maid Clara to arrange their current assignation. The maid had returned looking as flushed as Dara felt, and confirmed that Guise would dare the walls for a chance to meet the princess if she would provide sufficient distraction to give him the opportunity to reach her without being filled with spears.

And here he was, in the flesh. Firm beneath her hand and far more real than stories. Far more interesting. Thunder rolled outside, deep voiced and raw. She leant closer still. "You didn't just come here to tell stories did you?"

"I didn't, princess, not just to tell stories, no." Guise took her hand in his and stood from his chair. "It was on a night like this, in the gardens of this very castle, that Brother Sim murdered his way toward the high towers of Aramis." He led her to the window where he'd clambered into her chamber not an hour before. "Bloody handed Sim came, leaving the bodies of half a dozen men in his wake."

Guise slid an arm about her shoulder and she shivered beneath his touch as he guided her to stand beside him and watch the rain fall through the darkness. He held out his other hand to catch the drops, steering her gaze.

"Is that…is there?" Something caught her eye, still adjusting to the dark, something among the vegetation flailing beneath a storm wind…something darker…almost…man shaped. A lone guardsman?

"I—" Lightning flashed again and amid the shocking green

Dara saw a black figure, ragged and tall, half-emerging from the bushes that stood between the inner court and the gardens. The crash of thunder drowned her scream. "Oh God! It's him!"

"What?" Guise stepped back, staring at her. "What did you see?"

"Someone…someone's out there." She clung to his shoulder, heart thumping.

Pounding on the door, scarcely louder than the thunder in her chest. "Your highness?" The handle rattled but she'd bolted it earlier, before Guise climbed the rope.

"Tell him," Guise whispered. "If you saw someone."

"I'm fine." She called out. "I…I saw a man in the grounds, not a guardsman or one of the staff. I got scared." She sat in the chair Guise offered, trembling in her limbs and unsteady.

"I'll order a search, princess." The guardsman's voice through the door—Captain Exus. "I'll leave Howard to guard your chamber. Please set the main bolts."

"I'll do it," Guise whispered, and he hurried to push the two heavy bolts home into their housings. From beyond the door the sound of boots on stairs as her guardsmen hurried down to initiate the hunt. Dara felt safe now. The door would keep an army at bay and Howard would take some getting past too.

"I think the story's over." Guise returned to her, easing the tension in her shoulders with an expert touch.

"But you never got to the lie or told me the secret," Dara said, craning her neck to look back at him, behind the chair.

Guise shook his head, a sad smile on his lips. When he passed the cord beneath her chin she thought for a moment that it was a necklace, a gift.

"I'm the lie." A moment later the cord tightened choking the question off her lips. Her hands went to her neck and all thought narrowed to a single aim, a single goal, to draw another breath. And into that moment of silent, terminal, panic Sim whispered the secret.

Sim crouched behind the chair, safe from any clawing hands, hauling on the curtain cord until Dara's struggles ceased. Even then he kept the pressure, rising with the cord knotted between his straining hands. He knew how long it takes to kill someone in such a manner. The garrotte would have been quicker, but bloody, and his escape would be safer if he kept clean. In any case a wire seemed wrong for so royal a throat. Silk seemed…apt…for nobility.

Eventually Sim let go the cord, allowing the princess' corpse to flop forward, hiding her purple face, blood-filled eyes, protruding tongue. He took from his bag a copy of the royal servants' tunics and hose, changing into it without haste. He removed Dara's favor and hid the wound on his wrist beneath the cuff of his new uniform. A long blonde wig and a touch of rouge delicately applied with the help of a hand mirror to achieve the desired effect, and Sim looked every bit the serving girl. Disguise had always come easy to him. His childhood had served him well; when your sense of self is taken, it grows easier to become someone else. When you sell affection, it becomes easier to both understand love and be unmoved by it. The brothers had seen the killer in him at fourteen. He wondered how people less used to murder managed not to see it until it was far too late.

Sim straightened and went to the door. A device of one water bladder dripping into another acting as a counterweight had raised the rag figure amid the bushes, it would not take long to find, and the guardsmen would be back soon enough.

A drop of oil applied to the heavy bolts allowed each to be drawn back without alerting the guard outside. A couple more oil drops for the hinges and Sim set his four-inch punch spike in hand. He pulled the door open in a smooth motion and drove the steel into the back of Howard's neck, bringing him down in a clatter of useless armor.

Once Howard had been hauled into the room Sim collected the dining tray from Dara's chamber and closed the door behind him. With the tower guard thinned by Dara's alert, and suitably attired for one wishing to pass unremarked along the corridors of power, Sim took his leave.

He had served his purpose, the coin's purpose, Brother Jorg's purpose. Brother Jorg who he both hated and loved. Brother Jorg who found direction everywhere he looked, as if it bled between each word he spoke. And, with his task complete, once more Sim had a free choice of path. As free a choice as ever he'd been given in his eighteen years.

Half an hour later, on a dark and rain-swept highway with a good horse beneath him, Sim made his decision, pulling the reins once more toward the Roma Road that would bear him east and south toward the Appan Way, toward his brothers, toward another coin, another duty, toward the clarity of purpose in a world so lacking in direction.

In his wake, torn and flapping in the mud, the story scroll, its incomprehensible symbols smeared by rain, words and meaning running together, soaking away.

The story is done. Be glad that it wasn't yours and that, for you, the lie is still untold, the secret still unspoken.

FRIENDSHIP

-Silerian Trilogy-
LAURA RESNICK

"Friendship" is set in the world of my Silerian trilogy,
In Legend Born, The White Dragon, *and* The
Destroyer Goddess. *It takes place a few years*
before the trilogy begins and focuses on two important
secondary characters from the novels. This story
foreshadows a treacherous power struggle between
two sorcerers, portrays a relationship of mutual trust
that will be tested by fate, and gives you a taste of the
ruthlessness that characterizes life in Sileria.

T HE WATERY WALLS OF Kiloran's palace undulated smoothly around Najdan as he entered his master's lair. Hidden deep beneath the surface of Lake Kandahar, the waterlord's dwelling was imposing, luxurious, and maintained by sorcery. If Kiloran chose, he could loosen his control on any of the airy underwater rooms, allowing the icy lake to swallow them up—and drown whoever happened to be there. Entering Kiloran's home was a matter of trust if you were one of the assassins sworn to his service— and a matter of desperation if you were a supplicant seeking his help.

Upon finding Kiloran comfortably seated in conversation with a well-dressed young stranger, the assassin crossed his fists in front of his chest and bowed his head in formal greeting.

"*Siran*," said Najdan. *Master.* "I came as soon as I received your message."

"Najdan." The old waterlord, who was stout, coldly intelligent, and formidable, smiled and gestured for the assassin to join him and his young guest. "Allow me to introduce you to *Toren* Jimon."

The title didn't surprise Najdan. The young man's expensive attire combined with the arrogance of his attitude, apparent even at first

"FRIENDSHIP"

Illustration by OKSANA DMITRIENKO

glance, had led Najdan to guess he was one of the *toreni*—the landed aristocrats of Sileria.

"I am honored by the introduction, *toren,*" Najdan said politely.

The young man looked him over as if he were a Kintish courtesan, then said to Kiloran, sounding pleased, "Oh, this is excellent! He looks exactly the way I imagined an assassin would."

Najdan raised one brow and looked at Kiloran, whose face remained impassive as Jimon rose from his seat to walk in a circle around Najdan.

"The black tunic and leggings, the red woven sash…The unkempt hair of a *shallah*—he *is* a *shallah*, isn't he?"

"Yes," said Kiloran. He caught Najdan's eye, and the assassin could see that the old waterlord was amused.

"Of course," Jimon said with a nod. "He would have to be a *shallah.* Just look at the scars on his palms—from swearing bloodvows, yes? And that brutish face!" When Najdan gave him a cold glance, the *toren* fell back a step—then clapped his hands. "Marvelous!"

The *shallaheen,* Sileria's mountain peasants, were the poorest and most numerous of the island nation's disparate people. Although the assassins of the Honored Society came from all walks of Silerian life, the grinding poverty of the mountains drove many *shallaheen,* in particular, into this dangerous but lucrative vocation.

From the day he swore his loyalty in blood to a waterlord, an assassin's life belonged to his master and to the Honored Society. But since family ties were strong in the mountains, a wise waterlord nonetheless respected those bonds. When ordering Najdan to exact tribute, ensure obedience to the Society's will, or kill men, all of which the assassin did efficiently and ruthlessly, Kiloran had never required him to do so with his own clan. Then again, Najdan's clan was small, poor, meek, and submitted readily to the Society's will in exchange for Kiloran's favor.

"You are a magnificent specimen," the *toren* said to him. "I couldn't be more pleased."

"I am delighted to please your guest, *siran,*" Najdan said to his master. "Have you summoned me merely to be admired? Or is there work for me to do?"

Kiloran's lips twitched. "Now that you mention it, there is some work."

"I need someone killed," Jimon said baldly.

"Anyone in particular?" Najdan asked.

"An *Outlooker,*" the *toren* said, clearly intending to make an impression.

He made one. Najdan looked sharply at Kiloran—and was surprised to see that this was not news to the waterlord. *"Siran?"*

Kiloran nodded, his expression serious. "You heard correctly. An Outlooker."

"I don't understand."

"You don't need to understand," the *toren* said dismissively. "You just need to kill him."

Najdan said nothing, awaiting an explanation. Because there must surely be one.

The Outlookers were the occupying force of Valdania, the conquering mainland empire which had ruled Sileria for two centuries. The Valdani were powerful and greedy, the Outlookers were callous and brutal, and their emperor had outlawed the Honored Society and Silerian water magic. But Dar, the destroyer goddess who dwelled inside the snow-capped volcano of Mount Darshon, had ensured that Her home was not an easy one for foreign conquerors to control. Outlawing something was one thing, but enforcing the law in Sileria's mountainous terrain was quite another. And so the Honored Society, though heavily inconvenienced by the Valdani, continued to function much as it had for centuries, through successive waves of conquest and foreign rule.

But it was a delicate balance, one that relied on exercising good judgment and maintaining traditional boundaries. And one of those boundaries was that the Honored Society did not assassinate Valdani.

The slaying of an Outlooker would motivate the Valdani to work much harder at enforcing their will in the mountains and pursuing their emperor's goal of destroying the Society.

"The dry season was short this year," Kiloran said to Najdan. "And the rains have been good."

This seemed a feeble explanation for the extraordinarily foolish act that Kiloran apparently expected him to carry out.

No matter which mainland power held the coastal cities of Sileria's lowlands, the Society had always dominated the mountains by controlling Sileria's water supply. Through their power and magic, the waterlords created thirst and drought among the disobedient and those would who not pay tribute, and their might was enhanced by the practical skills of their assassins. The Society rewarded its loyal and submissive friends with a generous water supply—and by not inflicting terror and violence on them.

Sileria's annual dry season was the Society's most powerful and profitable time. Although always feared and respected, they were less easily able to impose their will in a year like this one, when the rains had come early and were still falling. Currently, almost everyone in Sileria had enough water, whether the waterlords willed it or not.

Even in a good year, the Society had to resort to other means of exacting tribute after the dry season ended, such as abduction, ransom, and killing. The blood extracted during the rainy season was how the Society continued to exert its authority and influence.

And in a bad year, as this one was, they must be bold and

innovative to ensure their own well-being.

Nonetheless…assassinating an Outlooker was foolhardy, not bold. The consequences could be costly and severe.

Yet Najdan could tell from Kiloran's expression that his master had already decided they would do it.

Kiloran said to him, "*Toren* Jimon has a difficult problem to solve. Recognizing the enormity of the favor he asks, he has offered us a generous gift, along with his sincere and lasting friendship."

Naturally, there would be coin involved; not even this young fool would come empty-handed to Kandahar to ask Kiloran to kill an Outlooker. But influence mattered more in the mountains than money did. For Kiloran to grant such an audacious request, the friendship Jimon offered him in exchange must be extremely valuable. Najdan wondered why. What made this pompous *toren's* loyalty worth taking such a risk?

"In addition to the bountiful rains," Kiloran continued, "we've had other misfortunes this year, have we not?"

They exchanged a look of acknowledgment.

"Yes, *siran*. We have."

The Honored Society was far more disciplined than the *shallaheen*, who were prone to constant clan wars and bloodfeuds, but the waterlords were allies rather than friends. And not always even allies, in fact.

For reasons that Kiloran had never shared with Najdan, and about which Najdan knew better than to ask, Kiloran had been locked for some years in a bitter, distracting, and occasionally destructive feud with Baran, a half-mad and wholly unscrupulous waterlord who inhabited a notoriously damp, abandoned ruin surrounded by a deadly, ensorcelled moat. Although much younger than Kiloran and insanely reckless, Baran was very talented and his power was growing. He had recently succeeded in taking over some of Kiloran's territory. This put Kiloran—and therefore Najdan—in a dangerous position, since it undoubtedly suggested to the other waterlords that Kiloran's strength might be waning, and these were not men to ignore an opportunity. Najdan knew that Kiloran had devoted much thought and attention lately to the problem of reasserting his predominance—and crushing Baran.

"Difficult times call for daring solutions," said Kiloran. "I have given due thought to the *toren's* situation, and I believe his desire to form a deep and lasting friendship with us represents an opportunity that makes his request one we should honor."

Najdan again wondered what qualities or advantages the silly young man possessed that were not apparent at this meeting.

"An opportunity," Kiloran repeated.

And Najdan, who knew that he served a shrewd man, as well as the greatest waterlord in Sileria, said, "As always, *siran,* you know best, and I obey."

"I felt certain I could count on you."

"I am honored by your faith in me, *siran.*"

"There is one thing…"

"Yes?"

"This business should be accomplished discreetly."

Najdan nodded. "I will find out where the Outlooker sleeps and do the work by night."

"Even more discreetly than that." When Najdan just looked at him blankly, Kiloran said, "It should never be known that a Society assassin was involved."

"Ah." Najdan nodded. "I am to disguise myself?"

The red and black colors of an assassin represented honor and ensured respect; but they also made him noticeable and clearly identified his allegiance to the Society. Kiloran hoped to escape consequences by obscuring the identity of the Outlooker's slayer.

Najdan did not relish masquerading as an ordinary *shallah*, but he could see the sense in it.

"Yes. I'm sorry to say that you must also leave your *shir* here. If anyone were to see it in connection with this work…" Kiloran shook his head. "That would be bad for us."

"I understand, *siran.*" With some regret, Najdan removed his *shir* from his sash and gave it to Kiloran for safekeeping until his return.

"Oh, I've never seen a *shir* before." Jimon glanced at Kiloran for permission. "May I?"

Kiloran gestured to Najdan, indicating that it belonged to him.

The wavy-edged dagger was an enchanted weapon created for him by Kiloran, fashioned from water by the wizard's cold magic. It was thing of beauty, as well as deadly. Even a minor cut from a *shir* took a long time to heal, and a wound inflicted by the unnaturally cold blade could seldom be staunched or healed. Yet, having been made for him by his master, the blade could not harm Najdan, and so it could be carried next to his skin, concealed and unsheathed, always ready for combat.

Najdan shrugged, which Jimon interpreted as acquiescence, and the *toren* picked up the dagger—then instantly exclaimed in pain and dropped it.

Having expected this, Najdan retrieved the weapon from the crystalline floor of Kiloran's enchanted water palace and placed it on the small table at his master's side. "Has no one ever told you that others cannot touch an assassin's *shir?*"

One of the reasons that every assassin of the Society valued his own deadly *shir* so highly was that no other could use it—or even touch it without pain.

"Yes, but I forgot," Jimon said stupidly. *"Ow."* He studied his hand, which he held awkwardly in front of him. "That thing is so cold it burns."

"Your hand may pain you for several days," Kiloran said, "but it will pass."

Evidently knowing better than to criticize the most powerful waterlord in Sileria, Jimon said petulantly to Najdan, "You might have warned me."

Najdan ignored the *toren* and kept his gaze on his *shir*. He could kill—and *had* killed—without it, of course. But he valued the weapon and used it well, so he would have preferred to take it with him. However, Kiloran was right. A *shir* was too easily recognized as the weapon of a Society assassin. And since each waterlord created *shir* in his own distinctive style, Najdan's dagger could, in particular, expose Kiloran's involvement in the slaying.

"I'll keep it safe for you," Kiloran said.

"I know." Najdan nodded, then asked, "Where shall I find the Outlooker in question?"

"I'll take you to him," said Jimon. "I know where he gambles and drinks."

"That should be sufficient," Najdan said.

Outlookers were hated in Sileria, but attacks on them were rare. So an off-duty one leaving a tavern in the dark, after an evening of gambling and drinking, should be vulnerable and unwary.

Kiloran said to Najdan, "I place this task completely in your hands."

"I will complete it quickly and quietly," Najdan vowed.

"I am confident that you will." Kiloran turned to regard their guest and said formally, "May our friendship endure all tests and never disappoint either of us, *Toren* Jimon."

It was both a promise and a warning, but Najdan didn't think the young man realized that.

AFTER SEVERAL DAYS OF wet, muddy travel, they reached Britar, a town that lay between the mountains and the lowlands. The Valdani fortress there accommodated a large contingent of Outlookers, and Jimon announced that his family had a modest estate nearby. The *toren* stayed in the family villa there, while Najdan was given quarters in an empty tenant cottage.

As agreed, that evening Najdan waited for Jimon outside the villa. When the *toren* emerged from his home, Najdan accompanied him on foot to the town, dressed in the humble clothes of a *shallah* and posing as a servant.

"How are your accommodations?" Jimon asked as they made their way to the tavern where they expected to find their quarry.

"Fine, thank you, *toren*."

In fact, the cottage was damp, drafty, infested with insects, and dirty, but Najdan was not prone to complaining, and he had come here to kill an Outlooker, not to enjoy his temporary quarters.

Jimon snorted and said, "All of the cottages on the estate are in a sad condition, I'm afraid. The place is rather neglected."

Najdan had noticed this. The estate was not large, the villa clearly needed repairs, and the land was not well tended. It seemed surprising that Jimon's friendship (and gold) had been enough to convince Kiloran to get involved in killing an Outlooker.

"But it's such a minor estate," Jimon continued, "my father says that it's not worth the money or attention it would require for improvements. So he won't help me."

"Ah, your family has other holdings."

"Oh, of course," Jimon said. "And my father regards this place as more of a burden for me than a *holding*. I inherited it last year from a relative on my mother's side. Having my own estate seemed appealing for a while, but now I don't know…Maybe I'll follow my father's advice, much as it galls me to say so, and sell it to some fat

Valdan who wants a country home."

"Your family does not live here," Najdan surmised.

The *toren* snorted again. "Dar, no!"

That would certainly make it much easier, he realized, for Jimon to act without their blessing—which seemed likely, since what landed family would want their son mixed up in the slaying of an Outlooker?

"My father has *never* been here, and even if he visited, he'd flee the place after just one night!" Jimon added, "Not that he could come here, anyhow. He's old and ill. Can't travel anymore. And he's used to luxury and everything being just *so*. He'd despise this place if he actually saw it." He sighed. "If I'm honest, I really *should* sell it."

"Then sell it," Najdan said, closing the subject. Or so he thought.

"But one gets attached and has reasons for staying…" Jimon was pensive for a moment, then his mood changed and he said angrily, "What a fool I was!"

Najdan resisted the urge to agree; regardless of what Jimon was thinking about now, he was a fool without question.

"By Dar, I *will* sell," the young man vowed. "When this is done, I'll put all this behind me, and—and—and I'll *laugh* about it!"

"May it be so," Najdan said politely. "And there are worse things than returning to a life of luxury, after all."

"Hmmm. Living with my family again," Jimon said without enthusiasm. "Back at Shevrar."

"Where?" he asked alertly.

"Shevrar. My family home. It's an estate in—"

"I know where it is," Najdan said. "It belongs to your family?"

"Yes."

"Ah." After a moment he asked, "You are the eldest son?"

"The *only* son. My parents had seven girls before they got me."

"Hmm."

And now Najdan understood why this young fool's friendship was worth so much to Kiloran. Shevrar, an old estate so large that even a *shallah* assassin knew its name, was in territory controlled by Baran.

It seemed unlikely that the father knew what the son was involved in, and perhaps he would never know. But, according to his son, he was old and ill. And Kiloran was patient. So rather than dismissing the youngster, he was cultivating the heir. When Jimon inherited Shevrar, he would be in debt to Kiloran. And the waterlord would use that friendship with the biggest landowner in Baran's territory to his advantage.

An opportunity, the *siran* had said. Now Najdan understood. Killing the Outlooker was worth a lot to his master.

So it was reassuring to find the man so easily that evening.

He and Jimon reached town, and as they approached the tavern Najdan could see it was frequented by Outlookers from the nearby fortress. He and the *toren* went inside, chose a table, and surveyed the crowd. Before long, exactly as Jimon had predicted, their man arrived, accompanied by several comrades, all of them wearing the gray uniform of the Outlookers. Their quarry ordered a large mug of ale and settled down to some enthusiastic and noisy gambling.

He was a handsome young man, about Jimon's age, and obviously popular among his companions. He laughed a good deal, both at himself and at others, and seemed good-natured about losing his money to better players.

Unfortunately, as a popular and sociable fellow, he was unlikely to leave the tavern alone when he returned to the Valdani fortress. And Najdan would much rather not kill *several* Outlookers; that would make discretion very difficult and the consequences of tonight's work more complicated.

On the other hand, this Outlooker was a thirsty lad and

drinking a great deal of ale. Perhaps that would suffice. Before long, he'd go outside to relieve himself in the dark. With any luck, he'd do that alone.

Najdan turned to Jimon, intending to suggest they leave quietly and wait outside, but the expression on the young *toren's* face silenced him. It held such intensity of feeling that he was startled. It had not occurred to him to wonder before now why Jimon wanted this Outlooker killed. Najdan's duty was to perform the work for Kiloran, not to pry into the motives of others. But now, seeing that uncharacteristically powerful expression on this vapid youngster's face, he was curious.

It was not his concern, though, so he dismissed this thought and quietly instructed Jimon to leave the tavern with him. The *toren* flinched slightly when he spoke, as if having forgotten Najdan's presence. As if having forgotten everything but the young man he was staring at so fiercely.

"What?"

"Let's wait outside," Najdan repeated.

"Huh? Oh…yes." Jimon nodded. "Yes, of course." But instead of rising, he looked again at the Outlooker.

"Quietly. And lower your eyes," Najdan said tersely.

Jimon ignored this and continued staring as they stood. As Najdan feared, the Outlooker felt that intense gaze, looked around to see what was intruding on his senses, and locked eyes with Jimon. The smile fled from his face, and he stared back at the *toren*.

Najdan had only a moment to wonder what had led to deadly animosity between these two fresh-faced young men—a gambling debt? a woman? a blood insult?—before the Outlooker, to his surprise, lowered his gaze and turned his back.

That was good. A confrontation or verbal exchange would have called too much attention to the business at hand. Najdan doubted

Jimon could be relied on to say nothing about Kiloran if questioned about the Outlooker's death. Fortunately, though, as long as the *toren* didn't attract attention tonight, such a problem was unlikely to arise. The Valdani imposed heavy taxes on Silerian aristocrats, but they wouldn't actively seek trouble with an important old family by questioning their son in this matter, unless he gave them a very good reason for doing so.

Najdan took Jimon by the elbow and guided him to the door. "Outside."

They stepped out into the cool, damp night, well away from prying eyes or curious ears, and Najdan said, "I will wait for him to come out to relieve himself, lure him into the dark, and finish this. It will be best if the Outlookers think someone wanted his purse enough to kill him for it, so I will take that—though it may be empty by the time he comes outside."

"He shouldn't gamble. He's terrible at it." Jimon's voice was breathless and tight. "I keep telling…Never mind." A pause, then: "How will you do it?"

"I have a *yahr* with me." Valdani law prohibited Silerians from bearing arms, but many *shallaheen* carried the *yahr*, a flailing weapon. It looked like a couple of short, thick sticks connected by some rope.

Jimon drew in a sharp breath. "You're going to *beat* him to death?"

"Keep your voice down," Najdan instructed. "Now that I have seen him, you need not remain, *toren*. I will deal with this business while you return home."

"You want me to go? But I…I…"

"Tomorrow morning, before I leave to return to my master, I will come to the villa to inform you that your request has been fulfilled."

"My req—*Wait*. I need to—to think."

"Think on the way home, *toren*. You should leave now." Najdan put a hand on his shoulder to turn him in the right direction for the journey home.

"No, wait. This is happening so fast."

Fast? As far as Najdan was concerned, this was the culmination of a long, wet journey in tedious company, and it couldn't be over soon enough. "Believe me when I say these things are best done quickly."

"I suppose you know what you're talk—"

"Shh." Najdan slid into the shadows, dragging the *toren* with him, when a man came out of the tavern, chuckling cheerfully, and walked a little unsteadily in their direction.

"It's him," Jimon breathed.

It was so dark, Najdan didn't take this identification seriously.

Jimon took a step forward, as if intending to approach the other man. Najdan grabbed his arm and yanked him sharply back into place, which made the *toren* grunt in surprise.

The stranger approaching them heard this. Speaking Valdan, he said, "Who's that?"

Also speaking Valdan, which he knew well enough for this at least, Najdan replied, "It's me."

"*Damn,* it's dark out tonight. I can't even see the path!" The man stumbled, then laughed again. "Oops!" He sounded relaxed and a little drunk. He obviously thought he was approaching a fellow Outlooker, perhaps even a friend. "Where are you?"

Squinting through the dark, Najdan still couldn't tell if this was the man he wanted. He could feel Jimon's tension, but that was probably fear rather than recognition.

Trying to get a better look, Najdan shifted his weight slightly—and Jimon said, "Stop!"

"Huh?" said the man.

Jimon tore himself from Najdan's grasp and stumbled forward

in the dark. Najdan heard the two men collide. Then he heard a gasp, some scuffling, and the Valdan said, "*Jimon?* What are you doing out—never mind. I'm going back inside."

"No!"

This was the man, all right. And now the *toren* was directly involved. Oh, well. Nothing to be done about it.

Finish it quickly.

"Jimon, *stop.* It's over."

"But I love you!"

Najdan withdrew his *yahr.*

"Quiet!" snapped the Outlooker. "What if someone hears you?"

"I don't care!"

"Let *go* of me."

Najdan leaped forward, his *yahr* making a soft whooshing sound as he swung it at the Outlooker's head.

"No!" Jimon cried as the man grunted and fell to his knees. "Stop!"

"*Quiet,*" Najdan ordered. So much for not attracting attention.

He struck the Outlooker again. The man fell to the ground and rolled onto his back, blood gushing from his broken nose as he groaned in disoriented pain.

"*Stop!*" Jimon flung himself between Najdan and the Outlooker, nearly getting hit by the swinging *yahr.* "Najdan, *no!*"

"Var..." The man lay gasping, blood flowing from his scalp. "V...V..."

"No, don't!" Jimon wailed as Najdan struck again. "I was wrong! I was *wrong.* Don't."

Najdan looked down at the unconscious, bloody young Outlooker, whose handsome face would be ruined even if he were spared now and managed to survive.

"Please, nooo! *Stop!*" Jimon begged.

But sparing the Valdan was no more Najdan's decision than coming here to kill him had been. With the death of an Outlooker on his head, *Toren* Jimon of Shevrar would be bound to Kiloran forever. It was what the waterlord wanted, and Najdan served his master—not a spurned lover who'd been too foolish to understand the difference between fantasizing about death and actually causing it.

Najdan struck twice more, finishing the job, then knelt and took the Valdan's purse. They had not yet been discovered, so perhaps the killing would, after all, be taken for a violent robbery.

And he knew now that Jimon would not be suspected, as long as they could get away from here quickly. Because both the *toren* and the Outlooker would have been very secretive about what was between them. Najdan minded his own business, but there were those in Sileria who'd kill two men over a thing like that—and even a fool like Jimon certainly knew it.

He dragged the weeping *toren* away from the corpse and into the dark before anyone else from the tavern came outside. He kept his pace fast, hauling the sobbing and disoriented young man with him. They traveled some distance from the body, and were shielded by the night, when Jimon yanked out of his grasp and turned on him.

"I told you to stop! How could you?" he cried. "What did you *do?*"

"I did what you asked," Najdan said. "This was the favor you purchased with your friendship."

"My friendship?" Jimon spat. "Do you think I'll be *friends* with—"

"Yes, I do," he said. "This deed was your choice, not ours. That you chose unwisely is your burden, not mine and not my master's. The bargain is made, and we have honored it. So will you. Because even *you* must know the consequences of betraying Kiloran."

"I don't want friends like *you*," Jimon said bitterly.

"Nonetheless, you have us now," said Najdan. "And you would do well to remember that in Sileria, a man's friends are always more dangerous than his enemies. Farewell, *toren*."

Najdan turned and left Jimon alone in the dark. He decided not to return to the cottage on the estate, in case the *toren*, in a fit of ill-advised vengeance, reported his deed to the Outlookers. With that possibility in mind, he thought it also best to be as far away from here as possible by dawn. This night had not gone smoothly, and there might be some complications ahead; but he thought that, overall, the waterlord would not be displeased with his work, and so Najdan got his bearings and, taking care not to be seen, headed north, in the general direction of home.

THE LONG KISS

CLAY SANGER

I have a special love for scoundrels.

Where the line between hero and villain gets blurry, anything is possible. That's what makes them such compelling characters. When you root for the bad guy you never know what you're going to get.

"The Long Kiss" is fundamentally a story about choices and consequences. Scoundrels by nature are well-versed in that equation. Staying ahead in that calculation is how they pay the bills, after all.

But sometimes ambition and deceit muddies the waters. Desire and desperation become perfect poisons. Duty and honor turn to guilt and wrath. Rising up and crumbling down, "The Long Kiss" is a tale where all of these collide in gold and blood.

Blackguards

S IX SHIPS, SIX MONTHS, and two thousand miles. That's how far Raddox Edorian, former Captain and sole survivor of the Blackfish, had to run until he finally felt safe. When he reached the City of Kos, nestled along a stretch of exotic eastern shore he couldn't pronounce, he thought that just maybe it was far enough.

Less than one in ten people here spoke his mother tongue. These people were a mix of Sundish and Pahji and other folk he was largely ignorant about. He couldn't tell them apart anyway. As far as Raddox was concerned, all the strange people that filled this howling city looked alike, and that meant they looked nothing like him. That suited him perfectly.

The aging mercenary stood head and shoulders taller than the average local. Men like him, burly pale-faced Westermen, were rare here which made them easy enough to spot in a crowd. It was those sort of people that held the price on Raddox's head. The people of Kos and all these other folk along the Sundish shores couldn't have cared less about him.

Haj'adann. That was the word he'd heard the locals use to describe men like him, westerners and northerners from Galadyr and beyond.

"THE LONG KISS"

Illustration by OKSANA DMITRIENKO

He didn't suppose they meant it politely. It made him laugh.

The City of Kos was good. Loud, busy, full to bursting. Fragrant and exotic. There was music here he'd never heard before. Food he'd never tasted. Women he'd never had. He even saw a great gray beast with a wizened little man on its back and a coiling serpent for a nose. *Yphant*, the locals called it. It dropped great piles of shit in the streets and boys with wicker baskets would come along to collect the droppings. Raddox found that comical. Little sun-darkened men pulled on the yphant's great flapping ears with hooked sticks to steer the hulking beasts like mules.

Raddox even saw a great fat man in purple robes and a silly hat accompanied by a tiny and hairy man dressed in a set of clothes that were identical in every stitch. The little hairy man climbed all over the huge fat man and sat on his shoulder squawking and clapping like a court jester. The speechless little fool even had a tail like a beast.

The fat man and the little hairy man danced and twirled for coins, singing loud brassy songs as they tottered up and down the streets. Folk here seemed to appreciate their talents. Raddox was not so impressed. The fat man's language sounded like two goats humping.

Kos was perfect. It was the other side of the world in Raddox's estimation.

If he went any further east, he'd be circling the world back home, he thought.

And there, he was a dead man.

RADDOX MADE HIMSELF AT home in Kos and the days turned into weeks. Back home, the world was full of problems. Big problems. War. Namely a war that he himself had been paid to start. Those things were no longer Raddox's concern though. He had small problems. Like a keeping a belly full of wine that outclassed his tastes and getting a regular bathing by beautiful women. That included finding a whorehouse that suited his liking, which he did. Though they didn't call them whore houses here. They called them *sunkiri damash*, which he understood meant pleasure house, or near enough.

He learned quickly that Kosian pleasure houses weren't like whore houses back home. They weren't dens for drunks and lechers. Here in Kos, visiting the pleasure houses was a classy, respectable pastime. Men of wealth and standing did that, and women too. Business was conducted. Deals were sealed. It was all very civilized. There was etiquette to be observed, or you'd find yourself in the street.

Raddox liked his wine and he liked his women, so he adapted.

On a jasmine-scented evening nine weeks after arriving in Kos, Raddox visited his favorite pleasure house, the Crimson Circle. He was still working on how to say the name in the local tongue, damnable and finicky as it was.

The madam, a smiling and polite hostess, always made him feel at home. She was aging, too old for his tastes if he was paying for it. She no longer worked the baths or the pillow rooms anyway, but she spoke his language. And she had a sense of humor. Raddox liked her.

She greeted Raddox with a kiss on each scruffy cheek and smiled.

"It is my Western Sun," she declared happily, taking him by the hand and leading him beyond the plush curtains into the parlor. "How do you fare this fine evening?"

"Well enough," Raddox replied. "I think I'm seeking Milaeka

tonight."

The madam tisked. "Milaeka is not in the house tonight. But…
there is a new girl."

Raddox frowned. He liked Milaeka best. She had talents he
truly appreciated and was more round and voluptuous than many
of these slender eastern girls.

"What's her name?" the expatriated mercenary asked.

The madam smiled. "Whatever you wish it to be."

"And what are her…. Talents?"

"Whatever you desire."

Raddox considered it, pondering the playful light dancing in
the madam's eyes.

"I'll take her," he said at last.

"Shall we discuss the terms?"

Raddox laughed. "If she's worth it, she's worth it. And I can
pay it." He was proud of that, of his wealth. Gold enough to last
five lifetimes, bought by blood and betrayal. Pockets full of gold
was the only thing he had left to be proud of, after all. Everything
else about him was a disgrace.

"As you will," the madam said with a respectful bow.

Raddox caught something then. A shift in her eyes. A sense
of tension, perhaps. Something not entirely warm and welcoming.

"What is it?" he asked plainly.

The madam realized then that he'd spotted her flicker of
misgiving. She cleared her throat and composed herself.

"She is…very expensive."

Raddox laughed. "Then she damn well better be worth it!" he
declared happily.

If there was a lie in her eyes, the raucous mercenary missed
it. The madam took him upstairs and to the bath and the woman
he desired.

———•———

THE ROOM WAS HOT and steamy from the bath, rich with
the scents of incense burning in nearby braziers and oils wafting
up from the marble tub. Raddox promptly disrobed, hanging his
clothes and sword belt over the back of a carved wooden bench.
He would keep them close. Raddox was at ease, but not foolish.

The door on the opposite side of the chamber opened and the
lithe, cat-like silhouette of a young woman came into view. Gliding
weightlessly on tiny feet, she breezed into the room and bowed
low before him.

She was young, very young. Bronze skinned, raven-haired,
with dark, almond shaped eyes. Silk veils draped her shapely form,
leaving little to the imagination. The girl was, as the madam had
represented, stunning.

"What is your name?" Raddox asked her and hearing his voice,
she rose from her low bow. There was non-comprehension in her
dark smoldering eyes. "Your name, girl. What is it?"

She offered a small smile and another bow.

Raddox chuckled. "You don't speak a word of the Galatti, do
ya?" Doe-eyed silence was her answer. That was good. It meant he
could dispense with much of the etiquette and pleasantries. As
elegant as Kosian pleasure houses were, they could learn a thing
or two from the gritty sex stores that were the brothels back home.

She gave him a brilliant smile and motioned toward the large
steaming bath. He nodded and stepped that way, sliding into the
hot water with a relaxing sigh. With a few graceful movements,
she disrobed and slid into the water beside him.

There she took up a scented sea sponge and rubbed it with a
rind of pale pink soap. Once the sponge was rich with lather she

began to meticulously bathe him.

Raddox almost liked this part best. It was soothing in a way that even the sex wasn't. She scrubbed and massaged his scarred, muscle-knotted arms and he closed his eyes, basking in the warmth.

"You're a damn sight better at this part than Milaeka," he commented after a bit.

The girl only looked back at him with sheepish, non-comprehending eyes. She said something in her own tongue, as if in apology, and continued to bathe him.

Raddox pondered that for a bit. Then he said, "I suppose…I suppose you can say things to a whore what don't speak your language you can't even say to a father-confessor, can't ya?"

The girl had no reply.

Raddox was quiet for a long while as she finished scrubbing and massaging him down. While he continued to soak his cares away, she left the bath and brought back a silver goblet and round-bellied flagon of wine. He drank without fear. The circle of runes tattooed around his neck had cost him a bloody fortune, but they protected him from poison, just as the little bald-headed Pahji mystic had promised. Raddox had even made him prove it, and sure enough, it was so.

He was a man with a price on his head after all. If he died from some assassin's poison with all that gold in his pockets, the bit he *hadn't* spent would do him no good. He'd paid it, just for the peace of mind of being able to eat and drink without wondering if every meal or cup was his last. As he filled his belly fearlessly with the little whore's wine, he deemed it, as he usually did, a price well paid.

Yes, if a man wanted Raddox Edorian dead, he'd have to earn it. With steel. And in that, Raddox was no easy kill. No easy kill at all.

He drank and he was in no hurry. He'd seen in the bath that all her parts were where they were supposed to be and he owned her for the night. She wasn't going anywhere and the rest of what he was after would be waiting for him when he was ready for it. So Raddox drank, drank until the wine made his face numb.

As he drank, his mood darkened.

"I'm a murderer," he said to her and a humorless smile twisted his mouth. "A murderer, and a killer, and a raper." Raddox laughed, a joyless sound. "I done worse than that, too."

She refilled his goblet, dutifully pretending to listen even though he knew she didn't understand the words.

"I remember this lad, Turro was his name. When we'd first hired him on, he comes to me back from some brothel one night. And he's covered in blood and he's crying like a babe. He says to me 'I done murder!' Like it was something…special. So I says to him 'Welcome, brother. Ain't we all.'"

At that, Raddox was quiet for a while. When he spoke next, his voice was grave and his eyes stared off into the distance well beyond the walls of the bath chamber.

"Back home, there's killin' and dyin' a plenty going on," he said. "I started a war. And boys is lining up to die in it now." He nodded. "Just like I was paid to do."

The girl refilled his goblet once more.

Raddox drank. He told her about it and she listened.

━━━•◆•━━━

ON THE DISTANT WESTERN edges of Outer Galadyr, there was always tension. Tension between the persistent growth of Imperial Galadyr and the native savages who dwelt there. Chief among them were a fierce and territorial people called the Tarqs. But between two kings reluctant to go to war with each other, there was peace, fragile as it might have been.

There were those, however, who felt the peace an unnatural, and unprofitable, condition. And such men set out to change the course of things in Outer Galadyr. Captain Raddox Edorian and the Blackfish were one such cat's paw thrown secretly into the gears by powerful and ambitious men.

Their mission was clandestine, as was their employer secret, known only to Captain Raddox himself and he kept that knowledge close and quiet.

Raddox and the Blackfish were to start a war with the Tarqs.

Making enemies was the sort of job the Blackfish excelled at. Raddox and his boys took to the wilds of Outer Galadyr to see it done and to bathe in the gold that would come with their success.

Not long after arriving in the frontier, with autumn in full flame, Raddox's scouts picked up the trail of one of the Tarq's savage princes. The Captain smelled the opportunity they'd been waiting for. He gathered eighty of his men and set out after the barbarian prince and his dozen riders.

Raddox and his vanguard caught up to the savages at Bitter Ford along the River Toreg.

The Tarqish Prince and his riders were watering their horses and stretching their saddle weary legs when Raddox and his van rode into view across the way. The Tarqs were skittish, seeing so many riders beneath a banner of Galadyr riding up on them in the wild. The savages held their ground and went about the business of watering their mounts and preparing to cross the river. They would yield the ford when they were done, but they would not be run off by outlanders.

"What do you think?" young Turro asked nervously. His horse, smelling the Tarqs across the ford, stamped and whickered.

Raddox smiled. "I think...we're about to get paid." He nodded to the rear of the van to Old Oliver, who took a dozen men and cantered off south down the flank, disappearing through the blazing yellow birches and alders. The remainder of Raddox's van held their ground at the top of the ford.

The Tarqs watched the company across the river with suspicious eyes. A member of their party ran back to his Prince, who was a tall lanky fellow with red hair and beard in long banded braids. He was stripped to the waist and knelt washing beside the stream.

Steering his horse down the bank, Raddox rode out to midstream, slowly and deliberately toward the Tarqs. The Prince and his men withdrew from the water's edge reaching for weapons, the Prince himself throwing a flowing shirt of iron mail back over his head as he moved beside his horse.

"Oy!" Raddox called out across the way. "Do any of you sorry cunts speak my language?" The scroungy mercenary smiled when the Prince himself bristled. "Are you son of the Graymantle King? Prince Vyan?"

The Prince cinched a belt with sword and axe about the waist of his chain shirt and spat in the river.

"I am, and I speak your tongue, outlander," he declared in clear and well-spoken Galatti. "What business would you have?"

Raddox's eyes twinkled. "A pleasure to finally meet you, Prince of the Tarqs."

Then the golden autumn air filled with the whistle of streaking arrows.

Three of Prince Vyan's men went down straight away under Old Oliver's hail from the south. The Prince himself took an arrow through the calf and two more of his men limped away wounded as well.

Men scurried for cover. Horses screamed and reared in panic. The chaos of battle set in.

"Boys!" Raddox bellowed. He ripped the spear from his stirrup and hefted his shield. "Have at 'em! Spare the Red-Haired Prince!"

With a laughing roar Raddox charged and the sixty men remaining in his vanguard came on with him. Horses snorted and dashed through the bubbling river, pounding across the ford in a thunderous wave.

Scrambling, desperate, out-manned, the Tarqs tried to reach their mounts to escape. Well-placed arrows cut more of them down, dumping them into the rocky river brush in choking bloodied heaps.

Raddox's howling horde was upon them as fast as they could gain their mounts.

A hulking yellow-bearded Tarq shivered Raddox's shield with a two-handed blow from a great iron axe. Twisting in the saddle, Raddox plunged his spear down through the Tarq's throat in a bloody tear.

To his right, a bald-headed Tarq wearing a black wolf-pelt on his shoulder unhorsed poor Turro and stoved his head in with a scarred old mace. Knobber from Gilder Bay put a spear through the brute's back and ended him.

As his men poured onto the Tarqs like an avalanche, Raddox swung down from his stirrups and stalked through the melee in search of the Prince.

Shin deep in the river, hobbled by the arrow through his calf, and bleeding from handful of cruel cuts, Raddox found the Prince hedged in by four of his boys.

A Tarq with a tattooed face and gory gash in the side of his head charged from the chaos to come at Raddox swinging a long handled axe. Raddox got his broken shield between the tattooed Tarq and the axe for two swings, recovered his footing, and shoved back with a brutal shield bash. The Tarq was unbalanced and Raddox rushed in low, bringing his spear up with a twist, knifing it through his enemy's leathers deep into his ribs. Grinding his blade in the savage's chest, Raddox drove him to the ground and finished him.

It was over as quick as it had begun.

Of the prince's twelve men, all but two were dead and the Prince himself was surrounded in a growing ring of Raddox's fighters.

"Enough!" Raddox roared. "Throw down or die!" Old Oliver's boys closed in from the south and bent their bows. Raddox's vanguard tightened the circle, bristling with cruel steel. The only sounds were the last moans of the dying, the screams of horses, the sigh of the wind, and the babble of the river over the rocks.

Prince Vyan spat a mouthful of hot blood and pitched his sword and axe into the stream in disgust. His last two men followed his example.

"Good," Raddox grumbled. "Get him up here." Once ashore, Bolbo cracked the Tarqish Prince in the small of the back with the butt of his spear and drove him to his knees. Wounded and stunned, the Prince of the Tarqs knelt and complied.

"You belong to me," Raddox told the Prince as he cast aside his ruined shield and stripped off his gauntlets. "I intend to keep you and ransom you back to your little cunt of a father, that is if he's king enough and has cock enough to come get you." Raddox made sure the furious Prince met his eyes. "Do you understand?"

The Tarqish Prince nodded.

"Tell them," Raddox ordered, nodding toward Prince Vyan's remaining men.

Eyes burning with hate, face streaked with blood and sweat, the Tarqish Prince did as his captor commanded. He spoke to his men in the tongue of the Tarqs and as he spoke they looked sickened and stunned. Raddox figured that meant they got the point.

"Send them back to your father-king," the mercenary captain ordered. "You tell them I'll trade your sorry hide back to him for ten thousand crown or its equal. Not a penny less. And you tell 'em, if he don't pay, then I'm gonna drag ya behind my horse all the way to Westergate, tar ya, string ya up in a tree, and set ya on fire. Divine help me so."

The Prince relayed this to his battered kinsmen.

"You're a good fighter," Raddox offered. "Some of your men was even fair fighters. But I'm gonna have a piss in your face anyway, just so your boys here know I'm serious."

Prince Vyan scowled and Raddox's men clamped down on him and held him firm as their Captain unlaced and proceeded to piss in the captive Prince's face. The Prince's surviving men howled in outrage, just as Raddox intended.

They seemed to get the message.

"Cut 'em loose," Raddox ordered when it was done. The two surviving Tarqs scrounged up a single healthy mount between them and rode off frantically back toward the northwest.

The wind shivered the forest again, bringing down another shower of golden leaves as the boys of the Blackfish finished off the enemy wounded and tended their own.

The gambit was only just begun, but whichever way it turned out, this would be the last big score for the Captain of the Blackfish. Soldiering was a young and lucky man's game, and Raddox Edorian knew he was fast running out of both.

———◆———

BY THE TIME RADDOX was done with his story, bath time was over and he was drunk and hard and ready to make the little bronze skinned doe weep. He groped and grabbed and she laughed and played, but rather than take him to the bed, she led him back to the wooden bench. Drunk and chuckling, he flopped down beside his gear and pawed at her.

She grinned and babbled at him in that meaningless language of hers and carefully, she pulled away, showing him gestures that seemed to indicate she was willing, but that she wanted him to wait a moment.

Raddox was drunk and happy and miserable, so he complied.

When she came back to him she brought a black silken satchel with her. It was decorated in a beautiful constellation of silver thread. She set the satchel beside him on the bench and began to meticulously move through its contents. The girl produced several little vials of ink and a quill adorned with a red and black feather.

Raddox laughed. "What's this about?"

The girl smiled. Reaching into the satchel, she produced a polished bronze mask. Giggling she placed it over her face, but it had no slits for eyes, mouth, or nostrils. Its surface was solid, and Raddox saw it was the face of a man, not a woman. There was something familiar in the shape of the face, but without eyes, beard, hair, and the tone of polished bronze rather than flesh, it eluded him.

The girl peeked out from behind the mask, grinned lustily, and set it aside.

She was half Raddox's size, if that, and he wanted to manhandle her like a doll. But she laid a gentle hand in the middle of his chest, gave his manhood a playful squeeze, and he played along, drunk and laughing.

She opened her three inkwells and dipped the quill in each. Then, with fluid and practiced movements, a mischievous smile on her face the entire time, she began to inscribe flowing calligraphy across his bare chest. The ink, so dark as to be almost black, but not quite, did not run in the damp heat of the room.

Raddox wondered what ridiculous Kosian love ritual this was and how long he'd be tattooed by the little girl's handiwork. Surely she was invoking the blessing of some little goatish love goddess before bouncing away merrily on his cock like she was paid to do. He chuckled and prattled on while she tickled his skin with her little quill.

"Oh, hell, did the boys love to torment that damn Prince," he muttered. "And they did. They fed him live rats and made him piss in his own face." Raddox laughed without humor. "Guess I inspired 'em, huh? And his father-king was gonna pay up too, if you can believe that. He was riding to treat with us at Grippa when that little cunt of a son of his tries to escape. Well…we couldn't have that, could we? So Old Oliver puts two arrows in the Prince's back and there wasn't nothing for it then but to take the hammer to his head and be done with it."

Raddox's face darkened, and his eyes grew once more distant, the little girl scribbling her funny sigils across his body all but forgotten. His grim smile was all teeth and no joy.

"The King of the Tarqs was mighty unhappy when he rode up to pay his ransom and found his son and kinsmen all dead. You shoulda seen his face when I says to him 'Your son was worth ten thousand…how much is *you* worth?'" The grizzled mercenary laughed, both sickened and amused by his own story.

"Ah, we set on the big gray-bearded bastard then. Set on him good. Killed half his men and kicked the gooseshit outta the other half." Raddox nodded, self-satisfied. "Then they got away…the King and his men we'd offended…Just like they was supposed to."

The girl offered no reply. She continued to scribble away with dexterous little flickers of her quill.

"Then the Prince's brothers, they just kept comin' south. Smashed right into Outer Galadyr, burning farms and sacking at Valnya. And that…was that. There was war then, whether anybody wanted it or not."

Raddox nodded. "A job done perfectly, I estimate. And so we

was heading home to get paid." He was suddenly very quiet. His distant eyes teared up and his voice got husky. "I got a funny feelin' about it, ya know? Like maybe what we done wasn't something the men who'd hired us could afford to let get out. And they're the sort o' men who can move mountains if it suits 'em."

A tear fell then. Just one. It rolled down his scruffy cheek and dripped from his chin to land on his rune-inscribed chest. The ink did not run, even under the salty tear.

"So I did a very uncaptainly thing to my boys," Raddox said. "I robbed 'em blind and I ran. Took everything I could carry and made for a port and a boat as fast as I could fly." He blinked the tears away and tried to laugh. "And I wasn't wrong. Misfortune done caught up to all my boys, one by one, and fast. Tall men got their war. I got my boys' gold. My boys got their deaths."

Raddox wanted to reach out for his goblet of wine. He didn't like feeling these things, and wine was a cure for that.

Only then did he realize he couldn't move.

There was no humor left on the girl's face as she finished the last rune with a flare of her quill. She stood up, naked and beautiful, skin glistening in the steamy bath chamber heat.

But Raddox felt suddenly cold.

Weight pushed in on his chest, making it hard to breathe. With each breath he let out, the pressure tightened, making the next one he took in smaller and smaller.

"Wha…." he wheezed, frozen as a statue as the girl produced a small, keen, curved knife from the black satchel, wicked as a barber's razor.

The runes inked on his flesh seeped into his skin, like glowing iron melting into ice, but cold rather than hot, dark rather than vibrant. No poison could take him, not with the runes of protection about his throat. There were few men he feared to face with steel in hand.

But this witchcraft, this was something he was wholly unprepared for.

Helpless, he watched as ghostly faces of his dead and betrayed comrades began to appear in the mist and the incense smoke. First one. Old Oliver. Then poor Turro. Knobber. Five Fingered Jack. They were there. They were coming.

His breath was gone. His lungs would not expand.

"What do you see?" the girl whispered to him flawlessly in his mother tongue, even though clearly he could not answer.

The ghosts in the mist pressed in around them as she took up the glittering, evil razor. They whispered to him in the flickering nightmarish gloom. "Welcome, brother."

Voice by ghostly voice, the chorus grew. Raddox would have screamed if he'd had the breath to do so. He looked desperately to the girl but found no more comfort there.

Taking up the little silver blade, she angled it along his jaw.

With a long, sweet final kiss, she began to cut.

———◆———

HALF A WORLD AWAY and many weeks later, Giori Dondain glided along the docks of Westergate like an alley cat. The hour was late and legitimate business was sparse. The groan of old planks, the creaking of ropes, the lap of the sea, the occasional bursts of distant laughter from the sailors' taverns. These were the only sounds.

Giori was accustomed to this environment and the lateness of the hour. Such was his trade, from his days as a humble knife-boy for the Harbor Rats to his more lucrative and recent days currying favor with the wealthy and powerful. There was no rough dock or darkened alley that intimidated Giori Dondain.

Meeting face to face with one of the Gray Sisters, however, was another matter. Dwelling on it too much slowed his pace and made his feet heavy, so he did his best to put it out of his mind.

The ship he sought flew beneath a Sundish flag and he could read the rolling foreign script on the fantail marking it as the *Silver Voyager*.

He walked up the gangplank like he owned the ship and the hidden shadows guarding the deck did nothing to bar his passage.

He found her waiting for him below in a chamber lit by a single lantern.

She was a tiny woman, a raven-haired beauty with rich bronze skin and dark almond shaped eyes. Her attire was simple, functional. She was the embodiment of stillness, seated at a small round table beside the pale glowing lantern. There were no guards with her in the chamber and no weapon in sight. That did nothing to ease Giori's sense of apprehension.

"It is done," she said softly, her voice touched with the accent of Valar.

"Are you certain?" Giori asked.

The woman smiled. "With the certainty of my own hand." Reaching down beside the table, she produced a box and slid it across to Giori.

With a nervous swallow, Giori removed the lid from the box and did his best to hide his revulsion. He'd seen his far share of violence, done his share of killing. Brutality and death were never pretty.

However, he'd never seen a man's surgically skinned face so meticulously tanned and mounted to a bronze mask before. That was a first, even for a scoundrel as worldly as Giori. The likeness of Raddox Edorian was unmistakable. Alien and lifeless, with bronze teeth showing between thin lips and empty bronze eyes showing through sleepy, half-closed lids, but it was the man, nonetheless. Pale as fallen snow and dead as a doll, the fate of Raddox Edorian was certain as far as Giori was concerned.

"We are…most pleased," Giori offered, putting the lid back on the ghoulish box. "All arrangements will be seen to, in good faith, as promised."

"Good," the tiny woman offered with a gracious nod.

"If we were…to need your services again, how would I find you?"

"You and I will never see each other again," the woman assured him plainly. "But if you have need of us, my Sisters will find *you*. As we did before."

"Understood," Giori offered with a forced, but charming smile. He swallowed and asked the hardest question of the night. "As… arranged…there are no means known to…compel Raddox Edorian to divulge secrets…even in death?" Most men would scoff at such a notion, but Giori knew it to be possible. He'd seen it, with his own horrified eyes. His employer knew it to be possible too.

The little woman smiled, radiant and beautiful, even in the pale lamplight.

"He who holds *this*, holds all the man's secrets," she offered, touching the tips of her fingers lightly to the gruesome box. "I assure you, no man's soul escapes the Long Kiss."

The price of such assurances was nothing short of monstrous. But there were men in this world who could pay such prices. Giori's employer was among them.

With that the little woman rose from behind the table, handed Giori his box, took him by the hand and led him back above decks to the gangplank.

"It has been a pleasure," the Gray Sister told him. Then, stretching up on tiny tiptoes, she kissed him on the cheek in parting.

For a moment, Giori's breath froze in fear, then he let it trickle slowly out.

The woman smiled, her eyes twinkling in the moonlight.

"Fear not," she said. "That is only a small kiss."

Giori, wanting no part of her kisses, Long or small, counted his blessings and shuffled quickly down the gangplank with his gruesome box. Before he was out of sight down the docks, the *Silver Voyager*'s rowers were underway and she was moving into the harbor, sails unfurling in the moonlight.

Neither she, nor the Gray Sister, would ever visit Westergate again.

Of course, neither would Raddox Edorian. Or his secrets.

THE WHITE ROSE THIEF

-*Tales of Annwn*-

SHAWN SPEAKMAN

When I finished writing The Dark Thorn, *I knew I would further explore its dangerous fey world of Annwn.*

"The White Rose Thief" does that. It is the story of Rosenwyn Whyte, a musician with a dark past, a woman possessed of talents that are coveted by the evil and powerful alike. A repentant thief, she is coerced to steal powerful magic from a creature thought dead. Of course, things are not as they seem. I wanted to look at how being born different could affect a person's life; I wanted to look at how those differences could push a person into a life they did not want —and possibly and ultimately save them.

I hope you enjoy the path Rosenwyn Whyte must tread.

THE FINAL NOTE OF the *crwth* died in silence, followed by raucous applause.

Rosenwyn Whyte lowered the stringed instrument and its bow, inclining her head in polite recognition. The audience cheered all the more. She sat upon a slightly elevated stage at the Raging Drunk, the largest inn and tavern in Annwn's northern city of Mur Castell, no other musicians accompanying her. Although larger than most, the Raging Drunk was like many such establishments she often played—smoky, loud, and the odor of crowded, unwashed humanity mingling with beer grown long sour. It attracted patrons from all castes, from the wealthy sitting in the upper balconies to the vagabonds who had managed to escape the notice of burly Byl Cornwyll, the owner. The Everwinter drove all of them inside, its snow and ice an indiscriminate hardship for all, while music and drunken fellowship offered the only solace.

The unnaturally long winter had been good to Rosenwyn though. Music helped people forget the terrible season, and music was her trade. This night, the crowd had been large. Money emptied from pockets to fill flagons with beer.

"THE WHITE ROSE THIEF"

Illustration by **ORION ZANGARA**

Not that Rosenwyn saw much of either.

"Yeh were a might amazin' again, Rosie," Byl Cornwyll said, having pushed his way from behind the bar through the crowd to tower over her.

"A great room, Byl, as usual."

The owner of the Raging Drunk grinned, wringing his large hands on a damp bar towel that hung at his waist. A nervous habit that made her smile. "That was one helluva rendition of *The Ballad of Gor Dwallyn*. Never heard its like sung. Found damnable tears in me eyes, ah did. Had to turn away."

"You are too big a man to cry, Byl," Rosenwyn said, smiling, tucking the crwth safely away within a padded carrying pouch.

"And yeh are too beautiful to play in holes like this," the other said, winking. "Do yeh have plans for tomorrow night? Another go? If these people do not see me ask, they will burn the Drunk down, ah swear."

"I will let you know later tonight," she said, massaging the stress from her hands.

"Yeh know where ah'll be."

Rosenwyn nodded her thanks. Byl made his way back behind the bar. He would pay her when most had left the common room— and beg her to stay one more night. She might accept. The Raging Drunk was one of her favorite places to play in all of Annwn. And Byl paid her better than most innkeepers, which meant she received more than just food and lodging. But not much more.

"You play with magic, love."

Still gathering her things, Rosenwyn turned. A man stared at her with piercing blue eyes, as bold as any hunter's. He was younger than her but that would not matter in his mind. She cursed inwardly. These were the moments she hated.

"It is a gift," she said simply. "And I work hard to improve upon it. Thank you for coming to the Raging Drunk. It helps keep me playing here."

"I am Aron McManus. May I buy you a beer?" he asked. "Better yet, a meal?"

There it was. Men could be so transparent sometimes. He prized her more for her status and appearance than the woman behind the music.

"If there is one thing I already get paid in, it's the necessities of life," Rosenwyn said, smiling her best to defuse the forthcoming situation. "And besides that, I see you coming from a town away, sir. Better for you to find another woman to entertain."

His smile became uncertain. "If I gave you the wrong impression, I apologize. You play lovely music but it pales to your beauty. One drink. That is all."

"Flattery will get you nowhere this night."

McManus darkened. "I think you misunderst—"

"Lady Rosenwyn Whyte!"

Both Rosenwyn and her suitor cringed as a fairy flew into their midst, its rainbow-hued gossamer wings a blur. The fey creature was no more than a hand tall, his naked body the color of damp ash. Rosenwyn did not care much for the fey. But she was pleased this one had interrupted a conversation that was about to become ugly.

Rather than talk to her though, the fairy hovered before the man and gave him a knowing grin that held no humor.

"*Crotchlove*, leave before this becomes painful for you," the fairy said.

"Fairy, should I squish you right now?" he asked.

"I will only say it once."

McManus turned crimson. "Look here, you little snit, no one tells me wha—"

"I know why you stand here still," the fey creature said, his tiny black eyes now appraising Rosenwyn. "Her hair, red as flame, a powerful shade to possess. The alabaster skin, as if it has never seen the tarnishing effects of sunlight. The blue eyes, so deep one could drown in them. That tiny mole by her sensuous lips. The sharp cheekbones and lithe figure. A worthy prize to lust after." The fey creature magically called forth a tiny sword that flared briefly and returned his gaze back to the man. "But if you do not leave us to our business, *whelp*, I will start with your sight. Test me, and you will never view another beautiful woman again."

The words held impatience. And certainty. The suitor glared, assessing his small foe; with the sword, the lightning-fast creature could be quite dangerous.

The man knew this. Rosenwyn hid her smile as she watched McManus' bravado diminish. "I beg your forgiveness, Lady Whyte," he said finally and, giving the fairy an angry last look, vanished into the crowd.

"Not that red is your natural hair color, of course," the fairy continued, his sword suddenly evaporating into nothing. "White, isn't it? Not that I care how adept you are at disguise. I rather like the red. Fiery."

Rosenwyn frowned, chill prickling her skin. "Who are you?"

"One who was sent to find you."

The chill became ice in her veins, her anger rising. "Who do you serve? That sword of yours might scare randy buggers looking for a toss in the sheets but it does not frighten me."

"If it did, my benefactor would be greatly unimpressed by your fabled prowess."

"Play your game," Rosenwyn said, grabbing her instrument and deciding another night at the Raging Drunk was not in the cards. "I have my own. And they will not be dictated by the likes of the fey."

"A redhead's birthright. The game is about to get more

interesting," the fairy said, blocking her path by flying in front of her to bow in midair. "I am Bazltrix. And I am here on the behalf of Lady Audeph Klestmark of Mur Castell, a woman in need of your help and great many talents."

"Never heard of her."

"She knows of you. *That* is what matters."

Rosenwyn hated being at a disadvantage. It was a part of her life though. Playing in taverns, surrounded by unknown people. Most of them simply enjoyed her music. Some had ulterior motives though. Bazltrix had scared off one such person but the man's motives had been easy to decipher. The motives of the fairy and his benefactor were not.

"What does she want of me?" Rosenwyn asked.

"That is for Lady Klestmark to share."

Rosenwyn appraised Bazltrix a moment. "Where is she then?"

"Outside," the fairy said, his charcoal face pinched with the gravity of his request. "Anonymity is a requirement. The Everwinter offers it best."

The tiny hairs along the back of her neck prickled warning. The area where the Raging Drunk conducted business was one of the safest districts in Mur Castell. Annwn had become more chaotic after the fall of Caer Llion though. Evil existed everywhere.

"To be alone on the streets of Mur Castell at night with an unknown woman and her fairy is not wise, I am afraid," Rosenwyn growled, already weaving her way past the flying creature. "I think your benefactor will have to find aid elsewhere."

"Lady Klestmark anticipated this," Bazltrix said, flying after. He removed something from a small cloth sack on his back. He then offered the item to her.

Curiosity trumping uneasiness, Rosenwyn accepted the item. She immediately wished she hadn't; a dark rage filled her as she held a small diamond spider, no larger than her thumbnail. It caught the candle and torchlight and glowed like the summer sun. It was a beautiful piece of art, symmetrical and flawless. There were only three in existence. And it was worth a fortune to the right people.

Its monetary worth did not matter to Rosenwyn, though. She gripped the spider, its legs cutting into her palm. The present world faded around her until all she could see was a past she had tried to escape, tried to forget.

This had once been her sigil. The Lleidr Corryn.

The calling token for a master thief.

"Unfortunately, someone else is not an option," Bazltrix sniffed with indignation. "I trust you are ready to go now?"

Rosenwyn cursed her luck.

———◆———

THE EVERWINTER SWIRLED ABOUT her as she left the Raging Drunk.

After having donned her fur-lined sable cloak and boots, Rosenwyn followed the fairy as he flew through the streets of Mur Castell. She pulled her cloak and its cowl close for warmth, the crwth on her back comforting as well. She had spoken to Byl briefly, sharing she would be leaving the inn for a while, telling him only what he needed to know. He had nodded, worry darkening his thick features as he frowned at the fairy, but he did not ask questions. She knew Byl well. He would undoubtedly send one of his kitchen boys to follow and watch from the shadows—a modicum of security.

Despite his nakedness, Bazltrix flew through the Everwinter seemingly unbothered by the elements, a silent black form in a world become white. She did not know what to expect from the forthcoming meeting. Her past had found her, one way or another, and there was no escaping it. Not from someone who possessed the Lleidr Corryn. Right now, even as she walked through the chill, there could be a hundred crossbow bolts pointed at her. Or none. One never knew. That's how these kinds of transactions happened. The life she had left behind long before the Everwinter began had been one of high reward with high risk. On reflection, it should have led to her death many times. Back then, of course, that thought had never crossed her mind. She had been young and impulsive, fearless and naïve.

She was older and more cautious now. She had left that life for one of music. Old memories were kept where they belonged—in the past. She had changed.

Fingering a dagger in her cloak's inner pocket with one hand and wearing a knife-ring on the other, Rosenwyn felt a stab of irony twisting inside her.

Some things never changed, it seemed.

At least there was no moon or stars this night to worry about.

"Where are you taking me?" she asked darkly. "I thought you said she was just outside."

The fairy either did not hear or was ignoring her.

She kept her frustration in check; it would not serve her this night. They eventually entered the primary courtyard of the city, so large she could barely see the other side. In summer, a market blossomed here, filled with colorful tents bearing produce, clothing, weapons, sweets, games, and other bazaar items. It was now a gray void. Directly across from her rose the ruling castle of Mur Castell, its walls tall, thick, and coated in ice and snow, torchlight flickering from various places giving just enough light to see by. Rosenwyn kept a keen eye on the fairy as he flew directly toward a massive stake that had been driven into the courtyard's stone. There, a figure stood, waiting.

Rosenwyn considered the situation. She didn't like it. The courtyard of Mur Castell had become a place of death. Earlier in the year, Caderyn Llewellyn, the lord of the great city, had burned a witch to death at the stake, retribution for the murder of his wife. The city had watched. Rosenwyn had not seen it, but she knew the tales and they chilled her. The fire. The screaming for mercy. The stench.

Its length charred, the giant stake remained as a gruesome warning:

Do not attack the royal family of Mur Castell.

While no one else appeared, it was an unsettling place for a meeting. And even as Bazltrix landed on the charred pole, a black stain amidst the Everwinter, the hooded figure by the stake did not move to meet her.

"Well met, Rosenwyn White," the woman said as the musician approached. "I am Lady Audeph Klestmark. I have to say, I am impressed. I could not hear you approach despite the snow and ice, your footfalls were so light."

"My craft often requires steady hands and steadier feet."

"And what craft is that exactly?" the lady asked with a hint of dark amusement. "A musician? Or a thief *unfettered?* No, do not answer. It matters not. I do, however, thank you for responding to my request."

"It felt like more a summons. One I could not deny," Rosenwyn said, fingering her hidden knife. "But you know that already."

"The diamond spider *does* possess that power."

Rosenwyn nodded, observing the other. There was not much to see. Like the musician, Lady Audeph Klestmark wore a cloak and hood, a tall, thin figure, cut like a dark blade. What light existed emphasized round eyes above sharp cheekbones, full lips, and a hint of black hair curled beneath her cowl.

"I am no longer a Lleidr Corryn," Rosenwyn asserted. "She was a master thief. And died long ago."

"You have many gifts, Lady Whyte, but playing coy in an attempt to deceive me is not one of them," the lady said coldly. "Do *not* be any more foolish than you have just been, *Spider Thief.*"

Rosenwyn had once been a favorite tool and done the bidding of many wealthy patrons, from lords and kings to merchant princes and their wives. No matter her outward appearance, Lady Audeph Klestmark was not one of them. They possessed a languid, indifferent air. The woman standing before her emanated an icy righteousness and a willingness to risk everything. Lady Klestmark would do anything to possess the thief's talents—as evidenced by the Lleidr Corryn. If the thief denied her, the woman would have her killed. Outright. Likely this night. And if not tonight, there were two men who would love to know Rosenwyn's location and they would finish the deed. Chill not born of the Everwinter infiltrated her. Despite her youthful appearance, the woman's shadowy gaze possessed a hatred so potent it could never be refused, especially not by a mere thief, retired or no.

For the first time in many years, fear gripped Rosenwyn Whyte. Real fear, as bone deep as the Everwinter itself.

"The Spider Thief lives, yes. I hate that she does."

"A first for everything, I fear, my dear," Lady Klestmark said with a small laugh, the threat behind her gaze gone as quickly as it had come. "You are also the Unseen Hand. The White Shadow. The Caer Ghost. Several other colorful names you have undoubtedly heard. The rich and powerful in all cities have different names for you. You are a legend, albeit a dubious one cursed aloud in private chambers or uttered in dark whispers upon the wind. And I have need of your legendary talents. I will pay handsomely for them, regardless of the token I possess."

"That part of my life is *over*," Rosenwyn said.

"The past." Lady Klestmark scoffed. "The past is always a part of our present, Lady Whyte. Do not be so quick to dismiss that fact."

"What does this have to do with?" Rosenwyn, steeled by anger again, tried to maintain some kind of control over the situation, but she knew what would happen if she refused the offer.

"As I said, I need your talents."

"For?"

"Finally we are getting somewhere useful," Lady Klestmark said. "A bit of background first though. The story of Saith yn Col. Once, the ruins were not ruined, rather a castle and keep called Caer Dathal where the first Druid Order built their home upon arriving in Annwn from those long-lost Misty Isles. The Druids worked hard at acquiring knowledge of all kinds. And people benefited from that. But when a dark faction overtook the order and tried to enslave Annwn, the most powerful fey of the Tuatha de Dannan gathered and destroyed that menace. The rebel Druids were killed. Caer Dathal of Old was destroyed in those battles, renamed Saith yn Col. It has remained that way since, a reminder of the danger excess power creates.

"The Druids who did not join the rebels were free to begin their order again, this time at Caer Dathal the New, where they live to this day."

"Then you want me to break into Caer Dathal and steal something that has been kept there from the days since it moved?"

"No." Lady Klestmark smirked. "I want something from Saith yn Col."

"I am a thief, not a ruins digger." Rosenwyn hated to admit still being a thief.

"Do you think for one moment I would need to acquire your

services if I could just visit the ruins of Saith yn Col myself and take what I desire?" Lady Klestmark said, laughing without humor. "Maybe you are not as bright as I have been led to believe."

Rosenwyn hated being mocked even more.

"Have you played your music at Caer Dathal?" Lady Klestmark asked.

"Several times." Rosenwyn's breath plumed on the air. "It is a beautiful keep. Arch Druid Aengus Doughal is always warm and welcoming. So too his Druids and students."

"You know of the grotesques that ward that keep then?"

"The gargoyles? Yes," Rosenwyn said. "They sit about the keep. I have never seen one move though. Probably just mummery, to scare visitors."

"Oh, they are more than alive, my dear. Caer Dathal of Old had similar magical creatures protecting its walls. They could not withstand the might of the Erlking and Tal Ebolyon's dragon might. The grotesques were destroyed like their rebel Druid masters, reduced to broken statuary and dust. All but one." The lady paused. "One grotesque survived, the strongest among them, and this stone creature has been there ever since, within the ruins of a keep he could not protect."

"I am to steal something from this gargoyle then?"

"He is named the Nix, a terrible creature, powerful and ancient." Lady Klestmark's gaze intensified. "It should have perished as the rest of his brethren. Caer Dathal of Old is destroyed; there is no need to protect Saith yn Col. Yet the Nix remains. He does not possess the power to leave his ruins, magic binding him to the former Druid keep. But I believe he is gathering more than just secrets from that age."

"If the Nix cannot roam free, how does he gather anything?" Rosenwyn disliked the fact she was already intrigued.

"No one knows. Perhaps a thief in his employ. Or a magic unfamiliar to me. Regardless, this task I ask of you will be dangerous for numerous reasons."

"I have heard those words before. All too often."

"Little is known about the ruins beneath Saith yn Col," Lady Klestmark said. "It will be fraught with peril. Less is known about where the Nix holds his treasures. It will be dangerous, even for one of the Lleidr Corryn."

"My price is steep then, perhaps too steep for one such as yourself." Rosenwyn stood straighter, showing her resolve. "You possess the Lleidr Corryn and you have a certain amount of power over me because of it, but no power over my price, which I and I alone set."

"Hear that, Bazltrix? She knows her worth." An icy smile crossed Lady Klestmark's pale features. The fairy nodded, barely interested, even as the woman removed a glove to reveal rings adorning every finger. "You are right, Lady Whyte. Jewels. Precious metals. Like these. These would be poor attempts at acquiring your talents. I wonder though, looking at you, knowing something of your past, if you would rather gain the ability to walk in the light—sunlight, moonlight, starlight—without others staring at you, hating you, or questioning you? Would that be an adequate payment for your services?" She paused. "What is the *price* for being human?"

Rosenwyn barely breathed. Lady Klestmark knew of her bane, the very thing that shackled her to the shadows. If she completed the charge, the reward would be a chance at something she had wanted since childhood.

A normal life.

"That is impossible," she whispered.

"Is it?" Lady Klestmark asked, just as serious. "Even Bazltrix does not know the full extent of my standing. With wealth comes power and with power comes opportunity. I know people. More importantly, I know the *right* people. There are those in my employ who possess magic. A great deal of magic." She smiled. "How ironic. The music you have replaced your former life with might be the very talent that undoes that past."

"Why would you say that?"

"Because grotesques are fond of music."

Rosenwyn now knew why she had been chosen. She had once been a master thief, true, but she was also a musician. The other two Lleidr Corryn were not.

It made sense.

Long moments passed.

"Not that I am accepting—because there *will* come a time when my death is more desirable than a job I am to take—but what am I to steal?"

Lady Audeph Klestmark smiled. Both women knew she had won her thief.

"The Grimoires of the rebel Druids, Lady Lleidr Corryn."

—◦—

LOST IN THOUGHT, ROSENWYN ignored the Everwinter chill.

She rode Wennyl eastward out of Mur Castell, cloaked in a black as dark as the Rhedewyr she sat upon. Wennyl had been the price of one of her first heists, a miraculous animal that had become her best friend, strong in ways normal horses were not, aware of her every mood and circumstance. Rhedewyr were difficult for humans to come by; if one lost its first rider to death, the horse usually died from sorrow. Some did not though. Rosenwyn and Wennyl had bonded upon meeting and they had been together ever since. The fey mount had carried her over much of Annwn, seen her through the most difficult thefts, and now the stallion moved through the snows toward the ruins of Saith yn Col, the elements barely a hindrance.

As Mur Castell faded behind her, she embraced the solitude of the peaceful road, senses always attuned to possible danger.

And thought about Lady Klestmark's offer.

From her earliest memories, Rosenwyn had been a thief. She did not understand the moral implications of such a life. Few four year olds needed to. She had learned them from the hardest of lives, to survive the river city streets of Velen Rhyd, to eat when others would starve. She rarely thought about her painful childhood—one spent stealing while evading the Red Crosses even as she outwitted older bullies and those who would try to exploit her abilities. But being summoned by the Lleidr Corryn token brought those memories to the fore, like angry slivers buried deep beneath her skin. Velen Rhyd was a threadbare city, barely able to sustain even its poor and, having lost her parents and older siblings to fire, she alone had survived. She hid the secret of her magic even then despite the fearful whispers on the streets. Halfbreed. Fey.

More witch than little girl.

No one back then knew her an actual secret. But children can sense truth without actually witnessing it. There was a reason she only ventured out at night. There was a reason she kept her skin covered. Her family had known. The night had replaced the family she had lost, become her first friend, camouflaging her unpredictable magic.

As she grew so did her thieving abilities, not because of the blood that flowed through her veins but because stealing ensured survival.

It did not take long for her to come to the attention of Vrace

Erryn. Young but already accomplished, he had trained Rosenwyn, shaping her like a master artist does a sculpture. Together, they had stolen from the capital of Caer Llion. Together, they had cheated Magwyn Mog within his spell-protected wizard warren. Together, they had taken a rare dragon egg from Tal Ebolyon just to watch it hatch.

And together they had become Lleidr Corryn.

Until the day Vrace broke her heart. Had tried to kill her. And she vanished from the game, beginning a new life as a wandering musician.

As far as she knew, Vrace and the older Rol Macleod remained in their trade. She had thought herself safe, far enough removed from that former life to escape notice from everyone, including the death the two men owed her for breaking the Lleidr Corryn vow.

Lady Audeph Klestmark had proven that thought wrong.

If she could find her, who else could?

Wennyl snorted, a ghost plume dying on the air.

"I know, boy." Rosenwyn patted the stallion's great neck, her annoyance matching his. "We will disappear again soon. I promise."

The path continued, the Everwinter a constant companion. The snow had stopped. No stars appeared, leaving Rosenwyn thankful. They possessed a light, no matter how faint, that brought the magic in her blood to life. Even though all parts of her skin were covered—including her eyes by darkglass goggles and a veil over her mouth—she had to be vigilant. It was a danger she lived with every day.

To be free of that curse would be worth one more theft.

If she survived.

As midnight came and went, the two companions came to a stone marker set along the road where another, smaller path intersected it, the marker's worn face covered in ice and snow.

Rosenwyn dismounted. She struck a match into life.

She could just make out the age-worn words chiseled on the stone sign.

– CAER DATHAL –

ROSENWYN GRUNTED. THAT CASTLE keep no longer existed. At least not in this part of the world. It had become Saith yn Col, home to one lone stubborn piece of rock.

"Easy part over," she said sarcastically.

Wennyl snorted and she remounted. They left the road for the smaller path, the forest closing in on them as if to strangle their passage. Rosenwyn ignored the feeling; unlike many thieves, she was not superstitious. The great oaks that suffocated the trail grew wilder the deeper they traveled, until frozen limbs threatened to unseat her. She dismounted then, sending her senses into the Everwinter around her, abilities honed to feel danger no matter its quarter. Nothing presented itself; no sound betrayed otherwise. With Wennyl quietly behind, Rosenwyn crossed over icy streams, the trail shrinking as it winded over small hills, until the ground flattened and the great oaks began to thin, the musician become thief-once-again finally viewing beyond her immediate vicinity.

She almost could not comprehend what she saw. Saith yn Col laid before her, the remnants of Caer Dathal of Old spreading into the distance. She gauged the situation from the forest. It did not look promising. The ruins were a black mess, the height of dead stone heaving out of the world making it difficult to measure the breadth of it all. She could imagine Caer Dathal then, the grand towers and buildings that had once filled the sky, the bustling, lively community, and pennants flying in the wind—all brought low by a battle waged centuries earlier. It spoke to the might of the Unseelie Court and the dragons of Tal Ebolyon. Many people had died, their remains crushed beneath. Caer Dathal of Old was no longer a place of learning; it had become a graveyard of stone and buried bone, a place where death had taken up ancient residence.

Only one tower remained, once probably the shortest. It had outlived its brethren, tall compared to the thief, its merlons ripped free but otherwise intact.

Rosenwyn took a deep breath, cursing Audeph Klestmark all the more. She moved Wennyl back into the forest, out of sight for anyone—or any gargoyle—that did not know of the fey horse's presence.

"Wish me speed and silence, old friend."

Wennyl stared back at her, his awareness mixed with fire.

She rubbed his nose, already looking back toward Saith yn Col. With footfalls light upon the frozen snow, she moved with soundless purpose. The last hours of night were upon her world, a clock ticking against her magical ailment, and while she shielded herself from the light it would not do well to linger, being exposed to the very thing that could alarm the gargoyle if her clothing and goggles failed. She strode the perimeter, not venturing into the ruins. Yet. If Audeph Klestmark was to be believed, gargoyles were perceptive creatures and the thief's continued anonymity would serve her best.

She crept into Saith yn Col as a ghost, ferreting its secrets. It had been many years since her last theft, but she found her skills right where she had left them, all too eager to be used.

It left her even more annoyed

The past remained, no matter her attempts to discard it.

Finishing her initial appraisal of Saith yn Col and not finding anything, Rosenwyn entered the short tower, grappling to its exposed top and dropping inside on cat's feet. But the structure had long been a dead shell, possessing nothing of interest. No treasure trove. And thankfully no grotesque. She then silently scaled the mounds of broken walls and buildings, searching outward from the center of Caer Dathal of Old in concentric circles, looking for any entrances into the rubble. That too yielded no results. She cursed silently. Saith yn Col was as unlike any situation she had entered. In that past, having accepted a job, she had always prepared, learning all she could. Surprises could get one killed all too easily and knowledge could be the key to living another day. But the destruction here wrought centuries earlier had left Caer Dathal of Old a formidable riddle, with none of the entrances and exits of her previous thieving forays had possessed.

Hating to admit defeat and her chance at a normal life, she leaned against a broken wall of the inner keep, considering her lack of options.

That's when her instincts tingled.

A lesser thief might have ignored them. Rosenwyn cocked her head, listening to an odd deadness on the air. Trusting those instincts, she shrunk down and moved over the ruins, quietly searching. It did not take her long to find an intact wall where the rubble had been moved aside.

Another wall—once part of the keep—met it. And where they intersected, a hidden maw of blackness waited where steps vanished into the bowels of Saith yn Col.

Massive footprints. Pressed into the snow around the opening. Unlike any Rosenwyn had ever seen.

Sign of the Nix.

And this was most likely the only entrance—and therefore the only exit.

Thieves abhorred such things.

Heart quickened, Rosenwyn retreated to crouch behind stones atop the ruins a short distance away, her eyes never leaving the wide hole leading to some unknown subterranean depth. Long moments passed. They became longer. Rosenwyn still did not move, thinking. The sky to the east began to lighten as a new snow fell. The day would soon be upon her. She fought the cold that threatened without as her thoughts turned icy within. Saith yn Col was an impossible task, she realized with real regret. She knew many a foolhardy thief, but few who would risk such a passage as that yawning gap. She simply did not possess enough information to overcome the terrible odds. Undoubtedly, the Nix waited for her below. A creature created to protect, it would have installed any number of physical or magical traps to protect Caer Dathal of Old.

Worse, the gargoyle could be waiting, right where true darkness first blinds.

Able to end her life easily.

No matter how much it galled the Lleidr Corryn, the situation was beyond her.

"Enough of this," she whispered, not happy having to convince herself of the truth. She was no coward but it had to be more equal than this.

She would return to Audeph Klestmark. This job was no job.

It was suicide.

That is when she saw the glowing eyes.

Rosenwyn almost thought it a trick of her imagination. In the feeble illumination of the night, even her eyes—eyes that had become as strong as any cat's—could not decipher what stared at her. The orbs looked like tiny lamps that floated in the dark, unblinking and unwavering.

"I see you are aware of me, Woman of Many Talents," the

darkness rumbled from within the entrance, the voice deep like stone grinding against stone.

Rosenwyn froze, torn between flight and intrigue.

"Standing still will not help you disappear," the darkness mocked.

"I did not think it would."

"Good. Now go. These ruins are no longer for the living."

Rosenwyn took a deep breath, bolstering her resolve. "Who do I have the pleasure of conversing?" she asked, fighting to keep her voice free of fear.

"I was wrong, in part. A *well-spoken* Woman of Many Talents," the voice digressed. It carried authority and something else. Curiosity? "An oddity in these broken wilds, that much I know." The Nix paused. "Tell me, Woman of Many Talents, should you not leave? This is where our conversation parts."

"Why do you keep calling me that?"

The eyes shifted in their tunnel. "Beauty is truth, truth beauty—that is all ye know on earth and all ye need to know."

"I was not prepared to meet a poet."

"It is not my own. Yet I hold it close." The eyes wavered as if leaving. "Go. There are warmer climes for your frail form than these stones." She did not move, willing the other to notice. "Do you woo death?" the Nix grated finally.

There it was. The threat.

At least the gargoyle had not left.

"I will not leave," Rosenwyn said. "Not until you step free of your home and truly reveal yourself. I have come a long way for that very thing."

The Nix grunted. "Unlike you, *I* was created with patience."

The eyes vanished. Rosenwyn waited but they did not return. She wagered the Nix would not be gone long. He would reappear.

Eventually. Curiosity ruled the creature. She had sensed it with every lingering sentence the gargoyle had spoken. And something else. Loneliness?

Rosenwyn slowed her adrenaline from the meeting and navigated back toward the forest. She needed to think. She had not expected to meet the Nix so quickly—especially a creature of such intelligence. It changed her approach in acquiring the grimoires she sought. Carefully exiting the ruins, she found Wennyl first, gathering a pack containing her supplies and a heavy blanket that would help ward off the chill while she built a fire. As the sky lightened in the east toward dawn, she did a quick visual of herself, ensuring no skin had become exposed during the night, and then sparked a small fire to life, its warmth chasing the cold that had followed her from Mur Castell.

The Nix did not appear throughout the day. It did not bother Rosenwyn. Thieves also possessed great patience. The gargoyle would emerge again during the day.

If he did not, she would be ready.

When night began to fall on Saith yn Col and the Nix still had not revealed himself once more, she pulled free her crwth and its bow from their case.

And closing her eyes, she began to play.

Rosenwyn chose *The Fall of Tember Tu*, the ballad describing the destruction of a mythical castle, beautiful quartz spires banded in silver brought low by the forces of dark midnight spawn. She poured all of her emotion into the epic song, building the tragedy of the city as well as the sorrow of two young lovers separated when the battle began. The Lleidr Corryn left her past behind then, a musician once more, letting her crwth and voice weave together in ways that had reduced the hardest men to tears. She bled her craft, the music infiltrating Saith yn Col. Rosenwyn felt the ghosts who now inhabited the ruins, and it made her sad that such grandeur could die in the world.

When the last note faded altogether, Rosenwyn took a deep breath and opened her eyes to the dying day.

"You are a mistress possessed of beautifully haunting music."

Suspecting her actions would bring the gargoyle, Rosenwyn feigned surprise and located him. The Nix sat regally tall on massive haunches where the forest met Saith yn Col, a stone dragon three times her height made from dark gray stone laced with tiny veins of silver. But unlike the dragons that flew over Annwn, the Nix appeared crippled, his long tail, wings, and left arm shattered, broken stone. His eyes burned bright though; no weakness stared at her. Power radiated from the ancient guardian. It remained a force to be reckoned.

A silver shield containing a single oak acorn winked from his left breast, reflecting the orange and yellow light of the fire.

"Thank you," she said simply.

The Nix looked into the branches of the frozen oaks, eyes lost to the past. "*The Fall of Tember Tu* had long been one my favorite songs. Poignant. Sorrowful. The cost of human loving in a world fractured by hatred." The gargoyle frowned. "The song took a new meaning when the stones of my home began killing those I was formed to protect. I have not heard it sung for centuries—and not as well sung. It is beautiful still but tainted with memory."

"I am sorry," Rosenwyn said. "I did not mean to cause you pain."

"The instrument you hold is also beautiful," the Nix rumbled, eyeing the crwth with interest. "I have seen its kind and yet have not."

"I have made modifications," she said. "Yes."

"You have added frets."

"Frets?" she asked, confused.

"Yes. Poet John Keats speaks of fret, I believe," the Nix said. "Fret is a word that came into existence in the Misty Isles, the world beyond this one. There are many such newly wrought words, apparently." The Nix thought on it. "The Heliwr of a century past brought me a book from his world, a book filled with poetry and song. The word 'fret' has two meanings though." The Nix gazed over the modified crwth. "I believe those raised areas along the neck of your instrument are of what he spoke."

Rosenwyn had made some changes to the design, true. As far as she knew, her crwth was one of a kind.

She found that she liked the Nix.

"I would like to hear you play again," the grotesque said. "It has been many centuries since I have heard music, longer from one so talented."

"Thank you."

"But first to serious matters," the Nix said. "Why are you here?"

The stone creature's sharp gaze daggered into her. Rosenwyn found it difficult to look away. "I am merely traveling. My grandfather would tell stories of Caer Dathal of Old's grandeur. The beauty. The prestige. The stories he told had been passed down from his fathers before him. I was hoping to view you as well as see…something…of that famous castle, to know those stories were real. You are more than I could ever have imagined."

"Stories have power." The Nix ignored her platitudes. "And shared stories grow in the telling, especially when those stories are told over centuries. Caer Dathal was beautiful, once. No longer. That beauty has vanished with time," the Nix said with a hint of anger. "And I am not a mindless beast as some of those stories make me out to be. I do not take kindly to strangers. Men and women and Seelie and Unseelie are all alike—they trespass to dig for imagined treasure or magical artifacts. I trust no one."

Rosenwyn returned her crwth and bow to their case. Pulling her cloak close, she stood much as she had against Audeph Klestmark—tall and strong. "I am not here to dig for artifacts," she said.

"My question remains unanswered with true honesty."

"There is beauty here," she said, looking toward Saith yn Col. "Even one such as you would seek it out."

The Nix squinted. "Go on."

"You are right about one thing: you are more than the stories suggest, a powerful presence amongst the bones of sorrow. And you are lonely," she said, hoping beyond hope she was correct. If she wasn't, she'd be soon dead. "Music brought you from your home, returned you to the light, my life's blood calling you from the shadows. I only wish to see your home and what remains of the beauty of Caer Dathal. If you wish to hear me play again, you will grant me this small request."

Rosenwyn had a hard time not holding her breath. If she lived. If she died. If the curse that had been upon her since she was a child could be lifted. Everything hinged on the next few moments. She had never been so reckless.

She had never so much to gain.

Eyes thoughtful, the Nix mulled it over. Rosenwyn prepared for the guardian to turn her away or, worse, kill her.

"It is a small price to pay for a song," the Nix mused.

She nodded. "True."

"I require your oath, your word, your promise, that your intent is not ill."

Rosenwyn had expected as much. "You have my oath as a musician," she promised, hating the sour taste of thief falsity on her tongue.

"What is your name, Woman of Many Talents?"

"Rosenwyn Whyte," she said. "And yours?"

The Nix bowed his head and then turned, ignoring the question. "Follow me."

He moved toward the entrance to the bowels of Saith yn Col, as silent upon the Everwinter as Rosenwyn had been. Giving Wennyl a last look, she followed. Rosenwyn marveled at the massive stone dragon, the fluidity of the rock that composed his body, the power in every silent stride. She had a hard time imagining how Caer Dathal of Old could fall with several dozen similar entities warding it. She suddenly wished she had met the Nix before the fall of the great Druid castle, unbroken by war and failure.

The grotesque did not look back to see if she followed. He simply vanished down his large staircase into darkness. Worried she would be unable to see where even the faintest light could not penetrate, she was surprised to find that every sixth stone comprising both walls and floors began to glow with a faint bluish-white light. The Nix strode in front of her, the illumination coming to life as he passed. Magic, most likely, of a kind she had only seen in the wealthiest houses. The hallway quickly opened into a grand hall, where massive pillars supported a ceiling lost to gloom. The Nix had brought her to his home, once a long banquet hall. She shivered. The ancient part of the keep had likely not been seen with human eyes for centuries.

A scent of parchment and ink mingled with the must of ages. With thief eyes, she began searching for the Grimoires of the rebel Druids. It would not be easy. Shelves as high as the ceiling stretched the length of the great room, filled with books, baubles, and items Rosenwyn had never seen before.

The grimoires were here. Somewhere.

"You need not wear the glass over your eyes, Rosenwyn Whyte," the Nix said, observing her. "You are safe from day and night's light here."

She hid her surprise. "How did you know?"

"It merely takes eyes to see."

She removed her goggles, thinking. The Nix could tell she possessed magic. He had deduced that and its trigger.

All of a sudden, she felt very transparent.

"I am Nicodemys Rothyn, First Warden of Caer Dathal," the Nix said, appraising her anew as if he could read her mind. "And I know there is more to you, Rosenwyn Whyte, than you have thus shared. Dragons covet their treasure. Trolls, the trinkets they gather from wayward travellers crossing bridges. Me? I was designed to cherish beauty in all of its forms, to keep it safe, no matter the cost. What do you treasure?" He paused, looking about him. "Despite these ruined halls, I still see beauty here. I protect it. I possess terrible secrets that should never leave these ruins, secrets so intrinsically powerful they could destroy Annwn and beyond. I protect as I was created—able to sense magic when it is close." He paused, looking down on her with sad eyes. "But I truly do miss from those former days of Caer Dathal's glory the music that filled these halls. The revelry. The joy. The laughter that kept the darkness at bay. And you, my dear, possess beautiful music."

"You know my secret," she said. "You know of the magic I carry in my blood."

"It weighs on you heavy, an anvil."

"I want nothing more than to be normal, to be whole," she said, unable to believe that she was opening up to one such as the Nix. "I suspect you know a thing or two about that. Wanting to be normal. Returning to what was once known."

The Nix glanced down where his arm should have been and then around the hall.

"Perhaps."

All of a sudden, she questioned the oath she had given to gain entrance to this ancient room of Caer Dathal of Old.

Could a person become more damned?

"This is your home now?" she asked, changing the subject.

"It is. Mine and mine alone, sadly. Once I lorded upon rooftops. Now?" the Nix dropped his head and looked away. "Long has guilt been my only companion. But guilt is not a true companion, is it? I am cursed with memory and it is filled with dragonfire and terrible shadows." He sat upon his haunches. "I suspect you know of this past of which I speak. Not everyone who walked these halls were evil. My kin and I were unable to keep safe those innocents who lived here. Now only I remain, evidence of past defeat."

"That must have been truly painful," she said, the other's pain tearing at her heart.

The Nix said nothing. Long moments passed.

The silence stretched and Rosenwyn became very aware of the other's scrutiny. She gazed about the room, letting her thief senses learn all aspects of it. She had a sudden thought—and a plan formed that she knew would damn her.

"You mentioned a book by a poet. A poet named John Keats, I believe?"

"Yes, yes I did," the Nix rumbled. He strode deeper into the hall. Rosenwyn followed. "The library under my care is a pittance compared to the grandeur of the Druid collection housed here eons ago. But I have managed to save a number of those volumes from their graveyard and acquire more by…outside means. I am fond of reading. When one lives eternally, reading can be the only solace."

With bluish-white light from the ceiling illuminating their way, the gargoyle and thief entered a part of the hall where one large shelf contained volume after volume. Rosenwyn was impressed. Books were not easily come by throughout Annwn, a privilege of wealth and, while she had seen larger libraries, this one held at least several thousand tomes. They came in various sizes and colors, all of them kept neat and orderly.

The First Warden of Caer Dathal of Old grabbed a book unlike any of the others, well made and bound in crimson leather, its cover filigreed with silver.

The Nix opened the book to a ribbon-marked page.

And read:

> *"Darkling, I listen; and, for many a time*
> *I have been half in love with easeful Death,*
> *Call'd him soft names in many a mused rhyme,*
> *To take into the air my quiet breath;"*

As the Nix recited from the poem, Rosenwyn sought the grimoires, books that would be like none of the others. She hoped they were here and she could end her search before he finished. It did not take long. High upon the shelf sat the objects of her hunt as described by Lady Audeph Klestmark—five books bound in black leather, their spines thick and left unadorned by text or title, the blank exteriors hiding powerful knowledge inside. They could be none other than what she sought.

The Grimoires of the rebel Druids.

"Beautiful," she whispered as the Nix finished reading.

"I continually return to this passage," the gargoyle said. "It seems John Keats knows me quite well. Although I am incapable of breath."

"And death, it seems," she offered.

The massive stone dragon said nothing.

"You have an impressive library here, Nicodemys Rothyn," she added.

"Thank you, Rosenwyn Whyte."

"You mentioned that you required 'outside means' to get some of these," she said hoping to keep her interest in the grimoires secret as her mind raced with how to steal them. "What did you mean by that? Can you not venture from Saith yn Col?"

The Nix grunted. "I am tied to the stone. I cannot venture abroad without leave from the Arch Druid of Caer Dathal. I will remain as long as this stone remains."

"We have a great deal in common," Rosenwyn found herself admitting.

"A great sorrow hangs upon you, a past where pain mingles with guilt," the Nix said. "It is easy to recognize because I know its source all too well. Did a lover do this to you? Or is this something else entirely, Rosenwyn Whyte?"

She shook her head, remembering her childhood.

"A man did hurt me. But he is nothing to me now."

"Something before this man then. When you were a child."

The Nix said it as though he already knew. Rosenwyn thought back to the day her family died. The lightning. The fire. The smoke. The screams. She alone had survived. The destruction of her home and her inability to stop it had created a guilt so deep it would always be there, right beneath the surface. Some memories could be carved into stone and hearts equally, for eternity.

"I will never be free of it," she said. "Like your own pain."

"But music helps."

It was not a question. Rosenwyn nodded.

"Then I hope you play music until your heart is healed," the Nix said.

Rosenwyn didn't have the heart to tell the Nix there was no amount of music in the world to do that.

"A song now, perhaps?" the gargoyle asked, all too eager.

Rosenwyn smiled, putting the past where it belonged. She

needed time to devise her next few moves and the Nix offered her time to do so. She grabbed the padded case from her back and pulled forth the crwth and its bow, moved to a block of stone that had fallen from the ceiling, sat, and began to play. She let the music flow through her and into her instrument, a continuous recycling of notes and emotion, each feeding on the other in a wave of creativity. Usually playing for dozens if not hundreds of people, Rosenwyn now played for only one and let the music take her elsewhere even as she tried to discover a way to be free of her greatest and worst curse.

The Nix closed his eyes, listening, his strong presence at peace.

In the middle of playing a third song, a light-hearted tune called *Fly, Fairy, Fly*, the Nix rose up suddenly on his hind legs, towering over Rosenwyn who stopped playing immediately, the peace he had found while she played replaced by a fire of anger so potent she could feel it vibrating the air.

"*Thief!*" the Nix roared.

And the very ruins shook with his fury.

———◆———

ROSENWYN CRINGED, WAITING FOR a massive clawed fist to deliver death.

It took her a moment to realize she yet lived, that the gargoyle had not killed her outright, that he hadn't finally discovered her secret in coming to Saith yn Col. Instead, the Nix frantically probed his subterranean home, every shadow and nook, ignoring her entirely and incensed beyond any rage she could believe the stone dragon to possess.

Thrusting her crwth and bow into their case, she madly scanned the area.

She saw nothing of what threatened the Nix or his home.

"What's going on?" she screamed.

"Thief, I know you are here," the Nix snarled, not looking at her. "I sense your magic. You *dare* enter my home, to steal. Show yourself and end this now, before Death becomes your assured reward."

Nothing. No one answered.

Not that Rosenwyn would think anyone that stupid.

The ruined gargoyle swiveled toward her then, suddenly dwarfing her, a stone cliff ready to collapse and kill.

"Accomplice! You know of what transpires!"

Rosenwyn shrunk to the floor, hands up and placating. "No! I am not! I have no idea what is going on right now!"

"Conspirator!" the Nix hissed. "*Liar!*"

Rosenwyn cringed and furiously tried to discover what was going on. The stone dragon cocked his head as if trying to discover a sound that was just beyond hearing. He gazed back at the library then toward the exit of the hall that led to the world above. His eyes sweeping the shadows, the gargoyle finally settled on Rosenwyn for a moment—a moment that frightened her more than any moment in her life before it—and he bunched like a cat about to pounce, the stone of his muscles filled with sheer power.

Then the Nix leapt at her.

No, not at her.

Over her.

In a single bound, the Nix tore toward the opening that led back to the surface. Rosenwyn inspected the shelves where the grimoires had been.

The books were gone.

And she had been used like a pawn in a chess game.

Cursing, she chased after the Nix, already replacing her goggles, the thief part of her become icy certainty seeking a reckoning. She now knew stealing the grimoires had never been her role. The books were gone, taken by someone else. She had been a mere diversion, put in direct conflict with the Nix to draw attention away from the real thief. She had been used. And she hated that more than even Vrace Erryn. Anger bolstered her resolve as she ran through the hall, up the steps, and returned to the Everwinter.

The snow of the previous day had given way to dark clouds wandering in an azure sky, allowing patches of early morning sunlight to reach Annwn. Rosenwyn found tracks almost immediately. They led hastily away from Saith yn Col, to the south where the forest thinned over a series of slowly rising hills. Rosenwyn could not see the Nix but she could hear him; it sounded like the gargoyle was tearing every icy limb free in the forest in his hunt. She wanted the stone dragon to find the thief. She knew what would happen.

She knelt. It was easy to follow the other thief; the fresh snow that had fallen more than aided her. The tracks were distinctive.

A small foot. Pointed boot.

Another woman had entered Saith yn Col and fled into the surrounding forest.

"Beautiful, did you miss me?"

She spun aside, turning to find the voice's owner. It took Rosenwyn a moment to place the young man from the Raging Drunk. Aron McManus. He had dressed more warmly during his travels from Mur Castell but the sly, arrogant smile remained.

He held a sword and, based upon his stance, knew how to use it.

"What the hellfire are you doing here?" she spat.

"You'll find out," he snarled and attacked.

Rosenwyn bounded backwards, her knives filling her hands as if by magic. McManus circled her calmly after his initial swipe, never taking his eyes off her, his footwork precise and practiced. He feinted. She ignored it. He thrust. She stepped lightly to the side. He was testing her, but she knew it. She held the knives with skillful purpose, the blades deadly extensions of her will. In her line of work, carrying a sword hindered her movements. She had been in many fights, most of them while Lleidr Corryn, and she knew she would have to be fast and precise to best the younger foe.

Already annoyed, his arrogance driving him forward, he attacked then, the sword a blur of efficiency. She backpedaled, waiting for the opportunity to strike back. It didn't take long. In his fury, he overextended his reach, if by a moment. She filled the void and slashed back, aiming for his neck.

But the blade caught his cheek instead, opening it wide.

She tried to escape his reach but he backhanded her to the ground, causing black spots to dance before her eyes.

He stood over her, his tongue able to stick through the bloody cut in his face.

"Bitch!" McManus roared.

Thunder drowned out the killer's anger then, filling the forest.

He barely had time to look up before Wennyl struck him with the galloping full force of his barrel chest, the fey horse maddened in his protection of Rosenwyn. The attacker flew through the air, bones broken. McManus' pain did not last long. He screamed once, then died bloodily beneath the fall of the Rhedewyr's flashing hooves.

Rosenwyn didn't spare the fool a second thought. She leapt onto the stallion's back and together they tore through the forest, seeking the Nix. He was not hard to follow. The path of destruction the stone dragon had left in his wake—the forest floor torn and shattered trees as big around as her waste—made it easy. She kept her wits about her though. She did not want to fall prey to another attack if Lady Audeph Klestmark had hired more than a killer and a thief.

Wennyl cleared the forest, following the havoc, until both

woman and horse burst from the trees into a long meadow that rolled over hills into the distance.

Nearby, the Nix tore huge frozen swaths from the ground

The body of Audeph Klestmark lay just beyond him, untouched by violence.

It wasn't until Rosenwyn realized the gargoyle lay fixated on someone else that she saw the old crone. The woman fled upon her own mount, trying to gain the safety of the forest through the meadow. A black speck flew at her side.

The fairy Bazltrix.

"Go after her!" Rosenwyn screamed at the stone monolith.

"I cannot go beyond the *boundaries* of Caer Dathal," the grotesque roared, voice thick with rage. "I am *chained* and cannot go after the witch."

"A witch?"

"Yes, Rosenwyn Whyte," the Nix grated. "A witch."

Rosenwyn watched as sunlight punctuated the hills, the snow-cover blinding as it reflected the sun. She then looked to the body. If Audeph Klestmark laid dead and not the thief, who did Bazltrix accompany in flight?

Her own rage replied to her question.

"If I help you, will that be proof this was not my intention?"

The Nix nodded with bearish ferocity. Rosenwyn dismounted. She sent Wennyl back into the forest and then walked in front of the gargoyle, throwing off her fur-lined cloak. The icy air bit her but she did not feel it, her thoughts elsewhere.

Instead, she removed her gloves and pushed up her sleeves.

Exposing her skin.

The moment she did that, the day darkened, the countryside become draped in pervasive shadow even as she began to brighten, her fair skin flaring with light. Closing her eyes, Rosenwyn focused.

The magic in her blood illuminated the countryside and all within it, the power that she kept hidden as a secret now fully exposed to the world and its elements. The light built until her skin writhed with it, power that filled her with dread and euphoria. Dark memories flooded her, of a time, as a child, when she stood at her window in a cloudless night—and moonlight bringing to terrible life the magic that would change her life forever.

Older now and having learned more about her curse, Rosenwyn still barely controlled it. It grew inside, a caged beast, and before it consumed her, she unleashed lightning upon the air, a swollen flood thundering through an obstinate dam. It blasted from her, into the earth, into the sky, into the morning. She sensed the Nix thrown away like a rag doll. The air sizzled and Rosenwyn concentrated on what her body had become, a gathering rod of sorts, capturing the sunlight and changing it into violence. The lightning arced and she sent it as best she could toward the fleeing woman and her fairy companion. As the lightning met the witch, a bright burst of wicked green flared, one not of Rosenwyn's making.

The crone vanished in an eruption of Everwinter elements.

When using her magic began to overwhelm her, Rosenwyn covered her skin anew, darkness swimming in her vision.

And collapsed, drained.

Silence more hollow than a graveyard followed, stillness so intense it rang in her ears. She breathed hard, fighting faintness. When she had recovered enough, she pushed up off the ground and focused on what she had done.

In the distance, the horse the witch had been riding lay unmoving.

Of the witch and the fairy, there was no sign.

The Nix untangled his stone body from crushed trees where the lightning had thrown him. "Woman of Many Talents," the stone behemoth growled a laugh, striding up to her. "I sensed your magic but I was not prepared for it."

"Are you hurt?" she asked.

"No," the Nix rumbled. "I have been struck by lightning more times than I can recount. It is nothing to me." He looked deeper into the meadow where the horse smoked. "You will have to approach with utmost caution. I cannot go with you. Be wary. The witch has guile and all too surely hates you for what just transpired."

Exhausted but determined, Rosenwyn nodded and mounted Wennyl. Both made their way to the horse's remains. The lightning had torn a hole in the mount's side, killing the mare instantly.

Having searched the area, Rosenwyn returned to the Nix.

"What did you find?" the gargoyle asked. "The grimoires?"

"No," she said, frustrated. She dismounted and went to the side of Audeph Klestmark. "The fairy is dead, reduced to black ash on the snow. The witch vanished though. The lightning threw her free of her mount but she regained her feet. The tracks led about twenty paces before they disappeared, like she never existed."

"Magic protected her and then concealed her passage. She will not be easily found," the Nix said, gently picking up the body of Audeph Klestmark with his remaining massive fist. "Come."

Rosenwyn nodded, the defeat like poison in her mouth and followed the great stone behemoth back toward his home. She first made certain the man from the Raging Drunk was dead. Aron McManus couldn't be more so. One eye stared up through the trees, the rest of his skull crushed beyond identification. Rosenwyn then went to the body of Audeph Klestmark where the Nix had laid her just outside the entrance to his lair. The wealthy woman stared to the side, her mouth agape. The thief checked over the body. She could not find a cause for the woman's death.

"You were attacked by this man here?" the Nix said, observing the remains.

"Wennyl finished him," she said.

"A fine Rhedewyr, a finer friend." The grotesque examined Audeph Klestmark then. "She was a vessel. And this was a plot," he growled.

"What do you mean by that?"

"Look upon her. Note what can be seen."

Rosenwyn did so. It did not take long to compare the difference from their previous meeting in Mur Castell—discarded gloves revealing fingers devoid of rings.

"Her rings are gone yet necklace and earrings remain," Rosenwyn observed.

"It means the rings held more worth," the Nix said. "And when it comes to magic and power, gems are priceless in the province of the witch."

"And the vessel?"

"This woman did not die, not by another's hand. No wounds. No bruising," the Nix said, inspecting the body. "An innocent. Housing a very rare evil. That evil overtook the body of this woman, similar to how a shadow infiltrates another shadow. Unseen. A witch, ancient, one whose body has long since decayed to dust yet the spirit lives on in a different body. One such witch even courted one of the rebel Druids of Caer Dathal. It is said she fled while my home—and her Druid partner—fell." The Nix looked into the forest as if the witch would be there. "And she would want the grimoires back. For their power…or something far more grave for Annwn."

"The grimoires of her fallen brethren," Rosenwyn said. "What have I done?"

"A terrible omen. No good can come of this."

Rosenwyn hated that she had aided the witch. More than she hated even herself.

"Tell me your role in this," the Nix rumbled. "With detail."

Rosenwyn did. She had no reason not to. She started with her childhood and the magic that she possessed—the same magic that had killed her family and plagued her life since that dark day. Talking briefly about becoming a Lleidr Corryn, she instead related her time as a musician—until the night when the man at the Raging Drunk had offered his company and the fairy intervened, leading to a clandestine meeting with Lady Audeph Klestmark and her promise to help rid Rosenwyn of her debilitating curse in exchange for the Grimoires of the rebel Druids.

"The man who tried to kill you," the gargoyle said. "He aided the witch. He was hired, under the supervision of the witch, to help deliver another vessel body. In killing this Lady Audeph Klestmark, you now have no lead to follow. This witch is devious. And she has her freedom." The Nix punched the ground, making Rosenwyn jump. He ignored her discomfort. "She stole dangerous knowledge," he said. "Quite possibly, the most dangerous books under my care."

"What makes them so dangerous?" she asked. "How can a set of books be that worrisome? They are only bound paper and ink."

"Books are quite possibly the most powerful items in the world, Rosenwyn Whyte," Nicodemys Rothyn argued. "These particular grimoires especially. They possess dark magic. That knowledge, in evil hands, could be a terrible bane on Annwn." The gargoyle turned to her, his dark eyes penetrating. "You were a part of this. I wish it were otherwise. I rather like you."

Rosenwyn thought the gargoyle about to attack. There would be no surviving.

"I did not sense the witch's magic," the Nix growled. "Because of you."

"My magic masked her magic."

The Nix nodded, still angry. "Do you wish to make amends?"

She realized she did. Nobody made a fool of her and lived to tell it. "I do," she admitted honestly. "Very much."

"Very well," the Nix said. "You start now."

"Start what?"

"You have power, Woman of Many Talents," the behemoth rumbled, his voice reverberating through the chill air. "It is powerful. You can also go where I cannot. You will become an extension of my will, for a time, until you have paid back the debt of your involvement. A Lleidr Corryn will become the White Rose." Rosenwyn was about to protest when the Nix raised his fist for silence. "Once, after the fall of Caer Llion, I had one such as you retrieve those lost grimoires from the private collection of the High King. In time, you will discover this witch. And regain what she stole."

"Where is that thief who stole the books from Caer Llion?" she questioned.

"Death comes all too soon in my presence, it seems."

Rosenwyn did not know what that meant. But if anyone could steal the grimoires back, it would be her.

"Do you accept this proposal?" the Nix asked finally.

"There may be a time when I am discovered. By those who would see me dead for abdicating my role as Lleidr Corryn," Rosenwyn said, hating the thought of confronting that part of her life. "In the past, I avoided Vrace Erryn and Rol Macleod by playing in a different town almost every night."

"Like the wind," the Nix said. "Constantly moving."

"Very much so," she said. "I can not guarantee others will not search for me here—and find you in the process. And all you possess. My life is tied to the master thief's token. They *will* come for me."

"The two other master thieves," the Nix grunted. "We will worry about them when the day of their reckoning comes."

The gargoyle said it so nonchalant she actually believed him. The Nix gazed at the dark clouds roaming their blue sky:

"Was I deceived, or did a sable cloud
Turn forth her silver lining on the night?
I did not err; there does a sable cloud
Turn forth her silver lining on the night,
And casts a gleam over this tufted grove."

"What does that mean?" Rosenwyn asked.

"That is a verse from a John Milton poem, my White Rose thief," the Nix said. "Another poet from the world beyond Annwn. The passage means not every evil turn is for ill if one is capable of perceiving it."

"That is quite appropriate, I guess," she admitted. "The sable cloud has entered our lives. But that same cloud has brought us together." She patted Wennyl who nuzzled her back. "Time to find the witch and end her *own* silver lining."

"I could not agree more," Nicodemys Rothyn growled.

Life had a way of changing course, like a swollen river escaping its original banks. It could not be fought, only accepted. Rosenwyn went to gather her things. If the Nix could endure the change in his role from gargoyle atop Caer Dathal of Old to living in its ruins, she could adapt and become something more.

She breathed in the chill and returned to the ruins.

And her new home of Saith yn Col.

A LENGTH OF CHERRYWOOD

-*The Vault of Heaven*-

PETER ORULLIAN

In some ways, this is an origin story for Jastail J'Vache,
a character from my series, The Vault of Heaven. But
you don't need to have read any of that to dive into "A
Length of Cherrywood." You'll see Jastail do some
dastardly stuff. You'll meet a few of his associates who
are altogether not nice. You'll also see that just maybe
there are reasons Jastail is the way he is.

I have to admit that this isn't a romp. This isn't
charming villainy. Or a clever heist. Or a bloodbath. The
ending surprised me. It's the kind where suffering stares
back at you from the page. Probably my horror roots
showing through. But there is one moment that shines.
And maybe a bit brighter for the darkness around it.

Blackguards

J ASTAIL J'VACHE CROUCHED BEHIND a thick patch of scrub oak and watched the woman washing clothes in the river. She hummed a tune as she worked, alone, unaware of him or his highwaymen hiding in a rough circle around her. Beyond the thinning trees stood a wagon, a hundred paces away. Too far for anyone to be of immediate aid. Jastail put a hand in his pocket, running his fingers over grooves in a short length of cherrywood. A reminder. Then, quite casually, he stood, revealing himself. "Greetings, my lady."

The woman's head snapped up. Her eyes wide.

"I've alarmed you." Jastail began to skirt the low brush, moving toward her. "My apologies. It's something of a hazard in my line of work, I'm afraid."

Insensibly, the woman gathered in the wet clothes and got to her feet. Jastail offered a wan smile at that. Such value for clothes belonged to the exceptionally poor. She began to back away from him, in the direction of her wagon.

"Come, don't fret yourself. This needn't go hard between us." He stepped into the shallow river, crossing directly toward her.

Just as she turned to run, he raised a hand and his men stepped

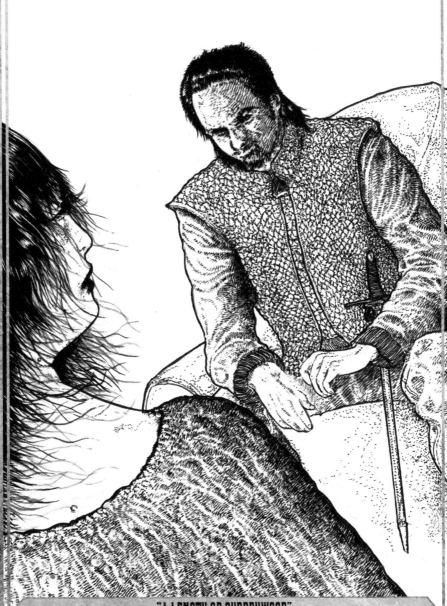

"A LENGTH OF CHERRYWOOD"

Illustration by ORION ZANGARA

from their concealments. The woman skidded to a stop, fell, and dropped the wet clothes.

Jastail reached the other side of the river as she scrambled to her feet and turned to face him.

"There, much better." He put on a smile of reassuring approval. "I think we have an understanding."

The woman glanced down at the clothes between them. He followed her gaze. The clothes . . . belonged to children.

Lawry, his newest man, laughed. "A neat prize. The lady and her loinfruits, besides." He nodded in the direction of the wagon.

Panic entered her eyes, and she shook her head. "No. No! Marcus! Highwaymen!"

The alarm echoed through the woods around them. And a moment later the sound of hurried feet came pounding through the brush.

"Oh, my lady." Jastail sighed. "If you'd only had a bit of patience. Now we've a hero to deal with. Let's hope he's sensible."

Jastail maneuvered around her, putting himself between the woman and her would-be rescuer. He drew his sword, holding it at an unthreatening angle. This Marcus came into view, and caught sight of the woman surrounded by Jastail's men.

The man held a smith hammer and a shoeing knife—he'd probably been tending his horse—and slowed as he surveyed the odds.

Good, at least he can do math. "Let me explain what you're seeing," Jastail began, planting his sword's tip in the dirt and leaning on it. "Your lady here was washing clothes in the river. Not usually a dangerous task, I'll admit. But today, it's bad fortune for you that *we* are here." He gestured with his other hand at his men.

"You won't be taking her." Marcus flipped his knife into a backhand grip—a pit fighter's grip.

Why couldn't I, just once, meet a man who sews or bakes?

Jastail bent and lifted a pair of trousers from the pile of wet clothes. "And who's going to watch the owner of these while you fight for your woman's honor?"

Worry crossed the man's face, and he cast a glance back toward the wagon.

"Dead gods," said Lawry, "let's get on with it."

Jastail's new man—first time on the road—started off to gather the little ones.

"Hold there," Jastail ordered, then fixed his attention back on the woman. "I need your help," he said with endless patience. "Marcus here is about to do an honorable thing. He wants to protect you from us. Perfectly understandable. In his place, I'd want to do the same. Love makes fools of us all. It blinds us to our real chances. It blinds us to the harm our heroism might do to others." He shook the wet trousers in emphasis.

"You want me to tell Marcus to let you take me." The woman's voice came with the monotone of the beaten. "You want me to tell him not to fight. Then you'll leave my family alone."

"Jastail?" It was Lawry, incredulous at the suggestion being made.

"I don't take more than I need," Jastail replied, and dropped the pants. "And remember we have a specialty." *Women—"wombs"—who can breed.* The little ones were both boys. He knew it by the clothes at his feet.

"The hell with that," Lawry exclaimed. "There's thirty full marks a head sitting back there. Easy pickings. If *you* won't take them, *I* will."

"Excuse me," Jastail said, raising a finger to the woman as he slid past her toward his new man.

He gestured for Lawry to join him in a short walk away from

the others. Twenty paces removed from the rest, he turned to face the man. "It's your first time on the roads."

"I don't see what that has to do—"

Jastail put his knife into the man's stomach with a short powerful stab, and yanked up, severing several internal organs. Lawry's eyes widened in surprise and pain before he dropped into the brush. Jastail wiped his blade clean on the man's shirt. Men who argue don't ever stop arguing. And they don't obey. With such men, he'd learned long ago to cut quick. Saved lots of pain later on.

Still, he paused long enough to offer over the body a line from one of the dark poets he'd learned to appreciate as a boy. "Each of us is walking earth, upright dust, consuming breath in ignorance."

Black verse. Like a good cool wine.

Jastail nodded a goodbye, and returned to the others, wearing his casual smile.

"Now," he said, taking a deep breath, "what will it be, Marcus? Can we be done with threats and heroism today? I'd really like to be on my way."

Marcus looked at the woman. "Jaryn?"

She returned a tortured gaze. Tortured, Jastail knew from experience, for her loved one. Not for herself. She'd already weighed the stakes and folded her cards.

Then Marcus shifted his gaze to Jastail. "If you take her, I'll follow. And I'll bring help."

"Of course you will." Jastail nodded to the fact with good humor. "And you'd have time to get your little ones someplace safe, so you can make an unencumbered rescue attempt. Quite practical."

In all the time Jastail had lain this type of ambush, only one man had ever successfully reclaimed the woman Jastail had taken. Good odds. And he didn't mind the game of it when a husband had wit and skill.

Marcus lowered his knife and hammer.

Jastail smiled apologetically—a touch of theater on his part. Then he put his hand on the woman's arm and began leading her northward. Their horses weren't far.

Marcus stood still as Nichols, Jastail's most seasoned man, passed by him. Then the would-be hero brought his shoeing knife up in a swift motion and plunged it into Nichols' kidney. A pit fighter's move. Debilitating. And lethal. Nichols cried out and fell.

Medi, one of Nichols' good friends, lunged at Marcus, blade and dagger slicing through the air.

Marcus shuffled back, avoiding the blades. He then closed fast, dropped low, and brought his hammer around hard on the side of Medi's left knee. The bones crunched as Medi's leg bent at an impossible angle and he fell. Marcus pounced, driving his hammer down on the man's throat, silencing his cries of pain.

Jastail pulled the woman away, clearing the area for the fight. *He has real skill.* Jastail nodded with approval, and smiled with eagerness.

The rest of his band formed a circle, caging Marcus in. But the man seemed unconcerned, keeping a fighter's crouch, and turning constantly to meet every eye. When he came last to Jastail, he showed a cold, reasoning expression.

"You won't harm her. She's your prize." *Good wit.* "And you're content with just the woman, which means you're a womb trader. You don't care for trafficking brats." *Damn, but I like this fellow.* "And I've a bit more skill than changing a horseshoe. I'll take my chances here, since I don't like them once she's gone."

A gambler, too. Jastail must have looked like he was beaming to his fellows, since he never could have imagined so good a contest coming on a minor highway in the south of So'Dell.

Jastail raised his sword. "You and I, then. For the lady's honor."

Marcus flipped the hammer up, spinning it twice, and caught

it again. He nodded.

The two began to circle, each feinting several times. Finally, Marcus stepped in with a clever combination of stab and swing. Jastail didn't fall for the dagger strike, anticipating the hammer from the other side. Good way to get an arm broken.

When the hammer came around, he wind-milled his sword and cut Marcus' upper arm deep. Blood soaked the man's sleeve with a spreading crimson.

Jastail hoped it wouldn't be so easy, and switched hands with this sword, shuffling his feet to a right-handed stance. His weaker side.

Marcus adjusted his grip on his knife, taking a standard hold. And did something surprising. Instead of circling in, he took half a step back and threw the dagger with a quick, flip of his wrist.

Jastail had no time to evade the attack. The knife sank into the meat of his upper chest. If he hadn't been ducking, it might have struck his heart or lung. He stumbled backward, as Marcus leapt forward, bringing his hammer down in a vicious arc.

Jastail spun, just escaping the blow, and brought his sword around with his momentum, forcing Marcus off-balance. As the two faced each other again, Jastail pulled the knife from his body and smiled. He loved to be surprised. And he loved to surprise others. He slowly tossed the knife back to Marcus handle first. The man caught the weapon and stared back in confusion.

"Again," Jastail said, and started forward.

Marcus crouched, looking more a pit fighter than before. Jastail rushed, feigning a sweeping overhand stroke, then lowered his sword fast and came in under Marcus' guard. The move put the man off-balance, and Jastail kicked him to the ground.

Before Marcus could roll, Jastail had his blade at the man's throat. A simple stab and the man would die.

"No, Da!"

Jastail looked up and saw two faces peering through the brush at the edge of the trees. But it wasn't mercy that kept him from killing their father.

"Let go your weapons," Jastail ordered.

Marcus looked at him a long time. Pride and defeat battled in the man's face. But not worry. Jastail wanted to meet more men like this. Marcus finally obeyed, and Jastail kicked the knife and hammer away.

"Thank you for the contest," Jastail said, bowing slightly. "A pleasant surprise. It hardly changes things for you, as it turns out. But you should feel good about your effort. And, of course, you can still come looking for us once you see to your little ones." Jastail bent, and quite earnestly confided in the man, "We're heading north and east to the river. I hope you'll take your chances again."

Sparing no concern, and ignoring his fallen men, Jastail left Marcus there. He paused only to take an article of clothing from the woman's wash—a child's sock. Then he gathered her with a gentle hand and led her from her wet clothes and family.

———•———

THE RIVERBOAT RANG WITH laughter and the sounds of dice and odds-makers calling numbers. Tobacco smoke lazed in the air, thick and sweet. Beneath it the sharp tang of brandy—the drink of choice—rose from countless cups and goblets. Serving men went shirtless, and could be bedded for a full realm mark. Serving women wore a bodice so thin they might as well not have bothered, and could be had at the same price. Gamblers' hands roamed to the delicate parts of servers and other gamblers as liberally as the drinks flowed. In the far corner of the riverboat's third deck, Jastail took a seat at the table of the boat's proprietor, Gynedo.

Back in this corner, behind a low wall, the din eased a bit. Gynedo smiled as he shuffled a set of plackards, and stared at Jastail from beneath a broad-rimmed hat.

"You think you're ready for this game, my young friend? You understand the rules?" Gynedo set the plackards aside and prepared himself a long-stem pipe.

Jastail nodded.

"We're not betting on coin value, you understand," Gynedo explained again.

It was a new game, something the gambling boss had conceived when money stakes ceased to hold his interest. That suited Jastail fine. More than fine.

Gynedo struck his pipe alight and eyed their third player, a raven-haired woman of perhaps twenty-five, whose smile suggested carnal appetites that involved instruments. She wore a black hat from which cascaded a thin curtain of black netting. The net-holes were wide, making her easy enough to see, but the black mesh gave her an air of menace and deceit. Lovely.

"Not even slave-stock," Gynedo said. "I have more men and women for the blocks than I can trade as it is. And that's messy, besides."

Jastail took a long drink of his brandy. "Wagers for this game are about the emotional loss of a person. Suffering, you might say." He grinned at the thought.

"And we bet a token of that suffering for each round we wish to stay in the game," the woman finished. She turned to Jastail. "Since Gynedo hasn't the manners to introduce us, I'm Fleur."

"Jastail," he replied. "Pleasure."

She held out her hand as a noble might, expecting a kiss on her knuckles. Jastail took her hand and made a slight bow.

"Just so," Gynedo confirmed. "I'm still working out a system to place emotional value on the items. For now, we'll take it by instinct and agreement at the table." He smiled around the stem of his pipe. "Three rounds, I think. Escalating value. Game will be Suits."

Suits was a simple three plack draw. Placks of the same suit could be added together to get a total point value. All cards were kept face down, and turned one at a time, in turn. Very little strategy, but a serviceable game given their purpose and wagers tonight.

Gynedo dealt out three placks to each of them.

Jastail turned first. A hawk with eight feathers showing. He then gently pushed a folded piece of parchment into the center of the table.

"And what do we have here?" Gynedo asked, a glimmer in his eyes.

"A letter," Jastail explained. "Written by a man awaiting execution for a crime . . . a crime that *I* committed."

There were false gasps from his table-mates.

"I orchestrated a bit of misdirection, and got him pegged for it." Jastail waved a dismissive hand. "Somehow, I was taken for his friend, and given the letter to deliver to his wife."

"What does it say?" Fleur asked, leaning in with anticipation.

Jastail looked at the letter, smiled. "It's filled with regret. Apology for petty wrongs. Declarations of love." He paused, considering. "It carries the sad realizations of all the things this man will never see or do again. He wanted to say all this to his wife, but they wouldn't let her visit him. The letter is all they'd allow."

Gynedo offered a low chuckle. "You should have saved this for a later round," he observed. "You realize, of course, that this token isn't just the suffering of the man. You've also prevented his wife from hearing his last, dearest thoughts and declarations of love. Your bet is double." He patted the table in appreciation and acceptance of the wager.

"You're a lovely bastard," Fleur declared. Her hand snaked beneath the table to cup his manhood. Jastail nodded thanks and gently put her hand back in her own lap. He knew the art of carnal distraction in a game of chance.

"My turn, then," Fleur said, turning her plack—a grey jay with twelve feathers up. She removed an emerald ring from her gloved left hand and placed it in the center of the table.

"There's a story behind this, I'm assuming," Gynedo said with good humor, "since I couldn't give a tinker's damn for a ring."

"Well, of course." Fleur cleared her throat dramatically, her face reminding Jastail of a young girl receiving her first kiss. "One of my former husbands ran a shipping trade. Profitable. Very profitable. Despite pirates and storms, we turned coin as though we minted it ourselves. A Soren Sea squall took one of our larger ships down. As an act of compassion, my husband not only made good on the lost freight with his customers, but gave to me 100 full realm marks for each crewman who died. I was to take that money to the spouses and families of those lost. 'You have decorum,' he said to me. I bowed gravely to the compliment, and went into the city and bought myself with that money this ring. It's lovely, don't you think?"

She smiled wickedly at Jastail and Gynedo.

"Suffering by omission," Gynedo mumbled, seeming to sort through the value. He was still refining his new game. "Those left behind had no breadwinner and no compassion money from their loved one's employer. I say it's good." He looked up and tapped the table again.

Fleur sat back, looking pleased with herself.

Gynedo turned his plack—a pine sparrow with three feathers. He reached into this pocket and produced a single, thin plug. He examined it a moment, as if he might not like to part with it. Then he solemnly placed it with the other tokens, making a show of it by doing so painfully slow.

Gynedo sat back. "Men and women stroll on to my boat every day," he began. "They come in two stripes. One has bags full of coin. And if this type leaves empty-handed, it means nothing to him. The other sort boards my boat with desperation in his heart. He hopes for a bit of luck. He hopes to turn a meager stake into meat and rent money, because not doing so means people who depend on him will go without."

"Then you must have bags full of coins like this," Fleur observed, leaning forward and fingering the coin.

Gynedo nodded. "But this one . . . this is one I took myself. And I took it with a cheat. The man had me cold with a high hand of triple draw. But I hate to lose. And it sets a bad precedent for me to be seen losing to a dock worker, of all things. So, I made a simple card exchange." He paused, his eyes distant. "The look in the man's face when he lost . . . I could see the ache of it. I could see those who depended on him losing a measure of hope."

Jastail stared at the coin, thinking of a line from one of his dark poets. "I'd have saved *that* for a later round."

They exchanged glances, silently agreeing that they'd all bought another turn. Jastail didn't hesitate to turn up his second plack. Another hawk. Ten feathers. He now had a suited pair. And he promptly produced a child's sock—the one he'd earned just a few days prior when he'd taken a woman by a quiet riverside. He shared the story of the article of clothing.

"Lovely," Fleur said.

Gynedo tapped the table again.

They continued around, each turning a plack, each offering a token. Jastail had the high hand when the third and final round came. But it was clear that both Fleur and Gynedo had dropped more suffering into the pot. He gave them both a long look, then reached into his inner pocket for his length of cherrywood. For perhaps the last time—should he lose tonight—he fingered the groove marks in the short stick. Then, he pulled it from his pocket and placed it with the rest of the wagers.

Gynedo eyed the token. Fleur looked aflutter with eagerness to hear the story.

"In Sever Ens, where I grew up, there's not much for a woman if she's not a soldier's wife." He smiled at dark memories. "My mother was *not* a soldier's wife. She wasn't a wife at all. And she couldn't tell me who my father was, because she didn't know."

"The wood belongs to your mother?" Gynedo asked.

Jastail shook his head. "Money was hard to come by. She was fifteen when I was born, and she struggled along until the day came I could help her earn a coin. I was six."

Gynedo sat forward. "Jastail?"

Fleur made a sound of delight at the story.

"Like anyplace, Sever Ens has its whoreboy trade." Jastail said it matter-of-factly. "But those are usually gangs of runaways, orphans, or snatched sons brought into the city from far places." He shook his head. "My mother started asking me to take meals with strangers who came by our shanty. 'A full, warm meal,' she'd say. 'Be grateful,' she'd say. And sometimes there was, in fact, a meal. But they were bugger meals. And just as often, the bugger bought me nothing."

He looked up at his two table-mates, and flashed a wicked smile. "After the first time, I found something to hold in my teeth when these meal-men set to their sport. It kept me from screams, which only ever earned me angry fists anyway. It helped me . . . suffer through."

Fleur removed her gloves and picked up the cherrywood, fingering the bite marks. Her expression held fascination and a glint of something Jastail had only seen in a woman at the peak of orgasm. She handed it to Gynedo, who wore a serious look as he studied the token.

Making the bet felt like pulling a knife slowly through one's own palm. It burned. Seared. But it exhilarated him to have the will to do something so personally painful.

He'd hate to lose the cherrywood. But he played to win.

Gyndeo placed the stick back at the table's center, knocked the table once rather weakly, and the round continued.

Gynedo won. He gathered in the pile of tokens, placing them gently into a felt bag. Fleur stood to go. As she passed Jastail, she bent near him, placing her face gently against his neck, and took a deep breath through her nose. *She's smelling me.* Then she ran the tip of her tongue over the delicate folds of his ear—a clear invitation—and returned to her room below-deck.

"It's an interesting game," Jastail remarked, as Gynedo settled him a firm stare.

"It's rough yet, but it'll smooth out." Gynedo gestured for Jastail to follow him into the small quarters just behind his rear-room table.

Once inside, the man closed the door, dimming the riverboat noise to a low roar. He came around to face Jastail square, and held out the length of cherrywood. "Take it."

"I lost." Jastail shrugged. Then he grinned. "Unless you cheated."

Gynedo returned a wry smile. "Not this time, I didn't." The smile fell away. "But I won't keep this."

"Why? Tender heart?" Jastail tried to push the length of wood away.

"You and I, we're not tender men," Gynedo said. There was no lament over the fact for either of them. "But a man who carries something like this is a man who has unresolved quarrels with his past."

"You sound like a priest. It was a wager, Gynedo, not a

confession." Jastail thought a moment. "And certainly not a plea for help. I have my poets for that." He offered a mild but genuine laugh.

"Then it wouldn't bother you if I burned it." Gyendo strolled to a lamp and removed the glass windbreak to expose the flame.

Jastail felt a tug of panic low in his gut. "I rather thought I could win it back at our next round of the game."

Gynedo began lowering the cherrywood toward the flame. "Snatching travelers from the road and selling them as stock on the blocks has grown tiresome, hasn't it? Oh, it's profitable, but hardly thrilling anymore for you or me."

Jastail spoke fast. "You think my holding onto the wood speaks of a weakness. A sentimentality, perhaps." He laughed. "Did I tell you I've completed my first stock sale to Bar'dyn out of the Bourne. Dead gods did that pay well. But, to your point, the risk was quite a thrill. One of every two men *die* trading with the Bar'dyn."

Gynedo looked unimpressed, and continued to lower the cherrywood. It was a hand-length from the flame now.

"Your new game has raised the stakes, too," Jastail quickly added. "You're right. I don't think much anymore about the wombs I gather for Bar'dyn buyers, though I like walking that line of uncertainty every time I meet with the beasts. No, when I'm collecting wombs, I think about what small token I might find to wager at your table." He gestured toward the gambling deck, where they'd just concluded their round of the new game.

Gynedo kept lowering the wood. "You should have won tonight," he said. "You lost because you put up a personal token. I'll modify the game rules to disallow it. Or maybe that'll be a separate game." He showed Jastail a moment's sympathy. "But I don't like to see a gambler with your potential chained by his past. It makes you weak. And if I know your weakness, I'll win every time." He stopped the wood's descent to the flame. "And you see, I'm a rather selfish bastard. I want the game to have real sport to it. I want to know I *could* lose. And unless you do something about this gods-forsaken wood, I'll find a way to beat you no matter what we play."

"I'm not quite sure how you'd manage that," Jastail said, smiling.

"Trust me." Gynedo lowered the cherrywood into the flame.

"Fine!" Jastail blurted, more loudly than he'd intended.

Gynedo smiled and pulled the wood away from the lamp with only a slight black sear. He tossed it to Jastail.

After a brief inspection of the scorching, Jastail placed the stick back in the pocket against his chest.

"Even bastards like us need to make peace with the past," Gynedo remarked, smiling conspiratorially, "or we'll never have the cool to play chances the right way . . . with the necessary indifference. Especially at high stakes."

Jastail returned the wisdom with a mock salute and shook his head, smiling, intending to heed every word the gambling boss uttered.

"And I'd stay out of Fleur's bed," Gynedo added. "She's a biter. She'll leave teeth marks in you like that wood you carry."

Well, maybe not every *word.*

JASTAIL DIDN'T BOTHER TO knock. He simply went into the home of his childhood. Such as it was.

It looked precisely as it had seven years ago, when he'd finally run from this place. He'd decided he wouldn't let his mother send him with men anymore for a *meal.* The room closed in tight. Suffocating. It was warmed by a fire over which a pot of beans was always simmering. Cow bones were tossed in for flavor—whatever could be scrounged from the butcher's waste barrel. And under the smell of the overcooked beans was the stench of armpits and unwashed skin.

In her chair beside the fire sat his mother, Lona. Her face told of a recent beating. She wasn't above *bedwork* herself if it came to that.

"My dying gods. Jastail," she exclaimed. "Come to your senses, have you. Returned home."

Jastail closed the door and took a seat opposite her near the hearth. Closer here, the beans smelled burned. He could also now see the small table beside her with its second shelf beneath. Lying there, covered in years of dust, was a volume of poetry by Tawl Tawminh. It was Jastail's book. One he'd forgotten when he fled this place. One of his dark poets. A line rose in his mind: *I hear secret convulsive sobs from young men, at anguish with themselves, remorseful after deeds done.*

"A visit is all. I'm not staying," Jastail said. He looked her over. Aside from the bruising, she didn't appear ill or underfed. "You look well."

She produced a coin bag hung down between her breasts on a leather strap. She jangled the coins within. "No complaints."

"You working alone?"

"Let's talk about you," she said, avoiding the question. "I've heard you ply the roads. Take folk and sell them on the blocks. That's gainful work. I imagine your purse is a might heavier than mine." She smiled, exposing a missing tooth. "I deserve some credit for that, you know. What you learned of *human wages* you learned from me." She eyed him. "Might even entitle me to a cut of your take."

Jastail laughed out loud. "I don't whore for you anymore, mother."

"Oh, lad. It wasn't like that." She waved a hand at him, as though he were talking foolish. "Each of us does what we must to get by.

If you can't swing a sword or keep a ledger, you do what's left and be grateful to those who pay."

Jastail gave a politician's nod of agreement. "You're wise beyond your years. Survival is more important than . . . well, than love."

"I see, you think I didn't love you. That it?" She put the bag of coins back into her blouse. "You come all this way to hear me say it. It'll make you feel better, I suppose, if I tell you I didn't want no baby when I was fifteen. Or that no good mother makes her little boy take a meal with a grown man who expects a little kindness in return for his generosity. Is that what you'd like to hear?"

Jastail glared at her. A hundred vicious things entered his mind. But he held his tongue until he found his smile again, and flashed it brightly. "You're a high breed bitch, all right."

She winked conspiratorially. "That I am, my boy. That I am. No one gives a good gods damn about me, and I give back the same."

He decided a little honesty wouldn't hurt. "I did love *you*. At first, anyway. You knew it. And you used it to convince me that I needed to go with that first meal-man. You said he'd want some kindnesses from me, and pay me for it." Jastail fell deeper into the memory. "You said that I'd do it if I loved you. Because we were starving, and we needed the scratch to buy meat. You sent me out with him, and a hundred more like him, asking me to do it because we were all each other had. Needed to do hard things to make our way, you said."

She nodded to it all, her eyes distant, wearing that particular frown of one hearing something entirely sensible. "Rough times in the beginning." Then her eyes focused again. "But look how far we've come, eh?" She grinned a wicked grin. "You doing hard trade on the road and no doubt flush with coin. And me? Well, I do better than most. Learned a thing or two, besides."

Rough times.

He regarded her for several moments. Damn hells how he'd looked forward to this. "Tell me these things you've learned. Educate your son."

She gave a coarse laugh, and rocked forward in her seat to share her secret. "A crew of five I have working the taverns and bedhouses. Young waifs. I pay one strong-hand to keep them from running, and to keep them safe from the kill-sex types. And I pay a second man to be sure the first doesn't get no ideas about taking my girls."

"Girls then?" Jastail said, feigning surprise.

Her devilish grin widened. "That's just what I call them. I offer the company of both lads and lasses. Payer's choice," she said proudly. "And I keep the crew small. No permanent home, neither. That way, I slide under the lawguards, who make examples of madams who set up expensive brothels with baths and lace. Hells," she laughed, "a few of my best patrons are lawguards. They get their turn free."

Jastail listened. All this he'd learned already for a few coins in a nearby tavern.

A silence settled between them. Just the low crackle of fire and warm smell of beans.

"You must have lost a few drabs, to learn that you needed protection," Jastail observed.

"Precisely."

"It's a good thing, then, that in all those times you sent me with buggers, none of them damaged me so badly I couldn't keep taking *meals*."

"Unavoidable risks, really," she answered, with a proprietor's tone. "I had no money for a strong-hand then."

"And you've operated all this while without any real challenge." Jastail sat back, speaking as though he truly marveled over her prowess and ability. "Until now."

She eyed him with suspicion. "How's that?"

"What I mean to say is, I've taken ownership of your working waifs." He flashed his grin again, mocking and bright.

His mother stared back a long moment, dumbstruck. Then her own devilish smile rose on her bruised lips. "A game? You're all grown up, and come to see if I can hold my own."

She produced a small knife with a serrated edge.

Jastail chuckled low over the threat.

"Don't think because I'm your mother that I won't use this." She spun it over the top of her hand in a deft movement he hadn't seen before. "Or that I don't know how. Now, what's the game?"

Jastail leaned forward, elbows on his knees, and spoke with dripping earnestness. "No game. Just doing what I must . . . to get by."

"You're an ungrateful whoreboy." She waved her dagger threateningly. "What you done back then ain't hurt you none. And it gave us coin to struggle through the lean years. What's wrong with that?"

He reached into his inside pocket and drew out the length of cherrywood. He stared at it a moment, then tossed it at her. She caught it with her free hand, and looked it over. Realization slowly bloomed in her face.

"What do you call it, mother? A 'bugger's bit'?" Jastail saw in his mind a rapid stream of men, their wanton nervous smiles, the sweat on their upper lips, their white puckered flesh.

Any bit of guilt or regret slipped from her face. "Poor boy. Carrying his little piece of wood around all his life. Thinks he had it rougher than most." Her expression hardened. "You're going to return my drabs, or I'm going to open you like a fall pig. Don't test me, Jastail." An idea lit her face. "And better yet, you and me, together. We could run quite a crew of drabs. You pluck 'em from the highway, I'll keep 'em on their backs."

Jastail shook his head and offered her an incredulous grin. "You're a high breed bitch, all right."

He leaned back and drew the curtain away from the windows once and let it fall back. A moment later, four of his men quietly entered the shanty house, steel drawn.

She stared at each man in turn, her eyes coming to rest again on Jastail. "What then? You going to kill me, take over my operation?"

Jastail noted that she hadn't lowered her knife. He shook his head as one might to shush a complaining child. "Absent gods, no. I'll be selling them to clients from the Bourne. They pay well for young girls." The boys he'd likely cut loose, leave them to their odds.

His mother shot him an angry frown, her lips drawing into a snarl. "That's bad business. I can earn a hundred times their sell-price in a few years, making them work the taverns." She calmed herself, adopting a negotiator's tone. "Let me keep on as I have. And I'll cut you in for one coin in three. That's more than fair. Hard to turn down a deal such as that."

He marveled at her tenacity. Maybe he'd gotten a bit of that from her. Again he leaned forward in his chair, to watch her face when he shared his next bit of news. "You won't have time for this nonsense anymore, mother. You see, the Bar'dyn prize something even more than *young* girls. Pay well for it."

He paused. The fire hissed beside them.

She'd already begun to nod, understanding, when he explained, "Wombs, ma. They pay handsomely for wombs. Girls will grow into their use. And you," he pointed between her legs, "bless you, you pushed me out at a tender age. There's still good bearing years in you."

He was almost too slow when she lashed out with her knife. Almost. He swayed back in the chair, and brought his arm around in a swiping motion to push the blade away. She recovered fast, and stabbed quick at his belly. He kicked out and knocked her down beside the pot of beans.

Casually, his men came forward, their blades pointing at her.

"Does selling me off make your ass hurt less, whoreboy?" She still held his length of cherrywood, and wagged it at him. "You're a weak mule. Here, take your bit. You're going to wear it all your days." She barked a single bitter laugh.

To his own surprise, he took the cherrywood from her hands, then motioned for his men to take her out. She thrashed for a moment, then put on an air of dignity that looked preposterous in her little shanty.

They exited quietly, leaving Jastail beside his boyhood hearth. He sat staring into the embers of the fire a long while, a strange mix of peace and hollowness in his chest.

He didn't hear the knock at the door. Or rather heard it distantly. The third time the knock came it was cracking loud, urgent. He got up to answer it, pulling the door back to see an overweight man in a leather smith-apron calling on his mother's home late in the evening.

Jastail's gut tightened. "Can I help you?"

The man didn't fidget from foot to foot. He didn't lick his lips or need to wipe sweat from his brow. He was altogether comfortable. This wasn't his first time calling at this door. He only looked at Jastail, then past him when the patter of feet came from deeper within the shanty home.

Jastail turned to see a boy, maybe six, maybe seven. The lad had a careworn look in his eye. A bit of fear, too. And he looked, for all the gods-forsaken world, like a young Jastail. *A brother. Did she have another child to replace me?*

The boy's face showed a hint of confusion when he saw Jastail, but a heartbreaking familiarity when he saw the man at the door. He glanced toward the hearth. "Where's mother?"

Jastail fingered the grooves in his length of cherrywood, feeling like he might lose his own moorings. He considered the words of one of his dark poets, but left them alone.

Instead, he stepped into the doorway, near the caller, and stared him dead in the eye. Just above a whisper, he said, "Don't ever come back here. If you do, I'll find you, and I'll use your own tools to brand the words 'boy bugger' on your forehead."

The big man managed a momentary look of defiance, but must have seen something in Jastail's eyes. He nodded once and scurried away.

Jastail went back into the shanty home, and quietly closed the door. The boy was staring at him, still looking confused, but now worry also showed in his young face.

Jastail shook his head. "There'll be no more meals with strangers. You don't owe anyone that sort of kindness anymore."

The boy's eyes filled with tears. He hung his head, and quietly began to sob.

A TASTE OF AGONY

-Dirge-

TIM MARQUITZ

"A Taste of Agony" is set in my upcoming fantasy series, Tales of the Prodigy that features my outlaw, eunuch assassin Gryl, the protagonist from my Neverland's Library companion story, "Redemption at Knife's Edge." Trapped in hostile territory just after the resolution of the Avan-Thrak war, Gryl lives off the land and the spoils of his once ally, the chaotic Thrak berserkers. When a chance encounter with a group of renegade Shytan knights offers him a chance at a warm meal and a few nights of relative peace, the possibility of coin in his pouch, Gryl finds himself unable to refuse. He soon learns, however, that no matter how far removed from the war he might be, the past is never far behind.

Blackguards

G RYL SNARLED LOW IN his throat, dispersing the wispy breath against his palm. After a sevenday on the hunt, he'd found his quarry…and more.

Crouched atop a gentle rise, the sullen droop of snow-burdened pines masked his presence. He glared through the swirl of white flakes at the chaos unfolding below. The clash of steel fractured the air like thunder, and the frantic shouts of men followed. Gryl had expected the Thrak berserkers—it had been their clumsy trail he'd followed— but the cluster of Shytan soldiers this far north was a surprise; a most unpleasant one.

His stomach grumbled, echoing mournfully inside the shell of his leathered cuirass. He'd been counting on the spoils of the Thrak to provide his next meal, but the appearance of the Shytan left a hollow emptiness gnawing at his guts. It had been many days since he'd eaten last. It would be even longer thanks to his former enemy encircling the two berserkers. Too weary to imagine the Shytan losing to the pitiful beasts, Gryl settled in to watch.

The largest of the knights wielded a serrated falchion, its edge dripping with ichor. While little more than a butcher's tool, he put it to

"A TASTE OF AGONY"

Illustration by OKSANA DMITRIENKO

fair use. He stood behind two of his companions, darting between them to carve chunks of wet flesh from the berserker's mottled torso. The Thrak howled, frothy spittle gleaming in its sharpened maw. Its blue-tinted flesh gleamed in the dim haze of light. Spatters of red and black dotted the whiteness at their feet.

The Thrak whipped its bone blade in a wide arc, an ivory halo blurring above its furred head as it brought its weapon to bear. The closest knights parried in tandem, leaning into each other to absorb the beast's fury, turning the blow aside in a clash of pale splinters. Their banded mail rang with the impact. The third took advantage and cleaved the life from the berserker's muscled frame. The Thrak would soon fall.

Its horde mate, however, would not meet its end so easy.

Gryl watched the second of the berserkers bury his blade in the unprotected neck of a knight. The man's head snapped sideways with a muffled *pop*, his eyes wide though none of his agony escaped his throat. His head tore free of his shoulders to the wretched dirge of ripping cloth, his braided hair writhing like serpents in the air. The head fell into the snow, gouts of red conquering the crystalline canvas in rhythmic spurts. The knight's body toppled after, stumbling sideways into his brother-at-arms.

Despite being off balance, the second knight managed a desperate parry against the berserker's follow up stroke. Bone clanged against steel, the man's arms shuddering as he was driven back, boots sinking ankle-deep in the snow.

The knight's companion—a twig of a boy, only just coming into his manhood—stood his ground and thrust a barbed spear into the Thrak's muscled side. The point sank between the berserker's ribs, but the beast turned, twisting the haft. Gryl watched as the boy struggled to pull his weapon free, but the spear was held immobile, caught in the Thrak's flesh.

"Hold him, Kel," the knight shouted, pressing forward with his broadsword.

The blade found meat, slicing into the berserker's shoulder until it *thunked* into bone. The beast roared, the sound setting Gryl's ears to ringing, and lashed out at the knight. Mountainous knuckles collided with the man's face. The sharp *crack* of broken bone sent him reeling. He spun about and fell to his knees with a shriek, hands clasping at his cheek and jaw. Gryl saw his one remaining eye whirling in in its socket, the other half of his face an oozing sea of ruby waves. A line of blood ran from the knight's ear. He was dead, but had yet to realize.

The Thrak grasped the spear in its guts, wrapping its gnarled fingers about the shaft and brought its bone blade around. The weapon sheared through the wooden haft with ease, leaving nearly a foot of wood protruding from its side. The Thrak paid it no heed. It rumbled a challenge and charged.

The boy's leverage gone, he stumbled backward and fell, wide eyes locked on the approaching berserker. His hands scrabbled for purchase but he could find little in the soft wetness beneath him.

Cold sickness washed away Gryl's hunger. He cast a wishful glance at the surviving knights only to see them focused on the other Thrak. They were winning the battle, but none had noticed their dwindling numbers. By the time they did, they would be down one more.

The boy—Kel—to his foolish credit, held his voice, though in bravery or fear, Gryl couldn't say. He sighed, realization souring in his throat. To leave the boy's fate in the hands of the knights meant the boy died. Gryl pulled his skullcap tighter across his scalp to ensure his scars remained hidden and sprinted down the rise.

He drew a throwing knife from the belt that crisscrossed his chest and whipped it underhand at the Thrak, just as it reared up, readying to bring its sword down upon the boy's head. The blade pierced the small of its back. Sharp as it was, the knife was nothing more than an inconvenience, the sting of a wasp to a giant. It sank less than two finger joints into the berserker's flesh, its handle quivering. It was enough to earn the beast's attention, though.

As expected, the Thrak spun about with a guttural bark. Gryl knew the berserkers well, years spent on the battlefield alongside the hordes. The slats of the Thrak's red eyes gleamed with rage as it spread the trunks of its arms in challenge. It went silent mid-roar at seeing Gryl, posed as though it were a morbid statue. Its upper lip peeled back in a confused sneer. Despite never having the knack of discerning one of the beasts from another, Gryl was certain this Thrak knew him, recognized him. Gryl closed in its confusion.

He reached out and clasped the end of the spear that jutted from the berserker's side. The Thrak's eyes followed Gryl's hand, seeming only then to grasp its danger. Gryl's free hand wormed its way into the beast's wooly mane, closing about the knotted mess and pulling the berserker's head down. The waft of rotten meat and rancid flesh flooded Gryl's nose, but he clenched his teeth and exhaled hard in defiance of the stench. At the same time, he twisted the spear in the Thrak's guts and drove the remnants of the blade upward into its chest until it grated to a halt. The beast shuddered and loosed a spray of bloody froth that peppered Gryl's cheeks, tinting his vision red.

The Thrak's eyes wavered and rolled in their deep sockets. It loosed a wet growl, a low rumble fading in the depths of its chest, before the last of its life spilled out warm across Gryl's gloved hand. Its full weight sagged onto the spear, and Gryl let go. The beast crumpled to the ground with a sigh, its gaze still locked on him. There was accusation in its sightless stare. Worse still, Gryl felt its betrayal clawing at his conscience, a sting he was not prepared for.

"You there…halt," a harsh voice called out, its tenor demanding obedience.

Gryl cursed his preoccupation with the Thrak, suddenly able to hear the crunch of booted steps at his back. He loosed his sword and swung it about, leveling it just inches from the nose of the approaching knight, bringing the man to a sudden halt. Blood dripped from Gryl's fingers, the warm fluid hissing as it hit the snow. He tightened his grip on the hilt to keep the tremor rattling down his arm from showing.

Shorter than Gryl, the knight stared up the length of the blade. His stained falchion held too low to defend, he forced a grin. Its glimmer never touched his dark eyes. Gryl gave the faintest of nods and backed away with measured steps, circling to keep the remaining knights and the boy in his sight. He lowered his sword but didn't put it away.

"That was impressive, stranger," the boldest of the knights said. The coldness in his tone was equal of the chill in the air. "Never seen anyone take out a berserker so easily." He shook the blood from his blade and slid it home in the sheath at his waist, ceding to the unspoken truce. "Name's Brant; sergeant in the 101st company of Her Imperial Majesty's Royal Army. And you are?"

"Gryl," he answered simply, following suit and sheathing his own sword. Though he understood little of the hierarchy of the Shytan forces, he knew well enough that five knights and a boy hardly made up a squad, let alone a company. "Where are the rest of your men?" He glanced about, though confident they were alone. He'd seen no sign of any others from his vantage atop the hill.

While the soldiers wore the traditional black and red of their land, the swooping raven sigil of Shytan stitched into their sleeves at shoulder and wrist, Gryl had seen more than enough discarded uniforms scattered about the countryside to have doubts as to the knight's sincerity. He'd almost taken a suit himself.

Brant glanced at each of the other knights in turn, a crooked smile forming as he turned back to face Gryl. He raised a finger to his roughened lips. "Shhhhhhh. We're on a secret mission for the empress." A sonorous chuckle followed.

Gryl said nothing, letting the laughter fade, the sharp edge to Brant's voice confirming what he suspected.

After breaking the backs of the Avan Overlords, the Shytan forces had pulled south to shelter for the winter, leaving the frozen northlands to the still-rampaging Thrak they could not bring to heel. Gryl had followed in the army's wake. While he dared only the furthest outposts in order to trade the baubles and coins he'd scavenged from the dead and the scalps of the berserkers, he'd tread a generous portion of the north since his freedom had been won. The only living beings he'd come across beside the Thrak were bandits or deserters, there being little difference between the two. These men could be either. Whichever they were now, Gryl was certain they were no longer beholden to the regimented forces of the Shytan.

Kel scrambled to his feet in the awkward silence. "Thank you, sir. I—"

"Shut up, boy," Brant told him, motioning over his shoulder with his thumb.

Kel hurried to do as he was told, moving to stand at their backs with a sullen pout. Gryl watched him until he settled in place, childhood memories stirred awake by the boy's meek compliance. He had known such fear himself.

All the while his thoughts churned, Brant's stare seared his cheeks. Gryl met the knight's eyes once more. The two stared without saying a word, hands hovering near their swords. There was no mistaking the knight's disapproval, though Gryl could only guess the source.

"It's okay." The smallest of the knights broke the standoff, stepping alongside Brant, though Gryl noted he kept a respectful distance. Not even the knights were immune to Brant's wrath, it seemed. "We're all friends, right? Gryl here saved your boy and took out a Thrak for us, right? That's good, yeah?" The smaller knight stared at Brant until he conceded.

"Yeah, Mihir, you're right." Brant eased his hand from his sword but the threat still glistened in his eyes.

The second knight joined in. "What are you doing out here?" He had none of Mihir's nervousness.

"Foraging."

"And *your* people?"

Gryl nearly smiled at having his question turned back on him. "Lived north with my tribe in the Ural Province until the Thrak came ashore. Most of my village—my family—fell the first night, before full dark even settled. Those who made it to dawn were scattered to the wind. I've been on my own since the last of my kin were swept away in the Avan retreat these moons back." He'd sufficient practice spewing lies since he'd made the new empire his home. This one was no more difficult than any of the rest.

The knight stared without blinking. Unlike Brant, there was no hint of the man's thoughts reflected in his features. Mihir, however, gave him no time to contemplate his options.

"He's one of us, eh, Damien? Shytan by blood, even if he is a *skeg*." His voice was smooth, its tone bathed in honey despite the prejudice that came so easily to his tongue. "There's no need for hostility."

Gryl nodded agreement with the knight. He was more than willing to play the role of snow nomad—however disrespected—if it brought peace and allowed him to go on his way. The more they dismissed him, the better. The tremor had crept from his arm into his torso, the mad dash down the hill having sapped the last of his energy. He would fight if he had to, but he'd rather not.

"I've no quarrel with you knights." He gestured to the berserker he'd killed. "I'll take the scalp I earned, by your leave, and let you be about your mission."

"Fair skies, skeg," Brant answered with a twitch of a smile, the words spewed with the force of a crossbow bolt.

"Hold on, eh?" Mihir raised his hands and inched up alongside the sergeant. "Couldn't we use another arm, what with Chase and Iggy eatin' dirt? A man who knows how to take down a Thrak especially, yeah?"

Brant's eyes snapped toward Mihir. There was no hiding the man's anger. "We don't need—"

"What about the mission?" Damien asked, the question drawing Brant up short.

"Please, there's no need to argue," Gryl said, jumping in, "I'm not looking for work."

"No?" Damien's eyes shifted to Gryl. "Then the gurgles in your belly must be from the last feast you gorged yourself on, eh? I can hear the thing from here." He motioned to the smallest knight. "Mihir here makes the best rat-gut gruel to be found this side of the sword line." A slight grinned twitched at his lips. "You might even make a coin or two."

Gryl just stared, saying nothing. Damien had the right of it. It would be another day or more before Gryl could trade the scalp for a meager sack of rations.

"You're serious?" Brant asked, splitting his gaze between Mihir and Damien. When they both nodded, he raised his hands. "Fine, but if this dhongy herder slits your throat in your sleep, don't come crawling to me for sympathy. And before you go offering the empress' tits, he's only getting one share of the bounty, and *only* if he earns it, you hear?" He shook his head and spun about, shoving Kel ahead of him. "Come on, boy. Let's fetch the gear."

"You with us?" Damien asked as Brant and the boy trudged off.

Gryl swallowed a sigh. He knew nothing of the men's mission or who they were hunting, but the promise of food called to him like a sweet dream. His stomach speaking for him, he nodded.

Damien returned his nod with one of his own before traipsing off after Brant. Mihir came over to stand beside Gryl.

"That one there is Damien Kartain. The call him "The Ghost" because of all the folks he's killed so be wary lest you want to spend all eternity haunting him." Mihir stood stoic for a moment before breaking into a wide grin. "Though really, he's not too bad. Brant's who you have to keep an eye out for."

Gryl forced a thankful smile, though it barely scraped his lips. He hadn't been looking for company, preferring his own.

As if Mihir understood, he changed the subject. "You'll like tonight's stew." He glanced about conspiratorially before leaning in close. "Found a mongrel buried in the snow not two days back. Skin was black from frost, but the insides were pink and moist." Mihir chuckled and waved Gryl on.

⎯⎯•⎯⎯

NIGHT FELL JUST HOURS after the group gathered their supplies. They shambled on until the gloomy light just barely illuminated the horizon, and Brant called a halt. Gryl had been given the pack of one of the fallen knights, which was little more than a couple of ratty tarps and rolled sleeping gear. The men had scavenged the weapons and personal effects of the dead, but they'd left the bulky armor and the extra pack behind. Mihir shouldered the largest bundle of gear, the others carrying the same as Gryl, which told him the Shytan were little better off than he was. They were subsisting off the land just as he had been.

The group sheltered on the leeward side of a small hill nestled at the feet of the Jiorn Highlands, which rose up at a shallow clip for miles on end before dropping suddenly to the Boric Sea beyond. Gryl remembered the sheer wall of stone as the Avan ships brought him to Shytan, a shudder passing through him. At the base of the hills, the knights formed a loose circle of makeshift tents around a hissing circle of emberstones. Soft, gentle heat wafted from the piled, gray-black rocks, but the stones cast no light. Were it not for the frosted sheet of the earth reflecting the ambient shimmer of the skies, they would have been swallowed by the obsidian night. As it was, any further away than a few arm lengths and the men became deeper shadows amidst the black.

True to Mihir's word, the gruel had been fantastic, though Gryl suspected the depths of his hunger held some sway. Regardless, he licked at the bowl, savoring every drop before reluctantly passing it back to Mihir.

The knight held a finger to his smiling lips and whispered, "Remember. It's our little secret."

Gryl nodded as Mihir went off to scrape the bowls clean with snow. He disappeared into the darkness, only his quiet humming and the crunch of his boots giving his location away.

Damien reclined on one of his tarps, the others set at his back to quell the slight breeze that snuck past the hills. He stared at the emberstones through the narrow slits of his eyes. His breathing, slow and steady, sent willowy tendrils of white drifting past his face. If he weren't yet asleep, he would be soon.

Brant, however, remained wide awake. Kel hunched close to the stones while the sergeant sat with his feet extended, his legs stretched over Kel's thighs, so his boots dangled off the other side.

The boy had said nothing since Brant had ordered his silence, and Gryl never once caught him even looking his direction.

Brant had no such compunction. He stared with intense concentration, a look that would have warranted his death were the circumstances any different. Gryl's gaze drifted over and over to the young boy as he fought the urge to challenge the sergeant for his boldness.

The vaguest of trembles shook through Kel as he huddled beside the emberstones. The twigs of his arms clutched to his chest, but there simply wasn't enough meat on him to ward off the cold. His eyes were dots of white in the gloom. There was no mistaking the sorrow that cast a pall across his features. Whatever circumstance had brought him to the company of these men had done him no favors. Gryl sighed. Shytan was no less cruel to its children than Avantr.

"He's a pretty one, ain't he, skeg?"

Gryl glanced up at Brant, swallowing his animosity in order to remain silent but there was no hiding his confusion. It took a moment before Gryl managed to grasp the meaning behind the sergeant's words.

"Kel here is like you—a skeg, but he's from Andral, not that I suspect it makes much difference to you folks up north. Might be a few less dhongy where he comes from but they make up for it with goats. Ain't that right, boy?"

Kel nodded, daring a fleeting look at Gryl before returning his eyes to the stones.

Brant lifted his feet and reached out, grabbing Kel by his collar. He tugged and the boy nearly toppled alongside him, the sergeant wrapping his meaty arm about Kel's shoulder. "We saved him from a horde of berserkers not long back, so now he's kinda like our little squire." Brant chuckled as he squeezed the boy tighter into his side.

"A knight in training, so to speak."

Gryl met the boy's eyes for just an instant before they fluttered away, a subtle hint of red coloring his cheeks.

"I see you watching him, skeg," Brant continued, "but don't be getting any ideas. Just because you both fell from frosty twats up north doesn't give you any special privileges. This here's my boy, nobody else's." The sergeant pulled Kel closer and stuck his tongue out, sliding it along the boy's jawline. The slightest scrape of growing stubble whispered to Gryl's ears just beneath the breathy whistle of Damien's snores.

Right then he understood the knight's hostility, and it sickened him. His stomach rumbled, not with hunger but with the sour churn of disgust.

Brant laughed and clambered to his feet, pulling Kel up with him. The boy's chin hung at his chest, the knight's arm still clasped about him.

"So you know, skeg, I'm a light sleeper. Anyone so much as rips a butt frog and I'll hear it, so don't you worry about nothing tonight." His chuckles shook the boy as he led him toward his tent—Gryl only then realizing there hadn't been one set up for Kel. "Hope you don't mind a serenade."

Gryl went to stand but a hand clasped at his arm. Fury warmed his cheeks, and he spun about to see Mihir standing behind him. The knight shook his head and mouthed a silent, "Don't."

Gryl reluctantly settled back, his fingers instinctively massaging the pommel of his sword as he heard Brant's armor *clunk* to the ground. Mihir dropped down next to him. He said nothing, but there was no collusion in the man's expression, which tempered Gryl's fury, if only slightly.

A stranger to the ways of sex, his manhood cut away by the Avan Seer who'd inducted him into the role of Prodigy when he was just a boy, Gryl had no sense of the sergeant's intent until he'd made it obvious. Brant had mistaken Gryl's empathy for the boy as desire. The posturing had been his way of marking his territory.

A quiet gasp sounded in Brant's tent and Mihir tightened its hold on his arm. Gryl hadn't even realized he'd tensed, his hand sliding to the hilt of his blade. He drew a slow, deep breath and let it ooze from his lungs. Fingers twitching, he eased his hand from his sword as he got to his feet. He nodded to Mihir, unwilling to trust his voice to speak.

Gryl went to his tent and slipped between its fluttering walls, crawling beneath the threadbare blanket he'd been given. The steady slap of flesh on flesh floated on the night air, Kel's muffled grunts almost a chant in stuttered rhythm. Gryl felt his scars worming across his skin, the sudden flush of his power begging to be set free. He clenched his teeth and covered his ears to silence the world. His hands still trembled, fury and weariness waging a war.

It would be many long hours before Gryl found sleep. His dreams were cruel.

———•———

THE GROUP WAS UP at first light and on the trail shortly after. Gryl said nothing as they made ready, gnawing on the salted meat Mihir had provided to break their fast. It was hardly a meal yet it might well have been a feast as far as Gryl was concerned.

Brant met him with a broad smile as he climbed out of his tent and went about his preparations, casting amused glances Gryl's direction at every opportunity. Kel had been just the opposite. He never once looked Gryl's way, his chin seemingly woven to his tunic. He hurried to get ready and shuffled off the moment the group started on. Gryl's anger, only muted from the night before, simmered as he fell in line. Though he still felt the tingles of weakness dancing through his skin, the gruel and rations had returned some measure of his energy. He glared at the back of Brant's head as they traveled, Damien and Kel bookending him at either side.

Mihir hovered close to Gryl, making small talk as though hoping to defuse his anger. It worked, to a degree as he blathered on about the *mission* amongst the more mundane topics. They'd set out from Cantor, Mihir said, a small fort set upon the sword line, the group charged with returning the head of an escaped convict, though he knew little more. The constant prattle of the knight's voice kept Gryl from dwelling on the sergeant and what he'd do to the man once he regained his strength.

The sun had crept nearly halfway across the sky behind its mask of gray and rumbling black clouds before Damien raised a fist to bring the group to a halt. Mihir's voice in his ears, Gryl hadn't heard anything until the talkative knight went silent. As soon as he did, a duet of raspy grunts resounded from somewhere ahead, distorted by the labyrinth of jutting, snow-covered stones that made up the gateway to Jiorn. The noise echoed through the afternoon still, striking a chord with Gryl. A tenuous hum danced inside his skull.

There were Thrak ahead.

Brant and Damien seemed to recognize it as well. They shifted their packs from their shoulders and eased their swords free of their scabbards. Gryl did the same, Mihir following their example a moment later. Brant handed one of the dead knight's swords to Kel, but it was clear he was uncomfortable with it. It looked overlarge in his hand, his forearm sagging with its weight. Brant was heedless of the boy's discomfort, though Gryl expected nothing less.

The sergeant crept along the narrow pathway between the sharpened stones that rose from the ground like fangs. The rest of the group followed, Kel hovering close to Brant despite the fear that stiffened the boy's spine.

They wound their way through the rocky maze until Brant dropped before a jagged outcrop, staring at something just over the other side. Gryl squeezed in alongside Damien and spotted two berserkers digging at the snow at the center of a tiny clearing. One's back was turned toward the group while the other sat facing them, though its view was blocked by its horde mate. They seemed oblivious to the world around them.

Brant raised a hand for the group to make ready as Gryl stared at the beasts, the pressure in his head growing. He had never seen the creatures so distracted before. He wondered if the Thrak were becoming as desperate as he had, scouring the land for sustenance as the Shytan population dwindled above the line, the populace either dead or having retreated. With only so much readily available supplies, he had to imagine the Thrak were beginning to burn through their food sources.

The sergeant gave him no more time to wonder. He slipped between the stones and charged at the berserkers, Damien and Kel in tow. Gryl hissed and ran after. Mihir was on his heels. The nearest Thrak stood and sniffed the air, whirling about just as Brant cleaved an oozing river across its chest. The beast roared and stumbled back, knocking the second one into the snow.

Damien and Kel dove on the berserker, flailing away with their swords as it lashed out at them with its claws, its bone blade swinging from a leathern hook at its belt. Brant and the other two drove it back, knocking aside its frantic attacks and meeting each with steel. The berserker bellowed, its voice echoing through the hills. The beast at its back scrambled and got its feet beneath it just as Brant hewed the leg of its companion.

The Thrak stumbled and fell to its knees, shrieking in rage and agony, spewing blood from the cavernous maw of its throat.

Damien drove his sword into the gaping hole and twisted, ripping the blade free with a grunt. The Thrak's scream melted into a wet gurgle. It fell back clutching at its spurting neck, convulsing as its life spilled from its wounds.

The second Thrak growled and spun. Without looking back, it darted up a step path that snaked its way up the hill.

"After it," Brant shouted, the shrill edge of laughter tingeing his voice. The knight barreled up the hill after the berserker, Damien right behind with Kel a few short paces to their rear.

A crushing fist seized Gryl's guts. His head throbbed, a sense of chaos warring for reason. He stumbled to a stop and stared after the fleeing beast, cursing his muddled thoughts. Mihir went to run past, but Gryl snaked a hand out and seized his arm, stopping the knight short.

The hum nagged.

"We need to help them," Mihir said, though he did nothing to shake loose of Gryl's hold. He remained silent for a short moment before asking, "What is it?"

Gryl ignored him, following the trail of the Thrak with his eyes. It had just slipped from sight behind a wall of rocky spires. Brant and the others were a short distance behind it, the berserker much lighter on its feet than its bulk suggested. Just as the knights and Kel dropped from sight behind the stone wall, Gryl's mind slid the pieces into place. His eyes went wide as he surveyed the terrain.

"They didn't draw their swords," he muttered, the words tumbling from his lips in a jumbled heap.

Mihir yanked his arm loose in a panic. "Tell me what's wrong."

"Thrak *never* flee," Gryl said as he slammed his sword into his sheath and bolted for the rocky face of the hill ahead.

"Wait," Mihir shouted at his back. "Don't leave me here,"

The words barely registered as Gryl leapt to the first of the rocks, his fingers clasping for leverage. Muscles screamed at the sudden exertion, flashes of pain spearing his shoulder blades as he scampered up the slick stones. The hum filled his head as he climbed, finally easing to a dull whisper as he grew accustomed to it. He had hoped to never hear its song again. The sound mocked him, as though laughing at his foolishness. He growled in reply as he made his way up the hill, each handhold an icy blade that threatened to rob him of his hands, but he pushed on.

His eyes traced the path he'd laid out from below, his body pulled along by the strings of his will, his fingers numb despite his gloves. He cared nothing for Brant and had no opinion of Damien, though the knight had offered him no offense, but it was Kel who drove him on. While death awaited the knights at the top of the hill, the boy's suffering at the hands of Brant would be a pleasant dream compared to what was to come.

A Thrak loosed a roar above and Gryl heard the muted clang of a weapon slamming into the steel of armor. The harsh grunt of a man followed, the berserker shrieking its displeasure.

The trap was sprung.

Gryl clambered up the last few horse-lengths of the hill leaving spots of blood and pieces of flesh in his hurry as he slithered along the rock wall. Time had run out.

He grasped at the ledge and pulled himself over the lip of stone that separated him from the scene below. His heart wailed at what he saw—what he had hoped to never see again.

An Avan sorceress stood at the center of a blackened circle, its lines drawn with the cooling ichor of a Thrak berserker, which lay desiccated and discarded in the snow just feet from where the sorceress chanted. Glyphs and sigils painted in red ran the length of the inside circle.

The woman preened, straight-backed and tall, confident in her superiority. Her purple robes clashed against the solemn whiteness of the hill, her shorn scalp glistening in the gloom. Gnarled hands traced invisible shapes in the air. Gryl's gaze fell back to the circle. It was a conduit, the sorceress amplifying her energies in preparation. It was the circle that had alerted Gryl to her presence.

His hands shook at seeing it, memories threatening to overwhelm him. He had been murdered within such a circle and reborn in its embrace, time and time again, the ritual purification feeding him with agony until he could devour no more. That was what the sorceress had in store for Kel.

Gryl glanced over at the boy. Kel had fallen to his knees, his hands clasping at trails of red that stained his tunic. To Gryl, the wounds looked shallow, but they were only the beginning of the boy's suffering if the sorceress had her way.

Lying beside Kel, Damien floated in pool of his own blood, clouds of steam billowing around him. A bone blade jutted from his skull. Its flesh-wrapped pommel quavered above as though a flag pole driven to ground. He was the lucky one, death having come swiftly to collect him.

Just a few feet behind them, Brant whipped his falchion overhand and slammed it, again and again, into the last of the Thrak's who'd fled. The butcher's block *thump* sang out against the rocky walls. Covered in blood, thick rivulets running down his frame, the sergeant kicked the berserker's carcass aside. He screamed at the sorceress, crimson streamers dangling from his lips as he stumbled toward her.

"I'll kill you, whore."

The sorceress only grinned, her fluttering movements stilling. Darkness welled about her hand as she held it out toward Brant. Before Gryl realized what she intended, bolts of ebony screamed from her fingertips. Nowhere to run, the sergeant reached out for anything to shelter behind.

His hands found Kel.

He yanked the boy in front of him just as the bursts of energy hit. Kel screamed, spears of blackness piercing his flesh. Held fast by Brant, he writhed beneath the virulent caress, skin peeling back in waves. When the spell broke, Kel tumbled from the knight's grip and slumped to the ground. Brant staggered off in a daze, wisps of black smoke wafting off him. After a few steps, he fell, as well.

The acrid scent of charred meat slithered into Gryl's nose as he launched himself at the sorceress.

"No!"

His voice echoed across the clearing though he hadn't realized he'd yelled.

The sorceress spun, surprise rippling across her features. If she recognized Gryl for what he was he would never know. His throwing blade punctured her eye, burying itself deep in the well of her skull. He landed just short of where she stood and drew his sword across her throat as he darted past. The sullen *whump* of her body collapsing sounded at his back as he rushed to examine the boy, his sword sheathed before the sorceress hit the ground.

Gryl's heart sputtered at what he saw.

Kel's clothing had been burned away to expose the entirety of his misery. Blackened pustules covered his exposed flesh like a swarm of giant beetles, their ashen mounds quivering as though possessed of a life of their own. The boy gasped when Gryl knelt beside him. His every breath, shallow and sharp, sounded like his last but still the next one came, and the one after that. Gryl cursed the boy's stubborn defiance and looked to his eyes. The lids had melted away, leaving nothing to hide the bubbled mass of ruin that sloshed inside the sockets. Gryl felt his own eyes well up, tears warming his cheeks as he looked down on the wreckage of the boy.

"Did you get her?"

Gryl's tears stilled when he heard the knight's raspy voice. He looked up from the boy to see Brant digging at the snow in an effort to sit up. While his skin had been scorched by the sorceress' spell, he had escaped its full wrath, hidden as he'd been behind Kel.

A low growl slipped from Gryl as he rose and went to stand in front of the sergeant.

"Well, did you, skeg?"

Brant struggled to his elbows with a grunt, still unable to see across the clearing to where the Avan sorceress lie dead. His dark eyes settled on Gryl. The sergeant's baleful smile was smeared with a layer of soot, but it shone through. Among all the myriad scrapes and crusted wounds, which covered his face, there was nothing there that resembled remorse.

Gryl grabbed the knight's throat, sinking his fingers in deep as he pushed the man to his back. Brant's eyes went wide as Gryl yanked his long dagger free, the blade shimmering in the reflected pallor of the cold north. The sergeant stiffened as the knife drew closer, but Gryl had no intention of letting him slip away so easily.

With the tip of the blade, Gryl split the sleeve of his tunic, opening it from his wrist to his elbow. As he peeled the fabric back, Brant sputtered against his grip, seeing the woven patchwork of scars revealed, but Gryl held him fast. Weakened by the sorceress' blast despite what he'd done, there was no escape for the sergeant. Gryl grinned at that thought.

He set the tip of the dagger to one of his scars and the mass squirmed as though a worm slithered beneath the skin. Warmth throbbed up the length of his arm. Brant struggled, his pulse pounding against his temples, face reddening. He cursed, but the words came out as phlegmy gurgles.

The blade sank into Gryl's savaged flesh and carved out a single line of scar tissue, a layer of skin peeling back beneath the knife with ease. It came loose in a ragged rectangle. Dots of red appeared on the meat beneath, but no blood flowed. Gryl speared the piece of flesh on the tip of his knife and shifted his other hand from Brant's throat to his jaw. He ground his thumb and forefinger into the joints as the sergeant gasped for breath, forcing his mouth open. A deft flick of his wrist spun the dagger about. Gryl slid the blade into Brant's mouth, driving the carven flesh into the back of his throat. The sergeant swallowed on instinct, the scar tissue sucked into his stomach with a retching gasp.

"You'll torment no more children."

Gryl pulled his blade free and shook the bloody spittle from the blade, releasing Brant. The knight coughed and clasped at his throat, desperately drawing in air.

"No!" Mihir screamed as he staggered up the rise to see Gryl standing over the sergeant. "Don't kill him."

"I hadn't intended to." Gryl laughed and slid his dagger into its sheath. "Death would be a mercy. He doesn't deserve such kindness." He spit on the knight and stepped away.

Mihir stood his ground and stared as Gryl returned to Kel. The boy still breathed, though that was hardly a kindness. Gryl reached beneath Kel and scooped him into his arms, waxen skin peeled away at the slightest touch. The boy moaned but unconsciousness was his sanctuary. He didn't awaken.

Brant thrashed in the snow, kicking up a mist of white powder and crystalline stars. Deep, guttural groans spilled from him as his fingers clawed at his chest, bloody streaks smeared across his armor. His wild eyes bulged, shimmering with an eerie, emerald hue. He stared unseeing at the billowing sky, drool splattering his lips and chin as he howled. The bitter stink of urine filled the air.

"What did you do to him?" Mihir asked, terror drawing a mask across his features. He stepped away as Gryl drew closer.

"I gave him a taste of agony."

Gryl started down the path, his burden hanging limp in his arms. Brant's cries swelled to shrieks that reverberated through the maze of stone. The sound followed Gryl toward the horizon, but with every step it fell further behind until it faded away.

Through it all, the boy breathed on.

WHAT GODS DEMAND

— The Blasted Lands —

JAMES A. MOORE

The Empire of Fellein has reigned in relative peace for hundreds of years. The legends told by the people speak of a First Empire and the greatest city ever known to mankind, Korwa. According to the tales Korwa was destroyed in the distant past in an epic battle so intense that it destroyed part of the world and created the Blasted Lands. There might be some truth to the legends. Not long ago explorers from Fellein found the distant Seven Forges mountain range, deep in the Blasted Lands and also discovered, to their surprise, that the area within that range is inhabited by people called the Sa'ba Taalor. The gray-skinned people from the distant realm have come to Fellein and, since that moment, a war has been building. Swech is one of the Sa'ba Taalor, chosen by her gods to hide among the humans and do the will of her deities.

Blackguards

T HE SA'BA TAALOR HAVE very few rules. First among
them, however, is never disobey the gods. That would never
happen with Swech.

Swech Tothis Durwrae served all of the Daxar Taalor—the gods of
the Seven Forges—without hesitation. She had her favorites, of course.
Paedle, who believed that wars could be won without the use of warriors,
and Wrommish, who believed that the body was the finest of weapons.

She agreed with both of the gods, and she served them as loyally
as any child has ever served a loving parent. Though if the truth were
to be completely revealed, she could have done without her current
predicament.

She was standing on a rooftop in a foreign town that she barely
knew, stalking one of the men walking below her, and wearing the
wrong body. She bore the flesh of a different woman; it was only her
spirit that remained unchanged. With a thought she could even change
her memories—as if she were moving behind a veil and watching the
world through someone else's eyes. Swech remained in charge of the
body at all times, the other woman was dead, killed by Swech when
she took the form—but she had access to a lifetime that had nothing

"WHAT GODS DEMAND"

Illustration by OKSANA DMITRIENKO

to do with her own. It was an enlightening experience.

The Daxar Taalor liked to challenge their followers, to sharpen them as a whetstone sharpens an edge, but there was a part of her that wondered about the wisdom behind their actions.

The city was Canhoon, often called the "Old Capitol." In appearance Canhoon was much like Tyrne, the Summer City. As Tyrne had been designed to look as much like Canhoon as possible that was not surprising.

Canhoon was a vast place that was ancient well before Swech was born. The city was, in fact, one of the last remaining cities left from the time of the First Empire, which had been destroyed ten centuries earlier. There was history in every stone building and in the timeworn statuary that lurked near every building and often atop the older structures. She moved among those frozen forms, flittering from one shadow to the next as she eyed her potential targets.

There were six men down there, and they moved together, but not for much longer she suspected. A few of them were armed, dressed in clothes that spoke of function, not wealth. Two, however, were dressed in finery, and of those two neither looked capable of fighting. One was old and heavy and walked with a pronounced limp, supporting a good deal of his weight in a walking staff. Her lip curled at the sight of him in an involuntary sign of disgust. Weakness was repugnant to her. Not the physical frailty of the man's form, but that he leaned on the staff as heavily as he did and that, likely, the four men dressed for fighting were there to defend him from any assault.

The Sa'ba Taalor learned to walk by the time they were six months of age. They were offered shelter and food and learned to speak at a young age. Not much later the training began on how to make war. There were seven gods in their land and all of those gods believed in war in its myriad incarnations.

Physical weakness was not something that could be avoided. In time all flesh fails. But mental weakness and emotional frailty were flaws that were either cut away or costs beaten out of the flesh as flaws are pounded from forged metal. The Sa'ba Taalor did not abide the weaknesses of the spirit.

"Do not make enemies you cannot defend yourself against." She whispered the words. Now was not the time to attack.

Swech ran her tongue over the back and then the front of her teeth, feeling the differences in the terrain of her mouth. These teeth were fine, she supposed, but they felt wrong. They were in just off from where she expected them to be. Her body was either resting in the heart of Wrommish or it had been incinerated when she threw herself deep into the volcano at the request of her god. She had been reborn into the new body, and it was sufficient, of course, but still not quite right. There were few scars on her body to tell tales of her previous combats. The Sa'ba Taalor were warriors, and each scar told a tale. The gods made demands and she listened, but the skin she wore now was almost unmarked. There were few scars and none that spoke of combat so much as they spoke of clumsiness. A scar on the hand where a knife has cut is not the same as a scar where a sword had kissed the flesh.

Her first name meant "soot hair," and it was a name that had always suited her appearance. Her tresses had been dark gray more than black for her entire life and she never much gave them any thought. Now her hair was a different color. She liked it well enough, she supposed but, like her teeth, the hair felt wrong.

Her hands were strong, lean and well muscled, with good joints and properly callused, but they looked wrong just the same, and her skin was unsettling pink in comparison to the light gray she had long since grown accustomed to.

The winds blew hard from the north and promised cold weather. Swech glanced in that direction but it did her little good. There were clouds gathering, a promise of storms to come. To the south Tyrne was gone, taken in a massive eruption of fire and molten rock only days earlier. Between the two towns a stream of refugees was makings its way to Canhoon by land and river alike, most carrying whatever they could and praying it would be enough. Swech had left a week before the destruction, warned away by her gods.

A great mountain rose where the city had been, birthed from the very fires that bled from it even now. She looked at it and smiled. Durhallem rose from those ashes. One of the gods of her people was now in place. She knew what would come next, what Durhallem would offer to the world around them, and she was pleased by that knowledge.

The world was changing and, as the Daxar Taalor demanded, she aided in that transformation.

The heat of the volcano mingled with the cold of the encroaching winter and gave birth to clouds.

The rains were already there, and as she blinked against the breeze she felt the first light droplets falling from above. The rooftop she stood on was at an angle. She made it a point to adjust her stance as the rains started in earnest.

Below her, in the streets and narrow alleys, people either ran for shelter or pulled up their hoods as they prepared for the rains.

"Which one?" she asked. Her eyes looked down on the crowds and Swech prayed for an answer from her gods.

What does distance mean to gods?

She closed her eyes and listened.

Wrommish and Paedle answered her together.

Sometimes the gods are kind.

"OF COURSE THE WORLD is changing, you old fool." The words were spoken without any enmity. "We've lost the new capitol and now the refugees from Tyrne overwhelm our town and fill the streets with their filth. If that isn't a sign of bad times ahead I don't know what is."

Lirrin Merath was an opinionated jackass, but he was also a powerful man. He had wealth and he had influence. He also had no intention of surrendering either, simply because the new empress was coming to live in Canhoon.

The man prattled on, waving his fat hands about and trusting that his hired guards would be enough to keep the beggars away. The gold on his fingers would have purchased a small house, but that hardly mattered. The important thing, as far as the old man was concerned was that he kept what was his.

Walking next to him, Arlo Lancey would have gleefully slapped the man senseless if he could have, but he was wise enough to know not to press his luck. Lirrin was an ass, but he was also the minister of land in Canhoon and as such he was a very powerful figure, even without his money and his guards.

Just of late land had become the most valuable commodity known to anyone.

"Lirrin, my friend, the refugees have only started." Arlo was not a minister. He had his own sources of power, but an appointment by the Council was not one of them. "We have a few of the Roathians, but only the start of them. When the people who escaped from Tyrne show up, the city will change, whether we want it or not."

"You don't need to tell me." Lirrin snorted the words as if trying not to laugh at a particularly fine quip. "I've already seen the desperation in some people's eyes. Tyrne is gone, but hardly forgotten." He scowled. "Her refuse is coming in like a tide of backed up sewage."

The winds picked up and Arlo raised his hood just before the faint drizzle became a proper downpour. They could have sought shelter, but nether of them much wanted to be where they could be easily heard, and so they continued on in the rains, preferring the added sounds to confound any who would listen in on their private conversations.

It was best not to discuss murder when others could hear the words spoken. The rain hammered down on their shoulders in a thousand tiny drumbeats. Arlo squinted against a rude droplet as it tried for his eye.

"I am for secrecy, Arlo, but we have reached a limit." Lirrin very nearly had to yell to be heard over the rains. He pointed toward the door to a tavern and Arlo nodded his agreement. There could be no discussion if they could not hear themselves speaking.

Within moments they were inside and grateful to be free of the deluge.

The Broken Oak sported a painted sign of a vast oak tree split in half, with four shields around the base and seven swords rammed though the tree itself. There was a legend about those very things, but Arlo couldn't remember it and didn't have time for childish tales in any event. The tavern was a larger place than they'd expected, reaching deep into the building and sliding far enough back that the back wall was lost in shadows and smoke. Between that shadowy depth and the front entrance squatted a collection of well-used tables and, at most of them, a few people sat locked in their own conversations.

Lirrin moved into the place as if he owned it, and headed for a table that sat hidden well in the murk of the large room.

The owner nodded in their direction and otherwise ignored them for the moment. There would be time for serving them after they'd made themselves comfortable.

Lirrin sat and gestured for his four bodyguards to stand close by but not too close. The four men managed to look suitably intimidating as they surrounded the table.

"Are they truly a necessity?"

"The lads? Of course they are. There are plenty hereabouts that would see me dead. I am not a popular man, Arlo. I am well hated by those with whom I do not do business. And right now that list is very long indeed."

Arlo already understood that, of course. The minister did not control the cost of land, but he did handle the paperwork involved in the sales. There were normally fees involved and he dictated what those fees might be. While he could not forbid a person from selling land, he could make the notion a very expensive one.

Currently, Lirrin was living a life of luxury and doing so gladly, but he also knew it might not last long now that there was a new empress and especially now that she was coming to Canhoon to live.

A flash of a coin and the barkeep came and took their order personally and then brought them their ales. When he was gone, Lirrin continued as if there had been no delays. He spoke and jabbed his fat fingers into the polished wood of the table to emphasize his words. "I have families coming here—entire families, mind you—that have nowhere to go. The messengers from those families have been coming to me and nearly demanding that they be allowed to purchase the houses they'll need, as if I have control over how quickly buildings rise."

"Well, they're desperate."

Lirrin shook his head and his jowls wobbled sympathetically. "No, they are scared and angry. And they think that coins alone will cover the cost of finding them new homes. The fact is that there simply aren't a thousand buildings waiting to be filled."

Arlo managed not to say anything that would have caused tension. There were ways around the problem, of course. Though there were few buildings waiting around empty, a few could have been found without too much trouble. Not enough, true, but for some of the wealthier families exceptions could be made.

Almost as if he could read minds Lirrin made a comment, "Not even a fortnight ago there were several lots that I could have used, but they were all purchased." He waved a hand. "Had I known then what was happening I could have charged a levy large enough to make the price impossible to handle, but the woman came through and made the deals before there was any reason to wonder about the future."

Arlo shook his head and made a face. There were reasons he was dealing with the old man across the table from him and mostly those reasons revolved around gold.

"Do you have a name for this woman? With a little persuasion, perhaps she could be convinced to sell the lands again. I have stonemasons waiting to start building as soon as the word is given. I have carpenters and a workforce that could be building even as we speak."

"Of course she has a name." The man's fat face twisted into an ugly mask of annoyance. "I don't recall it at the moment, but of course she has a name." Sometimes Lirrin played at being absentminded and sometimes he was sincere. For a few coins he would remember in the former. Arlo knew Lirrin's expressions well enough to know he sincerely could not recall.

A stray breeze caught the candle and lamp flames throughout the room and brought in a wave of fresh, cold air. Arlo looked toward the doors but saw no one cross the threshold.

He looked around the vast tavern again as he gathered his thoughts. There were four large men around them and he was grateful for that. The shapes around them were shadows, mostly, hulking shapes that loomed and fed themselves on mutton stew, or chunks of roasted meat. They were only people, and Arlo knew that, but as they spoke of dark things and deeds best not considered, those forms seemed more sinister than they should have.

Dark thoughts bred dark fears.

"Could the papers be lost?"

"Certain copies could be misplaced. Hers, however, are in her possession." Lirrin stared at Arlo as if he might be daft.

"A name, Lirrin. But give me a name and I can make this all better. You can have your higher levies and the families that pay the best can have their homes within a few months at the most."

Lirrin chuckled, his face taking on a particularly gourd-like symmetry as he did so. "Unless things change and drastically, we might not have to worry about that. These gray people everyone is talking about will see to it."

The Sa'ba Taalor. The name made Arlo's skin shiver. He'd not seen them, of course. No one had. But there are always rumors, aren't there? Giants. Invaders who were indestructible in combat from all he'd heard. One traveler he'd spoken to briefly told him they'd destroyed the Guntha by themselves, a hundred of them taking on over a thousand and winning. Actually, the man had said ten had done the job, but both agreed that had to be a case of the man mishearing what was told to him originally. If one of the monsters could kill a hundred soldiers, the empire was already doomed.

"That is a river I should rather worry about crossing when the time comes. Until I see these giants, I will continue with the daily business."

"Well then," The shadows spoke, soft and feminine. "You should wait no longer."

———— ◆ ————

SWECH WATCHED AND LISTENED and waited. The Daxar Taalor had told her who she should eliminate, but she waited just the same. There was no hurry and she had a constant desire to know more.

The two men were soft, both of them dressed in finery and perfumed. The older one she knew. She had dealt with him when Wrommish told her to buy the lands around the area. Four days ride into Canhoon, one afternoon spent counting coins, and four days back to the home she'd made in Tyrne before the gods decided it was time to destroy the city. Hardly an effort at all, but the Daxar Taalor wanted the land, and she claimed it silently in their names.

What the gods demanded, Swech was glad to do.

When she knew enough, Swech stepped from the shadows and made herself known. Her hair was pulled back, leaving her face free, but as had been the tradition when she first met the people of Fellein, she was wearing a veil that covered most of her face. In this work the shadows were her comrades and she intended to keep it that way.

Her attire was all dark, mostly black, with loose sleeves and leather breeches. She'd slipped free of her cloak and stood before the men in attire they surely thought better suited for a man.

"You are a Sa'ba Taalor?" The younger of the men was the one asking, but the four paid fighters immediately came to attention at the question.

The man sounded skeptical.

"I am."

The older man laughed, but there was no humor in the sound.

"I know you. I would know a northerner's eyes anywhere and yours are lovely enough. You're the very woman I was speaking of. You are the one who purchased so much land."

If he was trying to woo her with words his compliments were weak.

The younger one immediately smiled. "Truly? Perhaps we can reach an accord." Dogs ran for table scraps with less enthusiasm. He had a smile that showed many teeth, and too much of his gums. The Pra-Moresh smiled much the same way before they bit down and killed.

"The land is not for sale. Nor will I be paying extra fees."

The young man grew annoyed with her words. His smile wilted and became a confused scowl. He was pretty enough and likely expected her to swoon when he gazed in her direction. That was a problem with many of the people she'd met since coming to Fellein. They thought pretty faces and perfume made them attractive.

"There you have it, Arlo. The land is not for sale." Lirrin was the older man's name. He was old, and soft enough that he hired others to fight for him should the need ever arise. She resisted the urge to sneer again.

The other, Arlo, shook his head. "What a pity."

She knew their kind. They spoke lies and dressed them in pretty deceptions. Perhaps there were some among the Sa'ba Taalor who would not know the difference, but the god Paedle taught the purpose of lies, and how best to see them. Sometimes the finest battles were won with words as the weapons.

Other times….

"I have told you the land is not for sale. Was there anything else you needed to know?"

"Just your name." The younger one, Arlo. "Just that, so I can try to convince you again."

"You have no desire to convince me." She studied him carefully. "You prefer to know where I am staying and what name I use, the better to send your hired killers to take what is mine in the night."

Arlo blinked, and for one moment his true face was revealed. He was stunned by her direct words. The man was used to a certain level of respect accorded to his station, and thought himself too pretty to be so easily read.

"That's simply not true." He spoke softly and slid from his seat.

Behind the veil, Swech allowed herself a very slight smile.

"You would have me dead and take the deeds. The cost is less for you. Then you and your fat friend would make arrangements that profited both of you and left me a rotting corpse."

Lirrin made a disbelieving noise. She did not like him.

"You cannot speak to Arlo that way."

She didn't look in his direction, but kept her eyes on the pretty man. "I just did."

Lirrin spoke again and snapped his fingers. "I've a mind to teach you a lesson in proper behavior." As his fingers moved, so too his guards, who moved in a loose circle around Swech and eyed her without expression. All save one. The man to her right was trying not to smile and failing. He liked the notion of beating on a woman and likely felt it would be his place to do whatever he wanted with her when he was done.

"You would have your hirelings teach me a lesson? Or you would do it yourself, old man?"

She finally looked his way and Lirrin's face wobbled as he scowled. "I'll have it both ways, perhaps." His tongue licked across his lips. "I'll have my lads handle you, and I'll teach you a few lessons in civility when they're done."

The younger one actually seemed surprised by the comments. He was, perhaps, a little less likely to have others do his work for him.

Swech took a long stride to the left and brought her elbow around behind her, spinning her body to follow. The elbow struck the first of the bodyguards across his jaw and she felt the bones and teeth shatter under her assault. As the man was falling she grabbed the dagger he had at his side and pulled it from the sheath.

The man hit the ground and groaned as his broken face struck the floorboards.

The eager one came for her, bulling his way across the short distance. He had a few scars on his arms and though he was bearded she could see the remnants of an old wound on the side of his face.

As he reached for her, Swech dropped low and drove the dagger in her hand deep into his inner thigh. He yowled and staggered and tried to stand. She dodged to the left and drove her heel into his knee, forcing it to bend in the wrong direction. His screams grew louder as he crashed down, unable to stand on the ruined leg.

Blood flowed like water from the wound in his thigh. He would be dead before he could teach himself to walk again.

The third hired man shook his head and tried to back away, but Swech had a point to make. She reached for him and rammed stiffened fingers into his throat, feeling the cartilage in his neck collapse. In moments he was gagging and his face reddened as he tried to breathe through a ruined windpipe.

The fourth drove a fist into her side and Swech moved with it, feeling his heavy knuckles scrape across her ribs and drive into her stomach with bruising force.

Her arm came up from under and behind his elbow, and captured his forearm. He looked toward her, surprised by the move and then horrified as she bent her body and forced his arm to follow suit. For one moment he almost got away, but she turned her hip and felt his elbow break like a twig.

He could not make a noise. The pain, she knew, was far too large to allow him the luxury of a scream. Down he went, onto his knees, mouth open in a silent shriek of pain. She captured his head with one hand and brought her knee up into the side of his temple. When he fell the rest of the way to the floor his head was the wrong shape.

When Swech looked back at the table the old man stared at her with wide, frightened eyes and his hands clutched at his chest.

"What lesson will your men teach me?"

Arlo very carefully sat back down.

Around them the activity of the tavern had come to a complete halt, save for the moans of the broken and battered around Swech's area. Every person in the place was looking, and Swech shook her head. She could not understand these people. In the Taalor Valley a fight was not a spectacle very often.

"I—" Lirrin looked at her and shook his head. His eyes remained wide and stuck to her gaze, unable to look anywhere else apparently.

"You killed them!" Arlo shrieked. He looked at the bodies around her with a shaken expression and trembled where he sat.

"No. Some will live." She stepped away from table letting the two men contemplate both their actions, and the dead and wounded around them.

———✦———

ARLO TRIED TO KEEP his eyes on the woman but she faded away into the shadows of the tavern.

He also tried to breathe, but found he could not drink in enough air to help him.

Beside him Lirrin was pale and trembling, his eyes doing their very best to look everywhere at once. "Is she gone? Did she go away?" Five decades or more to his life and the bastard whimpered like a child having nightmares.

Arlo took comfort from the other man's fear. It balanced him and soothed worries.

Around them several of the patrons were staring at the dead and dying surrounding their table. Some looked upset, but less than he would have expected. This was a place where people came to talk and not be seen. The mess at their table was exactly the sort that guaranteed people got seen more than they wanted.

"We have to go, Lirrin."

"Go?" The calm surface was gone and the man trembled visibly. In all of his years of posturing it seemed the official had never seen bloodshed on that scale. It was possible, likely, even, that he'd thought himself safe from it, insulated by his hired swords.

"Yes, go. The City-Guard will be coming soon. We should not be here when they arrive."

Lirrin's thick fingers clutched at his sleeve and the man's round face wobbled as he shook his head.

"She might be anywhere, Arlo. We can't leave here. We have to wait for the guard. They'll protect us."

When he spoke his voice was cold and much calmer than he actually felt. Someone needed to take control of the situation. "We came here to discuss matters best not heard by the City-Guard or anyone else, Lirrin." He pulled his sleeve from the fat man's clutch. "We need to leave here. Now."

"What if she's still out there?" Lirrin nearly wailed the words and Arlo stepped away from him, embarrassed for himself and for the man he'd never respected but had at least considered a man.

"Come out of this, Lirrin! You're behaving like a child!"

That did it. Lirrin's head rocked back as surely as if he'd been slapped, and the wild fear in his eyes was crushed down.

For one moment Arlo thought he'd pushed the minister of land too far. The heavy jowls still quivered, but with a different expression on the mewling mouth buried in that face. His teeth were bared in anger for a moment before he calmed himself down.

"You're right. Thank you for that, Arlo."

"We must leave here. Now."

"Of course." Lirrin hauled his considerable bulk up and leaned heavily on his walking staff as he maneuvered around the dead and wounded. "Time to be elsewhere."

Outside the sounds of approaching figures could be heard past the closed door. They did not hesitate, but instead took their chances in the torrential rains.

If anything the storm was worse. The waters fell in sheets and the winds threw those sheets sideways, slapping open cloaks and making any attempt to stay dry a laughable failure. The City-Guard were stomping up the street, looking for any sign of who might be a danger. The man in the lead was unknown to Arlo, but he had the look of a seasoned veteran and his expression when he eyed the two of them was uninterested at best.

Arlo felt a slow bloom of shame in his chest. Even the City-Guard, who made less coin in a year than he did in a fortnight, looked at him with no real interest. He would have to look into hiring someone to train him in the finer points of using a sword. He had not so much as practiced since he'd done his required service to the Empire. He had just seen an unarmed woman ruin four men in a matter of seconds, and the sword at his side was never even considered as an option. It was an ornament to him, a sign of his status and nothing else.

He had to change a few things about himself, if he ever got the chance. The woman behind the veil, Lirrin said he knew her, that she was the one he wanted to deal with. She said she was one of the Sa'ba Taalor, the unholy terrors he'd heard about before. After watching how quickly she took down four trained men, he was beginning to doubt his earlier assessment of the assault on the Guntha.

The rains continued and Arlo had to shout to be heard over the constant deluge. "Did she seem like that when you permitted the land sales, Lirrin?"

"What?" The man was distracted, looking around at every alley as they moved along the wet cobblestones and sought a place where they could, once again, continue their conversation.

"The woman. Did she seem so damned…competent?"

"She was just a woman. I thought she was attractive enough. What did I care?" He shook his head and then went back to looking at every darkened corner. "As I said, I had no notion of what she was up to until it was too late."

Lirrin was crumbling again. Arlo could see it. Now that he was no longer among the public the fear was coming back and pressing down on the man. "We have to get inside! We have to find a safe place!"

They had chosen to meet in Old Canhoon, at the heart of the city, because many of the shops were closed at night and the chances of running across people who could identify them were slimmer when they were away from their homes. Now that choice played against them. The rains had come along unexpectedly and driven most of the City-Guard into hiding. The cut-purses were gone as well, but there was no place for them to easily hide, and they would be walking and exposed for longer than Arlo liked before they reached his home and safety.

He walked faster and then forced himself to slow down when Lirrin whimpered. The old bastard was lame, but he was also important enough that Arlo had to remember him.

Lirrin puffed along, his staff tap-tap-tapping along the cobblestones at a pace that was nearly frantic in comparison to his usual plodding steps.

Arlo bit back a demand that he move faster still, the words fading away as the now familiar sound of hard wood striking stone suddenly stopped.

He was ahead of the minister and he felt a deep and abiding cold creep through his flesh that had nothing at all to do with the rain.

He did not want to turn around. He was terrified by the notion. He did not want to see the older man dead or dying, but he had to see, he had to know, because until he checked he could not be certain if he was safe or in danger.

He turned and cursed under his breath.

Lirrin stood where he had been, his eyes bulging from the folds of fat around them. His face was red and growing redder and his hands reached out imploringly. The staff he'd been holding wobbled as if surprised, and seemed determined to stand on its own. Without the support of the old man's hand, however, it fell victim to gravity. The sound when it clattered to the street was loud enough to hear past the falling rains and the maddening winds.

Lirrin strained his arms forward but the rest of him did not move.

"Lirrin?" Arlo's voice was too small to be heard from more than a few inches away. "Lirrin what is it? Are you ill?"

The man dropped forward. He collapsed first to his knees, which gave a much louder crack of sound than his staff had, and he winced at the pain of impact even as his body shuddered.

Suddenly shorter than he had been, it was far easier to see the shape of the veiled woman standing behind him.

Even lost in shadows and rain, Arlo could see that she was a strong woman, her body well muscled, and almost as tall as he was. Arlo knew that he should have been able to take her in a physical challenge.

Should have been able to. His hand was only inches from his sword's hilt but he did not reach, did not attempt to draw the blade. He was far too scared for that. She had killed five men before his eyes and he had never killed even one in his life.

She was holding what looked like a fine metal thread in her hands. The thread spun into two metal rods, one held in each hand, the color of the metal ran from silver on either end to a deep red in the center.

Lirrin's neck vomited blood as the man tried to breathe and failed.

"You have walked away from your safety, Arlo." The woman's voice was muted by the rain, but not lost to him. "I was told that you should possibly live. That you might have value. What do you think of that notion?"

"Oh, yes!" His vision bobbled as he nodded vigorously, doing his best to keep a solid eye on the woman in front of him as Lirrin fell face first into a puddle among the cobblestones. The water around his head formed a reddening halo. "Yes! I can be very useful to you, I swear it!"

Her hands moved and the reddened metal strand wrapped around one of the rods in her grip. Her eyes never once moved from him.

She did not move closer, but the stance she took, the way she looked at him, carried a level of threat that nearly made Arlo soil himself. "My gods have said you could be useful to me. They have also said the choice is mine as to whether or not you survive. So tell me. How are you useful to me alive?"

"Lirrin was the minister of land! I'm in line to take his position should he die and—" He gestured at Lirrin's corpse. The halo was dispersing now, washing into a faint pink corona that bled down between the stones. "As you can see, he is very dead."

"You will take his place as minister?"

"Yes! Yes, of course! I would be his replacement!"

"And how does that help me, Arlo?" She was closer now. He didn't remember her moving but she was closer, her body in front of the corpse of dear, dead Lirrin. Arlo managed not to scream but it took an effort.

"I can help you buy more land, and keep your secrets! Yes! I can keep your secrets!" His voice had gone shrill again, but he could not stop himself. He could not make his voice be strong and confident when he was so certain he was about to die.

"I have already kept my secrets. You do not know my name and the only man who could have told you is dead." He listened to each word from her with a growing dread. She was right, of course. Lirrin was dead.

"Everyone needs allies. I can be your ally. Please let me show you how useful I can be to you."

She did not speak, but instead closed her eyes for a moment.

He raised one foot.

"If you run, I will kill you."

Arlo set his foot firmly on the ground.

———•———

THE DAXAR TAALOR WERE gods. It was exactly that simple. They had been a part of Swech's life since she first breathed and likely even before that moment.

They were the beginning and the end of everything that mattered in her world. When she was asked to throw herself into the heart of Wrommish, the fiery volcanic pit that pulsed with its own rhythm, she did not question the request, she simply obeyed.

Her body plummeted down into fire and she felt her skin and hair ignite. There was pain, of course, but there is always pain in life. She accepted the pain and was rewarded for her faith when she rose hundreds of leagues away from where she had been in the body she now occupied. Great Wrommish could ask anything of her and it was given. That was the way of the Sa'ba Taalor.

She looked at the pitiful man standing before her. She had warned him not to move and then she had waited with her eyes closed and listened to her gods.

He trembled. He stood before her and shook, his eyes wide and wet in the continuing rain. His hand scant inches from his sword and he never reached for it.

Had she not met members of the Fellein Empire capable of fighting, she would have been even more disgusted.

"Where I am from, you would be dead if you had not attacked me when you had the chance."

Arlo blinked and shook his head. "But I don't want to die." She read his lips as much as she heard him speak. The words were lost in the rains.

"When I come to you again, and I will come to you, you will do as I say. Do you understand?"

"Yes. Oh yes. Whatever you need." He looked so grateful she almost believed him.

"You say that." She stepped closer and he shook again. She was close enough she could have kissed him or bitten him and either way he would not have been able to stop her. Swech smelled his breath: it was as sour as the way he made her feel.

"You say that," she continued," and I know you think you mean it. You will change your mind later." Her hands moved quickly and caught his left hand in a strong grip. He flinched.

"No! I swear to you!"

"Do not swear to me. Swear to your gods."

"I don't have any gods."

Her smile was as cold as the rain.

"Listen to this name. Know it. Understand that to recite it means your life to me. Wrommish. Say it."

He looked at her for a long moment, puzzled. "Wrommish?"

"That is correct. Wrommish. Know the name. Keep it in your breast and keep it closely. If you do not repeat it to me when I see you again, I will kill you. Do you believe me?"

His sickly white face grew paler. "I do."

"Say the name again."

"Wrommish?" So weak a voice, so frail.

"Louder."

"Wrommish."

"Pray every night. Before you go to sleep, you must pray to Wrommish. Do you understand?"

"No."

"Before you close your eyes tonight, pray to Wrommish." She moved closer still, until the water that dripped from her veil fell across his lips as she spoke. "Thank him for your life. He is the only reason I have not killed you. Wrommish says you have not lost your usefulness."

"I will." He nodded his head slowly, but with very strong conviction. "I will. I swear it."

Her thumbnail scratched the top of his hand hard enough to scrape flesh and drawl a thin stream of blood. He was wise enough not to pull back.

"Before that heals, we will meet again." Swech let his hand go.

"I...Your face is covered. How will I know you if I can't see your face?"

"Look at my eyes. You will know me."

He nodded.

"You will say the name of your new god. Every night and when we meet. If you have not said your thanks to him every night, I will know. And you will die. Do you believe me?"

"Yes. Of course I do."

"This is good."

She stepped back from him, moving easily over the cooling corpse of the former minister of land.

"Now, Arlo. Go to your home."

He couldn't have run much faster. He turned from her and pelted his way up the road, panting and puffing after only a dozen strides. He was handsome enough in form, but he was soft and weak. A child of eight years could kill him with ease. At least if that child were of the Sa'ba Taalor.

"I have spared him, Wrommish. As you have asked. But he is so very weak."

Swech looked around carefully—always be aware of your surroundings—and then moved slowly away into the night. The rains would continue for the next few days, she knew that well enough.

For now she had to get to her home.

There was much that had to be done, and time was short.

Thunder rumbled from where Tyrne had once stood, a beautiful city crushed under the fury of Durhallem.

The gods made their demands and she obeyed without question.

TAKE YOU HOME

-Shadowdance-

DAVID DALGLISH

"Take You Home" takes place in the vast city of Veldaren, the major story hub of my Shadowdance Series. It also features the main protagonist of the series, Haern the Watcher. He's a self-appointed guardian of the city that keeps an eye on the various thief guilds, ensuring they follow the rules he's given them to keep the city in a state of delicate peace. He also tends to do some mercenary work on the side, so long as it isn't too distasteful. For those curious, this story takes place between books three and four of that series.

Blackguards

J ULIANNE SAT WITH HANDS folded across her lap, just as her mother had instructed, as their carriage rolled through the streets of Veldaren. The stone road was uneven and crowded, their driver lucky to keep them at a consistent pace for more than a second or two. The curtains were drawn, preventing her from seeing out, which left Julianne incredibly bored.

"Will we be there soon?" she asked.

"Your asking won't bring us there any sooner," her father said, head leaning against the side, cradling by his large hand.

"It won't be long," her mother said, casting an annoyed look to her father. She looked tired, dark circles underneath her blue eyes, her long brown hair lacking any luster as it fell past her neck. Julianne sensed the tension, and she prayed it wasn't her fault. Her parents had bickered about this trip to Veldaren for weeks, with neither seeming like they wanted to go. *Veldaren is dangerous,* her father had said over and over again. But her mother always countered with language of tradition, trade, contracts, things far beyond nine-year-old Julianne's understanding. All of it must have meant something, though, for her father had relented, and together they'd traveled south from Felwood

"TAKE YOU HOME"

Illustration by DAVID ALVAREZ & OKSANA DMITRIENKO

to the city of Veldaren.

Not alone, of course. They'd had their house guards, plus some servants, most of whom followed in the carriage behind them. The only strange addition was the man who sat beside Julianne to her right. He was a quiet man, having entered their carriage just before they drove through the gates of the city. She'd flushed upon first seeing him, for he was very handsome, his blonde hair cut to the neck, his blue eyes sparkling whenever he smiled, which was never enough for Julianne's taste. Whenever she could she peered at him, and she swore he was always watching from the corner of his eyes. Sometimes he ignored her. Sometimes he'd wink at her and smile.

The man was so charming it made it easy to ignore the long blades belted to his waist, to forget that she didn't know his name. Whatever the reason he'd joined them, Julianne had a feeling those swords were involved.

"*Get out of the way!*" she heard the driver shout, and the carriage lurched to a stop for the thousandth time that day.

Her father sat up, pulling back on the curtain so he could look out.

"Gods damn it," he muttered.

"Want me to take a look?" asked the blond stranger.

"It's probably for the best," her father answered.

The stranger pushed open the door and stepped out. The sounds of the city rushed in, louder than ever. She heard shouting, arguing, an intermixed bustle of motion and footsteps. The daylight was almost blinding, and she squinted and turned away. Wishing she could go with him, Julianne thumped her head against her door and lifted the curtain slightly. She was so short, she could only see the upper portions of the square wooden homes built on either side of the road.

Her mouth opened to ask again how long until arriving at their temporary home in the city when a shadow covered the door. She spotted a hooded man wearing a green cloak for the briefest of moments before the door ripped open. Instinctively, Julianne let out a cry and tried to scoot back, but hands were on her, a bag pulled over head. Her parents screamed, and she joined them as rough hands pulled her out of the carriage. Throat burning, she fought as coarse strings at the bottom of the bag tightened, choking out her cry. She gasped for air as her feet bumped along the stone, her tiny body easily carried. As the world turned brown, and then black, she heard the distant sound of swords clashing, coupled with the screams of men dying, dying just as she was now.

━━•━━

WHEN JULIANNE CAME TO, the bag was no longer over her head. Her eyes slowly opened and she fought waves of nausea in an attempt to gain her bearings. She was in an empty building, dark, dusty, and with a tall ceiling. Her last few moment of consciousness flickered through her, reawakening her fear. Letting out a gasp, she pushed her eyes fully open to take in her surroundings. Her gasp made hardly a sound, for a gag was tightly wound about her head and shoved into her mouth. She sat in a chair, hands tied behind her with a large piece of rope. All around her were men with dark clothes and long green cloaks. At their waists, tucked into belts and loose hanging sheaths, were daggers and swords.

"The girl's awake," said one of the four men, glancing over. He had a hood pulled over his head, much like the others. His face was badly scarred, and when he smiled at her, it was the ugliest thing she'd ever seen. Immediately she tried to stand and flee, without thought or reason. The binds held her down, and all she accomplished was rocking her chair from side to side.

Casually, as if it were nothing at all, that same man walked over and backhanded her across the face. Tears ran down as she cried into the gag, and she felt her right cheek starting to swell.

"No need to rough her up, Jack," said another of the men.

"Nothing says I can't, either," Jack shot back, and he winked at Julianne. "The rules of the job say she has to be alive when he gets here. I don't remember hearing she had to be dolled up and pretty, though...."

The way he was looking at her, smiling, filled Julianne's stomach with bile. As Jack took another step toward her the door to the warehouse burst open, and a fifth cloaked man rushed inside. His hood was down, his short red hair wet with sweat. He looked young to Julianne, easily younger than all the others.

"What the fuck, Lee?" asked the oldest of the five, a man with wrinkled skin and gray hair who leaned against the wall beside the door.

"The Watcher!" Lee shouted, turning about and kicking the door shut. "The Watcher's on our tail."

Jack took a step back, a hand dropping down to the sword at his side.

"How do you know?" he asked. "He drop in all nicely to tell you?"

"Fuck you," Lee said, wiping a hand across his forehead. "I found Kirby's body three streets over, and the Watcher's Eye was carved into his stomach."

"That doesn't mean anything," said the older man. "The Watcher's killed plenty of Serpents in his day. What makes you think he's looking for us?"

"If you'd let me finish I'd tell you," Lee said. "There was a message written with Kirby's blood in the dirt beside him. '*Where's the girl?*' it said. We're fucked, all of us, we're gods-damn *fucked!*"

Julianne's eyes were wide as they bounced from one man to the other, trying to make sense of the situation. Who was the Watcher? And why would these five be so scared of him?

"Let me get this straight," the older man said, as he drew his sword and stepped closer to Lee. "You found Kirby killed by the Watcher, recently killed I might add, and then you ran straight here?"

Lee's face, already pale to begin with, paled even more.

"Not…straight here," he said. "I ducked through a few alleys first. I'm not stupid, Stan."

The others drew their own weapons, and there was no hiding the frustration on the older man's face.

"Ducked a few alleys?" he asked. "You wet-nosed moron. Did you hang out a sign at the door asking the Watcher to come in for a mug of ale, too? Shit. We're leaving, now."

Jack gestured toward the door.

"What about our payment?" he asked. "If we're not here when—"

"We'll set up another meeting," Stan said. "Something we can't do if we're fucking dead. Have I made myself clear?"

"Perfectly clear," said a voice belonging to none of them. The men in the green cloaks froze, and in that sudden calm the intruder descended from the rafters. He was a swirling chaos of gray cloak and boots and flashing swords. He landed in their center, and though she never saw the hit, Jack fell backward, clutching at his neck as it gushed blood.

Then Julianne knew. The way the others hesitated to act. The way Lee let out a horrified scream as a large urine stain darkened his trousers. The way the intruder smiled beneath his dark hood, as if merely amused by the weapons they raised against him.

This had to be the Watcher.

Stan had the courage to lead the attack, and all but Lee joined in. The Watcher spun in place, cloaks whipping about the air. Julianne could not follow his movements, and it seemed neither could her kidnappers. The men were beaten back, one losing his hand, another screaming as a wound on his chest seemed to open on its own. Stan continued on, stubbornly refusing to be overwhelmed by the display, and then suddenly the Watcher lunged into him. Their bodies crashed together, rolling. When they came to a stop, it was the Watcher who stood, shoulders hunched, cloaks falling forward to hide his body.

His smile was gone.

"Get back here," he said, his voice a whisper that somehow Julianne heard with ease. She wondered a moment who he spoke to, then saw Lee flinging the door open to the warehouse. A slender dagger flew end over end through the air, stopping in Lee's neck. The young man let out a cry, then dropped to his stomach.

With that, it seemed the fight was over. The Watcher walked from body to body, checking for signs of life. Only Jack made noise, weeping as he clutched his bleeding neck. He lay not far from Julianne's bound feet, and the sounds he made, the way his whole body seemed to shiver, filled her with an overwhelming desire to vomit. Only the gag kept her from doing so.

Without saying a word, the Watcher leaned over Jack, curled a blade around his throat, and then cut. Jack's convulsions grew, but only for a moment. Then his eyes rolled back and he lay still, leaving Julianne's stifled weeping as the only sound in the warehouse. The Watcher sheathed his blades then turned to her, and she let out a muffled cry. His face…it was covered in shadow but for his mouth and lower jaw. The grim smile there, so cold, so determined, convinced her this man was not her salvation, but merely another kidnapper. Eyes widening, she kicked and struggled, desperate to free herself from the bonds as the man stepped toward her.

To her surprise, her display halted his approach.

"Calm yourself, Julianne," he whispered. "I'm here to free you."

That whisper…why whisper, when everyone was dead? She stopped struggling, though, for there was no use. Sniffling, she stared at the Watcher, wishing the gag was gone so she could plead with him. The man knelt down so that he was at her height, and then he touched his hood with his hand. It never moved, but somehow the shadows receded, revealing a handsome face, square jaw, blond hair, and pretty blue eyes. Julianne felt hope kindle for the first time in her breast. The man…the man from the carriage?

"Your father sent me," he said, as if he could read her mind. "Now sit still while I untie you."

He walked around her chair, pulling her gag free as he did. She spat several times, wishing she could get rid of the sweaty taste. Behind her, the binds on her feet and hands loosened, and with a soft cry she lurched from the chair and spun about. The Watcher stood there, eyes on her, ropes in hand.

"Take me to my father," she said.

"I will," the Watcher said, the shadows returning to his face. "But I still don't know who hired the Serpent Guild to kidnap you. If I take you to safety, the man or woman responsible may arrive while I'm gone. That means whoever wished you captured could do so again, and next time I may not be fast enough to save you. Do you understand?"

"I think," she said, though she didn't really. "What do you want from me?"

He gestured to the chair.

"If you're brave enough, I can put you back in this chair, and we can wait. When the other party comes, I'll put an end to it, permanently. I need you to trust me, Julianne. I'll understand if you want to leave…"

She thought of going through it all over again, of trying to sleep at night knowing whoever wished her kidnapped or dead still lurked in the shadows outside the window to her keep. Though it made her hands shake, she nodded.

"I'll do whatever it takes to keep me safe," she said. "Just tell me what to do."

He smiled at her.

"A brave girl," he said. "Your parents should be proud. Sit down in the chair and wait."

She did, crossing her arms to fend off the cold she felt despite the warmth of the warehouse. The Watcher removed his large, strange-looking cloak, setting it on top of a crate in the corner. After that he removed Stan's green cloak, checked it for blood, and put it around his neck. Once done, he dragged the bodies one by one to the same far corner where the shadows were at their deepest. Julianne watched with grim fascination. When he was done, the Watcher returned to her chair and stepped around back.

"Put your hands behind you," he said.

She did as she was told, and then she felt the ropes slide once more around her wrists.

"The knots won't be real," he whispered into her ear. "The moment you pull against them they'll come apart, so don't panic or do anything rash. I need you to trust me, you understand?"

She nodded, praying that she did.

The Watcher circled her, examining his handiwork. Apparently satisfied, he picked up the gag and moved to put it her mouth. Julianne turned her head to the side, and as much as she didn't want to, she felt fresh tears roll down her cheeks.

"Please," she said.

The Watcher paused, then tied the gag loosely around her neck instead, letting it hang down as if she'd forced it free.

"Remember," he said. "Stay calm, and no matter what happens, keep your faith in me. You won't die this day, I promise."

And with that they waited, the Watcher hovering over her as he stared at the warehouse's lone door. Julianne didn't know how long they waited, only knew it felt like forever. Her rear hurt from the hard wood, her back ached from staying still so long, but she knew she had to be patient. She was the heir to her family's numerous plantations, and as her mother often told her, suffering through difficulties was part of the life they must live. At last the door creaked open, and she straightened.

Armed soldiers entered, one after the other, until there were six in the warehouse. Her protector watched them with arms crossed over his chest, as if without a care in the world. Last came a man in a finely fitted vest, black pants, and dark hair pulled into a ponytail. A smile was on his face, a face so familiar Julianne could not contain herself.

"Uncle?" she gasped.

The Watcher glanced at her, mouth turned to a frown, and she shrank in her chair. Meanwhile, Uncle Ross chuckled.

"I must admit," he said. "Of all the family reunions we've had in the past ten years, this is my favorite."

The soldiers fanned out, two remaining before Ross to protect him, the other four surrounding Julianne and the Watcher from all sides. Julianne's panic grew, and she struggled to remain seated. The Watcher had just taken on five at once, but that was with surprise against men without armor. Now there were six, and these soldiers carried long blades and wore chainmail beneath their tunics. What hope could he possibly have?

"Good of you to join us," the Watcher said with that strange whisper of his. "Now hand over the rest of the payment."

Ross reached into a pocket, withdrawing a small bag of coins tied shut with a string. He tossed it underhanded, the bag landing near Julianne's feet with a loud, metallic rattle.

"It's all there," he said. "Now do the deed, or get out of the way."

The Watcher's hands drifted to the handles of his swords.

"Consider it done," he said. "You can go."

Ross shook his head.

"Not good enough, rogue. I want my brother's lands, and I want them without any fear of complications. Julianne dies, and before my own eyes. I'm not risking you squirreling her away to ransom back to my brother after I'm gone."

Julianne's eyes widened. Her father's lands? But what did that have to do with her? How did her dying help her uncle? The Watcher seemed to understand, though, and he slowly shook his head.

"Murdering your niece for a chance at an inheritance? You'd fit in well with the people of Veldaren, foreigner."

Ross shrugged.

"I'll consider that flattery. Now if you wish to keep breathing, this is your last chance. Kill the little bitch, or get out of my sight."

The Watcher drew his swords, and he placed one against the skin of Julianne's neck. She tensed, body shivering, teeth chattering. Trust him, he'd said, and she tried to do just that. Looking up, peering into the shadow that was his face, she saw him nod ever so slightly.

"Kill the bitch?" he asked. "If you insist."

The sword vanished from her throat as the Watcher spun into motion. Like a savage beast he flung himself into the soldier at her left, but unlike a beast he made no roar, no sound at all, just the chilling silence and ethereal movements as his body leapt through the air, swords like extended claws. That silence broke the moment he made contact, blood splashing, soldier howling in pain, Julianne screaming at the sudden ferocity as the other guards came rushing toward her with drawn steel. Not him, but *her*.

Julianne leapt from the chair, and true to his word, the Watcher's knots slipped open with ease.

"Watcher!" she screamed, running toward him. The man spun, green cloak twirling, and when he saw her he ripped it from his shoulders and flung it over her head.

"Drop!" he screamed, and she instantly obeyed. As the cloak hit the men behind her she fell to her knees, curled into a ball, and put her hands atop her head. Nothing but a blur, the Watcher sailed over her, twirling midair, and then she heard steel clashing against steel, shockingly close. Teeth clenched, she curled tighter, listening to the battle, listening to the pained screams of another soldier. Something hit her back, and she flung forward, rolling to spin around. It was the Watcher who had kicked her, pushing her away as one of the soldier's swords struck the ground where she'd been. Frozen with fear, she watched as her protector battled two-on-one, swords bouncing back and forth between his foes, and though he was outnumbered, it was clear the Watcher was the one on the offensive. The soldiers looked so sluggish in comparison, so slow and weak and baffled.

The first dropped, blood gushing from his neck. Another took his place, only to quickly find a sword through his eye. Uncle Ross swore, and it seemed he finally realized there would be no victory for him that day. The final soldier leapt back, trying to guard the path to the door as her uncle fled. He shouldn't have bothered. The Watcher slid about him like water around a stone, smooth and quick, and then the sabers slashed out Ross's ankles before he could finish opening the door. As her uncle screamed, the Watcher spun around, anticipating the final guard's rushing attack. Both blades curled around his chainmail, piercing through his armpits and deep into his body. The man froze for a moment, blood gargling from his mouth, and then he dropped.

Yanking his weapons free, the Watcher stood among the bodies, shoulders rising and falling as he breathed in deep. Drops fell from his blood-soaked sabers, and not a hint of his face was visible through the darkness of his hood. Even knowing his reason for being there, even knowing she was safe, Julianne found herself more frightened of him than ever before. He'd killed eleven men, and not a scratch was on him. The only sound now was that of Uncle Ross groaning in pain as he crawled to the door.

The Watcher knelt over him, and without ceremony or hesitation, he plunged one of his swords deep into Ross's back.

"Bitch killed, as requested," he whispered into her dying uncle's ear as he twisted the blade. "Consider yourself lucky to receive such a quick death. You deserve far worse."

The Watcher stood, cleaned his weapons on her uncle's shirt, and then retrieved his original mismatched gray cloak. Sweeping it over his shoulders and clasping it tight, he turned toward her. The shadow around his face receded, and she saw his blue eyes, and in them was a strange sort of sympathy.

"Come, Julianne," he said, hand outstretched. "You're safe now."

It seemed a strange thought, but though his cloak, his shirt, and his arms were all stained, there was no blood on his hands. Rising, she accepted it, and the Watcher smiled.

"Let's take you home."

SEEKING THE SHADOW

-The Book of Deacon-

JOSEPH R. LALLO

In The Book of Deacon's *setting the Northern Alliance and its southern neighbor Tressor have been at war for generations. Almost since the war began an assassin has stalked the northern lands, quickly becoming a legend among the people for both its skill and its elusiveness. This story takes place between* The Book of Deacon *and its prequel* The Rise of the Red Shadow. *It is the much-requested telling of how two of the most infamous figures in the setting first crossed paths.*

TALES OF ASSASSINS, MERCENARIES, AND ROGUES

Blackwing

I N A SMALL AND dark tavern in a forgotten corner of a kingdom once called Vulcrest, two men in heavy fur coats were drowning their frustrations in cheap ale. The tavern was lit mostly by scattered holes in the poorly thatched roof. From a hearth near the center of the room, a smoky fire provided meager warmth while roasting the remains of a wild pig, provided by one of the morning's patrons.

"Another!" growled one of the men, slamming his empty tankard on the table. He was a burly young man with a wooly brown beard and a face misshapen by his wont for fighting.

"For me, as well," said his drinking companion, an older and even more inebriated man in a rattier coat.

As the two men were the only patrons at the moment, the lull in activity had motivated the innkeeper to retire to a private room for the afternoon in preparation for the busier evening hours. That left only a mousy young barmaid to take orders and collect payment, a task for which she lacked the proper force of will to perform with any degree of success. The two men had been taking full advantage of the arrangement.

"I…I'm sorry, but that's your sixth, Carlisle," said the barmaid. She was addressing the younger man, but her eyes were held low to avoid

"SEEKING THE SHADOW"

Illustration by ORION ZANGARA

looking at him directly. "And Cassius, that's your eighth. Your tabs are both days old and awfully large. The keeper says I shouldn't give you any more until your bill is settled."

Each man gave the maid a hard look, which she still refused to meet.

"Now Belle," the older man began, "you would deny my good friend and your best customer the much needed salve of strong drink in this dark time of his?"

"You haven't paid in days, and the keeper…well, I can't—"

She was interrupted by a thump on the warped front door, finally heaved open after three attempts. A stranger strode inside and stamped the snow from his boots. He was tall and thin, dressed in finely tailored leather and fur more suited for a royal court than a nameless tavern. His skin was flawless and pale, neither baked by the sun nor marred by battle or blemish. He removed his fur hat to shake free its crust of snow and revealed short blond hair that seemed almost white in the dim light of the tavern. Despite the fact that the pair of drunken patrons and the barmaid turned distrustfully toward him, he didn't seem bothered in the least. The newcomer took a seat at an empty table, shrugging free a heavy pack. It struck the ground with the rattle of metal.

"Good afternoon, young lady," he said with a respectful bow of his head. "Might I trouble you for some brandy?"

"I'm afraid we don't have any brandy left, sir."

"Red wine?"

"Yes, sir."

He flipped her a silver coin. "A bottle please." He then turned to the two patrons. "Good afternoon, gentlemen. You were having a conversation. Don't let me interrupt."

"You aren't from around here," grumbled Carlisle. There was a quality to his voice that suggested he hadn't uttered a single word in the last few years without gruffness.

"Astutely observed, good sir," the newcomer said.

"Why are you here?" Carlisle said.

"I am a bit parched and badly chilled from my travels."

"But why are you *here*?" Carlisle repeated, a threat in his tone.

"I am a thirsty traveler. This is a tavern. Do I need a better reason?"

"Are you a trader?" Cassius asked.

"That I am not."

"Well, you don't look like a soldier."

"Another astute observation." The stranger turned to Belle, who perched on a stool, attempting to retrieve the requested bottle of wine. "Quite the savvy patronage you've got at this establishment, young lady."

Carlisle stood and rested his hand on the grip of a cudgel hanging at his belt, the end of it carved to reveal some kind of beastly creature. "You planning on joining the Alliance Army then? In the middle of training, maybe?"

"I'd wager a fair amount that I'm better trained than half of the soldiers at the front."

"If you're all that well trained and such, then why aren't you out there fighting?" growled Carlisle.

"Because, as you suggest, I am not from around here."

"Where are you from that you can't serve your time in the army?" Cassius asked.

"The mountains."

"This is Vulcrest. We're all from the mountains," Carlisle said, marching up to the man and pounding his cudgel on the table. *"Where are you—?"*

"You know something?" the stranger interjected, standing to meet Carlisle eye to eye. "I was warned when I came this way that

I would not be well received. It is thus a welcome surprise to find the locals showing so keen an interest in their fellow man. I find it heartening to see two complete strangers make so thorough an effort to become familiar with the personal history of a simple visitor. So heartening, in fact, that I feel comforted enough—no, more than that, I feel *obliged*—to ask you each a few questions such that we might each know one another as proper friends do."

"I don't—" Cassius blurted.

"Rumor has it the estate just outside town lost its owner last night."

"You know about that?" Carlisle said. The statement came as enough of a surprise to briefly push aside his violent intentions.

"It is why I came here, sir."

"To this village?"

"To this tavern. When I asked some townsfolk who might know more about the killing, they suggested there was a drunken lout in this very tavern who was formerly employed by the victim. Would that be you, or is it your friend here?"

Carlisle started to raise his cudgel again, but Cassius stopped him with a hand to the shoulder.

"You're treading dangerous ground, stranger," Cassius said. "Look at you. Prime of life. Claiming to be well trained. You ain't in the army, and you ain't never *been* in the army. We're at war, stranger. We need every warm body we can get to take his turn at the front line to keep those Tresson devils at bay. We each took our turn. Barely made it back and got the scars to show. No one makes it back looking the way they did when they left. You don't look like you so much as busted a lip in your life. Only way that happens for a man like you is if you deserted, dodged, or bought your way out. In any case, you're no kind of man at all." He pulled out his own cudgel. "I'd say it's our solemn duty to make an example of you."

The stranger didn't look frightened. If anything he looked disappointed. "You are planning to make an example of me…with *that* misshapen piece of *wood*?" he asked, vague disgust in his tone as he indicated Cassius's weapon.

"It don't need to be pretty to cave *your* pretty little skull in."

"Violence…" The outsider shook his head. "I have no specific objection to violence. It is regrettable, but it has its place. If you *must* spill blood though, don't you owe it to yourself and to the target to do so with dignity? Use a tool that pays honor to the fallen. A tool like this, for example."

The stranger drew a unique weapon from within his coat—the action performed with startling speed—brandishing a serpentine blade as long as his forearm. The gleam of metal and blur of motion were enough to convince his would-be attackers to retreat a few steps. For a moment no one moved. Even Belle, wine and tankard in hand, was frozen in place in the doorway of the storeroom.

"Gorgeous, isn't it?" the stranger said, turning the blade to catch the light of the fire. "Look at the cutting edge. Asymmetrical. Curving back and forth in ever more delicate sweeps until it reaches its point. This is a dagger designed by people who knew the value and sanctity of a life, so much so that it first served its masters in rituals and ceremonies." He sliced through the air twice, advancing as he did until the weapon was mere inches from their faces. They took a few more steps back until a stout support beam blocked their retreat.

"Look at the runes, the stranger continued. "This is an ancient invocation to the gods, requesting mercy and bounty in exchange for the blood that would flow. Now, look at the curves. Thirteen of them, diminishing toward a point sharper than a serpent's tooth. Unquestionably beautiful, and yet the shape has value in function as well as form. Each curve slices anew, like a separate weapon.

Each forward strike bites six times, each back strike bites seven. Each thrust carves thirteen separate slices into the belly of its target. Brilliant…"

"Now look at the hilt." He flicked the dagger toward them and each man dove aside. It twirled through the air and bit effortlessly into the beam, sinking a third of its length into the iron-hard wood. The drunks, now a good deal more sober, looked to the blade. "Made to resemble a coiled asp, its fangs needle sharp and curved toward the blade's tip. It is the one wholly artistic flourish, meant simply to intimidate." He glanced back and forth between them. "Effective, don't you think? Because if not"—he opened his coat to reveal the hilts of six similarly elaborate daggers and knives—"I've got many more fine examples."

In the stillness that followed, a stifled breath drew the stranger's eyes toward the storeroom. Belle still stood there with a bottle of wine and a clay tankard, her eyes wide and her hands shaking.

"You can put it on the table, young lady," he said. "And don't worry. I think the posturing has been put aside for now."

"You weren't lying about the training," breathed Carlisle, shakily returning his cudgel to his belt.

"I seldom lie. It is rarely necessary." He took a seat. Belle had set down the wine bottle, but after a casual inspection of the tankard had proved unsatisfactory she industriously swabbed at its interior with a rag.

"Who *are* you, sir?" Cassius asked. He returned his own weapon and lowered himself into a seat.

"I am many different things at many different times, good sir. Today I am a hunter, and my prey is a mysterious creature. A creature of the shadows." He smiled. "A shadow himself, if the rumors are true. They call him The Red Shadow."

There was a gasp and the shattering of hardened clay. Belle

stood rigidly, the rag still in her hand and the remnants of the tankard at her feet.

The stranger sighed. "Three men brandish weapons and the mug stays in your hand. Three little words, The Red Shadow, and it falls to the floor. It speaks volumes of his reputation."

"You think The Red Shadow was responsible for Sotur's death?"

"Sotur would be the local baron?"

"Yes."

"Then I have reason to suspect it. He was wealthy, from what little I've heard he was not overly popular, and now he is dead. Most importantly, no one I've spoken to has the slightest idea how it could have happened. I've been following The Shadow for years. He tends to leave things in such a state."

"The Red Shadow," Carlisle said. He stared blankly at the wall before him, rubbing at his stubbly throat as though genuinely surprised to find there was no slit. "I was guarding Sotur last night. I…The Red Shadow…he's…he killed a dire wolf. He killed a massive wolf the size of a horse, and he did it with his bare hands. Tore the thing's head off. Stained its fur with its own blood. Made the skull into a helmet."

"I know the stories. They would have me believe he is this supernatural thing, this demon that walks the world taking the lives of the corrupt."

"The Red Shadow has killed lords. He's killed other assassins," Cassius said. "No one has seen more than a flicker of the monster. He killed the second advisor to the king during a feast. *During a feast!* The man was smearing butter on his bread one moment and was slumped in his chair the next. He never even left the table."

"That's nothing. He killed Lord Marten the very first time the old man stepped into his new keep. He killed him while his own guards were showing him his own security measures," Carlisle said.

"As I've said, I know the stories."

"What makes you think you can find him when the Alliance's best men can't?"

"I don't have a high opinion of the Alliance's best men, but I also have an item that should allow me to follow him if I get close enough."

"You don't *follow* a thing like him! You *hide* from a thing like him," said Carlisle.

"This isn't the first time I've heard these words, gentlemen. And may I say that it never ceases to amaze me that the same people who would gleefully beat me to pulp for even seeming to abandon my army would caution me endlessly about seeking out a known murderer."

"You mustn't pursue The Red Shadow," Cassius said.

"Why would you try to stop me? Has this man not been a scourge of the Northern Alliance for decades?"

"*Death* has been a scourge for centuries. If you are going to hunt one of the two, death is the safer bet," Carlisle said.

"I'm not convinced there's a difference," Cassius added.

"The Red Shadow is a monster on the prowl. If you hunt it, you won't kill it. You'll just get its attention. Then it feeds on you instead of whatever it had its eye on. I don't want to be anywhere near the fool who would do such a thing," Carlisle explained.

"Be that as it may, I've got business with The Red Shadow that must be settled. There is a grave injustice that must be corrected, and I will not rest until I've done so."

"Then do it far from here. I've seen a slit neck before. Makes a hell of a mess, and my coat's stained enough," Cassius said.

"First I must find him, and as I've said, it is for that reason that I have come to this charming little establishment." The stranger paced to his seat, where Belle had returned with a fresh tankard and filled it from his bottle. She sorted through coins from her apron and counted out the change from his purchase. "Thank you. No, please. Keep the remainder. The service has been superb."

"What do you want from us?" Cassius asked.

Their visitor sipped his wine, wincing a bit at the flavor. "Information." He turned to Carlisle. "You say you were Sotur's personal guard last night?"

"I was. Everyone knows that. It was supposed to be Cassius here but the louse was passed out drunk. Look, why should I help you?"

The stranger reached into his coat and removed a satchel, which he upended onto the table. Two dozen silver coins clattered on the wooden surface. When the bag was empty, he tossed it down as well. "The usual reasons."

Carlisle eyed the small fortune on the table, his willpower visibly buckling. "I...even if I wanted to tell you something, I don't know anything. I didn't see anyone. I wasn't even there when the man died."

"Did you find him when the deed was done?"

"Yeah."

"Describe it."

"He was dead."

The stranger's expression hardened. "Care to elaborate?"

"What else is there? He was dead. Bled out all over the floor."

"What did the wound look like?"

"He had a bloody slit where his neck ought to be."

"Was it a clean wound?"

"I just said it was bloody. Does that sound clean to you?"

His benefactor sighed. "I can see I'll need to take a more direct role in the investigation. Do you know where the body is being kept?"

"In the baron's estate's infirmary."

"Has he been prepared for burial?"

"I don't think so."

"Take me there."

"How do you plan on getting inside?"

"If your susceptibility to bribery is indicative of the rest of the baron's staff, I don't foresee any difficulty."

Carlisle sat for a few moments, staring at the silver again. "I can't do this. I've got debts to pay and mouths to feed, but you are asking me to help you do something that might put my name in the mind of the bloodiest assassin in the history of the Northern Alliance. I'm not foolish enough to do that."

"Very well." The stranger turned to Cassius. "Are you?"

"Damn right I am," Cassius said.

"Cassius Whitmoor, you idiot! The Shadow will kill this lunatic for hunting him down, and he'll kill *you* for helping to find him."

"Maybe he'll kill *you*, Car. After all, *you* were the one on duty."

Carlisle lurched forward and attempted to grapple with Cassius. Having been denied a chance at violence once already, both men were eager for a second chance to let off some steam. For better or worse, they were still feeling the effects of the afternoon's libations and weren't the most graceful or effective combatants.

The stranger separated them and raised his voice. "Gentlemen, please! The Red Shadow won't give either of you louts a second glance."

"And why is that?" Carlisle growled.

"Because he is an assassin. Assassins kill *important* people, and they get paid handsomely to do it. Killing a drunken and ineffective guard and his still more drunken and ineffective cohort would be beneath him." He snatched his thrown dagger from the beam and gestured with it. "The common folk are safe as babes from the blade that kills kings."

"And you imagine you are safe for the same reason?" Carlisle asked. "You aren't concerned about the blade because you aren't a king?"

"On the contrary. The blade is of great concern to me, and I aim to be worthy of its bite, so long as its bite is worthy of me." He gave his weapon a final appreciative glance before slipping it into its sheath beneath his coat.

"You tie the language in knots when you talk, you know that?" Cassius said.

"I aim for artistry in my every endeavor. But enough delay." He finished his wine and corked the bottle, stowing it in an outer pocket of his pack. "If you mean to earn your silver, my good man Whitmoor, we'll need to be on our way quickly." He swept the mound of silver into two equal piles with a deft slice of his hand, pocketing the first. "Take your payment. You'll get the rest when I'm satisfied you've earned it."

"Gladly," Cassius said, messily clawing at the coins.

"Wait! What about me? I answered your questions!" Carlisle said, his eyes locked on the bribe that could have been his as it fell into his drinking partner's pocket.

"Here," the stranger said, snatching a coin from the table and tossing it to Carlisle.

"One silver? You must be giving Cass at least twenty!"

"Actions are so much more valuable than words, good sir. That's a lesson worth its weight in gold. Now if you will excuse me, I wouldn't want to keep a baron waiting."

THE REST OF THE late baron's family had fled the grounds on the night of his death for fear of sharing his fate, leaving the servants to watch over the sprawling residence and its former owner. It took three meager bribes to shift the loyalties of the staff enough to earn the stranger a private audience with their fallen master. Cassius led the way to a darkened room deep inside the late baron's estate and raised a torch. The infirmary was a frigid room with stone walls lined with cluttered shelves. It was discernable from the armory only in that the tools for drawing blood were accompanied by bowls to catch it. At the far end of the room was a slab, and resting in peace upon it was the former baron, respectfully concealed beneath a stained linen shroud.

"Odd that a baron would have an infirmary in his estate."

"Aw, the old codger said he wanted his estate built like a keep, made sure they put in a quarters for a squad of solders and an infirmary and suchlike," Cassius explained. "Guess he wanted to feel safe from invaders. Half a kingdom between him and the nearest border wasn't good enough. He even had a halfway decent healer, up until they made him send her down to the front. The butcher who runs the place now only knows how to pull teeth and cut off fingers and toes. Probably keeps 'em in one of these jars here…"

"Sound thinking. You would be surprised what one can do with a tooth and the right incantations."

"I wouldn't know anything about that stuff. All I know is when I die I'm going to make sure they keep a fire going wherever they lay me out," Cassius muttered, pulling his coat tighter. "Gonna spend a long time in the cold ground. The least you can do for a man is keep him from freezing before you put him in."

"It's just as well they didn't. With any luck the cold has kept the corpse fresh."

The curious stranger approached the body and turned down the sheet. The baron was a bloated and unpleasant man in life, and he was more so in death. He had the face and figure of a man who

SEEKING THE SHADOW   ⭢ 537

had never missed a meal; not fat, but with an overall pudginess that portrayed a life of ease. His beard was scraggly and gray, except for where it was stained brown by the dried blood of his murder. The stranger adjusted his gloves and gingerly lifted the end of the beard to reveal the wound that had claimed him.

"Bring the light closer," he instructed, leaning nearer to the slice.

As the flickering yellow light fell upon it, the strange newcomer almost seemed to admire the horrid slice across the late baron's neck.

"Oh yes. This is certainly the work of a fine blade and a steady hand. Look at the edge. It isn't ragged or torn in the least." He separated the cold-stiffened flesh on either side of the cut. "Straight to the bone in a single slice. There's no sign that the blade met anywhere but its mark. Where did they find him? In his bed?"

"Slumped on his balcony, I think."

"Dragged there perhaps? Was there a trail of blood, or merely a pool?"

"No trail. The servants made enough of a stink about cleaning it up where it was. If there was a trail, we'd still be hearing about it."

"Mmm." He pulled the shroud back farther to reveal the man's hands. "Spotless…no scrapes, no bruises. This man didn't have the chance to struggle. This was definitely the work of The Shadow." He restored the shroud and turned to Cassius. "Tell me about the baron."

"What's to tell?"

"I haven't noticed any mourners."

"I'm more surprised there aren't folks dancing in the streets. He squeezed his subjects dry, paid his servants and guards in copper, and squandered his money on damn fool things like his estate or mounds of jewels to keep that trophy of a wife interested."

"Did he have any sons?"

"None who survived the war. Just a wife and a daughter."

"Brothers?"

"Two."

"Younger, I assume. Otherwise one of *them* would have been the baron."

"That's right."

"And they are both alive?"

"Last I heard."

"Tell me about them."

"The middle brother is just as bad as him, only he doesn't have the title and didn't get the inheritance. His old man didn't leave him anything but the private hunting ground up north. He's practically a hermit, lives off the land and keeps his debtors off his back by having his brother accuse folk of poaching—whether or not they were nearby—then fining them."

"And the youngest brother?"

"As I recall, he didn't get land *or* money. But he's the richest of the lot, thanks to him starting an armory and supplying weapons and armor for the war effort. Rumor has it he's got his fingers in the black market, too."

"Have the brothers been informed of his passing?"

"How should I know? I'm just a guard. The steward would be the one to do that."

"Well then, where is the steward?"

"I think he had a meeting with the youngest. I expect they'll get to planning the burial and such when he gets back tomorrow."

The stranger paused to consider the facts, then reached into his coat to gather the second half of Cassius's silver coins. "Quickly, where is this hunting ground?"

"If you've got a fast horse and the weather's not too rough, just follow the road due north for a while."

"A while?"

"I forget how far. It's the only fenced-in piece of forest you'll see up that way anyway."

"Here is the remainder of your payment," he said, rushing for the door.

"Why the rush?"

"Because if the middle brother isn't dead yet, he will be soon. The youngest hired The Red Shadow to clear the way to the title and the estate."

He rushed out the door, heading for the outside. Cassius followed, trying to keep up.

"How do you figure?" he called after the stranger.

"I'm not a simpleton, that's how!"

"Are you going to try to save the middle brother?"

"He's already dead, or as good as, but if I move fast enough I just may reach him while The Shadow is still nearby!"

Cassius, not in the best of health, fell behind as his benefactor rushed through the estate to the stables and set about preparing his horse for travel. The stranger was mounting the steed when Cassius reached the door, thoroughly out of breath.

"Wait!" he gasped. "I don't even know your name!"

The stranger heaved himself into the saddle and spurred the horse out of the stable, calling back behind him, "That's just as well. It wouldn't have done you any good."

Cassius stood in the doorway and watched the bizarre outsider ride into the distance.

"Meh," he grunted. "Name doesn't matter anyway. If he's after The Shadow, by this time tomorrow he'll be dead."

———◆———

THE VAGUE DIRECTIONS CASSIUS provided turned out

to be accurate, if not precise. "A while" revealed itself to be half a day, bringing the stranger to the fenced stretch of woods well after sunset. Most of the trip had been through snow-covered plains, with the occasional farm invariably growing cabbage or potatoes. Due to hearty types of each being the only crops that would grow beyond the southern border region of the Northern Alliance, most of the population lived on little else. This was doubly true in areas with poor hunting, which described most of the north—that the Sotur clan had claimed the one patch of forest for miles dense enough for decent hunting indicated just how little they cared for their fellow people.

The fence around the property wasn't very imposing, being merely a row of evergreen branches and trunks driven at wide intervals into the ground, most still bearing their needles. They served as a marker and little else. What kept people from crossing through and taking advantage of the hunting ground was the penalty imposed by its owner if they were caught.

The stranger paid the marked boundary little heed. Dense clouds blotted out the moon and stars, as was frequently the case in the Alliance lands, leaving the forest shrouded in an almost impenetrable darkness.

"A moonless night...not the ideal time to be searching for a shadow," he uttered, his voice low.

His equipment included a lantern and a few more exotic methods for creating light, but at the moment the benefits of being able to see weren't nearly enough to outweigh the consequences of being seen. He moved forward through the inky woods as surely as he could manage. Unfortunately it soon became clear he wouldn't be able to rely upon the horse. The forest grew steadily thicker as he approached its center, and within minutes the low branches and high shrubs blocked the way too much for the steed to penetrate.

He dismounted and drew a shorter and simpler blade than the one he'd used to intimidate the guards. Such a weapon left him better able to put his final remaining advantage to use.

He dug into a well-protected pocket beneath two layers of clothes until his gloved fingers snagged, with some difficulty, a fine silver chain. When his grip was secure he tugged it into the open. A small leather satchel swung free from his pocket. He loosened his fingers and let the weight of the satchel draw the chain through them until it hung at its full length. It swung lightly, and when he whispered a few awkwardly phrased arcane words it swung a bit more. He closed his eyes and focused on articulating each unnatural syllable properly, though his untrained tongue tripped over them twice before the spell was cast in earnest; when it did the satchel tugged against the chain, angling out to the woods ahead.

"He's here." The man wrapped the chain around his fist and charged as quickly and quietly as he could in the direction it led.

Stealth was not an option. It was too dark to see more than a few steps ahead, leaving him at the mercy of every loose branch and boot-grabbing bush. Worse, the forest was silent, magnifying the noise of his own breathing and the crunch of his footsteps. There wasn't the chitter of a squirrel or the chirp of a bird. The woodland creatures were in hiding, all too aware of the danger lurking in the darkness. There was a predator in the woods.

Finally he reached a clearing and stopped short. A body lay face up on the ground. In the weak light the pool of blood looked black against the white snow, and the kill was so fresh steam still rose from the slit in his throat.

"Damn it," hissed the stranger.

He scanned the clearing. There were footprints, but they all seemed to belong to the dead man. None of the trees around him had dropped any of their snow, hinting that no one had hidden among their branches. The body was still warm and yet the trail was cold. He lowered his satchel and began the incantation.

The first word still hung in the air when a blow to his back sent him sprawling. His blade went one direction; the satchel went the other. He tried to scramble forward, but a weight dropped on his back and held him to the ground. The leather fingers of a gloved hand clutched his chin and pulled his head back. The stinging cold edge of a blade touched his throat. He gasped for breath but dared not struggle, lest he do the killer's work for him.

He sensed a presence beside his ear.

"You are alone," came a harsh whisper.

"Yes," the restrained man wheezed, his chest and mouth constricted.

"You did not follow my tracks. I did not leave any."

"No tracks."

"You did not follow the victim's tracks, because you came from the wrong side."

"Yes."

"You could not follow a scent, the wind is at your back."

"I didn't."

The next words were spoken with a force and harshness that simply wasn't human. "Tell me how you found me."

"If you kill me now, you'll never know."

"Neither will anyone else."

He swallowed. "You're holding a black blade to my throat. It isn't metal, it is stone. It was made for you by a gifted weaponsmith with the help of a fairy. You've used it for nearly sixty years and it still hasn't dulled. I know what you are."

The blade began to slide; blood ran down the man's neck.

"Five years ago you left a place called Entwell for the second time. I know these things because I was there. My name is Desmeres

Lumineblade. My father is the man who made that sword."

The blade stopped. "Why did you come here?"

"I came because you and I have business together, even if you don't know it. Let me speak. We both know if you don't like what you hear, there's nothing I can do to stop you from killing me."

His heart pounded in his ears. Warm blood dripped in fat drops on the snow. The weight lifted from his back and the blade pulled away. Desmeres moved slowly and deliberately, climbing to his feet and spreading his hands to his side to avoid provoking any rash decisions from the assassin.

"Speak," The Red Shadow said.

"May I retrieve a bandage to tend to my—?"

A bandage landed beside him, tossed from behind.

"Speak." This time the voice came from a different position.

Desmeres fetched the bandage and applied it. When it was in place, he turned. The assassin had backed into the darkness of the trees around the clearing. His presence was felt more than seen. There wasn't even the telltale gleam of his eyes.

"I didn't have much use for you when you were in Entwell. I knew you were the first to go and return, but I was still honing my craft. I make weapons, like my father before me. But a year after you left I got into an argument with him. I became irate that one of my weapons, one of my best, was in the hands of a green apprentice. Father believes that the purpose of crafting a weapon is to make a fighter as formidable as he or she can be. He said my weapon was elevating the apprentice to more than he was. I believe that a fighter and a weapon are two halves of the same whole. Perfection can only be achieved when the greatest weapon is in the hand of the greatest warrior. By holding my weapon, that apprentice was spitting in the face of greatness, preventing my sword from finding the hand that would do it justice. And though my father's sword is an undeniable masterpiece, in your hand it cheapens you. I've learned much since it was made. I can and have made better. My weapons belong in your hand and yours alone."

"You came this far, risked your life, to give me a weapon?"

"This weapon, and the next one, and the next one. You are the finest warrior the world has ever produced. Through you, my weapons can finally achieve their rightful place."

"You would help an assassin in his deeds."

"Let me make this clear. Your skill with weaponry is the only trait that concerns me. The rest is irrelevant. I will do whatever is needed. This is my purpose. Surely you can understand how important it is to serve one's purpose?"

The Shadow remained silent.

"I can do things for you. Things you and I both know you can't do yourself because of what you are."

There came a sound, something less than the swish of fabric, and from the darkness emerged a form. It looked to be a human, until Desmeres' gaze lingered upon the shadow within the hood. There was a pointed muzzle, the glint of whiskers, and the gleam of animal eyes. It was not the face of a human. This "man" of whom the whole of the north lived in fear was no man at all. He was a beast called a *malthrope*, with more in common with a fox than a human.

"Killed a wolf and wore its bloodstained skull as a helmet. You started that rumor, didn't you? Whispered it in someone's ear from the darkness. You have become the most feared figure in Vulcrest, and you've done it with your hands tied, because anyone who so much as sees your face, even without knowing your crimes, will kill you on the spot. You are a monster at a glance. I am not. I can speak to humans, and elves, and dwarves. I can mix with society. Meet face to face. I can *be* your face to the world, if you require. Whatever it takes to put my weapons in your hands. If either of us settled for anything less it would be a crime."

The assassin released a seething hiss, then snapped back to his main concern. "Enough about that. Tell me how you found me."

"Anyone can follow the crumbs. The mark of an assassin is unmistakable, but you aren't the only one. I found three before I saw a wound that might have come from my father's blade. From there I traced your path, found where you lingered."

"I know you were following me. I know you've come close before. *Tell me how you found me.*"

"The last few steps came from that satchel on the ground. I brought it from Entwell. Inside are a few precious strands of your hair, a few flakes of dried blood from an old bandage, and a pinch of soil from where you slept. Coupled with an incantation the gray wizard taught me, it draws itself toward you. Without it, I'd never have found you. Destroy it and neither I nor anyone else ever will again."

The Shadow stood silent once more. Desmeres knew the time for talk was nearly through, the killer's mind nearly made up.

"I don't know what you believe in, but I know you believe in something. You aren't an assassin for the thrill of the kill. The men and women who have fallen by your blade are, without exception, corrupt and deceitful. You are selecting people who deserve to die. Perhaps you wish to punish the wicked, perhaps you simply wish to ease your conscience. I don't know. What I do know is that if what you are working toward is truly important you are obligated to take every advantage offered. Anything less and you are turning your back on it. *Let me help you.*"

"…You would ask me to trust you?"

"You would be a fool to trust me, and I would be a fool to trust you. But I'm more than willing to live what remains of my life with a knife to my throat. I don't even care if it finds its way to my back."

He pointed to his fallen weapon. "As long as it is one of mine."

The assassin took two fluid paces toward Desmeres. They stood face-to-beastly-face, Desmeres's eyes locked on the predatory gleam beneath the assassin's hood. With a flicker of motion, The Red Shadow held one of the daggers formerly concealed beneath Desmeres's jacket.

"If I decide I have use for you, you'll see me again. If not"—the assassin held up the stolen blade—"you'll get your wish."

With those final words, The Red Shadow stepped aside, and in a blur of motion was gone. Desmeres adjusted the bloodstained bandage and breathed a long, slow breath. His eyes turned to the ground. In departing, The Red Shadow had snatched up the satchel and the fallen blade.

Desmeres smiled.

"And so begins the legacy…"

SUN AND STEEL

-Book of the Black Earth-
JON SPRUNK

"Sun and Steel" is set in same fictional world as
my Book of the Black Earth epic fantasy series. It
illuminates the origin of Jirom, one of the series' main
characters. This story explores the brutal nature of
this world, as well as the honor and duty that binds its
characters together.

THE AFTERNOON RAYS GLEAMED off the rusted sign above the Rearing Donkey. Crammed between a whorehouse and a *kafir* den, the tavern had the reputation as the worst dive in Pardisha. Jirom had only been inside once, and his decision not to return had been based mainly on a desire not to be knifed by one of the Donkey's prepubescent doxies who made their living rolling drunks and dumping them in the littered alley behind the tavern.

Three Moons had made the Donkey his newest home-away-from-home not long after the Company first arrived in Pardisha. Wherever the mercenaries went, their resident sorcerer was quick to put down roots, and that usually involved surrounding himself with a crowd of addicts and "free thinkers." And Jirom had been tasked with finding him.

He didn't want the assignment. He was a grunt at heart, but ever since he'd been promoted to squad leader his time was eaten up with even more responsibilities. He longed for the days when all he had to worry about was himself and the men beside him, and this town didn't make his job any easier. Little more than a pile of limestone and dried brick, Pardisha was one of several dozen independent satrapies strewn across the deserts of Isuran. Its ruler, Amir Dazo He'Jahana, had hired

"SUN AND STEEL"

Illustration by ORION ZANGARA

the Company to protect him from his ambitious neighbors. Six nights ago the Company had successfully defended the town from two of the Amir's rivals working in concert. As far as most of the brothers were concerned the mission was over, but this morning one of their patrols had detected a force of Akeshians approaching from the north. Jirom wasn't privy to the details. He only knew there had been some debate as to whether their contract required them to defend the town another time. Yet, in the end, Major Galbrein had granted their employer an extension in return for a renegotiated bonus, to be paid when Pardisha was safe. According to the rumors, the amount was staggering—if they lived to collect it.

Bracing himself, Jirom opened the tavern door, and almost bumped into a Company brother coming out. "Hillup," he said.

"Sergeant." The tall corporal nodded. His eyes were bloodshot. "You come to see Three Moons?"

"Yes. You heard?"

"Unta told me. I was just headed to the east wall. The major wants every able body up there in plain sight in case scouts are watching the town."

"You can be sure they are. Keep a sharp eye up there."

As Hillup trotted off, Jirom pushed inside. He had to squint to see through the dense smoke lingering over the clutter of tables and benches. A few locals were passed out on the floor—their pockets no doubt already emptied. A short, squat woman in a shapeless dress sat at the end of the bar puffing on a thin cigar. Jirom nodded to her, and was ignored, as he went to the door behind the bar. He loosened his sword in its scabbard and pushed the door open.

A green haze filled the tavern's back room, which was almost as large as the front of the house. About twenty people lounged around on cushions and divans, while a bald-headed youth with kohl-lined eyes plinked on a zither. A naked girl lay sprawled on the floor, either asleep or dead.

Jirom's quarry sat in a tall chair against the back wall, surrounded by a group of young lovelies of both sexes. Three Moons wasn't much to look at—a short, scrawny man with lanky gray hair and droopy eyes the color of old dishwater—but the brothers held him in awe for all the times he had saved their asses. They scared new recruits with tales of his sorcery gone awry, like the time in Yermin he drunkenly set the barracks on fire, nearly killing the entire Company.

Jirom tried to get the sorcerer's attention from across the room, but Three Moons stared at the ceiling without blinking. The air reeked of burning leaves laced with powerful narcotics. Jirom took a step inside, but stopped as three young men in various stages of undress surged to their feet.

"Who you do think you are?"

"Nobody invited you, tinman!"

"Take another move, and I'll cut you up!"

The addict making the last statement waved a thin-bladed knife back and forth. Jirom frowned. This was precisely what he'd wanted to avoid. "I'm here to see Three Moons."

"He's busy," one of the youths replied with a sneer that showed yellow, slightly-crooked teeth.

"You don't want none of this, man!" the knife-wielder yelled, now making stabbing motions with his weapon aimed at Jirom's chest.

"I need to talk to him," Jirom said. "Get out of my—"

He stopped as the knife-wielder darted forward. The youth didn't look like much of a threat, but Jirom's instincts took over. He caught the knife-hand by the wrist, twisted it backward until the weapon fell free, then he twisted a little more until he heard a satisfying snap. His other hand gripped the youth by his ragged collar and heaved him into the air. The room's windows were covered by wooden shutters. Jirom picked the nearest one and sent the youth hurtling through it. The clapping of the shutters broke up the party. Everyone looked at him, including Three Moons.

"Sergeant Jirom!" the sorcerer said with a smile. "Welcome to my dream."

"I need to see you. Alone."

The sorcerer nodded. "Begone, my children. Out into the world once again. Return to me with tales of wonder. And a little more *kafir* wouldn't be amiss."

His entourage left in a shambling, groaning herd. Three Moons found a cup on the floor, sniffed it, and poured something into it from a flask. He held it out. "Drink, Sarge?"

"No. The major sent me to find you. We've got trouble coming."

He outlined the situation with the Akeshians. Three Moons finished his drink and dropped the cup back on the floor. "I suggest we pack up and get out after dark." After a long belch, he added, "Preferably with as much booty as we can carry."

"You're not the first to make that suggestion, but the major wants plans for how we can defend this place."

"How in the six hells would I know? You should talk to the sappers. Ridder and Hance will have some ideas."

Jirom stepped closer until he towered over the magician. "You aren't hearing me, so I'll speak up. The major sent me to find you. I guess he wants you to cook up some of your infamous nasty tricks."

Three Moons rubbed his chin, a wicked gleam in his eyes. "Hmmm. Give me some time, and I'll see what I can come up with."

"We don't have time. Grab what you need and come with me to headquarters."

"Well, I don't know—"

Three Moons reached for his flask but Jirom snatched it away and threw it through the open window. "Now," he said, putting some growl into his voice. He had his own reputation among the brothers, and it wasn't for playing nice.

The sorcerer came along without any trouble.

A HAND SHOOK HIM out of a dream. "Sarge! You need to get up."

Jirom blinked and looked up. Longar stood over him. The light coming through the shuttered windows of the barracks house was pale gray. He'd been up half the night readying the town's defenses, which mostly meant patching the gaping holes that time and neglect had eaten into the outer walls. Given a few more months and access to a decent quarry, he might actually accomplish something. "What hour is it?"

"Almost second bell. The major's been asking for you."

He got up, buckled on his body armor and sword-belt, and looked around for something to wash the sticky dryness from his mouth. After a minute, he gave up on the drink and left the barracks.

Major Galbrein was waiting in his office, surrounded by the Company sergeants. "Did you find Three Moons?"

Jirom bit back a curse. "He didn't come find you? I put him to work on the problem. I assumed he would report in."

"Never mind that now. The Amir has demanded that we march out to meet the enemy."

Sergeant Skawl chuckled. "You've got to love this asshole. He figures if we get ourselves killed, he won't have to pay up."

"Are we?" Jirom asked. "Marching out?"

Major Galbrein shook his head. "Our mission doesn't include mass suicide. The latest scouting reports are in."

Jirom looked over the sheets of parchment handed to him.

"'Twelve hundred infantry. Six hundred light cavalry. Two hundred archers.' Sir, we can't handle this many."

"I know, but we're committed now." The major stood up. "I have to get back to the palace. Where are we on the town's defenses?"

"Not very far," Jirom replied. "But I'll go check on it."

"Good. Focus on the reinforcing the gates. The Akeshians won't wait long before launching their offensive."

His words proved prophetic. The Akeshians made their first assault an hour after full dark, aided by the full moon. They hit the northeast and west sections of the walls simultaneously. Jirom stood atop the southern gate with half of his squad. The other half was below piling stones against the gate's timbers in anticipation of an attack. Longar and Furuk stood next to him, watching the approaches.

The desert spread out beneath the walls in all its barren glory. Nothing but sand and rocks, and yet there was something hauntingly beautiful about the dunes at night with the moonlight dappled across their ridged slopes.

"We won't see the fucking sand-fleas until they've crawled right up our asses," Furuk muttered.

Furuk was the only one in the Company who actually hailed from this part of the world, and he was less tolerant of its natives than anyone.

Longar chuckled. "Sounds like you're talking from personal experience, Sweetness."

"Kill the chatter," Jirom said.

He turned as Three Moons climbed the stone stairs to the battlements, huffing with every step.

"Where's the major?" Three Moons asked.

"Probably on the north wall overseeing the defense, which begs the question: why are you here?"

Three Moons unslung his bag and set it at his feet. "Because this is where they'll attack next."

"Sergeant," Furuk said, pointing.

Jirom turned back to the wall. It took him a few heartbeats to see them, a column of shadows coming over a dune to the southeast. Moonlight glinted off helmets and the points of spears marching toward the town at a fast clip. "Elsig, go tell the major we've got company. Three Moons, what can you . . . ?"

The sorcerer pulled a small wooden box out of his bag and set it on the wall. He opened the box and took out a tiny wooden post, which he attached to the top of the lid. Hanging from the post was a thin membrane resembling a leaf or a slip of brown parchment.

"What's that?" Jirom asked.

"Just watch."

The sorcerer leaned close to the little apparatus and gently blew. The leaf-thing flittered and made a humming sound. Minutes passed, but nothing else happened except that Three Moons kept blowing and the Akeshians kept marching closer. They got within catapult range, but the south wall only had one working siege engine, a relic from Jirom's grandfather's time. It made a loud *thwunk* as it fired, launching a fifty-pound stone into the night air. A few seconds later, a cloud of sand kicked up in front of the advancing enemy. The Company sappers cursed at each other as they loaded the arm for another shot.

Jirom was about to check on the preparations below when he noticed a dark cloud in the southern sky, highlighted by the moon. Dread inched up his backbone as the cloud moved *against the breeze* to follow the enemy column. When it got over the Akeshians, it dropped like a swooping hawk. Distant cries rang out over the dunes. Three Moons broke into a victory jig.

Jirom tried to piece together what he'd seen and heard.

"Locusts?"

"Wasps," Three Moons answered with a guffaw. "Big, angry suckers. I wouldn't want to be those—"

The sorcerer stopped dancing and clutched the wall. Out on the dunes, a pillar of inky smoke rose from the enemy force. The cries of outrage had ended. A few moments later, the Akeshians emerged from the smoke, once again marching in formation toward the town.

"What happened?" Jirom asked.

Three Moons opened his mouth, and then ducked behind the battlements. Jirom lost his balance as the entire wall rocked like it'd been struck by a fleet of battering rams. A few seconds later, the catapult exploded in a shower of broken timbers. After he sent Longar to organize a medic detail, Jirom propped up the haggard-looking sorcerer.

Three Moons grimaced. "They've got a heavy-hitter out there, Sarge."

"Another wizard?"

"And not just any hedge wizard. Akeshian war-magi are bred to sorcery and trained up in fancy schools."

"So what are you saying? You can't handle him?"

Three Moons slid down on his haunches. "He's wielding High Magic, son. Not the backwater bayou stuff I learned at my grandpa's knee. The next time I pop off, he's liable to squash me like a bug."

Jirom rested a fist on top of a merlon. The enemy had advanced to within bowshot. Company archers sent a flight of arrows sailing into the column, but without much effect against the heavily-armored infantry. He didn't see scaling ladders or siege equipment with the enemy, but it was dark enough that he couldn't be sure. And he didn't have enough men to protect the entire wall. He estimated they could hold the gate for an hour, perhaps two, but he needed . . . .

Marching footsteps echoed down the street behind the gatehouse. Jirom turned, and almost couldn't believe his eyes. A small unit of troops in blue-dyed armor approached from the city center—the Amir's personal guard. Jirom could have hugged them all. He started mentally placing the new arrivals at different spots along the wall to shore up the defenses. He hoped they had brought some crossbows, which would put a dent in the Akeshian advance.

Three Moons leaned over the battlements. "What the hell?"

Jirom was turning as a clash of steel erupted in the courtyard below. He looked down in time to see one of the new arrivals split a brother's skull with a battle axe. The Amir's bodyguard had surged forward to envelop his men at the gate. Spears and javelins flew in the darkness, painting the street with blood as they slammed into flesh.

Jirom drew his sword and ran to the stairs when a titanic explosion, like the cracking of the world's foundation, burst behind him. His weapon dropped from his senseless hand as he hurtled through the air. He saw a bright green flash of light, and then darkness closed around him.

———— ·•· ————

DAWN'S RAYS STRETCHED ACROSS the cobbled square at the heart of the city. Its golden fingers walked across the row of bodies lining the western edge of the courtyard—Akeshians and Company men and locals all laid out together like family.

A bead of sweat ran down Jirom's forehead into his right eye, blurring his remaining vision; he couldn't see out of his left at all. After the explosion, he had awakened in the dark to find himself pinned under a pile of armored bodies. The gate was gone, completely destroyed except for its charred bronze hinges. He had been trying to pull himself free when a party of invaders had found him, bound him, and marched him here where a group of his brothers awaited, similarly tied and kneeling on the cobblestones.

As morning came, Jirom saw Major Galbrein arrive, escorted by a squad of enemy soldiers. The Company commander had a bloody compress around his head and one arm in a field sling. Every brother straightened up as the major stepped into the square, and Jirom joined them. If he was going to die today, he would die like a soldier.

The Akeshian command staff arrived with the major. A dozen tall men in shining mail, their scarlet scarves blowing from their necks. Jirom didn't see anyone who resembled a sorcerer, but then again he'd never known one before Three Moons. And where had Three Moons gone anyway?

Dead, probably.

A column of Akeshian crossbowmen entered the square from the north, escorting a big red-and-gold palanquin. An uneasy feeling crept into the pit of Jirom's stomach when the Amir got out of the litter and greeted the Akeshian commanders with polite enthusiasm.

Jirom tested the leather restraints binding his wrists. He had a knife hidden in his right boot, but waited as Major Galbrein was taken to meet the big-wigs. Jirom couldn't hear what was being said, but he saw the controlled rage written across the major's face. He wasn't surprised when the Company commander knocked the Amir on his ass in front of the assemblage, nor when the Akeshians dragged the major to a wooden block which had been set in the center of the square.

While the mercenaries shouted and cursed, they were forced to watch the beheading. The narrow two-handed sword of the Akeshian leader cut through the warm morning air, and the major died with as much dignity as a decapitated man could manage. This had all been for nothing.

Shouts broke out as a pair of brothers, Quarren and Skawl, broke free of their restraints. While they grappled with their captors, Jirom yanked his arms apart. For one terrifying moment, the cords held fast. Then, with a snap, he was free. He drew his knife and leapt to his feet. Many of his brothers had risen up as well, many fighting with their hands still tied. Jirom shouldered his way through the melee, his gaze locked on his target beside the execution block.

An Akeshian infantryman stepped in front of him, but Jirom spun around the point of the man's spear, slid the edge of his knife under the soldier's coif, and kept moving through the crowd with fresh blood running down his fingers. He drew back his arm as he reached his prey. The man turned, mouth agape, and Jirom drove the knife forward with all his strength. The blade punched through the mail shirt and sank to the hilt.

The Amir gasped as he glanced down at the handle protruding from his chest. Jirom smiled at him, and then lunged forward. He caught the nobleman's nose in his jaws and yanked back, tearing the flesh loose. Blood filled his mouth. A moment later, a hard blow landed on the side of his head, and the world tilted.

Gazing up from flat on his back, Jirom took a deep breath. The sky was a flawless azure blue. He grinned at the brown faces leaning over him. He was ready to die now. After fighting and scrapping for most of his life, a respite would be nice. If the gods were kind, he'd spend eternity under the shade of a nice fruit tree. Maybe he'd see his brothers again. Strong hands lifted him to his knees.

Blinking back against the pain in his temple, Jirom saw the Akeshian commander approach like a god of war with his beautiful two-handed sword. Jirom spat out the pieces of the Amir's nose at his feet.

"I am impressed, outlander," the Akeshian warlord said in a reasonable semblance of the local mercenary argot. "You fight like a lion. No fear at all. Nothing matters but the kill, eh?"

He looked at the rest of the Company brothers, once more back in custody, and lifted his sword. "All of you may have death, if you wish it. Or you may take the iron collar and live as a slave."

Akeshian soldiers armed with swords and collars went down the line of mercenaries, offering each the choice. The sounds of death and hammering iron echoed through the square. Jirom swallowed and wished he had a drink. The day was getting hot already, but with a cold drink in his hand a man could face anything. He started to laugh. It was only a chuckle at first, hardly even a sound, but it grew with each passing moment.

Then a shadow fell over him as the soldiers came to his turn.

THE BETYÁR AND THE MAGUS

S.R. CAMBRIDGE

When writing, I often take inspiration from real history, especially the history that often isn't read about that often. "The Betyár and the Magus" and the characters in it came to be because I started to read a lot about the Hungarian Revolution of 1848, a war for independence by Hungary against the Austrian Empire. Hungary was the victor in a series of early battles, and looked like it was winning, until the Austrian Empire allied with Russia for help. Russia, a formidable power at the time, brought it all to an end in short order. So I began to build a sort of historical-fantasy alternate-universe out of the Revolution, and what happened before and after. "The Betyár and the Magus" takes place six months after the end of the Revolution.

betyár (n.): a highwayman in 19th century Hungary
Outside Győr
Kingdom of Hungary
1850

M Y TEACHER JÓSKA BAJUSZ had died half a year earlier, and there was no fun in robbing the roads without him. You might imagine the life of a *betyár* to be all guns and riches and soft swooning women, but you wouldn't imagine the truth of it, the tedium, the long spans of night spent hiding and hoping for an unwary traveller to pass.

It was January, one of those days where the night steals in early, and unwary travellers had become a rare commodity. All I had to show for hours of waiting was a beard soaked through with snow, a sour mood, and half a *forint* from a shepherd who had been relieved, not afraid, when he realized it was a mere *betyár* who leapt in front of him.

People weren't frightened of *betyárok* then, not when there were worse dangers on the roads: Austrian soldiers, Habsburg men, who would name you a rebel and clap irons around your wrists before you could say *guten tag*. If you were lucky, you were held prisoner and conscripted. If not, you met your maker at the bad end of a firing squad.

I had been lazy with that shepherd, letting him go without even demanding one of his sheep, even though one of them would have fetched a good price. *But it wouldn't have been worth the trouble*, I told

"THE BETYÁR AND THE MAGUS"

Illustration by OKSANA DMITRIENKO

myself. *Sheep are stubborn.*

When Jóska was alive, before the war, I was never lazy, and never in poor spirits, even on the roughest of nights. With how much Jóska talked, I didn't have the chance. He was generous with advice, was Jóska, from the day he tried to steal a pig from me and instead decided to take me on as an apprentice *betyár*, although his habit was to begin with an insult before he got to anything helpful.

László, Jóska would say, *did your mother lay with a goat? It's the only explanation for that sad little beard of yours. Listen: if you apprehend a true Hungarian, then you take from him ten percent of what he has and let him go. That's what the churches do, after all. Frenchmen, Englishmen, take more. And if you rob an Austrian, take everything.*

Or, *László, you know there is a blind girl in Tata? There might be a wife for you, after all. Listen: you will rob many women. Treat them all with courtesy. The lady in her middle years, the one who was once a beauty, will respond best to romance. Speak kindly, look upon her as though you ache, and let your fingers linger on her throat. She'll be gladder to give you her coin if you give her a scandalous tale to tell other women about how she was nearly seduced on the road.*

The Russians killed Jóska during the battle at Segesvár. We'd come up with the brilliant idea to join up and fight for a free Hungary, Jóska and me. We ought to have stayed out of it. None of it had been fair. We had been winning, honestly *winning*, and then the Habsburgs got scared and said, *oh, Russia, please help us crush the Hungarians*, and Russia agreed and that was that.

Jóska had been hit with a spell from a Russian magus, some burst of terrible white-hot light that had ripped him open better and faster than a bayonet ever could. They were organized, those companies of Russian magi in the service of the Habsburgs. Always they attacked in formation. We had magi, too, but none so talented, none so regimented.

I'd knelt before Jóska as he struggled to speak, gurgling out blood and incoherent sounds in equal measure. His insides had glowed unnaturally and spilled on the earth. Tragic, truly, that a man who talked as endlessly as Jóska Bajusz should be denied the right to spit out a last bit of wisdom.

My hiding place for the night was one of the best spots Jóska and I had found along the well-worn road from Pest-Buda to Vienna: a hidden cleft of rock obscured by trees, a few paces from a bend in the road. A fine site for an ambush. It was easy for a wagon or a carriage to get bogged down in the deep ruts of the road when it was muddy. Always a fortunate thing, when that happened. You could appear before the poor stranded travellers with a benevolent smile on your face and act the solicitous saviour before you started waving your weapons about.

That's what I did with the Countess Almásy, Jóska had told me once. *Pretended I planned to help her when one of her horses fell injured on the road.* If he wasn't doling out advice, Jóska was going on about the time he robbed the Countess Almásy. I was fourteen and stupid when I first set out with Jóska, so initially I had believed him, but he told his Countess Almásy story so often and so inconsistently that it did not take me long to privately conclude it was horseshit designed to make me believe that being a *betyár* was more glamorous than it was.

Sometimes the countess kissed Jóska, having fallen in love with the handsome *betyár*, and wept because she would never see him again. (*It was my moustache*, Jóska had explained, stroking the black bristly mass of it. *Women love my moustache.*) Depending on how drunk Jóska was when he told the story, sometimes the countess was more lusty than loving. Once Jóska claimed the countess had told him she'd murder her old unkind husband and make Jóska her count if only he would leave his nomad's life to wed her.

When Jóska got into his Countess Almásy story, he always began the same way. *Once I charged before a carriage,* he would say, *a beautiful one, all white, and who should be inside but the Countess Almásy...*

Jézus, I thought. *László Sovány, you've gone sentimental.* Foolish, but on the night, quiet and windless with the snow settling about me like ash on embers, I longed to hear Jóska tell lies about the Countess Almásy. A strange listlessness had taken hold of me since Jóska's death. All I wanted, then, was a bed and supper and enough pálinka to make me forget that I had to think about what I would do next. *Half a forint is enough for that.*

Before the war I had been rich, in secret. Jóska and I had hidden the spoils of our robberies in places all along the road, in the houses of friends in Győr and Bicske and Komárom, but the Austrians had seen to my newfound poverty. After the war, after the Hungarians surrendered at Világos, Austrian soldiers swept over the country, *taking.* In the weeks it took me to get home, I went to each spot. In every case the money and valuables Jóska and I had spent years collecting were gone, replaced with abandoned or burnt-out buildings, or upturned earth. The friends were gone, too: dead, fled or captured.

I climbed down from my hiding place. On the road, I patted my coat and pockets to ensure my few possessions were still on my person: two pistols, a dagger, a paltry excuse for a coin purse. It would be a slow trudge back to Győr, where there were places I could lodge for the night. I was unused to life on my feet. I had sold Lánya, my horse, a week earlier, demoting myself from a mounted *betyár* to a lowly footpad. (*Listen,* Jóska's voice echoed in my head, *a betyár must always have handsome clothes and a fine fearsome horse, or else he is nothing but a common rogue.*) I regretted selling Lánya, having brought her to war with me, but it was time for her to go when I began thinking of her less as my faithful steed and more as tasty horsemeat.

It was then, starting that dreaded trek back to Győr, when I saw it: far off, faint, but unmistakable. *The light from a coachman's lantern*, I thought. Then: *oh, oh, thank God.*

Grinning, I drew my pistols, unmindful of the cold on my bare hands. I loaded each with powder and ball. I felt as though I had been buried but had clawed my way to fresh air, so great and so sweet was my relief. I had not spotted a proper carriage with a coachman in *months*. Before it all, before the revolution and the Russians and that horrible spell killing Jóska, the road was lousy with the wealthy, all of them ripe for a robbing. Afterwards, though, the rich seemed to have collectively determined that fashionable jaunts outside the relative safety of Pest-Buda weren't *quite* the thing when some cockless wonder of an Austrian could ruin your fun by deciding to detain you.

I stepped to one side, concealing myself among the trees. The light from the lantern grew closer, a pale beacon bobbing like a fairy-light through the drifting snow. I could hear the hooves of a pair of horses beating in time, squelching on the mud. *Jézus*, I prayed, *let them have gold and jewels and no guns and fearful dispositions.*

The carriage drew nearer. White, it was. *Just like the Countess Almásy's*, I thought, smiling. The coachman was a fat lump in a long winter coat, with a pouf of a fur hat and a wound-up scarf concealing his face. The horses were a matched pair of handsome chestnut Percherons, worth a fair bit more than poor battle-scarred Lánya.

It was time. I charged in front of the carriage, shouting, "Halt!"

The carriage stilled. (Part of me did notice, then, that the horses went utterly quiet, with nary a snort or a whinny from either to complain of such an unceremonious stop. However, this half-made observation did not pierce through the fog of my excitement.)

"Good evening, sir," I called, feigning cheer.

The coachman lifted the lantern, casting a yellow glow on me.

"Don't move," I said. "I am armed, and I'm aiming at you, but I have no desire to harm you unless you give me cause." I raised one pistol into the light so the coachman would see the gleam of the barrel. "I shall not leave you stranded. I'll have one horse, not both, and I will speak to your master or mistress inside regarding what else you might have for me."

The coachman did not speak, but he (if *he* is the right word; I'm not sure it is) dropped the lantern. It shattered on the carriage perch, leaving the road dark again, with only the snow-beaten light of the moon. The coachmen climbed to the ground, desultory, as though he were simply stopping to stretch his legs and not faced with a loaded pistol.

"Tread no further, sir," I warned.

The coachman did not listen, or perhaps he could not listen. I still couldn't see his face, just the hat and the scarf. Slowly, he went past the horses; his movements were more like *floating* than walking. By then a nervous knot had formed in my stomach, but I pressed on. "Stop now, or I *will* fire."

He stopped. His head tilted. Then he lunged at me, alarmingly fast, and I stumbled back and shot at him. The ball caught him in the thigh.

I could have shot him in the chest instead, if I had wanted. I was a good shot. Even Jóska couldn't make light of my skill with guns, so formidable it was. It even netted me something of a reputation during the war. Travellers weren't enemy soldiers, though, and I was no murderer. (*We are gentlemen,* Jóska would remind me, *not criminals.*) Rarely had Jóska and I encountered a target foolish enough to attempt to fight us, and on those occasions a careful shot to somewhere non-fatal would always quell the heroics.

The coachman's head fell back when he was hit, sharp and

soundless, like a puppet with its strings cut. None of the usual: no screaming, no doubling over, no cursing at me, no drip of blood from a wound.

I've killed him, I thought wildly. "Ah—" I said, stepping forward, but before I could say more, the coachman's coat spun, as though he and he alone had been caught in a brutal wind. His fur hat fell. Where a head should have been there was a black cloud of nothing. The scarf unwound and cascaded, in a spiral around him, to the ground.

A second later, there was nothing left of the coachman but a pile of clothes. The horses watched, still as statues and uncaring, and I *knew*.

There was only one piece of advice Jóska Bajusz had never delivered with humour.

László. Listen. Never, ever, ever try to rob a magus.

"Oh, *shit*," I spat.

In the next moment, I was frozen, and bathed in a dark blue mist. I tried to turn, to run, but my legs were rooted in the road. My hands were heavy like anchors; my pistols fell from my clumsy fingers. My tongue was a hot leaden weight in my mouth. Before, I had only known magic from the periphery of it: the graze of a spell during a battle, the lightning-storm smell that permeated the air when magi fought. The pure violence of this magic stunned me. My innards felt like they had together decided to all at once age and fail and die. My throat constricted; I could breathe only in thin streams. I couldn't blink. *Was this what Jóska felt?*

The carriage doors creaked open. First, I glimpsed old scratched boots, and the bottom of a ratty rough-spun cloak. Then the magus himself. His hood was down. His hair was long, tangled, and not the color you would expect on a magus: not white-blond, not blood-red, but an unremarkable peasant-brown.

He walked with a pronounced limp as he approached me, but he did not carry a staff like most of the magi I had seen in the war. When he stood before my trapped self, I could see that he was young. Eighteen or nineteen, at most. His face was ruddy. A few pimples dotted his chin. *My sort of luck lately*, I thought. *Dying at the hands of a crippled magus who's just out of short pants.*

But the magus did not kill me. He said, "You're no Austrian."

"Mmph," was my reply. It was impossible to speak.

He huffed impatiently, then pointed a bony finger at my throat and murmured a few indistinguishable words. *Horse's ass*, I thought. *You did this; don't get tetchy when I can't answer you.* Tendrils of smoke encircled my neck. I glared down at them, mistrustful, but my throat loosened and my tongue went back to normal. "Do I *look* Austrian?"

"No," the magus said. "You look poor."

"And I was hoping you and your carriage might be a step toward changing that," I said, adopting a jovial tone. "It appears I was wrong there, but, friend, no harm in an honest mistake. If you'll undo this spell and let me on my way—"

"You've ruined my coachman."

The magus gazed at the coachman's clothes, now speckled with fresh snow. He had bright blue eyes that belonged more on a guileless farm boy than someone who could kill you with a hand gesture. "That thing wasn't *alive*, was it?" I asked.

"Not like you and I are alive."

"So? You cannot wiggle your fingers and *magic* him back up?"

He sighed. "I see you have no understanding of how the Art works."

"I've had about five minutes of schooling," I snapped. It was true: I had no real family, not since I was small, and though I liked to read, every well-meaning attempt to put me in a schoolroom unfailingly ended once the Good Samaritan in question realized there was no keeping me from escaping formal education. "Somehow the nuances of magic weren't part of it."

The magus did not respond. He stared at me, calm and assessing, as though he were deciding what slimy creature he should snap his fingers to turn me into.

"Why would you even have a coachman? I've never seen a magus with a coachman. Or horses." You could tell a magus's carriage from the silent eerie way it travelled: unmanned, horseless, but lurching along with its wheels clacking and turning all the same.

The magus shrugged. "I've never seen a *betyár* with patches on his coat and holes in his trousers."

I ignored that. Jóska and I had once dressed in finery, since people had romantic notions of what *betyárok* should look like, but hunger had a way of making you not care about your threadbare clothes. "You can't fault me for attempting to rob you," I said. "It wouldn't be *fair*. I couldn't have known you were a magus."

"We live in unfair times," the magus said. His accent was from somewhere east of my own: the Carpathians, perhaps, or Transylvania. His voice dropped low. "You see, good *betyár*, I do not want *anyone* on the road to know what I am."

"I wouldn't—"

Before I could finish my sentence, the magus growled out more words I didn't know and held out both palms. Blue light, dark like the mist around me, arced from the magus's fingers and knocked me down. I howled, and tried to gain purchase on the ground, but the magic banded around my limbs and wrenched them back forcefully, as though an invisible strongman had pinned me. Trussed like a chicken, I craned my neck to look up. The magus loomed over me, the edge of his cloak tickling my cheek, his hands hidden in clouds of smoke, and the first thing I thought was *If I hadn't seen that damnable lantern, I'd be having beef and pálinka right now.*

The second thing was in Jóska's voice. *László, I should have made your pig my apprentice and made bacon of you. Listen: your pistols, your dagger, those are your weapons, but your words are your armor. Jóska Bajusz, you could sell a fur pelt to a fox: that's what the Countess Almásy told me of my charm. That's what you must do, if ever you cannot use your weapons. Use your armor. Sell a fur pelt to a fox.*

"Whatever you're doing, you're going about it wrong," I rasped.

If the magus heard, he did not show it. He lowered his hands, and an incredible pain shot through me, hot like fiery coals. From what I could see, my arms and legs appeared normal, but felt like they had been set afire. My chest burned, and I choked and sputtered before I managed to grind out, "I can tell you were in the war."

That did stop the magus. He balled his hands into fists. "And?"

Relieved, I took a gasping gulp of air, cold and sweet. "That leg of yours has to have been crippled by magic. Otherwise you could heal it, no? I would wager it was some Russian magus," I said, and again I remembered Jóska breathing his last. "Efficient, those Russian magi were, rows on rows of them casting God-knows-what at us in perfect time. It's a pity ours weren't so well-marshalled."

"*Betyár*, insulting me will not help you—"

"You thought I might be Austrian, and you were disappointed when I turned out not to be. You're travelling with the trappings of a wealthy man. You've a war wound. You're up to something—and I tell you, *magus*, you're going about it wrong."

The magus pursed his lips. He slashed one arm down. I flipped over, my limbs still bent and rigid beneath me. Snow seeped through my trousers and the skin of my ungloved hands, but, after the heat of the magus's spell, I welcomed it.

"My leg was hit at Segesvár," the magus said. "Scores of my brethren were killed, scores more wounded to the point where their magic was lost to them, and I was left with *this*." He glared at his bad leg with disgust, as though he wanted nothing more than to hack the thing off.

"I fought at Segesvár, too."

He met my eyes and snorted. "Is this where we embrace like old friends and go find some ale and regale one another with stories of our battles and sing songs of mother Hungary?"

"…Yes?" I said hopefully.

He raised an eyebrow, a touch peevishly. "I thought *betyárok* were meant to be clever."

"You can think me an idiot if you like, magus, but if it's Austrians you want to fall for your phony rich man's carriage, it's not men like what you're pretending to be that the *Austrians* want. I suspect you're out here, hiding who you truly are, because you're scheming some revenge on them." The east, where the magus's accent marked him as from, had borne the worst of the revolution. "Did they turn your home into a battlefield?"

The magus was silent.

I nodded at his carriage. "A fine carriage like that, a coachman, a pair of horses—to me, that says *here's a good law-abiding fellow who'll accept any king who rules him so long as his taxes don't go up.* For the most part, the Habsburg men aren't out here bothering noblemen. They're not the men an Austrian soldier would want to apprehend."

The magus paused, his mouth still pressed into a thin frown. "And what man *would* he want to apprehend?"

Yes, I thought. I had him. *I may taste that pálinka yet.* "Men like me. Former soldiers, rebels, *betyárok*. All the vermin that has to be hunted after a war." The magus was listening. I could tell by the way his magic seemed to drain from me, slowly, as his concentration shifted to my words. "Why, not a month ago the *betyár* Józef Szarka was arrested for making a toast to the thirteen martyrs of Arad in a public house," I continued. "And Artúr Marek was found outside Tata with his throat slashed." (Both Józef and Artúr were men Jóska had always dismissed as puffed-up peacock fools, not true *betyárok*, but he would not have minded me invoking their names in the service of persuasion.) "I had a-a friend who died at Segesvár. He always had the same advice regarding Austrians."

"Oh?"

"If you rob an Austrian, take everything."

The magus smiled, faint but satisfied. "You are offering to show me how to play the *betyár*," he concluded.

"Better than letting you kill me." My arms and legs were coming back to me, but I remained still, not wanting him to notice. "But there would be no *play* about it. You learn to rob the roads, you learn to do it for real." The idea of it was beginning to appeal to me. *Imagine the robberies you could pull off with a magus.*

He looked at me thoughtfully. "What's your name?"

"László Sovány."

"I haven't heard of you."

Listen, Jóska's voice reminded me, *it is a fine thing to have legends told of you, but remember you cannot eat a legend, nor spend it, nor sleep beside it for warmth in winter.* "Nor should you have," I said testily. "I imagine you've only heard of *betyárok* who are fools. It's no time to go around proclaiming yourself to be a *betyár*, not unless you want a swift death."

The magus nodded. "It's a generous offer you make, László Sovány."

"I'm a generous man."

"But I would rather remain on my own."

The magus raised his hands again, and that horrible blue smoke rose, but this time I was ready for him. I rolled and kicked out wildly, aiming for his crippled leg. I knew I'd hit my mark when the magus screamed and collapsed beside me; it was as though I had knocked one leg from a rickety stool.

The magus's hands went to his injured leg. I got to my knees and scrambled for my dagger. As the magus tried to pick himself up, I lunged forward and sliced along the back of his right wrist. I had cut him only lightly, but a runnel of blood dripped beneath the blade and onto the magus's cloak. "I'll give you a severed hand to match that lame leg if you don't stop trying to kill me," I said, through gritted teeth.

He winced, but then he laughed. "Old man, you're not as useless as I thought."

"*Old man*," I repeated, incredulous. I was thirty-three, not *seventy*. "Just because you're not even old enough to grow a beard—" I pressed the dagger down a little more. "You try to cast something and I start *sawing*."

"Peace, László," the magus said, his eyes fixed on his pinned hand. His words were even, but the look in his eyes was that of a frightened animal. "Let me go. I'll not hurt you. I promise." He held up his free hand in a gesture of supplication: something you would do if you wanted to show you were unarmed, but no comfort from a magus whose hands *were* his weapons.

I held the dagger in place. "Swear it on your mother's sweet soul."

He blanched at that, though it might have been from blood loss. But, from his look, I would have bet my last coin (and I did only have one) that his mother was dead, and his father, too. He had a loneliness about him that I recognized: a hollow, worn, burnt-out look that you don't see in people who still have homes and families. "Swear it, magus," I said.

"Very well," he said, sounding almost petulant. "On my mother's soul, I swear that if you now remove your dagger from my hand, and if you do not try to attack me or rob me further, I will use no magic on you."

I had hoped he wouldn't remember to put that bit in about me not robbing him, but I couldn't be picky. "Swear, too, that you will not *harm* me. I don't want you taking a swing at me, magic or not."

"And I will not harm you."

"Good," I said. I withdrew the dagger and instead held out my hand. He looked at it suspiciously, then shook it. To my astonishment, a ribbon of orange light circled our handshake, first cauterizing his cut wrist, then streaming over our fingers. It didn't hurt. Unlike the other magic I had experienced, this magic was warm and cozy, like a good wool mitten. *Binding the magus's word*, I realized.

I could tell the magus was irritated from how he yanked his hand away as soon as the spell released him. I stood up, but he struggled with his bad leg. After a moment, I sighed and held out my hand to help him up.

Just what Jóska did, I remembered. I had been on the way to Pest-Buda with a sow from a hog farmer who had hired me to bring it to market. Jóska had burst out with a pistol and demanded the pig. Jóska had not expected a skinny fourteen-year-old boy to strike back, but I had grown up stupid and feral, without learning much in the way of common sense. To me, fighting a *betyár*, even an armed one, had been preferable to a whipping from the hog farmer. We had fought until we were both as filthy as the pig. I even bit Jóska on his big hairy forearm. And, in the end, he had laughingly helped me up from the mud and told me I had the heart of a *betyár*. (The sow, rest its fat delicious soul, became our supper.)

Grudgingly, the magus took my hand, and I hauled him up. "Why are you smiling?" he asked me, as he inspected his crippled leg.

"I'm not dead, and I'm smarter than you," I said. "Fine reasons to smile, both." At his surly expression, I grinned wider. "You haven't given me your name, magus."

He drew his cloak around himself and stood a bit taller. "Krisztián."

"Truly? *Christian*, that means," I said, as I retrieved my pistols. "Are not all magi godless heathens?"

"Indeed we are, but my mother liked the name."

"Well, far be it from me to speak ill of a woman who produced a specimen so fine as yourself."

Krisztián's face was easy to read: he very much regretted his vow not to harm me. He pulled his hood up to cover his hair and hobbled toward the carriage. I cannot say what made me do what I did next. Perhaps I felt sorry for Krisztián, with that pathetic limp of his. Perhaps I was enamoured with the idea of having a magus's powers with me, of having my targets stunned with magic as I went through their belongings. Perhaps, deep down, I shared Krisztián's apparent desire to take revenge for the war. Perhaps it was simple: it was cold and late and I was weary and I missed Jóska. "Krisztián?" I called.

He turned.

"My offer stands, if you still want me to teach you how to rob the roads."

I could not see his reaction, not with that hood, but he asked, "There would be Austrians?"

I thought of all the treasures Jóska and I had collected, and all the ransacked places I had found when I had returned from the war alone. "There would be," I confirmed. "And it would be a shame, with your spells and my skills, if we didn't relieve them of their possessions, not when most of them have stolen from good honest Hungarians."

Even through the snow, I could see the gleam of Krisztián's smile. When, at last, he spoke, there was a bright note in his voice. "All right," he said. "I shall try it. But if I do not like learning to be a *betyár*, I will leave."

"Oh, you'll love it," I said cheerfully. "Guns, riches, soft swooning women. Now, can we *please* use your carriage to reach Győr? My clothes are soaked, thanks to you, and I long for a drink."

"No," Krisztián said.

"No?"

He looked glumly at the coachman's clothes. "The spell in that coachman was what held everything together. That's why I was furious. You destroyed *weeks* of complicated work with a single pull of a pistol's trigger. I cannot merely wave my hands and enchant the carriage anew."

"The horses?" *Please*, I thought.

Krisztián snapped his fingers. The beautiful chestnut Percherons vanished.

"What in *the*—"

"Those horses were not real, old man," Krisztián explained. "The carriage is, but now we have no way to move it. We shall have to walk."

I must have looked rather chagrined at the word *walk* because Krisztián sighed, muttered more strange words, and made a broad looping motion with one arm. This spell was yellow, the rich golden yellow of honey. Once it left Krisztián's fingers it broke apart and fell all about us like hundreds of humming fireflies.

But I felt nothing. "What is this?" I asked.

Krisztián frowned. "It's protection against the cold," he said. "I can feel it. It should warm you, like you're sitting before a hearth." He raised his hand to try again, but before he cast the spell, he began to laugh.

"What?"

"*I will use no magic on you.*"

"Obviously, I don't mind when it is *good* magic."

"No, that's what you had me swear. I cannot use magic on you, for good or ill."

"Oh-oh, *shit.* You *fucking* ass."

"It's not my fault, László," Krisztián said innocently. "You made me swear on my mother's sweet soul."

"Let's go," I growled. I turned away from the carriage and stomped up the road, my saturated boots squelching on the ground.

"*I'm* quite warm," he added, still snickering.

"Please be quiet."

We walked in silence for a stretch. The night was still snowy, still dark, and I still had a long way to Győr with only half a forint in my coin purse, but, even with my body aching from residual magic and my clothes sodden and ruined, I felt lighter. I had known the road a long time, the road Jóska and I had lived on: the pine smell of the trees, the scattered stars, the curves of every well-worn rut. There was something restful in that road when it was not walked alone.

Then Krisztián said, "László." For the first time, he sounded as young as he looked. "The rumours of *betyárok*, it is often said…" He hesitated.

"Hm?" I prodded.

"Well, you mentioned *women*. It is often said that a *betyár* has great luck with women."

I had to stop and hold my sides and gasp for breath, so hard did I laugh. It felt good, after he had laughed at me. "Now I see! That's why you're coming with me. Vengeance, yes, patriotism for mother Hungary, certainly, but there's no compromise to those if you happen to tumble a few lovely ladies along the way—"

"Never mind," he interrupted.

"Ah, Krisztián, not to worry," I said, coughing to hide a chuckle. "About women—well, let me tell you a story. Once I charged before a carriage, a beautiful one, all white, and who should be inside but the Countess Almásy…"

A KINGDOM AND A HORSE

-Valhalla Saga-

SNORRI KRISTJANSSON

"A Kingdom and a Horse" is set in the universe of my Valhalla Saga, which is pretty much 10th century Northern Europe because I'm not clever enough to build a world of my own. It contains the story of legendary Viking captain Sigurd and his trusty right-hand man Sven's youthful escapades in England. If your trade is to be looting and pillaging, you have to learn somewhere...right?

TALES OF ASSASSINS, MERCENARIES, AND ROGUES

Blackguards

Anglia, 963AD
Late summer

I
N THE DISTANCE, SHOUTS rang out and horses whinnied. The rhythmic clang of metal on metal told of blacksmiths hard at work, fixing armor and sharpening swords. Commands in a strange, woollen language carried over thatched roofs, river banks, and the heads of three young men hiding behind a thick hedge.

"Oh, great. *Now* what?" Thormund hissed, clutching a rough-spun sack.

Sven turned around and glared. "Now you shut up before you get us killed with your moaning," he hissed, bushy eyebrows knotted with fury. "And keep it still. If you move, it clinks."

"Should have just chopped it up," Thormund said. "Easier to carry."

Up ahead, Sigurd motioned for both of them to be quiet and scratched the few, stubbly hairs on his chin. "It's not about that. We need it in one piece. Now—there are twenty of them," he whispered. "They've only got one horse, but they're armed and armored. I could take about five, I think, but that still leaves too many for you." He turned and peered through the gap in the hedge.

"You think?" Sven hissed. "This is turning out to be a bad idea."

"It was *your* idea," Thormund growled, puffing up his bony chest

"A KINGDOM AND A HORSE"

Illustration by **ORION ZANGARA**

like a tiny rooster getting ready to fight.

"That's hardly my fault, is it?" Sven snarled.

"What? How is that not your fault? You're going to get all of us killed," Thormund said. "Now I'll never reach twenty summers."

"If you die it will be from cowardice, not blades," Sven said. "You've had no trouble avoiding a fight so far."

Thormund kicked out and connected with Sven's shin, just as a startled blackbird burst out of the hedge.

"Stop it." Sigurd glared at them. "You both need to shut up and think."

"He *kicked* me! Can we leave him?" Sven said. "Trade him for a pair of trousers, maybe? I'm sure the king will have him. For sausages or something."

"No," Sigurd said.

"Well, we can't go back." Sven glanced up at the keep. "We were lucky enough to get out."

"The river's too wide on the left," Sigurd added. "And there are too many people on the right."

"And we can't wait till nightfall, because they'll get news of the ship. So the only way is forward," said Thormund with a sigh.

Sigurd turned to Sven. "Impress me."

"Fine," Sven said. "Fine. I'll go. But you better be prepared to run." He slinked off towards the houses, hugging the growing shadows and hunching over.

Thormund slumped to the ground. "I hate this," he muttered. "We're all going to die. Stupid, stupid idea."

"The idea was fine," Sigurd said. "Get there, grab what we came for, get back before news of the ship gets to them. It's cost us quite a lot less than a full assault. Father will be pleased."

"If we get out of here alive, which is no guarantee."

"We will," Sigurd said, almost gently. "And you'll be back on the boat. He might even make you boatswain. Especially after Ormar died last week." Thormund studied the branch next to his face with great intent. Sigurd looked at his friend. "It was odd how he got his throat cut, wasn't it?"

"Girl musta had a knife," Thormund muttered.

"She may have. She'll have been very limber, too, to cut his throat from behind."

Thormund was about to answer when a clear voice interrupted. "*Hweart thed?*" Bright, innocent. A child's voice. Both men turned and stared. The boy couldn't be much more than five, and he was standing twenty yards away, staring at them. "Hweart thed?" he repeated.

Sigurd reached over and gently put his hand on Thormund's scrawny arm. "No," he whispered. "Too far away. He'll scream." Thormund eased the knife back under his belt.

Sigurd contorted his face into the biggest expression of surprise he could make.

The boy stared at him and giggled.

Sigurd smiled and slowly placed a finger on his lips.

The boy, eyes sparkling with understanding, did the same. Then he stuck his tongue out.

Sigurd Aegisson, captain's son and scourge of the north seas, stuck his tongue out further. The boy giggled again, and Sigurd motioned for him to come over. He glanced furtively at the hole in the hedge, then pulled back as if someone might have seen him. Delighted, the boy scampered over and crouched next to them, peering out onto the village square. When he saw the people there, he turned to Sigurd and Thormund. He opened his mouth—and hissed very quietly. "Sssh." Then he knelt next to them and smiled.

"Sssh," Sigurd repeated. Then he turned to the grinning Thormund. "Leave your blade be. If he lives, we get out of here. If we kill him, his kin will not stop until we're dead. But if you tell anyone I spared his life I will gut you like a fish. Understood?"

The smirk on Thormund's face vanished. "Understood," he muttered. "I wasn't going to—"

A woman's screech ripped through the village. "*Vykingr!*" she shouted. "VYKINGR!"

Moments later an odd shape dressed in what looked like five layers of the brightest clothes imaginable sprinted past the soldiers in the square, slapping a fair few of them in the process. "GET THE HORSE, YOU BASTARDS!" Sven screamed, lifting his knees high to avoid tripping on the hem of a stolen skirt. "RUN!!" He turned sharply and disappeared in between houses, vaulting over a waist-high fence.

The effect on the men in the square was impressive. Almost all of them grabbed their weapons and gave chase.

Behind them a woman screamed "AETHELRED!" Beside them the boy's ears perked up and he took off at great speed.

"Now!" Sigurd hissed. "NOW!"

Thormund did not need any encouragement. He squeezed out of the hedge and darted to the nearest oak tree, with Sigurd in pursuit.

Chaos reigned in the square. The fastest and the youngest were turning in between the houses where Sven had gone, but a number of them were still milling about in confusion.

Sigurd overtook Thormund and sprinted up to the next man he could find, grabbing him by the shift and screaming in his face, "VYKINGR!" Before the doughy soldier knew what had happened, Sigurd had spun him around and pushed him towards the road, on Sven's trail. Terrified, the soldier started running. Sigurd ran close behind him, staying at least partially hidden and inserting all the command he could muster into his voice, shouting "Vykingr" over and over. Two more soldiers joined, and before long they were barking encouragement at each other. Like a herd, the remaining soldiers caught on and started running.

When the last one ran out of the square, Sigurd turned and ran towards the horse, which Thormund had already saddled.

He greeted Sigurd with a smile. "Stopping for a chat, were we?"

"They needed some encouragement," Sigurd replied.

"Right. Shall we go catch ourselves an ugly woman?"

"Sounds good to me," They mounted up, Sigurd in front, and urged the stolen horse onwards. Over the sound of hooves on hard ground they heard the frustrated shouts of the townsfolk in their strange language.

"They bleat like sheep!" Thormund shouted.

"Sheep are smarter!" Sigurd shouted back.

Suddenly Sven burst out of an impossibly narrow space between a house and a tool shed, turning sharply and sprinting towards the edge of town. His clothes were ripped and torn, but he was grinning manically. Three young men ran hard on Sven's heels, but the fourth caught his foot, spun with complete lack of grace, and smacked into the ground.

"There!" Thormund shouted, and leaned forward on the horse to spur it on.

Sigurd's eyes narrowed in concentration. He took a deep breath. "Run, you bastard! Arms out, don't look back!" he shouted.

Sven stretched his arms out and sprinted for all he was worth.

Behind him, hooves thundered as Sigurd and Thormund approached. The pursuers looked up too late—a well-placed kick sent one flying, and the other two had to dive sideways to avoid being trampled.

Strong arms hooked Sven by the elbow, and he was airborne. He caught a toe-hold on the stirrup and swung his other leg over, grabbing hold of Sigurd's waist with both hands.

The town disappeared behind a bend in the road, and a frustrated scream suggested the pursuers had given up.

"Next time, let's rob a town that has more than one horse," Sven huffed.

"Nothing but complaints," Thormund muttered. The mare whinnied in agreement, and they rode on.

———•———

AN ENDLESS EXPANSE OF grass stretched out to either side as far as the eye could see. Up ahead, the road sloped up a hill, into a pine forest.

"No wonder these farmers have settled here," Thormund said. "It is the country for it."

"That's why they're soft," Sigurd said. "They don't need to defend themselves."

"Didn't," Sven corrected.

Sigurd smiled. "That's right. Thormund—do you have the sack?"

Eyes wide with panic, Thormund started patting himself. "The sack? Uhrm...what? No! Sven had it!"

Sven reached for his knife. "You lying pile of shit, I'll gut—" Then he looked up and saw the smirk on the skinny horse thief's face. "Not funny."

Grinning, Thormund produced the sack from underneath his shirt. "Here it is." The unmistakeable sound of seagulls punctuated his sentence, and he handed the sack over to Sigurd, who fastened it to the saddle horn.

"And here we are." Sigurd cupped his hands around his mouth and shouted, "Norsemen coming!"

"About fucking time!" a voice echoed from the forest. Seven men just...appeared, stepping out from the shadows of the trees.

"Your father is ready."

"My father is always ready," Sigurd replied.

"Did you get what you needed?" a big, broad-chested guard said, leaning on his spear.

Sigurd just grinned and rode past him.

It didn't take them long to clear the thicket and come out to the pebble-covered beach on the other side. His father's ship, *The Northman's Claw*, lay beached, and the men were sat around a cook-fire roasting something big.

"So that's what you do when the work is being done for you?" Sven hollered. "Sit around and stuff your face with the king's deer?"

Various levels of abuse and suggestions of where he could shove the hooves rang out from the men sat around the fire. Only one of them rose to his feet. Thick, silver-gray hair in a plait held together with gold wire snaked down over one shoulder. Sun-tanned and weather-beaten skin stretched taut over high cheek-bones, and piercing blue eyes stared at the boys.

Sigurd dismounted and grabbed the sack. "Here you are, father."

Aegir Njardarson took the sack and nodded. "You have done well," he said. "All of you."

Behind him, Thormund and Sven dismounted and grinned. Sigurd just stood there, ramrod straight. "Thank you," he said, but his father had already turned away.

Aegir's was the voice of command. "Everyone up. Push out. We'll have them on us sooner than you think. Carve up the meat, too. We're sailing." The men grumbled, but none of them hesitated, each one getting up and taking to his assigned role.

Thormund and Sven went to help push the boat out. The icy cold sea snapped at their ankles, then bit at their calves. "I swear, even the sea around here is softer," Sven said.

"Not soft enough," Thormund grumbled.

"You're just not fat enough," Sven countered, grunting with the effort of dragging the ship out and wincing at the sound of the hull scraping the pebbles.

Within moments, a cry came out from the watchers. "Soldiers coming!"

There was no shouting or cursing on the beach. Everyone simply did what they were already doing, just faster. As the seven watchers came running down the hill towards the ship, men were clearing up and jumping on board. Soon enough, Aegir's fighters were placing themselves on the twenty benches, grabbing oars, and stowing away sacks of loot.

In the midst of it all, Aegir Njardarson walked calmly on the shoreline commanding his men. When the time was right, he picked up a fist-sized stone, walked towards the longship, and leapt up into the bow.

Moments later, a wave of men crested the hill and charged down towards the ship—but too late. Strong arms were pulling on oars like they'd done thousands of times before, and the vessel slid effortlessly backwards and out to sea.

"They brought some friends," Thormund said.

"They probably heard Thormund the Destroyer was on the boat and didn't want to take any chances," Sven said.

"Halt," Aegir shouted. Commands were barked down the line, and the rowers kept the ship steady, out of arrow range. The Viking captain lifted the sack overhead. Then he stuck his hand in it and pulled out a glittering, finely wrought crown.

The mass of men on the beach shouted and shook their weapons, but there was nothing they could do as Aegir put the crown back in the sack, reached down and picked up the stone, and placed that in the bag too.

"No. He isn't—" Thormund began. He glanced at Sigurd, but

the young man's eyes were riveted to the figure of his father, of how his men looked at him, and how he stood in the bow, calm as a Tuesday morning.

"I reckon he is," Sven said.

"But why?" Thormund almost wailed.

"To piss them off," Sigurd said. "To make them too angry for reason. To make them charge us next time without thinking."

"To win," Sven added.

By the stern, Aegir Njardarson had started swinging the sack with the stone and the crown over his head. The clamour from the beach was raw now, men screaming the ugliest words they knew, invoking their god, *something*—and then Aegir let it go.

The sack sailed to their starboard side. It hit the water with an audible plop and sank out of sight immediately. Without needing to be prompted, the rowers on the port side pulled hard. *The Northman's Claw* turned in a half-circle and sped away.

"Glad that's over," Thormund said from his spot behind Sven and Sigurd.

"Over?" Sven said. "You should hear what we've got planned for Frankia!"

THIEVES AT THE GATE

JAMES ENGE

*The principal thief in this story is me. I stole the
world and characters for "Thieves at the Gate"
from Homer. It's always been interesting to me how
people like Odysseus (or Gunnarr Hamundarson or
whoever) could be decent, respectable guys at home
and murderous pirates abroad. This isn't really the
answer, but it's an answer.*

TALES OF ASSASSINS, MERCENARIES, AND ROGUES

Blackguards

WHEN THEIR FIRST CHILD was born dead, Odysseus and Penelope grieved, and Ithaca and the Cephallenian nations grieved with them. When their second child was stillborn also, Odysseus' father told him to get a new wife.

"Go back to your farm, old man!" said Odysseus, and went off to bury the dead baby.

After the third child took a few breaths and died, an assembly of Ithacan nobles came to Odysseus. Eupeithes spoke for the group, with his fair-haired son Alcinous standing at his side. He begged Odysseus to marry again. "We know how you love Penelope, and so do we all love her and honor her for her many talents. But if you have no heir, the lands conquered by your grandfather, Arceisius, may break away and we will be thrown back to live on our farms and flocks and the rocky soil of Ithaca. What a dreadful thing that would be!"

It would certainly be bad for Eupeithes, Odysseus knew. His lands, though large, wouldn't support a decent-sized herd of goats. Eupeithes was rich because he took money from the wealthy men of Cephallenia, promising to plead their cases with the king of Ithaca. Odysseus knew

"THIEVES AT THE GATE"

Illustration by **ORION ZANGARA**

better than Eupeithes how much treasure and blood it had taken to conquer the Cephallenian lands, and how much it still took to maintain Ithaca's rule there. He would've traded Ithacan rule over the Cephallenians for a decent plow. He was not about to throw Penelope aside for Eupethes' benefit.

But Eupeithes was rich, and the Ithacan nobles with him were important in more important ways. So Odysseus told them he would think about it, and didn't. Instead he went to play with his new puppy.

"Argus," he said reflectively to the puppy (who was his closest confidant, apart from Penelope), "if I were as good at siring children as I am at raising dogs, this house would be full of children. Herds of babies would darken the narrow plains of Ithaca, devouring all nursing mothers in their path."

Argus' dark clear eyes took on the tragic look of confusion they always wore when Odysseus said any sentence longer than, "Sit!" or "Seek!" or "Let's eat!"

"Never mind, fat boy," Odysseus said kindly. (The epithet was merely descriptive. At this point in his career, Argus resembled an overstuffed sausage with floppy ears and four alarmingly large feet.) "Let's eat!"

Relieved of his responsibilities as a state counsellor, Argus ran frantically to the kitchen, barking happily. Odysseus beat him there, but only by a hair. The puppy's legs were getting longer; Odysseus thought he'd be a good hunting dog.

"Keep that animal out of my kitchen!" shrieked Euryclea, as she did two or three times a day.

"You talk that way of my only son?" Odysseus declaimed, in mock-offended tones.

Euryclea gasped. "You're a fool, Odysseus: that's my opinion!" she said, when she could speak. "Your father Laertes was the only son of his father, and you are the only son of Laertes. The house of Arceisius is destined to yield only sons. If you persist in calling that dirty beast your only son, the gods will punish you by making it the truth!"

"And which god told you this, Euryclea?"

"It stands to reason!" Euryclea screamed. She rarely spoke at any tone other than the top of her voice, and Odysseus not infrequently felt the urge to clap his hand over her mouth and tell her to be quiet. But she had been his nurse when he was a child, so he let her run on. "Besides," she continued, "I thought you had given up this nasty hunting business. The last time you went hunting boar, the thing nearly took your leg off! Why would the gods let that happen, if they wanted you to go on hunting?"

"You worry too much about what the gods think, Euryclea. In the meantime, feed Argus, eh? He's turning to skin and bones as we stand here."

Feed Argus being one of the sentences Argus understood, human conversation became impossible in the face of a flood of irrefutable canine rhetoric.

Later, Odysseus went to see Penelope in her sickroom. She was ill with the fever that always comes after childbirth, but it hadn't dimmed her wits. He told her about his day. She chided him about teasing Euryclea, but she was unwontedly silent as he told her about the Ithacan nobles.

"They're right, you know," she said when he was done.

"They're not."

"You should send me back to my father's house," Penelope said, her face still pale from blood loss, "and take a new wife."

"No."

"You can set her aside if she gives you a son, and call me back. If you want to."

"No."

"I'd treat the boy as my very own," Penelope pleaded. "And I wouldn't be jealous of the woman."

"No."

"Why not?" Penelope asked reasonably.

"Because it's not your fault," he said, just as reasonably. "I've been with other women, you know. I've never had a son by any of them. If I had, I'd take him into the house and make him my heir."

"What will we do, then?"

For answer, Odysseus waggled his eyebrows lewdly at her.

Penelope laughed and coughed and laughed again. "I can't yet," she said at last. "I'm still bleeding."

"I'll wait. I'm good at waiting."

"Then I'll try to be, too."

When Penelope became pregnant for the fourth time, nobody ventured to advise the king on what he should do if the child was stillborn. This was because, if anyone seemed to be about to raise the subject with him, he would glare at them as if he were going to kill them on the spot. It had a way of killing the conversation on the spot, which was what Odysseus wanted.

In fact, he talked with few people, except Penelope, during her fourth pregnancy. He spent much of the time hunting in the hills with Argus, now a long, lean, dangerous-looking animal. The appearance was not misleading, as far as beasts of prey were concerned: Argus was the best hunting dog Odysseus had ever raised. But any man, woman, or child could tie the dog's tail in knots if they wanted to. When Odysseus wanted to find Argus, he rarely bothered going to the kennels; instead he would wander down the road to see which of the local children Argus was playing with.

Today was a deer-hunting day, and Odysseus had roused Argus and his hunting crew while it was still dark. They were deep into the hills above Odysseus' house by dawn. He had sent his crew ahead of him on a long curving path to scare up the deer and send them his way. Argus remained at his side to scent the prey and chase the animals down. Odysseus didn't use traps or gins to catch deer, nor did he hunt them with javelins. He had his great hunting bow with him, that no man but he had ever been able to bend.

The time came when he ceased to hear his hunters up ahead. This was not so very odd (they had to be quiet to avoid startling the deer), but it was strange that he didn't hear them a little later on. If they were driving the deer toward him, they were doing it with great subtlety. And he knew these men: subtlety wasn't among their many virtues.

"Go find them, Argus," he said to his lean dangerous-looking dog. "Find your friend Xenocles," he added, naming his chief hunter.

Argus barked happily and ran off up the slope, disappearing over the ridge in moments.

Odysseus waited a long time, but neither hound nor huntsman returned. Finally, he shook his head, put an arrow to his bowstring, and went over the ridge himself.

Following Argus' trail as best he could, he came to a place where, it seemed to him, his huntsmen must have stood; he saw blood staining the sparse mountain grass. His mouth tightened, and he went onward down the slope. He was now following not the track of a single dog but the path of many feet.

He came, at last, in midafternoon, to a hill above the sea-line. A ship was pulled up on the rocky shore below. Beside it a dozen or so armed men were herding a crowd of Ithacans, stripping them of their belongings and sorting them into two groups. The young and fit were sent on board the ship. Odysseus could see his huntsmen and their dogs—Argus among them—on the ship; the others were sent aside along the narrow beach.

Pirates. Odysseus had lived on an island nearly all his life, and he knew the type. He hated them the way a shepherd hates wolves. The men and women taken on board would be sold as slaves. The others would be killed, so that they could not raise the alarm. Odysseus guessed several were already dead; these were lying motionless on the ground, with dark stains in the raglike clothes the pirates had left them.

Odysseus set his feet firmly and took aim with his bow. He waited—his first shot must count for much—and at last released the arrow. It passed, dark-feathered, through three men, one standing, one kneeling, the other crouching. They fell, screaming, into the bitter foaming water of the shallows. At least, two of them were screaming—the third man seemed to be dead.

Odysseus now drew arrow after arrow and shot without pause. Only moments would pass before the pirates realized where he was standing and gathered together to rush at him. He must account for as many as he could before then.

Some god was guiding his arrows: each one wounded a pirate. Not all those struck were killed, but when the huntsmen realized what was happening they leapt out of the ship and struggled with the wounded men, their dogs fighting beside them (except for Argus who stood barking happily in the stern and looking around for his master). Three unwounded pirates were left to make the inevitable charge up the hill at Odysseus.

He unhurriedly took aim with a final arrow and shot one of the three men through the throat; the pirate dropped and rolled down to the rocky beach. Then Odysseus turned and ran swiftly back uphill. The two remaining pirates chased him, both intent on revenge, but not (as Odysseus anticipated) at precisely the same pace. One was faster than the other and, when he passed over the ridge first, Odysseus was waiting for him there and struck him senseless, using the great bow as a club.

Dropping the bow, he seized the bronze sword from the fallen man and waited for the last pirate, armed with a blade and a patient smile.

The last pirate, out of breath after climbing the hill, took in the situation at a glance and struck at Odysseus' head. But the unarmored Odysseus was much nimbler; the pirate's blade slashed empty air. Odysseus, now behind the pirate, stabbed him under his left arm. The pirate fell, bleeding and gasping, to the ground and lay there.

"Who…?" asked the dying pirate. "Who…are you…*huntsman?*"

Odysseus bent over the dying man. "You want my name so you can curse me with your dying breath? Very well, pirate. If anyone in Hades asks you who did this to you, tell them it was brave Odysseus, son of Laertes, who rules in Ithaca." Then Odysseus lopped off the man's head before he could say a word.

He then turned and, with a single thrust, dispatched the unconscious pirate at his feet.

"Artemis," he cried, "far-shooting goddess who delights in arrows, I greet you with joy. Thanks for my huntsmen and this victory with the bow. Remember, please, my wife in her childbirth; I will remember you with this praise and in another song also.

"Athena," he added, after a moment, "glorious goddess of the shining eyes, many-minded, unyielding in your will, aegis-bearer, city-savior, friend of heroes, I thank you for this victory with the sword. I will remember you with this praise, and in another song also."

A feeling of awe came over him and he turned. An armored woman with lightning-colored eyes stood below him on the slope, but she towered over him, even without her high-crested helmet (which she held in the crook of her elbow). "You put me second,

Odysseus," she said, in a clear voice ringing like a trumpet. "Suppose I don't like that?"

"Dread goddess," he said politely but firmly, "the bow is Artemis' own weapon, and my huntsmen are her servants. Also, my wife nears her hour of childbirth and is in Artemis' hands. But if I have done wrong I am sorry, and will appease you in any way you name."

"You never do wrong, Odysseus," Athena replied indulgently. "That's why many of the gods consider you inconvenient. Not I, though. Share out the spoils below and take the ship back home; there's news awaiting you there."

The goddess was gone, and the sunlight suddenly seemed a duller shade of gold.

Odysseus dragged the two corpses down the slope that led to the sea. His huntsmen and the other captives greeted him with shouts of triumph; by now all the pirates were dead.

"This victory is from the gods," he said, raising his hand to quiet them. "But we all fought; we all suffered. We'll treat the spoils as in war, each man to have a share. I take the ship as mine. Huntsmen, man the oars; you can come back for your shares later. You—" he recognized one of the townsmen "—Dictys, I put you in charge of the huntsmen's shares, and those belonging to the dead."

Dictys bowed his head, acknowledging the honor and the obligation. "What'll we do with the dead Ithacans' stuff, Odysseus of many counsels?" he asked.

"Take part of the spoils and give them a good funeral and give whatever's left to their families. If they've no family, buy offerings for Artemis and Athena; they've been good to us this day."

"And the pirates...?" someone asked. "We don't want their ghosts wandering around here."

"Bind their feet and put them on the ship," Odysseus directed. "I'll tend to them."

Soon Odysseus was out at sea with his crew of the living and his cargo of the dead. He never felt more alive than when he was at sea: his ship bounding among the bitter blue waves, the untraveled world gleaming on the horizon. He steered the ship far out to sea until they reached a current that set away from Ithaca. Then, he and the huntsmen dumped the dead pirates into the sea. Without a burial, their ghosts would long wander the wrong side of the river Styx, unable to reach their final rest on the far side. It was the ultimate revenge.

"Serve them right, the thieving, murdering bastards," muttered Elpenor, one of the youngest (and clumsiest) huntsmen.

Odysseus sat at the steering oar and said, "Home."

The huntsmen put their backs into it, and they were home soon enough.

There was news for the king, both good and bad. His wife had given birth to a son, perhaps in those very moments Odysseus was fighting the pirates far away, and the boy was as healthy as could be. Odysseus took the baby in his arms, called him Telemachus, and kissed him. Then he went to sit by his sleeping wife, thinking furiously.

For the other news had been very bad. King Menelaus' wife had been abducted by a foreign prince, and Agamemnon was already sending heralds to recruit the kings who had sworn to recover Helen if anyone kidnaped her. Kings like Odysseus.

That damned oath. It had seemed like such a good idea at the time. But perhaps there was a way out of it...

———•———

WHEN THE HERALD CAME to Ithaca, a month or so later, he found the house in mourning as if for a death. Nonetheless, he smiled. Of all heralds, he was the hardest to fool, and he had expected some sort of trick from the wily Odysseus. That was why he, of all heralds, had been sent here.

"Where is King Odysseus?" he asked the pale-faced queen, clutching her newborn child. "I am Palamedes, herald of the great King Agamemnon, and I have words for your lord's ears."

She said nothing but took him behind the king's great house and pointed.

Odysseus was there, his dress strangely disordered, with straws stuck in his red hair and beard. He had yoked a horse and a donkey as a team to pull a plow. But the plow was backwards. Odysseus followed the plow as the uneven team drove a crooked furrow through the rocky soil; he scattered something pale behind him, as if it were seed. The field around him was full of such crazy furrows, but nothing grew there.

The herald, who called himself Palamedes, went down to the field. He glanced down to examine the "seed" Odysseus was leaving on the furrows. It was sea-salt.

Penelope explained. "Each day he comes out here, yokes up his team, and plows a few furrows seeded with salt. He says he can grow pillars of the stuff."

The herald said nothing to this.

"We think it was the shock of the child being born," Penelope explained. "It was our fourth, but the first that lived. He has been like this since little Telemachus was born, refusing to even look at the baby, swearing that he will raise crops of salt instead of children, since all his sons have died."

The herald said nothing to this either.

"We hope he'll be better soon," Penelope said.

"So do I," the herald agreed.

He leapt up from the ground and snatched baby Telemachus

from Penelope's arms. As Penelope and Telemachus both cried out in dismay, the divinely tall herald gently set the baby down on the ground in Odysseus' path.

Odysseus kept driving the team for a few feet as if he neither saw nor heard the baby in front of his plow. But, as the herald had expected, Odysseus soon turned aside his awkward team and halted it. He walked around the plow, picked up the crying child and quieted it.

"Odysseus," said the herald, "I congratulate you on the sudden recovery of your wits. Give the child to his mother and come away; I have words for you."

Odysseus inclined his proud head and did as the herald commanded.

"A shrewd ploy," the herald commented when they were alone.

"It wasn't meant to fool you," Odysseus said, almost sullenly.

"Who, then?"

"Palamedes, perhaps."

The herald laughed. The sound went through Odysseus' head and the walls of his house and the mountains beyond, where the herdsfolk made the evil eye and prayed to be delivered from the watcher in the night, the thief at the gate, the ghost-leader: Hermes.

"You're hard to fool, Odysseus," said the god of messengers and thieves. "How did you know?"

"Palamedes is a tall clown with a good voice and not a single idea in his head."

"He has a pretty good memory, too," Hermes said, a little defensively.

Odysseus shrugged.

"You're not always kind to my people, Odysseus," said Hermes. "I'm the god of thieves, remember; I saw what you did to those pirates."

"And this is your revenge?" Odysseus demanded.

"No. I'm under orders to recruit you for the war effort against Troy. Athena wants you there; Zeus requires you to fulfill your oath." The god of tricksters smiled a broad alarming smile. "I do have a revenge planned for you, an especially fitting one. You'll know when it happens. But it won't interfere with your duties as a leader in the Greek fleet. Nor will it harm your wife and son, in case you're wondering. Athena likes them and, frankly, so do I."

Odysseus nodded. "Thanks, grace-bestowing Hermes."

"Now send a letter to the real Palamedes, who is asleep on board that ship in your harbor, and let him (and, through him, Agamemnon) know that you'll fulfill your oath. Set someone to raising troops and ships here in Ithaca and go straight to Mycenae. Agamemnon is preparing an embassy to the Trojans, and you're to lead it."

Odysseus' heart lifted at this news. "Then we might settle the matter without a war?"

"I doubt it," the god replied. "But if there's a chance in ten thousand, you're the man to make it happen, Odysseus. I'll see you again." Hermes dropped his disguise and stepped into the air with winged feet.

HERMES WAS RIGHT. THE embassy failed, and Odysseus did see him again.

Ten years later, Odysseus was steering a ship into the harbor of Chryse, an island-kingdom off the coast of western Asia. The sun had set: a liplike smear of red marked its passage in the western sky. There were only a few lights visible in the town, none along the harbor, and the lack of light made steering a safe course difficult.

But Odysseus wished there were less light still, since he and his sailors had come to sack the town. The Greek army in front of Troy was starving; they could buy no food from the neighboring lands, who all were allies of Troy, so they were going to steal it instead.

They beached their ships alongside some fat merchant craft that didn't seem to have night guards; indeed, there were no guards anywhere in the harbor. That was foolish of Chryses, the priest of Apollo who ruled the little island from his palace-temple, but perhaps he didn't realize that war, like fire, is apt to spread, and that war, unlike fire, can easily cross a stretch of water.

Odysseus sent men to take possession of the merchant ships and waited. When the moon finally rose, a blank bitter eye peering at them from over the eastern horizon, Odysseus turned to his second-in-command, Eurylochus, and said, "You know what to do. Jettison the cargo from those merchant ships, unless it's edible. I'll see you soon, I hope. But, remember, if the town rises and people start attacking the ships, don't fight them. Stand away from shore."

"But—"

"None of that, my friend. You may still be able to take us off, if the ships remain whole, but if the ships are burned we'll all die here."

"You don't know if Achilles and that crazy Diomedes have done what they said they'd do," Eurylochus complained. He hated to miss a fight, and it made him surly, an attitude Odysseus simply couldn't understand, although he pretended he did.

Diomedes and Achilles had landed with picked troops some distance up the coast. They planned to attack the priest-king's citadel and loot it. "It doesn't matter if they have," Odysseus explained to Eurylochus. "They're after glory. We're here for food, and we'll get it."

He jumped from the prow of his ship down to the beach and roughly half the men from all his ships formed up with him on the shore. They all had their orders, and he only needed to gesture to have them do as he wished. They crept behind him up the road from the harbor to the town gate.

There was only one guard on duty, and he was asleep. Odysseus killed him with a stab to the throat and gestured for his men to open the gate as quietly as possible.

A shadow that smelled like Perimedes was standing by Odysseus, and he said to it, "Take your men to the warehouses by the market; I'll take mine to the cattle-pens. See you back at the beach."

"Any captives?" the shadow whispered in Perimedes' voice.

"If you want to draft people to carry stuff for you, that's all right. But I don't want anything going on our ships that we can't eat."

"But ransom—"

"Ransom be damned. Go, Perimedes!"

Perimedes went, other bronze-armed shadows following at his heels. Odysseus went to get the cows.

It was the night before market day in Chryse-town, and there were a lot of cows in the cattle-pens by the market. But cows, unlike baskets of grain and olives, are prone to protest when wakened and moved in the middle of the night. That was why Odysseus had chosen this task for himself and his trustiest men: it was the more dangerous.

"This is more than we can carry on our ships," a shadow with Elpenor's voice whispered.

"Never mind," Odysseus whispered back. "Diomedes and Achilles are sending their ships around to the harbor to pick them up. We'll pass some cows off on them. If we have to leave some on the beach, so be it. We want as many as we can possibly take away. Unless you've developed a taste for corpse-fed dog."

By now there were sounds of fighting from the hilltop palace-temple of Chryse's priest-king. Diomedes and Achilles, and their men, drawing off the town's soldiery with their promised raid. Odysseus silently wished them luck and got down to herding the cattle.

They opened the pens, and merged the different groups of cattle into one large herd, then drove the herd down the main street in town. There was no point in being quiet anymore; they had to count on speed instead. But Odysseus and a few of his men hung back from the herd, in case they were attacked from behind.

And they were. They were passing by an alley when a spear flew out of the shadows and struck the face of one of Odysseus' warriors. The man fell dead to the ground. Odysseus didn't have a chance to see who it was as a crowd of armorless men armed with scythes and mattocks suddenly came at them.

Odysseus and his men closed together against the onslaught. Their peasantish attackers were determined and desperate to save their property, but they had never been trained to fight, they weren't armored, and their weapons were inferior. Soon enough the bravest of them lay dead or dying in the muck of the street and the wisest of them were fleeing away toward the citadel. The city beyond them was already marked with flame—Perimedes must have finished his mission and set the fires, as Odysseus had commanded. From now on, the men of Chryse would be fighting the flames or escaping from them; Odysseus didn't think he'd have to worry about them attacking his men anymore.

"We have to get poor Lycophron," Elpenor cried.

"Poor Lycophron's dead," Odysseus observed. "Let's get back to the beach."

"But they won't bury him!" Elpenor protested. "They'll leave him out for the dogs and the birds to feed on! His ghost will wander the world, homeless, unable to cross the river Styx!"

Odysseus was not interested in the welfare of ghosts—not when it conflicted with his own—but he could see that Elpenor's plea had moved his other men.

"Get him, then," Odysseus directed Elpenor. "I'll watch your back. The rest of you, get down to the beach and start loading our plunder."

They went gratefully: very grateful someone else was risking his life for the dead, Odysseus thought sourly.

Elpenor leaped over the fallen peasants and lifted Lycophron's corpse. He threw it over his shoulder and started back toward Odysseus. Then he stumbled over one of the bodies littering the street and went down among them.

Odysseus cursed Elpenor's clumsiness—it would kill him one day, Odysseus was sure—and ran over to help, but then he tripped on something: a stick of some sort lying in the street, twisting strangely in the moonlight. He looked back at it as he lifted himself from the blood and mud of the street. Then he spied the silhouette of a man emerging from the darkness of a side street. The newcomer's form was unclear, but he wielded an axe with a bright glittering edge, and raised it over his head.

It took forever for Odysseus to lift his hand from the muck—and it was empty,weaponless: he had lost his sword somewhere. Meanwhile, the axe-wielder moved swiftly. There was no way Odysseus would be able to defend himself. Then the writhing stick rose from the ground, tripping the axe-wielder. He went down on one knee. His face was in moonlight (and firelight) now, and Odysseus saw his expression go from clenched rage to cool bewilderment.

The writhing stick raised itself still farther from the ground. But it wasn't the stick that was writhing: there were two snakes entwined around it, and they passed in front of the man's face.

Instead of looking concerned, he lost all expression, his eyes closed, and he slumped to the ground.

A manlike shadow appeared, holding the stick upright. "No need to thank me, Odysseus," said Hermes' insinuating voice. "I always look after my people. I would have been glad to kill him for you, but he's one of mine, too. Constantly stealing his neighbor's livestock. Go now and take care of your sailors. They're mine now, as well."

Odysseus turned without a word. He helped Elpenor to his feet, and they carried Lycophron's body down to the town gate, where his men awaited the cattle milling about them. Perimedes' crew was standing there, too, laden with baskets.

"What are you waiting for?" Odysseus demanded.

Perimedes pointed down to the beach where a line of warriors had pinned the Greeks against the water. In the moonlight Odysseus could see Diomedes' leathery face and Achilles' almost girlishly pale one. They had looted the priest-king's citadel, as they had sworn they would. But the priest-king's guards had followed them back to the harbor. In the dark water of the harbor, beyond the clashing lines of bronze-armed warriors, stood the Greek ships--their way out of this, if only they could get to them.

"And if some of us don't, that's more room for cows," Odysseus said aloud.

"What's that?" Perimedes asked.

Rather than repeat himself, Odysseus said, "Stampede the cattle. Drive them into the backs of Chryses' warriors. We'll follow them up and finish them off."

Odysseus' men shouted as one. That was enough to start the cattle running and the men encouraged them with further cries, blows, and insults-unbecoming to any cow. They didn't have much distance in which to work up speed, but Chryses' warriors heard the cattle coming and fled before them.

The Greeks on the beach, laughing, divided to let the stampede pass. The cattle ran into the shallows of the sea and stood there, bewildered.

"Come on!" shouted Achilles, as Odysseus came up. "Let's go after them! We can destroy the whole force and take the island!"

"But not keep it, young warrior," Diomedes observed. "Odysseus, you are, as always, a man of many turnings."

"We came for food and we got it," Odysseus said, a little gruffly (for something was bothering him). "Let's go."

"You came for food," Achilles corrected. "We looted the palace storeroom and the women's quarters. We have Chryses' daughter and many fair royal kinswomen besides."

"They'll ransom well," Diomedes added. "Of course the money may not buy us much…"

"After tonight it will, I think," Odysseus conceded. "Kings will hear of the fate of Chryse and fear that the same may happen to them. They'll sell to us by day lest we raid them at night."

"All's well, then," said Diomedes, making it half a question as he stared into Odysseus' discontented face.

"Let's get our loot on board the ships," Odysseus said.

That wasn't a king's work so Odysseus turned away and spoke into the darkness, to a shadow he knew was walking there, although he couldn't see it.

"Hermes, intricate deviser, god of travellers and thieves, I see your vengeance at last. So I thank you for this victory and its plunder. Since I am one of your men, now, I will steal and lie and rob my way across the face of earth and sea until the gods grant me passage home. I will remember you with this praise, and in another song also."

Then the pirate-captain Odysseus turned back to lead his crews of thieving murdering bastards safely away, as the city of Chryse burned behind its violated gate.

HIS KIKUTA HANDS

-Tales of the Otori-
LIAN HEARN

"His Kikuta Hands" is set in Maruyama, the furthest city to the west in the Three Countries. It takes place behind the scenes of Chapter Five of Brilliance of the Moon. *I'd always wanted to expand these pages where a lot happens in a short space of time. Takeo feels he must take on the Tribe and demonstrate the ruthlessness he will need to be a competent ruler. The Tribe on the other hand don't believe, firstly, that he knows where to find them, secondly, that he will have the strength of will to deal with them. They are proved wrong.*

I N THE EAST THEY call him The Dog," the older brother said. "He lived with the Kikuta family in Matsue for months and was trained by Akio. The Kikuta master requested it. Apparently he is his nephew and has all the Kikuta skills and more."

The Kuroda boy, who was a great scoffer, scoffed now. "You all go on about his talents but I don't believe he has any. Why would he leave the Tribe if he had? My guess is he wasn't good enough, he couldn't take Akio's training and he ran away."

The man they were discussing was the new lord of Maruyama, by name Otori Takeo, though to them he would always be known as The Dog. Maruyama was the only great domain in all the Eight Islands to be inherited by the female line, an anomaly which infuriated many in the warrior class. When the last lady, Naomi, died in Inuyama, several of the clan's elders wanted to change the system quietly and install as lord someone from the Iida family, whose wife had a slight connection with Maruyama through marriage but not by blood, thereby saving themselves the trouble of finding the next female heir, for Lady Maruyama's daughter had drowned with her.

Now Otori Takeo had turned up in the city with a Shirakawa wife,

"HIS KIKUTA HANDS"

Illustration by ORION ZANGARA

Kaede, claiming she was the heir to the domain, in which he was supported by the Sugita family, senior retainers to the Maruyama.

"I told you to kill the Sugita boy," the older brother said.

"His father and the other guard took us longer than we expected," the Kuroda boy replied. "When we'd finished with them the son had vanished. We could hear Otori's horses; we had to get out of there."

There had subsequently been a huge and bloody battle in which most of the warrior class had been killed, including the Iida pretender, resulting in the Tribe not receiving payment for dispatching the two guards, an omission which annoyed Jiro's father immensely. Soon it would be the least of his worries.

The young men were chatting before training. If people thought about the Tribe at all, for very few even knew they existed, they probably imagined their skills came to them magically at birth. It was true that talents were innate but they were nothing without training. Hours were spent every day in gruelling routines to build up muscles needed for leaping, bare hand fighting, and garrotting; even the less common talents like invisibility and the *second self*, though they seemed effortless when they first appeared, usually just before puberty, withered away without constant practice.

Jiro's elder brother usually led the sessions. There were not many pupils—Jiro himself, three Muto boys, and two Kuroda: the scoffing boy and a girl who someone thought might have some talent, though so far there had not been much evidence of it. Mostly she was used to run errands and make tea. Jiro was interested in her as she was the same age as him, and he'd heard whispers in the kitchen where the women gossiped that she would be married either to one of the Muto boys or to himself. His older brother was already married to the only Muto girl in their generation.

They did not use names much, just the common ones: Taro,

Jiro, Saburo. When they became elders they would be given names that meant something to the Tribe. Jiro hoped he might be called Shintaro after the famous assassin who had died in the failed assassination that had brought The Dog to the attention of the Tribe. He was thinking about this as he began to limber up. It was already very hot. The training room had a wooden floor but the walls were plastered and painted white — if you could maintain invisibility against a stark white background, you could do it anywhere.

It had been believed that it was impossible for Shintaro to fail. He had murdered hundreds flawlessly throughout the Three Countries, yet The Dog had heard him and he had been apprehended. He had immediately bitten into the poison capsule, aconite encased in wax, which they all kept at the back of the jaw where the molar tooth had been extracted to make space for it. His death had sent shock waves through the Tribe, even as far away as Maruyama.

There were few families in the West. Their father feared they were dying out and wondered if they should not move east to Inuyama, but the years went past and he never made that decision. In Maruyama at least he was the sole ruler of his empire, even if it was a meager one. There was not a lot of work: the Seishuu clans of the West were an easy-going lot who settled their differences with marriage alliances, ceremonies, hunts, and feasts. The attack on the guards had been an exciting event — it was too bad they weren't going to get paid for it.

His brother cuffed him round the head, hard enough to make his eyes sting.

"Concentrate! Get to work! You're always dreaming about something or other. One day you'll wake up with a knife in your throat."

He faced up to his older brother, the Kuroda girl to hers. By the end of the session they both had bruised knuckles and ringing ears. He had been knocked down three times, the girl twice. He was seething inwardly.

The older brother said, "Hate me as much as you like. Hate your opponent, have no pity, and no hesitation." Then he went to the targets and loosed a few shafts. He was far and away the best marksman among them and loved his wisteria-bound bow and his eagle-fletched arrows.

Jiro spent a lot of time hating him but at the same time would die to save his life — in the Tribe that went without question. No one liked or had much affection for anyone else, but their loyalty was complete.

The girl gave him a quick glance. He thought he saw contempt in it, though maybe it was pity, which was no better. Her brother's back was tattooed in the Kuroda fashion. He wondered if hers was too. The thought obsessed him and he began to daydream about slipping the jacket from her shoulders and exploring the inked skin. He was at that age.

Maybe since she was the same age her glance showed interest.

Their skins were slick with sweat in the heat. The cicadas from the grove around the shrine were deafening. The thick woods cast dense shade on the rear of the house. It was on the edge of the city and, from the front, seemed a typical merchant's store where rice was fermented into wine, stored in casks and sold. The Tribe had the monopoly on its production in Maruyama, just as they had for the soybean paste that flavored everything they ate. Both had lately become more profitable than their other traditional trades of spying and assassination.

Behind the storefront were the living quarters, including several secret rooms and closets, and at the back were the indoor and outdoor training areas and the well.

Jiro lowered the bucket into the well, drew it up, and poured cold water over his head. He did the same for the Kuroda boy, admiring how the wet tattoos gleamed. Then he turned to the girl.

"Take off your jacket. I'll cool your skin."

She ignored him.

Inside the house the midday meal was waiting, trays and bowls set around the room. Their father was already taking up the wooden eating sticks. The men sat down. The girl went to the kitchen to eat with the other women. One of them said something to her that made her laugh.

Their father selected a morsel of grilled eel and ate deliberately and slowly, then he said quietly, "I've received a message from the Dog, and so have my colleagues in the Muto family, summoning us to consult with him tomorrow. I am a little surprised he knows about us and where to find us."

"What is there to consult about?" the Kuroda boy said cheekily. "Does he want us to tell him how we plan to kill him?"

"Will you go, Father?" Jiro asked.

Before he could answer the girl came from the kitchen and said, "Master, someone is here to speak with you. He says it is urgent."

Their father laid down the eating sticks and made a beckoning gesture. The man entered and fell to his knees. Jiro knew him by sight. He was of solid build with a plump face that looked dull apart from his glinting, deep-set eyes. He was from the Imai family and worked at Maruyama castle as a groom.

"What do you have to tell me that can't wait till I've finished eating?" the Master said.

Imai whispered, "There is a box containing records, made over the years by Otori Shigeru."

"Everyone knows Shigeru made records of everything, all his farming experiments and his crop yields." The Master drank his soup. "And all his failures. That would make a long list."

"These are different. They are of the Five Families, of the Tribe."

"It is not possible," the Master said. "Nothing has ever been written down. The structure of the Tribe means no one knows more than they need to, at any time, not even myself and the other Kikuta masters."

"Yet the records exist. They are in the current Otori lord's possession. His wife carries them hidden among her clothes, and she has begun making copies."

Jiro sensed his father's unease. The Tribe's power depended on secrecy, on the ability to strike without warning and disappear without trace. As he said, no one, even within the Tribe, knew everything. How could an outsider?

The Kuroda boy said, "It would not be difficult to steal the records or get rid of The Dog or, better still, both. Shigeru was a failure: this Otori is a weakling, we know that much."

Jiro's father smiled. Maybe he was a little uneasy but he was not yet truly concerned.

"May I?" said the Kuroda boy.

The Master nodded. "It will have to be tonight."

The girl spoke from the doorway. "He will hear you, as he heard Shintaro."

"He will not hear me or see me," boasted her brother.

No one slept that night at they awaited his return. At dawn there was a clattering in the street outside, men pounding on the gate. The two brothers and the girl fled over the roofs on the father's orders while he took refuge in one of the secret rooms. They went to a Muto house nearby. The girl and Jiro were quickly hidden away in a cavity in the wall while the elder brother donned merchant's clothes and went out into the town to gather news.

The girl said nothing but he could smell her fear and her grief, not for herself but for her brother who they both knew must be dead.

The house smelled of fermenting bean paste. Normally it would have made him feel hungry but now it nauseated him.

"Killed by the guards outside the wall," the older brother said when he returned. "Better than being captured." He had changed from his town clothes into a dull-colored jacket and leggings like that of a farmer, but he carried his bow and a quiver of arrows. "I am going into the country for a while."

"Is Father safe?"

"He was discovered and arrested."

The two Muto men looked at each other in disbelief.

"How…?" said one.

"It is not possible," murmured the other, his voice petulant. Jiro could see how slow and inflexible they had become. They thought they were invulnerable; they thought they could outwit everyone, but now Otori had appeared like a fox in a flock of ducks, and soon they would all be headless.

"You are not safe here," the older Muto master said. "It seems he has been informed about every house and its secrets."

"Someone has betrayed us," said the girl. "Someone from the Tribe." Her face was contorted with fury. "Wasn't he close to your family, the Muto, in the Middle Country?"

"Save the accusations for later," the older brother said. "I will deal with Otori." He embraced Jiro, an action so unusual Jiro feared it meant they would never meet again.

"He has offered to spare anyone under the age of sixteen," the younger Muto master said, his eyes on his own son.

"I would sooner kill them myself." The older brother spoke as if he were already the head of the Kikuta family, but he would die three days later and the following day his father would be hanged.

The older Muto master took poison, the younger fled with his son to the east.

"Your brother took a shot at him but Otori heard the bowstring," the girl said to Jiro. "His horse, who is as cunning as he is, heard it too. I could have told your brother that. Not that he would have listened to a girl. Now he's dead — he took poison."

Better than being captured.

"I suppose that means you are the last of your family," she said. "I wonder if I am the last of mine."

I am the Kikuta Master, he thought. It brought him not the slightest shred of consolation.

They had moved from house to house, from wells to lofts, escaping the slaughter that took place in their wake. Even their ruthless upbringing could not inure them to the shock of witnessing the extermination of their kin. He saw in her his own blank eyes, dulled wits, and numbed limbs. On their last night she crawled into his arms. At dawn he traced the Kuroda tattoos of the five poisonous creatures that covered her back; snake, scorpion, centipede, lizard, toad. She took her hands in his and pressed her lips to the line across his palms that marked him as Kikuta.

"We'll be married," he said dreamily. "We'll start again, a new family of our own, maybe in one of the other islands, free of the Tribe."

"No one is ever free of the Tribe," she replied.

Even as she spoke they heard Otori's guards breaking down the doors.

That was the moment when they should have bitten into the poison capsules, but neither of them did. Jiro waited to see if the girl would, and then he would follow, but she didn't. Perhaps she was waiting to see if he would. Then it was too late. Their bodies wanted to live and be joined again. Desire betrayed them into hope.

So they were brought into Otori's presence alive and forced

to their knees, their mouths held open with sticks and cords. He, The Dog, extracted the poison with gentle, Kikuta marked hands.

He had never been inside the castle before. There were fleeting glimpses of luxury in the cypress wood floors, the woven wall hangings, a smell of sandalwood, but the room they were taken into was unadorned, white walled, like a training hall. He knew instinctively that was what it was, and that Lord Otori, his Kikuta relative, trained here. And that The Dog could take on invisibility and not be perceived by any of them. And that he heard now the same soundscape that Jiro did, the tread of guards on the walls, street cries from the town, horses neighing in the water meadows, the surge of the tide against the rocks in the bay, just as he had heard the chock of the bowstring drawn by Jiro's older brother.

Jiro had expected him to be older, more brutal, more like a demon; this man was not much older than his brother, and there was a resemblance. You could see he was from the same family, perhaps a distant cousin. But he had an unexpected lightness to him, a dazzling, multi-faceted quality, very different from the dour single-mindedness that was demanded of the Tribe.

There were two other men, the senior retainer Sugita Haruki whom he knew by sight, and another man who looked like a monk, though he was dressed like a warrior. But it was Otori himself who loosened the cords that bound their wrists. He studied them both, saying nothing.

"So you are the last two," he said finally, with no air of pleasure or triumph, but something more akin to sorrow. "I will give you the choice I gave your relatives. You will renounce the Tribe and serve me, or you can die by poison or the sword."

He gestured towards a small table where the wax tablets had been placed in a celadon bowl. Next to the bowl lay a short sword with an unadorned handle and a blade so sharp it was almost transparent.

When neither of them replied he went on. "You are both young. You will find working for me has many benefits and rewards. Your talents, which I know are considerable, will be respected and put to use."

"Against the Tribe?" the girl said, her voice tiny and defiant.

"If I am to rule the Three Countries, and I intend to, I have to break the Tribe." He said it calmly, without vindictiveness, and smiled at them.

How did we misjudge him so? Jiro thought. *Why did we take him for a weakling?* The gentle demeanor, he saw, masked a complete ruthlessness. This would be a man worth serving. It would not be a betrayal: he was, after all, Kikuta. *If he commands me, I must obey.*

He felt desire to live flood through him. Never had the flow of his breath, the surge of his blood, seemed so precious. He looked up and into Otori's eyes, holding his gaze for a moment, before wrenching his own away, fearing the sleep the Kikuta could deliver. Certainly The Dog would possess that skill as he possessed all the others.

"They call you Jiro, don't they?" The Dog leaned towards him.

"Lord Otori," Sugita said in warning, taking a step forward.

The Dog gestured him to stay back.

"I already have a young man called Jiro in my service," he said. "He is about the same age as you, but of course not with the same talents. I need young people like you. Swear allegiance to me. I will give you your own name. "His voice was compelling and calm.

Jiro felt a weight lift from his shoulders as he drew breath to speak. His new life stretched before him. But with a movement of incredible swiftness, taking even Otori by surprise, the girl grasped the knife and stabbed herself in the throat. The blood, shockingly bright, vermilion, sprayed across his face and threw a splashed pattern against the white wall.

Jiro looked again at The Dog, saw the regret and pity in his eyes and felt tears spring into his own for everything that might have been. The girl reached towards him even as her eyes glazed. The sword fell from her hands into his.

"I'm sorry," he said, and used the blade before regret could unman him.

"Believe me, so am I," said The Dog, the last words Jiro heard before his sharp hearing finally failed, and his spirit fled after hers into the realm of the dead.

THE LORD COLLECTOR

-Raven's Shadow-
ANTHONY RYAN

*The following story takes place in the same world as
my novel* Blood Song, *the first volume in the Raven's
Shadow trilogy. I wrote it because I wanted to more
fully explore characters who appear in* Blood Song
and the sequels Tower Lord *and* Queen of Fire.
*Readers familiar with my work are sure to recognize
a certain pale-eyed, raspy voiced Sword Master of the
Sixth Order and those curious as to the origins of the
Tower Lord of the Southern Shore will find answers
here. The tale takes place at the mid-point of the
timeline described in* Blood Song, *a time when King
Janus, with typical ruthlessness, is in the process of
further consolidating his grip on the Unified Realm.*

WHERE ARE THEY, VARESH?"

Varesh Baldir was a tall man, somewhere past his fortieth year, thickset with a copious unkempt beard that partly concealed the weathered features common to those who eked a living from the shore. His heavy brows furrowed as he stared at Jehrid, eyes lit mostly with hate and fury, but also betraying a momentary flicker of fear.

"We counted near two score corpses on the beach after you lured that freighter to its death," Jehrid continued, sensing a fractional advantage. "I know the code as well as you. Blood pays for blood."

Varesh took a deep breath, closing his eyes and turning his face out towards the sea, hate and fear fading as his brow softened under the salted wind. After a moment he opened his eyes and turned back to Jehrid, mouth set in a hard, unyielding line, and his tattooed fists bunched, jangling the manacles on his meaty wrists.

Silence is the only law, Jehrid thought. First rule of the smuggler's code, drilled into him over many an unhappy year. *This is a waste of time.*

He sighed and moved closer to Nawen's Maw, an unnatural bore-hole through the rocky overhang on which they stood. Varesh's chain

"THE LORD COLLECTOR"

Illustration by OKSANA DMITRIENKO

traced from his manacles to an iron brace set into the top of a stone resembling an upended pear, a wide rounded top narrowing to a flat base. It had been carved from the pale red sandstone that proliferated on the southern Asraelin shore and made the buildings here so distinctive. One of Jehrid's first acts upon assuming his role had been to hire a mason to fashion the stones, insisting they be at least twice the weight of a man and shaped so as to allow them to be easily tipped into the maw. When complete, he had his men arrange them in a tidy row atop the overhang; a clear statement of intent. He had begun with twenty, now only five remained, soon to become four.

Jehrid rested a boot on the stone, glancing down at the waves crashing on the rocks far below. The terns had already begun to gather, wings folding back as they plunged into the swell, eager for the fresh pickings below. This shore had ever been kind to scavengers. The diving birds were the only sign of the six men he had already consigned to the Maw, Varesh's kin: four cousins, a brother, and a nephew. Last of the Stone Teeth, a brotherhood of smugglers and wreckers that had plagued this shore for more than three generations. Before kicking each boulder Jehrid had asked Varesh the same question, and each time the leader of the Stone Teeth had stood silent and watched his kin dragged to their deaths. Varesh's only child, a daughter of notoriously vicious temper, had fallen to a crossbow bolt when Jehrid led his company into the smuggler's den, a narrow crack in the maze of cliffs east of South Tower, crammed with sundry spoils looted from the Alpiran freighter they had enticed onto the rocks a month before. One of Varesh's cousins had allowed wine to loosen his tongue upon visiting a brothel in town the previous night, and Jehrid had always found whores to be excellent informants.

"My mother once told me a story of how the Maw got its name," he told Varesh in a reflective tone. "Would you like to hear it?"

"Your mother was a poxed bitch," Varesh told him, voice quivering with rage. "Who whelped a traitor."

"It's not natural, you see," Jehrid went on, his tone unchanged. "Nawen, or Na Wen to give him his correct name, was captain and only survivor of a wrecked ship from the Far West. A lonely old fishwife took him in, though he was quite mad by all accounts. Every day he would come here and chip away at the cliff with hammer and chisel. Every day for twelve years until he had carved a perfect circular hole through this overhang. And when he was done…well, I assume you can guess what he did next."

Jehrid stiffened his leg, tilting the stone towards the maw. "No-one knows why he did it, for who can divine the mind of a madman? But my mother was wise, and judged it an act of revenge, a desire to leave the mark of man on the shore that wrecked his ship and killed his crew."

He gave Varesh a final questioning glance. "Life in the king's mines isn't much," he said. "But it is life. I know the Stone Teeth allied with the Red Breakers to wreck that ship. Things must have come to a desperate pass to forge an alliance between hated enemies. Settle some old scores, Varesh. Tell me where their den is."

Varesh spat on the rocks at Jehrid's feet and straightened his back. "If I find your mother in the Beyond…"

Jehrid kicked the stone, sending it tumbling into the maw, the chain rattling over rock as it snapped taught. Varesh had time for only the briefest shout as he was drawn into the hole, bones cracking as he rebounded from the sides, followed by a despairing wail as he plummeted towards the crashing waves.

"Make a note for the Royal Dispatches," Jehrid said, turning to his Sergeant of Excise, a squat Nilsaelin recruited as much for his facility with letters as his skill with a crossbow. "Varesh Baldir, leader of the gang known as the Stone Teeth, executed this day with six of his cohorts. Execution carried out under the King's Word by Jehrid Al Bera, Lord Collector of the King's Excise. Append a list of the contraband we recovered, and be sure the men know I'll check it against stores."

The sergeant gave a brisk nod, wisely keeping silent. Like most of those recruited to the Lord Collector's service, he had quickly gained an appreciation for Jehrid's intolerance of even the most petty theft. "You are paid twice the wage of the Realm Guard for a reason," he had told their assembled ranks the morning he flogged a former Varinshold City Guard for helping himself to a single vial of redflower. "Greed will not be tolerated."

"Rider coming, my lord," another Excise Man called, pointing to the north. The rider wore the uniform of a South Guard, a youthful recruit as many were these days. The new Tower Lord had been punctilious in enforcing the King's order that his command be purged of the lazy and corrupt, though it left him in sore need of guardsmen.

"Tower Lord's compliments, Lord Al Bera," the young guardsman said, reining in and bowing low in the saddle. "He requests your presence with all urgency."

"Another wreck?" Jehrid asked him.

"No, my lord." The guardsman straightened and gave a wary smile. "We have…visitors."

———— ✦ ————

TOWER LORD NOHRIN AL Modral greeted Jehrid with an affable nod as he entered the chamber but failed to rise from his plain, high-backed chair. Although they were technically of equal rank Jehrid took no offense at the absence of an honorary greeting. He had known this man as captain and, later, Lord Marshal throughout his years in the Realm Guard and was well acquainted with his former commander's disdain for useless ceremony. Also, Al Modral was only two years shy of seventy and his legs not so sturdy these days.

The plainness of his chair, and the mostly bare audience chamber where he received visitors, were a stark contrast to the previous incumbent. Former Tower Lord Al Serahl had maintained a richly decorated chamber and greeted visitors perched atop a tall, throne-like chair, so tall in fact he required a ladder to ascend it. He had been a small man, narrow of face with a prominent nose, and Jehrid recalled seeing a resemblance to a suspicious parrot the day he and Lord Al Modral had walked in six months before, unannounced and bearing a warrant of arrest adorned with the King's seal. The full company of Realm Guard at their back had discouraged any unwise intervention from those South Guard present, despite the pleas of the unfortunate Al Serahl who screamed himself quite hoarse before tumbling from his lofty perch in a tangle of robes fashioned from the finest Alpiran silks. When Jehrid led him to the gallows, his clothing had been much more modest.

"It seems we have occasion to celebrate, Lord Collector," the Tower Lord said, gesturing at the three figures standing before him. "The Faith sees fit to lend aid to our cause."

Jehrid went to one knee before the Tower Lord before rising to survey the visitors. The tallest wore a sword on his back and the dark blue cloak of the Sixth Order, returning Jehrid's scrutiny with impassive pale eyes. His closely cropped hair was flecked with gray at the temples, and his features had the leanness typical of the Faith's deadly servants. Jehrid knew him from a best forgotten foray into Lonak territory, though he entertained no illusions the brother would remember the boy-soldier who stood staring in blank amazement as he cut down three Lonak warriors in as many seconds.

"Brother Sollis, is it not?" Jehrid greeted the pale-eyed man with a bow. *Deadliest blade in the Sixth Order,* he pondered as Sollis inclined his head. *Come south to battle smugglers. Does the King think so poorly of our efforts he begs aid from the Order?*

"This is Brother Lucin and Sister Cresia," Sollis said in a dry rasp, nodding at his two companions, both wearing the dun colored robes of the Second Order. Brother Lucin was a thin, balding man somewhere past his fiftieth year. It seemed to Jehrid that his apparently serene expression was somewhat forced, his features tensed as if holding a mask in place. Sister Cresia seemed to be little more than sixteen years old, honey blonde hair tied back from youthful features, her slight form concealed within robes worn with evident discomfort. Unlike Lucin, she felt no need for a false air of serenity, returning Jehrid's gaze with a barely suppressed scowl.

Second Order, Jehrid mused inwardly. *What use have we for missionaries here?*

"Our visitors come on a special errand, Lord Al Bera," the Tower Lord went on. "Regarding the Alpiran vessel wrecked last month. I was explaining you had the matter well in hand. You have finished with the Stone Teeth, have you not?"

"As of this morning, my lord," Jehrid replied. "Though the Red Breakers remain elusive. Perhaps another week of investigation will root them out. My agents are busy, promise of rich reward always stirs them to greater efforts."

"A week is too long," Brother Sollis stated. "With luck, our assistance will assuage any delays."

"The help of the Sixth Order is always welcome, brother," Jehrid replied before casting a pointed glance at the two missionaries. "However, I confess myself at a loss as to the aid offered by your companions. No offense, good brother and sister, but the hearts of the Red Breakers will not open to the Faith, regardless of how many catechisms you cast at their ears."

Sister Cresia's half-scowl twisted into a smirk, her voice betraying a faint note of contempt as she looked down, muttering "Got more than catechisms to throw at them."

Brother Lucin gave her a sharp glance, saying nothing, but the severity of his gaze was sufficient to make her lower her head further, sullenness replacing contempt. "My apologies, my lord," Lucin said to Jehrid. "My pupil is barely a week into her first foray beyond the walls of our house and knows little of the world or, it seems, common courtesy." He glared again at Cresia who kept her head lowered, though Jehrid saw her hands were now clasped tight together, quivering a little.

This girl's no more a missionary than I am, Jehrid thought. *What do they want here?*

"The ranks of my Order are filled with varied talents," Brother Lucin went on. "The missions test our bodies as well as our Faith. I myself was a hunter before I felt the call to don these robes."

No you weren't, Jehrid surmised from the briefest glance at the brother's spindly arms and lined but unweathered features. *I doubt you spend one more minute out of doors than you have to.* However, he merely nodded as the brother continued, "Sometimes my brothers in the Sixth have occasion to call on my tracking skills, when their own talents are otherwise occupied."

"We need to see the wreck," Sollis said.

"There'll barely be anything left," Jehrid told him. "A month of tides will have cleansed the shore of timber, and the sands of tracks."

"Even so," Sollis said, meeting his gaze, pale eyes unblinking.

Jehrid had been a soldier for twenty of his thirty-three years. He had fought Lonak, outlaws, heretics and, though he preferred not the dwell on it, Meldeneans, and knew himself to be the equal

or superior of most men he was likely to meet in combat. But this
one was different, for he had never forgotten seeing him fight.
Nevertheless, he had ever been a slave to his temper and resentful of
those who sought to stir fear in his breast, a long dulled sensation,
summoning ugly boyhood memories and unwise notions.

"May I ask," he grated, turning to face Sollis squarely, "what
interest you have in this particular wreck?"

Sollis angled his head slightly, expression unchanged apart
from a narrowing of his eyes. Jehrid felt his temper quicken yet
further at the knowledge of being assessed and, no doubt, found
wanting. Fortunately, the Tower Lord intervened before he could
give voice to any anger.

"It seems there was a passenger aboard," Lord Al Modral
groaned, levering himself out of his chair with difficulty, hand
trembling on the heavy staff he was obliged to carry these days.
Jehrid knew better than to offer assistance, the old man retained a
surfeit of pride and had a temper of his own. "A passenger of some
importance, eh brother?"

"Quite so, my lord," Sollis replied, blinking before switching
his gaze to the Tower Lord. "One King Janus is keen to recover."

"Every soul on that ship perished on the rocks or drowned in the
surf," Jehrid said. "The Alpiran merchants in town saw to the bodies
and did what they could to glean names from their belongings."

"The passenger we seek was not among them," Lucin stated
in an emphatic tone Jehrid found near as aggravating as Sollis's
appraising gaze.

"They're all dead," Jehrid repeated. "You come here on a fool's
errand..."

Lord Al Modral's heavy staff thumped onto the flagstones.
The old man's legs might be failing but his arm remained strong.
The echo birthed by his staff resounded through the chamber for

some seconds before he spoke again, "Brothers, and sister, the Lord Collector will be more than happy to escort you to the wreck and render any and all assistance required. Please leave us whilst we discuss other matters."

After the trio had made their exit the Tower Lord moved to the stained glass window set into the chamber's south facing wall. The window was the only vestige of the deposed Lord Al Serahl's love of expensive ornamentation, conceived to celebrate a battle, and an atrocity, he had taken no direct part in. It was a floor-to-ceiling wonder of expert craftsmanship, lead and glass of various hues rendered into an ascending narrative. At the bottom many ships sailed from a harbor, marked as South Tower by the lance-like structure rising above the docks. The middle panes depicted a vicious sea battle that failed to conform to Jehrid's memory. Most of the Meldenean fleet had been absent that day and the pirates hadn't been able to muster even a third of the ships ascribed to them here. Unlike the sea battle, the window's upper panes were entirely in keeping with Jehrid's memory: a city...burning. The late afternoon sun was clear of cloud today and painted the scene across the chamber floor in vivid detail, leaving Jehrid unable to escape its dreadful spectacle and the memories it provoked.

"More than ten years on," Lord Al Modral said, nodding at the window. "But it seems like yesterday sometimes. Then there are days when it's just a dim memory, like a fragment from a nightmare you can't quite shake."

"Indeed, my lord," Jehrid said, keeping his gaze lowered. He hated the window and had in fact petitioned for its destruction. The Tower Lord, however, had far too much respect for the arts to allow it.

"Before...this," Al Modral waved his staff at the burning city. "I recall a captain less inclined to anger."

"Ten years is a long time, my lord," Jehrid replied, resisting the impulse to close his eyes. Whoever had crafted the window had somehow managed to capture the exact shade of flame that had consumed the Meldenean capital, though fortunately, there was no art that could recreate the screams.

"Nevertheless," Al Modral went on. "I think the King would prefer his Lord Collector keep a clear and level head during this mission."

Jehrid blinked, forcing himself to focus on the Tower Lord. "Of course, my lord."

"They arrived unannounced, bearing missives from the Aspects of the Second and Sixth Orders, but no royal warrant. Curious, don't you think? Given that they come on royal business."

"Certainly, my lord. Sufficiently curious to require them to wait whilst we seek clarification from court."

Al Modral shook his head. "Life as a Lord Marshal taught me many lessons, Jehrid. Lessons you would do well to learn if, as is my fervent wish, you are to succeed me one day in holding this Tower. Today's lesson is twofold. First, the folly of obstructing the Orders, the Sixth in particular. Second, the value of information. I should like to know the identity of this passenger they seek, and the nature of their business on this shore."

Never reckoned him a schemer, Jehrid thought. *But the king gave him the Tower for a reason.* "I'll see to it, my lord."

"Good." The Tower Lord placed a hand on his shoulder as they turned and moved back to the chair, the old man more willing to accept aid now there were no witnesses. "And, if this passenger is still alive we know full well who holds them. With the Faith's help, mayhap you'll finally find what drew you back to this shore."

He settled back onto his chair with a sigh, his hand slipping from Jehrid's shoulder like a limp rag. "Do you think it'll be sweet when you finally taste it, my fierce and implacable friend?" he asked. "They say vengeance can be bitter."

"It could be wormwood and I'd still drink until my belly bursts." Jehrid stepped back, dropping to one knee before rising to deliver an impeccable salute. "By your leave, my lord."

———◦———

SHELTER BAY WAS A misnamed, rocky notch in the shoreline some thirty miles west of South Tower. It was formed of a hundred yards of beach flanked by tall bluffs. At high tide the sea became a fury of roaring breakers, churned up by the plentiful rocks lurking beneath the surface. They only became visible at low tide, a dark maze of jagged reefs making this such a favored spot for the wrecking gangs.

They had set out from South Tower the previous evening, Jehrid riding with twenty of his most trusted men. Brother Sollis rode with the two missionaries and a dozen brothers from the Sixth Order. They had camped in the dunes overnight before proceeding to the bay where, contrary to Jehrid's expectations, the tides had contrived to spare some vestige of the Alpiran vessel.

She had been named as the *Selennah* by the Alpiran merchants who came to lay claim to whatever cargo Jehrid might recover, an archaic term but within his grasp of Alpiran: *Voyager*. An old ship, but large and well captained, though not well enough to resist the lure of the wreckers' false lights. Jehrid assumed a junior mate must have had the watch when they neared the shore. A veteran sailor would have known better. Three of her arched beams rose from the waves like the bared ribs of some scavenged beast, all that remained of a freighter that had sailed the Erinean and beyond for three decades.

"And you found no survivors at all?" Sister Cresia asked, eyeing the wreck with little sign of the sullen frown she had worn throughout the journey.

"The sea is ever an efficient assassin, sister," Jehrid told her. "Though there were a few with their throats cut, fingers hacked off. Wreckers don't like to leave witnesses behind, or their jewelry."

Her features gave a twitch of mingled disgust and anger which Jehrid found himself liking her for. *Some sense of justice behind the scowl, it seems.*

"Best if we three proceed alone," Brother Lucin said, climbing down from his horse with a discomforted wince. "My…skills work best without distraction."

"The sand is bare, as I said it would be," Jehrid pointed out as Sister Cresia and Brother Sollis followed Lucin to the beach. The balding brother merely waved and kept laboring through the dunes. Jehrid watched the three of them approach the shoreline. For a time Lucin walked back and forth with Sollis and Cresia in tow, pausing occasionally to point at something on the sand before stroking his chin in apparent contemplation. Jehrid had never been one for plays, but he knew a performance when he saw one. *Tracker my arse.*

After some further mummery, Lucin came to a halt, turning his gaze out to sea. He stood still for some time, back straight and arms loose at his sides, seemingly uncaring of the waves lapping around his feet and dampening the hem of his robe. Abruptly, Lucin jerked as if in pain, clasping himself tight and doubling over. Sister Cresia came to his side in evident concern but he waved her away. Even from this distance Jehrid could see his hand was trembling.

"What is this, my lord?" the Sergeant of Excise murmured at his side, swarthy features bunched in suspicion.

"King's business!" Jehrid snapped, though in a low voice. "Still your tongue."

He watched Lucin say something to Brother Sollis before slumping with a weary shake of his head, kept upright only by Sister Cresia. Jehrid saw Lucin wipe at his nose before turning and raising a hand, now free of any tremble and pointing firmly west. It was too far away to tell for sure, but Jehrid could have sworn the brother's hand was stained with blood.

<hr />

THEY FOLLOWED THE COAST until the sky began to dim, Brother Lucin riding in front with Sollis at his side. Jehrid found it odd that Lucin barely glanced at the ground as he led them in apparent pursuit of the wreckers' trail. He had no guess as to where the brother was leading them; this stretch of coast was mostly bare of the caves or inlets beloved by smugglers, distinguished by tall cliffs and narrow stretches of shingle where only the most skilled or foolish sailor would seek to ground a boat.

Lucin and Sollis eventually came to a halt after ascending a steep rise over twenty miles from Shelter Bay. Jehrid trotted his mount closer as Lucin indicated a point a few miles ahead, a narrow channel cutting into the shore where waves broke on a series of tall sandstone columns, each shaped and honed by centuries of tides and wind so that they resembled a line of jagged swords.

"There," Lucin said.

"The Blades?" Jehrid asked, unable to keep the scorn from his voice. "You think the Red Breakers are sheltering in the Blades?"

"You know this place?" Sollis asked.

"Everyone raised on the southern shore knows this place, and they know to avoid it. It's completely unnavigable, even at low tide."

"The channel leads to a waterfall, does it not?" Sollis pressed.

"It does. Pretty enough place but the walls are too steep and damp to climb and free of caves, which is why it's of no use to the Breakers."

He saw the brothers exchange a glance before Sollis gave a small nod. "Not caves," Lucin said. There was a wariness to his voice, conveying the sense of a secret shared only through dire necessity. "Tunnels, built many years ago."

"By who's hand?" Jehrid asked.

"The Orders have a long history, my lord," Lucin replied. "And there are builders in our ranks as well as trackers."

"That farce you played on the beach," Jehrid grunted with a laugh. "Why not simply tell me of these tunnels back in South Tower?"

"We needed to be certain. And now ask for your discretion."

Jehrid glanced again at the Blades, the silent monolithic swords rising from ceaseless white fury. He recalled his first sight of them one frigid morning years ago, shivering at the rail as a large man pulled him into a warm hug and reeled off a list of foolhardy sailors who had ventured too close to this channel, among them his great uncle, dashed to ruin during a desperate gamble at evading the Lord's bounty-men. "That's how they kept law in those days," the large man had told him. "Put a bounty on our heads and set the scum of the fief on our tail. We fought a war to win this shore, boy, though you'll not find it in any history. Now we have a king, things are more civilized, but blood always pays for blood."

"What's in there?" Jehrid asked Lucin.

"Something that will remain hidden," Sollis stated before the tracker could answer. "With your assistance, for which the Faith will ever be grateful."

Jehrid had never been particularly scrupulous in his observance, but he had been raised in the Faith and the myriad dangers of a soldier's life had often found him holding to it with fierce conviction. Also, he had an obligation to honor Lord Al Modral's desire for information. "You know of a way in?" he asked Lucin.

———•———

WARY OF LOOKOUTS, JEHRID insisted they approach on foot and in darkness. This scarcely troubled the Brothers of the Sixth, who moved with an unnerving silence and sureness of foot, or his own men, well accustomed to finding their way across darkened country. Brother Lucin and his pupil, however, were not so attuned to stealth.

"Quiet!" Jehrid hissed at Sister Cresia as her foot contrived to find a rabbit hole, provoking a frustrated yelp. He saw her eyes gleam in the dark as she rounded on him, no doubt ready to deliver a retort, but a nudge from Brother Lucin was enough to still her voice.

Jehrid could hear the waterfall now, a low, steady rumble drifting across through the small copse of trees where they lay. The narrow but fast flowing river that fed the waterfall gurgled past fifty yards to their left, a clear track to their goal, but guarded. They were only the dimmest shapes in the gloom, wisely denying themselves a fire but well wrapped against the chill, four in two pairs on either side of the river, each hefting a crossbow and moving in tight circles, one never straying from the sight of the other.

"Easy targets," Sollis whispered at Jehrid's side, his bow already in hand, a gull-fletched arrow notched and ready.

"Wait," Jehrid murmured as Sollis turned to signal his brothers. "There's another. One you can't see. It'll be the youngest, small enough to be easily hidden. Kill these and he'll be blasting a horn a second later."

Sollis's lean features remained impassive, though a slight

tightness in his voice told of a marked impatience. "This matter requires resolution," he stated. "One way or another."

"Their prisoner, if they truly have one, will die the instant that horns sounds."

"The matter requires resolution," Sollis repeated in the same clipped tone.

Not here to rescue, Jehrid realized. *Only to silence.*

He returned his gaze to the sentries, then scanned the surrounding grassland. This was not his usual hunting ground. Smugglers and wreckers tended to keep to the east, close to the main roads leading to northern towns. *Where would he have put me?* he pondered, eyes roaming the dim country. *The falls are loud enough to mask all but the strongest blast. He would need me close...* His gaze came to rest on a small mound near the edge of the spray-damp ledge next to the falls. It would have been easily taken for just a clump of grass in the gloom, but the shape was subtly wrong, the lean of the grass not quite the correct angle for the wind. *He grows careless with age.*

Jehrid turned to his sergeant, nodding at the loaded crossbow in his grip and beckoning him closer. He lay at the sergeant's side and pointed out the mound. "You have it?"

The sergeant braced the crossbow against his shoulder, settling his cheek against the stock, fingers poised on the lock. "Clear as day, milord."

"He'll stand when the others go down. Don't miss." Jehrid inclined his head at Sollis. "As you will, brother."

Sollis raised a hand to make a series of complex but rapid signs, seven brothers immediately rising in response and moving to the edge of the copse. They crouched in unison, arrows nocked and bows drawn, all without the barest rustle or creak of straining wood. There was no further instruction from the Brother Commander, he simply drew, aimed and sent his arrow into the chest of the left-most sentry, the man caught in mid-fall by another arrow before disappearing into the grass with barely a groan. Six more bowstrings snapped as one and Jehrid had a scant second to witness the demise of the remaining lookouts before a slim figure jerked upright from the tell-tale mound, a long sailor's horn raised, back arched as he drew breath. The sergeant's crossbow snapped and the slim figure had time for a spastic final twist before collapsing from sight.

Jehrid surged to his feet and sprinted for the falls, sparing a glance at the sentries to confirm none still moved and coming to a halt beside the one with the horn. His features were pale in the gloom, youthful prettiness rendered slack and ugly in death. There was something familiar about the set of his eyes, the smoothness of his brow stirring yet more unwelcome memories. *Aunt Tilda's eyes,* Jehrid thought, scanning the boy's body. *A good mother would have spared him this.*

"Just a boy," a voice whispered at Jehrid's back. He turned to find Sister Cresia staring at the corpse, eyes wide and face white. Something glimmered in her right hand, something sharp judging from the way it caught the meager light. She blinked, noticing his gaze and quickly concealed her hand in her robe.

Jehrid crouched and lifted the boy's limp arm, pulling back the sleeve to reveal two black circles tattooed into the flesh alongside three vertical lines. "Two wrecks and three kills," he told Cresia. "Youth is not the same as innocence, sister. Not on this shore."

Brother Lucin led them to a notch in the cliff edge where a series of narrow steps had been carved into the rock, so weathered and softened by the seaward winds as to be barely visible. The climb down to the ledge below was short but not without peril, the damp steps and gloom making for some unnerving slips, though luckily there were none in their company sufficiently clumsy to completely lose footing, a deadly mistake judging by the roiling waves visible below. Sollis drew his sword and took the lead as they proceeded towards the falls, the cascade of water arcing down like a fluid glass curtain. The Brother Commander held up a hand to halt them in place and moved on alone, disappearing into the gloom behind the curtain. A second later came a faint sound of clashing steel then Sollis reappeared and beckoned them forward.

Behind the falls the ledge opened out into a grotto, much of it fashioned by hand judging by the worn but plain chisel marks on the rock. Sollis stood at the grotto's deepest point, running his hand over the rock as if in search of something. Another sentry lay nearby, sword in hand and blood streaming from a deep gash in his neck. Jehrid was impressed he had managed to draw a blade before Sollis cut him down.

Lucin moved to Sollis's side and peered closely at the rock, fingers probing for something. Eventually, he grunted in satisfaction and moved back, murmuring something to Sollis which Jehrid could barely catch, "Locks from the inside."

The older brother gestured at Cresia, leaning close to her as she came forward, his words too soft to hear above the tumult of the falls. Jehrid saw the girl give a reluctant nod before moving towards the rock, laying both hands against the damp stone, her form becoming still, face blank with concentration. She remained like that for some time, the two brothers standing by with evident impatience. Eventually Lucin moved to whisper a question at which the girl turned to him, face flashing anger as she voiced a harsh rebuke. Jehrid expected the brother to respond with some form of admonishment, but instead he merely sighed and moved back, gesturing for Sollis to follow.

"Our sister may be young," Lucin said, moving to Jehrid's side. "But is well versed in ancient lore regarding these tunnels. To open the entrance requires pressure in one particular spot. She'll find it soon enough."

Jehrid's gaze lingered on the girl, noting she had resumed the same statue-like stillness, her hands flat and unmoving on the rock. Abruptly she stiffened, leaning closer to the wall, eyes closed and head cocked at a slight angle. Her features betrayed a brief spasm before she stepped back, flexing her fingers, and a three foot wide section of rock swung inward to reveal a narrow passage. The sister stepped back, face paler than before though lit with a triumphal grin as she offered them a bow and bade them enter.

THE WIDTH OF THE passage would permit only one entrant at a time and Sollis insisted on taking the lead. Jehrid ordered his Excise Men to remain and guard the entrance before taking his place at Sollis's back, expecting some objection. However, the Brother Commander merely glanced at him and drew his sword before disappearing into the passage. Jehrid followed with Brother Lucin and Sister Cresia at his back. He had suggested they remain with his men but they merely shook their heads and fell into line, faces tense but, to Jehrid's eyes, not so fearful as they should be. The passage was dimly lit with torches set into the walls every twenty paces, guttering in the breeze from the entrance. The walls were roughly hewn, displaying only the most workmanlike skill in their fashioning. Whoever had crafted these tunnels had displayed scant interest in artistry.

Sollis set a slow pace, keeping his steps soft to prevent any betraying echo. Jehrid noted a slight downward slope and a gradual but increasing curve to the walls, indicating they were following a spiral course deep into the bowels of the rock. The curvature of the passage became more pronounced the deeper they went, obscuring the way ahead sufficiently for Sollis to flatten himself against the wall and move forward in a sideways shuffle. He stopped at the sound of voices, softly spoken but echoing well in the tunnel. There were two voices, both male, engaged in some form of argument, the words indistinct at first but becoming clearer as Sollis began to inch forward once more, now moving in a crouch, sword-grip reversed so the blade rested against his back. He stopped when the voices became clearer, turning to Jehrid with a questioning glance.

Jehrid felt his hand dampen with sweat, knuckles suddenly white on his sword handle. Two voices, older men, one he knew, though it had been many years since he heard it.

"…speak to me of promises," it said, a rich voice possessing the broad vowels of the shore-folk, but colored by a faint note of scorn. "Promises were made to me also. Promise of gold and jewels. Instead we risk much to scavenge no more than spices and silk. A tidy profit, to be sure. But hardly worth drawing the Lord Collector's eye."

"Gold will be forthcoming," the other voice replied. It was mostly toneless but with an odd accent, the vowels distinctly Renfaelin but the cadence similar to the harsh babble of Volarian sailors. "When you give me what I came for. And don't forget, without me you would have had no wreck to plunder."

Jehrid frowned in surprise as the other voice fell silent. *Since when did he ever fail to find a rejoinder?*

After a pause, the first voice spoke again, this time betraying a discomfort barely masked by angry defiance. "We've talked of this enough. She's mine. And she stays mine until you pay."

There came a sound then, so harsh and grating Jehrid took a moment to recognize it as a laugh. "What do you imagine you are, little smuggling man?" the second voice enquired when his mirth had subsided. "What cards do you think you hold? You are no more than a maggot feasting on the dead before the tide comes to wash you away. You have seen what I can do. Give me the woman unless you would like another demonstration."

A long, frozen pause. *Now for blood,* Jehrid decided. The insult and the challenge were too great to ignore. Jehrid could picture him standing there, face stricken with fury, fist no doubt clamping hard on a dagger, his other hand clutching a cudgel. 'The Dance of Hard and Sharp' he had called it; the traditional smuggler's fighting style. In an instant all would be chaos and confusion. The perfect moment to attack. Jehrid inched closer to Sollis, readying himself for the rush.

So it was with no small amount of shock that he heard the frigid silence broken by the first voice. "Bring her."

He's afraid. Jehrid found he had to contain a gasp of amused realization. *He's actually afraid.*

Footfalls echoed through the tunnel then another long pause, silence reigning until they returned. "Ah," the second voice said, now tinged with a tense anticipation. "I was expecting someone…older."

"She carried the amulet you described," the first voice said, hard and sullen. "Worthless bauble though it was."

"Show it to me." Another pause, then a satisfied chuckle. "Worthless to you perhaps, but not to her." The voice switched to Alpiran, coarse and harshly accented, but still fluent enough for Jehrid to follow. "*Isn't that right, my dear? It must have taken a remarkable effort to earn Rhevena's Tear at your age. Most don't until they're nearing dotage. Is your gift so powerful? I imagine not, since you remain bound by this scum.*"

A female voice, tremulous but also defiant, the cultured accent contrasting with her interrogator's grating vowels. "*Free me, and I'll be happy to show you.*"

"*Don't trouble yourself, honored lady. I'll shortly discover its nature for myself.*" There came the scrape of a blade being drawn as he switched back to Realm Tongue. "Hold her still."

Brother Lucin came forward in a rush, his steps drawing a loud echo from the stone, the bleached concern on his face betraying a desperate urgency. "He will do it!" he hissed at Sollis. "We cannot delay."

An enquiring shout came from beyond the curve; Lucin's footfall had not been missed. Sollis straightened, reversing the grip on his sword and glancing at Jehrid. "Secure the woman and take her out of here. Leave the others to us."

Then he was gone, blue cloak trailing as he charged from sight. Jehrid surged after him, the multiple echoes of the brothers' boots like thunder as they followed. Beyond the curve, the passage opened into a large chamber, near twenty feet across with bunks covering the walls and several side channels leading off in various directions. Standing in the center were three figures, an olive skinned woman of perhaps thirty years of age, her arms bound behind her back, and two men. The man on the right was of middling years and unkempt appearance, his wiry frame clad in ragged, threadbare garb.

But it was the man on the left that captured Jehrid's attention. He was older, of course. Hair now gray and thinning when it had once been thick and dark, face clean-shaven and lined with age, though he stood just as tall as Jehrid recalled and his waist seemed as free of paunch as ever. As expected, he had armed himself with a cudgel and dagger, swirling to face the intruders in a crouching stance, lips drawn back in a snarl, one that faded as he caught sight of Jehrid.

"Cohran Bera!" Jehrid called to him as he charged clear of the tunnel. "Stand and await the King's Jus—!"

He ducked as one of the Red Breakers sprang from the shadows on the left, something fast and sharp cutting the air above Jehrid's head. Another appeared on the right, axe raised to swing at Sollis and falling dead a heartbeat later as the brother's sword delivered a single expert thrust to his throat. The Breaker confronting Jehrid was clearly a traditionalist, coming at him with a cleaver in one hand and a cudgel in the other, aiming well-timed blows at his head and legs. Jehrid sidestepped the cudgel, swayed back to evade the cleaver and brought his blade up and down to hack through the Breaker's hamstring before he could recover for another swing. This smuggler was not easily cowed though, despite being forced to one knee and yelling in pain, he managed another lunge with the cleaver before Jehrid's sword point sank into his chest.

Jehrid spun, sword levelled at Cohran Bera, now moved to the center of the chamber, eyes locked on his. "You've grown," he said in a low growl before turning and issuing a shrill whistle. Only a bare second's delay then a tumult of pounding boots, a dozen or more Breakers appearing from the side tunnels at a run, all armed. Four went down almost immediately, tumbling to the floor as the brothers' throwing knives flickered in the torchlight. Those who managed to get close enough to exchange blows were scarcely more fortunate, most falling in the space of a few sword strokes though the momentary confusion allowed their leader time to run for the nearest passage, three survivors at his back.

Jehrid shouted in frustration, a familiar red tinge coloring his vision as he started forward. It was the woman's shout that stopped his pursuit, his gaze swivelling towards her, now standing rigid and head drawn back, the wiry man's fist in her hair, his other holding a thin-bladed dagger to her throat. Jehrid had time to catch Cohran Bera's final glance, oddly somber and lacking in hatred, before the shadows swallowed him.

"Oh no!" the wiry man barked, addressing his words to Sollis as the brothers quickly surrounded the pair, closing in with swords levelled. He jerked the woman's head back further, the edge of his blade pressing hard against her skin. "I require your consideration."

Sollis held up a hand to halt the brothers, lowering his own sword to take a single step closer. Jehrid noted Sollis's free hand twitch as it caught something that slipped from his sleeve. "Release her," Sollis commanded in a flat rasp. "If your life has value to you."

The wiry man replied only with another grating laugh. Jehrid frowned at the genuine humor he heard in that laugh, and the lack of any real hostility on the man's face. For all the world he seemed no more than a man responding to a particularly well executed prank. "Ask him," the wiry man said, nodding to Brother Lucin emerging from the passage with Sister Cresia at his side. "What value does his Order place on life? Did they bother to warn you what you'd find here? I'll wager they didn't."

It was Brother Lucin who spoke, face grim and gaze steady as he regarded the wiry man, his voice now possessed of a cold, unwavering note of command. "Kill him."

"Brother…" Jehrid stepped towards Sollis but the brother had already begun to move. His left hand seemed to blur, something small and metallic catching the light as it flew free. Jehrid shouted in alarm, knowing a killing blow might cause the wiry man's arm to tense with dire consequences for his hostage. Sollis, however, had chosen his target well. The throwing knife sank hilt-deep into the wiry man's wrist, the knife falling from his spasming grip. The woman twisted, tearing herself free and falling to the floor. Jehrid quickly moved to her side, sword pointed at her now prostrate captor.

His gaze met Jehrid's for a moment, bright with pain and fury, then softened as it shifted to the throwing knife embedded in his wrist, and he began to laugh anew.

"Kill him, brother!" Lucin commanded in a yell, his voice suddenly shrill with panic.

Sollis moved to the wiry man, sword drawn back, then stumbled to his knees as the floor shuddered beneath his feet.

"You put too much trust in these deluded mystics, master," the wiry man said, blood now streaming in rivulets from his nose. "Far too much trust…"

A great booming sound shook the surrounding rock, a jagged crack appearing in the floor, stretching the length of the chamber. Jehrid saw Lucin grab Sister Cresia's arm and drag her towards the passage as the chamber shuddered again, the floor becoming a jumbled matrix of cracks, the brothers reeling from multiple fountains of shattered rock. The wiry man was laughing again, writhing on the shuddering floor in uncontrollable mirth, blood now streaming from his mouth and eyes. Sollis lurched towards him, sword raised for a slash at his neck…and the chamber floor exploded, stone shattering all around into a fog of dust.

Jehrid had time to catch hold of the woman before the floor gave way beneath them, air rushing past his ears as they plummeted, swallowed by the welcoming dark.

───────◆───────

THE DOCKS ONCE AGAIN, his only reliable dream. It was always the same. The same pier, the same hour just before nightfall, every detail perfect and vivid even though the memory was over twenty years old.

He crouched behind a wall of stacked barrels in a quiet corner of the South Tower docks, peeking out at the end of the pier. There were people there, dim shadows glimpsed through twilight mist, four standing and one kneeling. The kneeling figure was bound, face concealed with a sack tied at the neck. Even so Jehrid knew whose face lay beneath the sack, *knew without any shred of doubt the face of the woman who knelt with head bowed in numb expectation of her fate. Just as he knew the name of the man who drew a knife and stepped to her side.*

He turned away then, knowing what was coming, reeling through the streets as his gorge rose to spill his guts on the cobbles. His treacherous ears caught the sound of a body tumbling into harbor waters, the splash carrying well in the clammy air. He ran, through the streets and the city gate and out into the fields beyond, blinded by tears, running until his lungs turned to fire and his legs gave way. He lay out in the fields until morning, and when the sun rose to wake him with its warmth, he got to his feet and started north. The road was long, and he grew to know hunger and danger as close friends for the wild country was ever rich in threats, but eventually, a thin, ragged boy staggered into Varinshold and sought entry to the Realm Guard.

"Has to be your real name, boy," the sergeant told him, quill poised over parchment, a somewhat wicked glint in his eye as he added, "King Janus wants only honest Guardsmen..."

He awoke to the taste of blood, iron, and salt stinging his tongue and provoking a convulsive retch as his senses returned. His dulled vision, hampered by eyelids that now seemed to be fashioned from lead, could see almost nothing save a faint impression of tumbled rock, though the sound invading his ears prevented any return to slumber; a muted but continuous, echoing torrent of rushing water.

"Not alone after all," a voice muttered nearby, a female voice, speaking in Alpiran.

It took a moment before he made her out, crouching in the gloom, on her knees, arms still bound and eyes pinpoints of light behind hair hanging in damp tendrils over her face.

Jehrid paused to spit the blood from his mouth, tongue exploring where his teeth had left a ragged impression on the inside of his cheek. "*Nor, it seems, are you, honored lady,*" he replied in his coarse but functional Alpiran.

She straightened a little in surprise, then spoke in accentless Realm Tongue that put his Alpiran to shame, "Would you mind?" She turned, crouching to proffer her bound wrists.

Jehrid realized his hands were empty, his sword no doubt lost somewhere in the fall. He fumbled at her bonds, grunting in frustration at his shaking hands, forcing himself to draw a series of deep breaths until the tremble subsided, though the cause was obvious. *He laughed. He bled and he laughed…He did this. He brought down the chamber.* The mystery of it all was absolute, but for one signal and reluctant conclusion: *The Dark.*

The woman gave an impatient sigh and Jehrid mumbled an apology, shuffling closer to work on the binding cord. The knots were well crafted and it took a protracted effort before the cord came loose. She issued a loud groan of mingled pain and relief, slumping forward with hands cradled in her lap, a soft curse coming from her lips. The words were mostly unfamiliar but he caught the name *Rhevena* among them.

"Rhevena's Tear," he said aloud, remembering the wiry man's words. "Goddess of the shadowed paths, is she not? Protector of the dead."

The woman's posture became guarded, her hand moving unconsciously to her bare neck. "I thought your people had no truck with gods," she said.

"Knowledge does not equal worship." Jehrid took a moment to flex his legs, confirming the absence of broken bones or torn muscles, though they did ache considerably, and his hands bore several painful scrapes. He levered himself upright, taking a closer look at their surroundings. They were in a narrow passage, the walls even more crudely made than the tunnel under the falls, dampened by a constant trickle of water. He stood at the base of a steep gravel slope, formed no doubt from shattered rock and providing enough of a break in their fall to prevent a bone-crushing landing. To the right the passage was completely blocked by fallen stone, leaving only the leftward course, illuminated by a faint, bluish light.

"Can you walk?" he asked the woman.

She nodded and got to her feet, ignoring or failing to notice the helping hand he offered. "Your comrades?" she asked, peering about.

Jehrid glanced at the wall of stone blocking the passage, then lifted his gaze to the black void above. *How far did we fall?* "I doubt we'll see them again," he said.

He took the lead, the dim luminescence growing as they followed the passage, the sound of rushing water increasing with every step. "You were held here for days," Jehrid said. "Have you any knowledge of these tunnels?"

"The route from my cell to the main chamber only. They were careful with me, my hands were always bound."

He found it odd Cohran would have exercised so much caution and restraint in confining her. Wreckers rarely took captives and the fate of those that did fall into their hands was never pretty. "*You are so dangerous then, honored lady?*" he asked, dropping into Alpiran once more.

She frowned and shook her head, gesturing impatiently for him to move on.

"*That man, back at the chamber,*" Jehrid persisted, halting to face her. "*He paid them to take you, didn't he? Paid them to wreck the ship carrying you. Why?*"

A mix of anger and grief passed over her face before she mastered it, meeting his gaze with stern resolve. "Did your father teach you Alpiran?" she asked, once again keeping to Realm Tongue. "You speak it with much the same accent. He told me he had been a sailor in his youth, learning many tongues and sailing to many ports. You have much the same face and the same bearing. He *is* your father, is he not?"

Jehrid found himself mastering his own surge of anger. "In name," he muttered, turning and continuing along the passage.

"And what is your name? You have yet to tell me."

"Jehrid Al Bera, Lord Collector of the King's Excise. At your service, my lady."

"Lord Collector…He spoke of you, said you would come one day. The thought seemed to make him sad. Now I see why."

Jehrid felt an abrupt need for a change of subject. "And your name, lady?"

"Meriva Al Lebra."

"Al Lebra is an Asraelin name."

"My father was an Asraelin sailor, obliged to forsake his homeland when he met my mother."

"Obliged?"

"She was a junior priestess to the temple of Rhevena in Untesh. Paying court to her required a certain…adjustment in his beliefs."

"He forsook the Faith for marriage?"

"For love, my lord. Has not love ever forced you to an extreme?"

There was a new note in her voice, clearly mocking but also gentle enough to remove any anger from his reply. "I have always found hate a better spur to useful action."

The passage soon grew wider and a dim glow appeared ahead, the pitch of cascading water deepening further. They found a body a few yards on, a slumped, cloaked bundle of twisted limbs. "May the Departed accept you, brother," Jehrid murmured, crouching to peer at the man's face, recognizing him as one of the archers who had taken down the sentries above. He was plainly dead, features drained of all color and his head pressed into his shoulder at an impossible angle. However, he had somehow contrived to retain hold of his sword.

"The Sixth Order," Meriva said, her tone soft but Jehrid could hear the fear it held. "You answer to them?"

"I answer to the King." He hefted the sword and held it up to the sparse light. *An Order blade*, he thought, seeing the tell-tale pattern in the steel, a facet of their secretive forging arts. *The strongest and keenest blades in the Realm. Doubtful they'll let me keep it.*

"Then why are you here with them?" she pressed.

Jehrid bent to remove the brother's scabbard from his back, a difficult task given the contortions of his body. "I came for the Breakers," he grunted, turning the corpse over and working at the buckles. "They came for you."

She made a small sound, half a laugh and half a groan. "To rescue me, no doubt."

"Their mission is their own." He tugged the scabbard free and buckled it on, around the waist rather than the back, sliding the blade in place. He straightened, staring at Meriva until she met his gaze, eyes shrouded and posture guarded, as if she might turn to flee at any second. "I will allow no harm to you," he told her. "But I will have the truth. Why do they want you?"

She sighed, her stance becoming a little more relaxed, though her gaze told of a lingering mistrust. "To hear the message I carry... Or ensure my silence."

"You carry a message? From who?"

She looked down, clearly fighting a deep reluctance. Jehrid stood and kept his eyes locked on her face. It was a favored trick when dealing with reticent informants, stillness and silence always stirred the tongue better than outright threats. "From the gods to the godless," she said eventually, raising her gaze once more. There was still fear there, but also an overriding defiance. "I have said all

I will say. Now, I suggest we move on. Unless you intend to stand and gawp at me forever."

He held up the only other weapon found on the brother's body, a hunting knife of good steel. "Do you know how to use this?"

She hesitated and reached for the knife, clasping it tight. "No. But I will, if needs must."

———◆———

TWENTY PACES ON THE passage opened out into a cavern, the ceiling lost to the darkness but the walls speckled with pinpoints of light, each no brighter than a match but combining to provide a clear view of the spectacle before them. A torrent of water arced down from the black void to continually replenish a broad pool in the center of the cavern. Jehrid saw there was a slow but definite current to the waters, his gaze tracking to the right where the cavern narrowed into another passage, water foaming as it was channelled deeper into the rock.

"There must be a fissure," Jehrid mused, gazing up at the cascade. "Siphoning off the river waters before they reach the fall."

He watched Meriva peer at the cavern wall, her fingers playing over one of the pinpoints of light, tracing dark tendrils across the surface. "Some kind of lichen," she mused. "Fed by the water and giving off light as a reward." She paused, then added something in Alpiran, voice pitched low in reverence as if she were reciting a catechism, "*May the goddess accept my thanks for her beneficence.*"

Jehrid was about to take a closer look at the channel on the right, assuming it led out to sea, and therefore might offer some avenue of escape, but paused when Meriva clasped his arm. She pointed at something in the pool, something limp and man-sized, trailing a blue cloak as it drifted in the shallows.

Jehrid plunged into the water and waded towards the body, heaving it over to reveal a lean face and graying hair. Sollis's eyes remained closed but his features twitched as Jehrid took a firmer grip on his shirt and began to haul him from the pool. *Still alive,* he thought with a certain grim resignation. *Of course he is.*

Meriva helped him drag the Brother Commander clear of the water and away from the damp rock fringing the pool. They rested him against a relatively dry patch of wall where Meriva pressed a hand to his forehead. "Chilled almost to the point of death," she said. Her eyes went to Sollis's right arm, his hand dangling from a twisted wrist. "And that's certainly broken."

Jehrid nodded agreement and reached for the brother's forearm, squeezing hard. Sollis came awake with a shout, trying to raise his right arm as it sought the empty scabbard on his back. He tried vainly to rise, ice numb legs giving way and leaving him flailing against the rock.

"It's all right," Meriva said, casting a reproachful glare at Jehrid as she placed a calming hand on the brother's shoulder. "We are friends."

Don't be too sure, Jehrid thought, watching the realization dawn on Sollis's face, the lean features tensing against the pain and a sharp calculation returning to his eyes.

"My brothers?" he said, gaze switching from Meriva to Jehrid.

"We found no others alive," Jehrid told him.

Sollis closed his eyes momentarily, face as immobile as the stone behind him. When he opened them again there was no grief, no sorrow, just firm decision. "I need a sling for this," he said, patting his broken arm.

Meriva tore a strip from the brother's cloak to fashion the sling and tied it in place, Sollis gritting his teeth against the pain as she pulled it taut. They helped him upright and moved to the channel at the far end of the cavern. Jehrid peered into the gloom beyond the foaming waters, seeing no ledge or other means of navigating such a treacherous passage.

"We could just jump in," Meriva suggested. "Trust the gods to see us safely free of this place."

Sollis gave a rasping grunt that might have been a laugh, drawing a scowl from Meriva. "They have preserved us this far," she said.

"Blind chance has preserved us," the brother replied, though his tone softened as he regarded the channel. "Though, in truth I see little option."

"The current is too swift," Jehrid stated. "And the course may well lead further underground before it reaches the sea. If we aren't dashed to pieces we'd most likely drown. And if we were to make it out, we'd find ourselves flailing amid the Blades in the dead of night."

He turned away from the channel, eyes roaming the cavern and finding a patch of dark a good way back from the pool where the glowing lichen didn't cling to the walls. He moved towards it, far enough until the shadows swallowed him. He could see nothing ahead, just blank emptiness, his hands finding only air as he reached out to explore the void.

"If we had a torch," he murmured. "A candle even. Just the barest flicker of light…"

And the black turned white. It was so sudden he found himself reeling, stifling a shout of pain and shielding eyes now streaming with tears. He blinked and cautiously looked again, finding the way ahead illuminated, a soft beam playing over the rock like a shaft of sunlight caught by a lens. The beam moved, revealing a tall, broad passage leading away from the cavern. Jehrid followed the course of the beam, tracking it back to Meriva, standing with her arm extended and light streaming from her hand, held out flat like a spear-point.

The Dark, he thought, feeling his mouth hang open in an appalled gape. *Free my hands and I'll show you...Light born of the Dark... This is impossible.*

His gaze shifted to Brother Sollis who seemed markedly less shocked than a servant of the Faith should be, standing back from Meriva with evident surprise but also a certain grave acceptance. *Perhaps he knew what he would find after all.*

Meriva walked towards Jehrid, arm still outstretched, the light beam bobbing as she moved. He saw a wary impatience on her face as she came to his side, avoiding his gaze and nodding at the way ahead. "I can't do this forever."

⸻ ✦ ⸻

SHE KEPT A FEW steps ahead as they moved, a slim silhouette framed by the light she cast forth. It gave off no heat, no threat that he could see, and yet Jehrid found he had to force himself to remain close to her as Brother Sollis struggled on behind.

There can be no room for the Dark in a Faithful soul, he recited inwardly, recalling a sermon from a Second Order missionary his mother had once dragged him to. *The Dark, as practiced by the Deniers who lurk in our midst, brought the Red Hand down upon us. Never forget this, and always be vigilant. Only evil can come of the Dark.*

There is no evil in her, he knew, watching Meriva guide them on, her impossible light playing over the jagged vault of the passage. *So then,* he wondered, his gaze going to Sollis's hunched form. *What truth is there in the likes of him?*

Meriva came to an abrupt halt, shoulders sagging a little and her light flickering as she tried to hold it steady. "Something there," she said in a strained whisper. Jehrid moved to her side, his eyes tracking the faltering beam to some kind of mound. A mound that glittered.

Meriva issued a pained sigh and lowered her hand, darkness descending as her light died, though the glittering mound was still visible, lit by the faint orange glow of multiple torches.

"Give the brother your knife," Jehrid told her, stepping forward and drawing the Order blade. "Stay behind us."

He paused to meet her gaze, seeing a great fatigue there and a trickle of blood falling from her eyes. She held his gaze for a moment, then blinked and wiped the red tears away.

"Does it hurt?" he asked her.

She smiled faintly. "It…tires me."

"Wasting time," Sollis grunted, taking the knife from her and moving on.

They kept close to the passage wall, though Jehrid knew their presence would surely have been betrayed by Meriva's light. The glow of the torches revealed another chamber as they drew closer, a crafted place like the one from which they had fallen, the floor worked to a smooth surface and the walls shaped into a circle. In the center sat the mound, glittering metal clustered around a tall stone column. Moving closer they saw silver plate stacked amid bronze figures and tangled jewelery, here and there the tell-tale gleam of bluestone, all shot through by chains of silver and gold, shining like gossamer threads.

"Gold and jewels," Meriva said, plucking a necklace from the mound and holding it up for inspection, three rubies set in a gold chain. "And still he wanted more."

"He was ever a miser," Jehrid replied. "And what miser doesn't want more?"

However, it wasn't the riches that most captured Jehrid's

attention, it was the seven-sided stone column about which they were piled. It rose from the center of the mound to a height of about twelve feet, etched all over with writing of some kind. Jehrid had learned his Realm letters at an early age, and could read Alpiran with sufficient effort, but these markings were unfamiliar, and the stone that held them clearly ancient. However, it did possess a form of decoration that made some kind of sense, a series of emblems carved into the top of the column on each of its seven sides. He began to circle the stone, finding each emblem to be different: a flame, a blazing sun, a book and a quill, an eye, an open hand…He paused at the sight of the sixth symbol, a figure holding a sword, deep holes where its eyes should be. *A blind warrior. Just like the one that sits atop the gate to the House of the Sixth Order, or the medallion every brother carries around his neck.*

"So the Faithful truly have builders in their ranks," Jehrid said, turning to Sollis.

Sollis said nothing, his stance unchanged and face as impassive as ever, though Jehrid noted he had managed to remove the scabbard from the knife. "There are six orders to the Faith," Jehrid went on, moving so he could view the final emblem, a snake and a goblet. "But seven sides to this stone."

Sollis merely returned his gaze and said nothing.

"These words." Jehrid jerked his head at the letters etched into the column. "What language is this? What do they mean?"

"It's Old Volarian," Meriva said. "The tongue spoken by the first Faithful to come to these lands."

"Can you read it?" he asked her, keeping his gaze on Sollis.

"It's been many a year since I had to." She placed a foot on the pile, dislodging a cascade of treasure as she leaned closer to inspect the letters. "The calligraphy is unfamiliar and the dialect strange. Far more archaic than any form I'm familiar with. But, I think…" She paused, lost in thought as Sollis and Jehrid continued to exchange stares.

"It's a narrative of some kind," Meriva said eventually, metal jangling as she moved to read more of the inscriptions. "Though it doesn't fit with any history I know, and much of the phrasing makes little sense."

"Read aloud what you can," Jehrid told her.

"'Armies clash beneath a desert sun…Blood flows in rivers, spilt by lies…The One Who Waits will face the Hope Killer's song…'"

"Stop!" Sollis commanded in a flat rasp, now turned so that his good arm was closest to Jehrid, shoulders lowered into a crouch, the knife now gripped tight.

"My lady," Jehrid said, backing away, sword levelled at the brother. "Please get behind me."

Meriva hesitated for a second, then rushed from the pile, scattering trinkets as she placed herself at Jehrid's back.

"Something that will remain hidden," Jehrid said. "At what cost, eh brother?"

Sollis gave no response, moving to maintain the distance between them as Jehrid fought down the unwelcome memory of his skirmish with the Lonak all those years ago. *Sword against a knife,* he told himself, trying to stir a confidence he knew to be misplaced. *And him half-crippled.* But the memory was compelling, and still he backed away.

"What do those words mean?" he demanded, playing for time. "What is this place?"

"It's my home," a new voice cut in, rich and vibrant as it echoed about the chamber. "And you were not invited."

Cohran Bera stood perhaps twenty paces away, cudgel in one hand and long-bladed knife in the other. On either side of him stood two Breakers, perhaps the only survivors of his once fearsome band, both armed with crossbows. Jehrid whirled to face Cohran, nudging Meriva behind him, still painfully aware of Sollis's proximity but knowing this to be the greater threat for the moment.

"Fifteen of your cousins died today," Cohran told him. "You bring the Sixth Order to my door and destroy what took a lifetime to build. Have you no words of contrition, my son?"

"Fifteen wasn't enough," Jehrid replied, feeling a familiar, unwise sensation building in his breast. *The dim figures at the end of the pier, the sound of a body falling into the harbor...* "And don't call me that."

"Deny your blood all you want, *my lord.*" Cohran's face contorted as he spoke the title, like an ardent Faithful voicing heresy. "But I look at you and see no difference from that vicious little shit I pulled from a hundred dockside fights. The King chose well in you, a man who delights in slaughter and calls it justice."

"As opposed to a man who slaughters innocents to build a pile of riches he'll never spend."

"Riches." Cohran's voice softened a fraction as his gaze went to the mound of plundered treasure. "No. Power, boy. Power enough to buy a king's boon. He promised me, you see. Back when the wars raged as he built the realm. 'Soldiers need pay,' he said. 'Bring me gold, and there will be no more bounty-men. Bring me enough and one day, perhaps, I'll make a lord of you.' And, when he'd built his realm, paying his guardsmen with the riches plundered from this shore, what did he do? Have the Tower Lord spout empty promises at me for twenty years until he could send you."

Liar! Jehrid found the accusation dying on his lips as long-held suspicions tumbled into place. Al Serahl's lengthy and corrupt tenure in the Tower, tolerated far longer than anyone could have expected. The smugglers and wreckers able to buy immunity from the South Guard for years whilst in the north even the most petty corruption earned a swift execution. *The King took a loan from the shore,* Jehrid realized. *And now considers it paid, in me.*

"Doesn't have to happen, boy," Cohran went on, nodding at Sollis. "With this one gone, there are no other witnesses to gainsay whatever tale you choose to tell." He turned, gesturing behind him where the torchlight played on a series of irregular steps cut into the stone, ascending to a ledge far above.

"It's a steep and winding path," Cohran said, "but it'll take you out of here. Keep the woman, if you like. I suspect she'll have little to say about all this. You have secrets of your own do you not, my dear?"

Meriva moved to Jehrid's side, face set in a mask of determined fury. "Yes," she said. "I have secrets, but this one I'll share."

Her arm shot out, straight and true, hand once again like a spear point. Jehrid closed his eyes as the light blazed forth, birthing an instant scream. When he looked again he saw the man on Cohran's right on his knees, crossbow forgotten as he clutched at his eyes, shrill panic and pain issuing from his mouth in a continual torrent. The Breaker on the left gaped at his fallen cousin for the briefest second, then at Meriva, his crossbow swinging towards her in a fear-born reflex.

Brother Sollis moved in a blur, doubling over as the knife flew from his hand, swift as an arrow as it described a perfect arc ending in the Breaker's skull, the blade sinking in to the hilt. The Breaker remained upright for a heartbeat or two, mouth twisting around gibbered words and an odd, puzzled frown on his brow. Before collapsing, he managed to work the lock on his crossbow, the bolt missing Sollis by a clear foot before rebounding from the stone column and skittering off into the darkness.

Jehrid saw it all in the scant seconds it took him to close with Cohran. The Breaker chief was shaking his head in confusion, eyes moist and bleary, but some brawler's instinct provided sufficient warning for him to duck the slash Jehrid aimed at his head. He growled and whirled towards Jehrid, club and knife whistling, a large man of middling years moving with all the grace and speed of a youthful dancer. Jehrid parried the knife, ducked the club and knew in an instant Cohran was doomed. He was a killer and a fighter, perhaps the most deadly ever seen on this shore, but he wasn't a soldier. He had never faced a charging Lonak war band or hacked his way across a Meldenean deck. He fought for status or money but never truly for survival. He had never seen battle, until now.

Jehrid anticipated his next attack with an ease that almost brought a laugh to his lips, the knife slashing at his sword arm whilst the club arced up for a strike at his chin. An attempt to stun and disarm, not to kill. Jehrid leapt and kicked before either blow could land, delivering the tip of his boot to the center of Cohran's face, nose and teeth breaking under the impact. Cohran back-pedalled, trying to gain space for a parry. Jehrid slashed the knife from his grip with a quick swipe of his looted sword and drove a second kick into Cohran's guts, doubling him over. He tried a final, ineffectual blow with the club, Jehrid catching his wrist and twisting until he heard a crack, the club falling from useless fingers.

He stood back as Cohran stared up at him, face showing neither anger nor defeat. But pride. "Quite a dance, eh son…"

Jehrid drove the iron tine of his sword into Cohran's temple, sending him unconscious to the floor. "Don't call me that."

He turned at the sound of an echoing scream, seeing the blinded Breaker sprinting away into the darkness, his cries continuing to resound through the caverns until they were cut off by a faint splash. *He found the pool,* Jehrid surmised. *Carried out to the Blades, blind and mad. Nawen's Maw would've been a kinder end.*

He went to Meriva, now on her knees, shoulders sagging with exhaustion. He placed a finger under her chin and gently lifted her face, now so streaked with blood she might have stepped from a slaughter pen. "Will you be all right?" he asked.

Her eyes flicked to Sollis, now bending to retrieve Cohran's fallen knife. "*Will either of us?*" she whispered in Alpiran. "*This place, those words. They were not meant for our eyes.*"

Jehrid straightened, watching Sollis as he stood regarding Cohran's prostrate form. For once the impassive mask had gone, a somber frown creasing the brother's brow. "He taught you to fight?" he asked after a moment, his gaze still lingering on the fallen outlaw.

"Yes," Jehrid said. "But war taught me more."

Jehrid detected a faint note of regret in Sollis's voice as he spoke again, "The pupil always steps from the master's shadow." Abruptly Sollis raised his gaze, all expression fading from his features as he briefly glanced at Jehrid and Meriva before gazing up at the winding steps with a critical eye. "Dragging him up there will be impossible. We'll bind him to the column, send your men for him later."

Jehrid gave a wary nod. "As you wish, brother." He bent to take Meriva's arm. "Can you walk, my lady?"

She sighed agreement and began to rise, then froze, her gaze snapping to the pile of treasure as it issued a jangling rattle, displaced metal sliding as something stirred beneath it. "No…" she breathed.

Something exploded from the mound in a fountain of glittering treasure, something wiry and dressed in rags, revealing pale flesh marked by many wounds, a feral grin shining in a face caked in dried blood. It screamed as it stumbled free of the pile; triumph, rage, and madness filling the chamber. A tremor thrummed through the rock beneath Jehrid's feet, both he and Sollis pitched onto their backs by the force of it, powdered rock spouting as cracks rent the chamber floor from end to end.

Jehrid saw the blind Breaker's crossbow lying barely five paces away and lunged for it, shouting in alarm as the rock beneath him lurched anew. The ragged thing issued another peeling laugh as a fresh crack opened to swallow the crossbow. Jehrid saw Sollis cast Cohran's knife at the laughing wreck of a man, but the juddering floor made it an impossible task, the spinning blade missing its target by a handspan.

The tremor faded as the ragged thing staggered, eyes tracking over them in evident satisfaction before settling on Sollis. Blood flowed from its mouth in a thick stream as it spoke, "Sorry to lose you so soon, brother. I always did find your cruelty so…entertaining." He sighed and raised his arms, head thrown back and his smile blazing anew. "I will miss this g—"

Something small and sharp streaked down from above, moving faster than any crossbow bolt or arrow, issuing a small whine as it sliced through the air to spear the ragged man through the eye. He staggered again, head swivelling about in confusion. Jehrid saw something metallic embedded in his eye, a dart of some kind, the needle-like point protruding from his skull as he reeled about, arms flailing like a drunk fighting imaginary foes. Another dart streaked down, a puff of red vapor spouting from the man's bony chest as it tore clean through his torso, drawing a piercing note from the floor as it rebounded and spun away into the shadows. The thing groaned and collapsed onto the mound, limbs soon slackening in death as blood streamed in rivulets across the gleaming metal.

Jehrid turned at a huffing sound, seeing Brother Lucin clambering down the crude stairway. Sister Cresia followed behind. "Brother," Lucin greeted Sollis on reaching the floor, a little out of breath as he moved towards the mound of riches, barely glancing at Jehrid or Meriva. Jehrid saw he wore a different face now, or more likely, felt no more need to conceal his true visage, free of any false serenity or deference. The face of a very serious man.

Lucin took a moment to survey the body slumped on the pile,

eyes lingering on the blood-caked features though Jehrid saw no flicker of recognition. His expression grew yet more serious as he raised his gaze to the seven-sided column. "All too real," he muttered before turning away, addressing his next words to Meriva in Alpiran, no doubt assuming that Jehrid couldn't understand his meaning. "*You have a message for me, honored lady.*"

Meriva took hold of Jehrid's proffered arm and hauled herself upright, wincing from the effort. "*Yes,*" she said, voice heavy with fatigue. "*The answer is no.*"

Lucin lowered his gaze in evident disappointment before inclining his head at the column. "*You read that, I assume?*"

"*Some.*"

"*Then I hope it provided an inkling of what your refusal will force us to do.*"

"*The decision was not mine. I merely carry the message. The Servants have spoken. Your war is not our war.*"

Lucin merely shook his head with a sigh. "*It will be.*" He nodded at Sister Cresia, now standing at the base of the stairway. Jehrid's gaze was immediately drawn to the brace of darts clutched between her fingers, darts that were identical to those that had dispatched the ragged man, though he could see no device on her that could project them with such force. However, any doubts that she had been the author of his end vanished at the sight of her face, bleached white and gaze fixed on the body laying amid the bloodied treasure.

"The first is always the hardest," Jehrid told her. She stared at him with moist eyes, no sign of a scowl on her brow. He saw that her hands were shaking.

"Sister," Lucin said with a note of impatience. "This matter requires resolution."

"No." Sollis stepped in front of Cresia, though his gaze was fixed on Lucin.

Jehrid saw Lucin's throat working before he found the nerve to reply. "Our Aspects are in agreement regarding the import of this mission…"

"Do not make an enemy of me, brother." The words were softly spoken, little more than a whisper in fact, but they seemed to linger in the air, caught by the cavern walls and repeated until they faded to a hiss.

A new voice came echoing down from above, the words indistinct but Jehrid recognized his sergeant's Nilsaelin brogue. "Lord Collector! Are you well?"

"Your men were kind enough to escort us," Sister Cresia said, the darts now vanished from her fingers and a distinct note of relief in her voice.

Jehrid's eyes tracked from Sollis to Lucin, noting how the elder brother's gaze was now averted.

"Quite well!" Jehrid called back, glancing at Cohran's still unconscious form. "Get down here! And bring rope!"

———✦———

COHRAN BERA STOOD GAZING out to sea, a breeze stirring his thinning hair. It was a fine morning, barely a cloud in the sky and the rising sun a bright shimmering ball on a mostly becalmed Erinean. He favored Jehrid with a fond glance as he came forward, then offered a respectful nod to Meriva. She failed to respond, arms crossed tightly beneath her cloak, face rigid. Jehrid had invited her out of courtesy, as the wronged party she had every right to witness the proceedings, though he had hoped she might stay away. *She has seen enough blood.*

Sollis, Cresia and Lucin could be seen on the crest of a nearby hill, all on horseback. The Brother Commander's arm still rested in a sling, the bones set and bound tight by the Fifth Order mission in South Tower, though the scabbard on his back remained empty.

"I'll get another when I return to the Order House," he said when Jehrid offered him the blade he had taken from the dead brother.

"I can keep it?"

Sollis shrugged. "It's just a sword, my lord. We have many." With that he strode to his horse and mounted up. Jehrid surmised this was the only farewell, or thanks, he was likely to receive.

"Cohran Bera," Jehrid began in formal tones. "You stand convicted of murder, theft, piracy, suborning the Realm's servants, and evading the King's Excise. Accordingly you will be executed under the King's Word in a manner deemed fit by the Lord Collector. As you have profited from the deaths of so many by casting them onto this shore, such shall be your fate."

He stepped forward and rested his boot on the pear-shaped stone to which Cohran had been chained, gaze fixed on Nawen's Maw as he tried to summon a face from his memory, one he thought he would never forget, One he hoped would be witnessing this event from the Beyond. And yet, though he strove to recall the dim figures at the end of the pier, seeking to stoke a hatred he had nurtured for more than twenty years, today he couldn't find it. *Why won't she come? Surely she would want to see this.*

"At least look me in the eye as you do this, son," Cohran said.

For a moment Jehrid found he couldn't lift his gaze, as if some invisible hand gripped him in place.

"You must have questions," Cohran went on. "Ask me and I'll tell you."

"You will earn no reprieve," Jehrid told him, still unable to meet his eye.

"I know. But perhaps I'll earn my son's regard."

Jehrid closed his eyes for a second, his boot slipping from the boulder, a great weariness pressing down as he stood back. He forced his eyes open and faced his father, seeing the fearsome wrecker now vanished, leaving behind the man he recalled from childhood, the prideful shine in his eyes as he beheld his son.

"Why did you kill my mother?" Jehrid asked him.

Cohran's smile faded slowly, the depth of his regret plain in the sagging, weathered features. "She was taking you away," he said. "She had grown tired of this life of danger and distrust, and fearful of the future. For she knew one day you would become what I am. She sold us out to the Tower Lord's men, not knowing they worked for me. She thought she was buying a new life in the north, with you. You know the code, Jehrid. Silence is the only law. And so I killed her, because my kin expected it, and because I needed to keep you with me…But you left anyway."

Jehrid's gaze returned to the stone, though he found he had no strength to lift his boot.

"It's all right, son," Cohran said. "Truth be told, I'd rather it was you than any other. Blood pays for blood. Let's get it done."

Jehrid was aware of the eyes of his men, all gathered to watch their Lord Collector's nerve fail. But still he had no strength today. Not for this.

"The ship you wrecked was called the Voyager." Jehrid turned to find Meriva at his side, face pale but determined as she stared at Cohran, suffering no reluctance to meet his eye. "Crafted in the yards of Marbellis near thirty years ago, funded by the honorable trading house of Al Lebra. For many years it was captained by my father and, when he became too old to bear the hardships of the sea, by my brother. He was a good man, an honest sailor who rose to captain at a young age, respected by his crew and loved by his family. When word reached him that I must sail to this shore, he insisted it be the Voyager that carried me, unwilling to trust the task to any other."

She stepped towards the stone, placing her foot on it, gaze still fixed on Cohran as she grated in Alpiran, "*I watched your scum slit my brother's throat, you piece of filth!*"

Jehrid turned away as she shoved the stone into the maw, hearing the rattle of chains and the crack of breaking bones. But no scream. *No,* Jehrid thought. *He never would.*

He waited for the faint splash, then turned to his sergeant. "Return to the Excise House. Double rum ration tonight." He glanced at Meriva, now staring down at the Maw as if frozen in place. "I'll be along directly."

He paused to watch Sollis turn his horse and ride away without pause, although his two companions lingered a moment. Jehrid found he didn't like the way Brother Lucin's gaze rested on Meriva, sensing far too much calculation behind it and experiencing a sudden wild desire to seize the brother and see him follow Cohran into the maw. Fortunately, it seemed Lucin sensed his intent for he gave an inexpert tug on his horse's reins and quickly disappeared from view. Sister Cresia loitered a moment longer, Jehrid gaining the impression of a smile as she raised a hand to offer a tentative wave. He waved back and offered a bow, seeing her laugh before she too rode from sight.

"It wasn't truly a man, was it?" he asked Meriva. "That thing we left in the tunnels."

She shook her head. "In truth I have never encountered its kind before. But I suspect whatever humanity it once possessed withered away long ago, and the world is enriched by its passing."

He nodded and pulled something from the pouch on his belt. "I believe this is yours, my lady," he said, holding up a small amulet; a single bead of amber set in a plain silver mounting. "Cohran…

my father had it in his pocket."

Her gaze finally rose from the maw, a small smile curving her lips as she took the amulet. "My thanks, my lord," she said, lifting the chain over her head.

"Rhevena's Tear," he said. "Am I wrong in assuming it to be worn by all those…similarly gifted?"

"Different gods have different servants, carrying different signs. Though we all endeavour to serve a common interest."

"An interest best served by refusing whatever the Seventh Order required of you?"

"Seventh Order? What's that?" He saw her smile broaden as she moved away, going to the horse he had lent her. "Will you escort a lady home, my lord?"

"Gladly. Though only as far as South Tower. I'm sure the Tower Lord will meet the expense of finding a ship to take you home."

"South Tower is my home now. At least for the time being. The House of Al Lebra has many interests here. It was my stated reason for coming. It would seem odd if I was to depart so quickly, don't you think?"

"Certainly." He mounted up and fell in beside her as they followed the clifftop trail towards the distant tower. "Tell me, have you ever heard the tale of how Nawen's Maw got its name…?"

Below the overhang the terns were already circling the spot beneath the maw, making ready to dive into the waves and claim the fresh bounty, for the southern shore had ever been kind to scavengers.

SCREAM

-Simon Canderous-

ANTON STROUT

Jumping from writing one series to the next is always

bittersweet. There's the excitement of new characters

and unknown tales to tell, but you're also leaving behind

familiar friends. Or at least friends you've tortured for

three or four books, anyway. Suffice it to say, I miss

the retractable bat swinging antics of psychometrist/

paranormal detective Simon Canderous and his semi-

heroic rise through Manhattan's terribly underfunded

Department of Extraordinary Affairs, but he wasn't

always a goody-two-shoes. Before the events of book

one Dead To Me, *Simon had to learn that 'with great*

power comes great responsibility' (thanks to years of

Spidey reading, natch), but in Simon's case it also came

with added financial perks from thievery too…

S O..." THE WOMAN SAID, drawing the word out with the long, slow hiss of a snake, her eyes dancing with mischievous curiosity. "What *is* your secret, Mister Canderous?"

The crowd of tourists and hipsters seated around us in Katz's chattered away like a gaggle of geese as they stuffed their faces with copious amounts of New York's finest deli fare. I, on the other hand, remained silent as I flecked crumbs of rye off my Ramones 'Gabba-Gabba-Hey!' t-shirt, much to the redhead's annoyance.

I wasn't in the habit of ignoring questions, especially when they came from someone as attractive as the woman who had introduced herself as Mina Saria as she slid in the seat across from me not five minutes ago. Then again, I usually didn't have gorgeous women tracking me down through some of my art dealing fences, either.

Her hawk-like eyes peered out from under bangs of dark red that was a color found more in a bottle than in anything in nature. When I didn't answer her, she sat back in her chair and folded her arms across her chest.

"What makes *you* so special then?" she asked, changing her tack slightly.

"SCREAM"

Illustration by OKSANA DMITRIENKO

"It's all in the hands, Miss Saria," I said, sliding off my thin black leather gloves and laying them on the smooth surface of the table.

"You've earned quite the reputation out there among the forgers and the fakers," she said.

"Have I?" I asked as nonchalant as I could, trying to mask the swell of newfound pride that rose up in me.

Mina gave me a single nod and a smile. "Yes. It appears they don't like how easily you see through their frauds."

"Sucks to be them," I said, flexing my fingers.

"Most people say you have to have a good eye to do what you do," she said. "Spotting forgeries."

"Well, there are *some* fakes you can tell right away by sight," I said, going for the bowl of pickles a waiter had set down before us, biting into its briny goodness. "For me? It's all about how it *feels*."

The fact that a bit of psychometric tinkering factored into it was not something my potential employer needed to know, but I couldn't help but feel that swell of pride again. This time I gave into it. And why shouldn't I? I had turned a near crippling preternatural power I could barely control into something that was proving quite lucrative among the arts and antique stores up and down Broadway. Not to mention classing up the walls of my newly acquired SoHo loft. Now my growing reputation had put this gorgeous redhead at the table with me, and that was far from something that normally happened in my day to day.

The woman's face was full of skepticism, but I said nothing and continued eating.

"Can you prove how talented you are?" she asked. I raised an eyebrow and she leaned forward. "I like to see things for myself. After all, my team and I want the best at our disposal. Please don't take offense, Mister Canderous."

"None taken," I said with a dismissive wave. "And please, call me Simon. As far as proof…"

The moment I had hoped for, which was why I had picked so notable a meeting spot as Katz's Deli. I gestured to the sign overhead. A red arrow pointed down at where we sat.

Where Harry Met Sally…Hope you have what she had! Enjoy!

Mina looked back down at me, so far unimpressed. "So?"

"We'll see about that," I said and laid my hands back down on the table.

It had taken what little control I had over my power to keep it in check when I had taken my gloves off, but now I gave into it and let the electric connection lash out as it always did, wild and barely containable.

Some objects in this world barely held a psychometric charge, but the fame of this film location saturated the entire deli, allowing me to focus all that raw power down and better direct my vision. My mind's eye filled with a thousand images in an instant. Every person who had ever touched this supposed famous table over the years flickered through my thoughts, and I fought to push through them, sorting as I went.

Like my own personal DVD player, I rewound through the images trying my best not to be pulled in any specific direction. When I caught the bright lights and camera equipment of the film shoot, I focused in until the familiar movie scene was upon me, seeing it from an entirely different perspective than I was used to from watching the film.

I had forgotten how 'Eighties' the Eighties truly looked, but the clothes of the extras were a perfect reminder. It was odd to see a young Rob Reiner directing an equally young Meg Ryan and Billy Crystal in the now famous scene, but one thing was immediately clear. The table I was reading was *not* the one actually being used in the filming. It instead sat about fifteen feet away in use by one of the film's grips to raise and focus a lighting unit on the actual film scene itself.

I had everything I needed and with a force of effort I pushed myself out of my mind's eyes. The strength of the vision held me transfixed in it longer that I would have liked, but with one final struggle I tore free from the historic moment. Gasping, I opened my eyes wide to find Mina Saria staring expectantly at me.

"Are you all right?" she asked. "You looked like you were stroking out."

I wasn't sure how long I had been in the vision, but by the way I was shaking and my head swam, it had been a bit too long. I grabbed my corned beef sandwich and began scarfing it down.

"Blood sugar dropping," I said between bites.

"Hypoglycemia?"

"Something like that," I said and fell back to eating, allowing me to dodge discussing it further, which was fine by me. Why my blood sugar plummeted while using my power was as much a mystery to me as it would be to her. It wasn't like I could just take the issue to my doctor to ask about.

When I was done eating, I licked the last few drops of mustard from my fingers.

"You want to tell me what that was all about?" she asked.

"Let's say this table was up for auction," I said, slapping my hands down on it. "As a piece of Hollywood history. First thing I'd tell you is that this table *wasn't* used in the film."

Mina looked up at the sign overhead and pointed to it. "It wasn't?"

I shook my head. "It wasn't even in the shot," I said.

"Bullshit," she said, and waved a waiter over.

A heavy set man in his late forties lumbered up to our table. His ring of what remained of his black hair was wild and curly, his eyes kind. He smiled at Mina.

"Yes?" he said, the hint of something European in his voice.

"This *is* the table from the movie, right?"

The man hesitated, then pointed to the sign overhead as Mina had, saying nothing.

"Be honest now," I added.

His gaze shifted back and forth between the two of us, then he cautiously looked around the room before leaning in to us, whispering.

"Yes and no," he said with some reluctance.

Mina looked annoyed. "Meaning…?"

"This is the *spot* where they filmed the scene, yes," he said, "but actually the owner took the original table off the floor long ago. It's in his home or the Smithsonian, I believe. Anything else?"

Mina shook her head and the man told us to enjoy our nosh and walked off to clear a table.

When I turned back to her, she appeared suitably impressed, and I tried to contain my smug smile.

"Well?" I asked.

The redhead looked me over. "All that from just the feel of the table, huh?"

"Like I said, it's all in the hands."

Mina leaned forward and held her hand out to me. "Then I do believe we have a deal, Mister Canderous."

"Hold on now," I said, moving my bare hands away from her by leaning back in my chair. "I didn't say I was ready to seal the deal."

"Oh?" she said, dropping her hand to her side.

"You haven't told me what you expect from me," I said.

"Just some light thievery and breaking and entering."

"I don't know what your contact told you about me," I said, pushing my chair back, "but I'm in the business of identifying fakes and forgeries, maybe perhaps keeping the occasional rare find for myself. Why would I steal for anyone's benefit other than my own?"

"Because it pays remarkably well...?"

I stood. "I'm not sure there's a price you can name. Sorry."

"Please, sit," she pleaded. "I work for the Metropolitan Museum of Art."

"Tsk tsk, Miss Saria," I said. "You want me to help you steal from your own job? What must your bosses think? I don't think any price you name is going to talk me into even going near the Met, sorry."

The first rule of Psychometry Club was 'no museums'. With my power and limited control of it, a location so full of history would drain me and leave me a flopping fish on the floor before I could barely make it past the main lobby.

"Thanks, but no thanks."

I turned away from our table and started toward the turnstile exit at the front corner of the restaurant.

"You misunderstand," she called out. "You wouldn't be stealing. Think of this more of a recovery."

I stopped and turned back to her. I leaned over the table, lowering my voice. "If this were legitimate, lady, you wouldn't be trying to hire *me*."

She paused as she collected her thoughts before once more speaking. "This is a delicate situation," she said. "You've indeed heard of *The Scream*, yes?"

Intrigue got the better part of me at the mere mention of the macabre piece of art and I slid back into the seat across from her. "Sure," I said. "Who hasn't? *Der Schrei der Natur*. The Scream of Nature. Gaunt fellow, pulling a *Home Alone* face slap on a long, haunting road. There are four versions by Edvard Munch."

One of Mina's eyebrows raised, disappearing behind her long, red bangs. "Impressive," she said.

I shrugged. "It's a sort of Holy Grail in art thieving circles. They've all gone missing at some point. Always recovered, I might add."

She laughed, but quickly regained her composure. "There are art thieving circles?"

"Not really," I said. "They're all too paranoid, but you get the idea."

She nodded. "One of them is currently on loan from the National Gallery of Oslo to the Metropolitan Museum of Art," she said, then her face fell. "Or was."

"*Was?*"

"You misunderstood me before, Mister Canderous," she said. "I don't want to hire you to steal it. It's *already* been stolen. We need your help retrieving it."

I sat back in my chair as I took her request in, surprised at the nature of it. "From who?" I asked. "From where?"

"As you said, it is highly sought after by the wrong crowd," she said. "Forgeries of it abound. We have some leads, but we need help if we're going to conduct our investigation in an expedient and covert manner. Time—forgive the cliché—is of the essence."

I shrugged. "So send the cops out, round all of them up."

Mina paused before proceeding, and when she spoke, I could see in her eyes the care with which she chose her words. "My higher-ups would appreciate some…subtlety in the handling of this," she said. "If we can recover the painting before it needs to be returned to Oslo, we can avoid a tangle with the Norwegians."

"There's something I never thought I would hear," I said with a chuckle, but Mina didn't laugh, her face remaining stern. "Sorry."

"An international incident would reflect poorly on our institution and the city of New York, Mister Canderous," she said.

"Years of diplomacy would be undone." She leaned in and finally let a smile cross her lips. "And be honest…wouldn't you like a chance at getting your hands on *The Scream*, even if it's only for a few moments? How many men can say that? Not to mention the service you would be doing your city…"

She had a point…more than she truly knew. Under the security of a museum's watch, *The Scream* was untouchable. But if I could find it with 'the someone' who had already saved me the trouble of getting it out of there, I just might be able to pull off this dream heist for myself. I'd check out whatever forgeries Mina had in mind, and if I came across the real one, I'd misdirect her until I could secure it for myself.

Mina studied my face, and when she saw me smile, she extended her hand once more.

"My services don't come cheap," I reminded her. "To validate the right painting, especially one as famous as this…"

"Price is no concern," she said, smiling.

I slid my gloves on and took her hand in mine, the sensation of my power dulled to the point where I was back in control of it now. I shook her hand with a wide and wicked grin. "Getting paid to steal *The Scream*," I said. "Who said crime doesn't pay?"

THE MOVIES ALWAYS MADE breaking and entering look oh so easy and yet it was anything but. Especially with three people watching. Luckily, they were also covering me while I knelt on the steps of a townhouse working the tumblers on its main entrance.

"Can you hurry it up?" Mina asked, her voice hushed under the rustling of wind through the leaves of the tree-lined Upper East Side cross street. "I would think after the first dozen places, you'd have mastered picking locks by now, Mister Canderous."

"Can the three of you kindly fuck off?" I asked, but kept my concentration on my tension control driving the pins under the shear line within the lock.

"Ooh, feisty," she purred, which seemed appropriate given the tight leather cat suit she had managed to squeeze herself into for our evening of burglaries. "I'm sure that mouth will do you well in prison."

"I can feel the three of you watching and it's not helping," I said, not bothering to look back at them. "It's like being pee shy."

"All right, let's all turn away," the one called Kreuger said. His voice sounded as heavy and thick as the man himself. I could picture him behind me, hulking and no doubt buttoning and unbuttoning his black leather coat as he had done a thousand times tonight so far, a habit that I found both annoying and distracting—even when I couldn't see him doing it.

I didn't appreciate Mina bringing along goons for this, but at least they knew how to keep watch so it was one less thing to worry about so I could get my job done.

"Hope you're faster with the interior alarm on this one," the other goon said. Meyers, I thought his name was, although he had spent most of the night watching me in silence.

"Much faster," I replied as the outer door finally clicked open with one last push against the tumblers in the lock. "In. Now!"

The long slow countdown of the alarm system arming beeped away. I ran in before the others could even move and slapped my hand down over the keypad. My psychometric connection snapped to, and my mind's eyes traced the history of the keypad's recent use.

A pale man with dark hair worked the numbers, but at a speed that seemed more than human. I rewound the instance over and over in my head until I could slow it enough to see the number he was keying in.

1337.

I pulled myself out of the vision, only a little shaky from the psychometric reading. Over the increasing tones of the beeping, I keyed the number in, silencing it. My hand shook from my power depletion and Mina held up several rolls of Life Savers.

"Here you go," she said. "I have a diabetic friend who swears by them."

I took a few and crunched them down, surprised at how quickly I felt better. By then she and her cronies were already moving through the dark interior of the townhouse. The main floor looked posh yet normal enough, but once upstairs the building had more of a museum vibe, the walls thick with art and the floor dotted with display cases filled with a variety of antique looking pieces.

"Who *is* this guy?" I asked. I slid my gloves back on, not wanting to trigger off anything in the townhouse by mistake.

"Just another eccentric collector," Mina said, stepping carefully through the room.

On the far wall of the main upstairs room hung *The Scream*, prominently displayed at the focal point as it had been at four of the previous places we had visited tonight. The four of us crossed to it, mindful of disturbing anything as we went.

Not every replica had looked all that genuine, but upon a cursory examination this one held up under my initial scrutiny.

Krueger and Myers kept back, but Mina settled in at my side, examining the painting herself.

"Well?" she asked, her eyes dancing with an anticipatory hope. "What can you tell me about this one?"

"We'll see." The painting itself had its own keypad alarm next to it. I pulled my gloves off, grabbed its code psychometrically to disarm the alarm. I reached for the painting, but before my fingers touched the edge of it, my power crackled to life like tiny jolts of lightning.

The visions associated with the other paintings tonight had varied. One had been reproduced in a loft in Chelsea while two others had been crafted in what looked to be a forgery operation downtown in the Bowery. Another had even been done by a museum staffer who had simply wanted to try his hand at duplicating the piece.

None, however, had screamed with the raw historical power of this one. Its journey to our country form Oslo flashed backwards through my mind's eye, but just seeing it back at the National Gallery wasn't enough for me, I realized. Experiencing this history didn't have to stop there…after all, how often was I going to get the chance to see the actual artistry and creation of a painting like this in action?

I pressed my power further, pushing back through the painting's history until its very creation. The tall, thin man I suddenly found myself as in the vision looked much like the gaunt figure in the painting, only with dark hair combed to one side and a thick mustache. *Edvard Munch himself.* He worked on the painting that would become *The Scream* where it stood alongside several others in a Berlin studio, and I marveled at the artistry unfolding from his—no, *my*—hand as the piece worked its way from swirls of colors to the end result of the painting. My cheeks hurt from the smile that had crept across my own face back in the real world. I had witnessed something no other human ever had—save Munch himself—and the sensation was truly overwhelming which, I realized, did *not* work to my advantage right now. I needed to pull myself out of the vision if I was going to trick Mina into thinking this was just another imitation. Once convinced, I could come back for it later, but first I had to return to reality.

Pulling my mind's eye out of the vision was harder than I imagined and took all my will, the effort driving a spike into the center of my brain to the point that when the connection broke, I stumbled back from the painting, shaking and on the verge of falling over.

Mina grabbed my shoulders to steady me, but I slumped to the floor anyway. I fished for the Life Savers in my pocket with still-shaking hands.

"What the hell was that?" she asked. "You look like you're going to pass out!" She turned from me back to the painting. "That's the real deal, isn't it?"

"That painting..." I managed to mumble through a mouthful of candy as I shoveled it in. Shaken as I was in my current state, I could barely speak let alone muster the guile to try to pull the wool over her eyes. I shut my mouth, and gave a simple nod.

"Are you sure?" she asked, glancing back and forth between me and the painting.

The sensation of being Munch was still coursing through me as I pulled myself up off the floor. "Pretty damn sure."

Like a tree on Christmas Eve, Mina's eyes practically sparkled. "Finally!" she shouted with a squeal, wrapping her arms around me. Her body shook with glee, and in a rush of adrenaline she pulled away, grabbed my face and kissed me hard.

If I wasn't already busy recovering from my psychometric hit, I might have been able to stop my connection from snapping to. Instead my mind flooded with unbidden images of Mina's private life. Images of all her previous art recoveries flickered through my mind, but as they flashed by one thing became abundantly clear.

I pushed myself away from her body, my lips pulling away from hers.

Her face was awash in confusion, no doubt having sensed the

psychometric connection.

"You don't actually recover art for the museum," I said through labored breath. "You find it, sell it, or keep it for *yourself*."

She backed away, her face changing from elation to something wicked—wicked, but confused. "How…how could you possibly know that?" she asked, rubbing her temple. "What did you do to me?"

"You hired me because I was good at finding fakes," I said. "What did you expect? I found the fake. It's you. Let's make something clear…I'm *not* going to help you steal this, Mina."

I reached for the alarm panel next to the painting and just managed to rearm it as a meaty hand closed on my wrist and pulled me away from it. *Myers.*

"And you wondered why I needed the muscle," she said. "Too bad. This could have become terribly lucrative for you, Mister Canderous…now it's just going to be terrible."

I stepped back from her. "I'm not getting paid, am I?"

"Paid in pain maybe—"

I turned to run, hoping to twist out of Myers grip, but he was stronger and quicker, twisting my arm behind me while Kreuger pulled back one of his fists and pistoned it into my stomach. The air went out of me, and all I could do was take it as Kreuger gut punched me over and over.

One thing became immediately clear: I needed to come up with something before they beat me into unconsciousness. There was no way I could take them both on. My only advantage here was my power, which frankly didn't seem cut out to be remarkably helpful in this particular situation.

Unless…

I needed to find an advantage somehow, but for that I realized I would need skin-to-skin contact to activate my psychometry.

Kreuger's next blow to my stomach had me barely able to breathe, but I managed to look up into his eyes and forced myself to speak.

"That...all you got?"

I kept my head up, daring him to strike me in the face, and he couldn't resist the target. The bone of his knuckles slammed into that of my jaw, the sensation jarring, but it gave me what I needed. A flash of Kreuger's life filled my mind's eye, lingering for a second then disappearing. I needed more.

"You're going to have to rough me up pretty bad with those meat hooks if you want me to be even half as ugly as you, Kreuger."

Another blow, another flash.

"I'd say you hit like a grandmother only that would be an insult to old people."

The blows rained down harder and harder, each one triggering my power. My mind's eye fought to make sense of the flashes, and like going through a kid's flip book, the images began to fit together into a cohesive flow as I sorted back through the thug's day. He might be busy beating me with his fists now, but hopefully Kreuger had not started his day leaving home empty-handed.

I kept searching his memories until at last an image of him strapping a thick, metallic cylinder to his belt hit me. It came to me in the vision just before I watched him leave his dingy Inwood apartment, concealing the tube with his heavy leather coat.

I pulled out of the vision and back to the present. Although I couldn't see the object on him now, it was the only hope I had.

As his next blow came towards me, I let my entire body go slack, my arms slipping out of Myer's hold as my full weight dropped to the floor. My knees screamed with pain as they took the impact, but I was already rolling myself forward, reaching into Kreuger's coat. Thankfully the cool metal of the cylinder was under there in its special holster, secured by an elaborate safety tie, but thanks to my vision I knew exactly how to undo it. I pulled the object free, rolled onto my back and pushed myself across the floor as I examined it.

A safety mechanism sat housed over the single button on the object. I flicked the cover of it off and pressed down. The thick cylinder telescoped out with a metallic *shkkt*, becoming a regulation sized steel baseball bat.

Myers stopped mid-lunge. Kreuger, however, looked more than pissed that I had taken his little toy and came on at a full on charge. I swung, catching him in the midsection with a meaty thud that doubled him over as I wound back and hit him again and again. After my third or fourth strike, Myers finally lunged into action to help, but I twirled the bat in his direction and poked him in the chest with the end of it, driving him back.

"Enough!" Mina called out.

Her voice held enough authority to make me pause and glance at her, while Myers helped Krueger stand. The men's eyes burned through me.

Their boss stepped forward. "Put down the weapon, Simon," she said, her voice calm but commanding.

I shook my head and raised the bat. "So you and your goons can kick my ass some more? No thanks."

From some hidden fold on her cat suit, Mina slid free a long, thin blade. "Suit yourself," she said. "One of us is leaving here with the painting, and here's a hint: it's not going to be you."

Thievery was the furthest thing from my mind. Survival was more my concern, and with three to one odds *and* a knife in the mix now, my chances were looking slimmer and slimmer.

"Fine," I said, backing myself further across the room from the painting towards the second floor windows. If only I had rolled myself across the floor toward the stairs. Stupid 20/20 hindsight.

"I don't care if that painting leaves with me, but I'm damned sure you're not taking it either."

Mina sighed. "Your funeral," she said. She flipped the knife around in her hand like a seasoned street fighter until she held it in an aggressive stance with the blade protruding underhand.

Mina and her two thugs started across the room, closing with me and approaching from three different directions using caution.

"I don't think so," I said.

Mina laughed. "No?" she asked. "And why not?"

I pointed to the painting. "I rearmed the alarm system, Mina," I said. "Now you might not be familiar with the finer points of them, but I am." She didn't need to know much of what I had gleaned about this set up had come from being psychometrically in the mind of the townhouse's owner. "In a sweet pad like this, you think the guy who lives here is going to skimp? No, he's going to go top of the line. You try to take that painting…you'll trip the alarm, the front door deadbolts, the windows shutter with steel plating. That sort of thing."

"So?" Kreuger asked with a growl. "We'll still beat you to death before anyone can get in here."

Despite the menace in his face I had to laugh. "I'm not planning on sticking around, guys," I said, raising the bat high. "Sorry to disappoint."

The three of them paused as I swung into motion, but they needn't have worried. None of them were my intended target. With my windup, I turned to the window and swung with all I had.

Glass exploded and fell to the street below as I worked the bat around the window frame, knocking away what I could of its jagged remains. I spun around to find my assailants closing with me again.

Mina raised an eyebrow. "You can't be serious."

I pulled another roll of Life Savers out of my pocket. Taking careful aim, I threw it across the room, toward *The Scream*. It wasn't a heavy enough object to do any damage to the painting itself, but it was enough to trigger its alarm. There was no siren or bells or whistles, but the slamming locks on the downstairs door and windows were enough to tell me it had gone off.

"You won't survive the fall," Mina said, a nervous desperation in her voice.

"I'd rather take my chances out there than in here with you lot," I said, and without waiting jumped into the open air just as the steel window shutters started sliding into place. I was in freefall.

I loved the townhouses of Manhattan, and this street lined with them shared a common trait I had noticed earlier—almost all townhouse streets were lined with trees. I had simply taken in their quiet rustling in the wind as a thing of beauty earlier, but now they were proving my salvation.

Not that the drop was an easy one. My body sailed from the window out over the sidewalk and into the trees next to the street. Branches and leaves poked at my face and eyes as I descended head first. I fell blind as my body exploded with pain, branches breaking some of my fall while others battered and bruised me the entire way down. The final freefall to the sidewalk left me stunned and aching, but I appeared unbroken, alive, and most importantly, not trapped inside with Mina and her thugs.

Already the sound of sirens echoed in the distance, getting me back on my feet faster than anything. I picked up the retractable steel bat from where it had fallen out of my hands.

Tonight had proved a bust, but at least I wasn't going to be busted. Plus I had this nifty new weapon, which I collapsed to its original size and slid inside my jacket before taking my first shaky steps.

"And this is why we only steal for ourselves, idiot," I muttered as I hobbled off.

By the time the rolling reds and blues turned onto the street, I was already rounding the corner onto Fifth Avenue. Shaken, I wondered if perhaps this was a wake-up call, a near miss that the universe had sent down upon me in the hopes I'd shape the hell up. At the very least it was clearly telling me I wasn't built for the life of a career criminal, which I guess I already knew. After all, I didn't look good in stripes or an orange jumpsuit, not to mention that my dating life would probably only get worse if I went to prison over something like this. The idea crept into my head that maybe this power could somehow be turned to something more constructive, to DOING GOOD…not that I had a clue as to the 'how' of all that.

Still, this was *The Scream* we were talking about, *the* Holy Grail of art thievery. Perhaps it wasn't the best painting to go cold turkey on, despite the close call tonight.

Never return to the scene of a crime, the old criminal axiom said, but it was hard to let go of such an opportunity, even after a failed first attempt…

My brain couldn't help but already start planning my return trip to the townhouse. How could I not? Most people would worry about dealing with the changes to a security system or new countermeasures being installed, but when you had psychometry on your side, all those changes are instantly knowable and literally at my fingertips.

Only next time there would be no bullshit stories, no false pretenses, and no partners in crime to get in my way. It wouldn't be about someone else or even the money a painting like that could earn me. In this case, the only way crime *would* pay was because something as special as *The Scream* didn't deserve to be bought or sold. No, it deserved to be appreciated, and as the sole person alive to have just experienced the painting's creation—save Edvard Munch himself, that is—I planned to appreciate the hell out of it on the space right above the mantle in my apartment.

Let the Norwegians be as pissed as they like. They had, after all, lost four versions of *The Scream* over the years. What was one more?

ACKNOWLEDGEMENTS

This unthinkable tome would not be in your grubby little mitts without donations made by the following rogues and rapscallions. We do not know how they came by such currency, and it is not ours to question.

Guild Masters

Mainon Schwartz, Shawn Speakman, Christopher Veach, Jim Thompson, Paul, Aron Dough, Stefan Gore, MihirW, Carrie Smith, John D Price III, John Carlisle, Jim Bellmore, Penelope Astridge, Matt Avella, Peastri, Jonathan Auerbach, Matt Gilliard

Master Thieves (of The Signed Page)

Danielle Hall, Kenneth Hayes, David Rockwell, Robin Carter, Tim Marquitz, Billy Vazquez, Mike Leaich, stef, TrashMan, Eivind, Dave Baughman, Eric Munson, Hannah, Midhun Mathew, Rhel, Damon, Stephan Ziegler, Connor McCarty, Jason, Andrew Monk, Steve Drew, Andrew Preece, Andrew Carrick, Tom Lewis, Andrew, Paul Lei Yik Liang, 'Super Green' Tim Parsons, Chappy Lu,

Bev C, Shelly McCann, Benjamin Rosenberg, Steve Irwin, Brian Horstmann, Larry Couch, T.J. Olson, Erickson Suarez, Estevon Dusek, Todd, Robin Crawford, Marquie, Joshua Villines, Jes Golka, T. Kay Erickson, Robert Cothran, Thomas, Mark Rollison, Cuong Trieu, Alexander Green, Jason, Yankton Robins, Nicholaus Chatelain, Kristina, David Christie, Oliver, Martin Jackson, Trevor Wissink, ROKJohnson, Rusty Baker

Monsters

Christopher A Buckley, Bitsy VonTrapp, Don Houdari Freeman, Sarah Wilson, Leigh Drusilla Lyle, Arne Radtke, Amelia Smith, Sean DeWoody, Fenecia Jones, Gregory Willmann, Joe, Benjamin Clay, Peter, Patrick Pfundstein, Scott Early, Jazion Keera, Matthew Cranor, Tana Wheeler, Fred Bailey, Chris Dent, Galit, gravebeast. zero, Park Anthony Rall, Gabriel Kellogg, Steve Acheson, Ray Pond, Andrew Taylor, Bill Silvia, Judd Arnold, GriffinFire

Upright Men (and Women!)

Kyle Burckhard, Douglsa Roemer, Eric Evilsizor, Rachel, Seth, Sally 'Qwill' Janin, Kathy Speakman, Curtis Wilson, Tony (ChronoNinja) K., Eric Myers, Ellen Sandberg, Brenda Snyder, SontaranPR, Ian Chung, Brennan See, Aaron Miller, Peter Hutchinson, Brandon Borre, Joe Parrino, Proof482, Dianne, Adam Scott, Ann Vergin, Lorri Lynne Brown, Tina Good, Mayestril, Joshua Tai, David Ramirez, Ivy Maturin, Alex Putnam, Matt Elliott, Joseph Lallo, Tracie Ashmore Kneeland, Calvin Li, Justin McKenney, Frank Bastian, Cody Spradlin, Jose Rojas, Chris Park, Tim Chambers, Robert Thompson, Timothy W. Long, Katrina L. Halliwell, Matthew Verish, Samantha Simpson, Joanne, Peter Nelson, Jason Peroutka, Harry Moran, Eric Schwartz, Jimmy Kimmel, Matt Damon

Knights of the Road

Kenny Soward, Joshua Hislop, Jason Breining, Sean Pfundstein, Donald Edwards, Naloth, Sarah Westphaln, Eisenhorn29, Jay Quigley, dgagnon99, Rodney Barnes, Brian Thomas, Rhiannon Rippke-Koch, Nicholas Watkins, Anne, Shawn King, Iván de Neymet, Simina A, Quek JiaJin, Elizabeth Gladys, Roman Poelzinger, Ven Sio, Robert Aldrich, Jason Plowman, Ferran Selles, Carissa, Greg Cueto, Anton Strout, Gunnar Rhonevaltir

Lone Wolves

Steven Nicoll, Andrew Clough, Leanne Ellis, Angela Spugnardi, Robin Allen, Randi Spears, Walter Bryan, Kent Holloway, David Jenks, Drae Corben, Patrick J McKernan, James Squeak Cawtheray, Joel Pearson, Owen Johnson, Ben Birkett, Eric DeFilippo, Joseph Fleischman, Jessica Furrow Allred, Jessica Meade, Kreniz, Ed Cooke Jr, Steven Diamond, Dylan LuciustheEternal Murphy, Daniel Hughes, Paul Walsh, Simon Bremner, Paquet Fabien, Ryan Lawler, Fiachra Horan, Jeremy Robinson, Bill Lovell, Aaron Markworth, Tad Ottman, Derek Christman, Nati, Moses Siregar III, Victor Morgan, Matthew Rogers, Todd Lockwood, Alex Ristea, Adam Parkinson, Kile, Kathryn Mergener, Josh Alderson, Melissa J. Katano, Ming Ming, Aaron Lindamood, Aditya Gajjar, Keith West, Ashley R. Morton, temp2264, Eric Wegner, David Tiggemann, Michael Ramm, Jeremy Freeman, Y. Lee, Christopher Buser, Kayla Wagner, Jamie Henderson, Martin Helsdon, Scott Maynard, Daniel Belanger, Andrea Pitman, Kyle Swank, Matthew Ashley, nama0011, Lira, Celyn the Raven, Jere Manninen, Melanie R. Meadors, Paul Tran, Jeremy Bokus, Wade Danielson, Rob Rhoden, John Leake Parsons, Alexandra Cenni, doublechocochip, Louie Clement, Thom Raymond, Michael, Bruce Bevens, Saturnine, Robert Coleman, Ashli Tingle, Tori Augustine, Frida Caspian Franzén, Brandon

Willey, Darren Tongate, Brian Eckfeld, Jeff Coleman, Jarod Devera, Ken Washington, Angel Fiszlewicz, Dan Tree, Heather K. Wertz Leasor, Jeff Cunningham, Jeffery Mace, Spencer Estabrooks, Ross Clifton, John Nock, Daniel Mayer, Liz Steinworth, Andy Holcombe, Matt Stevenson, Scott Nairn, Stephanie Lovell, Jeff Kapustka, Adam Holliday, Serge Lecler, Michael VanRandwyk, Ammon, Larry Heydorn, John Squire, Donald Cobb, Blake Tullo, Scott Whipkey, Steven Mentzel, Henry W, Jonathan Orton Gan, Travis McHenry, Chris Garrett, Ian Greenfield, Robert Napton, Sarah S., Derek Feddon, Eileen Birdsong, Ryan Leduc, Brian Sieglaff, Tim Albrecht, Cullen Gilchrist, Gregory S. Close, Vincent Menzi, Wayne McCalla, Roger McCray, Brian Koehler, Gerry Dupuis, Shaun Jurjens, Katie Filippello, Abdullah Shamsi, Elise, K Wirick, Paul Quick, Nilas Simonsen, Aaron Bevard, Vic Ayers, Kyle, Chris Huddleston, Ian O'Reilly, Neo Han Jie, Dave Robison, John Evans, Eric Gallant, Hade, Rodney, Ben Moser, Matt LeClair, Anthony Pennito, Dana Thoms, Erik Agerbjörk, Yago Gonzalez Rozas, Robert Soto, Justin White, Christopher Blaschke, Patrick Nelson, Amanda, Andrew Petty, Courtney Getty, Deborah A Wolf, Matthew Geoffroy, Chris Marr, David Jackson, Matthew Brown, Silentshot, Valkem, Luke Killam, Richard Cornish, Doug Eckhoff, Naomi, Eric Dooley, Brandon Gregory, Gabe Eggers, Sam Baskin, Steven Mitchell, AKASlaphappy, David Archibald, Burnnerman, Michael Tynan, Kirk Dougal, Balgin Stondraeg, Duncan MacKenzie, Stephen Brent McDowell, Kevin Kastelic, Ken Mann, Chris, Betsy Dornbusch, Nathaniel Vestri, Trevor Leong, Tracy W

Footpads
Shane Dunne, Rob Hayes, Nathan, Tyler Cummins, Bobby Seiter, Chandler, Nick Sharps, Sara Weiss, Gallant Knight Games, Torii Gardiner, Deborah, Robert Elrod, Nathan Gundlach, Ralph

M Seibert, Jeremy Rowland, Melanie C. Duncan, MMOGC, Michael Olsen, Jeffrey D. Pegues, Kyle Mahoney, Greg Hersom, Jake Grey, John Michael Davis, Paul Wittine, Jason M. Waltz, querysphinx, Allison Bistline East, Terrin, William Miskovetz, Maurice Forrester, Anne Burner, Steve Dean, Lori Joyce Parker, Jeff Jensen, Robert Johnson, Jeremy Hochhalter, Giulio Marchetti, Andreas Gustafsson, Rini Kirkpatrick, Michael D. Woods, Joshua Palmatier, Elizabeth Kite, Trevor Long, Stanley Wexler, Jim Foster, Sarah Webb, Doug Kirkland, Dong Ming, Tony A. Thompson, James Christman, Adam Cesare, Allison McDonlad, Eric Roberts, Dawson Cowals, Jenna Woginrich, Alysia Murphy, Ariane, Andrea Chilkiewicz, Carrie Pennow, Christine Cooney, Margaret St. John, Matthew Farnsworth, Jim Burzelic, Ashley Oswald, Robin Bayless, Jemma Kloss, ozog, Keith Strohm, Jeremy Cook, Loree Hansen, Kevin S. Haggerty, Arakas, Jim Reader, Ian Doyle, Robin Walls, Matt Stoecker, Adora Hoose, Ronnie J Darling, K Severson, Epper Marshall, Ryan Shumate, Chad B Thompson, Matthew Walker, Darren Lee, Drew Wolff, Kathryn Zinman, John Robertson, Stephen J. Shockey, Melicent Stossel, Lisa Herrick, Victoria Shade, KLH, Gopakumar Sethuraman, Mary Jo Schimelpfenig, Jessica Ernst, David Wu, Robert Cox, Lucinda Caughey, Jacob Magnusson, Debra Delorme, Mike Drobnack, Shean Mohammed, Annie Bellet, Tasha (Turner) Lennhoff, Katherine Pawlik, Malvinder Singh, Tom Narow, Erik Scott de Bie, Nick Sands, Jeff Pollock, Stephanie Piegzik, Julie Masters, Jeff Hotchkiss, Sharon Muffett, Patti Short, Mark Walker, Tracey Rose, Epheros Aldor, David Bowler, Barbara Soto, Bobby Hitt, Adam Pergande, Alex Shulman, Edward Bromley, Wendy, Diane Cutter, Johan, Carrie Mansfield, Steven T., Christian Lindke, Tyler M. Rhea, Tyson J Mauermann, Mark Wolfson, Jessica Wolf, James Enge, Andrew Berg, Pam Buchholz, Garett Lepper, Amanda Schiffer, Joel Sanet, Geoff Brown, Carol Berg, John Glen,

James Michael Mock, Marsheila Rockwell, Remer, Kevin, Deanna
Mercer, Gilad Bezalel Jaffe, Steve Ferrebee, Louis Marinos, Becky
B, Gary Lombardo, Brannigan Cheney, Jacqueline Hudson, Marty
Kagan, Craig Steven Herndon Jr., Daniel Nissman, Larry, Jean Rabe,
Tim Deal, Joshua Takashi, Philip Gelatt, Kai Hill, Stan MacDonald,
Gary Phillips, Kristie Strum, Jenn Ridley, Elizabeth Pittman, Rob
Cantrell, Heidi Wilde, Terry Harney, Lincoln Crisler, Brett Abbott,
Indi Go, cows, Inductor Guitars, Meghan Anne Merritt, John
Chingren, TheTygre, Hans Van de Berg, Yang Gao, Gini Koch,
Adam Selby-Martin, Andrea Montgomery, Rose, Kristen Johnson,
Crystal Kocher, NightsWatch, Korey, Steven Lord, KBKarma,
Thomas Brown, Sam Stuckman, Ducky, valathil, Doug Sturtevant,
Teresa, zeuslot, Kristi Weyland Taylor, Konstantin Koptev, Cody
Swatek, Jen Burns, Misty Massey, James Herbert, Jenny Langley,
Tyler Thomas, Adrian, Shannon Clark, Katrina 'Kitty' Goodwin,
Jo-Jo Taylor, David, Brandon Kanechika, Denis Davydov, Michael
Everly, PlatinumBlade00, Emme Hones, Andromeda Taylor, James
H. Murphy Jr., Andreas Flato, Arul Isai Imran, Katherine Socha,
Robert Knowles, Adam, Joe Schmoe, Joshua Kanapkey, Rob,
Randy Belanger, David Quist, Devan Lai, Matthew Koberlein,
Jerald Humes, Aaron Nguyen, Julia van Hees, Kevin, Anthony
Giordano, Todd V. Ehrenfels, Nate Miller, Cookie!, Abdul Gaffar
Chowdhury, Meg Lindsey, Dave Pherigo, Holly Early, J.S. Morin,
David Lamontagne, Michael Lapinsky, J.Rencher, Steven Schend,
Steph Kelley, Chris Janes, stlsully31, William Jones, Laura K. Deal,
Sharon Murphy Karpierz, Catalyst

Right Rascals

Susan Ferrara, John Wynn, Joshua Lowe, Jerome Lim, Chris
Slottee, Jude Hunter, Andrew Tudor, Sue Armitage, Louise
Löwenspets, Kerstin Fricke, Martha S., Kristi Callaghan, Sinead

McArdle, Carolyn Reid, Simon Dick, Joseph Dean, Trowby Brockman, Melissa Shumake, Melanie Eggleston, Kyle, Heather Blandford, Sean Huempfner, Adam Brockie, Jack, Andrew Fish, Elizabeth Crissey, Darren Murray, Stéphanie Verret-Roy, Dan Paddock, Jaclyn Tan, John Heine, Brian Kedersha, Rolf Laun, Kel George, Brandon Frere, Clay Dowling, Tomas, Joseph Hoopman, Derek Freeman, Greg Bennett, Stephen Giordano, Kevin Kelly, FredH, Robert M. Everson, Sean L., D D, Rob Crosby, DG, Jordi Gil, Andrea Milar, Chris Richards, Amanda Shore, Stuart Wilson, Kemtis, Daniel Gentle, Keith Hall, Rob Hobart, Daniel Andrisek, Christian Karl, Magdalena Fabrykowska-Młotek, Maximilian Klenk, Anu Pramila, Cato, Evan Hoadley, Markus H., Richard Eyres, Strella, John Lambert, Paul Bulmer, Angie Booth, Stephen Trainor, Joy S., Courtney, Jamieson Hoffman, Vibeke Koch, Bill Kte'pi, Leah Webber, Earendil02, Philip Overby, Richard Martin, Kaitlin Thorsen, Géraldine Zenhäusern, Cody Reichenau, Michele Kallish Price, Patrick Lahar, Brett Wehs, Miranda Li, David Salchow, Evan Williams, Carrie Williams, Eric Bishop, Mario Coto, Timothy Moore, Robert Zak, C. Brown, Fitzgerald Reist, Frank Michaels Errington, Cenica, Tammie Rice, gundato, Cindy Radvany, Jordan Charlton, Jay Kemberling, Delaura Serenity, Jeremy Hansen, David Annandale, Sverrir, David Scott DeSchuiteneer, Rob Karp, Andrew Jones, Jeremy Szal, Sonja Pieper, MavRk, Corbin Rapp, Matt Alexander, James Arnold, Susan, Wayne LePage, Rachel Ransom, Frank Skornia, James Reinhorn, John Ferrick, Michael Spredemann, eirik, Rob Holland, Michael Kaufman, Arun Srinivasan, Brad Justice, Bedrytski, David Sutherland, Amy C Smith, Jay King, justwes, Jesse Houwing, Jennifer Pol, Carl Clare, Dale Hanrahan, William Lee Peace Jr, Elizabeth Daly, Tomás, Misha Husnain Ali, Marj Crockett, Kenan, Lis Beasley, Katie Nelson, Adam Hoffman, Chris, Andrew, Jenny Colby, Daniel Williams, Dave LeGendre,

Jeffrey Davis, Kathy Messerli, Matthew Siew, wraith808, Jeremy Crigger, Timothy O'Flynn, John A, Carlos, Debra, Simon M Poon, Dion Graybeal, John Garrington, Preston Thomas, Tim, Magnus Sigurdsson, Janine Dhami, Dawn, Rod Fage, Steven Wilber, Jason Kuhlmann, Derek Roy, Lesley Ralph, Marmæl, Miranda Persaud, Revek, Shane, Alicia Smyth, Emma Lord, Georgina Scott, Gracjan Kaszyński, Harry Giovanopoulos, Jonathan Malnati, Amanda Moore, Jim Robinson, Joseph Asante, Lillith, Ryan Johnson, Daniel Minett, Robert Bullard, Jason Vierling, Margit Kaagaard, Chris Hammerle, Aldazar, Almudena Pumarega, James, Mostly Harmless, Richard Grayburn, Toea, Corey Shaw, Roxane Tourigny, Chris Ocano, Gary S Falk, Jeremy Kear, Robert Moric, Lawrence Schick, Davide Mana, Richard Tongue, Mad Martigan, Ian Magee, Bryant Kingry, Gwen, Mel Lafferty, Greg Dejasco, Maria Laura Montagna, Bernard Howell, Brenda Carr, Wayne Sklow, John Burt, Chyree Batton, Amber L Campbell, Syncytio, Tom Flahive, Santiago Hoyos, Doug Bailey, Jeff Montgomery, Richard Smeeton, Jasyn Jones, Jesica Swanstrom, Taylor Evan McNees, Donovan, John Hayholt, Andy Toye, Travis Gibson, Keith Nelson, Samo Korošec, Ian Wright, Tim D'Allaird, Wayne Naylor, Brian Berg, Emma, Andrew Turlington, John Idlor, Dominic, Fabian Monhemius, Carsten Deibel, Edward Potter, Justin Farquhar, Matthew Sylvester, Pablo Sorribes, Rebecca Lovatt, Mark Sergeant, Austin, Some Guy, Ian King, Manan Kothari, Jan Gehrer, Tera Fulbright, Marc Tassin, Joshua, Angeline Burton, Liang Gao, Jonathan Hollingsworth, Caroline Smith, Dreaming Isis, Graham Parkin, Rebecca Dornof, J.R. Murdock, Michael Cummings, Scott McKeon, Earl McElmurry, Gunnar Ingi Kristjansson, Ryan Cannon, Matthew O'Connor, Robert Jenkins, Pål Lövendahl, Simon Cornwell, milllcose, rcrantz, David Mandeville, ianquest, Robert Belus, Tor Andre Wigmostad, Justin Gallo, GMark Cole, Kris Johnson, David Long, Michael

Subin, Jenn Ong, Paul McMullen, Carol Guess, Scott, Paul V, Susan Erickson, Curmudgeon of Phoenix Rising, Greg, Elaine Tindill-Rohr, Jon Hughes, Evaristo Ramos, Clay Hanson, Marcel Guzman, Jason Colby, Andrew Michael Methven Skinner, Rick Whitesell, Michael Molnia, John Martin, Christopher Schroeder, Wil Asche, Michael Skolnik, Ryan Weaver, Roy Romasanta, Emily Smith, IdleDice, Katie Riley, Kevin Langevin, Donald Ferris, CH Wan, Stuart Renz, Dan Grove, Duncan Bain, Michelle Scharmack, Gökhan Akdeniz, Matthew McNally, Marc Collins, Rune, Euan Proffit, Ioannis Orfanakis, Jason Tilling, Matt Jebus Jones, Sarah Van Deventer, Duncan Rittschof, Brian D Lambert, John Brennan, Coliseo Films, Andrew Bailey, Andrey Akhmedov, Rory, Errin Carner, Justin Lance, Michael Downey, Austin Warawa, Arlene Penrose, Jonathan Dean, Jo Van, Ryo, Jennifer Shew, Jordan, Jen Woods, Gail Martin, WolfDC, Wee Tong NG, Nicholas, Doug Smith, Sascha Linder, Brian White, Drew Tipton, Joe Maron, Michael Fedrowitz, Adriane Ruzak, Alma Vilic, Arrowstorm Entertainment, Ryan Young, Roland Holacsek, Emiliano Tabarsi, Darkstand, D. Moonfire, Tony Fiorentino, Robert B II, Jeremy Jacobs, Mark E. Lein, Iain Riley, Meghan Normandin, Mitchel Rieth, Peter, Mitch Olsen, Caleb Flanagan, streakermaximus, René Tang, BowieFan65000, Svend Andersen, Caeldwyn, Kevin B., Samantha Attanasio, Teri Henderson Garety, Jon Newlands, David Jarrett, Sören Koch, Richard Pleyer, Emery Shier, John Frewin, Kevin Jacobson, Peggy Carpenter, João Beraldo, Fraser Gerrie, NightWind, Dina Willner, Alex, John Zanella, Daniel Goncalves, Greg Niehues, Psybernary, Marijn Hubert, Janice O'Connor, Craig Wright, Bellehound, Don, Darryl Miao, Jess, matthurlburt, Jacob Jensen, Christopher J. Gill, Celena, Parallaxe, Mark Davey, Akil Craigg, Colin Lloyd, DGSnyder, Jake, Vicki, Amber Ellis, Astrid Boehmer, Cathal Cooney, SwordFire, Martin Shaw, Patrick Devine,

Nathan, Paul Albrecht, Thomas Zilling—Tormented WoOS of
OOoE, Rukesh Patel, Cole Hurley, Herman Duyker, Tom Piggott,
Matthew DeWorken, behippo, Pineapple Steak, Jon Spengler,
Kevin Chan

Bung Nippers

Jennie Ivins, Jessica Moyer, Jan Waite, Juan Navarro, Shaun
Davis, Anna Davidson, Courtney Beard, Geoff Strayer, Don
Barnett, Michael J. Sullivan, James R. Vernon, Michael Bentley,
Benjamin Abbott, Elena Brefort-Moison, Courtney Schafer,
Carmen Brack, Eric Slaney, Verlene Landon, Ronald Lucero, Beck
Von des Welpen, David Weinstein, Alexandra Brandt, Christoph
Wagner, Richard Finn, kadymae, Jordan, Tim Mürphỷ, Katie Bruce,
Rachel Beyler, Wendy B, Martin Greening, Stephen Crawford,
Roger O'Dell, Robert Sauermann, Matt, Lou Anders, Stephan
Dinges, Sam Seah, Rockne Bender, Petr Dolejší, Michael Poretski,
Dard, Alyc Helms, Pasquale, Alan Stewart, Donald, Dan Weber,
Bone on Bone, Matthew Pearsall, Traci Loudin, Jill A. Alters, Seth
Lindberg, Morgan Baikie, Megan Walker, Alissa, Tommi Mannila,
Gabriel Fisher, George C. Cotronis, Gavran, Michael C. Fedoris,
omegadom, Joshua Antonishen, Tim Rosolino, Cody Dunmire,
Troels Damgaard, Dean Cooney, Nimrod Daniel, Rob Matheny,
Hugh Blair, JanThomas, Andrew Muir, RiTides of 3DG, Robert
Helmbrecht, Jacque Summers, Rob Aitken, Mikko Jauhiainen, Kofi
Tsamenyi, Josh Franks, William Ogier, Catherine, Ruth Stuart,
Matthew Bell, Chris Larson, Josiah Kalangie, Mary Garber, Recneps
Namthgiw, Berni Dunne, Krista Parker, Brian Mooney, Wes
Freeman, David Drew, Jake Nikirk, Jimmy Bruce, C.S. Loh, Will
Wight, Deanna Stanley, Derek Essique, Zach Hoskins, John Payne,
Petronila Esther Mandeno, Markus Krogh, Thorne N. Melcher,
Wiccan Hour Inc., Jon Beer, Alex Dingle, Donald J Bingle/54-40'

Orphyte, Inc., Al Clay, Brandon, Rachael, Chris Wilson, Kario, Brandon Zarzyczny, Dail, Andrew Rowe, Dan Brewer, Christine Bell, Tehani Wessely, Michael Tervoort, Angela Banks, Henrik Lindhe, Stephan Gieb, Dave Chua, Nicole Hall, Thomas Bull, Nick Kilburg, Laura C, Matt Pfaff, Arthur Cunningham, moorkh, Danny Whittaker, RP, Robert Tomaino, Donna Mould, MsMeglet, David Ting, Carla Moore, Jeff Coquery, Johan Rapp, Fırat Ender Koçyiğit, Michael Coward, Josh Garner, Jamie Manley, Colin Ngeow, Nicola, Sarah Uhl, Alice Leiper, Markus Henning, Nigel Phillips, G. Hartman

Pair O'Eyes
Michelle Strickland, Jason Aaron Wong, Mary Stephenson, Angela Meadon, AlphaCrimson, Briana Rose Chanin

ROLL CREDITS

Nods to Roger Bellini for his editorial assistance on select stories, to David Alvarez for the artistic layout of David Dalglish's "Take You Home" illustration (finishes by Oksana Dmitrienko), and to Shawn T. King, Ragnarok's designer, who makes all of this look so damn good. Also many thanks to Sarah Chorn of Bookworm Blues, Mihir Wanchoo, and Ragnarok's Editor-In-Chief, Tim Marquitz, for their assistance with the 271 open submissions we received. Last, Ragnarok staffers Melanie Meadors, Nick Sharps, Amanda Shore, Tyson Mauermann, Meaghan Mullin, and Ryan Lawler, thank you for manning the oars.

ARMAN AKOPIAN
Cover Artist
To see more: i-guyjin-i.deviantart.com

BRADLEY P. BEAULIEU
"Irindai"
Setting: The Song of the Shattered Sands (Sharakhai)
Find out more: quillings.com

CAROL BERG
"Seeds"
Setting: Sanctuary Duet
Find out more: sff.net/people/carolberg

RICHARD LEE BYERS
"Troll Trouble"
Setting: Balathex
Find out more: rleebyers.livejournal.com

S.R. CAMBRIDGE
"The Betyár and the Magus"
Find out more: twitter.com/SRCambridge

GLEN COOK
"Poorly Calculated Randomistics" (Foreword)
Setting: The Chronicles of the Black Company
Find out more: goodreads.com/author/show/13026.Glen_Cook

DAVID DALGLISH
"Take You Home"
Setting: Shadowdance Series (Dezrel)
Find out more: ddalglish.com

OKSANA DMITRIENKO
Interior Artist
To see more: huah.diary.ru (in Russian)

JAMES ENGE
"Thieves at the Gate"
Find out more: jamesenge.com

JOHN GWYNNE
"Better to Live than to Die"
Setting: The Faithful and the Fallen (The Banished Lands)
Find out more: john-gwynne.com

LIAN HEARN
"His Kikuta Hands"
Setting: Tales of the Otori (The Three Countries)
Find out more: lianhearn.com

PAUL S. KEMP
"A Better Man"
Setting: The Tales of Egil and Nix
Find out more: paulskemp.com

SNORRI KRISTJANSSON
"A Kingdom and a Horse"
Setting: The Valhalla Saga
Find out more: snorrikristjansson.com

JOSEPH R. LALLO
"Seeking the Shadow"
Setting: The Book of Deacon
Find out more: bookofdeacon.com

MARK LAWRENCE
"The Secret"
Setting: The Broken Empire and The Red Queen's War
Find out more: marklawrence.buzz

TIM MARQUITZ
"A Taste of Agony"
Setting: Tales of the Prodigy
Find out more: tmarquitz.com

J.M. MARTIN
Editor (Introduction)
Find out more: ragnarokpub.com

JAMES A. MOORE
"What Gods Demand"
Setting: The Blasted Lands Series
Find out more: jamesamoorebooks.com

PETER ORULLIAN
"A Length of Cherrywood"
Setting: The Vault of Heaven
Find out more: orullian.com

JEAN RABE
"Mainon"
Find out more: jeanrabe.com

CAT RAMBO
"The Subtler Art"
Setting: Serendib
Find out more: kittywumpus.net

LAURA RESNICK
"Friendship"
Setting: The Silerian Trilogy
Find out more: lauraresnick.com

ANTHONY RYAN
"The Lord Collector"
Setting: Raven's Shadow Trilogy
Find out more: anthonystuff.wordpress.com

CLAY SANGER
"The Long Kiss"
Find out more: claysanger.com

MARK SMYLIE
"Manhunt"
Setting: Sword & Barrow (The Known World)
Find out more: swordandbarrow.com

KENNY SOWARD
"Jancy's Justice"
Setting: GnomeSaga
Find out more: kennysoward.com

SHAWN SPEAKMAN
"The White Rose Thief"
Setting: The Annwn Cycle
Find out more: shawnspeakman.com

JON SPRUNK
"Sun and Steel"
Setting: Book of the Black Earth
Find out more: jonsprunk.com

ANTON STROUT
"Scream"
Setting: Simon Canderous series
Find out more: antonstrout.com

MICHAEL J. SULLIVAN
"Professional Integrity"
Setting: Riyria Revelations
Find out more: riyria.blogspot.com

DJANGO WEXLER
"The First Kill"
Setting: The Shadow Campaigns
Find out more: djangowexler.com

ORION ZANGARA
Interior Artist
To see more: orionzangara.com

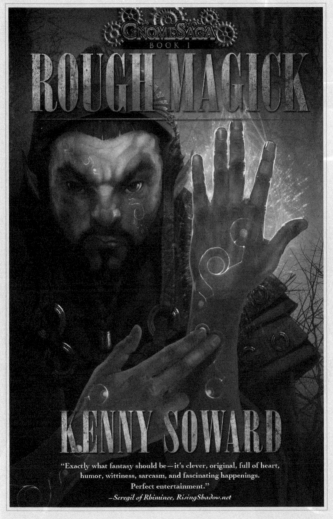

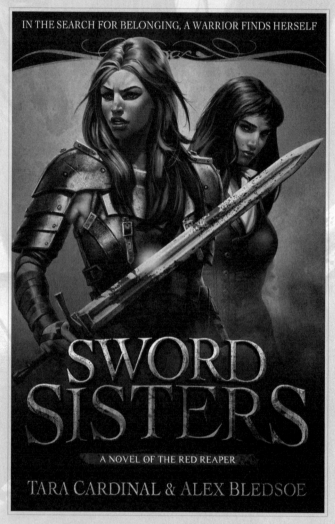